Hyndland Portrait

· a sequel to Pittenweem Sojourn ·

Nanzie McLeod

First published in the United Kingdom by
Nanzie McLeod, Glasgow

The author has asserted her moral rights.

British Library Cataloguing-in Publication Data.
A catalogue record for this book is available from
the British Library.

ISBN 0 9529527 6 9

Origination by Robin McCulloch
Printed by Bell & Bain Limited, Glasgow

Contents

Contents continued

Thanks to
Jean Reid, Jak Edwards and
Robin McCulloch
for their valuable assistance.

Thanks also to my four daughters
Kate, Esther, Sarah and Alice
for their support and encouragement.

This book
is dedicated to
my mother

Ann Cumming
1902-1980

A creative and courageous woman.

The author
Nanzie McLeod
at age 21

The Wheelchair

It was a Tuesday evening in April 1944 that the wheelchair arrived. Helen stood at the middle window in the sitting room, watching for it. She had no idea how it would come or what it would look like, but the idea of a wheelchair was exciting. Surely it would be a big help to her mother.

Helen cringed when she thought how silly she had been to dream that coming back to the city would make everything right again, imagining that the war would finish and her mother would be able to walk properly again. What an idiot she had been. At the age of twelve she should have had more sense.

Helen's mother, Annie, was still able to walk very slowly around the house if someone were there to support her, but the twenty four steps between her bedroom and the kitchen exhausted her, and she was pleased to drop into a chair as soon as she got there. The slow struggle to the fireside in the sitting room took even longer. Helen could see how her mother's strength and control had deteriorated in the few weeks since they had left Pittenweem. They had been living in the small fishing town on the East coast of Scotland since the start of the war and had now returned to Glasgow.

Annie sat in the deep leather armchair to the right of the fireplace with her back to the windows. She wore a shapeless tweed skirt and a loose grey cardigan. Her long face was thin and her lips were tightly pressed together as she knitted a brightly patterned Fair Isle glove.

Helen's grandmother, Mary sat on the other side of the fire. She looked much younger than her sixty-two years and had an aura of strength and energy. Although full-bosomed, she looked smart in a dark red jersey suit. She wore a discreet touch of lipstick and a long string of large ivory beads hung sensuously over her cream silk blouse. She was smoking a cigarette and a cup of tea sat on the small table beside her chair. Her long fingers tapped nervously on the arm of the chair, but she was strangely silent as she gazed into the coal flames.

A tramcar trundled up the hill and halted at the tramstop just outside the house.

Helen watched as two ladies stepped carefully down the metal steps, crossed to the pavement and walked purposefully away. Three men boarded the tram, all hurrying upstairs as if rushing to be seated before it started to move. Helen liked to observe the comings and goings of the local residents, though she could not remember paying much attention to people in Pittenweem. Here, most folk were formally and smartly dressed and each one looked as though his or her life was organised and important. Perhaps being grown up was like that. At twelve, she seemed often to be late, or losing or forgetting things, or generally finding herself in a muddle.

"No sign of your father yet?"

As Annie spoke, she looked over her shoulder with the slight smile and one raised eyebrow that Helen so admired. It made her mother seem composed and sophisticated. Helen had often practised that expression in the mirror, but both eyebrows went up at the same time and the effect was disappointing. She wondered how her mother could be so calm tonight?

She might never sit in that leather armchair again.

Surely she must be excited or worried? Perhaps sad?

Although Annie looked just like any other mother in her early forties as she sat there, she had suffered from disseminated sclerosis for some years. Walking had become progressively worse in the past five months. At bedtime, when only Helen was with her and Annie was tired, even walking was impossible and Annie would crawl on her hands and knees to the door of the sitting room, where Helen helped her to kneel on a rug. Then the daughter pulled her mother across the polished linoleum in the hall and into the bedroom. Annie was tall, but very slender and Helen was pleased to be useful and also to feel her power. She had always been interested in her own strength and muscular ability.

"Here it is, I think! Yes, there's Daddy getting out of a lorry...!"

"Well, run and let them in then."

Helen stood in the close outside her front door and watched her father and the lorry driver carry the chair up the sixteen steps from the pavement. It seemed very big and pretty heavy. They dropped it with a thump at the top of the stairs. After passing some money to the driver, who touched his cap and muttered his thanks, Bruce wheeled the chair slowly along the close towards her, grinning broadly.

The chair squeaked loudly and was much larger than Helen had imagined it would be. It had four wheels, two large ones at the front and two small rear wheels. The seat and back were cushioned in pale brown corduroy and the arms were padded with the same fabric.

"Here we are, Tuppenny, this should do the trick. This'll make a difference to yer lives, I'll bet. It's just like a big pram, isn't it. I'll give it a wee squirt of oil and get rid of that squeak. D'ye want to jump in and have a ride?"

Helen shook her head. It seemed important to her that the chair should be presented to her mother as her very own and not used as a toy. No one had suggested this to her but Helen felt this to be a serious and significant moment.

Her grandmother stood at the other end of the hall.

"My God! What a brute of a thing, Bruce. It's enormous. You'll need to be very careful of the paintwork when you go through doorways."

"Plenty room, Mrs Mackay, plenty room."

Bruce grinned, his teeth brilliant against the dark stubble which had normally received a second shave by this time. He whirled the chair round and pushed it through the doorway with speed, very slightly grazing the door jamb.

Mary Mackay tut-tutted three times, very loudly.

Helen felt the usual irritation welling up inside her stomach. She wished that her grandmother would be less critical, because her Father was putting himself to a lot of bother and expense to help them. She also wished her Father would just be a bit more careful.

Helen wanted to feel more fond of both of them, but it was difficult.

Mary Mackay followed Bruce into the sittingroom. The chair dominated the room and seemed terribly ugly to her. The whole situation was ugly. It was almost impossible for Mary to comprehend that her daughter could now hardly walk at all. Always quick to anger, she now felt consumed with fury, yet powerless to vent it on any one person. It was nobody's fault. Although Mary's relationship with her daughter had never been a close one, for their personalities were too different, she would not have admitted that she was disappointed in her daughter. But how very hard it was for the popular, energetic Mrs Mackay, well known in society and on the golf course, to have a daughter in a wheelchair! It was almost shameful. The maternal sympathy which she might have felt was blotted out by overwhelming emotion, embarrassment perhaps and anger certainly. Quite apart from the tragedy which it signified, this monstrous chair was a blot on the landscape. Mary had a fine and sensitive eye for furnishings and this awkward padded vehicle, which would obviously be a permanent fixture, ruined the look of the pleasant sitting room.

Bruce, apparently insensitive, spoke in his usual hail-fellow-well-met tone, his voice loud and staccato,

"Right, here we are at last, Annie. Sorry we're late, Lorry was a bugger. Broke down in the Gallowgate. But here we are now. Your new chariot! I must say it's quite a nice bit of engineering and I was lucky to get it. Old Nicholson helped me find it. I've done him a coupla favours in the past. D'ye remember old Nicholson at the Arlington?"

Annie slowly shook her head as she gazed at the chair with her quizzical half smile.

"It's certainly big enough and it looks very comfy, Bruce. Thank you. That should certainly make things easier for me. I bet Jessie'll be delighted."

Jessie came in daily to help her in the house. Annie turned to her daughter,

"How d'you like it, my wee lamb?"

Helen tried to sound enthusiastic.

"It certainly looks awfully…comfy."

But she felt the chair transformed the room that she had known all her life. It proclaimed change.

It shouted out that her mother was no longer able to walk. She swallowed hard and turned away so that no one would see the tears in her eyes.

As usual, Annie was positive.

"Will we try it out, then? Give me a hand to stand up Bruce: oh! wait, wait, not so fast though!"

Bruce with his usual strength and speed had overdone his helping hand. He was impatient and often too rough in dealing with Annie's painful condition. After her spasm of pain had passed and after Mrs Mackay's tut-tutts had died away, Annie settled herself in the chair.

"Oh! It's really wonderfully, tremendously comfortable. It's a long time since I've felt so supported and... just comfy. That's the only word to describe it. Thank you Bruce, you've picked a winner and I'm very, very grateful. I hope it wasn't too expensive."

"No, no. Not too bad. Anyway, it was a necessity."

It was the wrong thing to say and he realised it immediately and only made things worse by trying to unsay it. Helen and her grandmother both burst into tears and Annie shed a few as well.

Soon Annie took a deep breath and said,

"You know, I have to admit that it's really a relief for me to get into this chair. We knew it would come to it sooner or later, didn't we? Life was getting just too much of a struggle for all of us. Specially wee Helen there. Let's cheer up and have a cup of coffee and a bit of that apple tart I made today. Right, Helen see if you can wheel yer old Mum into the kitchen and I'll give you a hand."

"Watch the paintwork, Helen!" her grandmother admonished.

Helen made no acknowledgement of the warning. Of course she would watch the paintwork.

The handle was similar to a pram handle and the small rear wheels swivelled smoothly which made changing direction very easy. Helen had no difficulty in pushing the chair slowly through the sitting room doorway, then, with great care, negotiating the turn into the kitchen.

"Is it really quite nice to sit in, Mummy?"

"It's great! And you seem to be very good at driving it."

"It's fun to push. When they've all gone away and you're in bed, can I have wee shot in it, myself?"

"Of course, my darling. You can stop pushing me now. I'll need to get into the way of hurling it myself. Look how well I can make it go on the kitchen linoleum. It was harder to push on the carpet. I bet my arms get really strong after a few weeks. I wonder how Jessie will like it!"

"I hope she's not too wild when she pushes you!"

Jessie had a heart of gold and her laughter and unfailing willingness had been a wonderful help to the mother and daughter since she had come to work for them in February. However, she was not an ideal housewife, her ways were rough and ready and her slapdash methods left a trail of chipped crockery and singed towels. Perfection was not one of her aims and as she was usually in a hurry to finish a job, her favourite phrase was,

"Ach, tae hell, that'll dae fine the noo."

But Annie was willing to forgive her all her faults, for Jessie's optimism and breezy Glasgow humour were just what Annie needed at this difficult time. Now that her life was such a physical struggle, the ingrained family attitude to the maintenance and importance of material possesssions no longer seemed a priority. What did it matter if the crockery was chipped? And the personal care, which Jessie gave Annie was full of loving kindness and the patience which inanimate objects did not receive.

After the apple tart was eaten and duly appreciated, Helen was delighted to hear her father offer to drive his mother-in-law home to Charing Cross. It was always so nice when grandma and her father left, for they both talked nonstop about things that really did not interest Helen. Often after they had gone, her mother would whisper,

"Silence reigns again."

And then they would giggle. Helen found it so much more fun when it was just the two of them. Perhaps there would be something good to listen to on the wireless, or perhaps they might have a game of cards or just read their books. It would be easy to wheel her mother to bed tonight, although Helen would miss giving her mother the 'hurl' on the rug. For over ten weeks, Annie had balanced on the small carpet and been dragged by Helen over the linoleum. It was like a game and Annie usually shouted "Whee" as they turned the corner into the bedroom. Now Helen felt a quick pang of sadness because she would never do that again. It was a special thing that other daughters did not do for their mothers, and for a moment she felt a strong sense of loss.

That particular feeling had become very familiar in the last few months.

Helen roused herself from these thoughts in time to hear her grandmother say,

"Oh, I wasn't thinking of going home just yet, thank you Bruce. It's quite early, not even ten yet. I can get a tram at quarter to eleven."

Mary smiled charmingly as she spoke, but Helen's heart dropped.

"Are you sure now, Mrs Mackay? It's not out my road, you know. I've got to see a man in Bath Street at ten fifteen."

Helen listened hopefully, perhaps grandma would change her mind.

"No, it's very good of you, but I'll just spend some more time with Annie. I won't be over to see her again this week."

"Whatever you say, Mrs Mackay, but it would be no trouble and it'd get you home nice and early."

"I don't know, Bruce, it's a very kind offer ... but ... I wonder ... maybe I should just go."

How Helen wished that they would stop talking and go away. She knew her mother felt the same, for she heard her take a long controlled breath, almost a sigh.

"I wonder if your father will be home from the Art Club yet, Annie? I would accept a lift gratefully if I thought John would be home by now. I think he likes me to be there when he gets back."

Helen brightened once more and her clever mother chose the right words.

"Yes, I'm sure he likes to find you there when he gets in, Maw. You should just take the chance of a lift when it's there. I'll be fine tonight and I'll see you next week."

Ten minutes later the house was splendidly quiet and peaceful. The fire still burned brightly and they finished the last crumbs of apple tart and read their books until eleven o'clock.

What heaven!

Getting Annie to bed was certainly an easier and quicker process with the chair, but there was some regret in Helen's heart.

◊

Next day Jessie was absolutely delighted with the chair and immediately sat herself in it, rolling herself around the house, singing at the top of her voice,

"A life on the ocean waves, a diddle ay de dee, a life on the ocean blue, that's the life for me."

After five or six uninhibited minutes, she jumped out of the chair, rushed to the bedroom where Annie still lay in bed and apologised.

"Och Mrs Cornin', whit am Ah like? Ah'm soarry, hen! Whit a brass neck Ah've goat! Ye'll be wunnerin' if Ah poalish it ivry day. Ah'm awfy, awfy soarry. That wiz bluddy cheeky o' me tae dae that wi yer new chair, so it wuz."

"Not at all Jessie, you were enjoying yourself and you made

me laugh. You did! It's great to get some fun! There's nothing like a laugh."

Remorseful, Jessie wept a few tears and Annie's eyes were also moist, though she still smiled.

Then Jessie recovered and took charge again.

"Richt! whit's tae be furst, breakfast or a bed bath?"

It was a rhetorical question, for the bath always came first.

Once Annie was washed, dressed and sitting in her new chair, Jessie pushed her quickly and enthusiastically into the kitchen. Mrs Mackays' worst fears would have been realised for Jessie, with her genius for careless speed, managed to scrape the paintwork on each side of the bedroom and kitchen doorways.

After Annie had eaten breakfast, peeled the potatoes and accomplished one or two other chores in the kitchen, she announced,

"I'll retire now, if that's all the skivvy work done."

"Ah'll jist wheech ye through ben in a sec, hen."

Annie explained diplomatically that she must learn to be independent and it was good exercise for her to wheel herself around the house. However Jessie hovered behind her all the way to the fireside in the sittingroom, advising 'a wee bit to the right noo' and 'no' sae fast roon' they corners'. It was obvious she did not quite trust Annie's manoeuvring skills

"It's kinda like drivin' a tramcaur, Mrs Cornin', is it no'?"

"I don't know. I've never driven a tramcar."

This was met with gales of laughter and Annie thought how charming and satisfying it was to seem so witty and able to amuse her kindly helper.

◊

As Helen sat in the tram going to school that day, she thought a lot about the wheelchair and how it would change their lives. She could think of little else and would have liked to stay at home and see Jessie's reaction to the chair. She was sure that Jessie would sit in it and have a shot at whirling around the house. She hoped their ram-stam cleaner, as her mother called her, would be careful and not ruin the paintwork completely, It was not that Helen cared much about the scratches. It was just that grandma, with her eagle eyes, would get cross and go on and on about it and that would be boring. Helen was sure that Mary's anger, near the surface at all times, upset her mother and made her pains worse. Helen was becoming very intuitive about her mother's fragile condition and without analysing it exactly, she was aware that Annie seemed to have fewer spasms of pain when it was just the two of them in the house, for her father also often seemed to affect her mother's condition badly. Sometimes it was his thoughtlessness. His restless energy finding an outlet in almost constant fidgeting, he seemed unable to remember that his small habitual repetitive kick, if delivered to Annie's chair, would cause her spasmodic pain. Each time it happened and Annie had to ask him to stop, he was deeply apologetic, but Helen found it difficult to understand how he could not learn this lesson. Protecting her mother from unnecessary pain was a priority for her.

Helen often felt more fond of her father when he was not present and this morning she felt very kindly towards him. The chair would make life easier for everyone. It was not new of course. The corduroy was a little shabby, but that did not matter. What sort of person had used the chair before her mother? A man or a woman? She wondered if they too had suffered from disseminated sclerosis or perhaps polio, which was also a disease which landed you in a wheelchair. Perhaps the previous owner had just been old and weakly. One read a lot about elderly, weak relatives in books. They were generally grumpy and wealthy, but eventually became very fond of the young hero or heroine of the story and left them lots of money. She had read several books with a similar plot. She smiled to herself for her mother certainly wasn't elderly, weak, grumpy or wealthy.

Would she always sit in that wheelchair? Forever?

That was a thought that Helen disliked and quickly put from her mind.

Yes, it was good of her father to find a chair so quickly. How much had it cost? She had no idea and had little idea of the value of any sort of chair. She had never thought of chairs as having to be bought, they were just there in the house and new ones were never needed. She wondered idly what the big leather chairs had cost. The wheel chair, with its four solid rubber tires and braking mechanism must have been very dear, much more than a bicycle, certainly. Again she smiled to herself, for the chair was quite like a bicycle, a sort of cousin to a bike. Her bike was still in Pittenweem, propped against the wall in the shed. She did not miss it. She preferred walking to cycling and she absolutely hated when she was overtaken by a car. It made her flush and tremble and one might be overtaken three or four times on that half mile of road between Pittenweem and Anstruther. Certainly she would never dare ride a bike in Glasgow with all those trams and buses hurtling along. As she looked from the tram window, she shuddered at the thought.

◊

There was no doubt that Bruce Corning's visits, with his loud egocentric personality, created tension in the quiet female household.

The marriage had ended long ago, when Helen was still very small, and Bruce Corning, who now lived with his parents, was certainly a complex person. Perhaps he was the phenomenon known as a born bachelor. Blessed or cursed, whichever your point of view, by having an adoring, undemanding mother, whose unconditional, loving servitude was unlikely to be matched by any wife, Bruce retained a self-centred, boyish joy in his own abilities and pursuits. However, he was a decent and honourable man and, as Annie's condition had worsened, he had remained supportive, both financially and in various practical ways.

He visited his wife and daughter regularly, though his visits were brief and unpredictable. This suited Helen, who found his overpowering ebullience, his continous talking, his teasing and kidding very difficult to deal with. As he seldom listened to her mother or herself, he seemed to her to be uninterested in them, happy to remain oblivious of their lives. His presence almost always irritated her. Helen did try to be a proper daughter. She made many resolutions that next time he came to visit, she would smile more and chat in the friendly, relaxed way as she did with her mother. She knew she could be entertaining and make folk laugh. But the reality of her father's presence inhibited her. She sat in stony silence when faced with his seemingly self-satisfied grin and loud booming voice. In spite of her good intentions, the familiar hostility would bubble up and she longed for him to leave. No doubt her young, expressive face told its own tale, perhaps spurring her father to relate more tales of his own prowess, in an effort to gain his daughter's admiration. Who can explain the horrible circularity of life?

◊

Annie certainly found it easier to deal with the large pages of the Glasgow Herald as she sat in her new chair. She was never sure that reading the news was the best occupation, for apart from one or two items, it was all too depressing. It was good to see that the Government was considering a plan for a National Health Service, although Glasgow doctors sounded less than enthusiastic. These old traditionalists were giving the idea a 'cautious welcome' depending on 'its worth to the public' and of course 'its acceptability to the profession'. There must be 'adequate clarification and negotiation on many important points'. She suspected such an ideal might never materialise. Then there was news of extra clothing coupons, although the report was very confused as to the actual amount that each person would receive. Then there had been a monthly allocation of one pound of oranges per ration book since January. She had hardly believed that when she read it at first! But they had arrived in the shops as promised, and as long as one got there early and stood in the queue – and stalwart Helen had been near the front every time – you received these long lost treats. Not that they were the very sweetest or juiciest of oranges, but certainly very welcome. When Annie was first diagnosed as having disseminated sclerosis, her doctor had advised eating a daily orange. In spite of that being impossible, here she was still in tolerably good shape. Unlike the poor old world, she thought. Most of the news in the paper was concerned with the terrible fighting, the destruction and the carnage which was happening everywhere. Headlines gave monstrous figures of bomb tonnage dropped, ships sunk, casualties and deaths. The whole news page seemed to revel in this atrocious situation. What a waste of life and what a waste of energy. And money too! What was all this destruction costing, while ordinary people were hungry and cold and struggling? That article the other day had reported 1823 babies had died in Glasgow last year, due to bad housing and wintry weather. And we hardly knew what wintry weather was compared to the millions of poor starving Russians. What madness it all was.

She quickly turned the page to the ladies' section where middle class values still reigned supreme, with suggestions for elaborate ways of cooking the same old vegetables or transforming last year's costume with clever trimming.

Coplands were advertising two nice outfits.

**2 piece in Moygashel-contrast collar and piping on the sleeves.
£3.5s.4d   10 coupons.
Two-toned frock of Moygashel fabric. Design illustrated is in
mustard and nigger brown. New three-quarter sleeve.
£5.4s.6d   7 coupons**

They looked good in the fashion sketch, stylish without being
too extreme. Coplands had an excellent fashion artist, while
Pettigrew's ads tended to look rather outlandish. Daly's were
even more so. Of course some folk wanted the extreme styles. She
only hoped that they were not disappointed when their mirrors
did not reflect the wasp-waisted elegance depicted by the artist.
And what was Moygashel? Probably another name for rayon.
Perhaps a sort of linen substitute?

As Annie folded the paper up, a small ad caught her eye,

**OPEN AIR DANCING
IN KELVINGROVE PARK
Nightly 7-30 9-30
Entry 1/6
Allied Services uniformed 1/-
Spectators 4d**

That sounded a very pleasant idea. Perhaps still a bit chilly at
this time of year, though the weather had been good recently.
Probably they would be doing some of that wild jiving to keep
them warm. Poor cold spectators! But it was only fourpence and
how very nice to go and watch. She would love to see them herself. It could not be, of course. She must just content herself, sitting here in her chair, while they jived madly in the park.

Glasgow High School for Girls

When Helen had first returned to Glasgow from those rather unhappy years spent in Fife, she had several expectations. One of the most important was that she would meet a really special friend, the sort of friend that one read about in school stories, someone to share secrets and jokes, someone to swim with and perhaps share adventures with, just like those schoolgirls in books.

In Pittenweem, her friends had been nice girls, but somehow separated from her. They had no shared experience. They did not read the same books, nor had they ever lived in a city. The hurtling traffic, the enormous museums, the theatres and most importantly, her beloved Arlington Baths, were all outside their imagination. The Pittenweem children only knew of summer swimming in the sea and could not imagine the unique atmosphere of the Arlington Club. Helen thought it very special. It was like another home to her and she felt happy as soon as she walked into its quiet, dim warmth. Her dream was to take a friend there, who would share her enjoyment of swimming in the pool, lazing in the immense showers and swinging and jumping on the parallel bars in the gymnasium. That would be as good as any story.

Probably her best friend in Fife had been Jean Forgie. Helen and Jean had vied with each other for the position of 'top of the class' and had spent a lot of time together. Slightly older and taller than Helen, Jean had a bullying streak in her personality which damaged the affection that Helen wanted to feel for her. Sometimes Jean would grip Helen's wrist and twist her arm behind her back to force her into agreement in an argument. Helen accepted this occasional torture, but wondered at herself for doing so. She knew Jean could never be that ideal, 'very best' friend,

Jean had left Pittenweem some months before Helen did. Her parents had taken charge of a YMCA hostel in Dunfermline. Helen and her mother had visited them there the previous year, for the two mothers were friendly with each other.

On Helen's first day at the Glasgow High School for Girls she had been seated beside Jennifer, whose appearance certainly matched the descriptions of a best friend in those schoolgirl epics of Angela Brazil. Jennifer was tall and lanky, with short naturally curly hair and freckles. She looked as though she would find it easy to be harum-scarum, that necessary trait of the literary schoolgirl. At first Jennifer made the new girl very welcome. She smiled a lot and gave Helen a little description of each teacher as she came into the room to teach her subject. She was not charitable about the teachers, but she was quite funny. She had a way of looking sideways at Helen with a very meaningful expression and although Helen had no idea what she did mean, the mystery was intriguing. However Helen soon learned that Jennifer's personality did not make her fit for a best friend. She was a tell-tale, something that every honest schoolchild abhors. Even worse, she was a liar, for one day she spilt her ink over a jotter and immediately put up her hand to inform the teacher that Helen had spilt the ink. Helen was too amazed to say a word in her own defence and had to listen to the teacher's lecture about being more careful, especially with other people's property. After that, Helen noticed that Jennifer often twisted the truth in order to put other girls in the wrong. It was such a strange and horrible thing to do! Why did she do it?

Helen could not understand such dishonourable behaviour and when the opportunity presented itself, she moved to another desk. She had regrets because, without a doubt, Jennifer looked exactly like a girl in a Chalet School book.

By February she had met Khirstine, who was tall and mature looking, not a bit like a schoolgirl. She had a kind and sympathetic face with a beautiful smile and her voice was deep and lovely. She seemed very sure of herself. She was a few months older than Helen and seemed almost like a grown-up. Helen could not imagine her ever being nervous or making mistakes. Her beautiful writing flowed gracefully across the unlined page in perfect parallel lines, while Helen's writing was scratchy and slanted, with blots here and there. Surely Khirstine would always know what to do and where to go. Helen felt that she could rely on Khirstine. With her, she might not experience japes and rags like those girls in school stories, but she knew she could trust this friend and would always be safe with her. They always had lots to speak about and laughed at the same things.

Khirstine was a friend with whom Helen would keep in contact for the rest of her life.

In April Annie and Helen received letters from Jean and her mother, Clare, with the unexpected news that they were now living in Edinburgh.

Jean's father, who seemed a restless sort of person, had not liked the Dunfermline job and they had hardly stayed seven months before they moved. Annie certainly thought it a good move to take a thirteen-year-old girl away from all those young sailors in the YMCA. Annie did not even know of Jean's amorous friendship with a Polish soldier in Pittenweem when she was only twelve. Helen had been confided in and sworn to secrecy about this affair. She had worried about not telling her mother of the kissing and cuddling that Jean described, but she had found it hard to believe her friend's tales, comforting her conscience by deciding that it was all imagination

"That ancient broken down YMCA building was no place for a young girl and it was killing work for her mother. Not quite sure what the father's job was."

Helen thought her mother sounded unusually angry as she said this.

Now the Forgie family were in charge of something called a Camera Obscura. Annie had read of such a thing but had never seen one.

"It seems to reflect views of the city on to a sort of table. I don't quite understand it. I suppose people pay to go and see it."

"Yes, Jean says she takes the tickets at the door on a Saturday."

"Would you not like to go and visit them and see this Camera Obscura thing? You could get the train to Edinburgh for the day. And maybe Jessie could pop in for a couple of hours to keep me company."

Jessie chimed in,

"Och aye, let wee Helen go tae see her pal. She's needin' a wee break, an' me an'you 'll have a rerr time tae wursels, bakin' terts an' tellin' stories, eh? An' Ah'll bring the wee yin wi' me an' we'll get a good laugh."

Jessie had an adored baby, George, that Annie was always pleased to see. She considered him a very fine specimen, with his plump little body and mysterious smile.

However, Helen was still adjusting to living in a busy city, and the idea of coping alone with the train journey and a different town was too daunting.

"I think I'll just write Jean a letter. I don't need to visit her. Maybe they'll move again soon. Maybe they'll come to Glasgow!"

"Right enough, you never know!"

Helen realised that Jean was unlikely to be that best friend that she sought. Especially as best friends should be handy and not live at a distance.

◊

Because of wartime restrictions, school meals were rationed. On only one week in three could a child purchase a two-course lunch ticket, which had the five days printed on it, each day being ticked off when the ticket was presented at the dining-hall counter.

The following week the same child might buy twopenny and fourpenny tickets which could be exchanged for a bun or biscuits, which were collected in the dining hall, then the pupil returned to her own classroom to eat.

On the third week they were entirely independent and must bring their own food to school.

That first week, the lunches did not look at all appetising to Helen. The food seemed very different from the food at home: however a hungry schoolgirl will eat what is in front of her and it tasted better than it looked. Some days it was a meat course with pudding, other days it was soup and pudding. The soup was rather salt, the potatoes seemed watery and were never mashed properly, the meat was a little tough and grey. However, to Helen's surprise the puddings were very nice indeed.

In the following two weeks, each morning, Helen quickly cobbled together some bread and butter to take to school with her. She added two dried bananas from the health food shop, which looked strange, but tasted delicious with the brown National loaf that was the only bread available at that time. Most people complained bitterly about the 'grey loaf' and longed for the return of white bread, but Annie had always eaten brown bread and considered the National loaf 'not bad'.

Helen found it a bit of a rush in the morning to get it all ready and get herself out to catch the last tram that would take her to school in time. Her climb up the long steep Garnethill Street was usually accomplished at top speed and though panting slightly, she enjoyed that feeling of strength in her leg muscles

When Helen opened her untidy lunch package in the classroom, she saw people looking very hard at the bananas, though no one said a word. The other girls all had neatly folded little parcels of waxproof paper or smart lunch tins for sandwiches, lovingly prepared by their domestically organised mothers. Helen sat and enjoyed her messy bread and butter and chomped her dried bananas, wondering if she could improve her wrapping. How did they make those parcels look so perfect?

Her grandmother was in visiting one evening.

"How d'ye like those school dinners you get, Jewel?"

It was obvious from her tone of voice that she expected to hear the dinners were horrible and Helen was tempted to say they were scrumptious. Her grandmother often affected her in this perverse way, but honesty prevailed,

"They're all right. Quite tasty sometimes, not so good at others. The soup is…"

Helen made an expressive grimace,

"Not as good as your grandma's soup, I bet?"

"Oh, no, nothing like it!"

Here Helen's honesty was again tested. She was not fond of her grandmother's over-cooked soup either. Annie's soup was much nicer.

"But you'll have lovely desserts, do you?"

This was certainly a loaded question, asked with the sweetest of smiles.

"They're just quite plain, nothing fancy."

"Delicious though, are they?"

"Well no, not really delicious, mmm … just sort of ehm … I don't really know … all right, I suppose."

Annie saw that her daughter was in some sort of predicament and changed the subject by asking her mother to buy her some more Shetland wool from Smith's the next time she was in town.

Helen sat silently thinking of the school desserts. She loved them, but mixed with Helen's delight in these simple desserts was a secret sense of guilt. What sinful sweetmeats generated such worries in the heart of a twelve year old? Sometimes a piece of sponge had thin custard poured over it, but more usually it was a

milk pudding, semolina or custard, with a big spoonful of hot jam
in the middle of it. Throughout her life, Helen had adamantly
refused to eat milk puddings. She averred that she hated them.
They made her feel sick. They were a favourite with her grandfather, he liked them hot or cold, and there was nearly always a
'shape' of semolina or sago in the larder in her grandparents'
house. Now after turning her nose up at this nursery food for all
those years, Helen found that she really loved milk puddings!
Certainly those in the dinner school. If she saw that they were on
the menu as she stood waiting in the dinner queue, she felt a sense
of delightful expectation. It was a red letter day. Not only the
pudding, but the added jam was a problem for she knew that
Annie considered adding jam to semolina was unacceptable, most
definitely 'common'. How guilty she felt at enjoying those bland,
formerly rejected puddings. Swimming with jam! Although she
hated to hide anything from her mother, she could certainly never
admit to this secret delight. The guilt was almost too much to bear.

Helen awakened from her thoughts to hear her mother and
grandmother agree that it was too much for a wee girl to get her
own sandwiches every morning. The best idea was for her to
come to her grandma for lunch. It was only a five minute walk
from the school.

"Oh, but we're not allowed out of school till four o'clock,
Mummy."

"Yes, but I'm sure you could get special permission to go to
your grandmother's and then you could always get any messages,
if they were needed. That would be a help for you too, Maw,
wouldn't it?"

"Yes, that would be great. Save me going away down those
stairs for just a loaf of bread."

Helen had a strong mental vision of many plates of pudding
disappearing into the distance. It seemed too hard, that just when
she had discovered this delicacy, it was to be withdrawn. On the
other hand she would rather not eat bread and butter and dried
bananas every day for two weeks and her packaging skills
showed no signs of improvement.

"How would it be if I only went to grandma's house the two
weeks that I can't get dinners in school?"

Annie thought this was complicating things, but realised that
perhaps her daughter would miss the social side of lunchtime.

Mary thought it was a good idea. It meant that she was not entirely committed and would be able to spend a couple of days in town in the free week.

That is the arrangement that was arrived at with the school and Helen felt astonished that she could get what she wanted so easily. It seemed like a miracle. She enjoyed seeing her grandparents so often and the food was much tastier than bread and butter. Mary always tried to make something different. Then for one week, Helen could still enjoy those delectable milk puddings. Of course if playfully offered some semolina at her grandma's table, she was careful to shake her head vigorously, as always and say a very definite,

"No, thank you! You know I don't like that stuff."

Mary would laugh, but Helen suffered agonies of remorse. She hated to tell an untruth and she could hardly believe she was lying about milk pudding.

Adaptations

As Annie lost strength and became unable to stand, problems arose at bedtime when she was tired and had less control of her legs. When the time came that she could no longer stand at all, how was she to shift from the wheelchair to the bed, which was high in relation to the wheelchair?

The first time that she found that her legs would not support her, she just slithered off the chair and landed quite gently on the floor. Bruce was there that night and was strong enough to lift her up on to the high bed. The next night Mary and Helen managed it together, but it was not easy. Annie was still very thin, but she was tall, her legs were long and she was unable to make herself compact in order to help the lifters. Mary tut-tut-ed several times and everyone was breathless and rather cross by the time Annie was in bed.

The following night Helen was on her own and she struggled for ten minutes, trying to get her mother high enough to push her on to the mattress.

"Stop now, pet. We both need a rest and I think it's hopeless. The best thing is for you to make me comfy on the floor. You could bring the couch cushions through and I would be fine."

"I don't think so! I'm not going to sleep in a comfy bed with you on the floor. Maybe I could pull the whole mattress down on to the floor?"

"It's pretty big and heavy too. I would be fine on the cushions."

"I don't think so. Let's try again. I feel stronger now."

Whether Helen had discovered new strength or a more scientific method, or perhaps it was sheer determination, she managed to hoist her mother up and push her on to the bed, then fall on top of her laughing.

"We'll need to think of some other way to do it." Annie laughed too, but was appalled that her daughter should have this sort of responsibility last thing at night. She lay all that night thinking about it.

The next day was Saturday and as soon as she was up, Annie said,

"Right we're going to try an experiment while we're still strong and fresh. Bring that fancy box that your father gave you for Christmas."

Helen ran off to the kitchen and came back with the present which she had never quite found a use for. It was about the size of a log box, fourteen inches high with a base of perhaps fourteen by twelve. It was covered in brown patterned velvet and the hinged lid was padded. It was a roughly made object, but sturdy.

"Now put the box against the bed and wheel me close up to it and hold the chair firmly. Now I'm going to slide off the chair and kneel on the box and lean across the bed as far as I can, then you've to take the chair away as swiftly as you can, then come and grab me quick before I topple off the box. Then you should be able to chuck me on to the bed more easily from that height. But don't shilly shally on the way because I'm not sure how long I can balance there on the box!"

It all worked perfectly, though it was exciting. Annie certainly did not seem very steady or safe for the few moments that she must balance on the box, while Helen pulled the chair away. But Helen moved speedily, then jumped to position herself with her left hand under Annie's ankles and her right hand under her knees. Then a very little hoist was all that was required to get Annie up and on to the bed.

"Gosh that was really easy, Mummy! How did you think it up?"

"Well, we had to find a better way than last night, didn't we. You were excellent at tossing me on to the bed, I must say. It was quite dangerous and exciting. Now go to the foot of the bed and give me your hand."

Annie was lying on her left side, facing the edge of the bed. She reached out her right arm,

"Now take my hand and give me a long strong pull up!"

Helen stood at the end of the bed and grabbing her mother's right hand in her own left, pulled Annie to her knees, then swiftly moved to the front of the bed in case of a fall. Annie swivelled round on her knees until she had her back to the edge of the bed with her feet sticking over the side.

"Now push the chair in and I'll just drop backwards into it again. There! That was easy! That's a problem well solved."

Helen had reached out to help, but Annie was able to grip the arms of the chair behind her and lever herself backwards into it. She landed with a little grunt.

Helen laughed with pleasure,

"I can't believe how easy that was! It was like a little dance. Did you work that all out in your head last night? You're so clever."

"Well you're pretty smart yourself. You got the hang of it immediately and you knew just how much strength to put into your 'long strong pull'. I feel a lot better now that I'm more independent. It was a bit like a dance, wasn't it. It went so smoothly. That's because we worked in unison!"

"And we've made use of that box that Daddy gave me. It's been lying there doing nothing for ages. Now it's come in really handy."

The box was not a beautiful object and had come in for a fair bit of criticism.

"True. And the next thing is to teach Jessie our new method. She might not be just as nippy as you are, she's got a bit more poundage to shift, but she's very strong. I'm sure she'll be fine. I'll ask her to come back on Monday afternoon for a demonstration and she can bring George with her. He's such a wee entertainment."

Helen was always glad to see that splendid and enormous baby.

There was another adaptation that Annie must deal with. The bathroom was too narrow for the wheelchair and, as she could no longer walk, a baby's enamel pot was now kept in the bedroom. It was even more important that she was able to get in and out of her chair easily with Helen's or Jessie's help.

This method of getting in and out of bed would be used by Annie and whoever was helping her, for practically the rest of her life.

One evening when Annie's mother and Bruce were both there, Mary said,

"Don't you think a bath would help you with your pain, Annie? I'm sure Bruce and I could manage you in and out. Think how nice it would be to relax in a nice warm bath. You would be pleased to help with that wouldn't you, Bruce?"

"Oh, yes certainly, Mrs Mackay. If Annie thinks it would help her. I could arrange to come some night when I'm not too busy."

"What on earth would you be busy doing in the evening, Bruce?" Mary looked indignantly at her son-in-law, but Annie hastily intervened,

"I'm sure that's very kind of you both and it might make me feel a bit better. But you know Jessie gives me a thorough wash down every morning and I really think it would be an almighty struggle to get me into a bath and even worse to get me out. And Helen would need to put the kitchen fire on as soon as she got home from school to get enough hot water, too."

"Oh, I can easy do that, Mummy. I'm getting good at lighting fires."

Although Helen made the offer, she did not think the bath was a good idea.

She was more in touch with the realities of her mother's physical condition than the two adults. She knew how Annie must be propped with pillows in order to sit up in bed and even then she would slowly slip down. How could she sit up properly in the bath? She might just kneel of course, but then it would be hard to lift her out. However she said nothing. What dismayed her most was the loss of her mother's modesty and dignity. She hated the idea of people struggling to lift her mother while she was naked and vulnerable.

The idea was talked of and eventually implemented after two or three weeks, but as Helen had feared, it was not a success and was never repeated.

The Last Portrait

"There's a present for you!"

With a quiet look of triumph, Mary handed a lumpy parcel to her daughter.

"What on earth is it, Maw?"

"Open it and see!"

"Butter! Goodness, I never thought I'd see such a big lump of butter in my life again. Where did you get it? Not the black market, surely. I don't want to read about famous artist's wife jailed for profiteering... where did it come from? It's lovely butter, quite fresh."

Annie had sampled a small corner .

"Well I don't know whether you would call it the black market or not. There must be nearly a pound of it there and I have almost as much at home."

"Here, take it away from me before I eat any more. It is lovely butter. It's a treasure! But where did you get it?"

"I'll just put it away in the kitchen just now, the fire's so hot in here."

"The suspense is killing me!" Annie shouted after her mother, as she left the room, but Mary Mackay loved to be dramatic and mysterious and was happy to prolong the moment of mystery.

Annie determined to say no more and Mary came back and settled herself at the fire, then lit a cigarette before she started her story.

"You've heard me speak of Mrs Rayner at the whist drive, haven't you? Well I've found out what she does. She runs a canteen for the workers down near the shipyards. She was talking the other night about it. It was marvellous to hear her describe the immense pots of soup and stew she makes and the stones of potatoes that are peeled. Then gallons of semolina and vast boiled jammy dumplings. She has people to work for her, of course, but she seems to do a lot of it herself. She's so fat and wheezy too. She seems to have a problem with her throat. Her voice is constricted somehow. I don't know how she manages at all. Anyway I must have mentioned at some time or other that you never ate margarine on your bread, once the butter ration was finished and that seemed to affect her. She kept saying how sad that was, you 'being in a wheelchair and all'. Then last night she slipped me these two parcels, one for you and one for me. That was very kind of her, wasn't it. She wouldn't take any money either."

"It was very generous, indeed. We'll need to give her something. Maybe I could make a cake?"

"Well I think it would be coals to Newcastle when she lives in the middle of such plenty. You might make her a pair of gloves, though. You never know, perhaps she'll bring us something more another time."

"I know what I'm going to do tomorrow. I'm going to make myself some soda scones and have them with thick butter."

"Sounds delicious! I'm coming over to play cards with Mrs Carson round the corner tomorrow night, so I'll be in to collect my share. That'll make your father's eyes sparkle too."

The two women laughed together and Annie thought what good company her mother could be, when she was in the right mood.

"Talking of your father, he's got that commission that we hoped for!"

"That's wonderful. He'll be pleased. Is it a beautiful young girl or an ugly old man?"

"The latter I'm afraid, but he's a successful Glasgow business-man, so the money's fine and I know your father is pleased to be asked. I just worry that it's maybe too much for him. I see him failing, you know."

"Surely not, he was painting away fine last summer."

"Yes but his chest's been pretty rotten all winter. He will keep taking those damned Do-do pills and I don't think they agree with him."

"But they're supposed to help him! I don't suppose they can do him any harm, can they?"

"I don't know, but I hate the name, just always makes me think of 'dead as a dodo'."

"Yes, it's an unfortunate name, but p'raps if my father thinks they're doing him good, that's all that matters."

"Yes, you've said that before, but I can't agree. I just loathe that name. And I hope he has the strength to paint the portrait. This man is a leather manufacturer and seems to be very wealthy."

"Well that's always good to know."

The Food Office

Unsworth was the name of the neighbours who lived in the other ground floor flat in their close. Mr Unsworth had been very helpful at Christmas on their first night back in Glasgow. He had used his stirrup pump to good effect when the bedroom fireplace had caught fire, leaving little for the five enormous firemen to do when they arrived.

Mrs Unsworth had dropped in two or three times since then to visit Annie. Helen had not liked her much that first night, nor did she care for what she heard of her now.

"She sounds a bit girny, Mummy. She's not going to cheer you up much, if all she talks about are her problems. D'ye remember Mrs Walton that used to live there? I really liked her and all her family too, they were so nice and friendly. I wish they were still here instead of Mrs Unsworth"

"Yes I was very fond of them. I wonder where they are now? But poor Mrs Unsworth, maybe I make her sound worse than she is. I'm sorry for her, she's had a lot of trouble. It must be awful to lose a son in the war. He was only twenty-two, just ten years older than you are. Then her daughter in London doesn't seem to write to her much. She was bombed out so I expect she has plenty to struggle with, but a mother worries and gets lonely. Then her own health seems bad. She has some problem I've never heard of before, where her skin flakes off."

"That sounds terrible!"

"She says sometimes the bed is as if it's full of cornflakes!"

"Ooh! *Horrible!* I can't believe that. Does she look all right?"

"Yes she looks fine. Her face and hands are smooth. And I don't know why but she does seem to have an unfortunate number of bad encounters with shop assistants and tradesmen. Everyone she meets seems to be cheeky or dishonest."

"That's pretty peculiar."

Helen had not found anything but kindness in the shops and had a very good relationship with Milly, the young woman in the grocer's. Milly was blonde and pretty and very helpful about prices and amounts. She had taken a great fancy to the twelve year-old girl who did all the shopping and seemed to have complete charge of the household purse. Milly would point out any bargain or unusual treat and sometimes she slipped an illegal half pound of margarine into Helen's basket. The child had learned a lot from Milly and had been saved once or twice from making shopping blunders. Then the butcher, who remembered her as a very little girl before the war, was also friendly and always asked how her mother was and teased her about her long plaits. The lady in the dairy was pretty nice too, although the newsagent and the Post Office staff were snappy and abrupt, but then they seemed to be terribly busy, with all those newspapers to write names on all the and forms to fill in.

An idea struck Helen,

"Perhaps they don't like the way Mrs Unsworth speaks. I don't like it."

"D'ye mean her English accent? She can't help that. I expect she doesn't much like the way we speak, either. That wouldn't be nice or sensible to dislike someone just because of their accent."

Helen was all too aware of how speech can alienate people, for her years in Pittenweem had been hard partly because her speech was so different from the local accent. It had never occurred to her to try to change the way she spoke, nor had she ever confided her problems to her mother, but she remembered how she had been jeered at and ridiculed.

"She doesn't speak like they do on the wireless."

"No, I don't know if any ordinary people speak like that! But I suppose that's a posh London voice that the announcers on the wireless have and Mrs Unsworth comes from the middle of England. You know how the folk in Fife speak differently from Glasgow folk. It's the same in England, lots and lots of different accents in different parts of the country."

"I suppose so."

"Perhaps she's unfortunate in the shops she chooses?"

"Anyway I don't think it's just her accent, I think it's the way she says things, as though she knew better than you did and you weren't as clever or important as she is."

"Maybe you're right, my love, she does seem a bit superior sometimes. But really I think she's a sad wee woman. Perhaps I can cheer her up with some of Jessie's daft stories and she can certainly make me feel that my problems aren't the worst in the world. It's nice to have someone drop in now and again and she offered to shop in town for me if there was anything I needed."

"I don't like that skin flaking thing she has, it sounds so awful. I hope it's not catching. It couldn't be anything like...," Helen paused, for it seemed too terrible to say it, then whispered "... leprosy ... could it?"

Helen could hardly say the word, for in films and books, leprosy was the ultimate and most feared affliction. It was represented as highly contagious and incurable, final and fatal. To suffer from it separated you from the rest of society. There was no treatment and slowly parts of the body disintegrated or fell off.

Annie smiled reassurdingly,

"Oh, no, no, my darling. Nothing like leprosy. I wish I could remember what it was that she called it. Never heard the name before, but it's certainly nothing to be frightened for and we couldn't possibly catch it. Don't worry!"

Annie changed the subject quickly.

"One thing she was saying that I didn't know, was that schoolchildren are allowed extra clothing coupons for their growth. We'd better see about that, for the way you're stretching upwards, you'll need new clothes when the summer comes. Perhaps you could find out about it in the Post Office."

Helen's heart dropped. She hated going to the Post Office. There were two ladies there, an old one with a moustache and a young one that seldom stopped talking to other people as she served you. In fact the young one had twice made mistakes, giving Helen a postal order for the wrong amount one time and giving her wrong change at another. Helen felt stupid for she had not noticed the change at the time and so had lost a shilling. After that she started to pay a lot more attention when change was counted out into her hand. A shilling was certainly too much to lose!

When Helen screwed up enough courage to enquire about extra clothing coupons, she found that it was necessary to go the main Food Office in the Candleriggs to apply for them. What a strange name and where was it?

Glasgow's geography was still very hazy to the child and even Annie was not very familiar with that part of town.

"It's downtown certainly, I'm pretty sure." Annie said.

Where was downtown? Near Charing Cross perhaps where her school was and her grandmother lived? No, further downtown.

Near Coplands, perhaps? That was within walking distance of Charing Cross and familiar to her, but no, Candleriggs was much further downtown. Did she remember going to the 'Poly'? Oh yes, when she was a very little girl. Lewis's Polytechnic was an enormous exciting store with moving staircases and a zoo on the top floor. She remembered it very clearly, but she had no idea where it was. In those days she had just trotted along, holding the hand of an adult who knew where to go and she went where she was taken, like a little dog. Now she must set off all by herself into the city and find the Candleriggs which was even further away than the 'Poly'. It was very daunting. Most worrying was that no one seemed able to say exactly where the Candleriggs was. Her father certainly tried to explain and talked of the High Street, Argyle Street and the Trongate but Helen knew none of these places.

Mary Mackay was there that evening and at the mention of those familiar places she interrupted him.

"Oh Bruce! Maybe it's near where the Panoptican used to be? John and I went there quite often. It was a bit of a dump, but we saw some really good shows there, with people that became well-known afterwards."

She started to laugh, then shook her head and made an effort to control her mirth before she continued. "One time we were there with you, Annie, when you were just a wee bit thing, maybe twenty months or so. We were bang in the middle of the front row and you were sitting on my knee when a big fat man started to sing in the deepest voice you can imagine, it was coming right from the soles of his boots. He was singing "Asle-e-e-p on the De-e-p" and as he sang lower and lower, you suddenly shouted out "DON'T!". You had an awful clear wee voice and the audience roared with laughter and the orchestra all collapsed into giggles and couldn't play another note. The poor man had to leave the stage. What a furious look he gave us."

Bruce waited patiently while his mother-in-law told her story, but he did not smile and started to speak as soon as she had finished.

"Now you'll pass Stockwell Street and there's one or two streets after that before the Candleriggs, can't just remember the names, anyway, but don't ye cross the road there, or ye'll be heading down the Saltmarket."

Mary Mackay again broke in with a laugh,

"I used to wonder at my mother when she said 'all the comforts o' the Sa'tmarket'. It seemed to be such a terrible slum when I was a girl, just about the worst place in the town. I suppose it might have been swell at one time or other long ago, or perhaps she was being ironic, I don't know."

Bruce looked displeased, but again waited till she had finished.

"Now, Tuppenny, if you get to Albion Street, you've gone too far, The next thing ye know, ye'll be away along the Gallowgate and reach the works and I'd certainly be glad to see you and give ye a cup of coffee, but you won't find the Food Office there."

He laughed loudly at his own nonsense. Annie could see the puzzled look on Helen's face.

"Just try to tell her where to go, Bruce rather than the places that she's not to go. Where is it after Albion Street?"

"No, no ye'll mix the wee lass up. She shouldnae go as far as Albion Street."

"She's to walk east along Argyle Street past the Poly or better call it Lewis's because that's the name she'll see outside, nobody calls it the Poly now, I don't think. You'll recognise it when you see it Helen, I'm sure. A great big grey building on the right as you're walking along. Then she's to watch out for Albion Street on the left, is that it, Bruce?"

"No, no Candleriggs is before Albion. I'm pretty sure it is anyway. Never really walking around there myself, just driving past. The Food Office is a big building, too, though. You can't miss it, Tuppenny. Ye'll be fine."

Helen was not so confident and she was now thoroughly confused. What's more she was bored and had stopped even trying to listen or visualise the place that she must find all by herself.

Friday afternoon was a sports afternoon and as Helen did not play hockey, she could go into town that day

Helen had gone several times with her mother to the Anstruther Food Office in Fife. It was in a church hall and very easy to find, with one big wooden counter and two women in charge. The Glasgow office was very different. It was enormous when Helen finally found it. She had walked and walked along Argyle Street, passing Lewis's and looking at all the street names. Fortunately Candleriggs had not been difficult to find at all and she was quite enjoying herself, but her courage drained away

when she entered the vast hall. It was daunting, with many different counters and queues of people at every one. The place was
noisy and smelled stuffy and horrible and Helen had a strong
desire to walk out and go home.

She wandered amongst the people looking in vain for some
notice that might advise her which counter she must stand at. She
passed a man who seemed very angry and was shouting at the
official who was dealing with him. It seemed as though a fight
could break out and she ducked off in a different direction.

Who could she ask?

She decided to join one of the shorter queues and hope for the
best. The last person in line looked very old and very poor and
very sad. Helen was too shy to ask her if that was the right queue
for schoolchildren's extra clothing coupons. This line was slow-
moving and other queues seemed to be shuffling along much
faster. When the clerk left the counter for the third time to go and
ask about something, they all stood there motionless, as though
rooted to the spot. Helen looked at a large stain on the front of the
counter beside her. She had noticed it before and knew she had
been standing there for ages and had not moved an inch in ten
minutes The clerk returned and shook his head sadly and an old
bent man walked slowly away, stuffing papers in his pocket.
Helen suddenly realised that everyone in this queue was pretty
old. Surely none of these defeated old people had any schoolchildren in their lives. She decided to join another queue. That had
been a waste of time. She left that counter and walked further into
the big noisy hall. There were plenty of counters to choose from,
none with any explanatory notice that she could see, and all with
many people standing waiting, waiting, some more patiently than
others. She really should ask someone, but could not make up her
mind to speak to a stranger. Helen picked another queue at ran-
dom. She counted fifteen people standing ahead of her, *fifteen*, but
they were moving forward quite fast. When she was just three
from the head of the queue, again some problem arose and this
clerk went off too. He completely disappeared and was away a
very long time. Lots of folk had joined on behind Helen and the
queue was becoming so long that it was entangled with other
queues. With no one at the counter to serve them, the waiting
crowd started to grumble and complain. The murmurs grew
louder and louder and other clerks were looking over nervously.

"Where the hell has yon chap got tae, noo?"

"He's findin' oot aboot sumpin'."

"Ye'd think they'd know thur joab better'n that."

"He's jist went away an' left us."

"Is thur no' somebody in authority tae help us?"

"Jist left uz on wur onio."

"Disgraceful, so it is."

"Ye'd think we'd nuthin' else tae dae."

"Ah'm fair fed up hingin' aboot in queues a' day."

"An' Ah'm needin' tae catch the butcher afore he shuts."

"Ma boss'll be kickin' up stink if Ah'm no back soon."

"It's a bluddy shame, so it is, keepin' us standin' here."

"Ach well, ye know thur's a war oan."

This well-used phrase seemed to dissipate the disgruntlement and most folk smiled sheepishly, shrugging and mumbling 'Aye, aye' and nodding their heads or raising their eyes to heaven.

The clerk was never to reappear, but at last a senior official with an abrupt and irritable manner bustled up and took over. He dealt quickly with each person. When it was Helen's turn, he asked her to repeat what she was saying twice, leaning over the counter and lowering his thick black eyebrows. His intimidating expression scared Helen's small voice back into her throat.

"Extra clothing coupons! Is that what you're after? This is the wrong counter you've come to. Look! Over there by the wall, there's a notice on the counter, if you can read. NEXT please"

Helen felt thoroughly snubbed and joined yet another long queue. There was a little card on this counter that said 'extra clothing coupons for schoolchildren' but it was small and badly written in pencil and she felt she might have hunted all day for it and missed it. She wished she could go and tell that rude man about what a useless card it was, placed where no one could see it. She wished she could just go home.

When she finally reached the head of that queue, the lady was very nice, but was sorry to tell her that she had not all the required documents. Her identity card was necessary and she had not brought it. It took all Helen's grit and pride to avoid weeping. The fact that the lady was so kind and regretful after the horrible man, made it even more difficult. Helen managed to get out into the street before she wiped away a few tears.

She would just have to come back again next week.

Tennis and New Friends

When the Easter holidays finished, tennis replaced hockey as the Friday afternoon sport and Helen was keen to try playing it. Both her parents had been good players and she was pretty sure that was how they had met each other. Bruce took her to Lumleys sports shop on the Saturday and bought a racquet and tennis balls and also a very smart, divided skirt in navy wool. The lady had advised Bruce about the necessity for this garment and while Helen was not sure it was quite suitable, for it seemed too heavy and warm for running about, she was willing to be persuaded. It fitted beautifully, with deep pleats disguising the fact that it was divided. It was such a nice surprise to have this unexpected gift. Bruce had cleverly brought the clothing coupons with him, just in case. He could be very generous to his daughter and especially when an attractive assistant was encouraging him.

The playing fields were at Kirklee, which was a twenty minute tram journey from the school. Unfortunately Khirstine lived in Newton Mearns which was right on the other side of the city and she had decided not to play tennis. Travelling the extra distance made her day too long and she would probably join a tennis club closer to her home. Helen would have liked Khirstine's company and felt awkward and alone. Some girls were already good players and they went on the courts first of all, while the others were given a lesson in 'serving'. Helen loved it and felt she could be quite good, if she could just hit the ball a bit harder. She determined to practise. There was no chance of practising on the courts for any length of time as other girls were waiting anxiously for their turn. The teacher organised a game of basketball for the girls who were waiting, but this was unsatisfactory, for as soon as a court was available part of the team would dash off to play tennis. Helen did have ten minutes on the court and found returning balls across the net much more difficult than she had thought it would be. As the four girls were all beginners, it was not a proper game and there was a lot of giggling and running about retrieving balls. At three o'clock it started to rain and everyone huddled in the small changing room for twenty minutes until the teachers dismissed them.

It was less than a mile for Helen to walk home and everything smelled fresh and pleasant after the rain. New leaves were just beginning to burst out on the trees that lined the roads. She walked past large West End mansions, now mostly divided into service flats. They were shabby but still elegant and spoke of the wealth that had existed forty and fifty years ago. Many gardens had large brightly flowering bushes. Helen felt very happy, although she could hardly say that she had learned much about the game of tennis. She had forgotten about her new navy skirt while she was playing, but now it started to feel very heavy and much too warm as she walked briskly along.

She did intend to practise serving.

How she had missed Khirstine.

That night at bedtime she was surprised to see that the inside of her thighs were bright red and as she lay in bed, the skin became almost unbearably hot and itchy. She got up and showed her mother who explained that the cloth of her divided skirt must have 'burned' her.

"You were just running around so much that the woollen material has rubbed and irritated your skin. Go and put a cold wet cloth on the red bits for a while, then just pat it dry gently with the towel and put some talcum powder on it. What a shame, your nice new skirt."

Inwardly Annie was thinking that Bruce was so unfortunate. So often when he did a good turn, something went wrong. It seemed as if Fate were against him.

Helen did not sleep for a long time with the discomfort. She had never heard of cloth 'burning' your skin. It seemed very strange. She knew she would never wear that skirt again, which was a pity because she had looked so smart in it. Unfairly, she felt angry with her father for buying it. It was a waste of money and a waste of clothing coupons. As so often happened she was fully aware that she was being unfair to her father and made up her mind that he would never learn what a disaster it had been.

"We won't tell Daddy about the skirt burning me, will we?"

"No, I don't suppose that would do any good and it would make him feel bad."

"He spent a lot of money in Lumleys."

"Did he?"

"Yes, the racquet was nearly two pounds, then there were the balls and the racquet press and the skirt. Nearly six pounds altogether!"

"I expect he could afford it all right."

"I hope so."

"Don't worrry, if he can afford to smoke as many cigarettes as he does and drink a fair amount of whisky, I should think he'd manage to pay for some extras for his wee girl."

There was a bitter tinge to Annie's words. Their monthly allowance to cover housekeeping and Jessie's wages was only slightly over five pounds.

◊

Helen found that she could play perfectly well in a summer skirt from last year and each afternoon after school, she practised her service in the lane that ran from Clarence Drive to Queensborough Gardens. This rough and rutted lane separated the back greens of the Lauderdale Garden tenements from those in Polwarth Street. It was hardly ideal terrain for tennis practice, but it was quiet and handy. The only vehicle to use the lane was the bin lorry which serviced the back court middens and it came in the middle of the night. Bruce parked his car in the lane when he visited, but there were no other car owners in the whole block of tenements.

This large rectangular space in the centre of the tenements was strangely neglected. The sun only reached it in the height of summer and little grass grew in the damp, soot-sodden earth. Only one or two stunted trees had struggled to establish themselves. Not even weeds thrived. The wash houses were unused and derelict and only a few brave housewives hung out their laundry to dry. The bin shelters held old battered metal rubbish bins, filled mainly with ashes and vegetable peelings which started to smell as the weather became warmer. Yet there was a fascination for children in these large quiet spaces behind the tenements. It was pleasant to wander there. The rumble of trams and buses was distant and there were few grown-ups to warn against climbing walls or squeezing through the few bent railings that were left. Helen was familiar with all the lanes in Hyndland. One never knew what one might find, a friendly cat or a tiny magical garden that some keen horticulturalist had created in spite of the drawbacks.

There was one sinister feature in Helen's own lane, which always struck her when she returned from a walk. A complete tenement in Polwarth Street had been demolished by a landmine in 1941, at the time of the Clydebank blitz, leaving a gaping hole in the rampart of buildings. Helen thought the bomb site looked like a gap where an enormous tooth had been pulled out.

Forunately no lives had been lost, as the bomb had not detonated until the following day and everyone in the immediate area had been warned from their houses. Helen had been in Pittenweem at the time, but she knew the story well. Their neighbour at that time, Mrs Walton, had told how her daughter had come home very late from work and slept at home unaware that all the flats around were empty. When she had gone out in the morning, an air raid warden had exclaimed when he saw her,

"Where the HELL have you been? There's an unexploded bomb up the road!"

It was lunchtime before the bomb exploded and wiped out eight flats with all their furniture and the special small possessions which make a home.

Helen never passed this bomb site without thinking of Mrs Walton and the story of her daughter. She missed that friendly family. It would have been so nice for her mother to have them still next door.

Helen often tried to imagine how you would feel to lose everything in your life like that. All your clothes, books and toys. All the big things and every little unimportant thing, how terrible it would be never to see them again. She knew she would keep thinking about them ... her mother's special teaspoons that were round and unlike any other teaspoons she had ever seen, or the sitting room carpet where she had created games on the pattern, or the grandfather clock where she had made secret chalk marks inside, showing the distance that the weight descended each day of the week. Or, worst horror of all, what if her doll Topsy had been blown up! It made Helen shiver to think of that. Although she was twelve and too grown-up now to play with dolls, her brown velvet darling still held a special place in her heart. She had made some clothes for her and had many plans for splendid doll outfits. Anyway it was a mock terror to consider the loss of Topsy, for Helen knew that, if told to leave her house, she would have grabbed her doll first thing.

As there was no one to return Helen's tennis ball, she did a lot of running up and down the lane and had no practice in any aspect of playing tennis except serving. In this one area she became very proficient and on Friday afternoons found partners easily, because of her demon serve. Unfortunately she had little to contribute to the rest of the game. Apart from Fridays, she did not play a proper game and if it were wet that day, the visit to Kirklee was cancelled. She felt that she would never improve until she played more often. In the meantime she continued serving along the lane to invisible opponents.

She met two new friends, Tom and Greta, because of her constant tennis practice.

Greta wandered along the lane one Saturday afternoon and started speaking to Helen as though she had always known her.

"Would you like to go for a walk? What's your name? Why are you playing by yourself? Leave your bat and I'll show you a nice walk."

Helen was surprised and too polite to say no and deposited her stuff in the house before walking off with this strange girl.

Greta was thirteen and went to Hyndland Secondary school. She talked almost nonstop and there seemed an illogicality about her conversation. She jumped from subject to subject, giving unlikely little bits of information about herself, asking many questions, but seldom waiting for the answers. Almost immediately, Helen regretted having accepted the invitation to join her, but she was a kind child and felt she must now make the best of it. It looked as though she would not have to contribute much to the conversation. Occasionally Greta asked a question and immediately demanded the answer. As Helen had stopped giving her keen attention to the continuous chatter, her pause before answering would make Greta quite irritable. Also Helen was slow to answer because often she did not quite understand the question. Sometimes she was just surprised that after a ten minute monologue from Greta, she should be expected to speak.

It was an uncomfortable walk up and down the lanes of Hyndland, past the dusty bins of ashes and potato peelings, while Greta talked interminably, pointing out another gap site where bombs had fallen behind Dudley Drive, listing the number of people killed. Sometimes they clambered over walls or railings to stand on washhouse roofs and jump down onto midden roofs. Helen enjoyed that, for climbing was more to her taste.

As they walked, Helen became aware of the conversation returning frequently to some strange man that they might see. Greta sometimes called him a 'funny man' sometimes a 'bad man'. Helen tried to find out what she meant, but all that Greta would say was,

"We would run away if we saw him, run like hell."

Then she looked at Helen to see if she might be shocked at this word, but Helen hardly noticed it. She often swore to herself. She was more curious to find out what sort of bad man Greta was talking about.

The walk did not take them to any unfamiliar parts of the area. Helen knew every corner.

Eventually as the 'bad man' recurred again and again in Greta's talk, Helen became uncomfortably aware that they were in fact searching for this man, perhaps hunting for him! At that point she decided to act as irrationally as the girl did. Throwing good manners to the wind, she interrupted her companion in the middle of a sentence,

"Got to go home now and cook the dinner. Cheerio, Greta." And she ran off down Falkland Lane as fast as she could go.

Helen was determined that she would have nothing more to do with such a boring and strange girl, but it was not easy, for whenever Helen was practising tennis, Greta would wander along and start to talk and just would not go away. Helen's only recourse was leave Greta abruptly, announcing over her shoulder that she was going into her house now to help her mother. She was certainly not going walking with that girl again.

One day when Greta said,

"Can I come in and meet your Mum and see her wheelchair?" Helen was unable to summon enough rudeness to say no.

Besides, she knew her mother was curious to meet this girl who had become the bane of Helen's existence.

Greta was much more forthcoming with Annie and told her about the bad man who took little girls away and gave them sweeties and then undid his trousers. Expressionless, Annie listened to it all while Helen sat aghast, her mouth open in astonishment. Greta had never told her anything like that!! Fancy telling her mother all about it. What would her mother think?

Then Greta stood up and leaning close to Annie's ear, whispered something to her. Helen was dumbfounded. Her mother's expression did not change and she said,

"Is that so?"

"It's really true!"

"And have you seen this man yourself, Greta?"

"Oh no, but he's there nearly every day."

"Well I wouldn't worry about him too much, he sounds a poor soul. But never talk to any strange man you don't know, of course. That wouldn't be very sensible, would it? Now Greta, it's been very nice to meet you, but I am feeling rather tired now and I want to rest, so perhaps you'd better trot home. Your mother will be wondering where you are."

Helen quickly took Greta to the door and said goodbye.

"That was so clever, the way you got her to go, quite politely. I'm always rude to her. You're not really tired are you, Mummy?"

"Heavens no, but there was no getting rid of that girl without a bit of a shove. Sometimes it's quite handy to be an invalid, isn't it! I see what you mean about her. Poor thing, she's not very bright, is she? A bit simple really. Not someone you'd want to see a lot of."

"Definitely not. I wish Khirstine lived nearer. It would be lovely to see her at weekends."

"I was thinking maybe you would like to ask her and her mother over for their tea, some Saturday?"

"Oh d'you think they would come? That would be lovely. I would love to have Khirstine here."

"Well, we'll do that then. I'll write a wee letter to Mrs Thomson."

Annie thought it would be nice for her to spend time with this other mother. They could talk about their daughters. It was more than ten weeks since she had been out of the house and she felt that she would love to see a new face. She also decided to write to her old friend Nancy Little and invite her over sometime. Although they had never been special friends, she and Nancy had been part of the same crowd and had gone to High School and Art School together. It was a shame that her close friend from student days, Elsie, had moved to London. How nice it would have been to have a sewing bee each week as they had in the long ago, when they and the century were both in their twenties. It made Annie feel quite old to think of the changes that she had seen in the last twenty years. And yet at forty-two she was not old yet. Somewhat dilapidated, she thought ruefully, but she might have a few adventures yet, even though she was stuck in this chair. She could still think of things to brighten up Helen's life. The idea of a visit from the Thomsons had obviously delighted her daughter. She would think up a specially nice meal.

◊

Ten-year old Tom, Helen's other new friend, lived in a top flat in Lauderdale Gardens and his kitchen window overlooked the lane where Helen practised her serve so assiduously.

After looking down at her practising for three weeks, Tom, an enterprising boy, walked along the lane and smiled to her as he passed. Her reaction was not encouraging. Pittenweem experience had taught her that boys were usually rough and rude and best ignored. And she could see that this boy was younger than she was.

Ten minutes later he walked back and said "Hullo". Helen nodded and grunted and served another ball.

The following day he appeared again and ran to pick up the three balls that she had sent along the lane. She smiled politely, but not too enthusiastically, as she took them from him. Her experience with Greta had made her wary. Before serving again, she waited for him to walk away, but he stood still. He had screwed up his courage to talk and he could not have chosen a more fascinating subject.

"We've got a cat called Lucky and she's going to have kittens soon. Would you like to come and see them when they're born?"

Helen's eyes lit up and she relaxed her racquet arm and beamed at this boy. Of course she would like to come and see kittens!

Then Tom told the dramatic story of the accident that had happened to Lucky the last time she was expecting kittens. She had fallen from the kitchen window sill! Fallen three storeys to the ground and yet she had three lovely kittens the next day and they were all fine. What a wonderful cat! She certainly had the right name too. Would Helen like to come and see Lucky now and meet Tom's mum? She had a very fat tummy, the cat did, not his Mum. His mum had made ginger biscuits that morning and they were awful good.

This was irresistible and Helen dumped her tennis gear and went visiting in Lauderdale Gardens, where the biscuits were delicious and Tom's mum and the cat made a great fuss of Helen.

Tom was only ten, though 'nearly eleven' as he always reminded her and he was as tall as she was. He was certainly not material for that romantic encounter which Helen occasionaly dreamed about, but he was a really nice boy, although rather obssessed by planes. He often made her laugh. As far as Helen was concerned, their friendship was entirely platonic and would last until the summer holidays, when she moved to Fife with her mother and grandparents.

Tom suggested they go to the Saturday morning cinema at the Ascot together.

It was fun, but a very different experience for Helen from any previous cinema visit. It was so noisy and everyone was eating something. It became a regular Saturday outing.

There was usually a rather stupid adventure serial each week, and sometimes a short Western, then a cartoon and a film which was often about children. The film actress Jane Withers was in several of these films. She often played a horribly spoilt girl and played it very believably. Was she like that in real life, Helen wondered? By the end of the film, Jane's character was nearly always changed by the terrible things that had happened to her. Sometimes she was still unlikeable and finished up being spanked! That seemed very undignified to Helen. She thought she would need to be paid an awful lot of money to allow that to happen to her in public.

Sometimes Tom and Helen went scrambling around the wild places in Hyndland, finding wildflowers, climbing on walls and middens, speaking to stray cats and dogs, meeting other children who were following the same pursuits.

One Saturday afternoon Bruce took the two children to Byres Road for a glass of ginger beer in an Italian cafe. Helen liked that very much. It seemed to be what a daddy should do on a Saturday. Bruce did a lot of kidding and kept calling her friend Jim, but Tom seemed to enjoy it and just corrected him in a very loud voice, which made Bruce laugh even louder. In fact they were so noisy that other people in the cafe were looking at them. It was the first time that Helen had a faint inkling that her father might have enjoyed a son more than a daughter. This did not make her feel sad, it was just interesting and she promptly forgot about it until years later.

Of course her mother teased her about having a boyfriend and still in primary school. Nevertheless it was very nice to know some other child in the area. Khirstine lived so far away and the other girls in her class came from several different areas of Glasgow. There was no one who lived in or near Hyndland. She sometimes thought that it would have been more sensible for her to go to Hyndland Secondary School, which was just across the road. She would have been able to come home at lunchtime to help her mother and she would have known other children in the district. However her mother had wanted her to go to the more distinguished school, where she herself had gone. It was a bit posher and snobbier, Helen supposed.

Although Helen was quite interested in the opposite sex and the idea of romance, she did not feel quite ready for a boyfriend yet. Whatever Tom felt, Helen considered him only as a very nice companion, rather like a little brother. Khirstine had a little brother Bill, who said and did funny things, although he could be annoying too, his sister complained. Helen never found Tom really annoying, but Khirstine pointed out that it was different when you lived in the same house.

Almost as soon as they had made friends, Helen had been invited to Khirstine's house. It was quite an adventurous journey to Newton Mearns. First, Helen came into town by tram, getting off at Coplands, then she walked over Wellington Street and down the hill to Waterloo Street bus station. Khirstine had come into town specially to meet her and was waiting there. It seemed a long bus journey to Newton Mearns, but they had a really nice chat.

"What a long way you have to travel every day to school, Khirstine. I thought my journey was bad but it's nothing compared to yours. This long bus journey and then you've got to walk all the way uphill from the bus station to the school! Then up Garnethill! That's like two little mountains you climb every day. You must be really strong and fit but it must be horrible if it's windy and raining."

"Sometimes it is a bit miserable. I just have to do it, because that's the school Mummy wants me to go to."

Helen supposed that Khirstine's mummy must be a bit snobby too, just like her own mummy and they laughed about snobbish mothers.

Khirstine did not seem to let things worry her, but accepted life and made the best of it. She seemed to be calm and organised. That was one reason Helen liked her so much and felt she could always rely on her. Khirstine never grumbled or made unkind remarks as some other girls did.

Helen really liked Khirstine's house in Larchester Avenue. It was a bungalow with a large garden front and back. A dog and a cat greeted the girls enthusiastically when they arrived and Bill had two rabbits in a hutch that he took Helen to visit even before she took her coat off. There were also hens in the garden. How wonderful to have so many animals around!

Khirstine's mother was called Violet and was friendly and funny. Khirstine's dad was digging in the garden. It seemed to Helen like the sort of family that was described in books. She had always been searching for a real life family like this, but usually there were some imperfections.

"The poor hens are a bit bedraggled just now." Violet explained. "Last year we took them away with us when we went caravanning and we took wire netting and penned them under the caravan. They looked much better after their holiday and I expect we'll do the same again this year."

Helen tried to picture this scene. How had the hens travelled to the place where they parked the caravan? Inside the car or the caravan? She did not like to ask. Perhaps Violet was just making fun?

How relaxed the family seemed and pretty wealthy, too, for they had a fridge. No one else that Helen knew had such a luxury. When Violet opened up the fridge and brought out a jar of face cream, Helen was so astonished that she exclaimed,

"Fancy keeping your face cream in the fridge, Mrs Thomson!"

Violet laughed as she dabbed little dots of the cream all over her face, before smoothing it in. Pointing to the label on the jar, she asked,

"What does it call it? Cold Cream! So where else would I keep it?"

Helen felt slightly snubbed and still thought it was a strange place to store make-up.

There was a lovely tea of home-made mince pie and baked beans and Mr Thomson very kindly drove Helen all the way home again. Khirstine came too and Helen felt it had been a perfect day.

Bobby's Dog

S pring weather had arrived, then disappeared again. It was the end of April and as cold and gloomy as November. Dark rainclouds threatened, but never quite released the expected shower. Annie had noticed that this sort of weather was really bad for her. Her spirits and energy were as low as the heavy grey sky. Her hands were slightly swelled and her legs were repeatedly cramped with painful muscle spasms. Aspirins helped a little, but she was afraid of taking too many. The bottle advised that six a day was the maximum dosage and she stuck to that. Sometimes she watched the clock, longing for the time to arrive for her next two aspirin.

She knew that she might feel better if she did something more physical. Polish the brasses perhaps? But she hated the smell of Brasso. Perhaps she should have got Jessie to help her bake a cake, but Jessie was gone now and it all seemed too much effort. What else could she do? She felt listless and had no particular ideas to carry out. She felt she could not knit another stitch of Fair Isle for love nor money.

"I've just got no oomph today." She told herself.

She opened the built-in cupboard in the sitting room. There were various parcels and boxes that had not been looked at since before the war, probably. She could tidy it and perhaps there might be something of interest? But no, she could not face it and she shut the door again, before pushing herself over to the fire. She picked up the Daily Express which she had not looked at that day, but laid it down again. One glance at the headlines was enough. She really could not deal with the sadness and violence of the news. She wheeled herself to the window and amused herself watching the several people waiting at the tram stop. She recognised one or two that she saw regularly and had given them nicknames. One very smart little man she called the Boulevardier, for there was a touch of Paris in his good overcoat and jaunty hat. He marched very quickly up and down the street, doffing his hat and nodding, and his nod was almost a bow, to the various ladies that he met. He had now started to doff and nod up to Annie at her window. It was pleasant and friendly of him and she wondered what he would think of his nickname, if he knew.

How nice it would be when Helen arrived home. Only another hour or so to wait.

◊

Dinner was mince and potatoes that night, a favourite with Helen. The family tradition was to serve boiled rice with it and, when it was on the plate, to add curry powder and mix it all together. Helen had discovered that other families did not do this, but she loved it. After first eating the carrots in the mince, she mashed it all enthusiastically into an aromatic mound, patting it neatly with her fork. When she was little the mixture had been formed into the shape of a house in an effort to get her to eat. But that was far in the past and now she finished it up, always with the feeling that she could easily eat the same amount again. There was more in the kitchen but that would make a shepherd's pie for tomorrow.

They played cards after dinner, but it was plain that Annie was suffering.

"Your old Mum's a bit tired tonight. Would you feel lonely if I went to bed early?"

"No, of course I wouldn't mind, if you're tired. Are you awful sore too?" Helen was aware that her mother's legs were cramping more than usual, although Annie tried to suppress her frequent small grunts and gasps of pain.

"I'm feeling pretty rotten. I'll be fine tomorrow if I have a nice long lie down ."

"Do you want to go soon? It's only half past seven."

"Aye, I might as well go, I'm not up to much, But what will you do?"

"Oh I've got homework and there's my book to read."

Helen had recently discovered the pleasures of the 'Just William' series of books. She was able to borrow them from the small lending library in the newsagent's across the road. It was mostly well-thumbed murder mysteries and love novels that filled the shelves, but there was a small collection of children's fare, the Chalet School books and also several Tarzan adventures. Helen had eclectic tastes.

Annie was settled in bed and Helen had put more coal on the fire, when she heard the key in the front door. Her heart dropped.

It must be either daddy or grandma. They would go in and disturb her mother and she would have to make tea and there would be no peace to read with either of them talking nonstop.

It was Bruce and he had Sandy, the Forrester's spaniel, with him. The house was invaded by noise. The dog was straining to get off the leash, barking and panting, with its claws clipping and slipping on the linoleum.

"Mummy's just gone to bed. She's feeling awful sore tonight."

"She won't be sleeping yet, will she? I just popped in for a mo'. I brought wee Sandy out for a walk and I thought she might like a visit from him, he's such a grand wee friendly dog."

Helen's expression showed plainly what she thought of a visit from this fat, noisy dog. She followed her father into the bedroom.

"Well Annie, sorry to hear ye're not feeling too great tonight. Is there anything I can get you? Would a wee dram help?"

The words were shouted as the dog was off the lead now and racing round the room, barking.

Annie smiled and shook her head.

"No, thank you, Bruce. The aspirin will kick in soon and I'll feel better. What a dog that is. How do they stand the noise?"

"Oh he's just a wee bit excited. That's why I said I'd give him an outing, just walk him round the block. He's a rare wee fellow is Sandy."

"Looks as though a ten mile hike would do him good."

Just then the dog, inspite of its obesity, managed to scramble up on to the bed.

"Bruce! Get him off the bed."

Too late! The excited animal had peed on the quilt.

"Oh, my good eiderdown! Get him DOWN! That's horrible!"

Bruce had grabbed a towel from a chair and was scrubbing away at the silk quilt and the bedspread.

"That's it fine now, it was just a wee piddle. Fine an' dry now, ye'll never know the difference. Wee Sandy's just over excited. Never been in this house before have you, wee boy? Here we better get your lead on again, son."

Annie's face was dark.

"And I hope he'll never be in this house again."

Bruce continued the conversation for several minutes but found it heavy going. Annie was furious and silent.

"Well if you'll excuse me, I'll get away now. Bobby will be wondering where I've got to."

He put his hat on and turned to go.

"Bruce, what on earth's the matter with your hat?"

"Eh! What d'ye mean? What's wrong with it."

"What's happened to it? It's got a funny wee narrow brim!"

Bruce took it off and looked at it as though he had never seen a hat before.

"Aye, right enough, I'd left it in the hall and Sandy got at it and the wee bugger took a bite out the brim, just a nibble, but Peggy trimmed it up with a pair of scissors. Neatened it up, you know and she said it looked fine now. No one would notice. I think it's fine, is it not?"

He put it on and regarded himself in the triple mirror on the dressing table, leaning forward to look at his profile on each side and tilting his head.

"You'd better buy yourself a new one tomorrow, Bruce."

"Aye well, maybe you're right. It does look a bit skimpy. Och but it'll do me fine." He laughed heartily

"Bruce! Get yourself a new hat."

Bruce went off chuckling and Helen was pleased because her mother was laughing too and seemed to have forgotten about what the dog had done on the bed.

Helen decided that the homework could be looked at in the tram tomorrow and she still had an hour to read beside the glowing fire.

Horlicks

J essie had brought in a Glasgow Herald that day. She often went home with some small gift, perhaps some baking or a magazine, and she liked to return the generosity.

"Here, ye better get up tae date wi' the news, Missus Cornin'. It's the fourth of May an' things is hottin' up an' ye niver know, we'll mebbe get that bugger Adolf where he belongs. Sooner than ye think."

"Where does he belong, d'ye think? The madhouse?"

"NAW. He shud be in the jile, loacked up fur life!"

"Jail's too good for him. I should think he'll probably be executed, eventually."

"Is that right? Is that whit'll happen? Ah niver knew that." She sniffed," It's still too good fur'm, the bluddy wee bastard."

Annie smiled at her vehemence. She had noticed that although Jessie swore freely in her conversation, with bugger a favourite choice and often used in quite an affectionate way, the word bastard was a much more serious and damning epithet. Bastard was used sparingly and never lightly.

In half an hour, Annie was sitting in front of the sitting room fire with the newspaper, Though the leaves had burst their buds on the tree outside the window, it was still cold. She felt the cold much more than she used to. She realised she was hunching her shoulders and she tried to relax and did a few neck and arm exercises. Then she wriggled her toes and moved her legs as much as she could. Her knees were unwilling to straighten properly now, although there was still quite a bit of movement in them. She dreaded the idea of her knees being permanently bent but this now seemed increasingly likely as the tendons behind her knees stiffened.

A coffee was beside her on the table. She often felt that a whirlwind had seized her in one room and deposited her in the other, for Jessie was such a speedy worker, if a bit slapdash. From the kitchen came the sound of Jessie singing and banging her brush against the table and chair legs as she swept the floor. There were regular unexplained bangs and crashes. The pulley squeaked up and down. All Jessie's actions were vigorous and loud. Somehow Annie found the noisiness quite comforting. She knew that her mother would have hated it and constantly criticised the young woman. In fact Jessie would not have lasted a week with Mary Mackay. But Annie found her such a good-hearted, kindly, willing soul that she forgave her the loudness, quite enjoyed it in fact and was determined to overlook any breakages or damages. All these years she herself had been so damned careful of possessions, her own and other people's, and where had it got her?

She sighed as her eye travelled over the main newspage. She supposed she had better read it, but how violent and terrible it all was. Any of Jessie's small mishaps paled to such insignificance beside the destruction that was rife throughout the world just now.

AUSTRALIANS ADVANCE IN NEW GUINEA
US PACIFIC FLEET READY FOR JAPAN
GREAT ACTIVITY BY RAF BOMBERS
Frankfurt and Stuttgart attacked
30,000 BRITISH TROOPS EVACUATED FROM IMPHAL, CAPITAL OF THE MANIPUR STATE
unconfirmed report

What a terrible mess! All over the world! Everywhere across the globe. How was it ever to recover? Could it ever be the same again? How many human beings were in pain or dying at this very moment? How many were grieving for loved ones, lost forever. What sort of people planned and organised this mass killing and destruction? How could those in authority direct and arrange for people to kill and destroy other people? How could they justify the slaughter and still sleep at night? It did not bear thinking about. Not for the first time, she lectured herself on feeling depressed about her own situation. Here she was in a nice warm house with enough food and a comfortable chair to sit in and dear wee Helen and strong kindly Jessie to look after her and a husband who did his best and provided the necessary cash. Really she was very lucky. What right had she to complain about a few cramps and pains and being stuck in the chair?

Another article caught her eye,

SPECTACULAR BOMBING OF HAGUE BUILDING

Last night six mosquitoes swooped down on a house in The Hague, leaving it a blackened ruin after one of the most brilliant low-level precision attacks of the war ... British authorities received word secretly that the house stored thousands of documents of paramount importance to the Germans. The Second Tactical Airforce was asked to destroy the building and leave the nieghbours unscathed ...

Annie disliked the smug tone of this piece. They seemed to be gloating over the cleverness of this mission, but then there were all those other missions where no such care was taken and whole streets and their inhabitants were demolished. Anyway, she questioned if these pilots were really able to pinpoint just one building like that. And if they were, what would it be like to be a neighbour? Even if your home was not directly hit, she imagined the horror of six planes bombing the house next door. And then her scepticism took over and the phrase 'thousands of documents of paramount importance' made her laugh. Why were they there anyway? Did they really know which house they were in? Perhaps it was the house next door, that was so carefully left standing. Might even have been further down the street. And probably those documents were only important to some civil servant. They were probably just another piece of bureaucracy and might well have dealt with how much sausage meat was needed for the army in France or how many pairs of long drawers for the sailors in the North Sea. How could documents be important when people were being murdered? Perhaps there were no documents at all!

Then the word 'mosquitoes' caught her eye in another article but this time they were real insects.

The heading read,

NAZIS FLOOD PONTINE MARSHES

... besides utilising the floods as a protective barrier, Kesselring has heavily mined the Western approaches. Vast tracts of fertile land are now under water. Formerly this was one of the worst malarial plague spots in the world and mosquitoes are again breeding. Prisoners report a high incidence of malaria amongst some German units.

What a disastrous scene it painted. Farmers losing their fertile ground, other ground heavily mined and when would that be properly cleared? And now mosquitoes spreading malaria. The poor Germans. She could feel sorry for them, for no doubt they had wanted war as little as we had. Most of them could have had no idea how they would suffer in the war. They were just ordinary people trying to make a living from the land, which was now flooded and ruined.

Annie had no doubt that Germany would be defeated eventually and it all sounded as though big things would be happening very soon. Perhaps at last the war could come to an end, but how long would it take to clear up the mess?

She laid the paper aside and took up her knitting. The interminable gloves. Although the demand was tailing off now, of course, with the summer in sight. She felt that if she stopped knitting the gloves, she might never go back to them again. She would stockpile a few pairs for the autumn.

Jessie burst into the sitting room, as usual pushing the door open before she had quite turned the handle sufficiently

"Are ye comin' in tae peel they vegetables the now, hen? And did ye see any good news in that paper?"

"Not exactly good news, pretty horrible really, but I do think the end of the war must be in sight."

"Thank Goad fur that. Noo burl intae the kitchen an' stoor through they totties an' Ah'll gie this room the wance-over."

In the afternoon, when the house was quiet, Annie had another look at the paper and was relieved to find a paragraph that made her smile and had nothing to do with the war.

AMERICA'S CROONER OF THE MOMENT

... young Mr Sinatra is almost unknown here but in America ardent damsels send him neck-ties, while less ardent parties suggest he should be strangled by the gifts. The film "Higher And Higher" shows him to be an engaging natural youth with a fifth-class voice and no cinematic appearance at all ... although his singing leaves a vaguely pleasant impression. Whether or not Britannia will spend her coupons on neck-ties for Frank, only the future can tell.

Annie was sure that this newcomer would never oust her favourite, Bing Crosby.

◊

It was half past nine that night and the fire was burning low. Annie looked at the clock and said,.

"Don't think Bruce is going to show up tonight."

"It's not too late yet. D'ye want to go to bed soon? Are you feeling tired?"

"No, no, but I'll tell you what I'd like. I'd really love a nice cup of Horlicks, all frothy."

"I'd like that too, only not frothy."

Helen went into the kitchen with a feeling of reluctance, which she hoped her mother did not notice.

The Horlicks mixer was not her favourite gadget. It was a ten inch tall narrow metal container. Fitting closely into it was a metal rod, with a pierced disc fixed at one end and an unfixed lid at the other. The container was filled a third full of any milky drink, then with the lid put firmly in place, the plunger was vigorously pushed up and down for several minutes, resulting in much of the liquid being transformed to froth. Helen was not keen on the plunging process. It was hard work for something that seemed tasteless and useless to her. However, there were very few treats around and her mother enjoyed this and did not ask for it often. Helen liked her Horlicks made in an entirely different way and as she put the kettle on, she thought how nice it was that she could make her own just the way she liked it. And her way was much easier.

She put two heaped spoonfuls of Horlicks powder plus a few grains of salt into each mug, then added milk to this, mixing her mother's very thoroughly to a smooth paste, while gently stirring her own and allowing some lumps to form and remain in it. Hot water was then added to each cup and again she hardly moved the spoon in her own, allowing a nice crust of chewy bits to stay floating on the surface. The other cupful was thoroughly mixed before being poured into the metal tube. Then, taking time to fix the lid properly, which was not always easy, she started the labour that she dreaded. Up and down, up and down for ages, it seemed. It took a lot of effort. You could tell when it was finally ready because the noise changed.

Helen often used her imagination to make her chores more exciting. Her favourite subject at school was science and she would pretend that her work was in a laboratory rather than a kitchen. Tonight the pinch of salt was a significant addition of a rare chemical and was added with extreme care and the plunger was necessary to combine the ingredients of a new life-saving medicine.

Annie took her mug gratefully.

"That looks delicious, just what I was wanting! Thank you my darling." she laughed, "d'ye remember that night in St Andrews?"

"In the cafe, with the Horlicks that wouldn't cool down? And we had to catch the last bus and we couldn't drink it 'cos it just wouldn't cool, it was red hot..."

"It was like molten lava. How did they make it so hot? Yet we forced ourselves and our faces got redder and redder..."

"And you said we would just have to leave it... and I thought that was an awful waste."

"We did leave some of it in the end."

"Not much though. And we caught the bus. That was the night you were speaking to a young soldier in the seat in front of us."

"Oh yes, poor young fellow was only nineteen and trying to get to Kirkcaldy that night, but he had little chance, for the bus was only going to Leven. I was sorry for him."

"He was very handsome."

"How do you know? You seemed to be looking out the window all the time. In fact I thought you were asleep, for it was pitch dark and there was nothing to see."

"No, I was listening to what you were saying and I could see your reflection in the window and his too."

"So you had an eye for a handsome face even then, did you?"

"M-mm. And sometimes I just looked at my own reflection and thought what a funny nose I had and wished it wasn't so pointy."

"What a conceited wee thing! Anyway I think it's a very nice, pointy nose."

Skelmorlie

One morning towards the end of May, Jessie and Annie were in the kitchen. "Ah'm gaun doon the watter at the weekend, Mrs Cornin'."

"That's nice, Jessie. The weather's getting quite summery now. Where are you going?"

"Ah'm gaun in the train tae Skelmorlie, jist fur the day. Bella ma sister-in-law's goat a wee hoose, a nice wee flat it is an' I thought Ah'd take wee George an' show'm aff. Ah'm that proud o' the wee bugger."

She laughed self-consciously.

"Quite rightly so, he's a wonderful baby!"

"We wud get a breath o' sea air an' Ah wiz wunnerin' if wee Helen wud like tae come wi' uz. It wud be a wee treat fur her an' she cud help me cairry a' the stuff. Huz she iver been doon the Clyde? Mind you we'd be away early an' back late an' you'd need tae get yer mither tae come an' help ye, or mebbe Mr Cornin' would do it. Ah'm no' wantin' tae make things difficult, jist Ah thought the wee lassie might like a day oot at the seaside."

"Thank you. That's a very kind thought, Jessie. I'm sure Helen would love to spend a day with you and George. She's always talking about how clever he is. And we had a holiday in Millport at the beginning of the war and I know she loved it 'doon the watter'. I'd be delighted for you to take her away, but I'd need to see what other plans we could arrange. I suppose if the worst came to the worst, I could surely manage by myself..."

"Oh naw, Mrs Cornin', I wouldnae like you to be on yer lonesome the hale Setterday. Ah wouldnae enjoy masel, Ah'd feel bad, och, naw, naw, we couldnae leave a' by yersel'. Besides ye might pee yer drawers before we goat back."

They laughed.

It was arranged that Bruce would pop in during the morning and Mary Mackay would spend the afternoon here then leave early to give John his tea, before going to her usual whist drive at the Conservative club.

Annie would have been happy to spend more time on her own. The better weather suited her and she had been busy writing letters and tidying the sitting room cupboard.

◊

Helen waited until the tram passed the Kelvingrove Art Galleries, then got off at Radnor Street, which was a name she had always liked. It was a short street and she walked along it to Argyle Street then, turned left and continuing towards town, she passed the enormously tall tree that she glimpsed each morning on her journey to school. It seemed to be the only tree in Argyle Street and she wondered how it had grown alone there and if there had never been any other trees growing in the small patches of earth in front of the tenements. It was a very slender tree, as tall as the top flat. Helen wondered how healthy it was. What if it fell across the road one day and crushed buses and people? Her imagination of such a calamity made her quicken her pace as she passed it.

When she came to Kelvinhaugh Street where Jessie lived, she was very surprised at how wide the road was and how elegant the buildings looked. Because of Jessie's broad accent and uneducated grammar, Helen had relegated her in her mind to the group of 'poor people' who lived in small mean houses. She had read of these very small houses. Old Mrs Kelly, who washed the close and the front stairs each week, lived with her husband in a one-roomed house in Partick. It was called a single-end. Mrs Kelly said there were fifty four children living in that one tenement. There were three flats to each floor and some had two rooms, but Helen could hardly think how all those people could fit into one building. It seemed incredible and she felt very curious about these overcrowded houses, which were less than a mile away from her own home, where only seventeen people lived in the eight flats of the tenement and each flat had four or five spacious rooms. How did poor folk manage in such cramped places? Helen had supposed that Jessie would also inhabit this sort of cramped warren and she was looking forward to examining such a different sort of house. However when she turned in at number 28, the close looked very much like her own close at home, although it was not tiled and the staircase spiralled upwards, unlike the straight flights and landings in Hyndland.

Helen climbed to the first floor and Jessie opened the door and gave her a warm welcome.

Helen was astounded. The hall was much the same size as the one at home and she followed Jessie into a room that was even bigger and had a higher ceilng than her own sitting room! The ceiling had a wonderfully elaborate centrepiece and a deep ornate cornice. Three large windows looked on to the street. Jessie often spoke of 'hingin' oot the windae fur a blether' and one of those windows was open. That must be where she hung out.

Fancy Jessie living in such a swell flat! Were the other rooms as big? Helen longed to see around this flat that was so different from her expectations.

"What a nice big room!"

"Aye, it's spacey in't it. Gets cauld mind ye, in the winter. They windaes are bluddy drafty, but it's fine whin the sun's shinin'. Wur lookin' west here an' we get sun aw efternin, jist pourin' in, so i'is. If it's no rainin' that is."

She laughed and gave Helen a cuddle.

Helen wanted to ask about the rest of the house, but did not think it would be polite. Jessie was rushing around collecting various things in a basket for the journey, when another young woman came into the room. Like Jessie she was fat and rather untidy, but had a kind friendly smile,

"Aw, is this wee Helen that ye're aye tellin' me aboot, Jessie? Hullo Helen, Ah'm Maggie. Whit luvly long pigtails ye've goat an' ye're awfy blonde. That's no' oot a boattle, Jessie is it? That's the real Mackay, that is. An' whit a big tall wee lassie ye ur! Och d'ye hear whit Ah'm sayin'? Is that no a daft thing tae say, big tall wee lassie. Jessie'll tell ye Ah'm aye sayin' daft things an' ma tongue's niver at rest. In't that right, Jessie? An' ye're awa doon tae Skelmorlie the day, ur ye? Awa doon the watter! Ah hope it doesny rain. It doesny look like it the now. Anyways have a great day yous two and wee Georgy-Porgy as weel. Awfy nice meetin' ye Helen. An' you behave yersel the day, ye wee bugger."

The last remark was directed at the baby and accompanied by a sharp poke in the tummy which momentarily chased the smile from George's fat little face.

Helen thought that he must wonder sometimes whether his name was George or Bugger.

"That's ma cousin, Maggie. We share this flat, ye know. She's goat three weans, nice enough kids but noisy wee deevils an thur aye lookin' fur food. An' she's an awfy blether hersel. Worse than me, even! If ye kin believe that!"

Jessie's hearty laugh resounded to the tall ceiling. Helen was glad she had not asked to see the house. It must be quite crowded with two couples and their children. However this room was certainly much larger than she had expected to find.

Helen was forced to revise some of her views on 'poor people'.

The day in Skelmorlie was slightly boring for a twelve year old. Much of the time was spent in the small holiday flat with the adults chatting. George slept and Helen looked out of the window. When they went for a walk, just for a brief moment Helen smelled the salty seaweed smell that she had loved in Millport, then it faded. Helen realised that she had been hoping that this Clydeside town would be like Millport. She had such happy memories of that long ago holiday when she was only eight. But her experience of Skelmorlie could not compare with Millport.

Visitors

"What will we give them to eat?" The visit from Khirstine and her mother had been arranged for next Saturday and Helen was starting to feel nervous. Their life was so different from her friend's more conventional, suburban one. There was no daddy, no animals and her mother was in a wheelchair. While she happily accepted these features herself, it might seem rather strange to Khirstine and especially to her mother.

"Well I've been thinking about that and... maybe fish? Everyone likes fish and we could have it all prepared beforehand. You won't want to be cooking when your friend's here, will you?"

"I suppose not. How would we prepare it beforehand?"

Helen was used to fried or boiled fish which must be cooked and brought immediately to the table.

"Mmm, I've been thinking about that! I've remembered something I used to make that I think they would like. Wait and see. I'll teach you how to make it, it's quite easy, don't worry. And I'll bake something nice for our cup of coffee afterwards."

Helen decided to forgo her Saturday morning swim and was out early to buy haddock, bread and a tin of peas. Annie shouted after her,

"Make sure they're garden peas! They're worth the extra points. Don't want those other beastly floury ones.".

The fish shop was just across the road and, like other fish shops at that time, displayed its wares on a large sloping marble slab in a window, the lower half of which was open to the elements.To deal with the resulting low temperature of the fish shop, the three assistants were bundled up in many layers of jerseys under their overalls. With scale-spattered navy aprons tied over their many layers, there was no possibility of the smart feminine style that most other shop assistants aspired to, Wellington boots or sometimes wooden-soled boots were necessary footgear, for the floor was cold and hard and often running with water from a dripping hosepipe. Helen shivered as she waited in the short queue and thought this must be the coldest job in the world, for even on a mild sunny day like this it was freezing in the shop. She knew that catching the fish in the first place was also a bitter task, yet fishermen were working hard to keep themselves warm and they were out in the sun sometimes while these poor girls were standing filleting or just serving customers. She wondered why they did not get a job in a different kind of shop. Milly in the grocers had a much better time of it and had all the fun of weighing out sugar, slicing bacon on the machine and cutting up cheese with the wire cutter. Milly could chat to customers who were not anxious to return to a more acceptable temperature, as the customers in the fish shop were.

As she wheeled her mother into the kitchen, Helen wondered what they were going to cook. Only on Sunday was the kitchen fire lit to heat the boiler and Annie washed her hands at the cold tap, forgetting, as usual to put her brakes on until her chair started to slide away from the sink

" I'll never learn, will I?" she laughed, "Now first I'll do the baking and the oven will warm us up a bit. Light the oven please, and turn it up quite high to begin with."

The kitchen faced north and was never very bright or warm. The windows looked out at the dismal back green, the midden and the old unused washhouse. The six back greens of the Polwarth Street tenements, with their dividing railings, disappeared into the distance. The back of the Queensborough tenements faced south and were bathed in sunshine on a bright day. It made Helen rather sad to see the sun shining somewhere else, while she was stuck in a dull, cold kitchen. She often hurried through chores on a bright day and preferred the evening or a rainy day for working in the kitchen.

Today was different though and she felt very happy and excited to be preparing this meal for her special friend. She did not mention it to her mother, but she knew this kitchen was very shabby and old-fashioned compared to that Newton Mearns kitchen with its shiny white fridge, however she was sure that the food would be just as tasty.

"Put the kettle on, please, and fill it full, then pour some hot water into the basin in the sink and put that baking bowl with the sugar and margarine in it to soften. Now bring out the wee round Pyrex dish and butter it. Well, use margarine, of course."

Helen did as she was told, while her mother was cutting thin slices of lard and margarine into the flour to make ruff puff pastry. Annie had not divulged exactly what it was that they were preparing and Helen enjoyed the air of mystery about it all. They might have been magicians, weaving spells.

"We've always had this wee glass dish, haven't we, Mummy? I remember it in Pittenweem and even in Millport. You must have taken it there with you. And it's what we made the imitation marshmallow in, that disaster that was so tough we could hardly chew it, d'ye remember?"

Annie laughed,

"Oh yes, and you said it was the answer to the rubber shortage! Yes it's a handy wee dish. And I got it free! It was given away with the first edition of 'Woman' magazine. Can't quite remember when that was. Ages ago, but after you were born, I think."

"Free! That's amazing. You've certainly had good use out of it."

It had a lid and was used for casseroles and apple sponges, heating up cold food and practically all that was cooked in the oven, except for roasts. Helen liked the idea of things being well used. Suddenly she was struck by a terrible fear that she might break this precious dish. She would feel so guilty and what would they do without it?

"Now you can cut the two fillets into eight pieces and salt them, then curl the fish into little rounds and 'place' in the marvellous Pyrex dish. Then set that aside and help me here."

Annie rolled out the pastry and laid it in a round tin baking tray, with a layer of raspberry jam spread over it, while Helen beat up the marge and sugar till it was creamy. Then she mixed some dried egg and water in a cup, equal to two eggs. Annie insisted that both powder and water were carefully measured. She believed in scientifically exact amounts. The egg and flour and another spoon of water were added and well beaten to make a sponge which was then piled on top of the pastry.

"Now pop that in the oven. D'ye think that looks as though it will be good?"

Helen nodded enthusiastically as she licked out the bowl, although very little of the mixture remained. Annie had deftly wiped most of it out with her finger.

"Bring me the basin over now and I'll wash my hands again. Oh, how I hate to be sticky! And that warm water is gorgeous. Now bring out the good eggs, the ones from up North."

Two of Mary's aunts lived in the far North of Scotland and throughout the war, they had sent an occasional, very welcome box of eggs to their niece and sometimes a splendid cockerel which seemed to taste extra delicious. Annie and Helen had never met them, but Annie wrote to them sometimes.

"How many have we got left?"

"Three."

"That's fine, but we'll just need two. Now break them into a cup, then empty them into that little bowl. A wee pinch of salt now, a bit more than that maybe. Now add two cups of milk and switch it all up thoroughly.

Helen did as she was told and enjoyed doing it, but had no idea what it was for.

"Now pour that over the fish."

Helen hesitated, she wondered if her mother was joking.

"Go on, pour it over!"

Helen made a wry face but poured the egg mixture over the fish.

"Now if you put that into a very slow oven about quarter to four, it will be ready to eat at five o'clock. Will you remember now? It's got to be a cool oven or it'll go all bubbly, then dry up. Remember, just a wee flame. And don't put that face on, you'll love it and so will they. It'll be delicious. I see there's two tomatoes there. We'll cut them up and put them in as well. That'll make it a nice colour with the peas. See how the sponge is doing now. It must be nearly ready I would think."

Helen brought the perfect golden sponge out of the oven and her mother gently pressed the top with the tip of her finger.

"Yes that's fine. Now we'd better get my hair washed so that I look respectable for your swell friends from the South Side."

Although Helen had not said much, Annie had realised how impressed her daughter had been by the Thomsons' well-appointed home.

When the visitors arrived, Helen and Khirstine made a pot of tea for the mothers and then went for a walk.

Khirstine was surprised that Hyndland was so different from Newton Mearns. All these tall tenements in street after street

were a strange contrast to the neat little gardens, fronting bunga-
lows and semidetached villas in Newton Mearns.

"There must be lots of people living here!" Khirstine looked
along Falkland Street.

"I suppose there are quite a lot. We have seventeen in our
close. But down in Partick where the flats are much much smaller,
they have tons more people in each block. And lots of kids!"

"I wonder why they don't have real gardens in front of the
closes here. It's just grass with a tree in the middle. There's no
flowers."

But Helen remembered the sharp railings that had enclosed
the gardens before the war. It would have been very awkward to
clamber over them to work in the gardens.

Then she had a sudden memory of her mother's hat being
blown away at the top of Clarence Drive. It was years ago for she
had been very young at the time and her mother was still able to
walk normally. After she had chased the hat for twenty yards, it
had lifted high in the air, then deposited itself in a front garden
which was railed all around. Her mother had shrugged and
given up saying,

"That's it gone now!"

Helen had felt so sorry for the hat as it lay there in the garden,
just out of reach and it was strange and sad to think of that time
when her mother could run as other people did. She thought of
sharing this memory with her friend, but decided not to.

Khirstine said it might be fun to live in a tenement and have so
many neighbours. Her father would not need to work so hard in
the garden each weekend. He was always grumbling about it.
Helen thought it would be awfully nice to live in a real house with
flowers and vegetables and rabbits in the garden. Especially with
a fridge in the kitchen. Yet both girls loved their own homes and
would almost certainly have refused to exchange their abodes.

The meal was a great success and Khirstine was very
impressed that Helen took resposibility for cooking and serving it.

"Oh it was Mummy that did it all. I just had to pop it in the
oven and heat the peas. I'm just the assistant."

However she was pleased that Khirstine was impressed, for
Helen admired and looked up to her friend as someone who
seemed very grown-up.

◊

"Did youse have a rerr time wi' yer swell freends oan Setterday?"

"Yes, I think everything went off very well. Khirstine seems a very sweet sensible girl and I know Helen admires her and was a bit apprehensive that things wouldn't go right. The mother and I got on like a house on fire and the sponge turned out fine."

"Och yer sponges are aye light as a feather, Mrs Cornin'."

"Thank you! I'm afraid there's an awful lot of dirty dishes for you today. Helen hates washing dishes, but I should I should have made sure she did some of them…"

"Ach shite! Whit's a few durty dishes, hen. I'll soon crack through them, never worry."

" You're very good. But here, listen to what it says in the Herald today. 'Sir So and So, addressing the Commons today, said that the way in which the people of this country have accepted the restrictions which the Ministry of Food have felt it necessary to impose, is 'just amazing!'

"Bugger that! Fat chance we hud o' sayin' no tae them. Whit ur they gaun oan aboot?"

"That's what I was thinking myself. We weren't given much option, were we."

"Silly auld arsehole, so he is!"

They both laughed.

"And here, I see Coplands has some nice new materials in. I do miss going into town and seeing what's on offer. The fabric department has something called crepe satin beauté at four and eightpence ha'penny a yard, in four lovely colours. It's for lingerie."

"Aw, duz that no' sound awfy luxurious an' sexy, too! Crepe sa'in botty and is it meant tae cover up yer botty like?"

Jessie's peals of laughter at her own joke set Annie chortling too.

Raking

What does a child do on a very rainy day when all the chores are done, all the books are read, all the games are played? Ah yes, I hear my reader say, this could never happen, it would be an impossible situation to achieve. Nevertheless there are times when none of these occupations appeals and that is when a child likes to go raking through cupboards and drawers, finding long lost objects or discovering new ones, pouring over old cards and papers, examining each small discarded article which, deemed too important to throw out at the time, is now completely forgotten. It is like a treasure hunt.

In Helen's grandmother's flat in Renfrew Street there were numerous chests of drawers, sideboards, linen chests and deep mysterious cupboards. Mary Mackay had spent a lifetime collecting things that were interesting or useful, or might be useful at some future time. Most items had been purchased at a very moderate cost and often in wholesale bulk. For instance; two hundred reels of silk thread (from palest lilac to rich purple) were kept in a bureau drawer, and thirty perfumed cakes of soap (lemon, geranium and rose) shared a deep aromatic drawer in a Dutch chest with forty five compressed blocks of face powder (various shades from lily fair to deep rachelle).

Helen's own flat could not compare with her grandmother's for raking, of course. There were only three chests of drawers and they mostly held clothes or perhaps knitting wool or embroidery. One deep bottom drawer held the various art and music certificates which Annie had worked so hard to gain when a teenager. At her boarding school in the Lake District she had worked for a diploma which enabled her to teach art to primary children in England, though not in Scotland. It was a large and elaborately decorated piece of card and Helen felt a glow of pride when she came across it.

The kitchen table had two drawers, one for cutlery for which Bruce, when first married, had made wooden divisions to separate spoons from forks from knives. There was a special compartment for fish knives and forks to share. The other drawer had some interesting possibilities on a rainy day. There were neat rolls of string. No one in the family would ever have thought of cutting the string on a parcel. It would always be painstakingly unknotted and wound up into a tight little hank. There were bone egg spoons which were never used and therefore banned from the official cutlery drawer. A few boxes of matches, a penknife, some tie-on labels and sealing wax. Four brightly coloured individual jelly moulds lay towards the back of the drawer. Helen was sure that they had come free with some product before the war. She had been so excited the first time that she saw the shaped jelly turn out perfectly and sit quivering on the plate. If she rummaged right to the back corners of the drawer she found three little lead animals, a hen, a duck and a cow, all dressed in jackets and skirts. Those had certainly been free with cocoa, she knew. Just the thought of cocoa made her feel slightly sick, for she had been expected to finish her cupful each morning before she left for school and milk was never a favourite food with Helen. Then there were various kitchen gadgets, a corkscrew, a bottle opener, a pair of very blunt scissors, a metal instrument for making little fancy curls of butter for a genteel afternoon tea. Annie had shown Helen how that worked once. It was quite messy and took a long time and both agreed it was pretty unnecessary. With so little butter nowadays, it was silly to spread any of it anywhere except on the bread.

Also in the drawer was a splendid little Mouli grater. It could be clamped to the table just like the big heavy mincing machine, then cheese, carrots, turnip could be grated very finely. There was a wooden block to push the food down against the revolving drum as you turned the handle and it was a lot easier to use than the mincer. Helen remembered that she adored the raw carrot her mother used to grate. She never seemed to have as much of it as she wanted. Turnip was usually delicious but not always. They hardly ever used that grater nowadays, probably too difficult for her mother. And cheese, like butter, was in such short supply that one did not risk losing any of it on fancy gadgets. The last little metal kitchen accessory was Helen's favourite. It was for slicing hard boiled eggs. The hinged lid was composed of eight very fine wires, tightly strung. The cooked egg was placed on the egg-shaped hollow in the slatted lower portion of the machine. Then the lid was firmly pressed down and the egg divided into perfect slices! It was very useful nowadays when it was desirable to share one or two eggs amongst several people. Helen thought the little slices looked very elegant on the plate. There was another aspect to this wonderful invention and Helen often wondered if she were the only one to exploit it. When not busy slicing eggs, the wires could be plucked like a miniature harp and the sound produced was sweet and faery-like. The notes were all different, although not of course resembling a scale, nor even in an ascending order. After many trials, Helen had managed to find the correct arrangement for 'God save the King' and also 'The Bluebells of Scotland'. It was not easy. Mostly she made up little tunes for herself and often spent twenty minutes with her 'harp' The sound was so light that Annie was unaware of the kitchen music.

Sometimes if it was really cold weather, the sitting room was the warmest place to rake although the waist-high built-in cupboard in the sitting room was never exciting. It was rather too familiar, with games like Ludo, Tiddlywinks, Housey-housey and Snakes and Ladders. There were some small jars from long long ago, each one filled with a different dried pulse, beans, peas, orange lentils, split yellow peas. Annie had filled them for Helen to play at shops, before the war. Helen felt very nostalgic when she saw these. They were no use to her now, but she could not bear to throw them away, for she remembered how delighted she had been when she first saw them. She thought her mother so kind to use real food for her to play with.

Although there was much other clutter in the cupboard, it meant little to Helen and she soon pushed everything back and closed the doors. Annie had never cared to be too organised in her storage systems and had certainly not inculcated many rules of tidiness in her daughter.

The very best place for raking on a rainy day was the back room. It was quite a large room with one north facing window tucked far into a corner. It appeared really spacious, as it was almost empty of furniture, but it was a gloomy room, although Annie had papered and painted it in the days of her health. Apart from a small bedroom chair, a cakestand, two leather suitcases and the chiffonier, this room had remained unfurnished.

The chiffonier! Helen loved that word. She pronounced it shiffonneer and had no notion of its French roots. It was a solid piece of highly polished mahogany furniture with one long drawer and a double doored cupboard beneath. The drawer held five or six of Annie's watercolours of flowers and a few of John Mackay's etchings, some recipe books and also knitting and dress patterns. None of her friends had a chiffonier or had even heard of one. When she mentioned it once in school they had looked at her in astonishment, almost as if she had sworn. My dictionary tells me it means 'literally a ragpicker but also denotes a chest of drawers for odds and ends'. For Helen it was the perfect place to search through on a rainy day and she knew she would always find something new that she had never seen before or perhaps just something she had completely forgotten. The empty room was excellent for strewing her finds around and considering what she might do with them. Perhaps the fact that she could be sure of remaining undisturbed at her work enhanced the whole experience. There was a loneliness and a slightly scary atmosphere in the unused room that added to the excitement, although sometimes this atmosphere would overpower Helen. Quite suddenly, her imagination would start to throb and she would hurriedly bundle everything back into the cupboards and return to the warmth and company of the sitting room.

If Annie and Bruce had made a happier marriage, no doubt this room would have been Helen's and might have made a pretty and cheerful bedroom. It never occurred to Helen that her life might have been so different. She had no desire for a frilly feminine room such as one saw in Hollywood films. She accepted the situation she found herself in and enjoyed many aspects of it. Her resentments were not against the responsibiliites which she shouldered, so much as the time she considered wasted listening to her father and grandmother talking, talking without doing anything. She was sensitive to the underlying hostility of the adults without realising how much her own hostility aggravated the situation. She hardly discussed their shortcomings in her own mind and was only too pleased to dismiss them from her thoughts as soon as they left the house.

Tests

Helen's favourite subject was science. When she was eight, she had spent a memorable summer in Millport with the friendly Neilson family. Mr Neilson was an analytical chemist and his son, Jimmy, Helen's earliest male admirer, intended to follow in his father's footsteps. Helen had thought that she too would like to work in a laboratory and mix strange liquids and powders, then heat and transform them over a Bunsen burner. The magical process still fascinated her and her science lessons were particularly special, as she was taught in the same top floor laboratory as her mother had used and by the very same teacher, Miss Bates. This feeling of history and tradition particularly pleased Helen and was one of the good things about attending High School.

"Good Heavens!" Her mother had exclaimed, "Surely Miss Bates is not still going strong! She seemed ancient to me when I was your age. I remember we made a poem about her knitting socks for soldiers, something about 'socks as hard as rocks'. What little rotters we must have been. She was a poor plain woman even then. Who knows? Perhaps she had a boyfriend in the trenches who never came home and that's why she's never married and is still teaching. But everyone was knitting for soldiers in those days, scarves and mittens and even blankets. Poor souls, we had no idea what horror those men were going through in the cold and the mud. I hope all that knitting brought them some comfort."

Another much younger science teacher, Miss Rigg, often visited Miss Bates and the two had serious discussions. Sadly Miss Rigg was very small with the spinal deformity known as a hump. She was energetic and handsome and dressed as smartly as her handicap allowed. Her hair lay in perfect waves and she usually wore a bright scarf or a large brooch in her jumper with her overall unbuttoned, to show her finery. No doubt she was business-like when conducting experiments and she was totally unlike Miss Bates, whose meagre and faded brown overall seemed to be her only garment, perhaps she slept in it for all her pupils knew.

Little Miss Rigg had an aura of intelligence and alertness which verged on the overpowering. Some of the girls even whispered that Miss Bates was relieved when the other left the room and gave her peace.

One day Miss Rigg asked Miss Bates' permission to address the class. She explained that she was doing an experiment, not with chemicals, but with minds. She was helping in a nationwide educational survey and would ask some of the girls to help her. It was not like an exam. There would be no failing or passing, but they must take some tests. There would be no results, good or bad.

"Now hands up all those that would like to aid me. Don't be shy! You are just the age that I want and I think you would really find it quite good fun, girls. Some of the tests are rather like puzzles or games that you would do to amuse yourself on a rainy day."

Helen wished that Miss Rigg did not speak quite so like a teacher in an Angela Brazil book. She wanted to like her because she was sorry for her, but there was something about her attitude that distanced Helen from her. It seemed as if Miss Rigg might believe that she always knew best about everything. Helen expected she was like that because of her hump.

These tests sounded similar to the qualifying exam that Helen had sat at the end of primary school. She had enjoyed decoding the patterns of letters and numbers in that test. She supposed she must have been quite good at that sort of thing: she was placed in the top maths and science classes at the Waid Academy in Fife, before her return to Glasgow. Helen was first to put up her hand to volunteer and soon another nine girls joined her.

"Please come up to this lab tomorrow as soon as you have eaten lunch."

Just as Helen had expected, the tests were similar to the 'qually' and quite good fun. There was also written work, strangely asking questions about how you felt. Helen knew she had done well and when Miss Rigg asked her to come to the science lab the following week, Helen confidently expected to be congratulated.

"Now, Helen my dear, I really want to speak seriously to you."

The girl looked down at the little teacher who was wearing a black and red jumper, which Helen considered a bad mistake, far too bright and crude on the malformed little body.

"Yes, it's obvious you are having extreme problems with your handwriting, dear."

Expecting praise, Helen was taken aback, astonished in fact and there was that hateful 'dear', used by someone who was giving you a hard time. She was speechless.

"Now I think that we must work at this together, Helen. You will come to the lab on Tuesdays and Wednesdays to report to me, and every day I want you to do exercises to improve the strength of your hands. There is obviously tremendous weakness in the motor control of your right hand. I suggest you get a rubber ball, a nice, brightly coloured one would be good, and several times a day I want you to squeeze the ball hard in your right hand and keep on squeezing it for five minutes at least. It's very important. Do you read books at all?"

"Yes."

What Helen wanted to say was "Of course I read books, you stupid idiot, I read all the time. I've read all of Kipling's short stories as well as school stories and adventure stories, Just William and Tarzan and PG Wodehouse and loads of others. What do you mean? D'ye think I just read the Girl's Crystal?"

She did not say this of course and she did in fact read the Girl's Crystal and enjoy it, though always with a slightly guilty feeling.

"That's good, I think children can learn a lot from fiction. Anyway keep your nice, bright ball handy and just squeeze it as you read. Now I am looking forward to a great advancement here. We just need to work on strength and the control will come. Sadly, we only have a few weeks before the end of term, but I am very willing to help you. We might even keep in touch through the vacation. Now dry your eyes, dear and run back to class. I will see you here next Tuesday. Don't be upset. Anyone can develop a weakness, there is nothing to be ashamed of."

Helen's tears were of fury, indignation and frustration. How she would like to have spoken back to this teacher! Weakness! She had no weakness. She prided herself on her strength! She could lift her mother into bed and carry home heavy groceries. If Miss Rigg had allowed Helen to squeeze her hand instead of a damned rubber ball, she would have known how little weakness was there. She would have made the wee teacher shriek with pain. Silly bitch. Nothing to be ashamed of, indeed. She should be ashamed of wearing such a horrible bright sweater when she was such a strange shape. As Helen rushed down the many flights of stairs, her anger gave way to sadness and worry. Must she really go back each week and give up her lunch hour to listen to criticism and condescension? Was her writing really as bad as all that? Keep in touch through the vacation? Not bloody likely! It was all very upsetting.

Regretably, though a fine scientist, conscientious teacher and dedicated humanitarian, Miss Rigg had an unfortunate manner. Also, she was strangely ignorant of the fact that mental stress can affect hand-writing more than any physiological factor. In trying to help her pupil, she had added anger and indignation to a life already overburdened with difficulties.

◊

Although Helen was apparently very open with her mother about all aspects of her life, it was only now that Annie was starting to hear about the teasing and unhappiness that her daughter had suffered at Pittenweem school. How guilty Annie felt, but she comforted herself with the thought that Helen would now fit in at High School and have a happier time.

Nor had Annie ever guessed the extreme fears that Helen had struggled with in the Pittenweem house during the blackout, where many of the rooms were not curtained and the two of them had moved around those rooms in the dark. For the first time, Annie learned of the terror Helen used to feel when she went upstairs by herself at night to brush her teeth. How insensitive she had been, for all children do have fears of the dark. She wondered why she had not realised this at the time and marvelled at the pride which had kept her daughter's terror secret. Anyway they were now back in cvilisation, with electric light to switch on. Even in uncurtained rooms, the dim street lighting was sufficient to dispel fears and Helen was certainly past such childish worries now.

Annie knew that Helen liked to relay little anecdotes about what she had been doing. These were generally very positive and often amusing. No doubt Helen tried to entertain Annie and loved to make her laugh and she gave the impression of being very frank and open, but could there be underlying problems that remained unmentioned?

When Annie learned of her daughter's poor exam results, she realised that there must be many aspects of her daughter's life of which she was not aware. Helen must have found the move to Glasgow much more stressful than she had ever admitted. The school was suggesting that as Helen was young and her results disappointing, she should repeat first year. That seemed a good idea to Annie for surely their situation would remain more stable now and next year would have fewer problems.

George's Problem

Helen lay in bed, very unwilling to get up. She was feeling despondent, indignant as well. She could not forget Miss Rigg's criticisms and advice. It was so unfair. She felt that she was much stronger than most girls of her age. She had always taken such pride in her strength. She tried to forget that stupid suggestion about squeezing a rubber ball. What nonsense. She had no intention of following this ridiculous exercise. She wished that Miss Rigg could see her hoisting her mother on to the bed or pulling her through the hall on the rug. Yes, she knew her writing was pretty awful just now. Most exercises had the comment "Better writing, please!" written beside the mark. One or two even had "Poor writing!" Miss Rigg had been very kind and obviously wanted to help her, but that made it worse somehow. No one had ever criticised her writing in Pittenweem. These days she was always in a hurry and she found it hard to know quite how she wanted to write. Sometimes it was slanting forwards at a steep angle, sometimes straight up and down, almost backwards. It looked quite stylish to her when it slanted backwards, but it was hard work to do it that way and just too unusual and the teachers criticised it. She looked at the writing of others and it did not seem so very great. She did admire Khirstine's firm flowing hand, but she did not want to copy her exactly. Helen tried a different style on each new page, but none seemed right. Her hand would never move just the way she wanted, but she was sure that was not a lack of strength! Besides, she was always in such a hurry to get the work down. Especially if it were work that she liked and was good at: English for example.

Though none of Helen's examination marks were particularly good, some had been shockingly bad. She was practically the worst in the class in history and geography. This was a new and unpleasant experience for her. In Pittenweem, Helen had nearly always sat at the top of the class. Now although she had passes in English, French, maths and art, those subjects which required no study, her science and Latin were disappointing. She had lost her delight in Latin. She had really loved it when she first started at the Waid Academy in Anstruther. This ancient language seemed so steeped in tradition, for it was always a subject studied in school stories. At the Waid they were taught the old-fashioned way of pronouncing V as a W. She liked that. It was not difficult or embarrassing like French, where the accent was as important as the grammar and vocabulary. Saying W for V made it very special and you felt that you were speaking a foreign language. She and her mother often used the phrase *ita vero* to each other. It meant "Yes, indeed!" and sounded so definite with the v pronounced as w. They made each other laugh by saying "*Ita vero!*" unexpectedly. In High School, this pronunciation was not used and V was sounded as V. It took Helen a long time to come to terms with the change, because she really preferred the way she had first been taught. If she were reading aloud and pronounced the V wrongly, there would be giggles from some of the girls, then she would go back and blushingly read it again. Perhaps it was a small thing, but by sapping her confidence, it spoiled her enjoyment and somewhat changed her attitude to the subject.

She was young in the class and would repeat the year in the A class, which showed they had faith in her. That was something good and Khirstine was the only friend she would miss. However it was all a bit dispiriting.

"I don't feel too great this morning, Mummy. I have a sore head."

Annie looked closely at her daughter. Poor kid was obviously feeling a bit low.

"Do you want to take the day off? I don't suppose they're doing much work with the end of term in sight. And you'll see big George, Jessie is bringing him with her today. That's an education in itself."

"Yes and Mummy, I think I'll bake a cake later on."

Helen looked more cheerful already.

George lay naked on the sitting room hearth rug. It was the first of June and a glorious day.

Jessie had been changing the baby's nappy when the coalman had arrived, and she had left him with Annie and Helen to look after him while she stood guard in the kitchen, counting under her breath as the bags were emptied into the bunker. Not that she did not trust the small bandy-legged man, but mistakes could happen. As each of the six bags was dumped noisily into the bunker, the clouds of black dust billowed out over her newly cleaned kitchen and she tut-tutted regretfully.

"It's a shame ye didnae get here a bit earlier the day."

The coalman only grunted.

In the other room, Helen knelt beside the baby, gazing at him, saying nothing.

Annie was often puzzled that Helen showed no particular interest in the difference of the sexes or in anything to do with sex at all. She and her brother had searched out and shared all sorts of not necessarily accurate information on the subject at a much earlier age. It had seemed very important and very fascinating. Perhaps having a brother made a difference? Might Helen possibly be sharing knowledge with her friends? There was really only Khirstine. Greta was obviously not a candidate for confidences, for Helen did her best to avoid her company. How much did her twelve year old daughter know about the facts of life? Annie was aware that not only did Helen not search out information, but was quite skillful at steering the conversation away from anything to do with sex.

Now, lying in full view on the hearthrug, was a perfect specimen of infantile manhood, his sturdy chubby legs kicking. Annie was not sure how to use her opportunity.

"He's a great wee boy, isn't he?"

"Yes, I suppose he is." replied Helen.

"You don't sound very enthusiastic, darling,"

There was a pause before Helen spoke.

"I just think it's such a shame…"

"What's a shame?"

"Well his funny wee thing at the front. It'll be such a nuisance when he's walking about."

Annie kept her face straight,

"I'm sure he won't think it's a nuisance."

"But it will be. Fancy having to cram something like that into your knickers. I'd hate it. And it's such a funny shape."

Annie had no idea what to say and Helen continued,

"Perhaps it won't seem so big when he grows bigger himself and it won't be so noticeable. Poor wee thing. I'm really sorry for boys. I remember seeing that boy baby in Pittenweem when I was a wee girl. I didn't tell you at the time, but I was horrified. I thought the baby had a tumour or something and I couldn't even speak about it to you. I didn't know all boys were like that, it was only when I saw George, I realised that they must be all the same, poor things. It's such a shame and so unfair. P'raps it sort of modifies as they grow up and doesn't look so obvious?"

"No, it probably grows bigger."

"Oh dear, what a pity."

Annie was nonplussed and decided the time was not yet ripe for further sexual education.

Meanwhile George smiled smugly on the hearthrug, secure in the belief that the entire world worshipped at the shrine of his energetic little male body.

Summer 1944

June and the end of term was in sight. Helen was looking forward to returning to Pittenweem but Annie was more aware of the practical problems. If there were no possibility of taking the unwieldy wheel chair through to Fife, how would she manage to get about the house? When she mentioned this to Helen, the girl's face changed. She had taken the presence of the new chair for granted and Annie was sorry to see her dismay.

"But I thought we'd be taking the chair with us."

"I'm afraid it would be too big for that wee house. It would hardly go through the doors and grandma's got so much furniture…"

"What will we do, Mummy?"

"I expect we'll think of something."

That night Mary was visiting them.

"Oh yes, I've been thinking about that problem, Annie. I have a wee trolley that I think you might be able to use. If you could kneel on it, we could push you into the sitting room or out to the garden, then we could help you into a chair."

Annie expression was doubtful.

"If it's the trolley I'm thinking of, it's gey wee. Don't know if I could do a balancing act on it if I was being hurled around."

Helen shared her mother's doubts. Mary was optimistic, but then she had little to do with lifting or manhandling Annie.

When Bruce came in later that evening and assured them that the big wheel chair would certainly never go through the Pittenweem doorways, he was told of the trolley.

"Now what sort of trolley is it, Mrs Mackay? Would it bear Annie's weight?"

"Oh I'm sure it would. It's solid mahogany with big brass castors."

"I wonder what it was for. Have you any idea?"

Neither Annie nor Mary had any idea. It was just one of the many objects that Mary had picked up at an auction, thinking it might come in useful someday.

Mary started a story about some other artefact she had nearly bought at that same sale, a real bargain. When he found a chance, Bruce broke in to talk about mahogany and its wonderful properties. Wood was his business and he enjoyed displaying his knowledge of the different varieties. As each struggled for conversational space, the problem of how Annie would manage in Pittenweem was quickly shelved and only Annie and her daughter continued to worry about it.

◊

There were much greater worries afoot in the world.

"Things are fairly hotting up in Italy. D'ye think the end's in sight yet, Bruce?"

It was evening and Annie and Bruce were sitting at the window, drinking coffee and watching the passers-by. It was nearly ten o'clock but several Hyndland residents were strolling past in the long, light summer evening.

"Well, we have to hope so, but it still seems to be a bloody battle all over the world. Where's the wee one? Doing homework?"

Helen had served the coffee, then quickly retired to the kitchen to devour her latest book from the lending library, an adventure of shipwreck in the South Seas by H de Vere Stacpoole.

"No, it's a bit late in the day for homework. She's not done well in her exams, as you know, and she's a bit down about that, I suppose. She always did so well at school in Pittenweem. Anyway what was in the paper today? I didn't see one."

Bruce produced a crumpled Glasgow Herald and read,

"It says 'Kesselring has fallen back four kilometres in the Alban Hills and Valmontone and Velletri, twin pillars of German defence on road to Rome, have been captured … and the Eighth army are squeezing Nazi forces into an ever lessening space.' Awful fancy language but it sounds like good news, doesn't it?"

"Yes I suppose so. Of course the papers always make the most of anything positive."

Next morning Jessie arrived full of loud glee.

"Aw Mrs Cornin', in't it jist great. Thur getting' they Jerries oot o' Rome at last. Mrs McLafferty next door tae me, she's a pape ye know, an' she's that happy! She's jist waltzin' in the close an' tap-dancin' up'n doon the sterr. Here the paper tae ye. You read a' the wee details, while Ah pit the kettle oan. It's jist smashin' news in't it."

As she walked to the kitchen she was singing loudly, if not tunefully,

"Aye, w'ull hang oot the WAASHin' oan the SEEGfreed line." Annie ran her eye quickly over the page,

GERMAN EVACUATION OF ROME
Fifth Army completes task of liberation
Citizens of Rome strew flowers on Allied tanks

FIVE DAYS OF HARD FIGHTING IN ROUMANIA
ALLIED BOMBERS POUND FRENCH COAST FOR 200 MILES
SEINE BRIDGE WRECKED
ITALO-FRENCH BORDER HIT

Annie felt slightly sick and could read no further. There was news about the other side of the world as well, but it too was all about violence, destruction and death.

Then Jessie returned with the basin of water for the daily bed bath.

She treated Annie in much the same way as her baby son, talking non-stop as she thoroughly soaped then rinsed each limb, drying her thoroughly with a none too gentle touch, then turning her over swiftly to wash her back. Her homely flow of language was interspersed with exclamations of "Whit the hell" and "Och, bugger!" when she dropped the soap or spilled some water. Annie found it amusing and comforting.

"You'd think I was as light as a feather the way you throw me about!" Annie's voice was muffled in the pillow.

"Och aye hen, yer nae wecht at a'. Yer long'n lanky, no' like ma wee fat Georgie-porgie. He'll be some wecht when he's your age, Ah'll bet. Jist like his big fat mither."

"Och you're not fat, Jessie."

"Ah've niver iver been skinny an' that's the truth. Ah'm weel built, mebbe. Clyde-built, that's me." She laughed and Annie found herself quite cheerful again, what with the whirlwind bath and the articulate flow of somewhat vulgar Glasgow patter.

After breakfast Annie returned to the newspaper and saw a warning from President Roosevelt,

"It would be unwise to inflate in our minds the military importance of the capture of Rome. We shall have to push through a long period of greater effort and fiercer fighting before we get into Germany itself."

That was pretty pessimistic. Then in a small paragraph at the foot of the page she saw something which struck her as having greater significance than any other item.

INVASION NEWS

100,000 words per day will be transmitted from London's world news centre when Allied forces begin their invasion of Europe. The Ministry of Information will have at its command the greatest concentration of communication ever known.

Surely things were going to happen very soon.
She wheeled herself into the kitchen to peel the potatoes.
On the following day, the 7th June, the news broke.

ALLIES SEIZE FOOTHOLDS IN NORMANDY

Churchhill announced to the House of Commons that,
'During the night and the early hours of this morning, the first of a series of landings in force upon the European Continent has taken place.'

Later in the day he added,
"This operation is proceeding in a thoroughly satisfactory manner! Many dangers and difficulties which this time last night seemed extremely formidable are now behind us."

The Glasgow Herald reporter was dramatic and poetic and used the present tense for effect,
"An outstanding feature of the invasion is the landing of airborne forces on a scale which is far larger than anything seen in the world before. Guns are belching flames from more than 600 Allied warships. Thousands of bombers are roaring overhead and fighters are weaving in and out of the clouds as the invasion of Western Europe begins."

◊

The news occupied Annie's mind for the rest of that day. What a terrible slaughter must be taking place in Europe. This was the last big push. It was hard to believe that the war would ever stop. She felt very depressed, although the papers were all triumphant. Annie thought about the soldiers that would be killed in these last battles, how terrible to think that your loved ones were still in danger when the end of the whole stupid business was in sight.

What difference would the end of the war make to their own daily lives? Perhaps not a great deal. The blackout would stop at once, but what about rationing? Would food suddenly become plentiful again? Annie doubted it.

That evening, Helen was aware that her mother and grandmother kept switching on the news and talked continuously about the invasion, Normandy, airborne troops, 'the final push', but she hardly listened. It did not occur to her that this was an important time. The war had lasted so long that it might go forever. Of course she wanted it to end, but she no longer believed that the end of the war would bring back those distant good times, when fruit, sweets and ice cream were plentiful and her mother could walk again.

After Mary had dashed off to catch the last tram and Helen had helped her mother to bed, she glanced at the newspaper lying on the table. She ignored the shouting black headlines and turned to the Ladies' page. Pettigrew & Stephens were advertising the latest luxury housecoats. A fashion artist had depicted three models, each with enormous padded shoulders which accentuated the tiny waist. From this unlikely waist flowed an extravagantly full skirt which brushed the floor. How wonderfully unnecessary, yet elegant and desirable such a garment seemed to Helen, although she hated the big shoulders. Who would wear such a housecoat and when, she wondered? It would be nice to live the sort of life that required a housecoat. It was strange that they had short sleeves because they were described as 'comfy and cosy'. In Helen's opinion they were too tightly belted to be comfy and short sleeves were never cosy

The nicest one cost £5.13s.3d which was rather more than their monthly housekeeping allowance. Helen resigned herself to living without a housecoat for a very long time. Besides, it would be difficult to chuck her mother around while wearing that long full skirt.

Pittenweem Holidays

The Mackays travelled through to Fife by train in the third week of June. The house had been lying empty since Christmas and must be aired and the grass would be long enough to require a man with a scythe to cut it. Mary was anxious to be well prepared for her daughter's arrival, for she knew there would be more domestic responsibility to deal with this year. John tried to help, but he was not as strong as he had been. His cough was often bad at night, leaving him very tired in the morning. Also he was getting more forgetful. Mary, quick and energetic herself, knew she was impatient with him, but really he was another thing to worry about.

◊

Two weeks before Annie and Helen were due to go to Fife, Jessie arrived and went straight into the kitchen without her usual loud 'Cooee" and with no singing or banging. This silence was most unusual. Ten minutes passed and she did not appear. What could be wrong?

Annie called for her and she came running to the bedroom.

"Something's the matter, Jessie, what's wrong, my dear? It's not wee George, is it?"

Jessie sat down on the bed shaking her head and starting to weep,

"Wee George is fine but…"

"I'm very glad, but what is it then, tell me all about it."

It was a few moments before Jessie could control her sobs and Annie patted her hand.

At last she burst out,

"Ah'm gaun tae hiv tae leave ye, Mrs Cornin' Oh, an' Ah don't want tae… ."

More tears and sobbing interrupted her words and Annie waited, with a hollow feeling in her stomach.

"They're shiftin' ma man tae Aberdeen. It's a big step up fur Jim, a big raise too, fur he's a right good worker. An' he couldnae say 'no' onyway, because o' the war an' everythin'. But Ah'm no' wantin' tae move tae thon cauld place an' Ah'm no' wantin tae leave you, ma hen, an' who'll gie ye yer bedbath if Ah'm in Aberdeen!"

Here she started crying inconsolably and Annie wiped a few tears from her own eyes.

Eventually Annie spoke,

"Now I think that is wonderful that your husband is doing so well, you must be proud of him."

"Aye, proud! Ah'm proud but Ah wish we didnae hiv tae move an' leave you an' ma nice big flat an' ma mither an' a' ma freends. Ah'm awfy proud o' him, but Ah'm scunnered, an' a'. Whit a wurk tae get a' our stuff up therr when Ah'm *hatin* the idea an' no' wantin' tae move at a'. An' a' wur big furnicher 'll no' likely fit in some poky wee flat in one o' they auld granite tinements. He's stertin' the new job in August an' we'll get an extry week tae move, as weel as the Fair fortnight. They've been awful good tae 'm, but he's a grand worker, tho' Ah say it as shouldn't. An' he's wantin' tae go tae Rothesay at the Ferr, an' Ah couldnae enjoy Rothesay, goin' there for the last time ... an his granny'll miss wee George that much ... an' Ah'll be leavin' you all on yer lonesome ..."

Again she abandoned herself to grief.

Annie wondered how to comfort her, for she herself felt bereft at the news.

Life was so unpredictable. Had it always been like this? Or did war change things?

She did feel that no one would look after her quite as well as Jessie had done. They had been such good friends and Annie knew she would miss the cheerful girl terribly. If she voiced this, it would hardly comfort Jessie. Neither could she assure Jessie that someone else would be found to take her place. That would hardly be complimentary, though she knew it was the case. As usual, Annie tried to be positive.

"I think you should certainly go to Rothesay and please your husband and have a nice relaxing time to set you up for the removal. I'll be away in Pittenweem then, anyway, and you wouldn't be coming here. And wee George will love the beach, wading in the water and playing in the sand. And when you go to Aberdeen in August you can take him to the beach there every day and he'll get as brown as a wee nut. Aberdeen is a very popular holiday resort and you'll make friends with other mothers on the beach. There'll be lots of good things in Aberdeen, I'm sure. And I'll get Bruce to pay your wages for the holiday and that'll help with any wee extras. You've been so good to me. We all appreciate it so very, very much."

Now it was Annie's turn to break down. It had been a terrible blow.

◊

Two weeks later, after a last sad farewell to Jessie, Bruce drove his wife and daughter through to Pittenweem.

It was evening when they arrived and Helen helped Bruce lift Annie out ot the car and straight into bed.

"I'll just stay in my bed tonight. It's easiest.'

The next day Helen knelt on the little mahogony trolley and her father pushed it from the bedroom to the sitting room. Cornering was tricky with the fixed wheels and Helen, perched precariously, giggled nervously.

"That was easy now, wasn't it, Tuppeny?"

"Mm, I didn't really feel very safe. I don't think Mummy could balance properly.."

"Let's try it going out to the garden now. All right?"

He did not wait for her agreement and her knuckles were white as she clung more tightly to the side of the trolley. She was no longer smiling.

It was necessary to descend one shallow step at the back door and then cross over a few feet of very uneven crazy paving. When the trolley tipped at an angle as it went down the step, Helen cried out and quickly leaped off.

"Oh no," she shouted, "that's too difficult for mummy to balance on. It's no use."

"Well jump on again, sweetheart and just let me try pushing you over the stones."

She was very unwilling, so Bruce himself sat on the trolley, his knees clasped tight against his chest and suggested she try pushing him. She heaved and struggled but did not have the strength to move him over the rugged terrain.

"It's useless, Mummy could never balance and I'd be terrified she'd fall and then I couldn't begin to get her over the rough bits anyway. I'm not strong enough."

Bruce jumped up and bit his lip. Helen looked to see if he were angry, but he just seemed to be thinking.

"What would you do otherwise, Tuppenny?"

"I'd pull her on a wee rug, just the way I used to at night, before we got the wheelchair."

"Right then. Could you do that for the next week? And I'll get back to you with something better."

A suitable piece of carpet was found and for a week Helen pulled her mother back and forth between bedroom and sitting-room and sometimes, on a very nice day, she would struggle her out to the garden, bumping her down the step and over the rough crazy paving. Annie would usually partly laugh and partly groan at this point and say in a sort of Irish accent,

"Sure an' it's the rocky road to Dublin."

It was not ideal, for there was no suitable chair to lift Annie into in the garden and she would kneel or lie down on the grass, saying, with a rueful smile,

"I feel like a beached whale lying here!"

Quite soon she would start to feel too warm if the sun were shining, or too chilly if it disappeared behind a cloud. Then once more she must be dragged over the stones and up the step and into the house, where she could be helped into a chair and feel 'like a part of the human race again' as she said. She would apologise to her daughter for staying outside for such a short time, after all the effort involved but Helen enjoyed the whole process. It was good to use her muscles and she felt justified in ignoring what that silly teacher had said. Of course she was strong, brilliantly strong. Stronger than most girls, strong as a boy.

The following weekend Bruce arrived with a splendid little chair on wheels. It was the bucket seat from an old car and he had firmly fixed four pram wheels to it.

"Oh Bruce, this is so comfortable, almost better than my Glasgow wheelchair, I do believe. Thank you very much. It's absolutely marvellous."

"Well you mentioned how comfortable you were in my car when we drove through, so I just took the passenger seat out of an old Austin that was lying around the works, its engine was buggered, Then I spotted a wee lad with a four-wheeled carty and offered him ten bob for it. Wee bugger jumped at the chance. Then I cobbled it all together for you. Of course you can't push yourself around in it. That's the big drawback. You're not independent like you are in Glasgow, but I think the wee one will be able to manage it fine. Look, you have to tilt it on its back wheels to maneuvre it. Don't worry, you're quite safe!" Annie had given a little shriek as she was suddenly tilted backwards to a forty five degree angle, bringing her knees level with her nose.

" Right now, Helen, see if you can push that around the corners and through the doors in this wee house. Mind the paint-work now."

He winked at her.

Helen could do it perfectly and whirled it round and out of the sitting room door, then the careful double turn left into the narrow hallway then almost immediately, right again into the bedroom. Then she brought it back into the sitting room again and returned the front wheels to the floor with a bit of a thump.

"It's a great wee chair, Daddy. It's really easy to push."

"Slightly undignified with my knees up in the air and my feet dangling." Annie raised one eyebrow, "But tremendously comfortable. Real leather too, of course. Thank you, Bruce, It's a work of genius, so simple, yet just what we were needing. I really appreciate it."

Mary had not yet made any comment. Now she spoke.

"Of course it's quite a peculiar piece of furniture isn't it. It doesn't exactly enhance the room, however I suppose if it makes Annie's life easier, that's all that matters. I've certainly never seen anything like it before. Is it really comfortable, Annie?"

"Yes it couldn't be more so. I think it's a marvellous wee chair. I'm really delighted and grateful, Bruce."

She felt awkward at her mother's lukewarm reception of Bruce's kindness and skill. Yet she also felt sorry for her mother. The charming low-ceilinged sitting room, with its white-washed fireplace, chintz covered sofas, antique furniture and pretty china was her mother's delight and no doubt the useful but bizarre little chair spoiled the décor. But then any sort of invalid carriage would have struck a wrong note.

The Pittenweem bed was higher and the chair was lower than in Glasgow, but Mary had a small sturdy wooden stool in the coal shed that she had picked up for a shilling at some auction, thinking it would be useful sooner or later. With this stool Annie and Helen were able to use the same method of lifting in and out of bed as at home. The stool was smaller but Annie would cling to the brass bedstead while Helen wheeled the chair away, then rush forward to grab her mother and throw her upwards into bed. More strength was needed for the lift up and the deeper drop backwards into the chair was quite an adventure at first, but they both became used to it.

"You're quite brave letting yourself fall backwards down into space like that, mummy!"

"Aye, well I won't say it was easy the first few times, but I trust my wee girl to have the chair properly placed and 'at the ready' and you know, it's quite exciting! I'm beginning to enjoy it. And you're awful good at wheeching me up. I seem to fly through the air."

Although Mary would always dislike it intensely, it was a wonderful little chair and would do sterling service every summer for the next eleven years. It was easy to push it out into the garden and Helen liked to sit in it herself while she had her breakfast in the fresh air each morning before getting her mother up. She would set it out before she made breakfast and by the time she sat in it, the leather had been warmed by the sun and felt very luxurious.

On the third morning in Pittenweem, Annie had asked Helen why she was getting up so early. It was only seven-thirty.

"That's earlier than you get up during term time."

"I like to sit in the garden. It's lovely and quiet with just the birds singing. And I can smell the sea and read my book. Before grandma gets up, you know."

Annie knew only too well. Sitting reading a book in the garden was not considered acceptable behaviour for a young woman. There was always some chore that needed to be done.

"Will I tell you what I used to do? I'd make a cup of tea and take it up to her in her bed, with the Daily Express and then she would lie for another couple of hours and I would be able to read, or do what I wanted. And if you nipped along to the bakers and got the rolls, she would love a roll and butter and stay in bed even longer. And get up in a good mood."

Keeping grandma in a good mood was their constant, though not always achievable, aim.

Helen followed Annie's advice the following morning and throughout the rest of the summer. Mary was charmed and very grateful and usually stayed in bed till nearly eleven, enjoying the newspaper. grandad only needed a cup of tea before falling asleep again.

Meanwhile Helen, ensconced in the bucket seat on wheels in the flowery garden, munched two fresh rolls and homemade rhubarb jam, as she read of the adventures of three charming boys wrecked on a coral island. As she read, sparrows and blackbirds sang incredibly loudly all around her and the worries, disappointments and indignation of her Glasgow life started to fade from her mind.

Those wonderful hours in the garden! Though the weather was not always good that summer, the sun always seemed to shine in the morning for Helen. She thought it heavenly.

At nine-thirty she would get Annie up, bring her water to wash, help her dress and get her into her chair. Then tilting up the chair, Helen would wheel her mother briskly out to the garden, bumping the back wheels down the little doorstep, rattling over the crazy paving to the grass, where the chair was returned to its rightful angle with something of a thump. It was a week before Helen learned to use her own weight to counterbalance that jarring bump.

Annie always gasped a little on arrival in the garden. There was a certain degree of pain and discomfort in the short bumpy ride, but she would not complain. It was obviously something of a struggle for her daughter and it could not be accomplished in a more gentle or controlled way.

The sea and fresh air worked its magic on Annie too, as she sat knitting in the garden. She had started a pretty lacy jumper for Helen. She found the repeat pattern soothing and pleasurable and thought she might never again knit another pair of Fair Isle gloves. By the end of the first week, Annie and her daughter were brown and somewhat plumper, thanks to the rhubarb jam and the curds and cream that Mary made for her daughter each day.

Mary was an excellent cook and baker. The only drawback was that if something that she made were a success the first time, as the curds certainly were, she would continue to provide it until the recipient reached a stage of saturation. Any suggestion that a change might be advisable was met with reproach and hurt feelings leading swiftly to angry justifications.

"I thought you'd been enjoying it! You said you liked it before. So sorry you were getting fed up with it!"

Mary was touchy as dynamite and one never knew when she might explode.

However, Mary seemed determined to care for, even spoil, her daughter and granddaughter that summer. She was sixty-two now and still a very energetic woman. While she took nothing to do with the personal care of Annie, she asked very little of Helen, except to run errands or sweep the floor.

John, at seventy six, was certainly forgetful and was becoming rather a shadowy figure in the house, still spending most of his day in the upstairs studio. As always, he carried a sketchbook when out walking, but he no longer painted out of doors. The cumbersome weight of his tripod easel, canvas and paints was too much for him to carry. On colder days, he would chop up sticks and put on a fire in the studio for himself. Helen liked to see him chopping sticks. It reminded her of when he used to saw logs and she would collect the sawdust to make porridge for her dolls. But he did not use the saw nowadays and she realised sadly that he was quite an old man. As she watched him bend down stiffly to gather the kindling, she felt a pang of remorse to think that perhaps she was not as nice to him as she should be. They had been such good friends when she was little and now she was busy with her own friends, helping her mother, reading, swimming and there was never much time to spend with him.

Though John probably spent most of the time reading in his quiet studio, he did still paint and had asked Helen to sit for him sometime, when she wasn't busy. He was never insistant. The picture was of a fishergirl with a basket over her arm, always a favourite pose and always a good seller. But Helen, at twelve, was unwilling to sit for her grandfather and had so far avoided the task. It seemed a very boring occupation. She had modelled for him since she was four and then he had amused her with fairy stories and peeled apples. Now she was too old for those stories and apples were so scarce that Helen would nowadays certainly eat every bit of skin and the core too.

When John found the energy one day to replace a long-broken pane of glass, the evocative smell of the putty brought tears to Helen's eyes. As a child, she had adored playing with the grey, aromatic, plastic substance. As she watched her grandfather's slow movements, a great sadness overwhelmed her. It seemed that those old days, like so many other things, were lost and irretrievable. Intense feelings of sorrow and loss were not unknown to Helen. She had suffered from them regularly during their sojourn in Pittenweem but Annie had always cleverly vanquished her daughter's doldrums, by introducing a new handcraft or card game. Now Helen's sadness was aggravated by guilt. Surely she had neglected this special relationship with her grandfather. How unkind she had been. Watching him as he slowly climbed the stone stairs, she determined to sit for him and go walking with him, the very next time that he asked her.

◊

Annie had a pile of old newspapers beside her and was rolling them up to make fire-lighters. Although her hands were not as deft as formerly, she was pleased to see that she could still make the paper into a long tight roll, then wind it strongly around her hand, fixing the end through the middle, to make a firm knot. Four or five of these would start the fire without the help of sticks. As usual, she saw all sorts of interesting things to read that she had missed when the paper was new. A Glasgow Herald dated 21st June had black headlines that, as usual, shouted of strife in every part of the world.

JAPANESE FLEET
Decisive battle may be fought.

ALLIED ADVANCES IN BURMA

BATTLE ON THREE SIDES OF VALOGNE

ASSAULTS ON GERMAN OIL REFINERIES

CHERBOURG BLITZ
Land, sea and air.

RUSSIANS CAPTURE VIIPUR

RAF DROP RECORD TONNAGE IN JUNE

Annie grimaced at 'record tonnage'. How beastly to use such an abstract phrase with such glee and triumph. The word bomb was not used, yet how many people had been killed and how many homes and other precious possessions had been wiped out by this 'record tonnage'. A spasm of pain washed over her.

She picked up a more recent paper, dated 4th July. It was just as bad,

MINSK IS CAPTURED
AMERICAN OFFENSIVE IN NORMANDY
ALLIES GAIN CONTROL IN COTENTIN AREA
AMERICANS DROP 57,000 TONS IN JUNE

It was all too terrible. The Pittenweem house and garden were so quiet and fragrant. How hard to imagine devastation and horror in other places. And these incredible 'robot planes' that were dropping and exploding in London seemed almost supernatural.

There was mention of the reported death of Gigli. Two weeks previously, he had been banned from performing at a concert for British troops because of his alleged collaboration with the Germans. How sad that such a distinguished, world-famous man should have his reputation spoiled in the last weeks of his life.

By this time she had a mound of paper balls beside her. She did not want to stop. It made her feel useful and gave her some satisfaction to think of all this dreadful news being crushed and burned.

An even older paper from early June shrieked,

10,000 GERMANS DEAD AT JASSY

Annie swiftly turned to another page.

MAY HAD LITTLE SUN AND HEAVY RAIN

Well, they all knew that! It had been miserable. She turned to the women's page, always hoping to find a new recipe.

SAUSAGE AND BACON PIE
Short crust pastry, 4oz sausage meat, half oz diced bacon,
I reconstituted egg. 1tblsp flour, pinch of dried herbs, 1tblsp milk.

Annie was not excited by that one.

MINCE PATTIES
3ozs mince, 2tblsps mashed potato, I grated leek, I tblsp flour,
ketchup, I dried egg.
Drop small spoonfuls into hot deep fat and fry till golden brown.

She supposed this might be all right, though she was not sure about the grated leek. How did one grate a leek? She would prefer to put such a precious thing in soup. She started to laugh when she read the final sentence,

Any leftovers can be served cold with salad.

Was this irony? Only a magician might expect to have leftovers from three ounces of mince and two spoonfuls of potato!

On the next page she was amused by another item.

16,000 FARTHINGS STOLEN

James Brown, a checker with the LMS railway was convicted of removing the box of farthings from its rightful journey and hiding it away. This was not his first conviction. When found, the box was short of seventeen shillings and elevenpence halfpenny.

Helen walked into the sitting room just then.

"Helen, how many farthings are there in seventeen shillings and elevenpence halfpenny?"

Although Helen prided herself on her mental arithmetic, it was holiday time and she threw her mother a look of indignant astonishment and walked quickly from the room.

Annie sat there chuckling. Poor James Brown. Had he spent all those farthings in one shop? But surely no shop keeper would accept them as legal tender. Poor soul, he must have worked hard to get rid of his ill-gotten gains. Now he was in jail. Probably not one of the brightest lads. At least it had given her a good giggle.

There was a very nice summer coat advertised by Coplands. The drawing showed square shoulders which were not too extreme. It was of fine black wool marocain with a detachable white pique rever (complete rever underneath). It was *trés chic* and Annie sighed. Her old crottle coat hung in the Glasgow wardrobe. Harris tweed never wore out and anyway, she would never need a heavy coat again. She decided to stop her gloomy thoughts there and then. This marocain coat was disgustingly expensive at £18.5s.6d and 18 coupons, obscene when you thought of all the homeless and helpless people in Europe. She turned back to James Brown and his farthings to cheer herself up.

Old Friends

As she was collecting the rolls one morning, Helen was delighted to meet her friend Alison in the High Street. They had first met the previous October when Alison was visiting her aunt Alice, who was the Pittenweem butcher. The two girls had immediately found many interests in common and become firm friends. Alison lived in Dunfermline and they had written one letter to each other since Helen returned to Glasgow, but Helen's life had been too intense over these last months to keep up the correspondence.

Now they chatted eagerly, arranging to swim in the afternoon and to spend the evening drawing.

Helen walked home, smiling to herself. It was so nice to have a friend in Pittenweem. The years at school had been lonely. There had been Jean, but she had not been an altogether satisfactory friend. Helen knew that Alison would never bully her as Jean had.

She often thought of Jean and tried to imagine her in Edinburgh. They still wrote to each other sporadically, as did their mothers. Jean's parents were in charge of a strange thing called a Camera Obscura. It had been described to Helen but she found it difficult to understand or visualize. She could not imagine people coming to your house every day and paying to see views of Edinburgh. It sounded interesting and it must be good fun to take the tickets at the door, as Jean said she did. Perhaps Helen would go through and visit Jean sometime and find out exactly what a Camera Obscura was. Perhaps help take the tickets too. To travel to Edinburgh by herself was the problem. She had no ambition to go to a big city by herself. Here in Pittenweem, the streets were almost innocent of traffic, apart from the butcher's boy on his bike or the horse-drawn baker's van. One could wander along day-dreaming in the middle of the road. It was good to be back in Pittenweem again, especially as she did not have to go to school and the sun was shining and she had a friend.

It was going to be a very good summer.

◊

The adults listened religiously to the news each day at one o'clock and six o'clock.

Helen noticed that they almost always took the same position to listen.

Her grandmother sat in the big armchair, gazing intently into the fire, whether it was burning or not. Her slender legs were crossed and one hand gracefully supported her chin in the fashion of an Edwardian photograph, while the fingers of her other hand tapped impatiently on the arm of her chair. Often she might take a deep breath or perhaps tut slightly at some particular item of news.

Annie would carefully lay aside her knitting and fold her arms, tucking both hands out of sight, then turn her head to the side and gaze out to sea. Sometimes she would bite her lower lip with her large white teeth and heave a deep sigh.

John would have been called down from the studio to hear the news and was likely to be wearing his hat and muffler, as he usually did when he was working upstairs. He always sat with his back to the window, on the mahogony chair that his own grandfather had made around the time of Waterloo. He listened with his head bowed and his hands clasped between his knees.

Helen would leave the room while the plummy voice told of successful British and American encounters and German defeats in places all over the world. In spite of perfect enunciation, the announcer anglicised the unfamiliar foreign names in a way that would astonish and horrify the more globally aware modern listener.

If Helen returned before the news ended, she found them there, unchanged, sitting like statues, just as she had left them.

Helen had little interest in the war news and took advantage of the adults' preoccupation to read her book or daydream in some other room. Perhaps she might have felt more involved if any member of the family had been in the armed forces but, unlike most families, they knew no one on active service. There had been an Australian lad, a distant relation of Mary's, who had been killed early in the war. At the request of his family, John had painted his portrait from a photograph. Helen had liked the jaunty lop-sided hat he wore, but he had no reality for her. He had come from that unknown world called Australia and had died before she knew of his existence. He might as well have been a character in a book.

◊

Mary decided to have fish suppers for tea. Helen was really looking forward to that. There were two fish and chip shops in Pittenweem. The premises of the one near the end of the High Street were incredibly small. Each summer, Helen was newly astonished at how minute this thriving business was. Every cubic foot of the little cave was utilised. The deep-frying equipment was in a corner with the counter curving around it and the customers pressed together in the small remaining space. There was a fascination in watching the whole process. The chips were lifted out in a wire basket which was then thumped several times on the edge of the fryer to help drain the fat. The chips were thrown through a small door into a hot cupboard beside the boiling fat and that door slammed shut. Another door at the front of the cupboard opened for hot chips to be shovelled into the bespoke bags which were made in the shop, neat triangular pokes, with a little twist at the bottom. Helen thought she would like to learn how to do that. In fact the whole process of thumping, chucking and slamming little doors appealed to her.

"I think you should go to the other shop tonight, Helen. Taylor's is closer and they're supposed to do the best suppers just now. And she's a very nice woman."

Mary's word was law and Helen did not argue. She would go and buy chips for herself in the wee shop some other time.

Taylor's shop was long and narrow and as Helen stood at the end of the queue, Mrs Taylor caught sight of her. To Helen's embarrassment, she was called to the front of the counter and was served before the others.

"Noo jist wait there a wee minute, Helen,"

Mrs Taylor disappeared into the back shop and returned shortly with a magnificent bunch of mixed flowers from her garden.

"Noo, Ah ken yer mither's no' been sae strong-like recently an' Ah ken she pents picturs like her faither, so here's some bonny flooers frae the gairden an' she micht like tae pent thim. You gie them tae her from me an' say Ah wis askin' kindly fur her. Wull ye dae that noo, ma lassie?"

Helen was overwhelmed and said 'Thank you very much indeed' several times and returned along the High Street with the hot parcel under one arm and the fresh quivering flowers in her other hand.

The next day, John brought down a canvas from the studio and Helen helped her mother to set up her palette and the flowers in her bedroom. Annie stayed there painting all day. That night she said,

"I don't know what sort of job I've made of these flowers, but I've enjoyed myself tremendously. And you know what? I don't seem nearly so stiff and sore. It's done me good. I want you to go and thank Mrs Taylor tonight. You and Alison can go and have a bag of chips each and say thank you to her."

"I just hope you don't get cold sitting in that bedroom all day long." Mary looked cross as she spoke.

Later Helen asked her mother,

"Why did grandma seem angry?"

"Oh I don't know. Perhaps she's jealous that I'm not painting flowers from her own garden. Probably she thinks there's only one real artist in this family and I'm just wasting my time. Maybe I am."

"No, I think she's missing having someone to talk to. She likes talking so much."

"Maybe. Who knows?"

Wee Eileen

M ary looked at the envelope with a worried frown for a
few moments before she opened it.

"It's from Willie, John. I hope there's no bad news."

Willie did not write often and his letters often contained a
request for financial help.

However a smile broke over her face as she read.

"Isn't that nice! Willie and Eileen have been asked down to
London to a wedding and they wonder if we could look after wee
Eileen for a week, while they have a little holiday. Do you think I
could manage a little girl of four, John? I'm sure I could and Helen
will help me, won't you, my jewel? That would be lovely to have
her here, she's such a wee beauty. I've never seen a more beautiful
child, really I haven't."

Helen had not seen her little cousin for more than a year and
had not noticed that she was spectacularly beautiful. She had been
very sweet, with wonderful large, dark eyes, but she had seemed a
bit skinny for true beauty. Helen remembered the child being persuaded to sing just as she, as a child, had been encouraged to
mimic Mae West and Greta Garbo. The song was 'Jealousy'
entirely unsuitable for a child of three to lisp and Helen had wondered if wee Eileen had hated performing as much as she herself
used to hate it. She also considered it a bit stupid to call a child the
same name as her mother, necessitating the use of 'big' and 'wee'
at all times. It seemed to make life unnecessarily difficult. Helen
had few maternal instincts and the idea of helping to look after a
small kid did not really appeal. However it was only for a week
and Alison would have returned home by that time, so she agreed
to help, making herself sound quite enthusiastic and wondering at
the same time why she was doing that.

When wee Eileen arrived with her daddy she seemed very little
and very shy. Helen took her hand and led her into the garden. She
was not at all sure how to speak to such a young child, but she
remembered something she had liked very much herself when she
was wee. She picked a snapdragon flower and by squeezing the
back of the flower gently, it looked very much as though it was

opening up its mouth. As she manipulated the flower, Helen made it miaow like a cat and then speak in a tiny squeaky voice. It said,

"Hello little girl, what a pretty dress. I think your name must be wee Eileen."

Either Helen was a skillful ventriloquist, or Eileen was an imaginative child, for the toddler just fell into fits of laughter, then started to speak to the flower, asking its name, where it lived and if it was hungry. Helen made the flower respond correctly and the conversation developed as though it had been rehearsed. Helen was entranced by this imaginative child. What a sweet and amazing little girl!

When they went upstairs to unpack, Helen was delighted with the seven little summer dresses, each with matching pants and a little coat hanger. Surely it was only child film stars that had such a wardrobe. Helen knew that looking after her little cousin for a week would be just the greatest fun, almost like having a living doll.

Eileen was obedient and charming, with many quaint ideas and sayings. It was a delight to care for her and Helen liked bedtime best, when she washed the little face and hands and popped the frilly pyjamas on. Then they would stand at the back door for five minutes, listening to the noisy sparrows in the elder tree and sniffing the aromatic night-scented stock which released its pungent perfume at evening.Then Helen would bring her own beloved doll, Topsy (who had travelled to Pittenweem in spite of Helen's twelve years) to the tiny bedroom upstairs and tell Eileen stories about Topsy's life before she was Helen's doll. They were not exactly the same plots that her mother had told her when she was a little girl, for Helen disliked repetition and preferred to strike out in her own way. The four-year-old was fascinated by the doll, cuddling her as she listened to tales of her adventurous past.

Her lovable little cousin helped Helen discover deeply hidden maternal instincts as well as giving her the opportunity to employ those didactic skills, which until now had been mainly used for the benefit of her toys.

Eileen, on her part, was entranced by this cousin who was big and strong and kind, who could swim and jump off high walls, who had long fair plaits like a princess in a book. No other girl in the world had hair like that or could tell such good stories.

It is fair to say that the two cousins fell in love with each other that summer and in spite of the difference in their ages, would always remain close and affectionate friends.

One day the child had been upstairs by herself, when she suddenly came running downstairs and into the sitting room. Her grandma looked up, Eileen looked close to tears.

"Are you all right, my pet? I thought I heard a bang upstairs."

"Yeth, the wee bottle fell out de window!"

Mary was nonplussed,

"What bottle was that, darling? You didn't hurt yourself did you?"

Helen realised immediately what had happened. As is the way with neglected holiday homes, the bedroom window had no cord and the lower sash was always held ajar with a small medicine bottle.

"Were you trying to open the window wider?" Helen asked and Eileen nodded, her large eyes looking very worried. "And the bottle fell down into the street and broke? Is that what happened?"

Eileen nodded again.

"Well that doesn't matter at all, my little jewel." Mary's voice was deep and comforting, "As long as my wee girl wasn't hurt. Did my darling get a horrible fright?"

Eileen nodded and her lips trembled. Helen gave her a cuddle and at last Eileen spoke,

"I got a noffal big f'ight and den I looked in the mirror to thee if I wath pale…"

Helen bit her lip to stop from smiling. Annie, with a gentle quizzical look, asked,

"And were you pale, wee Eileen?"

"Yeth, I wath vewy pale."

Helen jumped up and left the room without looking at her mother, for she knew they were both close to uncontrollable giggles.

Annie later expressed disapproval,

"That child hasn't been helped to grow up properly. She shouldn't be speaking baby talk at her age."

"Oh, but she's so sweet and funny the way she talks."

"Yes, but she'll start school next year and other children will laugh and there's far too much fuss and nonsense made about her clothes. She's just treated like a little doll."

"I suppose that's true. But I do love looking after her."

Only once did Helen have a tussle with Eileen. It happened when the knickers matching a particular dress were not dry and the child had refused to wear any others. It was the only time she had been difficult, but she had been very obstinate. A lot of time and energy were wasted and Helen realised there was some truth in her mother's criticism.

Helen drew her little cousin several times and Eileen was very good at sitting still.

Helen had adored looking after this delightful little girl and the house seemed very empty on the day that wee Eileen returned to Glasgow with her parents.

◊

Helen felt reluctant to go swimming by herself, though probably she would meet acquaintances at the pool. It had been so nice to go swimming with Alison. They had such good conversations. When she was looking after her cousin, she had only swum once on a day that Mary had come to the beach. It was too cold for a non-swimmer to go into the water. Helen had found it fun building sandcastles and dams for Eileen. A younger child allowed you to play games that might have been undignified for a secondary school pupil.

Now a lonely summer stretched ahead. Helen's mind returned to her grievances at school. She remembered that silly teacher saying she was weak and the thought of repeating first year was boring and depressing. Yet again she would be a stranger in the class and must make new friends.

Only two days after Eileen's departure, there was a loud knock at the front door.

It was Vera, whose mother was related to the local bakers who made the delicious rolls. Earlier in the war, Vera had come to Pittenweem primary school for a short time. But as there was little likelihood of bombs dropping on Edinburgh, a city without industries, she had returned to Morningside, where her father was a minister. She was a pretty girl with beautiful red curly hair and she and Helen had been good friends for a couple of months before she left. Now she and her little sister, Jenny, would be staying in Pittenweem with her grandma and aunt for the next four weeks. It seemed just wonderful to Helen. Here was another friend for her holidays. They immediately went off for a walk to catch up on all the things that had happened to them both in the last four years.

Future Plans

Annie was in the sitting room scraping a big bowl of Ayrshire potatoes for the dinner. She had insisted that she could do a lot of chores, if the things were brought to her. Mary sat smoking a cigarette by the fire. The weather had turned cold and rainy.

"That's the good weather gone now and the unlucky Fair folk'll be drenched and frozen, as usual."

Sometimes it seemed that Mary delighted in gloomy prognostications.

Annie spoke her thoughts aloud,

"I wonder how poor Jessie is getting on in Rothesay and if the move to Aberdeen still makes her so unhappy. I expect she'll be fine once she gets there and settles in."

"Oh I think Aberdeen's a pretty damned cold place. Wouldn't like to be living there myself."

There was a pause, with only the sound of Annie scraping and the sticks in the fire crackling.

"I wonder what you'll do without Jessie, when you go home?"

"Just have to find someone else, I suppose. Won't be easy to replace Jessie though."

"She was loud though, wasn't she? And she was very careless with the china, I noticed a lot of chipped cups and plates."

"I suppose she wasn't perfect, but she had a very kind heart and we got on well together. We made each other laugh. I'll miss her a lot."

"I've been thinking, when I watch how good wee Helen is with you and how much she has to do for you…"

Annie winced at the words. She was very guilty at how much Helen had to do for her, yet she felt helpless to change it. Helen seemed determined to look after her and never complained. She was always there at the right time, nearly always anyway, and seemed to accept it all as quite normal.

Mary threw her cigarette end into the fire and said,

"Well, I think the two of you should come and stay with us in Renfrew Street. Your father and I have discussed it and he thinks it's the best idea and so do I. Helen will be near her school and I can help her look after you and she can help me with shopping. You'd have company and she wouldn't have so much responsibility. What d'you think? Bruce would be pleased too I'm sure, it would take a load off his mind. And his wallet."

Annie smiled but did not reply immediately.

"It's very generous of you to offer, Maw."

"I think it's the only thing to do, really."

"They were talking in the papers a few weeks ago about a Home Help system the government's trying to set up. Maybe that would be the answer, although it said there was a terrible shortage of domestic workers between eighteen and fifty.They were all involved in war work, I suppose."

"Och, the government! Nothing will ever come of that idea."

Hopeful as always, Annie did not want to agree with that statement.

She knew that the situation with Jessie had worked well and she was unwilling to relinquish her last shreds of independence. There was only one person in charge in any house where Mary was present. These weeks in Pittenweem had reminded Annie of her mother's unpredictable moods and domineering tendencies. She dreaded finding herself in her mother's power once again, even if that power had benign intentions. It might in the future be necessary to return to her parents' home but right now, she and Helen, with a bit of domestic help, could still deal with the world in their own home.

Annie thanked her mother again and said she would certainly think it over, but in her own mind she was sure a return to Renfrew Street could be disastrous. She was certain Helen would agree with her, but she would discuss it with her that night.

Suddenly, Mary jumped to her feet and rushed into the kitchen, which opened out of the sitting room.

"I knew it! I could smell it!"

"What is it, Maw? What's happened?"

"It's your father's burned the arse out of another kettle. Really! It's too bad! And they're so difficult to come by, these whistling kettles. What a nuisance. He's so forgetful."

Annie felt like smiling at her mother's colourful language, but knew better when Mary was obviously furious.

"Does it need to be a whistling kettle?"

"Och yes, because he would never remember otherwise. He'd just go away and leave an ordinary one to boil its guts out."

"But that one wasn't whistling or we would have heard it in here."

"No, because he fills it and then he forgets to put the whistle on."

"Well I don't see much point in getting another whistling kettle then ... surely an ordinary one..."

Annie should not have aggravated her mother's ire with that last remark, but she could never resist drawing things to their logical conclusion.

Marry tut-tutted loudly before she slammed the kitchen door shut and disappeared upstairs for the next two hours, where knocks and bangs and moving furniture defined her mood.

No, it would not be a good idea to move permanently into her mother's home. Eight summer weeks together in the Pittenweem house was about as much as they could all stand.

◊

Helen and Vera quickly renewed their old friendship and met practically every morning, and again in the afternoon. They swam in the morning, even if it were dull and windy, which it sometimes was. Then they would wear thick cardigans and take a 'shivery bite' of bread and jam to eat after the swim. Generally the weather was mostly sunny and dry, as it often is in that corner of Fife.

In the afternoons they usually played at Vera's grandmother's house and Jenny joined them. They did not meet in the evenings, as Vera had a stricter and earlier bedtime. Helen had mixed feelings about her mother's lax attitude towards her bed-time. She was pleased to stay up as late as she liked, but in other families and in books, children seemed to have a specific bed-time and she felt that this was perhaps more respectable.

Sometimes unexpected family demands meant that Helen and Vera could not meet as planned. As neither house had a telephone, Helen invented a method that seemed to have a touch of romance. Half way between the respective houses was an old wall beside the path. In a crevice in this wall, a small letter could be hidden. It was only a seven minute walk between the houses, but if there were a last minute cancellation of arrangements, a note could be left in the crevice and neither girl need continue her walk beyond that point. More importantly, she need not suffer disappointment nor that slight, but unavoidable, feeling of humiliation which attends a broken engagement. The two girls treasured this secret communication.

◊

Mary's great pleasure in the summer was to attend every church bazaar or sale of work in the immediate neighbourhood. Often Helen was co-opted to accompany her, which she did dutifully, though without joy. For Helen, as well as not seeing her friend, it meant an hour of standing around in a hot crowded room with nothing much of interest to do or see, although the overpowering perfume of sweet peas was almost always present and she loved that. The table where knitting was laid out for sale was probably the least boring. Sometimes there were dolls in elaborate outfits which reminded her of those far off days when she had poured over pattern books in the tiny house where her mother was visiting her friend Georgina. Such wonderful outfits had been illustrated in those books and Helen regretted that she had never made any of them. It was not exactly a sense of failure she felt, but a feeling of something as yet unaccomplished. The schoolgirl uniform and a frilly Spanish skirt had seemed particularly desirable, if slightly incongruous, for Topsy.

Georgina was always so kind and friendly and Helen loved her enormous striped cat, Ecky, who stood on his hind legs and pounded at the window to get in. That seemed such a long time ago. It was when her mother could still walk. Standing around at bazaars often seemed to make Helen's thoughts gloomy.

Soon Mary would interrupt these despondent memories and call her over to hold a big bag of fresh vegetables and also probably a bunch of flowers. She herself was laden with heavier bags containing articles which she had rummaged from the bric-a-brac stall. Mary adored the search and possible discovery of some really valuable piece, then the bargaining was also part of the thrill. She would later relate the adventure to her daughter,

"The woman was wanting three shillings, but I offered her half-a-crown and after humming and hawing a bit, she said 'all right' and gave it to me! But you know, I'm sure it's worth four or five pounds when it's cleaned up!"

"You know, Maw, it is a charity and you're supposed to be giving *them* money, not beating them down."

"Ah well, someone was just throwing it away, so at least the Church got something for it. I'm not going to sell it anyway. I like it myself."

To Helen, the conversations that took place after a bazaar were terribly similar, almost word for word. And boring. The good thing was that her grandmother was in a splendid frame of mind, much too good a mood to resent her daughter's remarks. Mary would spend the evening washing, polishing and gloating over her purchases. Annie would look forward to painting the flowers the following day. Sometimes the fresh vegetables included peas in their pods which were Helen's favourite. Everyone was happy.

Peas grew in Vera's grandmother's garden and the girls were encouraged to pick and eat as many as they liked! It was wonderful. Both Mrs Evesham, the grandmother, and Aunt Meg made Helen very welcome. They were pleased that their grandchildren had a friend to play with and there was a glass of milk and pancakes with home made jam for the girls every day at three o'clock. The house was a modern bungalow on the outskirts of the town and very different from any other Pittenweem houses that Helen had visited. Vera's Aunt Meg worked in the family bakery and most people seemed to think her cross and quick-tempered. Mary often complained of her manner in the shop but then she complained about most people. Helen always found Meg really nice and friendly. Meg had red hair like her niece, though it was faded for she was nearly forty. Helen wondered if people just expected red-haired folk to be quick-tempered. Vera was certainly not at all like that and probably Aunt Meg had to deal with a lot of problems in the shop.

The bungalow had a large attic where the children could play if it was chilly outside. Something between a ladder and a staircase had to be climbed to reach the attic, which gave a special feeling of privacy to their games. Adults climbed the stairs slowly and carefully, giving the children enough warning to return to reality. At twelve years old, there was just a slight feeling of guilt about imaginary games. Perhaps they were really too old to play at being pirates and ship-wrecked sailors? Of course little Jenny was an excuse to regress. Sometimes the games were more domestic and Jenny was Vera's child, while Helen was the nanny or the maid. This scenario gave Helen an idea.

"Why don't we do a concert? Let's make up a play and we can perform it in the garden."

Vera was immediately enthusiastic

"And I could recite a poem or maybe play the piano?"

"Yes and I could teach Jenny a little French poem I know. It's really easy and she would be so sweet saying it."

Work began on the French poem right away and Jenny was very willing to say the incomprehensible words in the dramatic manner that Helen required. What a great concert it would be.

◊

When the sea mist blew in or heavy clouds gathered on the horizon, Annie suffered.

In Glasgow, she had not thought of the weather affecting her condition so much, but here in Fife, with the wide visible skies, she realised that she was at the mercy of the elements. Sometimes her muscles contracted in a fierce spasm, at others she ached in her joints. She took her six aspirin daily and tried to hide her discomfort as much as possible, for it distressed her daughter and her father, though strangely it often seemed to irritate her mother. Annie knitted and painted and peeled potatoes and dealt stoically with her bad days. Painting certainly helped her, for the days that she set up her easel and a bunch of flowers were often calm and happy. Helen would look in to the bedroom and ask,

"You're not lonely in here all by yourself?"

Annie would smile and shake her head.

"Are you warm enough?"

"As warm as I would be anywhere else in the house."

It was not a cosy house. If the sun were shining outside, Helen was keen to take Annie out to the garden for she was a great believer in fresh air herself and never missed a chance to be out of doors. Annie always preferred to paint.

"I'm all set up here and enjoying myself. You go out and sit in the sun, though. Perhaps I'll come out later.

But Helen would probably not sit by herself for long before Mary found some little task for her.

Most days John went for a walk, usually along the seaside path, but occasionally into the country and Helen, remembering her good intentions, would sometimes accompany him. She still enjoyed listening to him, though occasionally he repeated himself several times. It was usually some subject about which he had strong feelings, Helen noticed. She felt so sorry for him. It must be horrible to be forgetful. His repetitions certainly annoyed Mary and she would tell him sharply,

'You've said that already, two or three times, in just the last ten minutes!"

John took this reproof mildly, muttering an apology for his forgetfulness.

But Helen felt very protective towards her grandfather and would never mention it, although she admitted to herself that it was quite irritating to have to make a reply to the same remark more than once.

Although forgetful, John was still very interesting when he talked about the past. Helen felt that if Mary had been kinder to him, she might have had more pleasure in his conversation.

Helen and John also went to the cinema some evenings, if Annie thought it was a film that both might enjoy. In this way they watched a wide range of films, some more suitable than others. Whether it was a good film or not, it was a companionable outing and the two of them would share a bag of chips on the way home.

As always, John loved listening to music on the radio, especially Beethoven. Helen, who had become so much more aware of classical music this last year, enjoyed listening too, although she thought it strange to see tears running down her grandfather's cheeks. The wonderful sound seemed to fill her with joy rather than sadness.

Helen thought longingly of their reliable Glasgow radio that did not run on batteries. Often and unexpectedly, the battery in the Pittenweem wireless would run low and the sound would start to fade away during a favourite programme. She hated taking the 'wet' battery up to the garage for re-charging. It was a heavy glass box with a wire handle which she kept shifting from her right hand to her left, as it bit painfully into her flesh. The fact that the liquid inside was acid was frightening, for if any spilled it might burn her skin or ruin her dress. And when the dry battery needed to be replaced, it seemed to be very expensive. Helen often thought how wonderful it would be to have electricity in the Pittenweem house, but that was just a dream. And when evening came, she found it difficult to imagine the little rooms without the friendly hiss of gaslight.

Each week Helen cut the grass. It was an old heavy lawn-mower but fortunately quite a small lawn, about the size of a moderate sitting room. There was a bench and a small table always there and deck chairs were brought out if required. There was also a very strange little chair made of pottery and fashioned to look as if made of rough hewn branches. It was quaint rather than attractive and visitors always commented that they had never seen anything like it before. It stood in a corner at the foot of the garden. It was never used, as it was much too heavy to lift. Also, it was bitingly cold to sit upon in even the hottest of weather. Nevertheless it was an important feature of the garden for Helen, just as important as the large half glazed shed that her grandfather used for painting on a windy day. That was referred to as the downstairs studio and Helen had spent many hours in that warm, musty space when she was younger, giving lessons to her toys, playing imaginary games and reading. Her mother had grown tomatoes and cucumbers there and Helen often thought she could still smell the moist dampness of the big leafy plants. Fifty years old and now somewhat dilapidated, the studio was a bright warm retreat on a chilly day.

While Helen enjoyed the different flowers and plants in the garden, she was never asked to do any weeding and was not at all knowledgable about the garden. Her tasks were more mundane. For example if one of the local horse drawn vans passed the front door at a time that the animal required to empty its bowels, Helen would be sent out with a pail and shovel to collect the excellent manure for the garden. No doubt she found this humiliating and was unwilling to do it, but like other children at that time, Helen had little concept of refusing an order, especially from her imperious grandmother. Apparent reluctance might have a softening effect on Anne, but Mary's command was law.

There was a much less embarrassing way of collecting enrichment for the garden. Each summer Helen and John, armed with a shovel and two large straw baskets, lined with newspaper, walked along the seashore path to St Monance, a mile away. Just outside the town was a tower, the remains of an ancient windmill, which, in the days when there was a salt industry in the area, had provided the power to pump up seawater. There was no longer a roof on the large stone building and the pigeons had made it their home for many years. It took little time to shovel up enough of the thick layer of guano that lay on the floor to fill the baskets. The 'pigeon pen' was brought home and diluted in several pails of water, then allowed to stand for a few days before it was spread on the garden. The stink was terrible. It pervaded the house and garden for over a week, but Mary asssured them it was the price they must pay for the flourishing growth.

Without making much fuss about it, Mary worked in the garden each day. The crazy path was kept free of weeds and the rambler roses were neatly tied up. There was a regular massacre of the snails who inhabited the old walls and soapy water was fiercely squirted at greenfly. Perhaps to amuse her family, Mary displayed a dark delight in this wholesale carnage. Annie laughed with the rest, but wondered at the possibilities of her mother's hidden violence.

Helen particularly liked the many perfumed herbs and shrubs in the little garden. Her favourite was the artemesia known as 'aippleringie' and she would seldom pass that unassuming plant without plucking and crushing a small pinch of its delicate fronds.

The Concert

Mary surprised everyone when she announced that she was going golfing. "I bumped into Mr Clark, you know he has the big licensed grocer's in Anstruther, and he was saying he never saw us along at the Anstruther course these days, so I've arranged to go tomorrow. I don't suppose you would like to come with me, John, would you?"

"No, my dear, I think my golfing days are over. A nice long walk or a game of snooker is about all I'm fit for these days. By the time I'd walked fifty yards I'd have forgotten where the ball was lying! No, you go ahead and enjoy yourself and give them my kind regards."

"That'll be nice, Maw. It's a long time since you've had a game. I hope you enjoy yourself."

Secretly, Annie was wondering if her mother was fit enough. She would never dare say it, but Mary had put on a lot of weight again and did not walk very much. She was still an energetic woman, weeding the garden and visiting her jumble sales, but a game of golf was different. There was no sitting down and resting during a game.

The next day when Mary returned from her game, she seemed only slightly weary. She lingered over her cup of tea and and showed no signs of preparing supper.

"Why doesn't Helen make the tea for us tonight, Maw. We'll just have some macaroni and cheese, will we?"

"It seems a shame to have the wee thing cooking, but my legs are a bit tired. Perhaps I shouldn't have gone after all. But it was nice seeing the old crowd again and my game wasn't so dusty either!"

"Helen would be cooking the tea if she were at home anyway. She just needs to double the quantities."

Helen was not as confident as her mother. It was different when it was just the two of them. Mary was so critical about everything. However the simple tea was produced successfully, amid many compliments from her grandparents.

Mary was up early the next day.

"I'm just going to put the boiler on, there's an awful load of sheets and towels needing washed."

Mary had always tended to have mammoth washdays during the summer. In past years Annie had been there to help with lifting hot water from the boiler to the sink, rubbing the dirtier things on a washboard, turning the mangle and hanging the damp washing to dry on the rope which zig-zagged across the small garden. There would be more mangling after the ritual of 'folding the sheets'.This required two people, two well co-ordinated people, to 'crack' the sheets'. Each took two corners of a sheet folded once lengthwise and standing just the length of the sheet apart, would bring their hands together as they raised their arms above their heads, then energetically opening and lowering their arms in unison, the result would be a loud, satisfying 'crack', similar to the crack of a whip. It was most important that they judged each other's actions and moved in unison, otherwise there would be no noise and the whole thing was a failure and must be repeated. If successful, the sheet was folded into smaller compass to be mangled once more, then aired on a tall wooden screen. Helen had watched this procedure over the years but had not taken part in it, as she was too small. She had no idea of the reason for the strange manoeuvre. Did it remove little folds perhaps? She could not tell and did not like to show her ignorance by asking. She had watched her mother help Mary in the past, though with less strength each summer. Now John must take Annie's place and he was sadly unco-ordinated. In fact he was useless. It was seldom that the sheet cracked when he was a partner and his wife's irritation would grow at each failure, until she became furious. Helen wonderd if it was absolutely necessary to do this difficult thing with sheets. Did other people do it? Whenever she saw the problems caused by grandad's inability she wondered why it must be done and what would happen if they were just folded and ironed.

Annie had dreaded the Pittenweem washdays for years and wondered why her mother did not just send the white things to the professional laundry, as she did in Glasgow. They made a very good job of them for a modest cost. Now she wondered why Mary should choose the day after a day's golfing for such a demanding task.

Helen was commandeered for mangle duty and ran up to leave a little note of regret in the wall for Vera. But she was rather looking forward to the whole business of the wash-day. It was something different. She remembered their days in Pittenweem and how much fun it had been to splash and slide in the old bath in the wash house, making the sort of mess that one could never make in a proper bathroom. That seemed so long ago, yet it was less than a year.

When it came to cracking the sheets, Helen was tested as a partner and was pretty good for a beginner. When it did not go right, Mary was kind and not at all cross, as she was with her husband. Poor John lacked domestic skills, for he was also ineffi-cient at holding a hank of wool while it was wound into a ball and Mary would shout,

"Tighter, John! Hold your hands further apart, for goodness sake. *John*, now you're letting it go all slack! Tut-tut, can you not hold it *tighter*."

Then almost immediately,

"NOT SO TIGHT! You're holding it far too tight!" and a shake of Mary's head was accompanied by her irritated tutting.

Then quite soon, without another word, she would snatch the hank from his hands and drape it over the back of a chair, to fin-ish winding it.

It seemed strange that the artist who could control his brush to paint such delicate details could not come up to scratch with these simple chores, but perhaps his heart was not in it.

The washday gave Helen another idea for her concert. The tall wooden airing stand could be draped with a bedspread to form a background to her stage and allow the actors to enter and exit.

◊

Little by little Helen's project built up in her mind. She had taken control of the concert and Vera and Jenny seemed quite happy to let her direct the operation.

In the shop in the market square that sold everything from china to kitchenware, from seeds to gas mantles and rude post-cards, Helen had caught sight of something which fascinated her. There displayed on the counter, was a bowl with many eggs in it. She knew the shop did not sell food and also such largesse as a baking bowl full of eggs was unknown at the time. She could not understand it. At last she plucked up courage to ask about them.

"Oh thae's chiny eggs, ma lass. If you pit them in the wi' the hen in 'er nest, it gies her the richt idea whaur to lay her ain eggs."

From that moment Helen wanted two of these china eggs for her play. She would jugggle them about and pretend to let them fall. She would never do that with real eggs. They were much too precious. She did not have an allowance, but she was easily able to ask for money without telling her mother what it was for.

"It's a secret, Mummy."

"That's fine, darling. Will I ever find out?"

"Oh yes, quite soon."

The following week, with the end of the holidays less than two weeks away, it was raining and the three girls were playing in the big attic at the bungalow. Jenny was at the other end of the large room and paying no attention to them. Their game had come to an end, or rather petered out, as these games tended to do eventually. Vera suddenly snatched a pillow from the bed and tucking it between her legs, said,

"When I put this pillow in, it's white and when I bring it out it's red. D'you know what I'm talking about?"

Helen nodded. She knew only too well, for menstruation is a messy business for an invalid unable to walk. Helen had dealt with bloody sheets and clothing for the last six months.

"Have you started yet?" Vera asked.

Helen shook her head.

"Neither have I."

Then with no more discussion, they returned to their childish games.

◊

Bruce came through for the weekend.

As usual, Helen looked forward to his visit, then very quickly started longing for Sunday night when he would go away again. He was his usual loud, jocular self and Mary and he chatted away as if they were the very best of friends. John stayed in his studio most of the day and Annie listened to the non-stop conversation and tried to hide the fact that she was in a lot of pain. The overcast sky was partly to blame.

Vera and Jenny were introduced to Bruce on Saturday and as usual, he concocted different names for them. Vera became Velma or Norma and Jenny was Jessy or Jinty. The two girls did not seem to mind, but Helen did and winced each time Bruce used the wrong name and her friends corrected him.

"Will we do the concert for your daddy tomorrow?" Vera asked on the Saturday as she left.

"Oh, I don't think we're quite ready yet, are we?"

But Helen knew she was not being honest. She did not want to perform for her father. His presence made her feel awkward and she could never relax and let herself go when he was around.. She did not know why. It was just the case.

Bruce had brought a letter for Annie. She tucked it into her pocket and said,

"I'll read it later."

She knew it would be from Jessie. That night in bed she read,

Dear Mrs Corning,

Wee George is walking and has lace-up boots and I'm that proud of him. The flat is alright but awful wee. Aberdeen is alright to and nice shops but I never know what there saying because they speak awful funny. Rothesay was wet but good fish suppers an we enjoyed werselves. Jim likes his new job an Im missing you awful. Do you ever get a bed bath now? George stumps along like a reel wee man now he is a lovely boy. I wish I was back in Glasgow with my mum and friends and you to.

With love from your dear friend Jessie.

Annie shed a few tears. That part of her life was behind her. Who would be looking after her next? Would she ever find another good-hearted, lively girl like Jessie again? Bruce said he was looking at the ads in shop windows. There was bound to be someone.

As Annie had suspected, Mary had overtaxed herself with golfing, followed by a washday. For most of the next three days she stayed in bed or relaxed with a book in the studio. She was irritable with everyone. When Annie suggested that she and Helen might prepare something for the next meal, Mary would snap at her and get up and do it herself with a martyred air.

Fortunately she had recovered for the next Saturday, when the concert was due to be performed.

The wooden drying frame was draped with a brown silk bedspread and Annie and her parents took their seats in the garden. It was a beautiful afternoon.

It would have been nice if Vera could have played the piano to start the concert, Unfortunately there was no working piano in the house, only the 150 year old, tinkling, rippling fortepiano that Mary had bought more than thirty years before, for five shillings. She had always meant to have it tuned, but suspected it needed a specialist and had never found one. It spent an elegant though unmusical life as a sideboard in the sitting room.

Helen had considered playing a tune on her recorder. There were quite a few tunes that she played by ear, but she knew that an audience might put her off. It was best to begin with Jenny's French poem. Helen had started to make a written programme but it looked so messy that she discarded it and decided to announce the details.

Jenny wore a pretty dress and with her fair curls, she looked very sweet. Helen stood half hidden in the 'wings', ready to prompt if required, and admired the scene and the audience as only a successful producer and entrepreneur can. The recital began and Jenny said her poem perfectly. Her accent was perfect too, or as perfect as Helen's tutoring could make it. The dramatic side of the verses was expressed in the last three lines, the first of which was whispered, the next spoken normally and the third shouted at full volume.

A Paris, a Paris, a Paris
Sur un petit cheval gris,
O pas, pas, pas.
O trot, trot, trot,
O GALOP O GALOP O GALOP.

That last line was very tricky with the swift change of vowel representing the horse at full gallop, but Jenny was excellent. What a clever wee girl. The adults started to clap furiously, but Helen held up a warning hand and shook her head. There was another verse.

A Rouen, a Rouen, a Rouen,
Sur un petit cheval blanc,
Etc, etc.

Again Jenny's enunciation was superb. The applause from the three adults was thunderous. Helen felt so proud of her little protegee and also proud of herself. She had worked hard at coaching.

Next came the play, 'The New Maid'. Helen took the title role and Vera was a Posh Lady with a Spoiled Daughter played by Jenny.

As soon as the play started, Annie realised that Helen had modelled her character on Jessie and on her coarser, careless side. The new maid spoke in a broad Glasgow accent and almost immediately started dropping and breaking things. She bumped into things, knocked chairs over and let books and other unbreakables drop. It was when she was offstage, behind the bedspread, that there was the unmistakable sound of dishes breaking. Then she would pop her head round the corner and apologise brightly,

"Ah'm awfy sorry, Ah think Ah've broke yer green vaise, Missus."

Then she would enter again and behave outrageously. Each time she exited there was the sound of more dishes breaking. It was well done and Mary and John were helpless with laughter. Annie rather less so. What was Helen breaking behind the curtain? Then she relaxed when she suddenly remembered a trick that Bruce had bought for Helen's Christmas some years ago. Five square metal plates, about the size of playing cards, which, when they were dropped on a hard surface, made a realistic sound of crashing china. Helen must have found them tucked away in a drawer.

As the maid was polishing the table, she stooped to examine an imaginary flaw. After rubbing it vigorously, she re-examined it, then looking towards her audience, exclaimed with a philosophic shrug,

"Ach tae hell, it'll dae!"

Annie's eyebrows rose. It was a perfect reproduction of Jessie's accent and philosophy but what other examples of Jessie's colourful language might Helen use?

The table was set noisily, with old cups and plates which Helen had found discarded in the wash house, Annie was glad to note. They were chucked and clattered and cutlery strewed indiscriminately amongst them. Vera sat with a wonderfully straight face, wincing when there was a specially loud bang. Jenny tried to hide her smiles behind clasped hands. Then Helen entered with a saucepan out of which she produced two eggs. Annie drew in a deep breath. Surely her daughter had not the effrontery to make use of this scarce commodity. A side glance showed that Mary was wondering the same thing. Soon Mary was laughing again as Helen juggled with them as though they were hot, dropped them on the ground, rolled them about the table, threw them in the air and only just caught them at the last minute. The audience was gasping with laughter. Vera was very good and continued to look disapproving, though it was obviously an effort but Jenny was laughing heartily. At last the play finished with one last crash offstage and Vera, with an admirably stern expression told the audience,

"The new maid must go!"

The concert had been a success and Mary and John both wiped their eyes after so much laughter. Annie was quieter. She knew that the picture Helen had painted had a lot of truth in it. Her daughter had not tried to be unkind, nevertheless, Annie could not laugh quite so wholeheartedly as her parents.

"Well, I must say," said Mary "no mystery about where that character came from. What an actress Helen is! I had no idea she had such talent. She was *wonderful* wasn't she, just astounding. She must have been observing Jessie all these months and she had her down to a T, she really did. Truly, I think she's a marvellous child. And the other wee girls did very well too. I don't know when I've had such a good laugh. What a great entertainment it all was!"

Helen thought it had been pretty great herself. Fancy them laughing as much as all that. It was very satisfying to make people laugh. She loved it!

They laughed again later when they learned the eggs were china.

The next day the concert was repeated in Vera's garden for the benefit of her aunt and grandma.

Acting on her mother's advice, Helen removed the word 'hell' from the script, for the Eveshams were church-goers. The ladies sat up very straight and smiled a lot, though they did not laugh as heartily as John and Mary had. It was surprising for them to see Vera's polite, rather timid friend acting in such a loud vulgar way, They had never met Jessie.

After the concert, there was lemonade and home-made biscuits and the girls ate peas from the vine for half an hour. Helen loved the whole process of standing in the sun amongst the fresh greenery, selecting a properly ripe pod, squeezing it in the right place to make it pop open, then the surprise of discovery! Perhaps nine peas were crammed together, flattening each other in the crush, or there might only be five little, very sweet, baby peas. The fresh pods were good to chew, too.

Standing there in the sunshine, Helen picked and ate and basked in the memory of her successful show, happy and satisfied.

Jessie's Successor

Bruce drove through the following weekend to take Annie and Helen back to Glasgow. Helen felt strange at first in the Clarence Drive flat, for the Glasgow ceilings were more than three feet higher than those of the Pittenweem house. Although she had not disliked the low ceilings in her grandmother's house, it was an exciting and charming feeling to have so much space above her head again. She kept looking upwards and enjoying it.

"Two women are coming to see you tomorrow, Annie. It wasn't easy. I found one advertised on a postcard in a shop window and I got the other one at the 'burroo'. Now if neither of them is any use, mother says you can have Betty until we find someone."

"Anything but that, Bruce, you know I can't stand that woman." Annie was emphatic.

Helen could see that her mother was tired and in pain after the journey, but she knew that she herself would start school in three days and they must find someone before that. Her father's face flooded with anger. He obviously felt he had done all he could and his wife should be more appreciative. His reply was loud and sharp and Annie winced as he spoke,

"You'll maybe just have to put up with what can be arranged!"

"Oh Bruce, I don't suppose I'll be lucky enough to find anyone like Jessie, but I'm sure one or other of these women will probably do."

She sounded exhausted and defeated. Helen wished her father would go away before a quarrel erupted.

"Well, a Mrs Kilmartin will be here at ten tomorrow and then Mrs Riley at eleven thirty. D'ye want me to come along and see them too?"

"No, no, that's not necessary. We'll manage fine. Perhaps you'll drop in at night to see how we got on?"

"Yes, I'll see if I can do that for you, yes, hmm, it'll be the back of nine though, I've got to see someone about ... yes, I should manage that. I'll just get away now, if you'll excuse me. I'm late for ... er ... You're sure you've got everything you need?"

"Yes, we're fine. Thank you for bringing us home. It was a lovely drive and I enjoyed seeing the harvest coming in."

"Right, I'll just get away then."

After the front door closed, Helen relaxed and started to unpack. She wondered why on earth he always asked to be excused.

"I was frightened you were going to ask him to stay for coffee, Mummy."

"I suppose we should have offered him one, but I don't think he was in the mood and I'm dead beat. You must be too, are you? I suppose Bruce has too much on his mind these days. No, I certainly wasn't in the mood, but really you should try and be a bit more affectionate to your father."

But Helen knew that Annie was just as relieved as she was to see him go. That air of tension when he was present was difficult. And just like grandma, he talked so relentlessly, mostly of his own affairs. Helen felt he hardly knew anything about her, for he never asked and she felt too shy to start telling him. There was never any chance, for his continuous speech seemed driven by determination or even anger. Grandma was the same, although she was more obviously cross about someone or something. Nothing seemed to be easy or relaxed when either of them was around. Helen wondered if they had been like that when they were her age.

There had been some very good times in Pittenweem that summer, but how nice and pleasant it was to be home again, just the two of them. How relaxed and cheerful and easy it seemed when it was only her mother and herself.

Helen did not let herself think about the problems of starting school on Wednesday, in another new class.

Mrs Kilmartin was young and thin with straight lank hair. Helen thought she looked very frightened when she met her at the door and invited her inside. Helen was disapponted not to be present at the interview and waited impatiently in the kitchen. After less than five minutes, the sitting room door opened and Mrs Kilmartin slipped out, looking more fearful than before. Helen saw her to the door and had no idea what to say. Would they meet again or not? The woman said nothing either and Helen guessed the interview had gone badly. What had her mother said? Annie was smiling her small enigmatic smile when Helen rushed into the sitting room. It wasn't she who had made the decision, it was Mrs Kilmartin. Her first words had been,

"Ah didnae know it wad be such a big hoose, Missus, wi' such great big flairs tae clean an Ah don't think Ah'd like tae waash such big flairs, missus. Ah niver knew it wad be sae big an' a' thae big windaes, tae. Naw, reely Ah cudnae dae it, missus. Ah'm awfy sorry, missus."

Helen looked disappointed but Annie shook her head and shrugged philosophically,

"Well, at least she knew her limitations and didn't waste anyone's time. Let's hope the next one is more courageous. Just as well it wasn't grandma's flat she saw. She might have fainted clean away at sight of the studio!"

Mrs Riley was older, about fifty and fat. A small squashed hat was perched on top of a mass of black curly hair and her shabby grey coat hardly buttoned across her buxom figure. She was not at all shy and sitting down without being asked, she immediately started to talk. She talked for fifty minutes, giving Annie no chance to ask her any questions. Helen waited impatiently in the kitchen to see her to the front door, but eventually the sitting room door opened and Mrs Riley whisked out by herself.

" I could hear her voice going on and on. What on earth was she talking about all that time?"

"I'm blowed if I know, she just rattled on and on about all her different relatives, some were having babies and some were dying. I just went into a sort of dwam and stopped listening. I doubt if that one would ever get any work done at all. Deadly boring … useless, I'm afraid. She would be here yet, if I hadn't lied."

"You didn't lie, did you! O Mummy!"

"I said I had someone else to interview shortly and she skedaddled."

"I wonder what we're going to do?"

"Don't worry, I expect we'll find someone soon. We might ask that wee woman that does the close, if she knows anyone.

What's her name again? Rita."

Rita was surely nearly seventy. She washed the stairs and close every Monday morning, wearing an old sack for an apron and kneeling on a pile of newspapers to protect her from the rough cold floor. Her thin grey hair was screwed into a small, tight bun and her voice had the screeching quality that Helen associated with witches. She seemed to Helen to be the epitome of a 'poor person' and she had more wrinkles on her face than seemed possible.

Rita did know someone. She was sure her neighbour Mrs Young would be glad to hear about a 'wee job' and she would tell her that night.

Helen was pessimistic.

"Maybe Mrs Young will be awful poor, like Rita, if she lives next door to her?"

"What d'ye mean 'poor'?"

"Well, you know how Jessie was rough and sort of common, but she wasn't poor. She had a nice house and a nice pram for her baby. Wee Rita looks awful, so old and everything … you know what I mean. For instance, would Mrs Young be wearing a sacking apron if she was working for us?"

Annie laughed,

"I think we could find her something better than sacking, if that's what's worrying you."

"I just always feel awful sorry for Rita."

"Yes, I know what you mean."

"And she said there were more than fifty children living up her close, so it must be…a bit slummy."

"We'll just need to wait and see what Mrs Young is like."

But Mrs Young was a well-spoken woman in her mid-fififties, very smart in a navy serge suit and matching felt hat. She struck Annie as a sensible woman, perhaps a woman who had known a very different life before she moved to a single-end in Partick. Of course she did not have Jessie's warm personality, but her grammar was certainly better and she was keen to start right away.

"There's only one thing Mrs Corning, I won't be able to work for you after Christmas, because my daughter is expecting a baby and she does war work and she's very well paid, so I'll be looking after the baby. I'm sorry about that, but I wanted you to know the situation and not feel let down later on."

"Oh I am sorry that you won't be more permanent, but I'm very pleased to have you just now and I hope you'll stay as long as you can."

Annie tried to hide her disappointment from her daughter, but it was depressing that this would be a temporary arrangement.

Mrs Young was very efficient and rather formal, even in the intimate sevices she performed for Annie. It was never suggested that her first name should be used.

"Fancy her staying next door to Rita!" Helen said several times. pleased that the new help did not look poor and bedraggled like her neighbour.

Bruce was slightly put out that neither worker he had found for Annie was suitable. For several weeks, he was inclined to ask suspicious questions about Mrs Young's background, questions that Annie had never thought of asking.

"Does she have a husband at all, d'ye know? This woman that's cleaning for you."

"She hasn't mentioned him so far, Bruce. I expect he's around somewhere. Or maybe she's a widow. She has a daughter."

"And d'ye know her exact address?"

"I know she lives in Fordyce Street, but I don't know the number. I'll find it out for you."

"Hmm, not a great area that, pretty funny crew around there, a lot of crime I believe. Does she seem all right, though?'

"I think you'd search a long time before you found a woman as respectable as Mrs Young."

"Is that right, now?"

"Oh yes, certainly. She's obviously used to better things. She was quite aghast that our house was without a special wee spoon in the tea caddy!"

He laughed at that.

"And can she lift you about, Annie? That's the important thing. Is she strong enough?"

"She's managed fine so far. She's about ten or twelve years older than me, I suppose. We get on well enough together, though not quite the same as Jessie of course. Jessie was one in a thousand. But I must admit this one is much quieter."

"Oh well, whatever you say. As long as you're suited in the meantime, that's fine."

After four weeks of repeatedly asking these same questions, he stopped, to Helen's great relief.

More Changes · Autumn 1944

To be back in Glasgow filled Helen with an inexplicable happiness. Even the awkwardness of being the new girl in a class, a class in which the majority had come up through primary school together, could not dull her delight in living in the busy, filthy city once again. She loved the friendly shop assistants and tram conductors with their broad Glasgow accent. She loved the fact that it was warmer than Fife, almost too hot in August. She loved swimming in the blue and transparent Arlington pool again, and not worrying about what might be lurking in the dark depths of seaweed beneath her in the Pittenweem pool. She loved the space of her Hyndland flat and the big windows where she and Annie would sit and make comments, admiring or otherwise, about the passing parade of Hyndland residents. Annie, usually so kind and sympathetic, could also be sharp and sarcastic. Sometimes her unexpectedly cutting criticisms made Helen laugh.

As well as her classmates, some of Helen's teachers were new this year. As usual, some were really nice and it was easy to dislike others. The form teacher was a wizened little lady with a sweet gentle manner which Helen distrusted. Mary was fond of the phrase 'too sweet to be wholesome', and that's exactly how Miss Walker struck Helen.

In the first week there was some form to fill in and somehow the fact became apparent that Helen's father did not share the same house.

"And does Daddy not live with you, dear?"

Although there might have been sympathy in her tone, Helen was sure that the teacher's small eyes lit up with an avid interest. She gazed keenly at Helen and seemed to wait for more information. Helen remained silent for she could imagine this teacher relaying this piece of gossip in the staff room with relish. Miss Walker would never be a favourite.

The morning journey to school was a very special time all to herself and Helen sat happily in the tramcar. She enjoyed a privacy in the tram that did not exist in Pittenweem, when at any minute she might be called upon for some small chore or errand.

Grandad sometimes beckoned her up to his studio, perhaps to pose for a drawing or a photograph or perhaps just to keep him company. Mary had friends dropping in most days and Helen was often expected to make a pot of tea for them. But she had spent more time with her own friends this summer and what fun the concert had been. Much of the holiday had seemed as though she were an irresponsible little girl again, rather than the woman that she had considered herself since starting secondary school. She blushed a little at the thought of playing imaginary games, surely she was too old for that. In spite of the good times in Pittenweem, she had missed those times of solitude that were a large and important part of her life in Glasgow. The twenty-five minute tramcar journey to and from school each day was a precious period of privacy, in which Helen enjoyed the luxury of uninterrupted thought.

As the tram trundled down Church Street, past the Out Patients' door of the Western Infirmary, she remembered that day in spring, when she had suddenly realised her own splendid separateness from the rest of the world. The idea had struck her like a brilliant light. That remembered realisation of self had seemed particularly vivid and important. It still did. She, Helen Corning, was a unique person, different from everyone else who had ever existed. She was herself and no one else. Each time the tram reached this point in its journey into town, her mind returned to that discovery which she treasured, though she was still unable to express its importance in any other way than,

"I am me. I am me."

◊

It was Saturday morning and two weeks since they had returned from Pittenweem. Helen had been to the baths for a swim, then collected the food shopping and now she sat munching a roll and jam.

"Milly in the grocers is an awful sweet wee lady, you know. She's always asking how you are and I really like her. The butcher's nice too. He remembers you and sends his regards."

"That's good, my pet. I'm glad. I know folk in shops can be pretty nippy these days. Difficult times."

"Well Milly is really nice. And funny too."

"Are you not missing the Pittenweem garden and going swimming every day?"

"Oh I like going to the baths. Not so cold and no seaweed. And it's great to be back here just the two of us. More relaxing."

Annie knew what her daughter meant. She was suffering much less pain in Glasgow. Was it because the damp sea air had affected her badly, or was it the continuous tension of living with Mary? She suspected the latter and had already determined that she would not accept the invitation to live with her parents after Christmas.

"What's Mrs Young like, Mummy? You never say much about her. I always used to like hearing about Jessie."

Helen had not yet met Mrs Young.

"No, she's not a character like Jessie. She's nice enough, I suppose. She does what's needed and no more. Not much talking and certainly no jokes, absolutely nothing naughty, no Silver Silk shite sheets for bare bums or anything like that!"

They both laughed. Silver Silk was the brand name of the toilet paper that they used and Annie had delighted Jessie by coining this vulgar phrase.

"You wouldn't tell her that rude Pittenweem thing."

"Which one is that?"

"Pee, po, piss, piddle, pump, toly, fart, turd." Helen rhymed it off with gusto.

"Oh no, never! We are both most circumspect. I don't really know much about her at all, except her daughter is going to have a baby, but she hardly mentions her. We don't have any chit-chat."

"Perhaps there isn't a daughter. Perhaps she just said that in case she didn't like working here and wanted an excuse to stop."

"Never thought of that. Maybe we'll get friendly yet. She's fine, really. I hardly know she's there."

"Bit different from Jessie!"

"Aye, you always knew when she was in the house right enough."

They giggled again.

"Have you not seen your boyfriend since you came home?"

"Who? Tom? *He's not my boyfriend*! I saw him in the distance once and we just waved to each other."

"D'you think that's the end of the romance?"

"It wasn't a romance, Mummy." Helen's eyes opened wide in indignation. "Anyway it was an awful rush on a Saturday to get the messages and then go to the pictures, And I was getting a bit fed up with all those cowboy films. I'd rather go swimming. He was far too young for me anyway!"

Annie switched on the wireless and some exquisite piano music flooded the room. As the vibrant melody of Chopin filled the air, Helen's face became withdrawn and intent. Annie had always known her daughter loved music, but this concentrated expression was something new. When the polonaise finished Annie spoke,

"D'you wish you could play like that?"

"Oh yes," Helen breathed.

"Very tricky, old Frederick C. I was never quite up to playing him properly."

Annie had studied piano for years and regretted that she had not been able to give her daughter the same opportunity.

"Were you dreaming you were Moura Lympany playing?"

She knew Helen admired the beautiful young pianist.

"Oh no. I'll never play like that. I was making up a dance in my head to the music. I'm always doing that. The dances just happen in my mind's eye as I listen to music that I like. But they don't happen for all music."

Annie had noticed that Helen had strict musical likes and dislikes and would walk out of the room when certain pieces were played.

"I never see you dancing these days. Does it only happen 'in your head'?"

"Oh no, I'm often dancing in the kitchen when I'm waiting for the potatoes to boil."

"Are you? And I never knew. What about starting dance lessons. You could go back to Miss Hopkins. That would be handy for school."

Helen made a face,

"That shouting lady that we hear from grandma's close? But I didn't like it when I went before, did I?"

"You were just a wee thing then and it wasn't real dancing, not proper ballet anyway."

"I'd be a bit shy to go there by myself."

"Blethers! I think you should just go in and see her after school on Monday. I don't suppose you'll remember the funny way you have to get to her place? Through the close, then up the stairs past the big fancy wrought iron lift, then out the back door to a sort of yard where there are three houses? It's not like anywhere else I've ever been, but don't let that put you off, I'm sure there'll be a notice to tell you. You should go next Monday and see what she says. Would you not like to do that?"

"But would we be able to afford it?"

"If my wee girl wants to dance, I'm sure we'll be able to afford it,"

After school on Monday, Helen dropped in to her grand-mother's flat to see if shopping was required. As she climbed the stairs, a window on the second floor landing was open. There was a deep drop to the back yard below, where rampant weeds had taken over. Helen sniffed the rank, but not unpleasant smell, that rose from this well of greenness. A tree as tall as the five floors of the tenement was filled with twittering city birds, mainly spar-rows. This immense and continuous sound of birdsong was unique in Helen's experience, something she associated with visit-ing her grandparents. Directly across from where she stood, beyond the deep garden, were the large windows of the dance studio. It was one of three private schools. The others offered typewriting and foreign languages. These one-storeyed studios were all that remained of the ground floor of a previous terrace. This once elegant terrace, long since part-demolished, was now isolated and hemmed in by the vast curving red sandstone ram-part of tenements that helped form Charing Cross. This remainder of another age lay hidden behind Albany Chambers to the south and Charing Cross Mansions to the west, and Albany mansions, where the Mackays lived, to the north.

As Helen stood gazing a figure came to the dance school win-dow and opened it wider. Was that Miss Hopkins? Helen could hear the piano tinkling. She felt very unwilling to enter this unknown territory. Perhaps she was too old at twelve? Too skinny? Too awkward? What if Miss Hopkins took one look and just shook her head sadly?

Helen followed her mother's instructions. Beside the ancient elaborate lift was a notice with a pointing arrow,

→ TO THE ENTRESOL

This sounded French and exciting. Helen could hear the old lift clanking high above her as she climbed halfway to the first floor. When she opened the back door from the close, more steps led upwards to the small yard, which must have been built on the roof of one of the large Sauchiehall street shops. Ahead of her were three doors, each with a flight of steps leading to it. What a strange and unusual place! There was no mistaking the Hopkins School of Dance for a crowd of little pre-school children, accompanied by their mothers, was just leaving the building, while taller girls entered, chattering excitedly to each other.

Just inside the front door stood a tall lady, Helen supposed it was Miss Hopkins, who was speaking into a wall-mounted telephone.

It was a very small entrance hall and very crowded and it could not have been easy for Miss Hopkins to hear the caller, as pupils and parents milled around her. Some were leaving, others arriving and all talked loudly. Helen felt sorry for the imposing lady who appeared somewhat distressed by the situation.

Helen stood hesitantly on the doorstep. She was tempted to go home, but Miss Hopkins had caught her eye and was smiling and looking enquiringly at her. By the time the phone call was finished, the small children had left and the others were in an inner hall, preparing for their class. Miss Hopkins shook Helen's hand. She had an English accent, extraordinarily big teeth and rather a large nose. Helen decided that she could never have been beautiful enough to be a ballet dancer herself. Also she was quite stout, although it was not a curvy stoutness like her grandmother's. Miss Hopkins seemed to be very straight up and down, whichever way you looked at her. She was not at all good-looking, but she had an air of dignified authority. She looked like a person that one might be just a little bit afraid of. However her manner was pleasant and she seemed to know what Helen wanted before Helen said a word. She explained that Helen must start ballet at the very beginning, grade one, and to begin with she would be in a class with much younger children.

"I expect you will feel rather tall amongst them, my dear. I'm very sympathetic about that feeling because I was always the tallest in my class and not always the best!"

She certainly seemed a very tall lady and so very straight up and down. No ins and outs at all, Helen noticed that even her legs were straight, not exactly fat, but the ankles were the same size as the calves. She had quite a masculine face, but she was elegantly dressed with a silk blouse and a pretty brooch.

Long ago, during the last war, when Annie had attended the Girls' High, Miss Hopkins had been the gym teacher and all the girls were terrified of her, but Helen thought she seemed really kind and nice.

Miss Hopkins left her for a moment, then returned with a short purple linen tunic with matching knickers.

"These should fit you nicely and you can settle up for them later, when you're sure you want to continue lessons. I'm afraid you may have difficulty finding ballet slippers, but ankle socks – or sockettes are fine in these difficult days. I look forward to seeing you next Wednesday, dear. The class starts at four fifteen."

It had all been very easy!

Annie was pleased that Helen had summoned up her courage and interested to hear about her old teacher. The fees were modest.

Next Wednesday, after school, Helen walked along Sauchiehall Street to Charing Cross, feeling pleasantly apprehensive.

Beyond the little entrance hall with the telephone was a slightly larger square hall, with hooks to hang coats on and two benches in the corner. A door led to a toilet, with a washhand basin and a beautiful WC, decorated with blue swans and reeds, similar to the one in her grandmother's bathroom. A set of double swing doors led to the dance studio and they also reminded her of the Renfrew Street flat. Another door was shut and she would later learn that it led into a spacious sitting room. What a strange little house it was. Did Miss Hopkins live here?

Two small girls were sitting on the bench, taking their shoes and socks off while their mummies watched. They could not be more than five or six. Surely they would not be in her class. Then a girl of around nine came in. Several more little ones arrived. How enormous Helen felt compared to these infants. She considered dressing again and leaving, but that would be cowardly. She wanted to learn to dance, didn't she? What if these tinies were all much better than she was? How humiliating. She felt her hands grow damp.

Helen followed the other children through the swing doors and saw the studio for the first time since she was a little girl of four. Though she had not been able to picture it previously, the room immediately felt familiar. Her eye fell on a bright green pottery rabbit. Yes, she remembered that rabbit clearly from all those years ago. It gave her confidence. On the wall opposite the doors were several large windows, with a broad sill. These were the windows that looked over towards her grandmother's building. On the right hand wall was a fireplace with a tall mantelpiece with more green pottery. An enormous gold-framed mirror which reached from floor to ceiling, reflected a large part of the studio. There were four chairs in front of the mirror, for mothers who wished to stay and watch their daughters' class. On the other side of the fireplace was a grand piano, very like the one in her grandmother's house. A lady, wearing a hat and sipping a cup of tea, sat ready to play. The wall to the left of the doors had a waist-high wooden barre, just like the ones that Helen had seen in pictures of ballet dancers at practice. On the last wall, there were wallbars similar to the ones in the school gymnasium. These provided a barre for those aspiring ballerinas who were as yet too small to reach the proper one. Miss Hopkins was stationed in front of the fireplace and smiled and beckoned them to come in and take their places.

"Hurry, girls! Come along now!"

An hour was never long enough to get through the work.

This was the third lesson of the term for the others girls, so Helen was already behind. However, as the others were so young, the class was not demanding. The biggest surprise for Helen was that ballet was danced with the toes turned out east and west. She had not realised this when watching those Hollywood films. She felt rather doubtful. It seemed very unnatural. Could Miss Hopkins be teaching the wrong sort of ballet? She learned 'first position' where the heels were touching and the toes must be completely turned away from each other, so that the two feet were in a straight line. It was difficult to stand up straight with the feet like this. In 'fifth position' all the outside of the front foot must touch all the inside of the back foot and you must keep your knees straight, too. It was really hard. She could just about do it, but it seemed bizarre and not really graceful. Several times Miss Hopkins said,

"Good, Helen!" and "Well done, dear!" but perhaps she was just being kind.

When it came to jumping, with the feet still in this strange position, Miss Hopkins exclaimed,

"Excellent!" and asked her to come to the front of the class to demonstrate.

Helen could not believe her ears. Those jumps had felt awkward and ugly and she was sure she was not doing them properly. What if she landed on her own toe? Or even fell over?

After the class, Miss Hopkins drew her aside,

"Helen, I hope you did not mind being in such a young class, dear. You did very well indeed and I'm going to suggest that you attend both grade one and grade two classes this term and take two exams at Christmas. I think you could do both grades easily and I won't charge for the extra class. Talk it over with mummy. The only extra expense would be the examination fees. Perhaps mummy would like to come in and speak to me about it, or perhaps phone, if she's busy."

Helen explained that her mother was in a wheelchair and that they had no phone.

Miss Hopkins looked nonplussed.

"Well, do tell her what I said, dear."

Helen realised that she liked being called 'dear' by Miss Hopkins.

That night Annie was dying to hear all about the first class, but Helen was strangely silent.

"Did you not enjoy it, my pet?"

"It was all right. It was different to what you see in the pictures. Not very graceful."

Annie raised her eyebrows.

Then Helen stood up and showed the strange positions of the feet. Annie had not appreciated that ballet was so stylised, either.

"Oh well, go for this term and see how you do. It'll maybe get more exciting when you get further on."

"She wants me to go to two classes a week, but only pay for one, and then do two exams at Christmas."

Annie smiled delightedly. Surely Miss Hopkins had recognised her daughter's potential.

"That's marvellous! It's very generous of her! She must think you've got something special and you're worth helping."

"I suppose so. She said, "Good, Helen!" two or three times."

It was difficult for Annie to know whether Helen was pleased or otherwise about the extra class.

A concert was just starting on the wireless and they settled down to listen to it.

As the orchestral music surged into the room, Helen relaxed into the deep leather chair and gazed into the distance, while Annie wondered what thrilling scenario and ethereal movements were taking place inside her daughter's mind.

Annie's Friends

Although Annie did not speak to anyone except Mrs Young during the day, she was not aware of feeling lonely. On bright sunny days she would sit knitting at the open window in the bedroom, where she could look up Clarence Drive towards the shops. There was a constant stream of passers-by and also usually a few people waiting at the tram stop. Many did not notice that she was there, for although it was a ground floor flat, the garden was five feet higher than the pavement and the window the same height above the garden. The tree outside the window was still in full leaf and Annie sat, hidden by the curtain of leaves. She almost enjoyed it more than the bright sun and constant breeze of the Pittenweem garden. Of course it did not smell so fresh and delicious as the sea air of Fife, but it was strangely peaceful and more interesting. If there were a shower of rain, there was a very special city smell of damp hot pavements which she enjoyed. If it became chilly, she could shut the window and wheel herself into the other room. It was good to be in a chair which she could move herself. Sitting at the open window made her almost part of the world again. Neighbours would wave to her and eventually several other regular passers-by waved too.

She liked to observe little day-to-day adventures.

For instance, the handsome young music teacher in the school across the road was always accompanied to the tram stop at four o'clock by a crowd of adoring teenage girls. When he boarded his tram, the pupils would stand and watch it disappearing up the hill with sorrowing faces as though all the light had gone from their lives.

She watched coal being delivered at the next close. What strength those two small coalmen must have. Time after time, each one would return to the street, where a third man had dragged another filthy sack to the edge of the cart, ready to be hoisted. Turning his back to the cart, the small Hercules in his studded leather back protector would shoulder the immense weight and climb the eleven stairs to the door of the close. When out of Annie's sight, he must mount the many flights of stairs to each floor, delivering four or five bags to each of the eight house-holds. How many stairs did they climb each day? And where did these wee men get their stamina and strength, she wondered? Were coalmen allowed extra rations, as fishermen and farm work-ers were? They jolly well should be. And extra soap coupons too, for they were black from top to toe.

The patient horse stood waiting. Now and again it would look back over its shoulder at the depleted cart, then turn and snort as if approving the removal of all these heavy bags from its load. After the last bag was carried in, the men stood there for a few minutes while tips were shared out. The horse was given some treat to eat, it looked like a pancake. The cart would then make the dangerous maneuvre of a U-turn in the road before the next tram or bus appeared Then it rattled off down the hill with a cheerfully trotting horse, who was no doubt unwilling to believe that they were headed for the coal depot to re-load.

Annie enjoyed watching the smartly dressed Hyndland ladies going off into town for the afternoon. It was wonderful how well these women could look after all the years of clothes coupons and shortages. Probably many of the older ladies had been wealthy enough to buy very good suits and coats which, with care, still looked like new, although perhaps they lacked the correct square-shouldered shape for the latest fashion. Annie considered that hats just now were particularly crazy, tiny saucer shaped confec-tions which were stuck to the front of the head. Really they looked too ridiculous on anyone over twenty-five.

Once, Annie, unobserved, overheard the fierce, whispered quarrel of an angry couple, as they stood at the tram stop. Should she move out of earshot? She decided her movement might draw attention to her presence and just sat quietly, enjoying the drama of their fury. When the leaves fell from the tree she would be more apparent and this sort of amusement would no longer be possible.

At the weekend, Helen joined her mother at the window and learned some of the nicknames that Annie had coined for the Hyndland residents.

There was 'the architect', a young man with a bow tie and a springing crop of hair. He always carried a drawing board or large sketchbook under his arm.

Then there was 'le boulevardier', always dapper, who now greeted Annie at her window each day.

There was 'Mrs Dirtylugs'. One day in the grocers, Helen had noticed that this lady's ears were far from clean.

There was 'Daphne's mother'. This woman had a deep, loud voice with a very English accent. One day last spring, Jessie had heard her shouting to her young daughter in the street.

"Aw Mrs Cornin', is that no' a sin, shoutin' at her wee gurl like tha'."

"What's she shouting, Jessie?"

"She's bawlin' oot "Daftie, daftie! C'meer daftie," tae her wee lassie."

"Oh no, it's all right, Jessie. That's the wee girl's name. It's Daphne, not daftie."

"An' whit sort o' bluddy name is that, fur Goadsake. Ah niver heard tell o' that name."

"I think it's a Greek name."

"*Greek*! It's a dam silly name tae gi'e a wean, if ye ask me."

One Saturday, when sitting at the window with her mother, Helen remembered some small errand that she had forgotten when shopping earlier.

"I'll just pop over and get that now. I think I could jump out the window. D'ye think I should?"

"If you want to."

So Helen, always fond of jumping from heights, sat out on the window sill, then pushed herself off and dropped the five feet to the ill kempt front garden. All the front patches in Clarence Drive were neglected plots of weeds and long grass. If there had ever been any horticultural ambition in the tenement dwellers of Hyndland, the removal of the railings for the war effort had extinguished it. Probably the exigencies of wartime existence left little energy for gardening.

As long as the weather was pleasant enough to have the window open, this was Helen's method of leaving the house to go shopping. It added a bit of excitement to the chore. Sometimes she forgot to take the front door key with her and her mother must wheel herself to the door to let her in.

"It's good exercise for me." Annie would say when Helen apologised.

◊

There was no whist drive on a Friday night and Mary usually visited her daughter.

"I saw Mrs Rayner today, Annie!".

Annie could tell from her mother's arch manner that she had a treat hidden away.

"And what black market delicacy has she produced this time?"

"Oh I wouldn't like to think it was the black market. I'd never do anything illegal and I'm sure it's all completely above board. It's just extra supplies that she can't make use of in the canteen."

"I expect that's the case. Well what is it? The suspense is killing me."

Mary produced and unwrapped a brown paper parcel and disclosed a large thick slab of chocolate about the same size as a telephone book. Annie and Helen both exclaimed with delight.

"It's cooking chocolate, but delicious. I have a slab at home for myself."

"I expect this cost you something."

"Yes, but not too much. It's a present for you."

It was a treasure and they were very grateful. Annie introduced Helen to the pleasure of eating brown bread and butter with a nibble of chocolate.

Two weeks later, Mary told them of some really beautiful men's suiting which Mrs Rayner happened to have for sale at seven shillings a yard and no coupons.

"I suppose this was surplus supplies for the canteen?" Annie asked, her face expressionless.

"I'm not sure where she got it, but it's very good quality, navy blue with a faint stripe in the weave and I thought it would make a school skirt for Helen. She's growing so tall."

"I suppose it's a good chance and it will be wide. I'll take a yard."

"Oh I think she wanted to sell the whole five yard piece."

"Five yards! Thirty-five shillings. That's more than I can afford, Maw. What would I do with it all?"

All her life Mary had been buying bargain goods in large quantities. She hated to miss a special offer, but Annie had never shared her mother's love of bulk purchases, nor ever had the money to indulge such a whim.

"It's really a bargain, Annie, and I'm sure it would all get used eventually and she'd probably take some of the payment in gloves."

"I thought I'd seen the last of those damned Fair Isle gloves!" Annie groaned.

The suiting was bought and as well as a skirt, Annie made a princess dress for Helen. It fitted her beautifully and made her look taller and more slender than ever. She did love the dress but no one else in school wore anything like it. It was too elegant and chic for a schoolgirl and too many comments were made about it for Helen's comfort. Mary suggested that a hand crocheted collar, a family heirloom, could be worn with the dress, but Helen had put her foot down at that. After several wearings, she refused to wear the dress to school at all.

She was sorry to disappoint her mother and sorry not to wear something which was smart and grown up, but she was adamant. Some girls in the class still wore gym tunics which really did not suit them once they had developed a bust. Helen was sorry for them, for she was sure their mothers forced them. Her fitted dress was flattering, but just too different from everyone else. She had had enough of being different in Pittenweem.

Annie had enjoyed using her sewing machine for the skirt and dress and felt that sewing was more interesting and better exercise than knitting. However once the garments were finshed, she returned to the gloves in order to help pay for the suiting.

Seeing Annie using the electric sewing machine had inspired Helen to try it too. While 'raking' in the chiffonier, she had found a large piece of jersey material in a pleasant ochre colour. She determined to make a dress for her mother's Christmas. It must be very simple and it must be a surprise. She also had an idea for an applique cushion cover which would have a picture of a girl and a little dog on it. The dog would be cut from a scrap of fur fabric that she had found also. She pursued these two projects in secret, although her mother knew she was using the sewing machine. Helen was not entirely satisfied with the results of her labour. The dress was rather shapeless and the dog was not as doggy as she had hoped, but Annie was appreciative of both and wore the dress for several years.

Illness

One Monday at the beginning of November, Helen wakened with a bad cold and a sore throat. She was obviously unfit for school and stayed in bed. However, as there was no one else there after one o'clock when Mrs Young left, she still had duties. There was food to prepare and also her mother to attend to. Annie felt guilty at these demands on her daughter. What if the child became worse? There was no telephone to summon help. However Helen, although coughing and miserable, was not too ill to heat soup or to help her mother in and out of her chair when required. After accomplishing the necessary chores, Helen would drop back into bed and quickly fall asleep again.

Mrs Young had suggested on the Tuesday that she could phone Mr Corning and let him know about his daughter's illness, but Annie was unwilling to trouble him. He seemed always to be so very busy. What could he do anyway? It was just a bad cold.

Helen's condition did not change, she slept a lot and complained that her throat was very sore. Annie tried to get her to gargle, but Helen had never gargled before and found her throat too sore to acquire a new skill. Long drinks of Robinson's lemon barley water diluted with warm water seemed to be the only thing she wanted. She continued to get up for short periods to help her mother when it was necessary, but she no longer ate anything.

Annie was worried, particularly in the middle of the night when she listened to Helen's stertorous breathing. What if it was more than a cold? Should she get the doctor? The following day, Helen helped Annie and seemed just as strong as usual when she guided her into the wheelchair or tipped her back into bed. Then after a drink of juice, Helen would settle back to sleep for another few hours.

Annie had always resisted the suggestion of living with her parents in the Renfrew Street flat, but with Helen's illness she started to waver. It seemed wrong that her twelve-year old daughter should be expected to take so much responsibility.

Surely a girl of that age had the right to stay in bed and be cared for, when she was ill.

Bruce's visits were always erratic and it so happened that neither he nor Mary came to Clarence Drive until the Thursday evening

Both were shocked that Helen was so ill. Bruce said that he would get the doctor first thing next morning and Mary reiterated the real necessity of having a telephone installed, making no secret of the fact that she blamed Bruce for having done nothing about it.

"Well of course, Mrs Mackay, it's not so easy to get one these day. Long, long waiting lists."

"Surely there would be no problem if it was for a house with an invalid. I don't think you'd find it difficult at all, in fact. Have you made enquiries, Bruce? It's absolutely crucial for Annie to have a phone and I don't suppose it would be such a very great expense, if that's what you're worried about."

Annie wished her mother would be quiet, for she could see that Bruce was becoming angry. It was obvious that Mary thought Bruce too mean to pay for a telephone and it would certainly be another expense to consider.

Bruce jumped to his feet and rattled his car keys in his pocket,

"Aye! Well I think I'd better get going now, Annie. I'll get John Hamilton to drop in tomorrow to look at the wee yin. Best in the morning, I suppose, when Mrs Whatsitname's here."

"Mrs Young. Yes, thank you Bruce, that would be good."

After he had slammed the front door, Annie gently protested,

"Really you shouldn't nag him about the telephone, Maw. He does pretty well and he gets little enough in return. I'm grateful to him for what he does do."

Mary breathed deeply and gazed into the fire, tapping her right foot in a quick impatient rhythm. Then lighting a cigarette with her usual deft movements, she drew in the smoke slowly then expelled it with some force,

"I was only trying to help. I think it's outrageous that you have no telephone. The two of you here, alone and helpless ..."

"I'm not exactly helpless!"

"You know what I mean." Her voice was dangerously deep.

"He has a lot of expense with the house and Mrs Young and ... everything."

"He seems to have plenty of money for his chain-smoking and his clubs and his whisky drinking."

Annie could not help laughing.

"You make him sound quite dissolute."

There was a long silence. Again Mary breathed deeply, quietly but noticeably, then rose and shrugged herself into her fur coat,

"I'd better get away back home in case your father's wondering where I am. I hope you're still thinking about coming to stay with us, I mean after Mrs Young leaves. I think it would really be best. In fact I think it's imperative."

After her mother left, Annie sat in front of the fire for a long time, thinking.

Imperative, that was a strong word. She did not much care for the sound of it. Bruce and her mother! Those two touchy, irritable people were the adults she must depend on. Why had her mother not made some gesture towards helping with the cost of a telephone? Certainly it would be a help to have one. Mary had owned a telephone for nearly forty years.

The idea of moving back to live with her parents seemed a very bad one. Imagine dealing daily with her mother's unpredictable temper. No, Annie could not contemplate that life.

Now she needed help to go to bed and she must waken Helen. What a shame. Perhaps they should move to Renfrew Street after all? Was she selfish to be so unwilling? But she knew that Helen was also unwilling.

Why had neither adult offered to help her to bed? That would have saved Helen from the task.

And why had she, herself, not asked either of them to help her to bed? The telephone had become the important topic, rather than Helen's health. How foolish they all were with their stupid quarrelling. Now the sick girl must be wakened and asked to deal with the bedtime routine.

Annie felt depressed and guilty as she slowly wheeled herself through the hall and into the bedroom.

Next day Doctor Hamilton diagnosed a bad cold and a throat infection.

"There's an awful lot of this around just now. I blame the lack of fruit in our diet. You're doing fine with the warm juice and a wee bit honey might help if you can find any. Take an aspirin if it's too sore. Is it pretty sore, dearie?"

Before he left, Annie asked him,

"You know, Doctor, Helen has to lift me two or three times a day. Is she fit enough to do that? Will she come to any harm, having to exert herself when she's under the weather like this? I feel bad about asking her to help me when she's feeling rotten, but I have to rely on her a lot."

"Oh she's a good strong girl, she'll come to no harm and I'll phone Bruce and let him know there's nothing to worry about. And you have assistance from that lady who let me in, she seems reliable and I'm sure Bruce will be a good help in the evening. And your mother lives close by too, doesn't she? No, no, don't worry about your daughter doing the odd little job. Probably another four or five days of that painful throat and then she'll be right as rain. And ye're keeping fine yourself, are you? That's good."

Annie was not so sure about Helen being 'right as rain'. She could see the girl had become very thin and still slept most of the time.

It was interesting that the doctor took it for granted that Bruce was there every evening, like a real husband. Did the other club members not realise that they were separated, with Bruce living with his parents? Well she would not be the one to blow the gaff.

One hour after the doctor left, Bruce arrived with his mother and Betty.

"Now Annie," Bruce's voice was clipped and dogmatic, "my mother has very kindly come along to help and she's brought Betty with her, so we can all give a hand."

Annie was speechless. What an unexpected visitation! Mrs Young stood in the background and she did not look particularly happy either.

"We'll go in and see the wee invalid first."

"She's sound asleep just now, Bruce!"

But she spoke too late, and Helen wakened to find three sympathetic faces peering down at her.

Her grandma Corning was very different from her other grandma. She seemed much older, more old-fashioned, She may have been pretty at one time, but she had long lost her looks and settled into being an old lady. Deep-set eyes above high rounded cheek bones, an indrawn mouth and sparse grey curls made her seem years older than her sixty-five years. Helen had seen little of

Jane Corning and hardly knew her.

Jane and Betty bustled into the kitchen where Betty filled the kettle and put it on.

Ignored, Mrs Young stood back. For a few minutes she watched in amazement as her kitchen was taken over, then she marched through to Annie in the sitting room.

"What's happening, Mrs Corning?"

"That's my mother-in-law and her daily help, Betty. They've come to help, so they say, but I can't stand that Betty."

"I didn't take to her myself. I think they were rather rude, coming in and never saying a word to me."

"Fancy! Is that what happened? Never a word! And what are they doing now?'

"I think I heard the older lady say something about a cold compress and that other one has the kettle on, filled to the brim."

"A cold compress? Is that what they're here for? What a nerve!"

In the bedroom, Jane Corning was preparing the bandages and comforting Helen.

"Now this is going to make you feel a lot better. This is what I used to do for your Daddy when he was a wee boy and had a sore throat. I'll be very gentle and quick and your throat will be all better by tonight. I'm just going to wind these damp cloths around your throat like this, there we are. Now another wee one, we'll soon be finished, dear."

Helen had a hatred of anything around her neck, never wore a scarf and always removed her school tie as soon as she possibly could. Also, she had been brought up with constant admonitions to 'change those damp clothes or you'll get pneumonia', 'take off your wet shoes or you'll catch your death of cold', 'is your hair still wet? Get it dried at once?' Now, when she was actually ill, her throat was being tightly wrapped in wet cloths! What madness was this? She had never heard of such a daft thing. Where was her mother? Did she know what was happening? It was inexplicable and frightening. She felt attacked and yet politeness stopped her from protesting as much as she wanted to. Where was her mother?

"I feel it's choking me." She whispered.

Bruce at the foot of the bed patted her knees,

"No, no, my wee lass, it has to be tight to build up the heat.

You'll feel a lot better soon, believe you me."

Helen most certainly did not believe him.

"It's horrible, I can hardly breathe or swallow. I don't like it at all. I don't want it round my neck. I want it taken off." The tears rolled down her cheeks and she felt humiliated and terrified. It had happened so quickly and where was her Mother?

Meanwhile in the sitting room, Mrs Young said in her quiet but determined way,

"Mrs Corning, as far as I know, cold compresses went out with button boots and it's your wee girl and it's your house and I don't think you should let something happen when you don't approve of it! "

"You're absolutely right, Mrs Young!"

"Will I wheel you through?"

"No, I'll go myself!"

Annie was already at the door of the sitting room and she rolled her wheels with more vigour than she had ever used before, whirling through the hall and bursting into the bedroom, pushing the door so hard that it hit the wardrobe with a bang.

Helen was crying hard and trying to loosen the bands about her neck, Mrs Corning looked dismayed and her hands were clasped below her chin, Betty stood back, biting her lip and Bruce with a half-hearted grin on his face was exhorting Helen,

"Come on Tuppeny, be a wee soldier now and bear up. It's not so bad as that surely now, is it?"

Helen nodded and whimpered,

"It's just horrible…!"

Annie took a deep breath and spoke in an assertive voice,

"Mrs Corning, please take those wet rags off the child's neck. She's very distressed, as you can see, and it seems cruel to make her worse than she already feels. No one asked my permission to apply this old-fashioned treatment to my daughter and I would certainly never have agreed to it."

Annie spoke loudly and clearly. Mrs Corning's pale round eyes looked at Annie and her head shook a little.

"All right, just as you wish, Annie, although of course…"

She stepped to the bed and worked swiftly to remove the compress. Betty stood beside her, glowering and untidily winding up the discarded bandages.

Helen stopped crying and gave her mother a wavery smile of thanks.

It was all very awkward and the Cornings and Betty soon left the flat with little more being said.

Mrs Young held the front door open for them and shut it behind them with a polite but definite click.

"Are you all right now, Mrs Corning? D'ye need anything before I go?"

"We're fine, Mrs Young and thank you. You gave me just the right boost at the right time and I'm grateful. I don't know why I let them treat Helen like that in the first place."

"That's all right, Mrs Corning, you're just too polite. Too much of a lady. I think we were in agreement about that crowd. Walking in here as though they owned the place! I'll see you tomorrow."

While Mrs Young could never take the place of Jessie, Annie appreciated her quiet dependability and regretted that she was not to be a permanent part of her life.

Ballet Exams

Helen attended ballet class on Wednesday and Saturday. As she learned other movements, she started to enjoy it more. For the approaching exams, they must learn a short simple ballet dance, also a folk dance and a short piece of mime. Although mime was a new word to Helen, she had been practising it all her life as she acted out her imaginary games. Miss Hopkins was very impressed with the mime that Helen gave of a woman trying on hats in front of a mirror.

One Saturday there was a young woman assisting at the morning class.

She was a strange gypsy-looking girl, with greasy dark curly hair and quite a strong Glasgow accent. It was difficult to judge what age she was, for her figure was plump and mature. She might have been fifteen or twenty-five. She was severe with the smaller ones when they made a noise in the changing hall and she corrected them sharply in class if they were not pointing their toes. She seemed a bit rough and common and an unlikely sort of pupil teacher in that refined middle class atmosphere. It did not help that her name was Helena.

Helen did not like her and dreaded being corrected by her, but Helena ignored her throughout the hour, though she smiled and clapped her hands when Helen practised her mime.

The following Saturday, Helen's heart dropped when she saw that Helena was again assisting. She was sure that 'gypsy' would come and criticise her

However, the dark girl only came to adjust Helen's arm gently, it had been held too high. She smiled as she did it and she had a lovely smile. Later she demonstrated a movement with beautifully pointed toes, Helen noticed. Then Helena danced one of the exam dances for the class to watch and Helen realised for the first time how the dance should look. It had seemed like a series of exercises before, but Helena's grace and interpretation transformed the simple steps. It did not matter that her hair was greasy and her hips were broad. It was a pleasure to watch her. Helena Bartholomew became our heroine's role model.

The following Saturday, at the barre, Helena stood beside Helen as she did her pliés. The young pupil teacher was nodding and smiling. Then she said,

"You realise that you are very, very good, don't you! Quite special, I think. You'll do really well in the exams, I bet. In fact I know. Good luck and work hard!"

She moved on to the next girl, leaving Helen feeling almost faint with delight. Had that amazing gypsy girl truly said those wonderful words to her?

She could not even share those words with her Mother, but gave a modified version.

◊

The exam date approached and there was the problem of what to wear. The rules were that examinees wore a tutu, but of course this was not always possible with wartime restrictions. Miss Hopkins tried without success to find another pupil who might lend one to Helen. She also suggested a newspaper advertisement might track down a second-hand one.

The difficulty and the expense of the whole thing appalled Helen. She knew her Mother could do nothing and she felt it all too impossible for her to deal with herself. A tutu seemed such an unusual and extravagant thing! Where could she get one and what would happen if she could not find one? Must she miss the exams?

Help came from an unexpected source. Her grandmother had been having lunch with her friend Mrs Horsland, whose husband was a director of a large department store. Mary was talking about her granddaughter's ballet classes and the problem of finding a tutu. Mrs Horsland said,

"Oh I'm sure we could help you out there. You know, we have *lots* of tutus in the store. They're for Santa Claus's fairy helpers and those fairies come in different sizes every year, so we have any number of dresses. They've been there since before the war and are dusty, but they clean up beautifully. Send Helen along on Saturday morning to speak to Miss Crerar and I'm sure we'll find something to fit."

Helen was taken to the basement of the big store and a tutu was found to fit her. It was very pretty with a scatter of sequins on the tarlatan skirt. It did not seem grubby to Helen, but Miss Crerar insisted that it be cleaned for her.

She would be able to take the exams after all. She would buy sockettes to wear rather than ankle socks. There were still no ballet slippers to be had.

The ballet dress was delivered in a big van and Helen opened the parcel excitedly.

Catasrophe! The cleaning had ruined the sequins and they had become melted little splotches on the pretty skirt. Helen wept. It had been fine before, though not pure white. Why had she not just grabbed it at the time?

There was no solution. She must wear it. Annie considered it was not really too bad. Helen thought it very bad.

She arrived at the studio on the day of the exams. How strangely quiet it was! Large notices advised

QUIET PLEASE, EXAMS IN PROGRESS

The pupils did not change in the little hallway as they normally did, but were brought into the sitting room. It was the first time Helen had seen that room. There was a gas fire, an electric kettle and quite a lot of furniture but no bed, so perhaps Miss Hopkins did not live here after all.

There was a church-like atmosphere in the school that day, with everyone whispering. If a child wanted to use the toilet, she was accompanied through the hall on tiptoe. It seemed that these examiners were very important people. Miss Hopkins made tea for them between exams and there was fine china and several kinds of biscuits, Helen noticed.

No one mentioned the ruined sequins on her dress and indeed most of the tutus looked rather the worse for wear. Each girl had a large square of cotton with a red number on it safety-pinned to the front and back of her bodice, which was far from attractive. Helen was number ten.

The usual pianist was there but without her hat.

Helen remembered the answers to all her theory questions and did her best, but she could not tell if the examiners, Mr Espinosa or Miss Berney were pleased or not, for they did not smile but whispered together a lot. A secretary sat at a table and marked down the marks and the comments that were whispered to her from time to time and she smiled at the children and looked encouraging, which was nice.

Mr Espinosa seemed very old and rather tired. For most of the time, he just sat in a chair with his hands clasped on top of his stick and did not seem to take much interest in the nervous girls in front of him. Helen wondered what the examiners were whispering about, for she was sure that he must miss many of the mistakes.

Miss Berney was tiny, lively, and extremely plump. A little 'butterball', her grandmother would have called her. She asked the theory questions and decided which exercise to do next. A blouse and cardigan, with a rather full skirt did nothing to improve her figure. Her voice was clear and pleasant and she was very kind when the little ones made a mistake, giving them every opportunity to correct it. Towards the end of the hour, she started to smile to Helen, almost as though they were old friends

When it was time for soubresauts and changements, Helen felt completely confident. She knew she could jump really well. When Miss Berney demonstrated the exercise, Helen was astonished at how high this fat little person could fly into the air and how silently her tiny pointed feet landed. She must have been a wonderful dancer when she was young and slim.

The children left the studio after the exercises, then returned one by one to show their ballet dance, a simplified sailor's hornpipe and the mime. Helen was last and found her knees trembling when it was time to re-enter the studio for her solo. As soon as the introductory chords were played, something wonderful happened. Her knees stopped trembling and she felt completely calm and ready to perform the simple examination dance. After her mime, Miss Berney looked especially pleased.

Helen had no idea how she had done, but Miss Hopkins smiled encouragingly to her and nodded enthusiastically.

Her second exam was on the following day and, knowing what to expect, Helen found it less daunting.

Miss Berney and the secretary gave her big smiles of recognition when she entered the studio but Mr Espinosa just sat there 'looking like a lizard' as Helen told her Mother later.

What had really impressed Helen was the way that Miss Hopkins had treated these people as though they were royalty. The friendly atmosphere of the busy studio was changed to one of tremendous respect and an almost fearful silence. Very strange.

Helen passed both her exams with honours. The remarks on the report card made one or two minor criticisms, but both reports commented on her excellent mime and *beautiful* feet.

Annie was delighted of course and not at all surprised, although she did raise one eyebrow at the beautiful feet. Helen's feet were strong and could point really well, but with the small curling toes and the bony instep, they were hardly beautiful in the classical sense. But those feet could certainly dance and Annie felt a sense of achievement herself, because she had encouraged her daughter to develop this talent. Even if Helen did not make it her career, ballet would teach her confidence and deportment and she would enjoy it and make friends.

Annie was absolutely determined that her own incapacity would never deprive her daughter of the education or pleasure that she deserved.

New Year 1945 · 351 Renfrew St.

Annie was sitting on a wooden kitchen chair at the foot of the first flight of stairs at 351 Renfrew Street. The decision had been made. Annie and Helen were moving to the Mackays' flat.

Bruce had brought one of his workmen to help carry her up to the top flat. Helen would come behind them carrying the chair, in case they needed to put Annie down before they got to the top.

The long continuing war meant that able-bodied men were in short supply and Charley was the youngest and fittest of the rather elderly fellows that Bruce employed. Charley's hollow chest and pale skin did not promise much strength or stamina.

"Will he be strong enough?" Annie whispered to her husband, when the man went out to the street to collect the wheelchair that had been brought in the small lorry.

"He'll be fine and dandy, don't you worry. You're long but there's not much beef on you and we can always have a wee breather if we need it. Helen's doing a fine job there. She's the reserve. Think you can carry that chair right to the top, wee Tuppenny?"

"'Course I can."

Annie looked at the stairs. Their marble facings were not as sparkling white as they used to be. She remembered how she used to dash up those stairs two at a time and come down three at a time. Then when Helen arrived, she had enjoyed her own strength, as she hauled the big pram full of shopping up the six flights. The stairs were shallow and easy to climb, but how strong and fit she must have been then.

Helen's chair was not needed, for the men found Annie quite light. They dumped her unceremoniously on the bed, then went to fetch the wheelchair.

Mary stood beside the bed and Annie noticed that her hands were moving nervously.

"Will that bed be all right, Annie? Is it soft enough for you?"

"It's absolutely fine, just very comfy, thank you.'

It was harder and lumpier than her own bed, but she would get used to it.

"Your father is just coming down in a minute. He's had a bad week with his chest and I told him to stay in bed as long as he could."

"I'm sorry to put you both out of your own bed."

"No no that's fine. He coughs so much through the night that we're sleeping in separate beds upstairs anyway. Are you sure you're all right? Warm enough? I'll just go and make a cup of tea for the men. Where's Helen?"

"She'll be helping with the luggage."

But Helen was by herself in the large empty studio.

Although she visited her grandparents several times each week and had known this spacious room all her life, it seemed different now that she would be living there.

She let the doors swing behind her and stood looking up at the high dark space above her head.

The studio, specially designed for an artist, incorporated the attic space. At its highest point, the ceiling was twenty three feet. There was a large north facing roof light and three windows below that, which were always kept heavily curtained. The unchanging northern light was necessary for John's painting and Helen liked the theatrical quality of the unusual toplight. People and objects looked different as soon as they entered this room.

On the west wall, a curving staircase of nine steps led to a landing which crossed the wall immediately above the fireplace. The landing led to a straight flight of six stairs, leading in turn, to the working studio or atelier, which projected over the lower floor of the top flat next door. Underneath the landing was a white marble fireplace, surrounded by a severe, black wooden mantelpiece. A cosy inglenook was formed by the landing and the stairs and a chintz covered couch and two armchairs were ranged around the fireplace in the inviting little alcove.

The flat was a fine example of the *Glasgow Style*, that architectural revolt against the carved woodwork and elaborate plasterwork of the Victorian interiors. The building was designed by J. J. Burnet and was built in 1898. In the same year and in the same street, the foundation stone was laid for the new Glasgow School of Art. Rennie Mackintosh, the brilliant young architect who had designed that strange and beautiful school would eventually introduce and popularise this new style to the wealthy and cultured of Europe. While his name would have great significance for modern architecture, there must have been a strong breath of change in the air at that time, for the Art School and the studio at 351 share many similarities of design.

Helen, entranced only by the size and unusual character of the studio, was ignorant of these facts, but her grandfather, who had taught in the Art School during the first war, must have been aware of the closely related details of the two buildings.

A high narrow gallery ran along the south wall from the upstairs door. It seemed to serve no useful purpose except that of symmetry, but it was an enchanting feature for a child to explore.

It was now after three o'clock and the immense roof windows still provided a dwindling light. A small fire was burning quietly, with only an occasional gentle, 'pop' from the gassy coal. So much empty air almost seemed to have a sound of its own. Helen held her breath and felt the silence pressing against her eardrums.

Helen was sure than no other girl at school had grandparents with such an unusual room. It was like something in a film.

The immense rooflight had made the problem of ensuring a proper blackout seem insurmountable, but Mary, always ingenious, had used a large thick velvet curtain draped along the edge of the landing above the fireplace, to enclose the alcove which contained the fire, the three piece suite and the small table on which the all-important radio stood. The result was a small brightly lit 'tent' around the hearth. After nightfall, the rest of the large room was utterly dark and one must move carefully through the blackness from the door to the velvet curtain. About eight cautious steps were needed before the safety of the bright 'tent' was reached. Then you could duck around the curtain and reach cosy safety. Helen found these steps in the dark petrifying, for any sort of monster or murderer might have been lurking amongst the furniture in the rest of that large unseen area. However these fears were immediately forgotten once she reached the curtain and was drawn into the oasis of warmth and light, where the wireless played and her relatives sat chatting.

Just now there was still enough daylight for her to revel in the whole room. Every corner was clear and safe.

She climbed to the landing and stood beside the grandfather clock, looking down at the familiar furniture. The round table that she used to swing on like a little monkey when she was two, the treadle sewing machine with its four drawers full of coloured threads, the desk which had so many delights in its large deep drawers that she could not remember them all, the carved wooden armchair fit for an eastern princess, the tall cabinet with the model of a sailing ship on top of it, the wooden dais covered by a Persian rug. A chair stood on the dais where Mr Tainsh must have been sitting to have his portrait painted. Would that really be the last portrait grandad would ever paint? That seemed sad.

Helen moved to the higher gallery. It was amazing to look down from here. She was always surprised and delighted at how different the room seemed. Almost like looking into a doll's house. She was practically at ceiling height here!

The clock on the landing ticked and the fire murmured. Both sounds seemed to accentuate the great silence of the unmoving air in that large space. Occasionally there was the distant, very faint grind and squeal of tramcars crossing the complicated tramlines at Charing Cross.

She had been sad to leave Clarence Drive and her feelings about staying in this flat fluctuated wildly, but in this very special quietness high on the gallery, she was sure she was going to love living here.

Shaking herself from her daydream, she realised she might be needed. Her grandmother was not sympathetic to daydreaming.

◊

Helen looked down at her mother in the unfamiliar bed. Annie's eyes were tightly shut and without opening them she said,

"Och, I think I'll just stay in my bed. It must be after four now and if I stayed here, it would save you putting me to bed later."

"Rubbish! You're not going to bed at this time of day! I think you have to get up. Grandma's made pancakes and I think she'd be disappointed if you didn't come and join the party."

Annie doubted if that were the case. She found herself deeply unwilling to face the return to her old home and was full of foreboding that this had been the wrong decision, but they had tried for weeks and it had seemed impossible to replace Mrs Young. Both Bruce and her Mother had been insistant that she should move to Renfrew Street. Finally she could resist no longer though she felt she knew she had been weak to agree.

"And I would be awful disappointed if you didn't come through to the kitchen!"

Annie opened her eyes and looked up, as Helen smiled and nodded wisely, as if to clinch the deal.

This bed was much lower than either of the other beds that Annie had used, so she and Helen required a few new skills in dealing with it. Instead of Annie dropping back into the chair from a height, Helen must now stretch forwards over the back of the chair and, hoisting her Mother under the arms, lift her upwards and backwards. Helen found this new manoeuvre strangely satisfying and Annie realised how strong and determined her daughter was.

Mary was very welcoming and made tea for everyone, serving it in the kitchen after noticing the state of Charley's trousers. Bruce and Charley each ate several of the newly baked pancakes.

When John joined them, he wore a large checked muffler and looked old and tired. He regarded Charley carefully. How thin and worn the man's face was. His body showed the results of a lifetime of toil and inadequate nutrition. John remembered similar small, emaciated workmen in the streets of Paris, where he had been a student in the 1890s. He had sketched some of them. He would have liked to ask this man to sit for him now, but it was an inopportune moment, with his poor daughter returning home in a wheelchair.

John knew that he had just finished painting his last portrait. It had to be his last, for he had found it very hard going. He was sure he had got the likeness well enough, but the colouring seemed to escape him. He seemed unable to mix the natural flesh tints that he sought. Even Mary, who really knew little about art, would come and criticise and point out places where he had made the skin 'too yellow'. Or so she thought. Though Mary was often quick to comment negatively on his choice of fabric, background or artefact, she had never before criticised his painting skills. Now, for the first time since his early youth, John felt a lack of confidence in his abilities. Yet he was afraid to listen to his wife's uneducated advice.

Fortunately the sitter had seemed delighted and paid his dues with apparent pleasure. John himself was less satisfied and decided he would never accept another commission.

In a few years, and he had forgotten exactly how many, he would be eighty. Surely it wasn't a disgrace to retire from his profession now.

"You're very quiet, John!" Mary broke in on his thoughts.

"Was I? I was just thinking I would like to make a drawing of this friend of Bruce's. I'm afraid I can't remember your name, sir"

"It's Charley, Mister." But Charley looked uncomfortable and wondered if the old fellow was making fun of him.

"Oh well this is quite the wrong time of night for that sort of thing, John. Mr McKay is an artist y'know, Charley, but he's getting a wee bit forgetful in his old age."

Annie felt furious with her mother. Why must Mary say a thing like that and humiliate her husband? After only one hour in her old home, how she longed to be back in her own flat.

Bruce and Charley left soon after that.

◊

The move to Renfrew Street seemed at first to benefit everyone, except Annie.

Helen was able to do practically all the shopping for her grandmother and her young legs could gallop easily up and down the stairs for small forgotten items. John took on a new lease of life with his granddaughter in the house. She would join him in his chilly upstairs studio after school. Usually, they kept their outdoor coats and hats on as they looked at books and chatted. Coal was short and often there was only a small electric radiator to warm them, but occasionally John would have a fire in the Dutch stove and then they would roast a few potatoes. Time with her grandfather was always special with all the illustrated books and drawings to examine.

As there was no way of blacking out the large rooflight, they left the atelier at dusk, but the days were lengthening all the time.

There were certainly benefits in the move to 351 Renfrew Street. School was only five minutes's walk away and Helen did not need to leave so early in the morning. Also she could walk quickly to her dance class and to the Arlington baths. Nor need she worry about hurrying home in case Annie was cold because of the fire needing coal.

Mary was relieved of many small physical tasks and was delighted to have the company, for she was an inveterate talker and was happy to talk to Annie for the greater part of the day.

But for Annie, it was not an improvement. She missed spending time alone and she found it less easy to be independent. Wheeling herself through the double swing doors to the studio was impossible without help. The doors could be latched back, but someone else must do this for her. When Helen took her into the studio, one door would be latched open and Helen would pull her backwards, pushing the other door open with her bottom, then whirling the chair round. It was a neat trick. Mary latched both doors back and let Annie push herself through. Mary seldom pushed the chair. She hated the cumbersome thing and could hardly bear to look at it. It seemed to represent all that was sad and ugly to her.

The bedroom that Annie and Helen shared was a pleasant south facing room, with rather too much furniture in it for easy movement. It was not a large room, considering the scale of the rest of the house, and as well as the double bed there were two chests of drawers and a Dutch wardrobe. The last named was tall and broad, the lower part having three deep drawers and the upper half a double-doored cupboard, displaying two shelves when opened. Folded on theses shelves were some of Mary's exotic and luxurious garments from the social years of the first part of the century. An impressive piece of furniture, the Dutch wardrobe made manoeuvering the wheelchair difficult and Annie grew used to her daughter's muttered imprecations. The chair passed between the corner of the wardrobe and the corner of the bed with less than two inches to spare and of course it was even more of a sin to scratch antique walnut than to damage paintwork.

Helen's heart dropped if her grandmother happened to be in the bedroom, for Mary's eagle eye made the girl nervous and more apt to misjudge distance.

The workings of an invalid's digestive processes are not always predictable and there were times when Annie must retire to her room quickly, with the warning to Helen,

"And don't linger on the way!"

Or she might say,

"A degree of speed is required!"

Then in her hurry, Helen would misjudge the clearance space and bump some object with the wheel of the chair. Mary would tut-tut loudly and jump to her feet.

How Helen missed their own uncluttered flat at those times.

One evening, when they were listening to the wireless, and Jack Buchanan was singing in his charming, uniquely husky voice, Mary said,

"He's done well, that chap, hasn't he. You know, it was his father that sold me the Dutch wardrobe in your bedroom."

Helen could hardly believe her ears. Jack Buchanan was a 'famous star of stage and screen', and her grandmother had known his father! She could not have been more surprised if her Mother had mentioned that Joan Crawford was an old schoolfellow.

"Yes, old Buchanan was an antique dealer," Mary went on, "I bought the blue Donegal carpet in the studio from him too. It was a real bargain. He seemed quite reluctant to sell the wardrobe at the time, and said if I ever wanted to sell it back to him he'd be glad to take it. I don't suppose he meant that, though."

Somehow, Helen felt more warmly towards the arrogant piece of furniture after learning that. Then another story added to her fondness for it. Some years before Helen was born, Mary had a grey Persian cat, an affectionate though spoiled creature. Like most of its tribe, it had the habit of claiming any box as a suitable bed. One day Mary had glanced at the top of the Dutch wardrobe and noticed that the lid of the hatbox which contained her latest and most expensive hat, was aslant. Furious, she realised the situation and with one of her impulsive and energetic gestures, sent box, hat and cat flying across the room. Helen felt sorry for the cat, but could not stop giggling when she imagined the scene.

◊

Annie certainly found the lack of privacy the biggest drawback of living at 351, for Mary was likely to join her at any time and talk.

At home, Annie had always been happy to spend time by herself. She never felt at all lonely and enjoyed reading, or knitting and listening to the radio. Mary, however, yearned for company and would always prefer conversation to anything that the BBC might offer, especially a conversation in which she was the chief speaker. Often when Annie was enjoying a play or an interesting talk, Mary would come into the room and, ignoring the radio, start to tell some anecdote or rehearse one of her many grumbles.

Annie found the interruption frustrating but, taking the easy way out, would say,

"You can just switch that off Maw, if you want."

"Oh, maybe you were listening to something special, were you?"

"No, no, it doesn't matter."

Annie had also been in the habit of having her own wireless beside her in the bedroom at night. Helen would wheel it from one room to another on a serving trolley. Annie enjoyed late night programmes and switched on again as soon as services started early in the morning. She did not sleep well and it helped to pass the night. Here, it was not practical to shift her mother's cumbersome set from one room to another and Annie found it a terrible loss. When she suffered cramping pains, a night without her wireless could seem interminable.

As usual, Bruce's visits were unpredictable. Although he and his mother-in-law often gave the impression of affability in their relationship, there was an underlying tension of which Annie was only too well aware.

"How's the wee yin, tonight? How's she getting on with that old typewriter I brought along? Is she studying the manual? Ye know touch typing's a great thing for a girl to learn. Very handy. Sometime in the future, she could even get a job with her old man out at the works."

Bruce shrugged his shoulders in his old tweed jacket and grinned at his daughter. Helen smiled an unenthusiastic smile, but Annie made no response to this prophecy, ignoring it completely. Her hopes for her clever daughter were more ambitious than a typist's job in the dilapidated Gallowgate firm of Turnbull and Co.

"She's been busy with her school work recently, but I might have a shot at the typewriter myself. My handwriting's gone all to pot these days.

"Aye, that's a good idea, Annie. You have a turn at it, too. Now, I'm a bit pressed for time tonight if you don't mind. I said I'd meet old Billy Cochran at the club, so if you'll just excuse me, I'll be getting away now."

Annie had already tried typing and though she was slow, she enjoyed it and was pleased to be able to communicate in this way. Her writing was now scribbly and uncontrolled. Her attitude to typing was typically relaxed and the recurring numbness in her fingers did not help her accuracy. If she made a slight error, she overlaid it with the correct word and if a more serious mistake occurred, she covered it up with a row of capital Xs.

The finished result was unconventional and not always completely legible. When sending off one of her typed letters, she would say philosophically,

"Oh, well, I suppose it's a bit of a mess and it won't be easy to read. Never mind. It's a lot better than my handwriting would have been. I expect I'll get better with practice. And the letter will seem longer, if they have to puzzle it out."

She had been writing down some of the stories that she used to tell Helen. Helen pounced upon a story about Topsy.

"I think the girls at school would like this, Mummy."

"Surely not. They'd think it was for babies."

"No! You've made Topsy quite grown up and awful funny. I could get them to pay a penny towards the war effort, if they wanted to read it. We're always trying to gather up money."

Quite soon there was one of the special weeks devoted to fund-raising and this provided a chance to introduce the Topsy stories. There was to be a class bazaar on the Wednesday and Helen had an idea of her own to make money. Amongst the many pre-war toys that remained in her grandmother's house was a tiny village made of colourful wooden blocks. These could be arranged in different ways. There were ten or twelve houses, a church with a spire, a Town Hall with a clock, a school and some stylized trees. Helen found an old cardboard box upstairs and after painting a background of blue sky and snowy mountains around the three inner sides, she arranged the village, using Seccotine to stick the little wooden buidings into place at the foot of the mountains. Disappointingly, the background colour sank into the cardboard and lost its first brilliance. Annie said it looked as though the mist had come down. Helen hoped that the general impression was of a Swiss village nestling amongst the mountains and decided to charge tuppence a peep.

A large batch of iced gingerbread buns was Mary's contribution to the bazaar.

The Topsy story was handed round, read and enjoyed. It would become a weekly money spinner for the war effort, earning nearly two shillings each week until the end of term.

Annie enjoyed writing the weekly story, but often wondered at twelve-year old schoolgirls being interested in such crazy, simplistic tales about a doll.

◊

There were regular visitors to 351. Their next door neighbour from Clarence Drive, Mrs Unsworth, visited each week, bringing the rations from the grocer in Hyndland. It had been her suggestion that she would do this and Annie was grateful. It was necessary to register with one particular shop to collect your rations and it had seemed a very final thing to Annie to move her custom from Hyndland to Coopers in Sauchiehall Street, where her mother shopped. She was not prepared to accept that her move to her mother's house was anything other than temporary.

Mrs Unsworth, never a very jolly visitor, seemed more positive and agreeable as she sat in the elegant studio and ate one of Mary's pancakes.

As usual, Mary put herself out to be charming and amusing and Mrs Unsworth seemed to respond.

She would always leave at exactly the same time, saying,

"Thank you so much for having me. I'll see you at the same time next week."

After she had gone, Mary would remark,

"That woman's like a clockwork doll, she comes and goes and I never know what she's thinking. It's very good of her to bring you the food though, isn't it. Very kind."

"Poor soul, I think she's had a hard life and she's lonely. Her health's not great. She has... psoriasis I think it's called, a very strange affliction. I'd never heard of it before. I'm sure she likes coming to this swell flat and hearing your stories."

"She looks fine to me. Quite smart in an ordinary sort of way. But what did you think of that hat?"

Nancy Little was another regular visitor. Her exact pronunciation and genteel ways were also critically commented on after she left. Helen thought her mother and grandmother rather unkind about Nancy.

"What in the name of the wee man was that crochet thing she was making?" Mary asked,

"It's a brassiere she's making for herself, I believe."

"A brassiere! What on earth is she doing that for? Could she not buy one?"

But brassieres were not considered necessities in the wardrobe of either Mary or Annie, although Mary had worn stays, boned and hooked, all her life. Annie had given up her stretch girdle some years before, when the struggle required to don it had become too much for her.

"The brassiere looked very neat, I thought." Annie smiled and Mary snorted.

"I'm sure it'll never look at her and I don't know how she can be bothered. And what did you think of that story about the woman she met in the train?"

"Well it was certainly very similar to the story you had just told her..."

"Yes, except her woman was much wealthier and wore a squirrel coat rather than a musquash..."

"Yes and she had five children, not four..."

"And had been married three times..."

They both laughed heartily and, Helen thought, rather unfairly. However she would notice in future that Nancy did tend to tell stories which closely mirrored the ones which had just been related, except that they were just a bit more dramatic, with exaggerated details. Nevertheless Helen was very fond of Nancy and looked forward to her visits.

As Mary cleared away, she said,

"Och, I like her fine and it's good of her to come and visit you so regularly. It must be hard to be a teacher and a mother. It's just she's so damned polite and all her geese are swans."

This was a phrase new to Helen and it appealed to her.

Nancy was divorced and, with her daughter Ruth, had returned to live with her father, a Glasgow factor. It was suggested that Helen might like to visit them in Dennistoun. Ruth, two years younger than Helen, would be delighted to see her, Nancy said. Helen was pleased to accept but wondered how she would get there. The idea of travelling around Glasgow by herself never seemed easy. Nancy was able to assure her that the tram at Charing Cross would take her right along Duke Street, and if she got off at Bellgrove Street, then she need only climb up Westercraigs and she would find Oakley Terrace. It sounded possible and Helen arranged to come soon.

◊

One Friday afternoon, Mary organised a card party. Mrs Rayner was invited and Annie and Helen were curious to meet this woman about whom they had heard so much.

"She's quite an ordinary woman, nothing special, really work-ing class, I would say." Mary warned them.

Mrs Ferrier was the fourth player.

"Will it be bridge?" Annie asked hopefully.

"No, no. It's solo we play mostly."

"Not even whist?"

"We get enough of that at the whist drives. They enjoy a wee bit of gambling, quite small stakes of course. Just a little flutter. It makes the time pass."

It was decided that Annie should sit on the couch, rather than in her wheelchair. It would make her more normal, Mary said. Annie was not sure about this, nor very pleased at the word normal. Helen transferred her from her wheelchair to the couch at lunchtime.

"I'm jealous that you're going to meet the amazing Mrs Rayner, Mummy!"

"Oh I'm sure she'll still be here when you get home. I wonder what delicious treat she'll bring us today?"

Mrs Rayner was in her fifties, dark, small and extremely fat, though well corsetted. Dressed entirely in black and with a surprisingly flirtatious little hat on the very front of her large head, she had several chins and no pretensions to good looks. With small close-set eyes and rather red cheeks, the most extraor-dinary thing about her was her deep, almost strangled voice. Annie had never heard such a strange rasping tone. Was the hoarsness due to some constriction in her throat, she wondered, or was it the result of years of shouting at staff in the hot canteen kitchen? The poor woman seemed to require a great effort to pro-duce the words and their harshness seemed to hang in the air for seconds after she had spoken.

When Mrs Rayner plumped herself down beside Annie on the couch, her greater weight affected the balance of the slimmer woman, who quickly grabbed the padded arm to steady herself.

It was all very friendly and Annie enjoyed the experience of holding a hand of cards again. When she shuffled the cards, the slight numbness in her fingers meant she was not as deft as before, but she had been such a master of cards previously, that she was able to hide any deficiencies. She smiled at the thought of her misspent youth.

At one point as they played, Mary held up her hand,

"Listen!"

"What is it?"

"SSH! Listen! Is that the siren I hear?"

The warning came from far away and was very faint, never easy to hear in that top flat. The sound was very different and much less terrifying than in Hyndland, where the siren was on the school roof, right across the road. The Hyndland siren shriek was deafening, almost painful in its incredible volume and its continuous unearthly howl seemed to announce catastrophe and chaos. Fortunately Mary was never to experience a siren at such close quarters, for she had never lost her feelings of extreme panic at the warning.

After listening intently, they all decided it could not have been that after all, and Mary was able to relax.

Soon, Mary again interrupted play with a dramatic gasp and a raised hand with a pointed finger,

"I'm positive I heard something. Are you sure that's not the siren this time? Away in the distance?" Everyone stopped breathing to listen and were again able to reassure her that there was no siren blowing.

Annie however now knew what the sound was. She was sitting beside it. It was the regular creaking of Mrs Rayner's corsets. With each breath there came a faint whining squeak from the lady's over-worked foundation garment. Annie felt it impossible to explain the noise to the company, yet wanted to set her mother's mind at rest. For a few minutes the frustrating situation filled her with a terrible desire to giggle uncontrollably. Fortunately the conversation became louder and the moment passed. Then Mrs Rayner shifted her position and the creaking stopped.

Mary and Helen enjoyed the joke that night when Annie finally told them. It would be referred to many times in the future. Helen had been a little disappointed that Mrs R was so very ordinary, but the story of her creaking corsets made up for it.

The half dozen eggs which Mrs Rayner had brought did not seem very exciting to Helen, but the adults were delirious.

◊

Helen was more confident in her school work this year, although history and geography still seemed obscure and boring. The history text-books spoke of battles and kings and queens in some unspecified vacuum of time long ago and held no interest for her. The geography text books contained lists of crops and fuzzy black and white photographs of mountains and lakes in far away countries. Perhaps if they had conveyed some idea of the vast size and infinite interest of our planet, Helen might have studied them more assiduously. She certainly loved stories of the South Sea Islands. Was it was a lack on the part of the textbooks that nothing in either subject grabbed her interest? Certainly it was her own fault that she often neglected to 'read the next chapter for Thursday', and thus fell further behind. The blank maps which were presented at the weekly tests seemed so very blank to Helen. She wondered how absolutely accurate one had to be in order to gain a mark. For instance, it seemed as though one might put Constantinople, (which appeared with irritating frequency in both history and geography test maps) anywhere within a quarter inch radius. In such a small map this allowed the possibility for quite a large error. Did one gain a mark if it was *roughly* in the right place? The rest of the map lay featureless and daunting. It all seemed too difficult as well as pointless. She pretty well gave up on those two subjects.

She loved English and the readings of Shakespeare in particular. It was always fun to act out the plays, though some girls were better at acting than others. Helen enjoyed learning speeches. Less enjoyable was the reading of a classic book around the class. That was a painfully slow process for someone who loved reading and a bad reader would make no sense of the nineteenth century prose. Helen read her books quickly at home, but then it was even more boring to listen to a familiar story fragmented and ruined by hesitant readers in class time.

They had read 'A Christmas Carol' in the first term and Helen was really sick of it for she had read it twice last year, first at the Waid Academy in Fife and again in Glasgow. It would never be a favourite for her. After Christmas the class started on 'Silas Marner', a strange choice for sheltered, middle-class twelve-year old girls, with its dark plot of epilepsy, false accusations, miserliness, crime, unwanted babies, drowning and general wickedness.

Helen's English test marks were good. Writing essays came easily to her, with her imagination and the wide vocabulary she had gained from her own reading, She particularly enjoyed a lesson from Miss Renwick, who took the class only once, when their regular teacher was ill. She asked them to write a story using all the words in a list which she gave them. At first sight, these words seemed to have no relation to each other, but suddenly Helen saw how she might combine them and Miss Renwick congratulated her on the unusual story she had written. It made it more exciting to find that, like Miss Bates and the headmistress, Mrs Tebb, Miss Renwick had been one of her mother's teachers.

English interpetation was fun and seemed to Helen just like commonsense. Most importantly, this subject needed no study.

Neither did Art, for her draughtsmanship was better than most.

Maths, science, French and Latin gave her no trouble as a reasonable standard could also be achieved with little or no study. Without application she would never gain very high marks, but with the false philosophy of so many school children, she felt it more commendable, even more noble, not to strive too hard. How much better to gain a reasonable pass mark without trying, rather than to swot really hard, then face the terrible ignominy of failing in spite of your hard work.

Though she could not have analysed this attitude of mind in words, it would stay with her until she left school. She would only realise the pleasure and satisfaction of hard dedicated work when she started Art School at seventeen.

It was a little boring to go over the same ground in Latin for another year, though she still very much liked the subject. She enjoyed the repetiton which was required to master the grammar, it was like reciting poetry. The idea of learning this classical language had always appealed to her for it was always studied by those exemplary children in books. She loved the illustrations in her text book of a Roman family in elegant flowing clothes, living in a villa overlooking the sea.

Shortly after they had moved to Renfrew Street, Helen asked her mother,

"Did you do Latin at school?"

"Oh no. I was far too lazy at school. I hope you're going to work much harder than I ever did."

"Hmm, Would you like to learn Latin now? I could teach you. It would be fun and good practice for me."

"Would you like to teach me Latin, my love? I hadn't thought of learning it, but I suppose it's never too late. All right. Fire away."

Helen bought a nice new exercise book at Mackinlays and started to teach her mother Latin. Annie was more amused than dedicated, but she learned her declensions and conjugations and wrote out the simple sentences that Helen made up for her. Perhaps it helped Helen with her Latin studies. It certainly fulfilled her desire to teach. It also gave the mother and daughter a small space of privacy, for when they were in their bedroom, learning Latin, Mary would leave them to it. The Latin lessons provided a quiet afternoon interlude for Annie and Helen.

Annie also noticed that she was very relaxed after a session of repeating 'mensa, mensa, mensam, mensae, mensae, mensa'. It was quite hypnotic.

Helen loved these quiet times alone with her mother. They were difficult to find for even when they had gone to bed at night, Mary would sometimes come in to their bedroom,

"I was wondering if you two were feeling any hunger about you? I could make you a wee sandwich if you fancied it."

The sandwich might be declined, but Mary would then lean on the end of the bed and talk for an hour. It could be amusing, but more often it was grumbles about old angers and resentments.

Helen would drift off to sleep but Annie, who had listened to her mother for much of the day, was a helpless prisoner of boredom.

Yet she felt sorry for this lonely ageing woman who had been for so much of her life an admired raconteur and socialite. It must be hard to accept that those days were gone.

Unkind Fate

Helen's feet had grown and she needed new shoes. Mary took her to Coplands and as she stood in the special foot-measuring machine looking down through the eyepiece at the X-ray picture of her feet, she thought what a lot of bones there were in feet. She supposed all feet were the same.

When the assistant brought out the right size of black lace-up shoes, Helen was horrified. They were like boys' shoes, big, clumsy and square-toed. Last year she had such prettily shaped, soft leather shoes with pointed toes, very comfortable and very grown-up. Helen had loved them and she looked in dismay at these ugly masculine shoes.

Mary was not favourably impressed either.

"Is that all you have?"

"Yes, Madam, things are getting so much scarcer and really you're lucky because that's the last size five in stock and we've *no* idea when the next delivery will be. And it would certainly be inadvisable for your daughter to continue wearing her present shoes, as they're really now much too small for her foot and could cause untold damage to the bones."

Helen listened cynically. This non-stop talking woman seemed over-dramatic. There were probably nicer shoes hidden away for special customers.

But it was getting late and Mary was flattered to be mistaken for the mother rather than the grandmother. Helen left the store wearing shoes which felt hard and heavy, looked awful and which she would always dislike.

The following Saturday, Bruce was visiting. He seemed less breezy than usual.

"Had a lot of worries this week with Singers. They promised me a whole load of wood, then the buggers reneged. Maybe they didn't get it themselves. I don't know. It's a big problem. If I can't get the bloody wood... works come to a standstill...Mhm. Aha yup..."

He made various noises that Helen translated to herself as meaning,

"Life is difficult, getting worse."

Then with one of his quick changes of mood, he jumped to his feet and asked,

"And how's my wee Tuppenny? Doing fine at school are you? C'm'ere till I see you."

He put his hands on her shoulders,

"My ye're getting near as big as your old man! Keep your shoulders back now, never slump, my lass."

Helen felt a wave of dislike at his touch and also at his implied criticism.

"Now, Annie," he always barked his wife's name in a specially sharp way, "I'm wondering here if the wee one doesn't have a slight cast in her eye."

He was looking steadily into Helen's eyes and she looked back at him.

"Surely not, Bruce. I've never noticed anything like that!"

Annie herself had a very faint, hardly noticeable cast in one eye. The sight in her left eye was slightly impaired, the aftermath of a bad infection when she was a baby.

"Aye, I'm afraid there's a wee problem there, right enough. Uh huh. Aye, let's see. I think I'll make an appointment with my good pal Davy Ferguson, he's a chap at the baths. D'ye remember him, Annie? Big eye specialist, best in Glasgow. Aye, she should see him anyway. Have a check-up."

Helen was too surprised to say anything.

Annie looked at her eyes that night,

"They seem fine to me, pet, but I suppose your father's right. A check-up won't do any harm and the specialist will let us know if anything's the matter."

Helen felt dismayed, but said nothing.

The appointment was made for the following Saturday and Bruce accompanied his daughter to an opulent house in Sauchiehall Street.

The doctor was very stern and serious. Belladonna was put into Helen's eyes and everything went blurry. The investigation required all sorts of lights and was quite interesting.

Another appointment was arranged and Bruce and Helen left, having learned that Helen suffered from astigmatism and might need to wear spectacles.

Helen felt glum as they walked away. How depressing. Spectacles! A broken front tooth and those horrible new shoes, what a guy she would be! No chance of a career in Hollywood with those unglamourous attributes. She tried to joke with herself, but was unable to share it with her father. That ideal of beauty and attraction that is the dream of most teenage girls, receded even further into the distance.

Even her father guessed her mood and suggested going to a cafe to cheer her up.

"I know a wee Tally's near the the Art Galleries. Great ice cream."

Helen found the misty world that the belladonna had created had its own charm. The tramcars looked extra colourful and seemed to shimmer along Sauchiehall Street in a weird way. When she mentioned this to Bruce, he offered her his arm,

"Just in case you stumble."

And they walked along companionably.

After their ice cream, they strolled back to Charing Cross through Kelvingrove Park. As they passed a large tree, her father asked Helen if she ever climbed trees.

"I love climbing, but I've never had a chance to climb a really big tree. It's the rocks at Pittenweem and the Billowness that I like to climb. And walls too. I love jumping down off walls."

"Well there's a fine big tree to climb over there, let's see you make a shot at it.'

Helen needed no second telling and was soon up above her father's head.

"Maybe you better not go any further up in case you get stuck!"

She came down obediently, but climbed several other trees that they passed on their way home.

Bruce and his daughter probably came closer to each other that day than they ever had before. Helen was pleased to show her skill and Bruce took pleasure in her strength and agility.

When they arrived back at her grandmother's flat, they were chatting in a relaxed friendly manner and had forgotten all about the eye specialist.

"Well, what did he say?" Mary asked immediately. She had waited impatiently for this important verdict.

"What did who say, Mrs Mackay?"

Mary was worried and angry and did not hide her irritation.

"The doctor, the eye doctor you went to see. Surely that's where you've been, isn't it? You've been away for a very long time! What did the specialist say about the child's eyes?"

Mary's irascible tone offended Bruce.

"Oh well, Mrs Mackay, it's just exactly as I had thought. There's a bit of a problem there. Astigmatism. She'll probably have to wear specs for a few years. P'raps not permanently of course, but certainly for the forseeable future."

The words rang like a knell in Helen's ears. She had not realised it was so definite. Why? When she could see perfectly well?

Just then Annie exclaimed in a loud voice,

"Bruce! What on earth has Helen been doing to her new shoes. Just look at them! They're all scraped on the toes. What a mess! Where the hell did you take her, to ruin a new pair of shoes like that!"

Unkind Fate had stepped in yet again to make sure that Bruce and his daughter would never have a fond relationship. Their pleasant afternoon was blotted and blackened. Bruce was angry with himself for allowing it to happen, furious at being reproached by his wife and humiliated in front of his mother-in-law. Helen felt guilty that her father seemed to take all the blame and even though she hated them, she was very ashamed of wasting her new shoes. Waste was the ultimate crime in those years of deprivation and she tried so hard never to waste anything

With a different relationship, the father and daughter might have shared their disgrace and enjoyed being in the doghouse together, but Helen and Bruce would never have that sort of empathy.

In spite of it all, Helen could not feel too regretful about her shoes, for she thought they looked no worse with scratched toes than without.

◊

For her thirteenth birthday in February, Annie gave Helen a small square parcel.

It was a Pond's presentation box with two white glass jars, one of vanishing cream and one of cold cream for cleansing.

It was a brilliantly chosen gift and Helen was thrilled and delighted. How very grown up to receive make-up! And from her mother! It was a statement that Helen appreciated deeply and the cream smelled delicious.

After she washed her face, she applied a little vanishing cream, such a magical name, and it helped her to forget her spectacles and her clumsy boyish shoes.

War News

Mary was at her whist drive and Helen was in the kitchen with her test tubes, making saturate solutions of sugar, salt, washing soda, anything that would dissolve. She was fascinated by crystals just now and had several labelled saucers laid out in the pantry, each at a different stage of crystal formation.

Annie and her father were in the cosy brightness of the black-out tent in the studio, waiting for the nine o'clock news to start.

John sat on the couch with his head bowed over his clasped hands. Sometimes he would be seized with a spasm of coughing and would bring out his handkerchief, blow his nose, then with a slight smile to his daughter, rub his moustache vigorously in a well-known gesture, before tucking the handkerchief away in his pocket.

"Are you feeling all right, Paw? Tired?"

He smiled quite brightly,

"No, not particularly tired, thank you. Just getting older, not so much use any more.

It was sad to see her father frail and failing.

"Oh well, you've just finished a successful portrait and maybe another will come along soon."

"I don't think that's going to happen, my dear. Don't think I'm strong enough any more and my memory lets me down, too. Took me all my time to get that one finished. It's the standing, y'know. I still enjoy a bit of sketching. I did a nice wee thing of Helen yesterday. I'll show it to you sometime. 'Fraid a pencil's all I'm fit for now. I just wish I could see an end to this damn war. Thought the last war would end all that strife. But no, here we are still, fighting, fighting, bombing … killing … I've seen it all before. And where did it leave us that time?"

He shook his head and sighed deeply.

There was little Annie could say. It did seem that the fighting had gone on and on and might never stop. It was happening all over the world and of course they only heard the more positive aspects of it. It was probably a great deal worse than the newspapers said. They would never really know how bad it all was.

"Where's your mother?"

"She's at the whist drive. It's Tuesday night, remember."

"Oh yes, of course, stupid of me…"

Mary played whist at the Conservative club every Tuesday, but John would often forget.

"There's a nice concert on later tonight, Paw. Beethoven and Schubert and some Chopin I think."

"Mm, yes, Beethoven and Schubert…"

These were John's favourite composers. How hard to think of them connected to the beastly Huns that were depicted in the newsreels and newspapers.

John looked up,

"As long as there's none of that brute Wagner's so-called music!"

John smiled as he said this, nevertheless he meant it. He hated Wagner's work and would never listen to it. Annie was glad to hear him make the slight joke. She wondered whether he objected to the actual sound of the music, or if Hitler's delight in the composer had coloured John's opinion.

The news started and although the announcer was trained to be calm and objective, he sounded almost hysterical and was obviously triumphant as he delivered news of the terrible devastation which the RAF had inflicted on Dresden. It had been a resoundingly successful attack, resulting in most of the city being razed to the ground.

The way that he gloated over this victory seemed particularly horrible to Annie. How many people had been killed and mutilated in such an attack? Pains ran up and down her spine and her legs started to cramp with the emotion that she felt as she listened.

When the war news was finished, her father shook his head and said very quietly,

"I visited Dresden when I was a young man. A very wonderful city. Exquisite. Marvellous buildings and galleries and paintings."

Neither of them spoke again.

The concert started and though she appeared to listen, Annie could not at first concentrate. Her mind reverted, as it so often did, to that first sea battle of the war out in the Firth of Forth. She had witnessed it from the garden in Pittenweem. Perhaps because it was the only action of the war that she had seen, it had affected her deeply

As the music of Beethoven poured into the studio, Annie felt herself relax. She looked over at her father. As always, he listened to the sublime sound with his eyes closed, the tears slowly rolling down his cheeks. He made no attempt to wipe them away and this seemed particularly heart-breaking to Annie.

When would the war finish?

◊

When Helen collected her new spectacles from Lizars, she walked home slowly. The woman had opened the velvet-lined case as if to delight her with some piece of exquisite jewellery but Helen was horrified. Round lenses, metal trying to look like tortoiseshell. How old-fashioned and unnattractive they looked, like something for an old lady. She tried them on and swiftly removed them. Yes, thank you, they felt quite comfortable. No thank you, she would not wear them just now. Tears were near the surface, but she determined not to show her sorrow.

"Let's see you in your new glasses, then."

How could her mother be so cheerful when her daughter was about to ruin any last chance of looking half human?

"Oh those are *very* smart. You look extremely intellectual, I think. Very studious."

That's the last thing I want.

"I don't like them. The floor looks as though it's sloping down a hill."

How stupid to wear ugly things like these and see the world wrongly.

"You just need to get used to them. It won't take long for your eyes to adapt."

I'll never get used to seeing a slope when I know it's flat.

"I can see perfectly well without them, better in fact."

"Yes, but the specialist thinks it's necessary for the good of your eyesight." Annie was beginning to realise how unhappy her daughter was. "You'll soon get used to them and forget you're wearing them."

I'll certainly never forget I'm wearing them. How can my mother say a ridiculous thing like that?

At school, there was a more honest reaction.

"You look so different!"

"I hardly recognised you!"

"I didn't know you needed glasses."

"Do you need to wear them all the time?"

"What a shame!"

"I think they look quite smart."

"Oh no, I don't, I'm sorry, but I don't think they suit your pigtails at all."

"Perhaps if you got your hair cut short, they would look better."

"I think they look all right on *you*, but I'm glad I don't need to wear them."

"Will you take them off for hockey and gym?"

It was Tessa that decided Helen looked like a professor. Tessa's self-confident, adult pronouncement was sufficient to make the name stick and Helen did not mind it too much. She was quite flattered in fact. Nicknames were unusual in the class and to have one added a little bit of interest to what had seemed like a disaster. Professor was quite distinguished.

Helen was known as 'the Professor' until the summer holidays arrived. By that time, Helen had started to develop a slight bony bump on the bridge of her nose. Her hitherto slightly tilted nose was changing to become a modified and feminine version of her father's rather noble feature. While this change did not bring her much joy, it had one major benefit. The despised spectacles irritated the bony bump and were returned to their velvet lined box forever.

VE Day

Helen travelled to Dennistoun to visit Nancy and her daughter Ruth. She jumped on the Denniston tram at Charing Cross and asked the conductor to let her know when they reached Bellgrove Street. Fortunately he was really friendly,

'Aye, don't you worry, hen. Ah'll tell you near the time we're getting' therr, an'pit ye aff at the right stoape. You sit jist inside therr an' Ah'll no' furget aboot ye, hen, you wi' they long pigtails doon yer back!"

It was quite a long journey and Helen saw parts of Glasgow unknown to her before. The great open space of George Square with its trees and statues was very surprising. It looked more like a foreign city. She must ask her mother about it.

When Helen rang the bell of number one Oakley Terrace, a maid answered the door of the imposing town house. She was quite old and wore an overall rather than a white apron, unlike the maids in films. Nevertheless Bridie was a real, live-in maid and had been with the family for more than twenty years. Helen was impressed.

In the entrance hall, a splendid staircase curved up to the first floor. Helen's first thought was that the bannister would be perfect to slide down. Of course that would be out of the question in this elegant establishment. What a shame.

Ruth came running to meet her and was not a bit shy, though they had not seen each other for years.

"Come on, Helen, come and see my doll's house."

Unlike her mother, Ruth spoke in a slightly Glasgow accent and completely lacked that affected gentility which attracted Mary Mackay's sarcastic comments.

What a pleasant time they had. The doll's house was in pretty bad repair. They washed the floors and windows and Helen fixed some of the furniture and promised to make curtains for the windows.

After nearly two hours, they climbed up the big staircase to the drawing room, where Nancy was sitting with some friends.

Bridie the maid was pouring tea from a silver teapot. Helen had read about upstairs drawing rooms, but had never seen one or expected anyone she knew to have such a thing. She realised now why Nancy was so polite and genteel. Surely one *had* to act like that in an upstairs drawing room with a real maid in attendance.

Helen was introduced as Annie's daughter. The three other ladies seemed to know her mother well and asked to be kindly remembered to her. They admired Helen's long fair plaits and the Fair Isle jumper she was wearing and agreed that – '… Annie was always so good with her hands and such a beautiful knitter'.

When the girls left this rarified atmosphere, Ruth asked Helen if she ever slid down bannisters.

"No, never. I'd like to, though. Are you allowed to?"

"Of course, come on."

They slid down and climbed and slid down again many times.

Helen could not believe her luck. Children in films often slid down bannisters and she had always wanted to try it herself. It was a wonderful experience! She would never find another one that could remotely compare with the Oakley Terrace bannister.

Helen visited Ruth several times that spring and became confident about alighting from the tram at the right place, without any help from the conductor. The doll's house blossomed and Helen put on plays in it for Ruth, as she had done years before for Elsie's daughters, Maureen and Eleanor, who now lived in London. The plays still tended to use that scenario which never fails to please, the Cinderella plot where an ill-used heroine triumphs in the end.

◊

One Saturday in March, Bruce brought Annie some purple rhododendrons.

"Saw these growing beside the golf course and thought you might like to paint them."

"Oh they're lovely, Bruce. That's very thoughtful. I haven't painted since last summer. I'll get started first thing tomorrow morning!"

Helen had never seen rhododendrons before or perhaps had never noticed them. She was entranced. They seemed such an exotic colour and shape to grow at this chilly time of year in Scotland. She could not stop gazing at them.

"Maybe you would like to paint them too, would you, my love?"

"In oils?"

"Why not? We'll get a bit of cardboard for you to try."

The following day the mother and daughter stayed in their bedroom painting. They enjoyed working together and while Helen's was very much a beginner's effort, she felt grown up using oil paints and revelled in the rich smell of linseed and turpentine. Just as in the summer, Annie felt relaxed after her day of painting, and determined that she would paint regularly in future. Perhaps she could get something good enough to send to the Royal Glasgow Institute exhibition in the autumn.

As Annie had feared, there were often disagreements in the Renfrew Street flat. Some fairly innocent remark of Annie's might easily infuriate her mother. Occasionally Annie would become tired of her mother's domineering attitude and bravely speak her own opinion. Several times, minor quarrels erupted into full blown rows. Annie would ask Helen to wheel her to her bedroom, John would retire to the safety of the studio upstairs and Mary, smoking furiously, would sit by the fire with a thunderous expression on her handsome face.

Several hours would pass before some sort of peace was restored and it would be a couple of days before a comfortable atmosphere returned to the house.

These dramatic encounters were unpredictable and to Helen often inexplicable. Why was Mary's anger always so close to the surface? And why did Annie make that one small provocative remark that was bound to upset her mother?

Helen had not learned the terrible potency of 'the last straw that breaks the camel's back'.

Annie would be upset and exhausted after one of these scenes, but strangely enough, the explosion of anger seemed to give Mary an injection of energy and she would be extra active for a few days, baking, cleaning and going into town for an afternoon's shopping.

Helen avoided these confrontations as much as possible, burying herself in a book in the kitchen when she heard raised voices.

By the end of March, after a particularly fierce argument with her mother, Annie had decided she must return to her own home.

She spoke to Bruce about it on the Saturday,

"Really I think it's too much for my mother and I know it's too much for me. I need to get back to my own place and I think it would be best for everyone. Especially Helen."

"Aye well, just what you say, Annie. I always wondered how it would work out. But there's still the big problem of who'd look after you at Clarence Drive."

"Oh, we'll get somebody. I don't care if they're useless, I need to get out of this house. It's affecting me. I'm in agony a lot of the time and I've lost the will to do the things that I could be doing. I'm not nearly as independent here as at home. My mother does-n't realise that I need to peel potatoes and make myself useful. She thinks she's helping me by doing it all herself and of course she's quicker, but ...oh well, I suppose she must find it all very difficult, too. And my poor father ... anyway Bruce, I've made up my mind, I'm sorry to be a nuisance, but I'm going home. As soon as possible."

Mary protested weakly, but she knew it was for the best.

Helen admitted to her mother that she was delighted. And relieved.

"You know every night before I go to sleep, I lie and worry about how I'd get you to safety if a fire broke out."

"Do you, my pet? And I never knew you were worrying like that. Och, you would soon dump me out my chair and I'd just slither down those stairs, if I'd had to."

But Helen knew that the reality of six flights of marble stairs would be painful and difficult, if not impossible.

She was glad that was one problem she would never have to deal with and so very pleased to be going home to Hyndland.

Mrs. Connell

B ruce applied to the Employment Bureau and was given
three names. "Here we are! This one lives in Dumbarton
Road, that would be handiest for the tram. Her name is
Mrs Connell. The others are quite far out, Yoker and
Knightswood."

When Mrs Connell walked in that Saturday morning, Annie
was sure she was a fourteen-year-old dressed as a woman.
Indeed she was very smart, with a wine red woollen suit and
black court shoes with matching handbag. Her little hat was
jaunty without being ridiculous. Slight and nervous, she certainly
looked terribly young. Could she possibly be a teenage girl posing as a married woman? Annie suspected the girl would hardly
be strong enough to lift her.

"As you can see, Mrs Connell, I'm out of action these days
and need someone to help with the house and also help me phys-
ically. I'm sure you're a good worker, but you're very petite and
dainty. D'you think you could manage to haul a big sonsy
woman like myself in and out of bed?"

"Oh I know I'm wee, but I'm awful strong, Mrs Corning. An'
I've got an awful lot of energy too, I can work from morning 'til
night...no bother."

"Well I only need you in the mornings, Monday to Friday. Do
you have any other jobs to go to, Mrs Connell?"

"No, but mornings would just suit me fine, you see I've got
my family to look after. And John, that's my husband, he's got a
really good job. He's a maintainance man in a big works." She
laid the emphasis on the middle syllable, pronouncing it to
rhyme with the first one. Otherwise her accent and grammar
were very correct, unlike Jessie's colourful patois. "And I just
thought I'd like to do something in the morning, now my wee
girl's at nursery school."

"My goodness, you don't look old enough to have a wee girl
that age!"

"Oh yes, Mrs Corning, I'm twenty-two and I've got a wee boy
in primary one as well. He's just nearly five. I would love to come

and work for you here. Your house is beautiful. You've got lovely things and I think we'd get on awful well, you and me. And I'd do my best to make everything nice and comfy for you. I really would, Mrs Corning. I'm not much of a cook, but I'm a right thorough cleaner and I love going messages and polishing floors. Just wait and see the shine I'll put on that green lino in the hall."

She shrugged her shoulders and closed her eyes as if thinking of some delightful treat in store.

Annie was attracted by the young woman's excellent appearance and touched and charmed by her eager and sincere manner. It seemed almost too good to be true that the first person she interviewed was suitable. But it was the case and Agnes Connell became an important and dependable part of Annie's life for many years to come.

◊

On her first day at work, Mrs Connell brought a basin of water to Annie in her bed and then, unlike Jessie, left her to wash, while she busied herself in another part of the house. Annie remembered how she had enjoyed those laughter driven ablutions with Jessie each morning, when she had been rubbed and scrubbed and tossed about. Well she must just get on with it herself now. In fact it was quite relaxing to kneel there and gently sponge herself. More dignified than the Jessie experience.

She could not hear a sound from the new cleaner. Where was she? What was she doing so quietly? Certainly very different from Jessie, whose heavy footsteps and frequent collisions with doors and furniture made her progress from one room to another only too apparent. Mrs Connell was even more silent than Mrs Young

When Annie was dressed and wheeled into the sitting room, it was obvious that Mrs Connell had not been wasting her time. The room was unfamiliar, for it had a bare and deserted look. No books or newspapers lay around, Annie's knitting was not in sight, in fact everything except the furniture had been tidied away. Annie could not guess where it could all be.

"My, you've fairly tidied this place up! What a speedy worker you must be! It looks splendid and what a nice fire burning there. But you'll need to tell me where things are. My knitting for instance and there was an article in yesterday's paper…"

Mrs Connell quickly lifted one of the velvet cushions of the armchair and there, neatly piled were all the Sunday papers from yesterday and one or two magazines.

It was an ingenious way of tidying the room that Annie had not encountered before. She suspected it would not add to the comfort of the chair, yet she did not want to criticise the girl on her first morning at work.

"Oh that's fine I'll know where to look. And my knitting?"

Mrs Connell went to the other armchair and lifted the cushion. Annie had to speak.

"Oh I don't want my knitting kept below a cushion, Mrs Connell, the pins might get broken or they might give someone a nasty jab in an awkward place. Besides, I need it where I can get at it easily and I really don't mind it lying around."

"Just whatever you say, Mrs Corning." But the girl blushed and Annie was sorry to correct her. She hoped that she was not too offended. No doubt the cleaner considered the room more elegant without all the different balls of wool required for Fair Isle gloves. Annie had not the heart to say that she would prefer not to have the newspapers tucked away either. For the many years that Mrs Connell continued to work for her, newspapers, magazines, bills. receipts, letters important and unimportant, even cheques were gathered up and stuffed below the chair or couch cushions, some of them never to resurface. It may seem that this rough and ready filing system would at least centralise all papers and it would just be a case of searching through the different piles for a particular item. Alas, it was never as straightforward as that. Of course, if Annie and her daughter had in the first place been more business-like, those important papers would not have been lying around to be gathered up and hidden. But Annie had always rather despised the over-organised and the too tidy. She was the wrong person to train her daughter in those skills and it meant that a great deal of time was wasted in searching for things. What Helen did develop was a fine disregard for chaos and convention, a useful skill for someone who must deal with the difficulties inherent in the unpredictable life of an invalid. She also had the knack of remembering just where she had spotted some particular article in the general clutter.

After the gentle correction, Mrs Connell retired to the kitchen and Annie wondered if she was sulking. However she soon darted back into the room and gave the lower sash of the windows a wash, then vigorously polished them with a duster. Her polishing extended to the woodwork below the windows and then to the skirting, the mantelpiece, the cupboard doors, anything that was wooden and shining. Everything was rubbed with an almost desperate energy. She put the strength of her whole body into her polishing and moved swiftly from place to place as though there were some dread deadline to meet.

"I'll do the upper windows later in the week, if that's all right, Mrs Corning. I'm just trying to do a bit here and there to make it as nice as possible. It had all got quite grubby, with you being away out the house so long. I'll soon get it nice, though. It's a lovely house and you've got really lovely furniture"

"My, you're an awful hard wee worker! I've never seen anything like it. No wonder you're so slender, you're using up enough energy for two people there. Would you not like to take a break and have a cup tea. I know I would like a cup of coffee and a bit of toast for my breakfast and I'd like you to join me, if you would."

"Oh Mrs Corning!" the pretty little face looked aghast, "I'd forgotten you hadn't had any breakfast! You'll think I'm terrible thoughtless. Oh I'm awful sorry, oh dear…"

"Never mind, I'm not starving or anything, just go and put the kettle on."

Annie smiled as the girl rushed from the room. She was so young, it was hard to believe she was a mother of two. She seemed to move at a superhuman speed, darting in and out of the room, always so quietly, like a little moth.

By Friday, Mrs Connell had lost most of her shyness and had fallen under the spell of Annie's personality. Annie was a good listener and was really interested in the lives of the people around her and Agnes, as she now wanted Annie to call her, had become quite confidential.

"We were married in November. We'd been saving up all year and my aunty has a wee boarding house in Blackpool and we were going to have our honeymoon there. Then did the war not start in September, but we just went ahead with our plans and it was a *lovely* wedding. I had a white satin gown, just what I'd always wanted, right down to the ground and a *gorgeous* bouquet of white flowers. I'll bring the photographs next week and show you. It was a dream wedding, everybody said that. Well, of course with the war starting, there were no lights in Blackpool, so it was a bit different to what we'd expected." She paused for a moment, obviously remembering that magical time. "But the sands were nice for walking, not too cold and there was hardly any other folk about. It was awful romantic, really. We went dancing in the Tower ballroom quite often, for my John's a great dancer, just lovely, so he is. He's not very tall, but then neither am I and we make a good couple. Oh, the way he can glide across the floor and whirl you round! He's always the best dancer in any hall and you know how difficult it is to get any man to dance, but he loves it. That's how we met at the F&F ballroom in Partick. We just danced together so well, it was love at first sight. He's not really what you'd call handsome, well I think he is, but my mother thought he was a plain wee man. She called him that when I first brought him home. Oh I was that angry at her for sayin' it! Spittin' mad, I was. But she likes him now and says he's a real good provider. So he is. And he doesn't hardly ever drink. Maybe just a wee whisky or two on a Saturday night. He doesn't go to the pub. We have friends in the close and we visit each others' houses and we're never far from home."

"That sounds like a very happy marriage and now you've got two lovely kids. You're so lucky that John is doing important work and not far away from home or in danger."

"Don't I know how lucky I am, Mrs Corning. I thank the good Lord every night for having John safe beside me. Hopefully it'll be all over soon and everyone will come back to their homes and loved ones."

"Aye there'll be a lot not coming back and I'm afraid we've got plenty of misery on the other side of the world to deal with yet. Everywhere has a hell of a lot tidying up to do after the bombing and destruction."

Their friendship developed quickly. By the end of the second week, Agnes was more relaxed and was enjoying Annie's humour. She had met Helen briefly on the day of her first interview and enjoyed hearing stories about her. She had not yet met Mary and was rather nervous about that.

Mary popped in unexpectedly on the Friday morning. She was wearing a smart suit and a dashing hat with feathers at the side though her long amber beads struck Annie as a little overdressed for a morning call. Then she realised that Mary was determined to make an impression on the new cleaner. Her mother often astonished her. Could it be that she also was nervous about meeting Mrs Connell, and had dressed in her best in order to bolster her own confidence? Her mother would always be an enigma to Annie.

Fortunately Mary took to Agnes immediately, saying later that she was 'a very pretty wee thing and seemed like an honest, hard worker. I believe your father would have liked to paint her in his younger days.' This was the highest accolade that Mary could bestow.

◊

HITLER COMMITS SUICIDE
3rd May 1945 Glasgow Herald

On German radio, after a dramatic roll of drums, Admiral Doenitz announced to the German people that their Fuhrer, after fighting to the last breath in his body, had fallen at his post, defending his country against the scourge of Bolshevism.

Annie and Agnes were sitting drinking coffee, strangely silent. There was little to say about this dramatic news. At last Agnes spoke,

"Last night, it said on the news that the Russians were awful near him at the end, Mrs Corning. D'ye think he was frightened of them?"

"Well, after what he did to them, I certainly think he had reason to be frightened. They might have torn him to pieces."

"What would have happened to him if he hadn't... done that to himself?"

"I suppose he would have been tried and executed eventually. But there was never much chance of him reaching a court. Not if ordinary soldiers got their hands on him first."

"What an awful long time the war's been going on, hasn't it."

"Aye, a long weary time."

"You know, Mrs Corning, I can hardly remember what it was like in peacetime!"

"It was another world."

"But I think things'll get better now that Hitler's out the way."

"I certainly hope so."

The End of the War in Europe

For Helen the end of the war seemed strangely unexciting. It just seemed to happen. Hitler was dead and the Allies were in Germany. All of a sudden there would be no more bombing and soldiers would start to return home. Perhaps if someone in the family had been in the forces, there would have been more joy, more drama. Her old dreams seemed childish now. The end of the war could have no effect on her mother's condition, nor could it stop grandad from getting old. The rationing of food and sweets did not change. The only change as far as they were concerned was the ending of the blackout. Lights could be put on in every room in the house now, if needed, though the heavy curtains in the sitting room were still pulled across at night, for warmth and privacy. Helen had got used to going through the rest of the house in the half dark and she continued to do so, often in a state of undress.

When she visited her grandparents on a Sunday, there was no longer any need for the little tent around the fireside and she missed it. It had been friendly and cosy.

◊

On VE night, crowds of people passed up and down Clarence Drive, laughing and shouting to each other. Annie was listening to the description of the crowds in London on the wireless. The number of people sounded quite frightening and the noise was incredible. The announcer was beside himself with excitement.

"Pull the curtains back and let's watch the folk passing, Helen. Would you not like to go out and see what's happening in Hyndland? Join in the excitement?"

Helen shrugged unenthusiastically.

'I think you should take a walk and see what you can see. It's a pretty special night you know. Hopefully there will never be another one like it"

Helen put on a jacket and reluctantly went out.

Was this what they had been waiting for all these years? All these rotten years of worry and deprivation. She felt grumpy rather than triumphant as she wandered down to Airlie Street, where a small crowd was gathered on the piece of waste ground there. Two men were trying to get a bonfire lighted, without much success. Someone had a fiddle and was playing Scottish music, but the sound was thin, disappearing like vapour amongst the high tenement walls. It sounded very sad to Helen, not at all triumphant. However most people looked very happy, standing around chatting and laughing. Two or three small children were dancing in a circle. Helen stood for five minutes watching the unsuccessful fire-makers, but she felt conspicuous standing by herself. Soon she walked quickly away from the groups and turned up the hill towards the bowling green, then walked down her own lane and home.

'You didn't stay out long."

"Nothing much to see, really."

Annie wondered if her daughter was lonely. Her nearest school friend lived a mile away. Perhaps she had made a mistake in sending Helen to the Girl's High. If she had gone to Hyndland Secondary, she would have had more friends in the area. She always seemed happy enough with her books and her knitting. There was her dancing class and she had a friend to go swimming with just now. Her class-mate Olive accompanied her to the Arlington twice a week. They seemed to be close friends, but Olive lived in Old Drumchapel, on the outskirts of town and was not around for companionship on a night like this.

Helen had poked the fire and settled down with her 'Just William' book. She was smiling gently to herself. She had recently moved her patronage from the small lending library in the Clarence Drive newsagents to a larger establishment on Hyndland Road and both she and her mother were enjoying its wider selection of authors. After Helen had devoured all the Tarzan and Chalet School stories in the newsagents, nothing much was left except romance, cowboys or crime. Now the two of them could share the humour of P G Wodehouse or the cold chill of M R James ghost stories. When Helen had been ill last year, her mother had read aloud the charming stories of Wee McGreegor by John Jay Bell. Usually Helen preferred to read herself, but her mother's Glasgow accent had added greatly to her enjoyment of these pawky tales.

◊

It was June and Helen had just finished exams at school. She was amongst the top few in English and everything else was fairly satisfactory, except history and geography, which showed the usual dire results. She also had her grade three ballet exam that month and she would be taking part in the display that Miss Hopkins held for her junior pupils each year in the McLellan Galleries. Her class was performing a Welsh dance which was also to be part of her exam, and she would join the younger pupils as they danced the waltz, polka, eightsome reel, lancers and the Grand March. Helen was unsure of the last item and hoped it was simple, as they had never rehearsed it. Although she knew the McLellan Galleries well because of visiting the annual RGI exhibition of paintings and sculpture, she had no idea how it could be used as a place for a dancing display. Would they climb up the wonderful marble staircase to the halls where the paintings were hung? Where would people sit to watch? Or would it be some other part of the building that she had never seen? She was not particularly excited about her first performance. The Welsh dance was very simple, with little possibility for interpretation. There was also the drawback that she was taller than the other girls in her class. Not quite so different now since she had moved to grade three. She knew Miss Hopkins had another display later that month, a proper one on the stage of the Athenaeum. Miss Hopkins had given her a ticket to attend that evening performance, but she was not sure if she would go.

She had a faint memory, not a very happy one, of dancing on the Athenaeum stage, wearing her nighty and carrying Topsy. She had been a very little girl then and was distressed that she could not see her mother in the audience.

The grade three exam was less daunting than the first two. Helen knew what to expect this time and the fact that she had a new ballet dress helped a lot. She had been given the address of a seamstress in the Cowcaddens who made them. It did not have the complicated structure of a traditional tutu, but it was pristine white and hung on the bedroom door, fascinating and magical. Each night, Helen lay in bed gazing at the layers of tarlatan and tulle shimmering in the soft glow of the street light.

Perhaps Mr Espinosa was too tired to come to Glasgow this time, for Miss Berney was the only examiner and she gave Helen a welcoming smile. Once again Helen was astonished and dazzled by the neat little feet and marvellous jumps of the plump Miss Berney. The examiner must have been equally impressed by Helen's jumps, for once more she passed with honours and the crit card specially mentioned her ballon, beautiful feet and excellent mime. When Helen learned that ballon meant the ability to jump high in the air, she was particularly pleased, for Miss Berney was obviously an expert.

The Facts of Life

As Annie and Agnes Connell became closer, Annie confided her worries about Helen. "You know, Agnes, she's thirteen now and I have no idea what she knows about the facts of life. I've tried over and over to bring the conversation round to it, but she is a genius at changing the subject. It's as though she doesn't want to speak about it."

"She knows where babies come from though, does she?"

"Oh yes, of course. She's known that since she was four or so, though I remember she was unwilling to believe that humans were just the same as cats and dogs and monkeys. I think she hoped I'd made a mistake at first. Then she took it in her stride. But she's never asked the next question of how does the baby get in there? I remember my brother and I were always wondering and asking and trying to find out long, long before we were thirteen, more like eight or nine probably. When did you first find out?"

"Well it was my big sister that told me all about it when I was about eleven. She was getting me prepared for my periods starting. Has Helen started yet?"

"Yes, just the last few months, but she knew all about that through helping me. I never know if she's just not curious about the whole business, or maybe she knows already and is embarrassed to discuss it with her old mum. Or perhaps she's afraid to find out. I'm sure they must talk about sex at school. What I worry is that she'll hear some daft half-true story from some other kid and get it all wrong. I certainly feel she shouldn't be ignorant at her age."

"Oh no, she certainly shouldn't be ignorant. That's where danger lies and she's quite a big tall grown-up girl now. And she's not got a sister to go around with, like I had and you're not able to be out and about with her either. I wonder what we could do?"

Annie was touched by the fact that Agnes had immediately taken on joint responsibility for the problem.

"We've got a wee book at home. Maybe it would be no use but I'll bring it tomorrow and you can see. John was given it when he joined the army at the beginning of the war, that was before they realised he was needed at home for the maintainance. It's just a wee thin book with advice for the young soldiers. I'll bring it tomorrow and let you see it."

The following day Annie looked at the book but decided it was not really quite right for her daughter.

Next Monday morning, Agnes arrived and she was smiling broadly,

"You'll never guess, Mrs Corning! What a coincidence! I canny believe it myself."

Her usually correct speech was slightly forgotten in her excitement.

"See, it's just exactly what we're looking for. It's so strange...one of the Sunday papers, next week it's starting... they're going to do a special sex education supplement for young people. There was a big article. John read it out to me because I was telling him about your problem, and doctors and nurses and psychiatrists have all got together to write this so that there won't be so much ignorance on the subject. And it's all awful modern and up to date, although I don't know if these things change all that much. But just fancy that! Now could that not be better timing? Next week!"

"It seems miraculous really." Annie was thinking that Helen would be furious if she knew that John Connell and maybe others had been discussing her ignorance.

"Which newspaper was it?"

Agnes looked blank for a moment.

"D'ye know I forgot to ask him! But I'll soon find out. It wasn't the Sunday Post but it might be the News of the World or the Sunday Express."

'It wasn't the Express because we had that."

"It must have been the News of the World then."

Annie's heart dropped. It was such a rag of a paper. Sex education sounded more like a big selling point than a serious endeavour.

"We'll see. Is it not an awful scandalous sort of paper?"

"Well it does have some terrible stories in it. You can hardly believe them. But it has a good women's page and recipes and there's an awful nice fashion contest that I do every week. You've to choose the outfits that are most stylish and there's a big prize. Never won it right enough."

They both laughed but Annie made sure she would read the educational article before she passed it to Helen.

"We can try our hand at the fashion competition too, then."

◊

Helen thoroughly enjoyed the Babies' Ball in the McLellan Galleries. It took place in a large hall on the ground floor with a gallery running around it. Miss Hopkins looked very splendid in a beautiful black silk skirt and a dark green satin blouse. Though there were lots of parents upstairs and downstairs and it seemed like hundreds of well washed, well-behaved little children. She looked very happy and not at all harassed. Many folk wanted to speak to Miss Hopkins and she managed to deal with everyone with a calm and pleasant smile. She had to muster the correct group for each item and keep the programme flowing smoothly, visit the dressing rooms at intervals to deal with small crises, and signal to the three piece orchestra at the beginning of each dance. She seemed to be everywhere at once, yet always charming and dignified. Helen was very impressed and realised that it would have been easier to have a stage, where one could direct it all from the wings, rather than walk swiftly back and forth all the time in the large ballroom.

It was obvious that the children were enjoying themselves, though occasional weeping broke out. It was inevitable with so many young children.

The three and four year olds were in their little purple romper suits with purple or pink ribbons in their hair. The five and six year olds were in ballet dresses and the older classes were in a variety of costumes. The outfit for the Welsh dance was surprisingly theatrical, with an emerald green skirt, black cape and tall witch's hat. Helen helped with the smaller ones in the Grand March which was really easy and quite good fun. She danced a polka with a girl in a clown's outfit and waltzed with a little elf. There was a tea break for the adults, while the children sat at long tables and demolished a feast of sandwiches, biscuits, cake and jelly. What a lot of organising had gone into this event. Helen had never imagined it would be so much like a party. She helped serve sandwiches, jelly and trifle to the younger children and worried that their tutus might suffer from spillage, but there were no serious accidents.

After the break, the older pupils danced an eightsome reel then the lancers. Three or four of the advanced pupils gave solo performances. There was tap dancing, which had little in common with the movements of Fred Astaire or Jack Buchanan. Helen hoped these might improve in time. Helena Bartholomew did a wonderful Hungarian gypsy dance, full of fire and whirling skirts. It suited her beautifully and Helen was enthralled. Perhaps she would be allowed to dance a solo dance some day.

After it was over and she had changed to a summer dress, Helen felt quite tired, an unusual feeling for her. She wondered if Miss Hopkins felt tired. She certainly did not look it. Her smile never flagged as she accepted congratulations, collected hoops and tambourines, organised costumes into hampers, thanked the musicians and the staff. Her black marocain skirt flowed elegantly around her ankles, as she strode back and forth, her back straight, her hair perfect, her blouse uncrushed. Helen did see her accept a cup of tea from one of her assistants with a look of great gratitude and sit down for three minutes to drink it. Helen wondered what age she was. She must be a lot older than her mother when she had been her teacher at school.

◊

Annie did not find it easy to get Helen to read the newspaper the following week. In fact the article was disappointingly mealy-mouthed, but at least it had introduced the subject. In spite of Helen's reluctance to discuss it, Annie felt that they had made a start and she could return to it in more detail later. The little soldier's book was also there to be perused, but Helen left it lying, unread.

The fashion contest fascinated Helen much more than the article on sex. She made her choice of the smartest outfits and sent off her coupon and postal order with that certitude of winning which always accompanies the entering of competitions.

Annie was wrong to think that the girls in school would talk about sex. There were probably a few who were knowledgeable, but mostly they were as ignorant as Helen. They were certainly interested in romance, as depicted in the novels of Georgette Heyer, and they all looked forward to a hazy happy marriage in the distant future, but certainly for the girls in Helen's set, sex was almost non-existent. The word 'sex' was not bandied about as it now is. No doubt there were references and suggestive allusions to sex everywhere, but these might not be apparent to the ignorant. And though Helen read many adult books, most of them skirted around the subject in a way that seems quite incredible today. The Hays code had made Hollywood films squeaky clean as a result of the scandalous and orgiastic epics of the earlier era. Suggestion and innuendo were still present in films and radio, but often so subtle that one who was completely innocent was unlikely to understand. Helen was aware that there was something she knew nothing about, a rather strange something. There were times that she felt embarrassed at some remark that she could not understand. But she was not a curious child and was content to take her world at its surface value and not search for that dark area that lay beyond rose-tinted Romance. Surely she hardly guessed how closely the two were linked. Certainly most of her friends in school were still quite happy to stay in their childish imaginings. Like Helen, if they guessed at the existence of sex, they accepted that it was just one of the many aspects of life beyond their understanding at the moment.

Once, when Helen had complained about Miss Heyer's young heroines always finishing up with much older husbands, her friend Tessa had asserted that she certainly wanted to marry an older, *experienced* man. Tessa did not give her reasons or her expectations of such a man and no one asked her to explain. Helen was certainly amazed at this ambition and not a little puzzled. Her own ideal was a boy and girl romance, a first and only love that consisted of kisses and hand-holding and lasted a lifetime.

Were all of the first year pupils at the Girl's High quite so innocent and incurious?

No, there was Ariane, but we will meet her later.

Holidays Again

"Well, Tuppenny, school holidays again. Ye'll be delighted, I expect. Friday you finish, is it?"

Helen had just told him that they finished next Friday, but her father liked to repeat facts several times, she noticed.

"Yes, well, that works in just dandy, because my friend Bobby is off to St Andrews next weekend. It's his holidays too, you know, and if we can get away sharp on Saturday, I might manage a wee round of golf with him, before I get back to the grind in Glasgow. Your poor old man doesn't get these long fancy holidays that kids and schoolteachers get. He's got to work, bring in the pennies, ye know."

"Oh that's nice that you can manage a break as well as take us through, Bruce. You wouldn't really like to be a school teacher, yourself, though. Would you? Even with the long holidays?"

"No fear! Dealing with all those rotten wee buggers. They're a wild lot. No no, I could never do that sort of job. I'd lay my hands on them. I might *murder* one!"

"Oh, surely not, Bruce!"

"Ah well, some of the things Bobby tells me...right wee hooligans...don't know how he puts up with it."

"He'll have a belt to help him, I expect.'

"Aye and doesn't he just know how to use it."

Helen shivered. There was no belt at the Girl's High and she was very happy about that. She had been belted four times in her life. The fear and humiliation had exceeded the actual pain, but far, far worse than anything else was the feeling of injustice. In each case she had been punished for some small misdemeanour committed in ignorance. The resentment which a child feels against unfair punishment will last a lifetime.

Annie spoke,

"My folk are going through on Wednesday."

"Fine. That's just great. Can ye get your packing all done for Saturday, Tuppenny? I'll call for you nice and early, Saturday morning."

"What sort of time is early, Bruce? I thought maybe Mrs Connell could come and help us get away."

"Early? Oh well, probably not 'til eleven thirty or twelve. We'll see."

Annie sighed quietly. That probably meant one o'clock or two.

On Monday night, Mary broke the news that she and John would not be going through until the following week.

"It's Mr Tainsh, the leather man. His portrait has been so much admired by his friends that he would like one of your father's sea pieces, Iona preferably. Maybe two pictures and he wants to look at etchings, too. He's coming on Thursday, so we'll have to postpone our trip. We might get through next Monday."

"*Two pictures*! That's very nice news. The leather business must be doing well, in spite of the war. Maybe because of it? P'raps you'll hire a Rolls Royce and come to Pittenweem in style."

"That'll be the day. No, there's plenty bills needing paid and the rates will be due soon."

£80 was the annual rate for the Mackay house – high, partly because the flat was used as a business and partly because of its value. In these last few leaner years, Mary grudged Glasgow Corporation every penny of that tax.

"But it's a shame if you have to put off coming through as well. I'm sorry about that, but you and Helen could never manage alone. The house is always damp and needs a lot done to it after the winter."

Annie said it didn't matter. However, she had an idea. Why not go through next weekend as planned and take Agnes with them? Though he had not said so, Bruce was no doubt staying till Sunday night with the Fosters in St Andrews, and he could drive Agnes home again. She was sure that John Connell would look after the two children for a couple of days. Agnes could save Mary a lot of work and earn some extra cash. Besides, she would enjoy seeing the wee house she had heard so much about. The East Coast would be an adventure for her.

Predictably, both Bruce and Mary found various arguments against the idea when Annie propounded it. But for once, she had her way and Agnes was thrilled.

Agnes looked very stylish in a green costume when she arrived on Saturday morning.

"My goodness, you look like a fashion plate! What a smart

suit. Of course with your lovely figure you make everything look good. 'Ye'd set a dish cloot' as they used to say."

Agnes smiled with pleasure.

"And don't worry, Mrs Corning, I've got my old duds here in the case and I'm all ready for action. Is there any lino to polish in Pittenweem?"

"Yes I think we'll find you some lino and Mansion polish to keep you happy. Need to get the place warm and dry first though. We'll save the polishing for dessert."

Agnes laughed. She always showed a warm appreciation of the slightest of Annie's jokes.

"Now, Agnes, my husband isn't here yet and heaven knows when he'll get here. He'll have met some chap in the Gallowgate, no doubt and got talking. I just want to warn you that about halfway to Pittenweem, something is very likely to go wrong with the car. Oh don't worry!" Agnes had looked quite dismayed, "Bruce will open up the bonnet and gaze at it for a while, muttering to himself, then after frowning and tinkering a bit, he'll jump back in, smiling broadly and tell us it's all fixed now. And we'll continue our journey."

Agnes stared at Annie as though she were a fortune teller. Annie nodded.

"Just you wait and see."

Bruce arrived at one o'clock and he and Helen carried Annie out through the back court to where the little green Austin was parked in the lane. He was in a very jolly mood and mentioned this helluva funny fellow he had been speaking to in the Gallowgate. Annie caught Agnes's eye and pressing her lips firmly together, raised her eyebrows. Agnes said nothing, but opened her mouth.

Soon after they had driven through Stirling, Bruce grunted.

"D'ye hear that, Annie?"

"I don't hear anything except the engine."

"That's what I mean. I don't like it, Annie. Not one little bit. Nup. Something not too good happening in there, I'm afraid. A very funny knocking. Listen to that! Can ye not hear it? Not good news, I'm afraid."

He pulled over and got out and lifted the bonnet. Annie spoke over her shoulder to Agnes and Helen in the back seat.

"What did I tell you?"

After ten minutes of mumbles, interlaced with swears, and twice restarting the engine with a deeply worried expression, Bruce took his seat again with a happy grin on his face.

"All fine and ready to go again. I thought we'd had it there for a while. Bit of a bugger with your mother and all that luggage in the car, wee Tuppenny. Don't know what we'd have done. Eh? All's well that ends well, but we might easily have been stuck here for a *long* time. Were you a wee bit anxious, Mrs Connell?"

"Oh, no, I wasn't really worried at all, Mr Corning, because Mrs Corning told me the car would likely break down at some point, but you would manage to fix it all right, in the end."

"Did she, by jabers? Did she tell you that, indeed?"

He was silent for many miles after that. Annie, expressionless, gazed calmly at the passing countryside. Agnes and Helen nudged each other and exchanged a look in the back of the rickety little car.

Summer 1945

When the car arrived at 54 High Street, each occupant looked out with very different thoughts. Until they reached the familiar door, Annie had not realised how much she dreaded returning to the demanding company of her mother. Also the recurring memory of the sea battle, never far from her mind, flooded back unbearably. Five years later and only now, after these last months of horrible devastation, was Europe no longer at war, though other parts of the world were still suffering violence and bloodshed. She sat, staring straight ahead, numb and listless, longing to return to Glasgow.

Agnes was astonished and disappointed that it was such a small house. She had expected something imposing, more like the fine middle-class villas of the Clyde coast. This low red-roofed cottage with dirty little windows was disappointing.

Helen was full of delight. Another summer holiday starting! She looked forward to seeing old friends, swimming and perhaps staging another successful concert.

Bruce had no particular emotional reaction. He was hungry. He was pleased to have brought them through successfully and once he had eaten, he would soon be with his friends in St Andrews.

The luggage was unloaded and Annie was lifted into the bucket seat on wheels.

She had forgotten how comfortable it was. Helen tilted it smartly back and whirled her round and into the house, with something of a magician's showmanship. Annie's mood changed and she laughed as she shouted over her shoulder,

"This is really a marvellous wee seat, Bruce. So comfy"

Bruce smiled happily.

"You know ladies, I wouldn't say no to a bite to eat. It's hungry work driving and y'know what sea air does to you…"

They had brought soup and rolls and Agnes quickly heated some for him. Helen opened the back door and exclaimed over the length of the grass.

"It's like a hayfield out here!"

Normally her grandparents would have hired a man with a

scythe to deal the winter's growth before she arrived.

Agnes was surprised when she saw the interior of the house. It was far bigger than she had thought from that first glimpse, outside. The ceilings were certainly low, but the kitchen and the three other rooms downstairs seemed quite spacious to her and there were two bedroom upstairs. The view of the sea was beautiful beyond her imaginings. She had never seen a house quite like it and she was charmed, though it was very dirty after a winter of neglect. She could hardly wait to change out of her smart travelling outfit and get started.

"Delicious soup, Annie. Just what I was needing. Now I think ye're all settled here? Yup. Fine and dandy? Great. It's getting on a bit now, so I'll just leave you ladies to it and get away up the road. I'll be back tomorrow, probably a bit later on and take you home, Mrs Connell."

"Are you going away now, Bruce?" Helen saw that her mother had that dangerous, still expression on her face.

Bruce's reply was cheery.

"Aye, I think I'll just get away now, Annie, and ye'll be fine now, won't ye? Ye're not needing me cluttering up the place and Bobby'll be wondering where I've got to. I'll see you about four or five tomorrow. There or thereabouts."

Helen could see that Annie was far from fine. Helen would have been quite pleased for him to go. Was there going to be a row? Annie's voice was quiet but determined.

"I didn't think you were going to bring us here and just dump us, Bruce. There's a lot to be done and I can't be much help. Surely you could at least put the fire on before you go. All the bedding has to be aired."

Helen thought her father looked very much as she remembered the schoolboys in Pittenweem school, when they had been brought out to the front and asked about some misdemeanour. He shuffled his feet and looked out at the sea.

"Well, I know Bobby was expecting me earlier than this."

"Well we were expecting you earlier in Glasgow."

"Aye, aye. I know that fine."

He stood there, looking sideways, biting his moustache, rattling his keys in his pocket, It seemed to Helen that he waited for Annie to relent and just say it was all right for him to go, but she said nothing.

"You see, I did promise Bobby…"

"Bobby, Bobby." Her voice rose and Helen knew that a quarrel was imminent. Why had her mother not just let him go when he wanted to?

"You seem infatuated with that man. You'd think the welfare of your own family would be more important to you than that wee, fat self-important boozer. I don't know what you see in him."

Usually Bruce's anger would have swiftly overtaken his wife's, but to Helen's complete astonishment, he said,

" Aye, well, I'll stay just now and get a fire going for you."

For nearly three hours, Bruce, Helen and Agnes worked at the little house, cleaning the sitting room first, then draping blankets, quilts and pillows around the fire. Agnes washed floors and Helen washed windows. Bruce carried in coal, chopped sticks. A pleasant working atmosphere developed.

Annie remembered the Valor heater and Helen went to the shops for paraffin.

"That wee heater was a life-saver in those bitter winters of the war. And if you take the accumulator up to be charged, Helen, the wireless will be working for my folk coming thro' next week, if the rest of it hasn't gone to pot, that is."

Helen had forgotten many of the drawbacks of the house and thought for the thousandth time how wonderful it would be to have electricity in this house.

Bruce popped out for a few 'supplies'.

"I phoned Bobby when I was out. Told him I'd be up later on and I'll have a fish supper here with you folks before I nip over the hill. By the way, I just got a wee bottle of sherry to warm us up after our labours."

"That's very nice and thoughtful, Bruce and the house is clean and warm and comfortable now, too. Thank you. The three of you have worked so hard and all I could do was knit, but I've finished the fingers in *the last pair of gloves* I'm going to make this summer. I'm really fed up with knitting them. I feel as if I've made *thousands* of pairs. And I'm fair looking forward to my fish supper!"

Helen intercepted the smiling look that Annie and Bruce interchanged. Perhaps love was not present in that look, but kindliness, approval and familiarity. Momentarily, Helen wondered what life would be like if her father played a larger part in their lives. She could not imagine it and had no desire for more of his company. Was she an unnatural daughter, she wondered?

As all the work was done in the house, Helen wandered out to the garden and started to pull up some of the long grass. The 'lawn' was roughly the size of her sitting room at home and she could not make much difference to it, but it was fun to pull up the long stalks and make a pile on the path. It would turn into real hay.

Bruce came to the back door.

"Just be careful, Tuppenny, you can sometimes cut your hands pulling grass. Take care now."

She felt a surge of anger. How she hated to be warned about what she should or should not do. She particularly disliked it when her father or her grandmother warned her. They sounded so know-it-all. She continued hauling up handfuls of grass. How could grass harm you? She would clear a big enough space for her mother's chair and bring her out in the morning.

Suddenly, Helen felt a little tired. She stood up and it was as though she had eaten something which disagreed with her. She felt bad, not sick, but not just right. She tried to take a deep breath but found she could not. She was only capable of short shallow breaths. Something was wrong. There was no pain, but her body would not obey her. Just then Agnes came out to the garden.

"I don't feel very well, Agnes. I feel sort of funny."

"Oh come away into the house, Helen and sit down, dear. Or wait, I'll bring a chair out here."

Within seconds, Agnes had a kitchen chair outside and Helen sat in it.

"You're awful pale, my dear. What d'ye think's the matter?"

"I don't know."

Helen was no longer in control of her breathing. It was as if a wicked magic spell had been cast and the muscles controlling her chest no longer belonged to her. She could only take little gulps of air into her lungs and she lacked the power to breathe them out again. It was terribly frightening. She felt dizzy and gripped the seat of the chair to keep herself steady.

Agnes brought Bruce out to the garden and the two of them looked at her anxiously. How she hated to cause a fuss and be the centre of attention. Bruce felt her forehead which annoyed her intensely.

"Aye, she's hot, a wee bit of a temperature."

"Oh Mr Corning, what will we do?"

Their obvious anxiety added to Helen's own fears.

How suddenly it had happened. What was it?

"Where's Mummy?"

Bruce brought Annie out and she held her daughter's hand, while Helen struggled in vain to fill or empty her lungs properly.

"We must get Doctor Armour, Bruce. *At once.* He's in that corner house in Anstruther. You know where we heard the canaries singing one time. Please hurry."

"I'll drive along right now.'

"Hurry."

Helen looked at the worried faces. Did they expect her to die? Would the doctor come in time to save her? She was pretty positive she would not die, she was only thirteen and though she felt horrible, surely she did not feel as bad as dying must feel!

Bruce returned with the doctor in less than twenty minutes. By that time the attack had faded and Helen was breathing almost normally again. She felt exhausted, but relieved and happy to fill her lungs deeply once more.

As she lay on the couch in the sitting room, it all seemed like a bad dream.

"Yes, I'm afraid that was a very typical asthma attack, no doubt she had a bad reaction to the grass seed. She's never had a similar episode before? No? And she might never suffer another one, though thirteen is often the age for an onset of this condition. However, I would be hopeful that she'd grow out of it. Most children do. She should avoid grasses and other irritants of course and does she take much exercise? Oh excellent, swimming and dancing are the very best things. Good. Now take it easy for a day or so and let someone else mow your lawn."

The doctor was kind and confident and set their mind at rest.

"I'm so glad you were here, Bruce. What if you had gone away?"

"Aye, aye. Just as well I was on the spot. Are ye feeling hungry now, wee yin? Could you eat that fish supper?"

Helen thought she could and Bruce went off to buy four suppers and some ginger beer.

By the time they had eaten, everyone was in a very good mood, joking and laughing. Helen had almost forgotten the asthma attack. She felt fine and when Bruce suggested they all have a glass of sherry, she was enthusiastic.

"Oh I don't think Helen should have any." Annie had not forgotten her terror at the child's difficult breathing.

However she was over-ruled and Helen enjoyed a modest glassful.

"Aye we just need a wee bit music now. Pity the wireless is kaput."

"I could play the piano." said Helen.

Her mother's eyebrows rose. The ancient fortepiano had never played in her lifetime. It did duty as an elegant sideboard, but its days of providing music had been long gone when Mary had bought it nearly forty years ago.

However, Helen set about her preparations and after removing the miniature Chinese cabinet, the two tea boxes and the three ornamental bowls from its surface, she opened up the small keyboard and put a chair in place.

'First, I'll play my own composition." She announced.

Annie was astonished.

With rhythm, panache and dramatic movement of head and hands Helen managed to give a tolerable impression, if one dismissed the actual sound produced, of a maestro at the keyboard. Many films had provided her with the model. No discernible melody issued from the instrument, only tinkling echoes and rippling ghosts of long gone musical notes.

No doubt the sherry helped the illusion, but her performance seemed almost miraculous, and yet so very far from music that her audience started to laugh.

Spurred on by their appreciation, Helen jazzed up the tempo, until everyone was giggling helplessly. Bruce quickly refilled every glass and Helen continued to play the non-music. How happy she was to make people laugh. It was the best thing in the world.

Next they tried singing, and with a more restrained use of the keyboard, and a steady beat, one hardly noticed that the accompaniment bore no relation to the song.

It was a hilarious evening and Agnes wiped the tears away several times.

"Oh Mrs Corning, what a rare night we've made of it. Mr Corning is such a good laugh and Helen... I'd love to hear her on a real piano?"

Annie smiled and nodded, but thought a real piano might have been a disappointment.

"Well I'll get away up the road now, it's past ten o'clock!"

"Bobby will have given you up by now, I expect."

"No no, They're late bedders, the two of them."

"Will you be all right to drive, Bruce? You've had a lot of sherry."

"Och, sherry's just a lady's drink. Many's the time I've driven further with half a bottle of whisky in me. It helps yer concentration, ye know. That's a well known fact. Anyway it's too late to see another car on that road over the hill."

"Well, go carefully."

"Aye, see ye all tomorrow."

It had been such a good evening. Helen could hardly believe it. She had never seen her parents so much in accord and she was proud that she had kept them all laughing so helplessly.

She hoped she would never have that horrible breathing problem again. Surely it was unlikely.

But Annie lay for a long time worrying. What if Helen grew worse and needed nursing? Who would look after her wee girl? She knew that asthma could be a crippling disease.

Disappointments

Helen wakened with a slight cold the next day. "Best not to go swimming with that sniffle." Annie was relieved to forbid swimming, for what if cold water brought on another attack and Helen were taken ill at the bathing pool? Annie knew nothing about asthma. John had always been wheezy and chesty, but he had never experienced anything like that.

After the Mackays arrived, Helen's cold worsened, though she did not feel ill. Swimming was forbidden, but after her daily chores were accomplished, she ran down Calman's Wynd to the old harbour, the Thell. There, she climbed and jumped over the smooth, colourful rocks and pools, rediscovering the familiar sensation of a being giant, able to leap over a miniature landscape of lochs and mountains.

The Mackays owned the ruined building adjacent to their house. It had been bought for a song many years ago, in order to preserve the privacy of the garden, which it overlooked. There had been plans to reconstruct it at one time, but these had not materialised. Annie had grown vegetables in the garden belonging to this other house, during her stay in Pittenweem. Now only rhubarb and weeds survived. As in the rest of the town, gardens were at different levels and old walls supported and divided small patches from each other. The wall into their other garden was much the same height as the window sill in the Glasgow flat and Helen enjoyed jumping down into the neglected garden. Helen went off by herself and practised jumps from this wall, backwards jumps, sideways jumps, far-out jumps, turning in mid-air jumps. After each jump, she clambered quickly back up for there were three perfectly placed toe-holds in the stonework of the wall. Almost as much as the sensation of flying through the air, she enjoyed the challenge of climbing the wall. She worked hard and continuously, ignorant of the excellent bone density she was building for her old age.

Since the asthma attack, both her mother and grandmother were apt to regard the girl as a semi-invalid, watching her carefully and forbidding her to do anything too demanding. They might have been surprised to know just how she spent her spare time, but her jumping wall was hidden from the house.

She was a strong active girl who revelled in physical prowess and longed to swim, but the stupid cold lasted for days. The asthma attack seemed like a bad dream.

Annie again received a bouquet from Mrs Taylor in the fish and chip shop. It was even larger and more opulent than last year. She was set up with paints and easel in her bedroom and once again realised how well she felt while plying her brushes. Was it the actual painting that relaxed her, she wondered? Or was it the fact that she was alone and safe from her mother's constant small talk? Whatever the reason, she felt much better and decided to do a smaller painting next time. She reassured Helen that she would get as much fresh air in her bedroom as in the garden. It was certainly draughty enough.

Annie decided to paint marigolds or American Pillar roses next, much simpler than this daunting magnificence of delphiniums, campanula, larkspur, monkshood, stock, floribunda roses, honeysuckle. How gorgeous, but it was too much! Where did one start? Mrs Taylor must have an amazing garden.

Two nights after she had started the large painting, Annie awoke suddenly in the middle of the night as if an electric shock had jolted her awake. What had the doctor said about avoiding irritants? No specific irritant was mentioned, but almost certainly flower pollen was one, for it made many people sneeze. And there in the corner of the bedroom was Mrs Taylor's enormous bunch of flowers. Annie could smell them distinctly. How thoughtless and selfish of her to keep them in the bedroom beside her sensitive child. What should she do now? As she lay there, the perfume became stronger and stronger. The air in the little room must be saturated with all the evil essences that the flowers could produce. Should she waken Helen and ask her to remove them? Perhaps a sudden awakening, plus handling the blooms themselves would bring on another attack? Annie lay and castigated herself for not having thought of this danger before. Eventually she realised that nothing could be more calm and even than her daughter's breathing, as she slept there. If Helen had suffered no ill effects after two nights of exposure to the flowers, surely she was alarming herself unnecessarily. Annie tried to calm down, but sleep did not come again. She felt very guilty.

◊

The crowds of the Glasgow Fair had vanished. So had Helen's cold and she had been swimming a few times, though the weather had been poor. Disappointingly, none of her other friends had visited Pittenweem. It had been quiet and a bit lonely. However Nancy Little and her daughter Ruth were coming to stay in a boarding house in Pittenweem for a week. Helen was looking forward to teaching Ruth all those jumps that she had invented. A tomboy like herself, Ruth would thoroughly enjoy such an occupation.

When John Mackay heard that Mrs Little was coming to visit them, he looked rather disturbed.

"She won't be staying here in the house with us, will she?"

"Oh no, Paw. She's staying in Mrs Kennedy's boarding house at the back of the town."

"Ah well that's all right. It's not that I dislike her. I'm sure she's a very nice woman. I just find it uncomfortable, the way she fixes me with her basilisk eye as she talks. I feel impaled and unable to escape. Have you happened to notice that habit she has?"

Annie laughed,

"Yes, she does have a bit of the ancient mariner about her. But she's a decent sowl and she's had a tough life, poor thing. She's been a very devoted visitor. And Helen gets on well with her wee girl."

"That's very nice for you and Helen to have company and I'm pleased, however I expect I'll be playing snooker in Anstruther most nights this week."

Helen met them at the station and as soon as the luggage was taken to the boarding house, Helen started Ruth's education in wall-jumping. The two girls spent nearly three hours assiduously climbing the wall, then jumping off it again in the various different ways that Helen had invented. Ruth was an excellent pupil and they reluctantly stopped only when supper was ready. Ruth promised to continue practice immediately after breakfast next day.

John had cleverly caught the 6.45 bus to Anstruther when Nancy came to visit Annie that night.

"The train journey seems to have tired Ruth out completely. I asked her if she wanted to join me tonight and see Helen for an hour or so, but she just felt like going to bed. So unlike Ruth! Of course she'll read 'til all hours, I expect."

Helen felt the first stirrings of conscience. Could she have overdone the jumping lessons? The answer was 'yes' and poor Ruth's aching legs kept her in bed next day.

She had recovered by the following day, and assured a remorseful Helen that she was ready to jump again any time, though not for so long and best not to mention it to her mother.

In the morning, Nancy, Ruth and Helen went together to the swimming pool. Nancy hired a deck chair and settled herself with knitting, novel, sketchbook and pencil, hat, parasol, shoulder shawl, vacuum flask of coffee for herself, lemon barley water for the girls and a small tin of biscuits. Helen was very impressed with these supplies. All eventualities were provided for.

When she described Nancy's foresight at home, she found that instead of reflecting her own admiration, Annie and Mary were apt to be scathing about such personal comforts. Mary was particularly catty, but Annie was also sarcastic. Helen could not understand this attitude and decided that when she herself was too old to swim, she would sit on the sands in a deck chair, with book, knitting, and a flask of coffee.

Thursday was a beautiful sunny day and Nancy astonished both girls by changing into a swimsuit and having a brief dip in the icy pool. Helen found it amazing, never having thought of Nancy as athletic in any way and certainly considering her long past an age for swimming. At forty-two, she was not the oldest person in the pool by many years, but she seemed to Helen such an unlikely swimmer. Nor was she an impressive swimmer, but the fact that she had entered the water at all seemed almost miraculous to Helen.

How wonderful it would have been if her own mother could have gone swimming with her and watched some of the tricks she had invented in the water. She could hardly remember her mother swimming.

By the end of the week Helen had another nasty chest cold.

What a nuisance it was to be ill during the holidays. Friday was the last day of Ruth's holiday and they had not played together that day, in case Ruth caught her cold.

Nancy came down at night for a last evening visit. John had not been quick enough to catch the early bus and stood there, dressed in overcoat and muffler, shifting his weight from one foot to the other. Nancy was telling one of her long stories and appeared to direct it specially at John, though the anecdote could hold little interest for an elderly artist. Her eyes seldom left his face, though the banality of the plot hardly justified the drama of her delivery. Every few minutes John dragged his eyes away from Nancy's compelling gaze, to glance at the clock.

Annie was sorry for him and could think of no way to help him escape. Those pale mesmerising eyes of Nancy's were concentrated on his face, as though telepathy were required to substantiate the integrity of her tale.

Finally he broke the spell by clapping his hat on his head and muttering that as it was such a fine night, he would just walk along the road to Anstruther.

Helen was in her bed, coughing but not unhappy, for she was sucking Victory V lozenges, as she read Coral Island for a second time. Those three young men, Ralph, Jack and Peterkin seemed like such nice boys, such staunch friends. What adventures they had. Helen really loved the idea of being ship-wrecked on a beautiful island, especially swimming in the lagoon She had read Robinson Crusoe when she was eight and the difficulties and possibilities of adapting to the exigencies of shipwreck had delighted her and fuelled many of her imaginary games. The exotic allure of whispering palm trees, and surf beating on the reef of some remote South Pacific island would remain with her throughout her life.

At nine o'clock, Nancy heard Helen coughing.

"Has Helen had a chest rub, Ann?" Nancy never called her Annie, " I always think a chest rub last thing at night is a great help. You'll have Vick in the house?"

Mary was about to say it wasn't necessary, but Annie thought it a good idea and said there was Vick in the bedroom.

When Nancy left the room, Mary, who was surprisingly secretive and possessive about the non-public rooms of her house, said,

"It's all just curiosity, you know. She's just *dying* to get a look at that bedroom. I hope it's reasonably tidy."

"It's fine and I don't think it's just curiosity, Maw. Give her some credit. I know she's very fond of Helen. It'll help the kid, I'm sure."

"Hmm. But I could easily have rubbed her chest, if she needed it."

Helen was surprised when Nancy came into the room and immediately laid aside her book. She liked her mother's friend.

Perhaps Nancy's eyes did wander over the furnishings and disorder of the room, as she applied the strongly aromatic ointment, but it did not stop her doing a thorough job. Far too thorough for Helen. Nancy believed in continuous and energetic friction and Helen's back and chest were rubbed and rubbed, until Helen thought she might not be able to stand it any more. In spite of genteel pursuits of crochet and knitting, Nancy had rather rough hands and Helen had never been so harshly handled. Her skin started to burn, but gratitude and shyness sealed her lips. On and on the determined rubbing went and Helen became hotter and hotter. She supposed that the heat was part of the cure. Previously she had only had a gentle application of the ointment and it seemed to provide its own heat. She remembered as a child, having the pink cottonwool wadding, called Thermogene, applied to her chest. It had created the same unbearable heat, until she demanded that it be removed. Helen intensely disliked extreme heat. She wondered how she could politely ask Nancy to stop, but she could not find the courage. Presumably Ruth was used to this sort of agony, poor girl, but if Ruth could stand it, she supposed she could too. She longed for it to stop, which of course, it eventually did.

"Now I hope you feel nice and cosy, dear and you'll have a good, sound sleep now and feel a lot better in the morning. Night night."

Nancy tucked the bedclothes tightly around her, another thing Helen hated, and left the room quietly.

What a very nice, kind lady she was, but Helen felt like a hot coal. An unhappy, glowing, flaring ember. She pushed the bedclothes off. Would she ever cool down again? Her chest and back felt sand-papered. She would get up as soon as Nancy left the house, put her mother to bed, then stand at the back door, smelling the night-scented stock in the chilly air and listening to the sea. Perhaps then she would reach a normal temperature.

Some days later, Helen was still coughing badly and had lost her usual healthy appetite. She accepted that swimming was out of the question for she tired easily. One evening Mary came into the bedroom where Helen was reading the Mowgli stories for the third time.

"I noticed you hardly took any scrambled egg at tea-time and I thought this might be nice for you to sup."

On a tray was a saucerful of peeled, chopped tomato, lightly salted and with a touch of pepper. There was a teaspoon to eat it with. Helen thought she had never tasted anything so delicious. It was exactly what she needed. How very kind her grandmother could be.

"Would you like some more, my jewel?"

"Oh! I would love some more, please."

Over the next few days, Mary plied Helen with many saucers of prepared tomatoes and the child never tired of the fresh sweet taste. The tomato diet seemed to do her good, for she quickly started to eat other foods and recover her strength.

Helen would always feel tremendously grateful to Mary for introducing her to this delicacy. Throughout her life, lightly seasoned raw tomatoes would be Helen's chosen food, when she felt under the weather.

The memory of her grandmother's solicitude that summer helped her deal with Mary's difficult personality at other times. Although she appeared seldom, there was certainly a generous and caring person under that temperamental and critical exterior.

Walking Boots

"I hope that damned wind isn't going to wreck my holly-hocks." Mary glared at the sky as if her displeasure might quell the elements. It was a bright sunny day, but an unusually brisk breeze blew from the south and Annie had been wheeled back into the house. Helen would have kept her mother in the garden all day, but the wind had repeatedly blown Annie's hat off. Finally she had insisted on returning inside, saying, as she was rattled over the crazy path,

"You can get *too much* of a good thing, you know!"

Helen had gone swimming. As she walked swiftly to the swimming pool, the wind blew her fringe back from her brow and fluttered her short skirt. She loved a day like this, with the white-tipped waves and clouds scudding across the sky. She supposed it wasn't quite the same if you were stuck in a chair.

John had returned from his daily walk. He sighed deeply as he sat down on the chintz covered sofa and took off his hat. After smoothing the scant white hair, he replaced his hat and sighed again.

Annie looked affectionately at her father. No doubt he was frail, but he had been gone for more than two hours. Had he walked all that time?

"Did you have a good walk, Paw?"

"Very, very nice. I went up the country and it wasn't nearly as blowy up there. The trees give a lot of shelter. I'm a wee bit tired out now, though."

"That's Helen back from her swim. She'll make you a nice cup of tea."

She coo-eed for her daughter and Helen bounded in, then disappeared to put on the kettle.

John laughed quietly,

"Indeed, I do feel a bit weary. Must be getting old."

Mary came into the sitting room in time to hear the last remark.

Irritated by the wind rattling doors and windows, she spoke sharply,

"I don't know why you want to go tiring yourself out with such a long walk. You've been away for hours! You should have more sense. Where on earth did you go, anyway?"

"Oh, up the back of the town and into the country," he spoke vaguely, waving his hand in that direction, then added, after a pause, "I think..."

"You *think*? What d'ye mean you *think*? Did you go up by the station?"

"No... no, I came back by the station road."

"Did you go round by Balcaskie?"

"No...eh...well I believe I did. But yes, maybe I did. I'm not just quite sure."

" Surely you can remember where you've been all this time."

"I did pass Grangemuir."

"Did you pass the 'cheepin' gate' You'd remember that surely?"

This was another entrance to the Grangemuir estate and a peculiarity of the gate structure made a chirping sound when anyone walked past.

"That's right, I did, yes, and I passed the end of the road to Kelly Castle before that."

"What a ridiculous long walk you've had! You must have gone out of Pittenweem by the Taft Hill and gone away round past Abercrombie, That's what you did, isn't it?"

Annie wondered why her mother felt the need to cross-question John. He was safely home now. It did not really matter where he had been. Probably later in the day, he would remember something. Mary's inquisition unnerved him and Annie sometimes wondered if his forgetfulness was entirely unfeigned. Perhaps it was a protection against his wife's aggressive questioning?

"Did you meet anyone you knew when you were out?"

"I believe I spoke to an old farmer, but I don't remember his name. In fact I don't think I've ever met him before."

Mary breathed deeply in and out, then turned away in disgust. Annie smiled inwardly. If John were really trying to annoy his wife, he was brilliantly successful.

Helen brought in the tea with a slice of bread and jam. Strictly speaking, John was not allowed jam, because of his late onset diabetes, but it was reckoned that, with so few sweet things available these days, a smear of home-made jam would not hurt,

"John!" Mary suddenly exclaimed in a loud dramatic voice, making him spill a little tea in the saucer. "Would you look at the mud and dirt you've brought in! What a mess on the rug! And the lino, too. Look at it! You've surely been tramping through ploughed fields. And what on earth have you got on your feet?"

John extended one leg and slowly waggled his foot from side to side.

"Well I'm pretty sure they're boots, but I could be wrong."

He threw a humorous glance at Helen. Although partly hidden by his full white moustache, his mouth was well shaped and expressive. Helen was reminded of her childhood, when she thought him the funniest and kindest man in the world and not a bit old. That was only a few years ago and suddenly she felt very sad and sorry for him. Tears came into her eyes and she left the room quickly.

"Good Heavens, John. Those are never your boots! They're like a *ploughman's* boots! And they're far too big for you. I wonder you can walk in them. How the devil did you come to be wearing some other man's boots? Did you exchange boots with the farmer you spoke to?"

"I did think my feet seemed heavier than usual, today. I just thought I was getting tired. My word, that's a very strange puzzle. I see what you mean, but I can't understand it. They certainly don't look like my boots."

Again he stretched out his leg in front of him and regarded the boot with a little laugh. Annie laughed too, but Mary was in a fury.

"Of course they don't, because they're *not* your boots! It's no laughing matter. Where on earth did they come from? Working men's boots!"

Annie had started to giggle.

"Big clumsy brutes! Where did you get them? Can you not *remember*?"

John frowned and shook his head slowly,

"I'm afraid I have no idea! It seems a very strange, inexplicable matter, doesn't it? Perhaps one day we'll find out the answer. Or perhaps we'll never know."

John had always been philosophical.

"I'll certainly find out where they came from and that right soon."

Mary fumed into the kitchen and her mood was easily discernible by the noise of crashing pots and pans.

"It's a real blustery east coast day today, isn't it?" John was looking out at the sea.

"Yes, it is. A bit too blustery for my taste. But Paw, you'd better take those boots off, they're making my mother awful angry and there's more mud going on the rug."

"Yes, you're right, m'dear."

He was fumbling with the laces when Mary stormed back into the room,

"Get those awful things off your feet at once, John. I've just remembered. Your own boots were being repaired and you went along to collect them from the bootmaker this morning, before your walk, D'ye remember? And the idiot's given you the wrong ones. And *you*! Fancy you never noticing. You're worse than he is. Take them off. At once! I'm going along there right now. What an idea! Giving you some farm labourer's boots."

"I don't suppose he did it on purpose, Maw."

Mary ignored Annie's remark. Her anger had already reached white heat.

"And how you didn't notice it yourself, I'll never understand."

Uncharacteristically jamming her hat on her head without glancing in the mirror, Mary slammed the front door behind her. She quickly returned with the correct boots, but did not deign to describe her interview with the unfortunate cobbler.

The following week, Helen was in the butcher's shop."

"Is Alison coming to visit you this year?" she asked Alice, the butcher.

Alice replied, her grammar and pronunciation very exact, her speech slow and sing-song, rising sharply at the end of each phrase, as if constantly questioning. Helen knew no one else who spoke quite like that.

"I'm afraid my niece won't be here till next month, Helen. The family is attending a wedding soon and then my sister is having a wee operation, nothing serious, but Alison will be required to help her mother at home. Are you missing her? I think the two of you are awful good pals, aren't you? I'm sure you'll be missing her."

"Yes I wish she was coming sooner."

"Because you both love your swimming and you could be dancing in the Market Place, too. I always sit at the window on a Tuesday and Thursday and watch the young people dancing. It's awful nice. You could come along yourself, though, Helen and have a wee dance."

"I'll just wait till Alison gets here."

"Maybe you'd be shy on your own, would you? Now I thought I'd pop in and see your mother tonight. I'll be making shortbread and I know she likes it."

Annie and Alice had always stayed friends, though Mary Mackay often had stormy confrontations with the butcher, accusing her of short weight and other wicked practices, sometimes removing her custom to the other butcher in town for months at a time.

Alice arrived that night, looking very smart. Helen normally saw her in the shop, her sleeves rolled up above her muscular forearms and her blood-stained striped apron wrapped tightly round her ample figure. Now a navy suit with a pale pink blouse fastened by a large gold brooch transformed her. Her speech was different too, even slower than her normal measured syllables. Perhaps when visiting, time was less precious than when conducting business. Helen was fascinated and determined to try and reproduce that unique speech. Alice's words flowed smoothly and unhurriedly.

"And how are you keeping Annie? There's a wee bit shorty I've brought you. Made with butter, but don't tell anyone."

"Thank you very much. Is that why yours is better than anyone else's?"

Alice smiled her placid smile and her always rosy cheeks flushed a deeper pink.

"But how *are* you feeling, Annie? Not too much pain I hope."

"Och well, I suppose I could be better. A few aches and cramps today with all that low cloud. But I expect there's lots of folk far worse off than I am."

"You've got a fine wee daughter to help you anyway. She's always willing, isn't she."

"Yes and as a matter of fact I need her to help me right now if you'll excuse me for a moment. When you've got to go, you've got to go."

"Quite right. You just take your time. *Oh my goodness*! I thought Helen was going to turn you tapsel-teerie just now…"

Helen had tipped the bucket seat up on its two back wheels as usual, but Alice had not seen this alarming procedure before.

Mary came in with the tea things.

"My, your granddaughter's a strong girl, isn't she, Mrs Mackay and so good to her mother."

"Yes, she is and always willing, too."

"That's just what I was saying to Annie."

Later that evening, a mystery was revealed by Alice. Mary had told of the iniquitous shoe repairer who had given the wrong boots to her husband.

"And did Mr Mackay not notice? Were they not uncomfortable to walk in? Fancy him walking all that way in boots that were too big!" Alice's voice soared even higher at the end of each sentence, then leaning forward, she whispered the conspiratorially. "However, I can tell you a bit more of the story. Those boots that Mr Mackay took for a walk up the country, were Mr Smith's boots. My brother-in-law, you know."

The previous year, Alice's sister Lizzie, a maiden lady in her late forties, had surprised the town by marrying Jack Smith, a well-to do farmer in his sixties. After years of housekeeping for Alice and making potted meat and boiling bones in the back shop, Lizzie had become the mistress of a large, well-furnished farmhouse two miles north of Pittenweem. Alice missed her, but took a certain pride in her sister's new status.

"Yes, Lizzie phoned me and asked me to collect Jack's working boots, but when I went over the street to get them, they couldn't find them! Well, I was very surprised. Then Mr Harrison looked again and brought out a pair of boots and he said they were the *only ones* he had in the back shop, but I said at once, 'No, no. Those are never Mr Smith's workboots. Those are dress boots for a gentleman. Look how fine the leather is, Mr Harrison!' So he put them away again. But that afternoon, he brought over the correct boots to me at the shop and just muttered something about them being 'mislaid'. It seemed very strange to me at the time. But fancy that now, when you think of it, those boots were walking just in the right direction for their own home!" The others laughed, "They were, you know! Just like a horse knows its road home, because Jack told me later that he had met Mr

Mackay at the road-end that same day and had a good blether with him. I think those boots must have known where they were going!"

When they had finished laughing, Mary said,

"Oh well, I must tell Mr Mackay that story when he comes in. He'll get a good laugh, I'm sure. He's away to Anstruther tonight, for a game of snooker. But I hope he takes the bus home, for those are Glasgow boots he's wearing and they might easily get lost in Fife."

◊

Helen did not spend so much time with friends that summer. Alison was only in Pittenweem for a few days. They packed a lot into the short time, swimming each morning at ten o'clock, going to the cinema twice, picnicking at Balcaskie and taking the boat trip to the May Island.

They had taken milk in a lemonade bottle to the Balcaskie picnic, and on the way home, each took turns to shake the remaining milk vigorously for five minutes, optimistically hoping to make butter. Helen thought how nice it would be to present her mother with a pat of butter. Alas, something the size of a pea floated in the warm smelly milk and Helen poured it away in the garden.

"All that effort wasted!" Alison said regretfully, but Helen was philosophic,

"Never mind, the exercise would be building up our muscles."

"I suppose so."

Muscular development was perhaps not such a desirable goal for Alison.

Irene Black, a pretty Pittenweem girl and a keen swimmer, accompanied them on the excursion to the May. Irene's older brother, Billy, had been in Helen's class in primary school.

It was a sunny day, with slightly choppy water and the small fishing boat danced over the small waves in a way that delighted the girls. Though they clasped the nearest support firmly, they smiled almost continuously throughout the forty minute voyage. They had not taken swimming gear with them as several people seemed certain there was nowhere to swim on the island. But when they discovered a large pool amongst the rocks, translucent and perfect, Helen had no doubts about what they must do.

"We don't need swimsuits. Who's going to see us?"

They all agreed it was a glorious sensation to swim naked.

Even Billy's assurance, on their return, that the Lighthouse telescope "could see a' points o' the island " failed to spoil the memory of that unique and delicious swim.

◊

Helen kept hoping that Vera and little Jenny would come to visit their relatives in Pittenweem. She had plans for another concert.

Vera's Aunt Meg was in charge of the baker's shop and when Helen collected the rolls each morning, she asked if there was any word of their coming, but Meg always shook her head sadly. As the summer advanced, Helen realised there would be no concert that year.

In spite of wartime shortages, Meg had been able to create magnificent wedding cakes which were always displayed in the shop window for a few days before the ceremony. Helen was full of admiration for these white sugar edifices, some of them quite large, with the different shapes and curlicues which adorned them. She had no idea how those little shells and whorls were made. It looked difficult.

Hiroshima

Glasgow Herald, 7th August 1945
ALLIES INVENT MOST POWERFUL BOMB IN THE WORLD
The Western Allies have invented an atomic bomb which it is believed
will help to shorten the war against Japan. One has already been
dropped on Tokyo, with more than 2,000 times the blast power of the
10-ton bombs dropped by the RAF on Germany.

Glasgow Herald, 9th August 1945
NAGASAKI RAZED
A second atomic bomb has been dropped and it is believed that a large
part of the city of 250,000 no longer exists.

Annie sat in the sunny garden. It was very hot and the sea
was impossibly blue. North Berwick Law and the Bass Rock
seemed to float on the horizon. How calm and idyllic it was with
the flowers and birds around her. Yet on the other side of the
world there was black destruction and death. These were the
most enormous explosions that man had yet caused, not the
greatest that the world had known, for nature could be even
more powerful and dreadful than man. But what a decision to
take! To wipe out two cities and most of their inhabitants quite
deliberately. How could men dressed in smart suits and uniforms
and sitting comfortably around a table, coldly decide to order
such a catastrophe? And how could nice, educated young men
push the button or pull the lever, or whatever they did, with the
knowledge that they rained destruction on hundreds of thousands of ordinary people? How could they do it? How horrible it
all was and now the authorities said they were unsure of the
effect of this new bomb. Possibly a million were dead and the
aftermath might last years. Perhaps it had been the only way to
end the war, but she found that hard to believe. It was difficult to
picture the scene in that distant unknown land. Much more difficult than visualising the damage in Europe. The people looked
different of course, with their unfamiliar features. They were
small and fragile and though many wore Western dress, some
still dressed in the traditional way. It was an entirely foreign culture. Had this fact made it easier for the authorities to drop that

terrible unknown bomb on them? And yet she knew quite a lot about these faraway people, about their cleverness and fine artistic sense. She was familiar with many Japanese artefacts. Mary had several eggshell thin, china tea sets, with finely drawn flowers and butterflies, exquisitely delicate. She also had a very different tea set of heavy Satsuma pottery, fired many times and decorated with richly coloured three dimensional dragons and fierce samurai warriors. And how many yards of fine vibrantly coloured silk, bought at a ridiculously low price, lay folded away in Mary's wardrobe? Would she ever make use of it all? Then there were the patterned paper parasols that every family used in the summer. Also the exquisite paper fans. In the Kelvingrove Art Galleries, the Japanese section showed incredibly tiny detailed carvings of jade and ivory, as well as terrifying masks and luxurious kimonos. What a rich exuberant culture it seemed to be. Helen used to be fascinated by the transformation of the small shrivelled leaf which changed so magically to a brightly coloured flower after a few minutes' immersion in water. But these were all luxuries, delightful but unnecessary. What about the everyday things in Japan? Houses, warm clothing, cooking pots, food, those possessions so vital and so precious to the owner? Had all these things been destroyed or contaminated? Contaminated was a word Annie had hardly known before the war. At first it had been applied to the aftermath of poison gas attacks. Now it was used about the areas destroyed by these terrible bombs. Contaminated! It was like a medieval curse. Poor faraway people. Contaminated. It made them sound like lepers. It would be horrible to believe that they been chosen to suffer because they were so far away and unknown. They certainly seemed to be fierce fighters for, in spite of their wonderful aesthetic sense, their history and culture were war-like. There were terrible stories of their cruelty to prisoners, but perhaps that was propaganda and what lies were they perhaps told about the cruelty of the West? Annie hardly believed much of what she read. As always, it would be the women and children and old people that would suffer.

Annie tried to imagine how their own family would survive such an attack. It was beyond her, just too horrific. Surely this was the dreadful finale of the war with the world returning to some sensible balance and ordinary people allowed to get on with their ordinary lives. It certainly would be very hard for many for a long time. And so many were gone forever.

Tears blurred the bright scene around her, as she thought how very lucky she was and told herself to 'snap out of it".

Annie threw the newspaper away from her and leaning dangerously over to the side, recovered her knitting from the grass. Best to keep busy.

◊

In spite of the articles in the News of the World and her mother's several subsequent attempts to introduce the subject of sex, Helen continued to ignore its existence. However romance was often on her mind and she dreamed of meeting some nice boy on holiday, someone to go swimming with, perhaps even hold hands with, in the cinema. Young couples wandered around town each evening, eating chips and laughing. It looked friendly and desirable and some of them were not much older than she was.

As Helen sat on the garden wall one day, a tall boy appeared in the garden next door. This garden was on a lower level than the Mackay garden. Perhaps the surprise of his sudden appearance or perhaps the fact that she was above him gave Helen courage to speak first.

"Hullo, are you visiting the Andersons?"

"Yes. They're my grandparents."

He had a nice accent, obviously a well-brought up boy, though he did not appear particularly pleased to see her. He was a couple of years older than Helen and at that unfortunate age where custom demanded schoolboys still wear short trousers, while his stage of growth made long trousers desirable.

"I'm staying with my grandparents too. My name is Helen. What's yours?"

She astonished herself with this speech. She had imagined a very different first meeting with a boy. Still he did not smile. Perhaps he would ask her to jump down into his garden? She had done it many times to collect a wayward ball.

"David Brown. I live in Edinburgh."

"Oh."

"I think my tea's ready now."

"I'm going to practise my jumping."

They hesitated a moment, then both turned away, David to

return to his house and Helen to walk along the wall to the next
door garden where her jumping wall was.

It was not a memorable meeting and their paths would not
cross again for many years. However Helen felt that she had
spoken to a boy, and that was some sort of achievement for a
pupil of the Girls' High.

Three days later she met another boy over another garden
wall. He was a couple of years younger than she was and this
somehow removed the awkwardness from their meeting.
Romance was obviously not an issue.

Gordon was also visiting his grandparents. Almost the first
thing he said was.

"Can you draw trees?"

Helen thought she probably could.

'Well I'm making a model theatre and I've written a play and I
need a forest scene. Could you do that for me, d'ye think?"

For the next week they worked together in his grandparents'
house. Gordon had built the stage and now needed backcloth
and side flats. Helen found she was quite good at making a sinister forest scene. She had never realised the three dimensional
possibilities of a model theatre. She painted a backcloth with a
castle in the distance, then another with a little town surrounded
by mountains. Gordon was most appreciative and thought her
brilliantly clever. Helen, though not achieving quite the standard
she hoped for, was quite impressed herself.

Gordon was not a swimmer or a wall jumper, nor did they
visit the cinema or stroll around in the evening eating chips.
None of those companionable things that Helen had imagined
was shared, but they had a lot of fun together. Gordon's holiday
came to an end before there was any performance in his theatre,
but that did not seem to matter. Creating the scenery had been
sufficiently satisfying.

Annie teased,

"Another younger man in your life! My daughter, the baby-
snatcher."

"Mummy! He was just a friend."

Clothing, Food and Sex

Helen returned to school with good intentions. She would work harder and not leave homework to the last minute. She would not use the morning tram journey to learn poetry that must be recited that day. Also, she would try to make some special friends in her own class. She had found no one to replace Khirstine, who was now a year ahead of her. Sometimes Helen joined her old friend at lunchtime for an enjoyable half hour in the more senior classroom, but she felt that the other pupils looked at her askance. She was no longer a member of that class and was seen as an intruder. And when she returned to her own classroom, someone was bound to ask,

"Where have you been?" with more than a touch of implied reproach.

It sometimes seemed that she was almost as much an odd man out in High School as she had been in Pittenweem.

In Fife she had often felt superior to rural children, separated from them by her command of English, her wider experience and her general knowledge. Now, in Glasgow, she felt inferior to her classmates for a variety of reasons. Getting hold of the right text book was still a problem for her. Books were in short supply and if a particular one was not available at the nearby educational store of Mackinlays in Sauchiehall Street, it was difficult for her to find the time, the money and the daring to venture into town to search further afield. Often she was late in acquiring the necessary book and must ask to share it in class. This lack of text books led to her falling further behind in the usual subjects of geography and history. The fact that these books seemed boring and uninteresting on the occasions when she did see them did not inspire her to go in search of her own copies.

On a more personal level, Helen was dissatisfied with her own ironing skills and was sure that her blue uniform shirt was never as perfectly smooth as those smart shirts of her fellow pupils. Her packed lunches, hastily made and wrapped in any scrap of greaseproof paper she could find, looked rough and amateurish beside the dainty lunch boxes prepared by loving maternal hands. Perhaps these minor deficiencies were not as obvious to her fellows as they were to Helen, but no doubt there was a snobbishness and a feeling of elitism amongst many of the girls. A withering sideways glance could say as much and be as hurtful as a cutting remark.

The friends she had made through sharing the same tram route home were serious minded and scholarly. While she continued an acquaintance with them, Helen started to spend more time with Moira, Margaret and Anne, more light-hearted girls, less dedicated to school work, who were happy to welcome Helen to their 'crowd'.

The tallest and prettiest girl was Anne who, like Helen, wore her hair in two long plaits. Her hair was thick and dark and even longer than Helen's. They were the only girls in the year with this rather old-fashioned style and it formed a bond between them. Anne hated her long hair and only wore it because her mother insisted. She often muttered darkly about getting scissors and 'chopping it all off', while Helen felt that her plaits were an important part of her personality. She could not imagine herself without them. Her father believed long hair might be sapping her strength and regularly suggested she should have it cut. Helen thought this idea ludicrous and no doubt her opposition to her father's opinions fuelled her determination to keep her hair long.

Anne intended to be a doctor, which seemed very grown-up and ambitious to Helen, who was happy to let the future take care of itself.

Helen quickly found that she could make these girls laugh and a day was wasted that she did not bring them to helpless giggles at least once. These fits of uncontrollable laughter were not always confined to the leisure periods and teachers were surprised to find that the quiet new girl could be disruptive.

Helen had also developed a special friendship with another girl in the class, Olive, a very good-looking girl, for Helen was always attracted to the beauty which she felt she herself lacked. She too was a member of the Arlington Baths and they went swimming every Tuesday and Thursday after school throughout that year.

Olive and Helen spent many hours together each week, leaping in and out of the pool, creating new graceful swimming strokes, enjoying the wonderful old-fashioned showers, where one was bombarded by two hundred and forty sharp needles of hot water. They chanted songs together in the echoing shower room. The Song of the Volga Boatmen was a favourite and they beat out the rhythm enthusiastically on the marble slabs which separated the shower stalls. No one remonstrated with them for their rowdiness. Almost always they were the only swimmers, for the club seemed strangely deserted. The silence and lack of other people gave the girls a pleasurable yet exciting feeling of being trespassers. After their swim, they climbed upstairs to the gymnasium where an ancient rowing machine and massive parallel bars suggested a game of pirates. The various sizes of Indian clubs might also be utilised for attacking imaginary natives. Their visit would finish in the reading room, where a beautiful fire was always burning and where the Tatler, the Sketch and the Illustrated London News showed pictures of windblown Royalty at the races and misty debutantes in ball gowns, suggesting an unknown life of luxury and romance in distant, sophisticated London.

Olive lived in the small village of old Drumchapel and after their swim they would walk to Charing Cross station for her train, sometimes treating themselves to a bag of chips. As school rules stated *there must be no eating in the streets,* ties and hats were stuffed into their satchels before they bought their small tasty snack.

Their conversation was often about food, mainly sweets and cakes which had been in such short supply for so very long. Faint memories and longings were expressed. Helen fondly remembered marzipan walnuts and Olive sighed over trifle and real cream.

Strangely, although these girls of thirteen, nearly fourteen, were spending hours of intimate time alone, none of their conversation related to sex. Sex might not have existed as far as they were concerned. Nor did sex feature in Helen's conversations with Khirstine, when clothes, cooking and animals were the favourite topics. Even romance was hardly ever discussed with any of her friends. Helen would have enjoyed a conversation on that subject, but hesitated to instigate it.

When Moira had a birthday party, they played the game of Murder. Helen wonderfully enjoyed it, relieved to find that other girls of her own age still indulged in games of imagination. It was an all girls' party and did not offer the opportunities that a mixed party might no doubt have offered when the lights were extinguished.

Certainly Helen was aware that some unknown situation existed, some hazy something beyond romance, something *not discussed*, though adults acknowledged it and joked about it. She felt unwilling to find out too much about this dark, unspeakable subject, happy to continue basking in the warm pink glow of male-female relationships as depicted in films and stories, in the always fashionable plot of early misunderstandings and hostility, eventually wiped away and succeeded by chaste kisses and cuddles.

She was happy to remain ignorant.

This stubborn attitude was the brick wall which Annie encountered when she tried to extend her daughter's education, for Annie worried about Helen's lack of knowledge and apparent lack of interest in sex. She discussed it with Agnes.

"I don't know what to say to her, Agnes. I don't know how much or how little she knows. I suspect very little. She is adamant about not getting involved in any sort of conversation about sex and can always wriggle out of it by changing the conversation. I suppose she is embarrassed. And of course she can always make some excuse and leap to her feet and disappear out the room, leaving me sitting there like a knotless thread, just when I've been leading up to it so carefully. She's a wee devil."

"D'ye think she's read any of those newspaper articles or the wee book I brought?"

"I doubt it. I know where they are. She folded them very carefully and put them away in the top drawer of the wee chest of drawers. I suspect she's never looked at them since, but I could be wrong of course. They should really give some lessons on sex in school, though I can't imagine those sedate unmarried ladies that I remember even thinking about it, never mind talking about it except for very obscure references to flowers pollinating. I suppose they did think about it, though few of them married. P'raps that was due to the Great War, of course. I just don't want my daughter to be ignorant about something so important."

"No, that would be bad, Mrs Corning.Though mind you, I didn't know much when I married John. Just things the other kids said at school. Mostly rubbish, really."

"Yes, that's what I want to avoid for Helen. There's so much nonsense talked and I don't want her to get the wrong idea about it all."

"You shouldn't worry too much. I think she's an awful sensible girl. Did I ever tell you about the night John and I had our first wee party? It was just after the honeymoon. Oh Mrs Corning, there were six of us, three married couples and they'd just come in for a wee refreshment and we were sitting around chatting and laughing and there was a nice fire blazing, when suddenly I realised that those other men there knew exactly what I looked like with no clothes on! Oh I was so embarrassed. And I knew what they looked like! Oh, I blushed scarlet and I could hardly hold my glass steady. I didn't say a word for half an hour. Not a cheep. I don't think anyone noticed at the time, but I felt that stupid."

The two women laughed, but Annie was rather sad to think that this girl, who looked hardly older than Helen, had two children to care for and must go out to clean other people's houses. She certainly hoped that Helen would have a career and not settle down into domesticity too early.

◊

Shopping for food was Helen's entire responsibility and she enjoyed many aspects of it. Her mother had been a regular customer at the Clarence Drive grocer and butcher, and several assistants remembered Helen from her early childhood, before the war. Annie had also been a regular customer at a quaint little fruit shop on the hillside opposite the shops in Clarence Drive. It was one of several wooden huts built when the Hyndland tenements were first constructed, nearly fifty years previously, These huts had been part of the administrative side of that immense structural undertaking and though no doubt considered temporary at the time, were still well utilised by the community.

Adhoc groups of steps, some of concrete, others roughly constructed of wooden spars, led up the earthy slope from the pavement to each hut. Children generally avoided the erratic steps, preferring the challenge of climbing the steep incline. Clumps of grass and weeds were scattered over the hillside, and in wet weather, a small stream cascaded down, creating miniature ravines in the packed earth. Those sheds contrasted strangely with the other side of Clarence Drive, where the solid, custom-built row of shops was crowned by a red sandstone balustrade and fronted with a broad, well-swept suburban pavement.

Helen thought the huts looked as though they had grown on the rough hillside, like old mushrooms. She liked to gather up impetus and rush up at the steepest part, then more decorously descend the steps, once her basket was full.

The upper one of the three huts housed an electrical business, necessary in such a densely populated area where wartime shortages meant that old equipment was constantly in need of repair. The lowest, a tiny cubicle of a structure, was a shoe repairer, also vital to the comfort of the community, when shoes must last for years.

The fruit shop, central and largest, had been a thriving little business before the war, with constant jam-making, beetroot boiling and cabbage pickling in the back-shop, the perfumed steam continuously pouring into the surrounding atmosphere.

Helen could still remember that time vaguely. Nowadays there was no cooking and little variety in their wares. Occasionally there would be an unusual item that sparked customer's interest. Everyone longed for change and few could resist an unexpected fruit or vegetable. Perhaps there might only be one or two boxes of the novelty and it would sell out within a very short space of time. There was an almost telepathic communication amongst the Saturday shoppers.

Helen's pleasure was to buy something unexpected and surprise her mother, for even if she were not sure what to do with it, Annie would know.

One Saturday morning, there was a box of green tomatoes on the fruit shop counter.

Helen remembered the time in Pittenweem when her mother had wrapped green tomatoes in tissue paper and ripened them in a drawer for three months. Ripe tomatoes at Christmas had seemed miraculous.

But there were only a few left and as Helen was waiting behind several other customers, she shifted from one foot to the other, peeping anxiously around the large lady in front of her. Would there be any left by the time it was her turn? She longed to produce green tomatoes from her basket with a magician's flourish, when Annie asked,

"Any treats today?"

There were only four small ones left and Helen bought them immediately.

Annie was suitably impressed.

That afternoon she said,

"Are you ready to try an experiment? I heard this recipe on the wireless."

Helen nodded. She loved the word experiment.

"Well, first, put the kettle on. Then wash half a cup of rice and put it on to boil."

"With salt?"

"Of course. About half a teaspoon should do. We've got an onion all right, haven't we?"

"Yes."

"And an egg?"

"We've got two."

"Just need one. Keep the other one for Sunday's Yorkshire pudding. Now I'll chop the onion and you put on the egg to boil. And pass me the green tomatoes, please."

Helen was completely puzzled. What on earth were they making? It was sad to see the tomatoes chopped up.

"Now put a bit of that dripping to melt in the frying pan and add these onions. Not too high, don't let them burn, just cook gently. I think the rice must be ready to pour. Just leave it there to strain for a moment. Now add the tomatoes to the onions in the frying pan and stir it up, but very gently. Now just a light sprinkle of salt and pepper. Good. That's the stuff."

"What are we making, exactly?"

"Just wait and see. Now add the boiled rice to the frying pan. Go on, it'll be fine. Just take my word for it."

Helen had looked her disbelief.

"Now stir it all together very gently and I'll shell the egg."

Helen stirred, but her face showed she was not convinced. This all seemed very unusual.

"Right, put half the rice on each plate and half the egg on the top. Now doesn't that look exciting and I think it smells delicious."

"I suppose so." Helen's tone made it clear she was not convinced.

However as they sat eating it in the sitting room, Helen admitted it was absolutely delicious.

"I've never, never tasted anything so good in my life before – it's so unusual! It's smashing! It's gorgeous! But I could eat it all over again! Couldn't you?"

"Yes I suppose it was a modest helping for a hungry teenager."

"And you had less than I had."

"You need it more than I do. But that was a good idea of your old Mum's wasn't it! It's called 'Savoury Rice' ."

"I wish we could have it again soon, but I might never see green tomatoes again."

"We could try it with red ones."

But though they tried it with various other vegetables, somehow it was never as tasty as with the green tomatoes.

Fog

Mary was visiting Hyndland on the first foggy night of the year. The day had been cold and murky until six o'clock when Mary had left home, but by seven the atmosphere had become thick and sulphurous.

"I suppose I really shouldn't have come out tonight, Annie. It didn't seem so bad earlier and I wanted to bring those meat patties along for you. They'll do your dinner tomorrow night. Unless you're maybe feeling peckish tonight?"

Annie smiled and shook her head. Her mother showed her love by providing food and was never happier than when watching her cooking being eaten and appreciated.

"Thank you very much, Maw. That's good of you to come away out in a night like this and we'll really enjoy them tomorrow. I don't know what you do to them to make them so tasty. See what it's like outside now, Helen."

"I must say I think the wee touch of dried sage does help the flavour." Mary looked pleased.

Helen pulled back a corner of the heavy curtain and looked out, "Brr, it's really cold and I can only see a wee fuzzy blur where the streetlight is. I can't see the lamp post at all. Here's a tram coming and I can hardly see the lights inside it, just a faint glow. Now it's disappeared in a moment. There's a motor car too. I can hear it and it's going very, very slowly. It's *really* cold and it smells all smoky out there."

She coughed as she pulled the curtain back into place, but she thought it looked exciting. If she had had a companion, a boyfriend perhaps, she would have loved to go out and walk through that thick yellow fog which transformed the familiar streets, making them unrecognisable and romantic.

"Oh, that's fine if the trams are still running. I'd better not wait too late tonight, Annie. Your father will be worried and he was coughing a lot when I left. Fog's the devil for him, of course. I dread it."

Helen listened hopefully. Annie had taught her a new card game called Newmarket. Although they only gambled with matches, it was fascinating. Perhaps if Mary left early there would be time to play a few hands before bedtime. But once Mary started talking, time meant nothing to her and it was after ten thirty when Annie said,

"D'ye not think you should be getting on your way, Maw? The trams'll maybe stop early tonight, ye know."

"My goodness! Is that the time? It surely can't be as late as that already!"

Helen smiled inwardly. Her grandmother was *always* surprised at how late it was and always used much the same words to express her surprise.

After Mary left, they played cards for 'just half an hour' before bed and Helen won a satisfying number of matches.

It was nearly midnight when Helen wheeled her mother off to bed.

"You'll never get up in time for school tomorrow."

"Och yes, of course I will."

The fog lasted for three days. The traffic was disrupted and people complained bitterly about the filth that settled everywhere, but Helen enjoyed the unusual environment. Fog was exciting and made a change in the humdrum daily life and she was amused by how dirty her face was at the end of the each day. Later when she washed her fog-bound clothes, she found great satisfaction in how filthy the water was.

The following week was cold and bright and the fog forgotten. Mary arrived on Wednesday night and seemed particularly vivacious.

"Wait till I tell you about my adventure the other night in the fog!"

She was still struggling out of her coat as she spoke and Annie twisted round in her chair to look at her.

"Nothing unpleasant, I hope?"

"Well... no. Not exactly unpleasant... not at all... perhaps unusual, you could say. A bit of an adventure, I suppose."

Mary sat down at the fireside, brought out her cigarettes and put one between her lips. Her movements were leisurely and slightly affected. She searched unsuccessfully through her handbag for matches with a muttered "damn", then caught Helen's eye and nodded towards a newspaper on the table. Helen jumped up and passed it to her. Then, very deliberately, Mary pulled a strip from the paper, folded it twice, pressing the edges quite exactly, then stretched forwards and took a light from the fire. After inhaling deeply, she vigorously beat out the flaming spill, just before it burned her fingers. With infuriating tranquillity, she blew the smoke out in a slow, controlled stream, threw the charred ashes into the fire, and turned to look mysteriously at her daughter, her cigarette dramatically poised in her graceful hand.

"Come on Maw, we're all agog and the suspense *is killing us*. What happened to you in the fog?"

Again Mary inhaled and again sent the exhalation towards the fire, where the smoke merged with the general exodus up the chimney. Mary smiled a quiet secret smile. How she revelled in the tension of a dramatic pause.

Helen thought she overdid it.

At last she spoke.

"Well, last week, you know I hoped to get a tram, but I wasn't sure if I would or not. There was a man standing out there at the stop, so I thought there must be one expected. He was tall, but of course I couldn't really see him properly, for it was like pea soup. We stood for about five minutes, then he spoke and said,

"I'm not sure if we may have missed the last tram."

And I was pleased to hear he had a very nice cultured voice. Just a slight accent. Might have been Highland, I thought. He seemed to be wearing a sort of cloak, but I couldn't make it out properly in the murk. There seemed too much cloth for an ordinary coat and what with his gentle accent, I decided he must be wearing an Inverness cape. He seemed quite gentlemanly, almost like a Highland laird. That's the impression I got anyway. I told him that there were usually trams until the back of eleven, but as nothing was coming and it was cold, he suggested we might walk on to the next stop, where we had a chance of two trams Yes, I see you think that was a bad idea, but don't worry, nothing bad happened. Not really. And I couldn't very well say 'no' to this Highland laird, as I thought. Well, we walked to the top of the road, but never a tram, so we kept on walking along Hyndland Road. I don't think there were any buses running that night. I was hoping that we wouldn't get caught between two stops if a tram did come, but they'd been going so slowly ... and anyway I think they might have stopped on a night like that.

Nothing came and nothing came and it was terribly cold so we kept on walking and walked and walked. He kept up a fair speed, too, with his long legs and his cape billowing out behind him. We got to Byres Road and then away down Church Street and still nothing. I wasn't a bit frightened, because we were having quite a nice conversation and I told him about visiting you and Helen and he had been at some place or other that I didn't quite catch. He did have quite a strong country accent, but an acceptable one. He really seemed very respectable. Well, anyway, by this time we were past the Art Galleries.."

"My goodness! That *was* a long walk with an unknown man at eleven o'clock at night!" Annie exclaimed.

A flicker of irritation passed over Mary's face at the interruption, then she continued,

"Anyway… just beside the bowling greens, we heard a tram in the distance. Was I glad? He was fairly striding along and the pace was a bit much for me. We waited at the stop and I think the fog there was thicker than ever and we were frightened the driver wouldn't even see us, so the Highland laird, as I still thought he was, stepped right out to the tramlines to flag him down. Fortunately it stopped all right… but…"

Mary paused for breath, pursing her lips and rolling her large brown eyes meaningfully.

"He let me get on first, of course, and I was going to say goodnight before going inside, but he jumped on to the platform and immediately leaped up the stairs, like a gazelle. I thought he probably didn't want to have to offer to pay my fare. But no wonder he skedaddled, for as he disappeared upwards, I saw that it wasn't an Inverness cape at all but the oldest, shabbiest raincoat you could imagine, draped round his shoulders, with the sleeves tied round his neck And you should have seen the bottom of his trousers! They were frayed and ragged up the back of his legs, well above his ankle, nearly to his knee. He was a *tramp*. Or he certainly looked like one. And that's what I had been chatting to and walking through the fog with for more than a mile! Poor soul, too. I think he must have known better days. Just imagine though, me walking all that way chatting with a tramp! I should have offered him a shilling. I bet he wouldn't have said no to it, either."

They all laughed at her adventure and it was referred to throughout the evening. There was no doubt that Mary seemed to attract unusual circumstances and she could always make a good story even better in the way she told it.

After the first laughter had died down, Annie said,

"I wonder why that poor down-and-out was in Hyndland so late on a foggy night? And I wonder if he's got a bed to go to?"

But they would never know the answer to those questions.

◊

It was a dark November day and though the fog had not returned, a heavy blanket of cloud stretched over the city of Glasgow. The low pressure was affecting Annie badly.

"Can I fetch your aspirins for you, Mrs Corning?"

Agnes's pretty face was full of concern. Annie was obviously distressed, though she bit her lower lip to stifle her groans. The back of her neck and shoulders were stiff and aching, her calf muscles were cramped and irregular spasms of pain shot through her legs. She had struggled with the discomfort for hours and felt exhausted.

She shook her head with a small. grim smile.

"Thank you Agnes, but I've had my dose for this morning. Better not take any more till three o'clock. I just wish the rain would start."

"And would that help you?"

"Aye," this was said on a sharply indrawn breath as another cramp overpowered her." I seem to relax when the rain starts. I don't know why. I mentioned it to the doctor, but he just smiled kindly."

"I don't think that doctor's been much help to you, Mrs Corning. He never comes in to see you and I'm sure he could give you some stronger pills."

"Och, maybe it's my own fault. Not sure I want to get too dependent on pills and maybe get too dozy and lazy and not want to do anything. And you never know what pills are doing to your insides."

"Well I think he should help you more. What about massage or something like that? Maybe that would do you some good? I worked for a lady once and she had massage to help her sore back."

"Mmm. Not so sure I want anyone pummelling me about. Not up to it, I'm afraid"

But she remembered the rough handling Jessie had dealt out. That had been very enjoyable.

"Well you think about it, Mrs Corning. It's not right, you suffering like that."

"I'll be fine when the rain comes on."

And in twenty minutes, just moments before a fierce downpour started, Annie felt her entire body relax.

"I'm afraid it's awful wet for you going home, Agnes."

"I don't mind that Mrs Corning, when I see you're a wee bit more easier like. You're fine now, aren't you? I wouldn't have wanted to leave you before, when you were so bad."

"Ye're an awfy guid wee wumman and yes, I'm almost hunky dory again."

The immediate change in her condition was like a miracle, but the long struggle had left her tired. After Agnes left, Annie leaned her elbow on the padded arm of her chair and, with her head on her hand, slept for an hour.

High School Teachers

Helen adored her new form teacher, Elizabeth Crichton. Most girls in the class felt the same. Miss Crichton inspired devotion. Perhaps it was her enthusiasm for her subject. No doubt she loved literature and taught it well. Perhaps it was the absolute attention which she gave when speaking to a pupil. She would listen carefully and her reply would have none of that patronising tone employed by so many of the teachers. As well as unfailing kindness and integrity, Elizabeth Crichton had a quick wit and enjoyed making her pupils laugh. It is not surprising that most of the girls in the class developed a schoolgirl crush on their form mistress. Also, there was a shyness and modesty about her personality which added to her charm. She seemed unaware of the general admiration and was not spoiled by her popularity.

It was not her beauty that dazzled the girls, although she had a fresh complexion, large white teeth and a lovely smile. Thin, and with a nervous speed in her movements, she invariably wore a baggy tweed suit and plain blouse under the voluminous black academic gown which, apart from those who taught science and gymnastics, all teachers wore at the High School. Though scarcely forty, Miss Crichton had no pretensions to style or glamour. Heavy duty stockings and sensible brown lace-up shoes did nothing to diminish the size of her feet and her frizzy, grey hair was dragged back into an unfashionable bun on the nape of her neck. By afternoon, wayward wisps and strands of curls had escaped the severe hairstyle, giving her an appearance of untidy vulnerability. Was it this air of defencelessness which inspired the strongly protective feelings to be found in most of her pupils?

Because of the love she inspired, the girls yearned to transform her appearance, dowdy as it seemed to them. They often discussed just how they would advise her, probably changing her manner of dressing entirely. Perhaps a smart wool dress might enhance her slender figure and they must certainly cut her hair. Much finer stockings and court shoes with medium heels would flatter her feet, and just a touch of powder could modify that high colour that sometimes flooded her cheeks. They were sure she had the possibility of beauty and, with their counsel, could be *immensely* improved.

Ah, how lucky teachers are to remain ignorant of their pupils' conversations.

Though Miss Crichton's perceived needs were part of her appeal, and many girls felt almost maternal towards her, her personality was what bound them to her.

Was she aware of how many girlish hearts beat faster when she entered the room and smiled her 'Good Morning'? Other teachers might be popular, but none generated the same degree of emotion as Miss Crichton.

Miss Myron, the French teacher, was also much admired, though never loved in the same way. Hardly a pretty woman, the French might have labelled her *jolie-laide*, she obviously took the greatest interest in her personal appearance. Her hair was short and always faultlessly waved, her make-up was so subtle as to be invisible and her clothes were not only chic, but memorable. Forty years later, when those schoolgirls had become mature matrons, they were able to describe and visualise the various stylish *ensembles* that Miss Myron had worn as she explained the intricacies of the past historic and imperfect tenses. Indeed the memory of fashion details outlasted points of grammar in many minds. A favourite outfit was the leaf green suit with elbow length sleeves, showing glimpses of a tucked, egg-yolk yellow blouse. Then there was the deep purple tunic effect over a finely pleated dress of ochre wool. A smart brown tweed suit, with a short fitted jacket, had very special buttons. With that suit she wore a silk scarf of rich autumn colours and tied with unique Parisian chic. A simple grey dress was transformed to something wonderful by the addition of a large silver brooch, Where other teachers wore their academic gowns as a type of disguise, Miss Myron never allowed her gown to detract from her outfit, for she wore it negligently dropping off the shoulders, often slipping down as far as her wrists.

Helen wondered where she found such clothes. Perhaps she had bought them in Paris, before the war? But they looked too new. Perhaps she knew a clever little French dressmaker or even made them herself? Surely there was no shop in Glasgow that sold such beautiful, unusual clothes. It was a puzzle. Her shoes and stockings, too, were always exquisite. She was like a fashion model, who had accidentally strayed amongst the out-dated ladies of the Girls' High teaching staff.

◊

At home Helen was becoming very accustomed to cooking simple meals when she came home from school. Annie had pre-pared vegetables earlier and with a few hints, Helen would work in the kitchen by herself, then bring the meal proudly through to the sitting room, where they ate beside the fire. Her cooking was reasonably successful and Annie was always appreciative with, very occasionally, only a minor criticism.

"Just a *spot* more salt in the potatoes next time perhaps, d'ye think? But they're fine and those chops are cooked to perfection and the mint sauce is *delicious*."

Or another time,

"Maybe cook the cabbage a minute less next time, so it's not too soft, but what nice haddock it is this week and you've fried it beautifully, my pet, golden brown and crunchy on each side."

Whenever possible Annie determined to give her daughter encouragement, rather than criticism. Her own mother's belief in the necessity of non-stop criticism as a teaching tool had taught Annie the power of praise. Her suggestions were offered tentatively and generally she was as enthusiastic as the kitten of Helen's youth, eating up every morsel on the plate with obvious enjoyment. No chef can ask for a better incentive.

Rationing continued and there was little variety in the food, but in a way that made it easier for the thirteen year-old to cope. She became confident with tried and true dishes and sometimes strayed from her mother's advice, considering, rightly or wrongly, that there were easier and better ways. Annie was wise enough to let her daughter get on with it by herself.

Helen had other things to do in the kitchen while the pots boiled. Sometimes she had a poem to learn for the following day and would declaim it, striding up and down the large empty kitchen, focussing on the range as her audience. Her performance was much more dramatic than she would ever dare give in the classroom. With little more in the kitchen than the cooker and the table, there was space to practise ballet steps, though the worn linoleum was not an ideal surface.

One day she had used a piece of torn paper bag to transfer a light from the front gas ring to the back and then amused herself, burning it to ashes. Next, she tried burning other pieces of paper, brown wrapping paper, a piece of cardboard, newspaper, butter wrapper, interested in the different flames and smells produced. Then she burned a short length of string. It produced no flame but it smouldered and smoked and gave no sign of dying out. The string was thick and strong enough to remain straight and with its glowing tip, it looked like a thin little cigarette. Helen had never considered smoking herself though, apart from her mother who had 'given up' on the day that war was declared, everyone else in the family smoked. How would she look if she were smoking a cigarette, she wondered? She held the piece of glowing string in an elegant hand, and waved it about casually, just as she had observed her grandmother's graceful flourishing throughout her life. Next she placed the unlit end between her lips. She felt there could be no harm in this, as of course one could not inhale the smoke. She was just *pretending* to smoke, though the glow made it quite realistic. After removing and replacing the string from her lips several times, the ash had grown sufficiently long to require that next well-known movement – the tapping with the forefinger over a suitable receptacle to dislodge the ash. She found an ash-tray and accomplished this part of the ritual. Her little pretend cigarette was hilarious and, as Helen often did, she laughed at herself for doing such a crazy thing. Nevertheless it was quite satisfying too. It was a grown-up and elegant occupation and though her hands could not compare with Mary's perfectly manicured ones, hers were quite pretty and graceful as she waved the string about. Probably one of the few pretty attributes she had, she thought glumly. Very importantly, she wasn't breathing that tarry poison that her mother spoke about into her lungs. Her mother had described her own youthful days of practising smoking in the bathroom, feeling terribly sick, but persevering nevertheless. Well, here she was, having all the fun of smoking and she felt just fine.

The string was in her mouth when she tested the potatoes and found them ready to pour. Unfortunately by the time this task was accomplished, the string had become so short that a wisp of acrid smoke drifted into her eyes and that was *very painful*. Helen had never experienced such agony before and splashed cold water on her eyes for a long time before she recovered.

This bad experience did not stop her 'smoking' each day as she made the dinner, though she never allowed the smoke to sting her eyes again. She practised string smoking for many months and neither Annie nor anyone else ever found out about this eccentric hobby. An ashtray containing unexplained threads of ash and two-inch lengths of burned string possibly escaped the notice of the busy housekeeper. Perhaps she dismissed it as beyond her understanding. In Agnes's eyes, Mrs Corning and her daughter were wonderful, if sometimes inexplicable.

In later years, Helen thought this substitute smoking had been rather a good thing, for it had carried her through the period of foolishness when she might have started to smoke in earnest. Of course finding money to buy cigarettes would have been a problem, for although Helen had control of the household purse, it was a slender one, with little enough for the necessities and she was strictly honest with the housekeeping money.

Though it must be admitted that, if feeling specially hungry in the grocer's, she might, on occasion allow herself a small edible extravagance, to which her mother's attention was not necessarily drawn. A modest slice of Madeira cake or perhaps a jar of Heinz Sandwich Spread (the latter never spread on bread, but eaten with a teaspoon) were her favourites.

Miss Arthur

"**N**ow Annie, d'ye think this massage caper would do ye any good? If you're sure, I'll speak to Bob Hamilton about it. But Zander Thomson had massage, you know and he thought it was a right waste of time and cash too, of course. Not that I'm worried about that, if you really think it'll help you much."

"Oh Bruce, I wouldn't expect you to pay for it. I would see to that and my mother would help me. I've no idea whether it would be any use or not, but sometimes I just feel hellish. I don't know if it could do anything at all for my legs, but I think my shoulders and arms are stiffening up completely and I'd hate not to be able to do the few things I still can do."

"Right, right you are, Annie. I'll see Bob about it and see what he suggests.'

"Thank you, that's very good of you, Bruce."

The following week Annie received a letter from Mary Arthur. It was beautifully written on very good writing paper.

"Here's a letter from the masseuse. I think she must have had this paper since before the war, it's so thick and smooth! She says she'll be here on Friday evening at six o'clock and I've to be in my bed. Goodness I'm not keen to go to bed at that time! I can always get up again after, I suppose. She says the treatment will last an hour. I'd better have a second wash and clean nighty and sheets. It's quite a lot of work for you and that'll be every week. I'm not sure about this at all. I hope it's worth it."

"I wonder what Mary Arthur will look like?"

Helen had great hopes that the massage would work wonders, imagining a strong, athletic young woman successfully manipulating her mother's limbs, perhaps straightening her legs.

On Friday, after an early meal and a second wash, Annie lay in her pristine bed at quarter to six. Helen combed her hair and settled her pillows.

"It's a bit of a damned nuisance this, if you ask me. I feel like a complete invalid. It's going to cost a fortune in laundry bills too, clean sheets every week."

"Och, the top one never gets crushed. We'll only need one clean sheet for the top and put the used top one underneath and that'll be fine."

"I suppose it would."

Annie wondered where her daughter had acquired such saving ways. It must be the wartime shortages that had educated her. Or perhaps she had inherited parsimonious genes from the Corning side of the family.

It was a shock for Helen when she opened the door to a small elderly woman. She was dressed in a pale blue coat and hat that exactly matched her watery, slightly red-rimmed, blue eyes. She extended her hand,

"I am Mary Arthur, dear. Mrs Corning is expecting me for a massage."

Helen had never shaken such a strong, cool, dry hand before.

Before Helen left the bedroom, Miss Arthur had removed her outdoor clothes, donned a white overall over her grey skirt and pale blue blouse and placed a large tin of Johnson's baby powder on the bedside table.

In the kitchen, as she thoughtfully smoked a piece of string, Helen decided that the talcum powder was just right for Miss Arthur. She was a *powdery* sort of person. That blue that she obviously preferred to wear was known as powder blue and her pale cheeks had a powdery look to them. Her hand was powdery. What age could she be? She looked old and hardly strong enough for her job.

Helen imagined her drenching Annie in powder before gently massaging her in a ladylike way. The letter, her clothes and her voice were all very genteel and old-fashioned. Powdery.

It reminded Helen of a funny story that Annie had told her once or twice, chuckling delightedly at her own joke, although Helen had never quite understood it. Annie sometimes quoted it still, if the context seemed right.

The story concerned a nasty little boy who was rude and insulting to a fairy, until the fairy could stand it no longer and waving her wand, she shouted at the child,

"Poother doon!"

She was a Scottish fairy and pronounced powder as 'poother'. The punchline was that when the fairy shouted,

"Poother doon."

And the boy poothered doon!

Then Annie would start to giggle and her amusement made Helen giggle, although the vision of the boy turning to a little pile of powder did not strike her as at all funny.

Adults sometimes had a strange sense of humour.

But somehow she could imagine that little pale old lady in there 'poothered doon'.

In fact, Miss Arthur was still in her fifties and very strong and at that moment she was giving Annie a most thorough treatment, a right 'going over' as Annie later described it. The masseuse had worked particularly hard at the 'nodules' as she called them, which had developed in Annie's shoulders and neck.

"No wonder you've suffered a lot, my dear! But we can certainly make a difference here. It will take a few weeks and it will be hard work. Perhaps a little bit painful... *but we'll do it.*" She sounded determined and Annie tried to suppress her exclamations, for what Miss Arthur was doing was certainly very sore.

She had started with Annie's hands, then her arms, and then her legs, trying to straighten them as much as Annie could bear. Next, turning her patient on her side, Miss Arthur worked on her buttocks and back, then settled to the hard work on those nodules in her shoulders. She dug and pinched and squeezed until Annie, with a regretful smile, asked her to stop for a moment.

"I think maybe I've had enough for a first session, Miss Arthur. You must be tired too, you've worked so hard yourself and goodness, look at the time! You've been here nearly two hours."

"Oh, I do hope I haven't over-tired you, Mrs Corning. I just felt I could help you so much."

"And you certainly have. I feel wonderful, but absolutely exhausted."

"Well just rest now and I'm so pleased if you feel a bit better, my dear. I'll see you next week at six."

The front door softly clicked behind her before Helen realised she was leaving. Helen had gone into the sitting room and buried herself in a PG Wodehouse book, for it seemed that Miss Arthur had settled in for the night.

"D'ye want to get up now Mummy?"

"Oh no, I never want to get up again. What a strength that wee woman has. You'd never believe it to look at her, would you."

"Did you not enjoy it, Mummy? Was it sore?"

"It was no picnic, but I think it did me an awful lot of good. She certainly seemed to know what she was doing. But I feel like a chamois leather that's just washed every window in the block. Inside and out."

Helen laughed,

"Would you like a drink? Bovril or Horlicks?"

"Horlicks would be nice. Did I tell you they were suggesting Bovril sandwiches in the paper the other day. D'ye fancy that?"

"Ooh no!" Helen made a horrible face.

"You won't be lonely will you, if I just stay here in bed?"

"No! I've got a great book to read. It's so funny."

Miss Arthur would visit every Friday night for the next twelve years and though Annie often grumbled at having to wash and change and go back into bed so early, there's no doubt her general condition was helped by the weekly massage. Anne's arms and shoulders improved tremendously and she felt a great release of tension in her back and legs. She returned to an awareness of the positive potential of her body, which the fear of pain had inhibited in the last year. She started to stretch more, move her legs as much as possible and regularly wriggle her toes throughout the day. Although low pressure weather still affected her badly with cramping and spasms, she felt much stronger and better in the interim periods.

Just as Mrs Connell had done, Mary Arthur fell under Annie's spell and became devoted to her and her daughter. The Cornings adopted Miss Arthur as a sort of maiden aunt, though her old-fashioned conventionality, her extreme gentility and her increasing deafness would often try Helen's patience.

Three weeks after the first massage session, Nancy and Mary were both visiting Annie. Nancy had just finished rather a long story about her sister having an unsatisfactory massage.

"But you seem to think it's doing you good, Annie, don't you?" Mary asked her daughter.

"*Indubitably!*" this was a favourite fun word of Annie's. "It's made an enormous difference to my neck and shoulders. Her hands are so strong and she's squeezed the life out of my nodules. It's great!"

"What on earth are nodules? I've never heard of such things." Mary was never easily impressed.

"Sort of knotty bits in your muscles, I believe. Too much tension that produces them. Too many Fair Isle gloves, if you ask me. Miss Arthur says I should cut down on the knitting."

"That's a pity. I've got five people at the whist drive *clamouring* for gloves."

"Too bad. I'm retiring from knitting those damn things. I'm *fair seek* of them."

Annie's tone was humorous but the swift tapping of Mrs Mackay's right foot showed she was displeased. Her face was expressionless as she gazed into the fire breathing deeply.

Helen came in with a pot of tea and some biscuits that Nancy had brought.

"I must tell you of an embarrassing experience I had last week." Nancy started another story. Mary's face remained stony.

"I was in the fruit shop and I saw a very nice big cabbage and asked "How much is that cabbage?" and the woman weighed it and said it was eleven pence! Can you believe it, eleven pence for a cabbage! I said it was much too dear and she replied, 'Aye it's a terrible price, int'it. It's no fur the likes o' you an' me."

Nancy's accent was authentic and everyone laughed, especially Mary. Nancy was proud of her position in society and the story was so much against herself, which was unusual with her stories.

"What on earth were you wearing that day, Nancy?" only Mary had the nerve to ask such a question.

"Well, truthfully, I know I was rather shabby that day. I was wearing my old wolfskin coat. Father bought all his daughters wolfskin coats because he always said a good wolfskin was superior to other moderately priced furs and so much harder wearing."

Mary interrupted her,

"But I've always heard wolf smells when it gets wet?"

"Oh no! I've never noticed that myself, Mrs Mackay, anyway I've had mine many years and it's done sterling duty, but I think I'm going to treat myself to one of the new beaver lamb coats which are in the shops just now. They say this will be a cold winter and I get so chilled on that long tram journey to school."

"Good idea. It's been cold enough already." Annie encouraged her.

Helen was listening carefully. A wolfskin conjured up ideas of Red Riding Hood.

The two visitors had laid their coats on the couch and Helen looked over at them curiously. Certainly Nancy's was a bit mangy and raggy round the edges. She tried to picture it as an animal slinking through the forest. She knew her grandmother's opulent coat with its vivid silk lining was grey squirrel, though somehow she had never connected that coat with small woodland animals. What a lot of squirrels would be needed to make a big coat like that but it suited her tall grandmother. Then she wondered again about the wolves. All she knew of them was her grandfather's stories of Russia, where starving wolves might chase a crowded sleigh across the frozen snow, then one unfortunate person, probably a serf, would be thrown out for the wolves to eat, sacrificed to save the others. That was only one of her grandfather's many gruesome stories. She had always loved them.

Helen had never thought much about fur coats and at no time wished for, or even thought of one for herself. Fur coats were for old ladies.

It was lucky that she could not read her mother's mind. The conversation that evening had reminded Annie of her own musquash coat, hanging, unused, in the wardrobe. As she lay in bed, she decided to have it re-modelled for Helen. It might be quite expensive, but it would be a lovely Christmas present for her daughter.

A Typical Weekend

Helen often thought of her Pittenweem friend Jean and was pleased when Annie received a letter from Clare Forgie, her mother. As Annie read, her eyebrows rose and her mouth pouted.

"What does she say, Mummy?"

"Well!" Annie had a special way of saying that word that Helen enjoyed and she shivered with anticipation.

"First of all, they've moved again. Some wee town in Fife, I've never heard of. They've bought a shop there, a grocers and Mr Forgie has stayed in Edinburgh to be a bookie!"

"What's that?"

"It's to do with betting. But that's not all. Jean has left school…"

"But she's not even fourteen yet!"

"Her mother's going to have a baby and needs her at home to help. What nonsense! Really! Why on earth does she need her at home? What a shame. She always said she was going to make sure Jean had the education that she had missed herself. And Jean was always clever at school, wasn't she? It's ridiculous."

Helen tried to imagine a life like that with a baby and a little shop to look after. It might be quite fun for a while. Just as she had enjoyed staying up late and drying dishes in the Dunfermline Youth Hostel when they had visited the Forgies years ago. Then they'd moved to Edinburgh and Jean had helped her father with the Camera Obscura. Helen regretted not going to see that strangely named object, for she could not imagine what it was like. Too late now. It seemed as though her friend had experienced a lot of things. Perhaps they were as important as the things you learned in school. Annie spoke again,

"The baby is due any minute and she says she hopes to visit us next year sometime, if she can manage. Well…"

Helen thought her mother said that last word in a very special way. It sounded final and defeated.

It was a cold Saturday morning and Helen was glad to have finished the shopping and sit close to the fire while the soup heated for lunch.

She was specially jubilant that day for she had bought 'treats' in both the grocers and the fruit shop.

"Taste and try before you buy", Millie in the grocers had whispered with a wink, as she cut a paper thin slice off the long brick of processed cheese and, with a quick glimpse over her shoulder at the manager, passed the morsel over the counter to Helen.

Helen thought it delicious. It tasted so different from the mousetrap cheese that they had been eating for years and Millie's secretive manner added to the excitement.

Then the fruit shop had a wonderful and immense consignment of small hard brown pears. It was unheard of to have so many boxes piled on the counter and all over the floor. There was hardly room for the customers to stand. Helen could not believe her ears when she was asked how many pounds she would like.

"How much are they?"

"Thruppence a pound."

She examined the money in her purse.

"Could I have four pounds of pears, please."

Her voice was faint with amazement at asking for such a large quantity, Perhaps they would refuse! And if they did give her so many, it would cost a whole shilling. But what an opportunity. She mustn't miss it. There was so little fruit available and she loved pears. She remembered old Mr Murray across the road in Pittenweem, who always invited her into his garden in the autumn and picked a big bag of delicious little green pears from his tree for her.

When the assistant had weighed out the pears and emptied them into her basket, Helen sighed her relief and hurried home. She hoped her mother would not think it too extravagant to buy four pounds. But Annie hardly ever criticised her daughter's shopping skills and was much more likely to exclaim at her cleverness.

That had certainly happened today and Annie had loved the cheese. Perhaps she was less enthusiastic about the pears, but she was delighted for her daughter to have them.

'You don't think I bought too many, do you."

"No, of course not. I'm just delighted you were sensible enough to grab them when you saw them. Not sure if they would agree with my old tum, so you just eat them up yourself. I think they'd go well with a lump of cheese."

Helen looked puzzled.

"Yes, fruit and cheese are delicious eaten together. You should try it."

And when Helen tried it, after her soup, her enthusiasm was unbounded.

"This is gorgeous! I'm going to take this for my packed lunch next week and I won't need to make myself any bread and butter. In fact I'm going to eat just cheese and pears together for the rest of my life."

"But all the same, I think a bit of bread would stop you getting too hungry by four o'clock."

"Is Daddy coming today?"

'I expect he'll look in at some point. Don't know when."

"Is there a concert on the wireless this afternoon?"

"Yes, a really nice one at two o'clock. Mendelssohn and Beethoven. And talk of the devil, here's your father."

She had heard the sound of his car gunning up the sharp incline in the lane. Bruce always arrived with a flourish. Helen looked at the clock.

"Twenty to two. I'll make his coffee right away and maybe we can get him out of here before it starts."

"Now don't be unkind. Try and be pleasant to him. Is there a wee bit of that shortbread left for him?"

"I suppose so."

"Away and let him in and *be nice!*"

As usual, Bruce was hail fellow-well-met, greeting them loudly, asking them how they were doing, and without waiting for a reply, immediately informing them, very regretfully, that he couldn't stay long for he had to see some fellow in Byres Road at three and there was a wee message he had to do for his mother before that. And his car was acting up again and he couldn't rely on it. He was really sorry. They would have to excuse him this time.

Helen handed him his coffee and shortbread and listened to his loud continuous voice with no expression of any kind on her face.

"You won't be playing golf today then, will you?" Annie managed to get a word in after ten minutes.

"No, I'm afraid that's out today. Was bloody busy at the works this morning, all manner of things goin' tae hell. But tomorrow should be fine. I expect Bobby and I'll go down to Gailes for the day. Get a bite of lunch. See if they've any of their special whisky under the counter. Bobby likes that y'know. Ha ha. He really likes his whisky, does old Bobby."

For quite a few moments, he laughed the strange, strangled laugh that Helen disliked so much. Helen wondered why he did not notice that he was the only one laughing, though her mother smiled politely.

"And how's the wee yin doing these days? Been to the baths this week? That's good, it's the best exercise and it's a great social life, too."

Helen could not agree about the social life for, apart from the maid and the scowling baths master, she and Olive were usually the only ones there,. Sometimes an ancient lady would shuffle past in her slippers, wrapped in a sheet and towels and heading for the Turkish room. The expression these old ladies bestowed on the girls was never friendly.

"Oh I used to have a beezer time at the baths when I was a kid!" he continued, "I loved the rings and I was always climbing up on the trapeze platform, and if you got one of the rings you could swing away out far and fly over nearly to the other side o' the pool. It was strictly against the rules of course. Ye got suspended if old Sadler caught ye. That was part of the fun. Used to jump off the balcony going up to the gym too. My, those were great days."

"And were you ever suspended, Bruce?"

"Eh? Och yes, manys the time I got a fortnight's suspension. Aye, a wild wee devil, that's what I was. Great days though, great days. So how goes the enemy?" He glanced at the clock on the mantelpiece. "Aye, time enough yet."

Helen also watched the clock. Nearly two. Was she impolite enough to switch on the wireless, while he was talking? No she could not do it.

"Ye know, Tuppenny...I was thinking...!"

He gazed intensely at his daughter for several moments without speaking and she found it embarrassing. She waited for him to speak. He looked as though he might ask her something important. Perhaps some question about her own life? And perhaps he might just listen to the answer she gave. Or perhaps he might comment on how grown-up or how pretty she was? Not that she considered herself pretty, but surely her father thought so. How she longed to be admired by someone other than her mother. Masculine admiration would be particularly acceptable.

She held her breath.

He grinned happily and nodded his head as he spoke,

"Aye, wee Helen, ye've got a fine sturdy pair of legs on you."

Fury and disappointment filled Helen's heart: 'fine sturdy pair of legs' indeed.

It was hateful.

'Sturdy' was so far from what she wished to be. What a word to use! She was rather pleased with the shape of her legs and considered them to be almost a glamorous feature, her only one. Now he had demolished that small conceit with such a mundane word as 'sturdy'. It was a horrible word.

She jumped up and switched on the wireless.

Bruce, unaware that he had insulted his daughter, when almost certainly meaning to pay her a compliment and convinced that he had done so successfully, raised his voice to be heard above the announcer.

'Aye, Bobby told me a hell of a funny joke the other day. It was about an Irishman, a policeman and a prostit..."

"*Bruce*! This might not be the best time for such a..."

"Oh, aye, right. Got ye. The wee one. Sorry, I'd forgotten. Well anyway he's a helluva funny bloke, Bobby. Specially when he's got a dram in him. But I'm not spending so much time at the house these days. Och, one or two things have happened. I think his wife's not so pleased to see me these days. Maybe I wasn't friendly enough with her friend. I don't know."

"Surely not something as simple as that." Annie wore her ironic smile and one eyebrow was slightly raised.

"Och, I don't rightly know. I'm not going to talk about it."

Just then the exquisite music of the overture to a Midsummer's Night's Dream floated in the air. Helen had turned it up quite loud. Bruce talked on and on as though the sounds did not exist. A golf game of the previous weekend was minutely described, with bad luck and good luck for each hole detailed. Or so it seemed to Helen. She gazed into the fire and no longer made any pretence of interest in her father's talk.

"Now, tell me Helen, do you really like that sort of music that they're playing just now? It sounds awful monotonous to me. Ye see I like a good tune and that doesn't seem to me to have

much... melody about it. I think melody's the word I mean. D'ye
not agree? I think my favourite music is Paul Robeson singing
'Ol' Man River'. Now that's real music. What a voice that lad has.
Magnificent. D'you not think so Annie? D'you like that sort of
twiddly stuff they're playing just now? D'ye not think a talent
like Paul Robeson has that stuff knocked into a cocked hat?"

"Oh there's no doubt Robeson has a marvellous voice, very
talented certainly. But there's all sorts of music in the world and
we all have different tastes, I suppose."

Helen wondered how her mother could keep so calm, while
Annie kept an anxious eye on Helen, hoping she would not say
something really rude. Annie could see signs that her daughter
was losing all patience with Bruce. She sat there like a smoulder-
ing volcano. She might just lose control of her temper suddenly
and completely, in the way that normally mild-mannered people
sometimes do. John Mackay was like that. Long-suffering and
equable most of the time, he was capable of an unexpectedly
fierce rage. Surely Bruce would go soon, but he seemed unheed-
ing of Helen's simmering fury.

When Beethoven's first piano concerto was announced as the
next item, Annie looked at the clock and said,

"What was it you had to do for your mother, Bruce? You'd
better not leave it too late if you've to meet that man at three."

Helen smiled wanly at her, looking like a drowning person
who has been thrown a lifeline.

"Aye, aye, ye're right, Annie. Better get a move on. mother
always complains I forget about her wee messages. But it's easy
to get caught up with folk. Y'know there's some folk that'll
blether on for hours. Yes, I'll just get away now, if you'll excuse
me. Leave you to your music, if that's what you call it. As long as
you like it. Blowed if I can see what you enjoy about it. And you
like that man Bing Crosby too, don't you, Annie? Boo boo ba
doom stuff. Can't stand'm myself. God knows what people see in
that sort of rubbish. Well, right, I'll get away now if there's nothing else I can help you with. Fine? Right I'm off. I doubt if that
shop'll still be open for my mother. Anyway! Can't be helped.
Now cheerio, folks. I'm away. Don't shift now, Tuppenny, I'll let
myself out. 'Bye."

Helen stayed by the fire, having shown no sign of shifting.

"I thought he would NEVER go."

"You should have seen him off the premises."

"Huh."

"I was frightened you were going to throw him out by the seat of his pants."

"I wish I could have."

"Anyway let's enjoy the music, now."

They relaxed to the magical sounds and not another word was spoken for nearly half an hour.

In the charming repeating phrases of the Rondo, Helen roused herself from her own complicated thoughts, as she noticed her mother smiling and shrugging her shoulders and moving in her chair in time to the music.

"I just love this bit." Annie whispered, " It makes me think of a little horse trotting and dancing and galloping along.".

Helen smiled too. She was happy to think of her mother dancing, even a little bit.

◊

Sunday morning was a lazy time for Annie and Helen in the winter months. What was the point in getting out of their warm bed too early? It just meant putting on the fire and they were going to read for most of the morning anyway.

Helen went into the cold kitchen and as quickly as possible, made two cups of cocoa, bread and butter for her mother and cheese and two pears for herself. Rushing back and tumbling into the warm bed again seemed delicious.

She had visited the lending library on Hyndland Road the previous morning and collected another four books, a PG Wodehouse, Thorne Smith, Angela Brazil and an omnibus of short stories.

"What does omnibus mean, Mummy? I thought it was just a bus."

"I suppose it means a collection. I'm not very familiar with it being used this way myself. Should be good. Lots of well known names amongst the authors. It might be a bit grown up for you."

Helen bridled.

"I've been reading Kipling for years."

After they had eaten they settled to their books, but Helen was disappointed to find she had read the schoolgirl book before. The titles were very similar and she had made a mistake. She started on the omnibus. The stories were short and varied and she read three with great enjoyment.

The wireless was playing music quietly in the background.

The fourth story was not as straightforward as the others. Helen was a bit puzzled and re-read part of it, although it seemed as though it should be simple enough. A young girl was living in a flat in Paris. She was desperately short of money and very worried. Then she went out and met a man and brought him home to her flat. Perhaps he could help her? The girl seemed to be struggling with some problem that Helen could not quite grasp. The girl was unwilling to do what she felt she must do. The girl's uneasiness transferred itself to Helen as she read and she realised that she was face to face with that dark something beyond romance, that unknown naughty thing that she, Helen, had always avoided understanding. The girl in the story left the man in the sitting room, while she went to have a shower, which seemed to Helen a very strange thing to do when you had a visitor. There was only half a page left to read and Helen stopped to wonder about it. She did not understand this story and perhaps she did not want to finish it? As she paused, the music on the wireless caught her attention. An orchestra was playing the sensuous and passionate *Valse Triste* of Sibelius.

Although Helen could not have expressed her feelings, the music seemed to define the hothouse sexuality of the story she was reading far better than the printed word.

After the piece finished, Helen lay quietly for a few minutes, then finished the story which provided no unwanted information, for the man had left the flat by the time the heroine had finished her shower.

Although the story could hardly be said to have advanced Helen's sexual knowledge, the addition of Sibelius' music at just the right moment had opened her mind to some of the unknown possibilities of life.

Though she could not have explained, Helen thought the *Valse Triste* badly named. Nor would her opinion change as she grew older and wiser, for rather than sadness, the music seemed to express the potency and mystery of sexual love.

◊

By 11.30 Helen reluctantly left her warm bed and set about Sunday's tasks. First she put the fire on in the sitting room, then the fire in the kitchen range which was never easy to start. Today she would need hot water for the weekly wash. At night, she

would have a bath and wash either her own hair or her mother's.
The shampoo advertisements shouted "Friday night is Amami
night", but Sunday suited her best and once a fortnight seemed
to be often enough. Helen hated the name Amami for some reason and still used the Evan Williams camomile shampoo that
Annie had used for her fair hair since she was a small screaming
child. Helen felt embarrassed to remember that badly behaved
child. She could still remember feeling compelled to shriek continuously while her mother struggled to calm her and wash her
hair and she blushed when she thought of it. What a spoiled little
beast she must have been. So different from her little cousin
Eileen, who was such a well-behaved, biddable wee girl. Helen
looked forward to seeing her at her grandmother's house later
that afternoon. Wee Eileen came with her daddy each Sunday
and the two cousins played imaginary games together in the
large flat, which had so many possibilities for adventure with its
large cupboards, high balcony and two staircases. Seven years
older than her cousins, Helen managed the scenario of the games
they played, but she had no false dignity and fully appreciated
the fact that playing with the younger child gave her an excuse
for enjoying childish pastimes. These happy hours of Helen's
regression would continue for several years to come and were an
important outlet for her.

After Annie and Helen had eaten lunch, they went into the
kitchen, where Annie prepared potatoes and turnip for the
evening meal. As Helen washed the clothes, she decided on the
game she would concoct with Eileen that afternoon. Bed linen
and towels were sent to the laundry so Helen's pile of washing
consisted of two school shirts, two nighties, underwear, stockings
and hankies. Clothes were not changed as frequently in those less
fastidious days before washing machines were commonplace.
Mary had bought a washing machine before the war but Helen
had never seen it used. It just sat there in the corner of her grandmother's kitchen. Perhaps it was broken.

Apart from handkerchiefs, Helen really enjoyed washing
clothes. Oxydol soap powder was sprinkled into the hot water,
then beaten into foamy bubbles. It smelled very pleasant and it
was good to plunge her hands into the deep water, especially in
cold weather. There was extra satisfaction when the clothes made
the water particularly dirty, as happened this Sunday after the

recent foggy weather. When the water turned grey and murky, it made the task seem very worth while.

"I wonder what sort of treat grandma will have for you this afternoon?"

"P'raps she'll bake some bread."

"Mm, or pancakes maybe?"

"I always think we should only have pancakes in Pittenweem, to use up the milk when it's gone that horrible solid way in the warm weather."

"But it's delicious to drink like that. I could fine go some just now."

"Ooo no!" Helen made a face and shuddered.

"And crowdy cheese too. Delicious." Annie's voice was teasing.

"Ugh!" She did not share her mother's pleasure in milk products.

"But you must admit sour milk makes delicious pancakes."

"I suppose so. But I nearly didn't eat them the first time I saw grandma mix in the smelly milk."

"Ah well, perhaps it's an acquired taste and one day you'll find you just love sour milk."

"That day will never come."

◊

It was after six when Helen returned from her grandmother's.

"You know, Mummy, Eileen's such a sweet wee thing! She had a lovely dress on today, with an embroidered yoke. And you know how she always hides under the stairs in the studio when I arrive and grandma has to pretend to me that she didn't come with her daddy today? Then I've to pretend to be so disappointed and say loudly that I'll just go home again? Well, today I walked out the studio and opened and closed the front door as though I really had gone home and the poor wee soul rushed out from behind the curtain and was nearly crying. What a shame. Anyway she soon cheered up and grandma had made gingerbread and it was deelicious! I ate a lot and I brought some home for you."

"I hope you didn't eat so much as to put yourself off your dinner."

"Not bloody likely, chum!"

Annie raised an eyebrow, but smiled in spite of herself. It was a popular saying.

The Sunday night routine was a tight schedule. It had become established and would remain unchanged as long as Helen was a schoolgirl.

After making Annie comfortable and putting coal on both fires, Helen brought out her homework. Her good intentions of dealing with homework earlier in the weekend, had unfortunately not been realised. It was usually an algebra problem, an ink exercise. There might well be other things to study, which she ignored, but the ink exercise was mandatory. Helen would first work it out in pencil, then copy it neatly in ink. She had no problems with second years maths and it was just a straightforward job. She worked with one eye on the clock because the roast must be popped into the oven at 7.45.

Meat was rationed by price. One shilling and fourpence worth of meat per week was allowed for each ration book. Part of this allowance must be taken in either corned beef or Spam. Annie always took corned beef. Perhaps Spam was tasty, but she did not care for the sound of it. There were certainly many jokes made about it in newspapers and on the wireless. The phrase 'Spam fritters' seemed to make everybody laugh, though no doubt some people ate them. Annie had decided it was best to buy some small cheap item, chops or mince perhaps, early in the week, with the remainder of the allowance sufficient for a modest roast at the weekend. It was a very small roast, but if there was one shilling and threepence worth of meat still due on the two books, the butcher might very well cut a roast costing one shilling and tenpence, or even two shillings. Thus the customer benefitted considerably and the butcher was glad to sell a more expensive cut.

The roast might be lamb, pork or beef, depending on what was available and on the time of year. Lamb was accompanied by a tin of garden peas and mint sauce. With pork, there must be cabbage and hopefully some stewed apples. Sometimes these were dried apples which tasted a little woolly, Helen thought. With beef there was Yorkshire pudding and mashed turnip. However, Helen had decreed that she liked Yorkshire pudding so much that she wanted to have it, whatever the roast was. Annie agreed that was a good idea, for it would help to eke out the meal.

After Helen finished her homework and the meat had been cooking for twenty minutes, she put her mother to bed.

Next she put on the kettle for the vegetables and beat up the Yorkshire pudding while her bath was running. The potatoes, turnip and pudding all cooked while she had her bath. Then, in her nighty, she made the gravy, poured the vegetables and brought the dinner into the bedroom on two trays. They enjoyed their dinner, sitting up in bed, finishing it with a few minutes to spare before the deep and thrilling voice of Valentine Dyall announced his 'Mystery Theatre" by which time the light was out and they were both cuddled down in bed, full of delightfully scary anticipation.

It was an operation of exact timing and Helen prided herself on serving the meal, really hot and as near nine fifteen as possible. It was a routine which she demanded of herself, for Annie would not have asked as much of her daughter. Helen saw it as the climax of the week and was particularly proud of her Yorkshire pudding which swelled into a different sculptural shape each week.

Kelvin Hall

"How d'ye fancy a jaunt to the Kelvin Hall again, wee one?" It was seven thirty on the second of January and Bruce had arrived unusually early that night.

"You don't mean just now, do you, Daddy?" She had enjoyed the quick visit last year and hoped that they might go again and spend longer this time.

"No, no. On Saturday. I'll tell you how you can help me out here. Wee Christian Turnbull is keen to see the circus and her mother's bringing her up to town. Now if you came along with me, you'd be company for her on the roundabouts and suchlike. She's a poor wee thing, you know. There's nothing of her, just a wee skinnymalink."

"Well her mother's a wee skinnymalink too, isn't she!" Annie said.

Her tone was unfriendly. Clive Turnbull owned the chemical business in the Gallowgate which was run by Bruce and his father and brother. Clive had suffered a stroke in his early fifities and now led a retired life in Rosneath, a small town on the Clyde. The Turnbulls were the elderly parents of one daughter, Christian, who seemed to be a delicate child. Bruce was often asked at short notice to drive down to their home to discuss business affairs but was often drawn into more domestic matters. Annie felt that the Turnbulls made very good use of Bruce and she and Helen resented the fact that some of Helen's toys and games had been given to Christian. Helen particularly regretted a large horse on wheels, complete with saddle and harness, a present from Campbell Horsland when she was four. Although she would never play with the horse again, it seemed hard that she should lose her possessions to a family that were far wealthier than her own. It might have been easier if her toys had gone to some poor child who had nothing.

As her parents talked, Helen thought of the day last year when Bruce had taken her and his father to visit the Turnbulls. They had driven first to Helensburgh, then along a twisting road past Rhu. It seemed like a long way. The Turnbulls lived in a large, comfortable house with central heating and a live-in maid. Christian had a real nursery, with a washhand basin, always a sign of luxury to Helen. She also had a frilly Hollywood-type dressing table, many expensive dolls and several shelves of books. It was certainly the room of a wealthy child. But there was only one thing that Helen adored and perhaps coveted. It was a musical box, shaped like a large round cake. On top, it had a charming working model of four furry little rabbits sitting around a table in a leafy arbour. Tiny flowers grew amongst the surrounding foliage. As the music played, the mother rabbit moved around from child to child, serving supper to each one. It was a most beautiful old German music box and Helen had never seen anything like it and would have loved to hear it play several times, but was too shy to ask. She was entranced by it and would never forget it, often visiting it in her imagination.

Now as Helen visualised that busy mother rabbit, she suddenly laughed out loud.

"What are you thinking about?" her mother asked.

"Oh, nothing,"

But she was picturing the photo that had been taken that day in Rosneath. Her father and her grandfather were not big men, yet the Turnbulls seemed small beside them. Helen was sitting in the centre of the photo, nearest to the camera, and her long teenage legs made her look enormous compared to everyone else in the picture, a sort of giantess. Christian sat beside her, a little smout, with stick thin legs. Then Helen had a sudden vision of the Kelvin Hall, with her tall self perched on some boring infantile roundabout, circling sedately round with that skinny child beside her. It was not a pleasing picture and quickly brought her back to the present.

"What age is Christian now?" she asked her father

"Now let me see. Nine or ten I think, can't quite remember."

"I don't expect she'll want to go on things like the Whip or the Waltzer, will she? She's a bit young."

Helen had particularly enjoyed the Whip the previous winter. As the small vehicle speeded up to hurtle around each curve, her long plaits had flown out at right angles to her head, adding to the thrill and also attracting the smiles of several people in the watching crowd. When she had told her mother of this exciting phenomenon, Annie had shivered at the thought that if Helen's hair had caught on something, she might have been scalped. But that gruesome thought only added a grisly fascination to Helen's memory of the exhilerating experience.

"Oh I'm sure ye'll have a rare old time the two of ye. She's really a great wee girl. Great sense of humour. You'll like her. And we'll see the circus, too. I've to book seats for that. My, I always loved the circus and the clowns and horses when I was a wee lad."

Annie could see that Helen was far from thrilled. She was unsmiling and her lower lip was prominent.

"You get on fine with Ruth, don't you." Annie tried to catch her daughter's eye. "And she's younger than you are."

"Ruth's eleven, nearly twelve and anyway, we've always been friends."

"It'll be fine."

Helen's face showed no sign of agreement.

"Aye, I think the two wee ones will hit it off just dandy. I'm really looking forward to it."

Bruce, shrugged his shoulders, rattled his keys and nodded his head wisely.

Annie looked at her husband with disbelief and some pity.

It must be nice to be like Bruce and believe that things would always turn out just the way he wanted.

The visit to the Kelvin Hall was not a complete disaster, for Annie had urged her daughter to be kind to them all and hide her feelings as much as she could. So Helen was aware of acting a part for the whole afternoon and she enjoyed that. At first too, she had a sense of excitement when they entered the immense echoing Kelvin Hall, with its varied sounds of music and voices disappearing into the vast roof space. The warm surges of hot sugar-scented air, alternating with unexpected cold draughts, created an environment unlike any other that she knew. It was neither indoors nor outdoors! Her coat seemed too heavy, yet she was glad she wore it.

They passed a stall with a row of slowly wagging clowns' heads, their obscene, gaping mouths turning from side to side, searching for the ball that someone might drop down their throat.

"Five balls for thruppence, sir. The little ladies might be lucky. Lovely prizes! Prizes for everyone. Five balls for thruppence!"

Helen hurried past. Those clowns looked horrible.

They passed the Whip and Helen looked longingly at it, but it was nearly time for the circus to start and they must make their way through the crowds to the other end of the hall.

As they hurried along, Christian saw a little roundabout with miniature cars, buses and motor cycles and was insistent that she must ride on it. Although she was warned that they would be late for the circus, nothing would change her mind. To Helen's astonishment and embarrassment, this slip of a girl had a very loud voice and was not afraid to use it to get what she wanted. She also insisted that Helen accompany her. The adults quickly gave in to the determined child and Helen accepted the inevitable, although she considered even Christian was too well grown for the miniature vehicles. The younger girl crept into a small red bus and sat happily behind the wheel, whirling it about madly, even before the roundabout started to revolve. Helen felt astonishment that the girl could be so childish. Cringeing with embarrassment, Helen, too tall to fold into any of the cramped interiors, took a reluctant seat on a tiny motor cycle, her knees near her chin and her lower lip proclaiming her mood.

Her previous vision of herself, too old, too tall, too obvious and very bored, on a trundling roundabout was horribly realised. It was even worse than her imagination had painted. She determined to ride no more infant roundabouts ever again, no matter how loudly that odious child roared.

From the first moment, Helen disliked the circus intensely. They had reached their seats at the very last minute, excusing themselves humbly, as they pushed past the bony knees of unhelpful people. The music was loud and strident and the arena smelled unpleasantly. When the clowns appeared, Helen found them stupid, yet rather frightening. They were so unpredictable and they came too close. Then the acrobats were nerve-racking. What if they made a mistake? What if the trapeze artists fell? Helen felt anxious and could hardly bear to watch. The poor elephants looked so sad, as though they wished to be somewhere else, and only the horses seemed full of life. Even they needed a bigger space to gallop. Helen was glad when it was finished.

Back out in the cold, noisy hall, it was suggested that Helen and Christian share a horse on the traditional roundabout, the one with poles like barley sugar. Large and splendid, it seemed the typical symbol of every Hollywood funfair. Helen mounted a fine spotted steed and as this roundabout was judged to be safe and gentle enough for the timid child, Christian was set in front of her. Helen held her closely. It was a surprisingly large horse and Helen felt her first moment of pleasant anticipation that afternoon. Christian, however, took cold feet before the machine started and was lifted down, weeping bitterly. Helen was soon glad about that, because holding on was much more exciting and difficult than she had thought it would be. How awful if she had let Christian fall off! It made her flush to think of it.

Bruce gave Helen money for three consecutive turns on the Waltzer by herself. It seemed daunting to ride it alone, but it was wonderfully enjoyable, filling her with mad, helpless dizziness and she adored the experience. After she descended the steps from the moving platform, she suddenly fell over! Jumping up again immediately, she was pleased to find that the others were not in sight to witness this. What an idiot she felt, but she was able to laugh at it later when she told her mother.

There were many possible rides and sideshows that Mrs Turnbull considered unsuitable and immediately rejected. She shook her head at the Ghost Train, the Whip, the Big Wheel. She did not approve of rolling pennies down the little wooden slides or playing any of the games, though Bruce had a try at the rifle range and Helen threw rings at the hoopla stall. No prizes were won. It seemed as if the afternoon was going to be very boring

Christian rode alone on one or two of the juvenile round-abouts for, in spite of her pleadings, Helen was adamant and would not join her.

"I'm just too big. My legs are too long."

And the adults could not disagree.

Bruce took Helen on the Ghost Train, leaving the other two looking helpless and forlorn.

The small unprotected car rattled along in a dim dustiness, stopping suddenly at intervals,when a bright light would flash, disclosing a skeleton or a coffin or some other supposedly fear-some object. It was a rickety little seat and its lack of safety was what frightened Helen most. Occasionally some long strands of something soft would brush across her face. That was horrible. Especially when she thought of how many other unknown faces those strands had brushed against.

They looked at the side show called Niagara Falls. Helen was

not impressed. She could still remember the wonderful and terrifying water displays that she had seen in her childhood at the
Empire Exhibition. Those memories made this little waterfall
seem paltry.

Another sideshow proclaimed,

DIORAMA
GREAT MOMENTS OF HISTORY DEPICTED

All the chosen moments were highly sensational and mostly
drenched in blood. The Battle of Waterloo, the Destruction of
Pompeii, the Fire of London, the Sinking of the Titanic, even the
Colliseum with fighting gladiators, unnaturally large lions and
cowering Christians were realised in a series of three dimensional
scenes behind glass, like little stage sets. Each scene contained
many, small, roughly-shaped human figures in various agonised
postures. There was a degree of ingenuity in the composition of
each scene and the lack of skill in the modelling of individuals
was balanced by a fair degree of nudity.

Mrs Turnbull hurried her daughter through the tent quickly,
but Helen really enjoyed it and kept the others waiting outside
while she inspected each scene closely. The variety of costume
and also the lack of costume appealed to her.

After they left the Kelvin Hall, the largest indoor space in
Britain at that time, they walked the short distance to Byres Road
to find a tearoom. It was dark and wet, but it was nice to smell
fresh air again. Mrs Turnbull talked in her high pseudo-English
accent, while Christian complained and whimpered most of the
way. Helen felt she had been dutiful long enough and strode out
as fast as she could, leading the way by a few yards. She was
amazed at how this little tyrant could rule her mother and also
rule Bruce. Christian never asked if she might have something,
but shouted out that she wanted it and never said 'please'. And
she got it! What a spoiled child. It was astonishing how the adults
rushed to get her what she wanted. Helen made a secret vow that
never again would she be forced to spend time with this unpleasant girl.

Christmas 1945

A nnie had given up her idea of remodelling the musquash for Helen's Christmas. The furrier's estimate had been too expensive. She asked Agnes to buy a Coty powder compact and Helen was thrilled with that. Bruce had been advised that a nice shoulder bag would be a good idea and he had chosen a tan leather bag. Helen was delighted with her surprise presents.

Glasgow Herald, 2nd January 1946

FIRST BANANA CARGO ARRIVES

The first consignment of bananas to arrive in Britain for five years was given a splendid Civic Welcome in Bristol yesterday.

When her fourteenth birthday came along, Annie broke the news that there was no surprise this year.

"I know what I want to give you, but you'll have to buy it yourself!"

Very slowly, a few luxuries were coming into the shops and Annie had seen an advertisement for Clark's shoes that she liked very much. She thought they would be just what Helen needed now that she was going to one or two parties. These shoes were called Flattabacks and were of black suede. They had a low heel and an ankle strap. When Helen saw the picture that Annie had cut out, she thought them very glamorous. It was a lovely present and she bought herself a pair of Flattabacks in Byres Road on Saturday. They were like something that a teenage girl in an Andy Hardy film might wear and like nothing she had ever had before.

Quite soon after that she was asked to a party. What would she wear? She was at an awkward stage. As tall as she would ever be, but very thin. Neither a child nor a grown up. Most styles were for adults, too sophisticated and with detailed draping. She was realist enough to know that she would look silly in anything like that. The fashionable exaggerated shoulders were something she hated on anyone and especially for herself, with her broad swimmer's shoulders. Yet those delightful shoes demanded a splendid frock.

"I could try making you something, if you think that would do." Annie had somewhat lost her confidence, for her last essay in dressmaking, the dress of men's suiting, had hardly been worn, "I'm sure there's some nice fabric in the chiffonier. Bit ancient maybe, but see what you think." Helen brought out a length of soft green printed crepe and decided it would be just right.

"I'll need a pattern. You can go to Coplands and pick something you like. I think Simplicity patterns are best."

Glasgow Herald, 16th January 1946

An exhibition of paintings by Picasso and Matisse will shortly open in the Kelvingrove Art Galleries. A storm of controversy has burst over these modern works in London. It will be interesting to see what reaction they provoke in Glasgow.

◊

On Saturday morning Helen went into town to the big department store. It was the first time that she had been there by herself and it took some time to find the right floor to buy patterns. The store was housed in two separate buildings, one facing Sauchiehall Street and the other backing on to Bath Street. Stairs and corridors cobbled the two buildings together but, because of the rising terrain, the floors of the two buildings were not on the same level. As there were separate lifts in the front and back part of the store and flights of stairs heading in different directions, it was quite a complicated environment. On previous visits, Helen had followed her grandmother without paying much attention to her surroundings. Now she must work it out for herself.

She felt rather like an explorer as she climbed stairs, took lifts and wandered around departments that she was sure she had never seen before.

Always unwilling to ask for directions, Helen was at last forced to apply to a stern old lady behind a counter. She often found adults unhelpful, not even polite, but this assistant smiled immediately and was very nice indeed.

Helen followed the complicated directions and found the fabric department, which looked strangely empty. Some shelves had different coloured bales of striped pyjama cotton piled on them.

Here and there, a few pieces of patterned, silky stuff were draped artistically to look like dresses. Although the war was over, choice was still very limited.

Helen soon located the tall counter where large pattern books were laid out for inspection. There were several different titles, Weldon's, Vogue, Simplicity and others.

It was fun looking through these books at all the patterns. She had not realised that you could buy patterns for men's clothes, underwear, fancy dress and even toys and doll's clothes. She could have looked at the books for much longer, but the store would close at one o'clock. She determined to return here soon. There was a section in the Simplicity book for Teenage Girls and although Helen had never really thought of herself as a teenage girl, it seemed to be what she was looking for. She chose a pattern for a dress with a scalloped neck and hemline that looked right for a party.

When she left the fabric department, she felt a moment of panic because she could not think where the front of the building was. However, she soon found a corridor with windows on both sides that looked familiar and after descending a steep flight of stairs, she found herself in the tearoom where she had been taken so often by her mother and her grandmother in those distant days before the war. What a relief. Then more stairs down to the ladies's dress department. Then a flight of stairs at a different angle brought her to the ground floor where stockings, gloves and handbags were sold. She knew the last flight well, for it had several portraits in gold frames hanging beside it. One was a particularly splendid full length portrait of an officer in full Highland dress uniform. These were portraits of members of the Horsland family, who owned Coplands, and Helen felt proud that they had all been painted by her grandfather.

◊

Annie was rather daunted by the dress pattern when she saw it.

"It looks very complicated to make, darling. I hope I can manage. Even cutting it out won't be easy, all those scallops and you'll have to do that bit, you know."

"Oh, we'll both manage fine." Helen spoke with the confident voice of ignorance.

Although Helen would never have admitted it to her mother, the dress was not really a success. The scallops did not lie as smoothly and perfectly as they had in the fashion drawing. It wasn't a failure, but it was too fancy. Helen blamed herself for choosing it. She determined that the next time she bought a pattern, she would look more carefully at the shape of the dress and the way it was cut, and not let herself be led astray by a pretty drawing.

She wore the dress and her new shoes to a splendid party. It was held in a beautiful house in Jordanhill and was a birthday party for Dorothy Sloan, whose family owned the large Glasgow dairy. The food was unlike anything available to normal mortals at that time. Exquisite dainty sandwiches with such tasty though unknown fillings, crisp and shiny sausage rolls, shortbread, treacle biscuits, cream sponges, eclairs, tiny iced french cakes and a large moist chocolate cake. Helen had only read about chocolate cakes like that and it tasted more wonderful than she had dreamed. It was an experience that she would never forget and she came home with the new dress fitting her very tightly.

Although Dorothy was not a special friend, Helen had always found her a very pleasant girl, ever ready to laugh and chat and not snobbish or catty, as some of the girls were. Dorothy had a little sister, Margaret, who was fascinated by Helen's long plaits.

"Did it take you an awful long time to grow your hair so long? I would like to have long hair too but mine's curly and never grows beyond my shoulders."

"But you're so lucky to have naturally curly hair! I've always wanted naturally curly hair!"

As Helen said this, she realised she was not completely honest. Naturally curly hair was certainly seen as the acme of beauty, but Helen was quite satisfied with her long straight hair. Anyway Margaret was pleased with this answer.

After the party, Helen held Dorothy in respectful awe. Did she have those cakes every week? Helen would have loved to ask for the recipe for the chocolate cake but was too shy.

Snow

Glasgow Herald, 21st January 1946

In spite of the inclement weather, the Students' Charities' Week, first to be held since 1940, has had a splendid success with a collection of £23,610. Previous record was £17,300 in 1930.

CONTINUED COLD SPELL PERMITS
WINTER SPORTS IN GLASGOW

It had been very cold for five days before that unforgettable Thursday morning when Glaswegian citizens awakened to a city engulfed in snow. No one could remember snow so deep. Everything was brought to a standstill.

"Who could recognise that as Clarence Drive out there? It looks like the depths of the country."

Annie was still in bed and Helen had pulled the curtains back to let her see the incredible, pristine world outside.

"Isn't the tree gorgeous, Mummy, with the snow piled up along the branches. There can't be any wind or it would blow away."

"It's truly wonderful. I don't expect wee Agnes will be able to struggle up from Partick today."

"That doesn't matter because I won't be going to school, will I. It's just like a holiday and I'll get the fire on and we'll have a lovely day, knitting and reading and listening to the wireless."

"Uh huh? But perhaps there are trams running at the top of the hill, where it's level?"

"Oh, I don't think so and I'm not going up there to find out."

Helen was not to be deprived of her unexpected holiday.

"I think it would be a good idea for you to clear the front steps though. They must be impossible and dangerous."

Helen made a face, but later found that she quite enjoyed the task.

"It was lovely outside, not really cold at all out there, in fact I'm far too warm after all that hard work. It was really easy to do, though each shovelful had snow about nine inches high. I liked the way it flew into bits when I tossed it aside."

Just then Agnes arrived, full of apologies for being late. As the school and nursery were closed, she had taken her children to her mother's house.

"But I hardly expected you in this weather, Agnes. What a busy morning you've had and that struggle up the hill, too. I'm delighted you're here, but I think you should have a cup of tea and then get back home again for your kids. Helen's here to look after me and it won't make any difference to your paypacket."

Helen put on wellingtons and an extra pair of gloves and went out for a walk. How quiet and bright it was. All the noise and dirt of the city had disappeared beneath the blanket of snow. There was no traffic at all and only the newsagent was open.

She wandered down Clarence Drive and along Airlie Street where some boys were having a snowball fight in the spare ground where the bonfire had been on VE night. She quickened her pace. Flying snowballs could be painful, even dangerous. When she was around the corner she made a few snowballs herself and taking a shortcut down a lane, she flung them satisfyingly at wash houses.

It was another new experience when thick snow started to fall again. The flakes landed on her lashes and lips. There was a special smell in the air and the flakes seemed flavoured with this same smell. She had never heard anyone speak of snow smelling, but there was no doubt it did have a particular, pleasant aroma which seemed to manifest itself high up in her nose, just under the bump.

"Perhaps that's what the bump's for," she smiled to herself," a snow-smelling bump. It's good if it's useful for something, for it's not pretty."

Soon the front of her coat was pure white and she returned home.

"Goodness, you're like a snowman! I'm glad you're back. I was wondering if you'd got lost in this blizzard. Thought I might have to send out a St Bernard to find you."

Helen looked puzzled, for she had never heard of the clever mountain dogs with their little barrels of brandy. She settled by the fire and enjoyed the tale her mother told of those canine saviours.

Helen was colder than she had realised, but after she thawed out, they both sat at the window and watched the snow fall.

Annie sighed,

"Don't you just love watching it as it falls. It makes me feel as though I'm floating upwards as the flakes go downwards. It's a lovely sensation. Just drifting upwards continuously, I could sit here and watch it all day. D'you have that illusion of travelling up and up and up...?

Truthfully Helen could not say that she did. She tried and sometimes she almost felt it or thought she did. She wanted to, but almost immediately she would once more have the impression of travelling downwards, down and down in company with the snowflakes.

By lunchtime, some of the shops were open and those who had reasonably suitable clothing were out and about.

At six, when it was dark, Helen had been sitting still long enough and decided to have another walk.

"Where will you go this time?"

"Oh just round about, I suppose. I'll go up the hill. There are a few people passing now.

Helen walked up Clarence Drive, crossed Hyndland Road and walked up Prince Albert Drive. On her right, just behind the Hyndland road shops was a vacant piece of ground. Half of it lay level with the pavement but the rest rose steeply to meet the pavement in Crown Road North. No one had sullied the area with footprints and it lay there invitingly. Helen walked boldly across to the centre and whispered into the cold silent air,

"Come unto these yellow sands...and then take hands"

She looked around quickly and no one was in sight. She was quite alone.

Again she repeated the poetry which she had recently learned in school. Her voice was louder this time and she strode through the deep snow as she recited the entire passage.

"Curtsied when you have and kissed, the wild waves whist,"

Next she struck out in a different path and declaimed the verses in a proper volume to carry over the snow. Her voice echoed back from the tenements very satisfactorily. Next she climbed the less steep part of the incline and ran down and across the level area as she shouted the poetry triumphantly. "Foot it featly here and there; And, sweet sprites, the burden bear."

It was wonderful! She had not realised she had so much voice, for people were always telling her to speak up. Her footprints now criss-crossed the whole area. It gave her a unusual feeling of power. No one else dare leave their spoor on her land! Just then she noticed a dainty line of little pawprints leading into the bushes. Some impudent cat had trespassed! However, Helen could always forgive a cat.

After practising her dramatic skills, she looked at the snow covered hillock. What a pity she did not have a sledge. She wondered if there was anything in the house that she could use? Yes there was, and she hurried home through the now trampled snow. She had remembered an old papier mâché trunk with the lid partly off. It lay in a cupboard with very little in it. She would ask if she could use that.

"Oh of course!" Annie said, "But are you not coming home soon? You're absolutely soaked."

"No, I'm fine. The snow isn't cold at all when you're jumping about in it. It just melts when I come inside again. See you later."

The trunk lid was light and not easy to direct as it slid down the little hillside, but she laughed when she rolled off into the snow. Climbing up the hill again was just as much fun as sliding down. Helen was aware that if anyone saw her, they might think it strange that she was playing all alone in the dark, but she didn't care. Perhaps others would not have been so pleased with the old trunk lid, nor would they have thought it was fun to shout poetry into the night. When alone, she could do just as she liked. The entire piece of ground, with the footprints and sledge marks showed how much she had been enjoying herself and how much exercise she had taken. It was almost as much fun as swimming. It was a night of light-hearted girlhood that she would always remember. Helen would experience a great deal of deep snow later in her life, but never again would she find such pleasure in it. In the future, there would be times that snow would seem to be an unbearable handicap, even an enemy.

◊

Annie was enjoying using the typewriter. Typing was essential, for her handwriting was pretty ragged now. She sent long amusing letters to Mary's old aunts who lived up north. They still sent eggs regularly and sometimes a cockerel. She had no idea how old they were, but Mary was in her mid sixties now and they were obviously older. What sort of house did they live in? She imagined it would be pretty primitive. How were they managing in this terrible weather? What did they use for fuel? Wood? It was difficult to imagine such isolation and how strange never to have met these kind relations. She knitted gloves and a scarf for each of them. Annie watched Helen as she parcelled these up.

"We'd better register them, so we'll need to put sealing wax on the knots of the string."

Helen looked up in surprise.

"Do we really need sealing wax?" Sealing wax seemed to her like something ancient, the sort of thing that was put on legal documents of long ago.

"I'm afraid so, if we want to register it. There might be some in the kitchen drawer."

Helen was intrigued by the whole business of melting the wax and applying it to the knots of string. It seemed like some nine-teenth century Dickensian ritual.

◊

Annie felt that, if her condition did not worsen, her life was pretty good. Helen seemed able to cope well with her extra duties and also swim and dance, and was comparatively happy in school and doing quite well. Though her mother and Bruce were unpredictable and often domineering, they were always there.

She determined not to consider the possibilities of bad health that might await her and just take each day as it came. Keeping herself occupied seemed the most important thing. She was lucky to have quite a lot of company.

Agnes was an energetic little treasure, who was devoted to both Helen and herself. Nancy Little visited regularly, as well as Mrs Unsworth next door. Khirstine's mother had come over twice, though it was a long journey from Newton Mearns. Then Helen's friend Tessa had brought her mother, Margaret, to visit. They lived in a flat in Ruthven Street, just off Byres Road. Annie described Margaret to Mary,

"...quite a vivacious wee buddy, very unlike her daughter, who looks superior and critical most of the time. What's more, I sometimes see Helen with the same sort of expression on her face and I told her I don't want to see it again. But I don't think she's as friendly with Tessa as she was, though I suppose they come home together on the tram."

"I would certainly put a stop to the friendship, if you don't like the girl."

"Oh I couldn't do that! You can't interfere in a daughter's friendships. And I don't exactly dislike the girl. I'm rather sorry for her, with such doting, ambitious parents. I think they've stuffed her up with too much idea of her own importance and that doesn't make her popular. They'd be better helping her to lose a little weight. Helen has to choose her own friends and no one lives close to us except Tessa."

Mary grunted,

"Well I'm having a difficult time with your father these days. That damned exhibition at Kelvingrove. Picasso, or whatever his name is, the one that puts the two eyes on the same side of the face. John never stops going on about what rubbish it is and how madmen have taken over the art world and dealers are tricking the public and making a fortune. I wish he'd never gone to see the damned things. He can't talk about anything else. I'm fed up to the back teeth with Picasso. Still, I'm sorry for John too, he's very upset. But surely no one will ever take that sort of nonsense seriously."

Annie felt sorry for her father, but could offer no comfort. Fashions changed and the Pre-Raphaelites, who had so much to do with her father's education at the Royal Academy, had fallen into disrepute and were now sneered at. Perhaps in another eighty years, Picasso would be a laughing matter.

"You should encourage him to go to the Art Club and they can all complain together."

"But some of them actually say that they *like* these daubs and that infuriates your father even more!"

◊

In March Helen suffered influenza for the first time. She was in the grocers on Saturday morning. Milly was arranging the various small packets on the counter. As often happened there was an extra packet of margarine.

"I know yer Mum likes to bake an' we've plenty marge this week, hen. Helen! Ye're lookin' a wee bit peelly-wally, Helen: are ye all right?"

As she spoke Helen grabbed the counter and shook her head. She felt very peculiar. In a moment Milly was round the counter and beside her, holding her arm, It was a great comfort to feel her strong hand.

"Here you, bring a chair oot here, quick. Wee Helen's no weel."

The girl was glad to sit down, though very embarrassed. She was the centre of attention in the small crowded shop. Four assistants and five customers were looking at her.

"I'll be fine in a minute." Her voice sounded as though it belonged to someone else, someone far away. Someone said something about a girl fainting. Helen knew that was nonsense. She certainly had not fainted.

Milly hovered over her,

"Now you just sit there 'til ye're feelin' better, my love. Ah bet it's that nasty five day 'flu ye've got. The papers are sayin' it's ragin' thro' the city,. Now just sit there as long as ye like and then ye can get away home and straight into bed. An' would ye no' take a tin o' Granny's tomato soup an' that'll save ye cookin'.'"

Helen nodded a weak consent and the tin was added to her basket. In a few minutes she stood up.

"Are ye sure ye're be able to carry that home, all right? I'll come across the road with you."

"No, no, I'm better now, thank you."

But she was far from better and lay down as soon as she got home. It was a difficult weekend for both of them. Annie hated to disturb her sick girl, yet needed practical help at regular intervals. She was unwilling to suggest making food, and spent rather a hungry two days. Helen was only thirsty and had no appetite at all. The tomato soup was certainly a good idea of Milly's. Annie wished there had been two tins, but bread and cheese and a tin of sardines kept her going until Agnes arrived on Monday morning.

"Oh I wish I'd known and I could have come up and helped, Mrs Corning, and saved wee Helen."

"Never mind, we've survived and you're here now and if you get me up, we'll leave her to sleep in peace."

Helen seemed only to need sleep, but it occurred to Annie that if she had been seriously ill, pneumonia perhaps, there was no way that Annie could summon help. Mary was right. They really should have a telephone.

That night she lay worrying.

Suddenly she told herself to stop being silly. If a real emergency arose, she was far from helpless, she could always drop out of the bed, get down on the floor and crawl to the front door, then out into the close and ask her next door neighbour for help. Hopefully such a situation would never arise but should it, oh poor Mrs Unsworth! The thought of her expression gave Annie a quiet fit of giggles.

Agnes came in the following weekend to help and by that time Helen thought she could take some dry toast and a cup of Bovril, which was her diet for the next week.

"What I'd really like is a chopped tomato like grandma made in Pittenweem, but I know I can't have it."

There would be no tomatoes until early summer when the first of the Scottish crop arrived in the shops.

The Harris Tweed Suit

W hen Spring arrived, Annie felt that Helen should have some new clothes and spoke to Bruce about it. Something other than a school uniform, she thought.

"Well whatever you want. I'll take the lass out and buy her something, but y'know I'm not much use with clothes, not in my line at all. Especially not for a young girl, too. What sort of thing d'ye think she needs, Annie? Does she know what she wants?"

"I suppose she'd like a complete change from her school uniform, something a bit smarter for the weekend. Maybe a little suit or something. See what you can get. Probably there's not much choice."

Perhaps the half remembered moygashel two-piece advertised by Coplands last year was in the back of Annie's mind but she was really quite vague about what her daughter might require, and though the thought of new clothes appealed to Helen, she herself had no idea what she might like or need, It was unfortunate that Annie had mentioned a 'little suit' for the phrase was firmly fixed in the mind of both father and daughter as they set off for town, though neither could visualise just what sort of little suit Annie might mean.

Coplands was the first place to go. The well-corseted assistant produced three suits. Bruce felt completely ignorant and Helen looked at them in dismay. Each one looked like something an old lady might wear, dark and tailored and unattractive. Bruce looked at her to see her reaction. His mother wore suits like these and he certainly could not imagine his fourteen-year-old daughter wearing one. Fortunately not one fitted properly.

The assistant spoke in a carefully correct accent,

"Of course we do not hev a great deel of choyice these days, sir, we mast jast take whot is sent. Perhaps, if you caired to call next week, we maight have nyoo stock and something more syootable for a young gell."

Helen was so fascinated by the woman's voice that she hardly listened to what was said. They left hurriedly.

"Well, wee yin, where d'we go now?"

"C&A has some nice stuff."

"Oh I think your mother meant something a bit more special than that. That's a cheap jack sort of place is it not?"

"Oh no! I've bought nice dresses there for me and Mummy."

"Well anyway let's try Pettigrews, my mother likes that store better than Coplands. In fact she said we should go there first"

But Pettigrew's suits were no more alluring than Copland's, quite similar in fact, definitely falling into the 'old lady' category.

"What about this one here? Dalys, is that what it's called?"

"I think it's an awful expensive shop, Daddy."

" Oh, in that case, we better give it a miss. Don't know about you, tuppenny, but I'm ready for a cup of coffee. It's thirsty work this buying clothes. Y'know, I just wear the same things for as long as I can, myself. Look at this jacket, it's twelve years old if it's a day. Nothing wrong with it, is there? I hate all that trying-on stuff and all that smarmy telling you how great you look. I've no time for those wee counter jumpers. Could never do a job like that, no, no. Just say anything to make a sale. Got to watch them. Watch them like a hawk. Remember that now, Tuppenny."

Helen had not yet tried anything on, but she said nothing and they went into a little café in Cambridge Street for a cup of coffee.

"I know where we'll go next. My mother goes to Watt Brothers sometimes. We'll try there. We better not go home without a new suit!"

Helen had never heard of this shop and was not prepared to approve of her paternal grandmother's choice.

"If they don't have anything nice, I think we should just go home then."

"Oh no, we'd better not show our faces without a new suit. Your mother would be furious."

Helen knew that was nonsense. Her mother would not be at all angry if they could not find what they wanted. Then she realised with a start that she herself did not really want a suit. What sort of suit would it be? And when would she wear it?

Helen felt cross with her mother for suggesting the suit and irritated by her father's continuous talking and illogical remarks. Spending time with him always wore down her patience, then her anger made her feel guilty. It was Saturday morning and she wished she were at the Arlington having a swim instead of this stupid shopping.

In Watt Brothers, there were again three suits. Two dark 'old lady' ones and one in green Harris tweed. It was a very nice colour and Helen tried it on.

"Now that's a really smart outfit, I think!" Bruce was smiling broadly and nodding his head.

The assistant was young and pretty and enthusiastic.

"Doesn't it fit beautifully! And Harris tweed is so hard wearing, sir, it lasts forever."

"Oh yes, I know that. It's wonderful stuff, isn't it." He sounded so enthusiastic, smiling broadly and nodding vigorously,"Never wears out at all, I believe."

Helen was less impressed, for though the colour was pleasant, the fabric was rough and scratchy. And with the padded shoulders and the skirt shorter than she would have chosen, she thought she looked very square in the mirror. Also her black stockings looked wrong with the green suit.

"Is the skirt not a bit short?" Helen asked.

"No, that's the very latest length, dear. All the new garments are getting shorter these days. You'll see just how attractive it is when you're not wearing your school stockings."

As Helen stood there wondering if she liked it or not, she realised that her father was now paying for the suit! And paying quite a lot of money. She was not sure she wanted it at all, but it seemed to be too late! He was asking about a blouse to match the suit, which was thoughtful and generous, she knew, but what if she hated this suit? She felt powerless.

A Vyella shirt blouse with small green checks was brought.

"Oh yes," her father enthused, "that's really nice, that's just the ticket. We'll have that one, Miss. Right you are."

More money was counted out. He had spent nearly ten pounds on things she did not want. The blouse also had square shoulders and was quite short and would never stay tucked into her skirt. She hated blouses like that.

"Now we'll get some nice stockings and that'll be you all set, smartest girl in town, I bet."

He seemed so happy and he was spending so much money, what could she say? She tried to smile gratefully, but her face did not feel as though it smiled.

At the stocking counter he bought beige woollen stockings.

"Better have something warm. It's still pretty chilly out there, eh wee yin?"

He winked and grinned happily and again paid what seemed to Helen an enormous amount for a pair of stockings. She knew she would never wear those thick, old lady stockings.

Helen sat quietly beside her father on the top deck of the yellow tram gazing at the parcels on her lap without enthusiasm. Bruce lit a cigarette,

"I think ye're a tired wee lass, are ye? Aye, it's a terrible business, shopping. Clothes are the worst. Still you won't need to go again for a long time. That'll see you through. But y'know, I quite enjoyed it when we finally found all the right things. I bet your mother'll be pleased. That's a really first class outfit. Ye could be wearing that suit until you're thirty, I bet. Great stuff that Harris tweed. You might even turn it when it gets shabby. My mother got the tailor to turn her old tweed coat very successfully. Looked like new again. Cost about as much as a new outfit to get it done right enough, but that handwoven cloth never wears out, y'know."

At home, Helen donned her new garments and Annie appeared suitably impressed and grateful to Bruce. It was not exactly what she had had in mind, but she said nothing, for it was a good suit, warm and hard-wearing. She hoped Helen was pleased with it. She would never learn quite how much her daughter disliked it.

The suit, however, was dutifully worn each Sunday when Helen visited her grandparents. She always felt very *square* in it and never became accustomed to the roughness of the fabric. Many of the games that she played with her little cousin necessitated clambering under furniture or sliding down stairs and Helen was always happily aware that this demanding usage was helping to shorten the life of the indestructible tweed and hasten the day that the suit might be discarded.

Visitors

Annie received a letter from Clare Forgie in May. "Listen to this, they'd like to come and visit us with the new baby. It's a nice idea, but where on earth would they sleep?"

Bruce had the answer. His mother had a bedroom suite, left to her by the old aunts in Kelvindale. She had intended to sell it but Annie was welcome to it, if it was any use. The back room was still empty, except for the chiffonier.

Bruce smiled brightly,

"I'll get the lorry and a couple of men on Saturday afternoon and bring it round. I know you'll like it, and mother will be pleased you're taking it. And wouldn't this be a great chance for the wee yin to move into her own room. She's a big girl now. You would like that wouldn't you, Tuppenny? A nice bedroom all to yourself? It's a complete suite, you know, and *very good quality*. Now isn't that a rare idea."

Helen looked at him thoughtfully. She considered it a stupid suggestion. How would her mother manage without someone there to help her turn over through the night? What if Annie suddenly felt ill? And what would happen to late night, whispered conversations and laughter? What about shared breakfasts and reading in bed at the weekend and Sunday night dinner with Mystery Theatre afterwards? How little her father knew of their life together.

Annie worried that she would be landed with old worm-eaten furniture.

However, Agnes and Helen gave the room a thorough clean and when the suite arrived and was put in place, it looked very nice. Helen realised it was pleasant to have a spare bedroom. That room had always seemed a little frightening in its emptiness.

The suite was of oak, not mahogany as Annie had feared. The dressing table had a large mirror and there were little drawers as well as large ones. Helen had to admit she liked it, although she had no desire or intention of sleeping in the room.

Though Annie thanked Bruce, she grumbled when he had left,

"It's a bit of an old wreck, isn't it, only worth a few pounds. I expect Jane was glad to get rid of it."

Helen could not really agree with her mother and for the first time wondered if Annie was quite fair to her mother-in-law.

◊

Jean's visit was exciting and Helen looked forward to it. What would they talk about? Would they still get on well together? Would Jean have to look after the baby a lot? How much looking after did a seven month old baby need? There was the problem of feeding the visitors. She had never had folk staying overnight before. They would be there for three nights. What would they want for breakfast?

The Forgies arrived late on Friday in a taxi, with a lot of bags and parcels and a little pushchair for baby Cathy, who was bigger and less attractive than Helen had expected.

Helen and Jean took up their friendship as though they had never been apart. Helen thought Jean looked different, older and not like a schoolgirl any more, and of course, she was not, which seemed rather sad.

Jean had a lot to do for her mother and the baby. She was sent off to fetch this and that every five minutes, while her mother fondled Cathy and chatted to Annie. Helen wondered why Mrs Forgie did not go and get things herself, as she was perfectly able to walk. Her own mother would never have expected her to to run back and forth like that. Annie was careful to think about all the things she needed at one time and not make unnecessary work.

Helen unpacked the bag of food they had brought with them and was not impressed. There was despised Spam, a pound of sausages and two half pounds of margarine. Extra margarine was something Milly often gave Helen and there were already four half pounds in the cupboard. Clare had also brought six eggs, which were always welcome, a tin of salmon and two packets of biscuits. It would certainly help to feed them, but what would Helen do with the Spam? So many jokes had been made at its expense on the radio that somehow it no longer seemed like proper food.

Clare Forgie sat and chatted for three hours after she arrived. At forty one, she had decided that she needed a nursemaid for her baby and while Jean fulfilled that role, Clare could sit still and do as little as possible.

Annie watched her in astonishment.

In only one way did Clare exert herself. She washed the dishes after each meal. As soon as the meal was finished, almost before, Clare would gather up the dishes and rush into the kitchen to put the kettle on. It was as though the dishes might melt away, if they were not made clean again very quickly! It almost seemed as though the food was eaten *in order* to dirty the dishes, that they might be washed, dried and returned to the shelf. Washing dishes had never been Helen's favourite occupation. As she had so many other household duties, the weekend's dirty dishes were usually piled up for Agnes to wash on Monday morning. Clare always insisted that Helen come and dry the dishes, while Jean looked after Cathy. Helen could not refuse. Washing dishes was Clare's only contribution to the daily chores.

Helen found it boring that the baby was the centre of attention most of the time. Jean was constantly employed, for the work involved in washing, dressing, patting, soothing and amusing little Cathy was never-ending. Most of it seemed unnecessary to Helen. Cathy cried petulantly if not immediately given what she wanted. Perhaps some babies were lovable, but Helen found this particular one a great nuisance.

When Annie exclaimed enthusiastically about what a very fine baby Cathy was, Helen spoiled the moment by saying,

"I expect she will be quite pretty, when she grows some hair."

It was a relief when Clare decided at nine o'clock that she was tired and must go to bed and take the still whimpering Cathy with her.

Later, just as Helen was lifting her mother on to the bed, Annie said,

"I think that woman's arse is stuck to the chair with Seccotine."

They both collapsed on the bed, giggling helplessly.

As the backroom bed was a single one, Jean and Helen slept on cushions in the sitting room floor, which was great fun. Helen had only once slept on the floor before and she enjoyed it.

They chatted until one o'clock, when Jean fell asleep quite suddenly.

Next day, Annie said to Helen,

"I think you should take Jean into town today. You could go to Lewis's on the subway. And you could get one or two treats for

us, while you're there. Their bread's so nice and maybe some
cakes, too. And you never know what else you might see in the
Poly."

Helen looked at her clever mother. She knew that the suggestion meant Jean would have a day off from nursemaiding.

Clare also looked at Annie.

"But how will we manage here without them? When will they
get back? Will you be all right without Helen? And I've got the
baby to look after, too."

"Och yes, you'll be back by three or thereabouts, won't you,
girls? We'll be *fine* 'til they get back. We'll surely manage between
the two of us. We're both grown women. And we'll have a nice
tea waiting for them when they come home. We'll think of something tasty."

The girls enjoyed the walk to Byres Road. The trees were just
beginning to show their green buds and Jean exclaimed over the
large mansions that they passed.

"You're lucky living in town. I really miss Edinburgh and I
miss going to school. I really liked school in Edinburgh. There
was an awful nice boy in my class. I wrote him a letter but he
didn't write back. Kingskettle is such a funny wee place, all cottages. And it's quite lonely, there's not many girls my age. Of
course the shop is quite good fun. People speak to you and tell
you gossip and I like weighing out the sweeties and sugar and
flour and putting the tins neatly on the shelf. It's better than
looking after Cathy all the time."

"D'ye think your wee sister is a bit spoiled?"

"Oh, she's a spoiled wee rat."

They laughed, then said nothing more for a while.

It was Jean's first trip on a subway and she was amazed and a
little apprehensive as they descended the stairs to the strange
narrow platform.

"I've never seen anywhere like this before and what's that
smell? It's quite nice, but it's really strong."

Helen could not tell her what the smell was, knowing it only
as the particular aroma of the subway, and accepting it as such.

The walk from St Enoch's was exciting with so many trams
and buses in Argyle Street.

"How do you know when to cross the road? It's a lot busier
than Edinburgh!"

"It's a lot bigger, Jean. Lots more people."

Helen spoke confidently, though she had not visited Edinburgh since she was five.

The ground floor of Lewis's was busy, as usual on a Saturday morning. Jean was fascinated by the escalators and wanted to come down again as soon as she had gone up. They went up and down three times before Helen insisted they go and look at all the other interesting things.

Even in those difficult times, Lewis's Polytechnic had a wonderful selection of goods for sale. The girls wandered from floor to floor and Helen enjoyed Jean's astonishment. They watched a demonstration of jewellery making. The girl had a sheet of brightly coloured plastic film, which she cut into small squares, which she then cleverly folded and threaded together to make a pretty necklace. It was quite cheap and the girls bought some, along with instructions. Another plastic article was called a rain-mate and it was to protect your head in the rain. When not required, it folded up into a small space and could be kept in your pocket. Jean was terribly enthusiastic about this and bought one for her mother. It might be a good idea, but Helen thought it looked far too ugly to wear. She would rather have wet hair.

A hairdresser was demonstrating a waving lotion and asked for a volunteer. To Helen's astonishment, Jean stepped forward and sat down in the chair *in front of all these people watching*. She gave a small secret smile to Helen, who could not believe her eyes and quickly escaped to another part of the store. After the treatment was finished and the curls combed into place, Jean joined her again. Helen did not think the curls an improvement, and said nothing. Neither girl ever again mentioned the incident.

Back on the ground floor, it was getting busier and busier. The girls bought bread with seeds on top, jam doughnuts and small iced fairy cakes.

Just as they were leaving, a woman stopped them and asked if they would like to buy her product. She was wearing a tray strapped to her shoulders like the ice cream tray that a cinema usherette carries, This was a very special offer, she said, fresh pineapple slices covered in chocolate! The girls looked at each other. It seemed too good to be true. What an incredible, exotic and delicious luxury to find! It was expensive at ninepence a slice but what an opportunity. They bought four slices and set off for home triumphantly.

"Your Mum said you never know what you might find in the Polly and she was right!"

Clare was very pleased with her rainmate and immediately put it on. Helen wonderd how anyone would wear such a thing in public.

Annie was delighted with all the treats,

"I never imagined in a thousand years that you would find something as unusual as *chocolate covered pineapple slices*. I'm absolutely flabbergasted."

Jean looked puzzled, but Helen was used to her mother's strange extravagant expressions. She felt sorry for her friend, for Jean's mum was a quiet country sort of person, while Annie was such an interesting one, always ready to make a joke or have a good idea.

"Are you all hungry? I've made something different for us tonight. Something I've always wanted to make. It's called toad-in-the-hole."

There was a silence. Neither Helen or Jean had ever heard of this dish, nor did it sound appetising.

Clare had watched it being prepared with misgivings, thinking the sausages would surely have been better fried.

But it was a wonderful success. Everyone enjoyed it and wished there had been more of it.

Then the great pineapple delicacy was produced.

Alas, alas, under the chocolate coating, the pineapple was mouldy and inedible. It was a terrible disappointment and Helen regretted the money wasted on it.

"D'you think she knew it was mouldy when she sold it to us, Mummy?"

"Well...maybe she did and maybe she didn't... but probably she did."

Helen felt stupid and angry and careless as well as disappointed and she burst into tears.

"You're not to blame, darling. Sometimes these things happen and we're disappointed and it's best to put it all down to experience and forget it as quickly as possible. Now get out your jewellery kit, the two of you. I want to see how these necklaces are made. It's a wonderful colour. I'll help Clare dry the dishes.

There are only a few. Cathy can sit in her little pram and watch and be a *good girl*."

Annie gave the baby rather a stern look which seemed to have an effect, for Cathy sat quietly, while the girls worked at their new craft, which was not as easy as the demonstrator had made it seem. When the necklaces were finished, they discovered that, though they looked nice, they were not very comfortable to wear. Helen was reminded of the wonderful string of melon seeds that her grandmother had made for her long ago. It, too, had been very jaggy on the neck.

"Now Clare, I think *tomorrow*, you and Jean should have an afternoon off. The Ideal Homes exhibition is on, perhaps you would like to see that. The tram goes right to the door of the Kelvin Hall and Helen and I can take care of Cathy for a couple of hours."

Helen was speechless. What was her mother saying? This was a *terrible* idea, but it was too late to protest, for Clare and Jean were delighted to accept and were already planning the things they would like to look at.

When Helen put her mother to bed that night, she was silent and scowling.

"Now Helen, I know you're not mad keen to look after that wee spoilt besom, but if you put her in the pram and take her for a walk, I'm sure she'll fall asleep for an hour or so. I just felt I had to have a break from that woman. She never stops talking and it's such inane nonsense. I can't think why I was ever friendly with her. Perhaps her brain has become fuddled with having the baby. Maybe it's all the moving around from one place to another. Really, her husband sounds like a madman and of course it's always her that has the burden of work to do. And I bet they're not settled yet, for I don't expect he'll make his fortune as a bookie. Then off they'll go again somewhere else. I am sorry for her, but she's not treating Jean properly and if I don't get a rest from her constant tongue-wagging, I might say something I'd regret. You and I will manage fine with that wee brute for a couple of hours. Maybe teach her some manners. She's probably quite a nice kid, if she's treated like a human being."

Helen was laughing now and quite looking forward to teaching some manners to the 'wee brute'.

"And was that just a Yorkshire pudding mixture round the sausages? It was awful good."

◊

They had a really amusing time with Cathy the next day, rolling a ball across the floor to her and showing her a book of farm animals with the proper noises to match. Then Helen held up the baby's toy rabbit and made it speak and sing in a funny little voice. Cathy was completely fascinated. Annie was also amused at her daughter's performance. What a family of performers they all were. She herself enjoyed making people laugh and Mary loved to hold an audience enthralled with her dramatic stories. While Mary's own personality was always an integral part of her tales, Helen had the actor's gift of eliminating her own persona and creating a new character. The rabbit was charming, but naughty, and Annie could never forget Helen's depiction of the new maid in the concert last summmer. Perhaps her daughter would become an actress? That was a hard life, unless one found early success.

When Helen took Cathy out in her pram, the baby pointed to cats and dogs with pleasure and when she fell asleep on the way home, Helen was quite sorry. Babies could be fun, if you could get them away from their mothers.

Clare and Jean had a wonderful time at the exhibition and had bought all sorts of kitchen implements, something to make fancy butter curls, a vegetable slicer and an egg slicer, rather like the one on which Helen could play 'God save the King'. She would have liked to try Clare's egg slicer, but hesitated to ask. There were yet other gadgets, but Helen never discovered their purpose.

In private, Annie commented that all those things would likely finish up, forgotten, in a kitchen drawer.

It was soup and Spam sandwiches for tea that night and Helen realised the sense of Annie's advice to choose corned beef, rather than the bland luncheon meat.

Helen had gone to school before the Forgies left next day. When she returned at four the house seemed wonderfully, delightfully quiet and calm.

"Well, they seemed to have a great time, Helen. Thank you for being such a help. Not easy having house guests, is it!"

"Not when there's a baby. Are all babies as much work as that?"

"She was fine yesterday afternoon, when we had her to ourselves, wasn't she? It all depends on how you treat them. I must admit you were a bit of a spoiled besom yourself! Always screaming if you didn't get what you wanted. Even louder than Cathy I would say."

"Oh! Surely not! Was I? That's terrible. I can still remember shrieking when you washed my hair. I think I felt I *had* to. I'm really ashamed. How did you stand it?"

"Och, I suppose it was all my fault in the first place. Too soft! And I was quite fond of you, in spite of your beastliness. Anyway, you've turned out fine now, haven't you? Hardly spoiled at all, I would say, in fact a very nice girl and I'm proud of you. Give us a kiss."

"Even though we have a spare bedroom now, please don't let's have any more house guests for a long time."

Dancing

Helen came home from dancing with exciting news. "This year I'll be dancing with older girls in the display in the Athenaeum! Miss Hopkins wants me to go to an extra class on Thursdays to learn the dances that the elementary class is doing."

"That's great. You'll be performing on a real stage, will you?"

"Yes and I'll be with girls my own age and the dances will be real dances, more exciting than the lancers and polkas at the Babies' Ball last year. Is the Athenaeum the same place that I did the Goodnight dance when I was a wee thing long ago?"

"I suppose it is. I hope I can manage to be hoisted in to see you perform."

"Of course you'll be there. Daddy will take you."

"Well, you'd better be a bit nicer to him."

Helen's face remained expressionless and she stopped breathing for several moments. It was the equivalent of the deeply indrawn and expelled breath of her grandmother's displeasure. Though less obvious, Annie was aware of this unspoken statement. Fortunately it seemed a sufficient gesture and did not lead to prolonged sulking, as in her mother's case.

There was beginning to be a lot of discussion these days in America about the problems of teenagers and their bad behaviour. Annie read these articles with interest, for she remembered finding life difficult and unhappy when she was fourteen. She had felt her mother very unfair, but perhaps she too had been difficult. When she was sent to boarding school at fifteen, she had gained tremendously in self-esteem. Her abilities in art and music had been appreciated and developed by the teachers and she had found popularity amongst the other girls with her wit. Most importantly, she had stopped believing she was so ugly that no one would ever be friends with her. Was Helen going through any of the unhappiness that she had suffered? It did not seem as if she were, though of course they disagreed at times. Occasionally, maternal scoldings and reprimands were necessary, but Helen had so many responsibilities and unpleasant tasks unknown to other girls of her age, that Annie was more likely to overlook carelessness or minor misdemeanours. Helen was still so young in many ways, yet sometimes she astonished her mother with her adult practicalities.

Their relationship was certainly much closer than Annie had ever enjoyed with her own mother.

As Annie thought about this she realised that she herself was developing and maturing almost as much as Helen. She smiled at the thought that the two of them were growing up together. They shared the pleasure of discovering new words or facts and often Annie was able to regress and take part in the mad giddy moments of her fourteen-year-old daughter. Their greatest pleasure was in making future plans together, perhaps for something as simple as a meal. Imagining what might go wrong was part of the fun, and a possible chaotic outcome would bring them to helpless laughter.

◊

In a strange way, Annie's incapacities gave her a power that she had not possessed before, a protection against the domination that Mary and Bruce had exerted over her. She must make decisions that suited her alone and use her ingenuity to solve problems arising from her condition. Her aim was to live as normally as possible. Helen was a willing partner in this struggle, but Annie was also determined that her daughter would not become a victim of its demands. Helen must have a good education in order to become independent financially. Annie blamed herself for not having acquired a training. How wonderful if, in spite of her handicap, she could earn real cash. She constantly thought of how she might do it. Knitting gloves was certainly not the way.

First and foremost, Annie determined that Helen should have just as much fun as any other girl of her age, marriage and a family too, if she wanted that. The time would come when Helen would have more outside interests but Annie tried not to look too far ahead. She realised the unpredictability of her disease and she must just do her best, for it was no use worrying about that unknown future.

She stifled a small grunt as it occurred to her that *everyone* has an unknown future. Fate is always ready to hand out surprises, some good, mostly bad. Capricious Fate! Look at poor Clare Forgie, what a fragmented unsettled life she had been landed with. When first married, they had lived in the Falkland Islands, where Jean was born. Then they had constantly shifted from one place to another. Now they were in Kingskettle. Yet Clare was delighted to spend money on kitchen gadgets which might make her life easier, more elegant. Surely Annie's own life was better and more real than that. She certainly hoped that she would do more honourably by her daughter. What future was there for Jean serving in a little shop in the wilds of Fife?

Annie was sure that Helen possessed some special and wonderful qualities. Though her school work was only average, some of it poor, Helen had something that Annie lacked, the determination to achieve what she set her mind to do. She had tremendous energy, which was Bruce's gift to his daughter. His strength and energy were phenomenal, almost a handicap to normal life.

She supposed all mothers felt a deep faith in their children's potential. Her own mother certainly felt it about her brother William, though probably not about herself. Annie involuntarily smiled her ironic smile as she considered that, at forty-one, William had not so far justified that faith.

Apart from these practical attributes, Annie was sure that Helen had some deeper quality, some inner creative force that she recognised, but could not name. Ever since she was a small child, music had inspired Helen to express this inner life in dance. Annie remembered the record that first revealed the child's reaction to music. It was *In the Hall of the Mountain King* which contrasted with *Anitra's Dance* on the reverse side. Three-year-old Helen had leaped and rushed and followed the changing tempo of the first, then interpreted the sweet grace of the second in a way that had astounded her mother and grandparents. Though joyfully spontaneous and unselfconscious, yet there was control and it was difficult to believe that the child had never before heard either piece. Nowadays Helen still danced when some favourite or dramatic music was playing on the wireless. She would quickly wheel her mother to one side of the sitting room, push back the furniture and dance just as unselfconsciously as she had done when little. She would dance for an hour and only for her mother. This happened only occasionally At other times Helen would sit very still, listening with a look of rapt concentration, as she imagined how she would interpret the music.

Annie thought it would be marvellous if Helen could use this talent, this *obsession*, to make a career for herself.

Sadly, there was little money for the arts in Britain just now and she had read that the chorus girls of Sadler's Wells Ballet required wealthy parents to subsidise their accommodation, their travel, even the special shoes, which wore out so quickly. Did Helen dream of being a ballerina? She did not speak of it, though she often poured over Arnold Haskell's book about ballet that Mrs Horsland had given her last Christmas. And she idolised Vera Zorina, the film star ballerina, but she also adored Esther Williams and Johnny Weismuller for their swimming abilities. She was still such a child.

And of course, a career in ballet meant London and then who would look after her? It was just a pleasant fantasy. The future was too dark and foggy to worry about.

◊

The tennis season arrived and on Friday afternoons Helen and her classmates took the tram along Great Western Road to Kirklee Road where the playing fields, generally rather damp, awaited them. As Friday afternoons seemed to be popular with the rain-clouds, there was often a lot of hanging about and little tennis. A weekly session was hardly enough to learn any sort of skill and Helen had lost her enthusiasm for the game. Many girls had joined tennis clubs nearer their own home. Helen would have liked to play more basketball, but the few games at Kirklee were disorganised and desultory, used only to employ the time of those waiting for a court to become free. That is how it appeared to Helen, but she would have been the first to admit that she was dreamy and often knew less about what was happening, than other girls did. She was never unduly worried by this.

The solitary walk home from Kirklee over Victoria Circus and down Sydenham Road was still the best part of Friday, for there was the delightful knowledge that school was finished for the weekend.

Helen did not spend much time in study and Annie was told little about approaching school exams. She often spoke to her daughter of her own less than brilliant schooldays and advised her to be more sensilble and less lazy than she herself had been. Helen listened politely to these exhortations, then returned to her knitting or her latest library book. She had no worries about passing those exams which did not require study and the others did not interest her.

Ballet exams were approaching, but these did not worry her, either. The theory with its question and answer format needed study, but there was a certain poetry in the questions and the answers were logical. Helen diligently practised pirouettes and other exercises in the kitchen, while waiting for the potatoes to boil.

Being on a stage in a real theatre was more terrifying and nerve-racking. Sometimes the thought of it would make her screw her eyes tightly shut and give a shrill little squeak of pleasure and say,

"Oh, just fancy! The Athenaeum! I wonder what it will be like?"

One night Annie asked,

"What sort of dances are you learning in the bigger class?"

"We're learning two dances, and neither is like ballet at all. One is a bit boring, to tell you the truth, with different names for things, not in French like ballet. We walk in a circle a lot and when we put our arms up above our head it's called 'high V' then there's 'low V' too. I think we're supposed to be like people on a Greek vase. Miss Hopkins often smiles to me and says, "Very good, Helen!" but I don't particularly enjoy it. I don't feel I'm doing it right and I think we all look a bit soppy."

"It sounds very Isadora Duncan?"

"Does it? I think the other girls wonder who I am, suddenly appearing in their class."

"And what's the other dance like?"

"It's gorgeous music! I think it's called a mazurka or maybe a czardas and it's real ballet music, though I think we are going to wear boots to dance it, for it's a sort of Russian peasant dance. It's not really ballet either but *I love it*. You know that Crakow Wedding ballet that we saw long, long ago, the first time I ever saw ballet? Remember? Well it's quite like that. Remember how they clicked their heels together up at the side? We've to do that and it's not too difficult!"

"Wonderful, pet. I'm looking forward to seeing you *so* much."

More Guests

"**P**oor Miss Arthur. I think she's a lonely soul. She 's been very good to me, never stinting her time on a Friday night and bringing us presents. How about asking her for a meal?"

"All right, what would we give her to eat? Maybe she's fussy."

"Now I wonder why you say that? People always like to be fed. I think she would appreciate it. And we could have some other people too. How about Tessa and her parents? It would be a nice way to say 'thank you'. They've had you to tea and Tessa's mother has visited me. And think of the beetle drive, you really enjoyed that, didn't you!"

Helen made a wry face, for Annie was teasing. Twelve of her classmates had been invited to Tessa's beetle drive. Some may have enjoyed it, but for Helen it had been a disaster. She had grumbled when she came home.

"You've no idea how boring it is to keep throwing the dice to try and get a three for an antennae or a one for a leg and they had *six legs*. Do beetles have six legs? Anyway you have to get a one *six times* to finish your beetle, then you move on to the next table and *do it all again*. I'd rather wash dishes. When I think of all the good games we could have played or even just chatted...I never want to hear the sound of dice rattling ever again."

The invitations for the meal were given out for the following Saturday and all accepted. Then there was the menu to decide.

"People always like soup. I think we'll have lentil. Maybe Milly could get you a few ham bones. Then fish baked in custard is easy and it can be cooking away nice and slowly. It was a success with Khirstine and her mother. Maybe we could make an apple sponge for dessert. What a shame we can't get cream. Milk will do fine. I'll tell you another thing we could have, potato croquettes!"

"I've never heard of those."

"You'll like them." Annie promised.

What Annie had forgotten, or perhaps not quite realised, was that Miss Arthur was very deaf. It had not been so obvious in the close interaction of a massage. Around the table in the spacious

sittting room, with the various competing voices, the clatter of
cutlery and some degree of noise from the passing traffic, the
poor lady was at a terrible disadvantage. Margaret, Tessa's
mother spoke out in her authoritative teacher's voice, but the
deep and quiet tones of her husband were on a wavelength quite
difficult even for those with much sharper hearing than Miss
Arthur. Tessa, who suffered from no schoolgirl shyness, spoke at
length in a self-confident drawl, not easy to pick up. Helen and
her mother, both blessed with excellent hearing, were used to
conversing quietly together with no need to 'project' and were
unpractised in dinner table speech. Miss Arthur's faded blue eyes
moved from face to face, obviously struggling, and failing to
follow the conversation, her smile flickering on and off at inappropriate moments.

Annie tried to include her, but the others seemed unaware or
uncaring of her isolation.

Otherwise, the meal went very smoothly, for the food had
been prepared before anyone arrived and kept hot. Only the little
toast squares to serve with the soup needed to be made at the last
minute. Helen enjoyed hearing the exclamations of pleasure,
when the soup was brought in. She had thought it unlikely anyone would want lentil soup. She really enjoyed the croquettes
and wondered why her mother had never made them before. The
apple sponge was delicious.

For the first time, Helen enjoyed that feeling of hospitable
achievement, that pleasure in making people welcome, happy
and well fed, which was so much a part of Annie's personality.
Helen would learn to share this trait and use it for the rest of her
life.

After the meal, it was suggested, probably by Margaret, that
they might enjoy hearing Tessa recite, for she attended elocution
lessons. Though Annie was less than enthusiastic and knew it to
be an unsuitable entertainment for her hard-of-hearing friend,
she politely agreed that they would all *love* to hear Tessa say her
piece.

Helen cringed at the thought of standing up to recite in a
sitting room and the thought of listening to it was almost as
appalling.

But Tessa seemed not at all nonplussed and stepped off the
carpet to the linoleum to help the acoustics. Then, fixing her eye

on the picture rail, she clearly declaimed the poem, in a voice entirely unlike her familiar daily one.

There was a slight scatter of embarrassed applause, in which Helen did not join. She was too sorry for her friend, though truthfully Tessa showed no signs of requiring pity.

"She's very good, a great deal of potential." Annie spoke heartily, if insincerely, "Would she like to be an actress d'you think?".

She had thought it ridiculous for a girl to be encouraged to speak in that unnatural way. She had sometimes wondered if elocution would help Helen to find a bit more strength in her voice, but she would hate her to use those dramatic pauses and anglicised diphthongs.

"Oh, *never!*" Margaret exclaimed, 'I expect Tessa will have an academic career, probably study the classics, you know."

"Indeed? Well, she's certainly talented, I would say." Annie smiled sweetly.

George, Tessa's father nodded and leaning forward confidentially, asserted in his low, inaccessible voice,

"Yes, she really is very, *very* talented and I can tell you she hasn't yet used *half of her brain!*"

Annie looked at him, wordless. Only Helen noticed the sardonic raised eyebrow that she so coveted. How many minutes had she spent in front of the mirror trying to achieve that subtle expression of disbelief. She stood quickly and started to clear the plates from the table. Tessa jumped up to help.

In the kitchen, Helen asked if her friend did not feel shy standing up and speaking like that.

"Oh, no. I know I'm good at it, so I don't worry."

This remark seemed sensible, if a bit conceited. Yet, without quite knowing why, Helen still felt the recitation had been unacceptable. She knew she could never do it herself. Was performing on a stage more acceptable than in a sitting room? Helen thought it was.

"I'm going in for the British Empire Shakespeare Society competition next year. You could do it too."

"I don't study elocution though."

"But you've got quite a nice voice, when you speak up. You should try it."

Helen had always felt that Tessa considered herself superior in every way, and she took it as a compliment that the suggestion was made at all.

In the sitting room Margaret was taking the opportunity of Tessa's absence,

"You know, Tessa is now studying the piano and she's so good, so very, very good. We're just thrilled with her progress."

Annie was tempted to mention that Helen had gained honours in four ballet exams, but it seemed more dignified to refrain from competing in the proud parent stakes.

"Oh, yes!" she said, politely.

George again leaned towards her, making it even less likely that Miss Arthur would catch any of his words.

"I must tell you, Mrs Corning, that she was playing Beethoven's *Für Elise* yesterday and I realise she may not have the experience or technique of Moura Lympany but I do believe Tessa's interpretation had a very special quality that I certainly found superior, really more *sensitive*.

Annie murmured "I'm sure." and gazed into the fire.

They all gazed into the fire, until Miss Arthur suddenly jumped to her feet and said, very formally,

"Thank you so much for having me to tea, dear Mrs Corning. It was a delicious meal that I shall always remember."

She kissed a surprised Annie's cheek and darted from the room.

The others left soon after. Margaret also kissed Annie, who had no gratitude, saying when they were gone,

"I don't know why they want to kiss me, with their old papery cheeks!"

Cheek-kissing and hugging were a minor part of the family behaviour.

"Well, I certainly enjoyed the meal myself, jewel. Did you?"

"I did indeed. The apple sponge was scrumptious and the croquettes… can we have them again tomorrow?"

"We'll see. And did you enjoy Tessa's recital?"

Helen made a face.

"Why does Miss Arthur always wear pale blue? And I'd no idea she was so deaf. That was a shame. I don't think she heard much at all."

"P'raps not, but maybe just as well." And Annie told of Tessa's musical powers according to her parents and they laughed about that for a long time.

"But did you notice? I don't think Miss Arthur even liked the food much, because she left a little bit of everything on her plate, soup, fish and sponge. That was rude."

"Oh that's an old-fashioned thing to do, to show that you've been given more than you need. It's supposed to be a compliment and she ate most of it."

"Damn silly if you ask me. What a waste! And I think it's rude."

"Or it might be an even older superstition of leaving a small offering to the gods."

"Well I just think it's rude and a waste of good food."

The Athenaeum

At the last class before the dress rehearsal Miss Hopkins told the girls to go into her sitting room and find their costumes.

Helen was always happy to inspect this room. It was large and cluttered with many parcels, suitcases and boxes as well as a great deal of old-fashioned furniture. Photos and paintings covered the walls and beside the gas fire stood an electric kettle to provide regular pots of tea. As there was no sign of a bed, Helen knew that Miss Hopkins must have a house somewhere else. She had never been sure whether this was her home or not.

Near the window were two large hampers, out of which Miss Cleland, the assistant teacher, was producing colourful and voluminous skirts. After shaking them briskly, she spread them over the backs of chairs. Helen hoped the dust would not start her sneezing, or worse still, an asthma attack. Fortunately the asthma had not recurred, though she often sneezed furiously several times.

Peasant blouses were also produced from the hampers and the girls crowded round to try them on. There was a little head dress of coloured ribbons for each girl. Helen was just setting one on her head, when Miss Hopkins drew her to one side and said,

"Don't take that one, dear, I want you to wear this one."

Helen could not believe her eyes. There must be some mistake.

Miss Hopkins was holding a high tripartite head-dress, edged with sequins and glittering with mock rubies and pearls. Abundant ribbons hung from either side. Helen felt confused. Her eyes and mouth were both wide open and the other girls were stock still, looking at the magnificent crown.

"You dance the Czardas so nicely, Helen, I want you to be the leader. I'll keep this just now and bring it to rehearsal, as it's rather unwieldy to carry in the tramcar."

How magically can self-esteem be transformed with just one show of complete confidence from the right person.

Helen walked from the studio and crossed the road to the tram stop in a haze of delighted disbelief. Did Miss Hopkins really think she was as good as all that? She should not even be in that class! She was in a lower grade than the other girls and yet she was to be the leader! That marvellous headdress would certainly mark her out from everyone else on stage. Surely she must be pretty good if Miss Hopkins was making her the leader. How fantastic it seemed. The other girls had looked at her in disbelief. She was not at all nervous, for if Miss Hopkins believed in her, she must be good. Perhaps her mother was right in thinking she was special. It was all too incredible.

Just wait until she told her mother!

◊

The night at the Athenaeum was all she could have wished for. Helen had been glad to find that it really was a proper stage in a proper theatre.

She helped Bruce carry Annie in at the side door of the elaborate building in Exchange Square. The auditorium was still empty and she sat in the middle of the front row.

"Well I've certainly got the best seat in the house. Very comfy, too."

"You'll be all right, will you?" Helen asked anxiously

"Right as rain, my pet. I'm going to enjoy myself and you're going to steal the show, I'm sure.

Helen did not believe that, because all those older girls had studied for years and could dance *en pointe*, which seemed such a miraculous thing,

The stage was bare and inviting. Dark, empty and silent, the space seemed waiting to be filled. Tightly shutting her eyes and hugging herself, Helen gave her usual small, stifled crow of delight. The nervous excitement that stimulated her every muscle was never a handicap for Helen, but filled her brimful of energy and anticipation.

No fears marred her enjoyment of the actual performance, which went smoothly, except for one small hitch. The decoratve handkerchief which she deployed throughout the dance caught momentarily at the back of her head on the hairpins securing the magnificent head dress. She freed the handkerchief almost instantly, but did she lose that look of confident joy while doing so? She would never know.

Summer 1946

The grass was cut when Helen arrived in Pittenweem. Mary warned her repeatedly not to go sniffing any flowers in case she had a recurrence of her asthma. The delicious perfumes in the garden were a large part of Helen's summer happiness and it is unlikely she obeyed her grandmother. Did Mary realise that her dictatorial orders often had the effect of making the denied pleasure seem extremely desirable. Often, when Mary lit a cigarette, she would advise her grand daughter,

"Now I sincerely hope *you'll never start smoking!"*

Which remark would make Helen want to rush off and light up a fag immediately. Only once in her lifetime would Helen ever sample a real cigarette. In the meantime she had found her own substitute, though string was beginning to lose its charm.

◊

In July Annie received a letter from Bruce and looked very serious as she read it.

"What a shame, Mrs Corning has taken ill on holiday and is in hospital. It's a stroke, but Bruce seems to be optimistic and says she's not too bad. Unfortunately he and Willie have to get back to Glasgow to get the works started again."

"What age will she be now?" Mary asked.

"About ten years older than you, I think."

Mary was a very active sixty-four.

"I don't hold out much hope then. Once you're in your seventies…and she's always seemed frail and elderly to me."

"Well we'll hope for the best, for how would those three get on in that big flat without her? Old Corning's older than my father, in his mid eighties now."

"And yet you told me he still swims at the Arlington and goes to the office every day?"

"Aye, he has to keep an eye on the boys and see they're behaving themselves."

"That's *ridiculous*, they're in their fifties!"

"It can't be easy, I wouldn't think. He seems to be a domineering old devil and as mean as all get out. Bruce is always complaining that he can't get new equipment, or get things done the way he wants, for his father keeps such tight purse strings. When Bruce went there to work at first, his father wanted him to labour alongside the men but, sensibly, Bruce refused and pointed out he was a trained engineer who could maintain and improve the machinery. Then he had to fight for the workshop he needed. Yet he won't say one word against his father. He's a great one for 'honour thy father and mother' et cetera."

The next letter was sad and brief. Jane Corning had died before her sons could return to the East Coast on the Saturday. Bruce was heartbroken that he had not been with her at the end.

"This will be a terrible blow for Bruce. I'm really sorry for him. He was absoluted devoted to her. She was his ideal of womanhood and of course he was her little god on earth. I wonder what he'll do now? It'll change his life, I'm sure."

Annie's intuition was uncannily correct, though she would not learn about that change for many years.

Although it was the first time that Helen had encountered death, she was strangely untouched by the demise of her paternal grandmother. She found it sad, but inevitable. She had seen little of Granny Corning and not always in the happiest of circumstances. Compared to her other vivid and powerful grandmother, she hardly knew her Granny, who had always seemed like a very old lady to Helen. Death was what happened to old people. Because of her lack of sympathy with Bruce, she was unable or unwilling to understand his loss in the same way as Annie could.

Helen was required to write a letter of sorrow and condolence to her father. After two hours of staring at a page with only the heading and 'Dear Daddy', Annie dictated the letter, and in much kinder tones than Helen might have used.

It would be interesting to record that this first experience of death encouraged Helen to think more philosophically, perhaps religiously, but this would be untrue. Her thoughts, as usual, were mainly divided between the practicalities of her mother's well-being and the employment of her time once she left the house and its domestic duties. Certainly, when listening to music, her mind drifted into deeper poetic waters, but death and a possible hereafter played no part in these imaginings. She tried hard, if not always successfully, to dismiss any belief in the supernatural.

Although her fantasies about dance and romance were a rich part of her character and a wonderful release, Helen's responsibilities had made her pragmatic and fatalistic. Added to this, she had a strong awareness of the present moment and the need to enjoy it and make the best of it, for soon it would be lost, never to return.

The Waddell Family

T here was a knock at the door one afternoon and Helen was surprised to see a crowd of strangers standing there, all smiling happily as though they knew her.

"Now, I think you must be wee Helen grown up into a big tall beautiful girl. Is that right? Am I not right?"

The speaker was a plump, friendly lady, with a round face made memorable by flashing, rather prominent dark eyes. Her voice was loud and had an Edinburgh lilt.

"I'm Isobel Waddell and you won't remember me, but away and tell your granny or your mum that Isobel Lumsden's here. They'll know who you mean, though I've not seen either of them for donkey's and I'll send these three men away down the shore just now, and we'll have a good blether. On you go boys, away down the harbour! And amuse yourselves now! And come back for me at four. Now don't forget, four o'clock. We've to get back to Mrs Kennedy's for our high tea! And don't be late."

The latter part of this speech was shouted along the High Street, and grew in crescendo as Isobel's sandy-haired husband and two sons obediently wandered off into the distance.

This was obviously a forceful and overpowering lady, though Helen was not too overpowered to notice that the older boy might be a suitable companion for herself. Was this the summer that would produce a boyfriend? And was this the one? Tall and stalwart with spectacles and a mass of blonde hair, he was certainly a possibility and the only one to date. Lots of girls at school went out with boys and had even received their first kiss! At fourteen, she was without any friends of the opposite sex and with no apparent chance of meeting any. Though not a constant worry, it was dispiriting and a problem which she pondered occasionally. Not exactly a failure perhaps, but she lagged behind those other girls and might never catch up. Some of them were certainly fatter or sillier than she was, and not much prettier, so why was she minus a boyfriend?

Annie and Mary greeted Isobel with great enthusiasm. While Helen made tea in the kitchen, the gusts of laughter and conversation from the next room seemed particularly loud. She had never heard quite such an uproarious afternoon visit. Isobel's voice was predominant, but the other two were obviously enjoying themselves very much.

Isobel Lumsden was one of Nature's supreme jesters, only happy when she had the whole company laughing helplessly. Because of her wonderful delivery and sense of timing, she achieved success where other would-be jesters might have failed. With an infectious laugh, marvellous body language and an unending fund of anecdotes and funny stories, some more vulgar than others, she commanded the attention of any company in which she found herself. Within the first five minutes she would almost bully them into enjoyment. A larger than life personality, her kindness and ability to appreciate the humour of others, not always attributes of the dedicated story-teller, made her irresistible.

Helen learned that Isobel had grown up in Pittenweem and her sister had nearly married Annie's brother, Willie. Some hitch at the last minute had stopped that. After this story was told, Isobel winked at Annie and said,

"But there's time yet for our families to unite, for I've got a big son to get rid of and you've got Helen. Ye never know what the future'll bring."

Helen thought this a bit strong and escaped to the kitchen to make more tea. When the men returned from the harbour at four, they were invited in and Helen made yet more tea for Abe, the husband, and Jack and Lindsay.

If it sometimes seemed that the men of Isobel's family must be long suffering, they did not show it, though they spent a great deal of their holiday waiting around while she charmed and entertained others. No doubt they listened to many oft-repeated punch lines, but were noble enough to join in the ensuing gales of merriment.

They were a very attractive family.

Helen was now able to inspect the older boy at close quarters. In spite of the sad defects of spectacles and a pronounced squint, he seemed acceptable as a first boyfriend. He was fifteen and at that awkward stage of adolescence when grey flannel shorts seem inadequate for the large bony knees growing out of them, but he was polite and joined in the conversation. He looked suitably unhappy when his mother described how '*marvellously* well Jack had done at school,' with prizes and scholarships right and left. He was going to study law.

The fact that he was clever impressed Helen particularly.

Apart from accepting a cup of tea and a scone from her with mumbled thanks, Jack at no time appeared to be aware of Helen's presence. She was relieved about that, for she was wearing a dress from last year, as brief and uncompromising as his shorts.

John Mackay came down from the studio and joined them. He often seemed serious and sad these days, but he shared and enjoyed the hilarity as much as anyone, which surprised Helen.

The sitting room seemed overcrowded, but very jolly and Helen thought how lucky it was that these people had come on holiday just now. Mary was in a great mood and Annie was wiping tears of laughter from her eyes.

They were like a 'family in a book', that Holy Grail for which Helen was always searching. It was arranged that Helen would join them to go swimming next day. They talked of taking a picnic to Elie beach in the afternoon and later in the week, they intended to sail to the May Island and they certainly hoped that Helen would come with them. It seemed almost too good to be true.

And always there was that remote possibility of romance.

Perhaps Jack would fall in love with her?

That would be pretty nice.

Perhaps he was her future husband?

Unlike her friend Tessa, Helen believed in the ideal of first love and Jack Waddell appeared to be excellent and innocent raw material. It seemed unlikely that this stereotypical schoolboy had ever asked a girl out on a date and he would almost certainly be as inexperienced in kissing as she herself was.

The unfortunate Mrs Kennedy must have watched her high tea congeal, for it was after six before the quiet, long-suffering Abe finally insisted they leave.

Helen would learn that Isobel chose to ignore the passage of time.

Helen and Jack had very little conversation. On their first swim, he had criticised her crawl technique, which she thought a bit rich, as he employed only the breast stroke himself. Also his diving left a lot to be desired. However she and the younger boy,

Lindsay, quickly became very relaxed with each other, really like brother and sister. She found him an interesting, thoughtful boy, determined to be a doctor. He often made surprisingly adult remarks for an eleven-year-old and had a whimsical sense of humour. He made Helen laugh when others did not see the joke. Jack's humour was more direct and bawdy like his mother's. Annie and Mary also enjoyed blue jokes and Helen was used to this, but, while not a prude, she had a slight puritanical streak and particularly liked a joke which was funny without being 'rude'. Sadly, there were so few un-rude jokes that were funny.

◊

Although the dreams of romance failed to materialise, Helen spent a wonderful fortnight with the Waddell family. The parents were charmed with the shy, well-behaved girl,

"So unlike our two rough brutes!" as Isobel often said, though Helen saw how Isobel looked at her boys with adoration.

Being part of a family which was determined to enjoy its holiday, was a wonderful and unusual experience for Helen. The Waddells had a more carefree attitude to money than she was used to, and with her two 'siblings' she enjoyed the relaxed holiday spirit which threaded everything the Waddells did. On their outings she was treated as a protected child, with no responsibilities or duties. Abe certainly spoiled her on every occasion. It was a different life.

Of course, at intervals each day she was still needed at home to help her mother and to complete a few chores for her grandmother. She accomplished these duties as speedily as possible, for the Waddells always included her in their elaborate plans for excursions, not all of which came to fruition. If Isobel met some old acquaintances in the High Street, and she seemed to know everyone in Pittenweem, the conversation might go on indefinitely. Each one of the group would remember yet another anecdote and laughter and shouts would echo from the town clock to the West Wynd. Isobel seemed to generate noisiness and it was easy to locate her, because of this. Her husband and sons would be lounging patiently somewhere in the vicinity. Abe always welcomed Helen's appearance and used it as a lever to prise his wife from her cronies.

"Here's Helen ready to go to St Andrews now, Isobel. We'd better get away and not be too late getting back."

Isobel would give Helen a bright smile, then turn and continue talking to her friends for another ten minutes.

Even in St Andrews, they were not quite safe. More than likely Isobel would bump into a long lost relative in South Street, or even meet a neighbour from Edinburgh. She knew people *wherever* she went and she talked to all of them. Talked interminably, it seemed to Helen, while the sun was shining and the pleasures of the Step Rock pool were waiting. Helen did not have the patience of the Waddell men. She supposed she should be used to hanging around listening, for both Mary and Bruce were inveterate talkers, but Isobel was even worse.

Helen would never understand why people would rather talk than *do something*.

Her impatience would fill her with guilt, for Isobel was so kind and loving. Surely she could wait around without irritation, as the boys did. Helen felt a lot of guilt these days. Since the Waddells had erupted into her life, she had spent much less time with her mother and skimped what she did for her grandmother. Nor had she accompanied her Grandfather on his daily walk or on his occasional visit to the cinema. After the Waddells returned to Edinburgh, she would be more dutiful.

The trip to the May Island was terrific, because there was no one else there for Isobel to speak to. It was a beautiful day for a sail, calm and hot. Mary had made the picnic, with a choice of salmon, egg and tomato or meat paste in Evesham's rolls. She had also baked gingerbread. It was a feast superior in every way to the ones provided by Mrs Kennedy at the boarding house. Helen agreed with the boys that ginger beer was the best drink when you were thirsty.

They walked all over the May Island, with Abe pointing out things that Helen had not noticed on her previous visit. On the cliffs, myriads of various and noisy seabirds perched and soared. Seals were basking on distant rocks. Underfoot the thickly matted thrift grew everywhere, giving the impression of walking on a soft mattress. Care must be taken to avoid the eider-duck nests, which lay scattered on the ground, so well camouflaged as to be almost invisible. A large, unattractive mother duck flew out, almost from under Jack's shoe, leaving her eggs unattended. After that they were all more careful where they trod. Helen worried that the eggs would be spoiled or eaten by some other bird, before the mother could return.

There were hundreds of puffins, a bird which Helen had never seen before. She was charmed by them and fascinated by their swift, fluttering flight.

"They really are like little parrots, aren't they! And they look as though they were just learning to fly and it was *awful* hard work for them. P'raps they're frightened to go slowly in case they fall, just like learning to ride a bike.

Helen had few good memories of learning to ride a bike.

◊

One afternoon the Waddells were visiting Annie and, as usual, making plans.

"Now we mustn't lose touch again, Annie. It's just daft to lose touch after such an awful long, long friendship. Isn't that right Abe? Isn't that right, boys? Don't you agree? Now it's far too long to wait 'til next summer in Pittenweem so they'll *need* to come and visit us in Edinburgh and see our wee house and the garden, too. The garden's just wonderful. Abe's a marvellous gardener. Aren't you, Abe? Now admit it. Ye're better than anyone else in Greenbank Road. The garden at Sunnybrae is renowned throughout Morningside, isn't it Abe? He's famous, y'know. So *when* are you and Helen coming through to see us, Annie?"

"Well that's very nice of you to invite us, but I think it would be a bit too difficult, really. Why don't you come through and visit *us*?"

"Now that would be a splendid idea, wouldn't it Abe? We could bring a picnic through some Sunday and it doesn't take long to drive between the two cities, does it Abe? I don't really know. How far is it? How long would it take, I wonder? Anyway it doesn't matter how long, We could get away really early and have a nice day of chat with you. That would be lovely, wouldn't it. It's years since I've been in Glasgow."

Her speech flowed on, her questions all rhetorical, her enthusiasm immense and infectious,

Helen thought it would certainly be fun to have a visit from them, although she doubted if Isobel could ever 'get away early'. Then Lindsay, taking swift advantage of a pause in his mother's speech, said the strangest thing that Helen had ever heard.

"If we came to Glasgow, we'd need to keep our car windows closed, in case they threw knives in at us!"

Helen looked at him. He seemed perfectly serious. What on earth did he mean? Helen was ignorant of the gang warfare which, encapsulated and exaggerated in the book *No Mean City*, had blackened Glasgow's reputation in the pre-war years, and which was once more rearing its ugly head in the outlying districts.

People throwing knives through car windows!

It seemed impossible. Helen tried to imagine any place in Glasgow where such a bizarre thing might take place. Certainly not in sedate Hyndland, Jordanhill, Broomhill. Hillhead, Pollokshields or Lambhill. She had visited all those respectable places with her mother. Then surely none of Mrs Connell's friends in their spotless little flats in Dumbarton Road, no one could believe they would throw knives. She imagined the busy pavements of Byres Road, Sauchiehall Street, Argyle Street with throngs of people hurrying about their business without any thought of throwing knives. Even where her father's works were in the Gallowgate, which was the most dilapidated and impoverished place she knew, even there she had walked beside her father, with no fear of violence.

Lindsay's parents smilingly tut-tutted at him and shook their heads, but neither of them seemed puzzled at such a strange remark.

She must ask her mother later for an explanation.

The fortnight passed without one sign of romantic interest from Jack. In a way it was a relief, for Helen could relax in the carefree family life, paying no more attention to Jack than politeness demanded.

On the day they were to leave, Jack and Helen were sent to collect some books for Annie, from the boarding house. They were alone in the house and Helen wondered if perhaps Jack might choose this opportune moment to kiss her. In view of his previous lack of interest, it seemed unlikely. She now rather dreaded the idea. Nevertheless it was a chance which had not occurred before and it was a last chance.

He did not kiss her, but sat at the piano and played. Nothing could have enhanced him or imprinted his image more deeply on Helen's heart, for Jack was a very accomplished musician. After some beautiful Beethoven and Schubert, which enthralled Helen, he broke into mad jazzy pieces whose speed and brilliance also delighted her. Helen was snobbish about popular music and hated 'swing', but she was unfamiliar with the tunes and rhythms of traditional jazz and these immediately appealed to her. She could have listened to him all day. His playing cast a spell over her.

Helen had found the hero on which to bestow her worship.

Jack jumped up from the piano stool, gathered up the books and said.

"We'd better get going or I'll get the blame for being late. Dad's always hoping to catch the last ferry. That's at six thirty and if he misses that, he has to go the long way round by Kincardine Bridge. Of course we *will* miss it. We always do. Mum blethers so much. Come on, hurry up, Helen."

Jack was right. On that last day, Isobel held hilarious court throughout Pittenweem. Abe's gentle requests and patient reminders were, as always, ignored and it was after six when she popped in to see Annie and nearly nine before they set off, via Kincardine Bridge, on the long road home to Edinburgh.

For the next three months Helen's thoughts were filled with Jack and his wonderful piano playing. As the weeks passed, even the squint faded into insignificance.

The promised visit from the Waddells never took place.

By November, Helen had transferred her adoration to another older, more handsome, more worthy, even more unattainable member of the opposite sex.

Mixed Feelings

The Waddell's visit made a strong impact on Annie. She had to deal with very mixed feelings. It was obvious that Helen was having a wonderful time on her outings with the family and, of course, Annie was delighted to see her daughter enjoying herself. Although Helen usually seemed happy to spend time alone, it was a more normal childlike experience to be taken places and have other children there to share in the fun. Annie wondered if it might have been better if she had had another child. Would a sister for Helen have helped to make life easier for all of them? Annie certainly had happy memories of her brother, when they were young, though sadly things had soured in later life. Who could tell?

She could understand the attraction the Waddells exerted and she was not surprised that Helen accepted their tempting invitations. Annie herself was cheered when Isobel popped in to see them. She was so vital and vivacious and, above all, so kind that one could forgive her non-stop chatter. Most of it was very amusing, though surely Abe must sometimes long for peace. He seemed to take it all in good part. He must be an unusually patient chap.

Annie had to face the fact that she felt slightly hurt that Helen had become so involved with the Waddells and, yes, she was rather jealous. It seemed as if Helen spent little time in the house nowadays, dashing home, dealing with chores and then dashing out again and there was no knowing when she would come back. If her return was later than expected, Annie had probably been sitting in discomfort for some time. It was very unlike Helen to let this happen. Of course Isobel was cavalier about time-keeping and the child had no power to force the Waddells to bring her home. There were several times that Helen had rushed in breathless, saying,

"Are you all right, Mummy? I'm so sorry..."

But probably it had not been her fault.

Annie recognised her own jealousy and knew she must fight it. She had always known a time would come when Helen would make a life of her own. Theoretically, she had determined to encourage this and deal with it sensibly and unselfishly, but the reality was difficult.

Mary's grumbles helped her to find strength.

"Is Helen going away *again* for the *whole afternoon* with those people? We've hardly seen her all week and I was wanting her for some messages. She forgot to get the potatoes this morning. And we need more bread and the baker's'll be sold out by the time she gets home, I expect. And where've they all gone this time? They're forever gadding about. What restless folk they are! I hope she's not late back again, with you sitting waiting and needing to 'go'. I wish I could help you, but I'd never be strong enough."

"Aye, we might both land rolling on the floor." Annie smiled hopefully.

Mary just grunted,

"Well, I think she's neglecting you. You should give her a bit of a talking-to. She's got to learn."

"No, Maw, she's having a nice holiday and she's always sorry when she's late. She can't help it, if they keep her late. She's usually very conscientious. I'm *really* pleased she can take some time off and forget all her responsibilities, though I'm sorry if she's not doing as much for you as she should. I'll speak to her about that and you should send her right back out again, if she forgets a message. But I think it's *great* that she's had a chance to go to the May Island and be driven around and get taken for picnics with other kids for company. I can surely deal with a wee bit of waiting around."

Her feelings were not as firm as her words indicated, but she knew she must convince herself as well as Mary.

She decided that she would paint the next day. That made the time pass quickly. There were some lovely roses in the garden and she would try a small 14x10 canvas and send it in to the RGI. Perhaps she would be lucky this time and sell it.

◊

Next day, when Helen set her mother up with paints and easel, Mary asked,

"Which roses will you paint, d'ye think? There's the ramblers and the New Dawn. The American Pillars are lovely but they have terrible thorns."

"Is the New Dawn the pale pink one you got from Mr White in Anstruther?"

"Yes, it's very pretty."

"Is that the man that grows the delicious tomatoes, grandma?"

"Yes, he's a *wonderful* gardener. You should see his flowers, and the vegetables are astonishing. And his strawberries are bigger than any I've ever seen."

"Would you say he had a green thumb?"

"Well, my jewel, I think he's got two green thumbs for he can grow anything!"

Annie added,

"Sounds as though he's green right up to the elbows!"

Everybody laughed.

Though Helen was terribly fond of Isobel, she thought her mother was much funnier and did not need to try so hard

It was a pity that Annie could not read her daughter's mind, but she found it easier that day to watch her daughter dash off to the swimming pool with the Waddells. What an idiot she had been not to start painting sooner.

"My, that's a terrible rose, that. It's like struggling and fighting with a tiger!" Mary complained as she brought in a bunch of the American Pillars.

Annie laughed at the picture this conjured up, but Mary had been quite serious and looked offended.

"It really is tigerish, you know! I'm ripped to pieces!"

But she started to laugh too. It was always good to hear Mary laugh. This would be one of her 'good days' when nothing seemed to annoy her. Those days were few and welcome, for they made a difference to the whole family.

◊

John inspected his daughter's finished painting, made a few criticisms but was hardly enthusiastic. His standards were high and he was not a natural teacher.

However Isobel loved the painting and wanted to buy it.

"What would you give me for it?"

"How about a fiver? "

"Done!"

"It's a bargain, Annie. I love it. You've had a lot of work and I could never do that myself! I can't draw a straight line."

"Och well, I enjoyed doing it and I'm glad it's going to a good home."

"I'm going to hang it in the sitting room and it'll always remind me of this holiday and dear wee Helen. Mind you, we hardly ever use the sitting room except to play the piano, but never mind, we'll see it sometimes."

As usual, Isobel's remarks generated laughter.

As Helen had gone for a walk with her grandfather that day, Annie described her daughter's dancing success.

"She was so astonished to be given a leading part! And I must say she danced wonderfully, so full of vigour and expression. She seemed to *glow* with the pleasure of dancing. Though I shouldn't be saying it, of course, but she did knock the others into a cocked hat. Even the more advanced pupils seemed half-hearted compared to her. But then I'm her mother and rather prejudiced, no doubt. Bruce thought she was wonderful too, though he always manages to say the wrong thing, poor soul."

Then Isobel admitted that she did recitations to audiences at the church and at other small community gatherings.

"Oh, I'll bet you're a *big* success!" Annie said, though Mary sat silent and unresponsive.

"Well, they do seem to like me! I wear my mother's old fox fur and a funny wee hat and as soon as I come on the stage, they all start to laugh. Even before I've said a word! I just stand there and look at them and they laugh and laugh. It's just daft wee monologues I do, y'know the sort of thing. I send off to Manchester for them. There's an awful funny one about a bridge foursome and I'm the woman that everyone dreads to play with because I know *nothing* about the game ... it's a scream. Then there's one where I'm standing at the bus stop…"

Abe's voice was seldom heard, but unusually, he broke in.

"It's always a sell-out when Isobel's on the programme!"

"Och it's not really, but they seem to like me fine. I just love *treading the boards!* Maybe I should have been on the stage. D'ye think, Mrs Mackay?"

"Yes, quite possibly you should have had a stage career, Isobel." Mary's voice lacked enthusiasm.

Annie said nothing, but thought to herself that if Mary had pursued tragedy and Isobel comedy, they might have done very well, indeed.

What rivals they would have been!

Annie felt a degree of relief when the Waddells returned to Edinburgh, It was as if a whirlwind had passd through their lives, but she had survived it. She wondered if perhaps Helen felt the same. Her duties no longer need be skimped or accomplished at high speed and she seemed content to take her daily swim alone, or immerse herself in a book as often as possible. Then there was the interminable jumping off the wall that had over-powered Ruth last year. Annie hoped all that jumping was not harmful for her daughter's young bones.

◊

Bruce drove them back to Glasgow via Kingskettle to visit the Forgies. They had no map and the little town was not easy to find. No one seemed to think it worthwhile to signpost such a small village.

It was only a short visit and Clare sat chatting in the car with Annie, while Bruce went for a walk and Helen helped Jean look after the shop. Not many customers came for Helen to serve, but she stacked some tins on a shelf and weighed out quarter pounds of sweets. It was not as much fun as she had thought it might be.

Autumn 1946

T he leaves were thick on the ground when Helen came in from shopping one day. "Oh, Mummy, I saw such a *terribly* handsome young man in the close just now! He was *gorgeous*. He was so tall and oh I don't know ..." words failed her.

Annie was amused at her daughter's unusually extravagant reaction.

"Was he visiting or delivering something, d'ye think?"

"Oh no, he wasn't a deliveryman, he had a nice coat and hat on and he was *so handsome!* And he held the door open for me politely, but he was awful grown up."

The last phrase was said sadly.

"In his twenties d'ye think?"

Helen nodded sadly.

"A bit of a Methuselah then, but you're growing up all the time, too."

"Not fast enough." She sighed deeply. " I wonder if I'll ever see him again."

Two days later, on Helen's return from school, Annie announced triumphantly,

"I've found out all about your handsome stranger."

The girl's face lit up as Annie continued.

"He's a medical student from London. He's here for two years and he's staying with Mrs Beaton who lives above Mrs Unsworth. I think he's a friend of the family. He's a very nice boy who studies hard and hardly ever goes out. He's twenty one, his name is John Hennington and *he doesn't have a girlfriend.*"

"Fancy him staying just upstairs! And how did you find all that out ?"

"Aha, your old mother might be stuck in a wheel chair, but she has her methods!"

"But really, how *did* you find out?"

"Just asked Agnes to invite Mrs Unsworth in for a coffee. Who needs a detective, when you've got Mrs Unsworth next door?"

Annie felt content as she watched her daughter sit dreaming happily by the fire.Those feelings of worry and jealousy that

Annie had experienced in Pittenweem, seemed to have faded. Of course, jealousy was easier to squash when the rival was only a dream, There was no danger of romance, though obviously Helen was smitten with his good looks. The medical student was hardly likely to pay much attention to a fourteen-year old.

Annie could not remember if she herself, at fourteen, had ever dreamed romantic dreams about the opposite sex. No doubt growing up with a brother produced a less idealistic view of the male. But Annie was a romantic and hoped that Helen's high expectations might one day be fulfilled.

She knew she must be prepared to spend more time alone and learn to deal with it as her daughter went out into the world. She would keep busy, preferably doing something that made money. She wished she could think what that might be. The Waddell family had certainly been an entertainment for her, as well as for Helen. And she had sold the painting!

◊

"Has Helen spoken to him yet?" Agnes was also a romantic and keen to know the latest developments.

"No, she's met him in the close two or three times, but she's too shy to smile."

"Och, the wee soul!"

"I saw him myself yesterday, from the window."

"And was he handsome?"

"Oh very. Very tall and elegant."

"He sounds like a real heart-throb! D'ye think she's forgotten about that boy in Pittenweem?"

"I'm afraid poor Jack's got the dooral ding." They laughed.

"I think she should just smile to him the next time they bump into each other in the close. That was how I met John at the F&F ballroom. I just smiled to him as he walked by me. Then he asked me for a dance and that was it, we never danced with anyone else that night and we were married two months later. She should just smile to him one day."

Helen was thinking the same thing and gathering her courage to do it. On Saturday morning she informed Annie,

"I'm going to smile today."

"Are you? That's good."

"Yes, he always goes out about half past nine on a Saturday and I'm going to put my coat on and open the front door a wee bit and listen for Mrs Beaton's door shutting. I'll give him five seconds to come down the stairs and then I'll just walk out when he reaches the foot and *then I'll smile to him*. I might say 'hullo'. No, I'll just smile. I hope. I feel all trembly. I don't know if I can do it."

"Och, of course you can!"

But she couldn't. Yet again they looked at each other and passed on. The swing doors at the front of the close were hooked back, so he did not even have to hold the door open for her.

"You should have thought of that and unhooked the doors earlier!" Annie smiled, but she saw Helen was not in the mood for jokes.

The next night Annie said,

"I've got an idea. Why don't you go upstairs and ask Mrs Beaton if she's got a postage stamp she could let you have, as you've a letter that must go tomorrow and no stamp."

Helen considered this.

"But I don't have a letter to post."

"Well you could always write one, couldn't you. It needn't be a long one. You haven't written to Jean for ages. Or you could write to Jack Waddell, maybe."

This was greeted with a snort of derision.

"I could write to Jean. But would I really need to have a letter?"

"Yes, I think you have to have a real letter in your hand. And Jean would love to get a letter, poor girl."

"Would it not seem funny wanting a stamp on a Sunday night?"

"Where else would you get a stamp on a Sunday night?"

Helen wrote the letter and with much trepidation, climbed the stairs to the first floor flat and rang the bell. Like their own, it was a pull bell and her first attempt was too gentle. Nothing happened. Her next harder tug produced an embarrassing amount of noise as the bell tinkled endlessly on its wire. She thought it would never stop.

John came to the door and greeted her with a very friendly smile!

When she had explained her errand, he went off to find Mrs Beaton who brought her daughter. They seemed terribly pleased to see her, though they did not ask her in. They knew all about her and asked how she was enjoying school and how her mother was keeping. Then John came back and stayed with Helen while the two ladies searched for a stamp. A few stilted sentences were exchanged, but the silences were friendly and he smiled a lot. It was so much more than she could have dreamed of and she floated downstairs in ecstasy. Now they could smile to each other whenever they met. And they could meet any time that Helen chose to wait at her front door and pounce!

Who knew what might happen in the future?

What a brilliant mother she had.

An Old Friend

"I had a phone call from an old friend today. He wants to come and visit you." Mary poked the fire as she spoke. She had a sort of genius for adding unspoken disapproval to any action. It was obvious from her vigorous attack on the large lump of coal, that she was unimpressed by its quality.

Annie watched with that slight offence that belongs to the houseowner whose visitor has taken upon themselves to poke the fire.

"I'm intrigued, Maw. Who can it be?"

"D'ye still get your coal from Sprott?"

"Yes. Of course."

Coal deliveries were still scarce and irregular and, as with grocers and butchers, one must register with one particular merchant.

Mary grunted.

"So who is it that wants to visit me?"

"Can you guess? See if you can guess."

"I'm sure I can't. Just tell me."

"Well, it"s Andrew Gamley! He phoned me yesterday. He hasn't been too well, you know. Mentally I think. Melancholia. He's never recovered from his wife's death. They just lived for each other, those two."

"That would be very nice to see him again, though I'm not sure that seeing me in a wheelchair would cheer him up much. I always loved his watercolours. I thought they were marvellous."

Mary's foot started to tap and she was silent for a few minutes, never caring to hear of the merit of any artist, other than her own husband.

"So when is he coming? D'ye want to bring him for a meal? Some nice food might do him good!"

"No, no it would just be a flying visit. You know that last year the Queen chose one of his pictures for her calendar. Did you know that?"

"*Did she*? That was quite an honour! Fancy that! You'd think that would have helped him, given him a boost, you know. It should certainly make a big difference to his career."

"Well he's an old man now, of course. Nearly as old as your father. Late seventies, anyway. Evidently, the Royal approval came too late, for Chatty had died by then and she was the only one he cared about."

"Who's Chatty? That's a funny name." Helen had come in with a pot of tea.

"I was just telling your mother about this old artist friend. His wife's name was Chatty and she *was* a bit of a chatterbox, very sweet but not the brightest... anyway, they seemed to adore each other...just lived for each other... he's coming to see your mother on Saturday."

Annie broke in,

"The Gamleys used to come to Pittenweem every summer. Watercolours were his thing and *very* nice too. Delicate and lovely. That's one of his on the wall there."

"Of course he never sold much, Annie, did he. Never made much of it at all, poor soul, for all his supposed talent." Mary shook her head and glanced coldly at Annie,"They seemed to be happy enough, but they were always *terribly* hard up. Every half-crown, every shilling counted."

"Tell Helen what they did when he sold a painting."

Mary smiled,

"Well, in those days, paintings were usually paid for in guineas and Andrew would give all the notes to Chatty, though I don't suppose there were many of them. Anyway she got the notes for the housekeeping. Then he would take the silver, the half-crowns and florins, probably shillings too and go into the studio, where all the canvases and frames were stacked against the wall, and then he would *throw the handful of silver into the air,"*

Mary demonstrated with a dramatic gesture.

"And let it land where it would! Then when the hard times came along and they hadn't a penny left, they would search behind paintings and under furniture, all over the studio, He said it was such fun to find a shilling! They were always a bit mad, the two of them."

Helen laughed delightedly, while Mary smiled at the knowledge that her own husband's successful career had removed any possibility of the Mackays ever scrabbling in corners for small change.

"And now he's sold a painting to the Queen to use for her calendar or Christmas card or something!" Annie added to the story, but Helen thought very little of royalty.

When Mr Gamley arrived on Saturday, Helen thought he looked terribly old. Her own grandfather was still very upright and the brisk walks which he took when fit enough had kept his colour good. This man was grey and bowed and terribly sad.

"Oh, Annie, Annie, I'm truly sorry to see you like this, my dear." The voice was weak and tears brimmed in the old man's eyes.

How could Annie reply? She had known it would be an uneasy meeting.

"Oh well, you know… I could be a lot worse, Mr Gamley. And I get plenty of help from my family and my daughter is marvellous…"

"I believe you suffer pain for much of the time. I am so very sorry. Pain is a terrible affliction to bear. And I remember you as such an active young woman in Pittenweem, too, with your swimming and your tennis. Golf and dancing, as well. And now to be so completely helpless, when you're hardly forty. What a tragedy! A terrible, terrible tragedy. Fate can be so cruel. You must often despair. Do you, Annie? Surely you must despair. Often and often."

"Well not *too* often, I hope." It was all more lugubrious than she could have imagined and Annie's sense of humour was never far from the surface, "And of course I'm not *completely* helpless, I can still peel potatoes and suchlike and I'm afraid I'm forty-five now."

But Mr Gamley's sad eyes had turned towards Helen,

"Yes and your devoted young daughter, far too young to be so heavily burdened with care. What a fearful handicap for a little girl of her age."

Helen was about to reply indignantly, but was stopped by a look from her mother.

Annie's heart fell lower than before, How long would this visit last? She tried again,

"I was sorry to hear that you've not been so well yourself recently, Mr Gamley."

"No, no. I've not been myself ever since I lost my dear wife. Life has seemed very empty and pointless and of course these are sad days we're living in. Everything is changing. I'm afraid all the good days are gone for ever."

"But I believe I must congratulate you on selling your painting to the Queen. That is indeed a *great* honour."

"I suppose so, but I expect it was a case of choosing the best of a bad bunch. Let's face it, paintings nowadays, look at them! Daubs, nothing but daubs. I know John will agree with me. Isn't that right, Mrs Mackay? There's a terrible, terrible madness in the art world. Sad, very, very sad. It's all changed now." He sighed deeply and shook his head, then turned to gaze to the fire.

Annie glanced at her mother for help.

"Oh, John would certainly agree with you there, Mr Gamley. He's very upset by these confidence tricksters from France and the way the dealers are bamboozling the public and making a fortune, but I think you would like a cup of tea now, wouldn't you? Helen, my jewel, run and put the kettle on and I think Annie has baked something nice for us, Mr Gamley. Shortbread is it, Annie? Yes, I thought so, it smells delicious. Can you smell it too, Mr Gamley?"

But there was no response. He seemed mesmerised by the flames.

Helen was glad to bound off to the kitchen and leave the uneasy silence which had settled on the sittingroom. Even Mary felt daunted by this poor miserable man and remained silent.

Apart from the small sounds of the fire and the muffled traffic outside, there was only the ticking of the cuckoo clock, which seemed to Annie to accentuate and extend the silence.

Bruce had given Helen the clock last Christmas. He had remembered that, as a child, Helen had loved the cuckoo clock in a St Andrews restaurant, insisting on waiting for the bird's next appearance, and the next, and the next.

Annie thought it kind of Bruce and was impressed that he had remembered, but Helen had lost interest in cuckoo clocks in the intervening years. She thought this clock quite ugly and it kept very bad time. At first, she had tried to improve the latter defect by adding small scraps of putty rubber to the pendulum, using trial and error until the clock was less inaccurate. Her success had given her more affection for the clock, but one night, as they listened to a concert, Annie pointed out that during the quiet passages of music, the loud ticking was an unpleasant distraction. Helen agreed and the cuckoo clock was stopped. Only at weekends, when Bruce was liable to pop in for a short visit, and his visits were very short these days, was the clock started up again, for Annie had said,

"It was very kind of him to remember and he'd be hurt if it wasn't working. My goodness, what a little demon you used to be in the Tudor Café. We couldn't *drag* you away and we missed our bus more than once, because of that damned cuckoo."

"Why did a two-year old not do as it was told?"

"Believe me, you roared the place down and made so much fuss! Sheer embarrassment made us give in!".

Helen found it difficult to believe she had ever been like that.

When Helen brought the tea and shortbread, Mr Gamley seemed to waken from his daze and took his cup and saucer with a bright,

"Thank you, my dear, this is most kind."

He took no sugar, but stirred and stirred his tea interminably.

Mary watched him with a look of irritation and Helen feared she might tut-tut and bid him to 'stop that nonsense', as she most certainly would have ordered her husband to do. Helen passed the shortbread, but Mr Gamley shook his head,

"No thank you, I'm not at all hungry. I've no appetite these days. I'm sure it looks very nice, but I don't want any. Annie, I must apologise for giving you all this trouble and keeping you up. I feel very bad about coming and annoying you like this. I expect you would be resting just now and here I am come to disturb you."

"Oh, I'm quite tough you know. I'm not an invalid and I'm delighted to see you, I don't usually take a rest and I love having visitors."

"Nevertheless, I think we should be getting along soon and not trouble you any more today, don't you agree, Mrs Mackay? And John will be wondering where you are too, I expect."

"No, no, he knows where I am. Let's enjoy our tea first, at any rate."

Helen could see that Mary was on the edge of anger and only clinging to civility with difficulty.

Mr Gamley took a small sip of tea. When he put his cup back in the saucer the china rattled. It seemed very loud in the quiet room. Again he withdrew into his dark inner world and gazed at the flames. He continued taking tiny sips and noisily replacing the cup each time. Helen heard her grandmother inhale deeply through her nose, then utter a muffled tut-tut.

Annie murmured a few trite sentences but Mr Gamley paid no attention. It seemed impossible to fill the silence.

Then Annie noticed that he had become more agitated, looking up at the high mantelpiece and behind him towards the windows, smoothing his hair and fiddling with his collar. Annie motioned for Helen to take his cup from him. Looking startled he gave it up without a word. Then, shifting in his chair, he brought out his handkerchief and unfolded it, then re-folded it, less neatly, glancing over his shoulder several times as he did so.

Annie caught Helen's eye and with a brief frown and a flick of her eyes towards the cuckoo clock, mouthed the words,

"Stop the clock."

Helen caught her meaning and moved quietly to obey.

With the clock silenced, Mr Gamley seemed to relax, and sat back more comfortably in his chair. He smiled to Annie, then let his eye wander slowly round the square room, until he caught sight of his own picture. It was a watercolour of young trees on a breezy Spring day and a favourite of Helen's. He looked at it for a long moment, smiling slightly.

Mary started to tell a story of some mutual acquaintance at the Art Club. As usual, she was articulate and witty and Helen and her mother laughed appreciatively. Probably Mr Gamley heard nothing, but he sat smiling politely, with his eye returning several times to his own painting.

"How long will it take to get back to Charing Cross?" He suddenly asked, just before Mary's story ended.

Next, almost like a young man, he jumped decisively to his feet.

"Perhaps we'd better get going right now, Mrs Mackay! It's been wonderful seeing you, Annie and I hope to see you again, sometime, if we're both spared. And I do hope your condition doesn't worsen in the future. We must hope for the best. Goodbye."

He was out of the front door in a moment and Mary, struggling into her coat, almost ran to catch up with him.

"Do you really think the clock ticking was affecting him. Mummy?"

"Well, he seemed better when we put it off, didn't he? Poor soul. He's a sad fellow. It shows you there's worse things than having legs that don't work. Imagine, he seems to see the black side of everything."

"I'm awful glad you're not a bit like that."

"Am I not ?"

"*Not at all*! You're always finding something to cheer me up, when *I* feel sad."

Annie felt a glow of satisfaction, because of course there were many times when she did feel low. She was glad she could hide it from her daughter.

◊

Annie had at last managed to gather enough money together to have her old musquash coat remodelled. She presented the large parcel to Helen at the beginning of December.

"You might as well have it as soon as possible. I was going to give it to you for Christmas, but I'll get another wee something for you, then. I hope you like your coat and get good wear out of it. It should make you feel grown-up."

Helen smiled delightedly, but her heart dropped. She knew what the large parcel would be and a fur coat was the last thing she wanted. Nobody of her age wore a fur coat. She kept a pleased face, as she opened the parcel. It must have been difficult for her mother to pay for it. It had been styled with the large square shoulders, still so fashionable and so much hated by Helen. It looked horribly like Nancy Little's new beaver lamb coat. Helen slung it on and went off to see herself in the bedroom. It was depressing. First the Harris tweed suit and now this, another outfit that made her look square and had cost a lot. And where and when would she wear it? But she must just hide her feelings. She supposed she would wear it sometime or other, but she hoped she would never meet John Hennington when she had it on.

Golf Lessons

B y early May it was particularly warm, with temperatures in the mid seventies. Mary arrived one evening, in a state of dramatic agitation and slapped a copy of the Glasgow Herald down on the table.

"Have you seen what's in the papers today? About the meat ration?"

"Yes. I heard it on the wireless. They're talking about reducing it from one and fourpence to one and threepence."

"It's *disgraceful!* Who would believe *that we won the war*? I don't know how we've *managed* so long on *so little*. And now we're to get *less*. It's *monstrous*."

"It's only a penny less."

Mary gazed into the fire, her face still and furious, her toe tapping out an angry rhythm.

Helen wondered, as she often did, why her mother had made that remark? It was bound to annoy Mary and seemed like pouring oil on a fire, rather than on troubled waters. Resignedly, she went off to the kitchen to make tea.

After Mary went home, Annie read through the newspaper. Coplands advertised a hand-made, pure silk, lace-trimmed nightgown for seventeen pounds, seventeen shillings and one penny. And Brittany was welcoming tourists back this summer. Were there really many folk around these days with enough money to consider such expensive luxuries? And must those curled darlings subsist on one and fourpence worth of meat each week, just like everyone else? It was a funny old world.

Reading the Glasgow Herald the following week, she looked with disbelief at a prominent headline.

PALESTINE'S FUTURE IN THE BALANCE
FINAL SOLUTION LIES IN PARTITION

What a very unfortunate phrase some ignorant reporter had chosen.

◊

Bruce stood in the middle of the sitting room and gave a preliminary waggle to an imaginary golf club, before he took several practice swings, the vigorous exertions interrupting and affecting the rhythm of his speech.

"My... it's a great game, golf, isn't it, Annie... you used to enjoy it, didn't you? Getting out in the fresh air and ... whackin' that ball, never knowing if ye're goin' to have a good day or ... not. I thought I had it beat last autumn but nup!... Swing's gone all to hell again since January... S'pose that's what makes you keep on trying, isn't it, Annie? Ye just cannae tell how yer game'll go. Some days you send that damn ball flying right, straight down the fairway...other days, ye can hardly hit the bloody thing! Fascinating! I just love it... It's a bugger, but I love it. Such magnificent exercise...out in the fresh air, too. Everyone should be out playing golf...D'ye know these big bugs in the church are trying to stop the Sunday golfers? *Can you credit that?* No golf or cricket on a Sunday, That was in the Herald the other day. I couldn't believe my eyes. But here, is it not time the wee yin learned how to handle a club? I think she'd be good at it, d'ye not think so, Annie? She'd soon get keen, too. I bet she'd love it."

Smiling slightly, nodding or shaking her head in agreement at each rhetorical question, Annie had watched his repeated, manic practice.

"You'd need to ask her yourself, Bruce. Not sure where she'd find the time. Golf takes a lot of time and her life is pretty well filled up. Where would she play? No ladies allowed at Killermont, are there?

"No, no, we've managed to keep the fair sex out, so far. It's always been a man's club and we'll certainly try and keep it that way. No, she couldn't play at Killy, but we'd think of something. Your mother was fond of the game, too. Hilton Park, she played, didn't she? Quite a nice wee course there. Ah, here's Helen now."

Helen had been to her Saturday dance class and, as it was such a beautiful spring day, she had taken the No 3 tram to the terminus and walked home over University Avenue. She had walked quickly and her cheeks were flushed. Her mind was on food.

'We've just been thinking it's time ye learned to play the fine old game of golf, my lass, it's such a *grand* game. Will yer old man take you up to the Glasgow Golf Club tomorrow and get you started? Eh? Would you like that, eh?"

"Golf?" she said blankly,"Tomorrow? I can't go tomorrow, I'm busy all day."

"Oh! Aye! Right. I didn't know ye'd be busy."

Helen had been taken off guard and her downright refusal had disconcerted Bruce in his enthusiasm. Annie felt sorry for both of them and suggested,

"Maybe next Saturday afternoon would be better, Bruce. Helen hasn't had time to think about it, yet. I'm sure she'd like to go though, wouldn't you, Helen?"

Annie's particular steady look conveyed to Helen that the outing was mandatory. She muttered,

"Yes, that would be nice, Daddy."

"Aye, right. You see it would get you out in the fresh air and I'm sure you'd enjoy it. It's a great game. Will we do that then, Tuppenny? And maybe you can wear that smart green suit I bought you? Now I'd better get away down the road or Dick'll think I'm not coming."

When he left, Helen looked sternly at her mother,

'Why would I want to learn golf? When would I have time and where would I go to play? All the courses are far away and I don't know anyone that plays golf. I'd rather swim, any day."

"No, I agree it's not very practical, but just go anyway, it'll please your father. He's awful keen to show you what a marvellous game it is and you only need to go a few times. You never know, you might fall in love with golf, just as grandma did. She hated it to begin with. Thought it would be more fun to hit the ball as *often* as possible, but she became a mad keen player and very good at it. Won lots of silver cups. And you never know who you might meet!"

The last remark was one which Annie, always optimistic, often made.

Helen's protruding lower lip did not hold out much hope for an interesting golf experience.

◊

The first hour of the visit to Killermont took place in the club's dignified entrance hall and consisted of standing around while elderly men talked to Bruce. One after another, they tottered up and he greeted each one with apparent delight. Was he really as pleased to see them as he looked? Helen was infuriated that they all spoke of her in the third person. All made similar comments, though in various ways.

"And is this your wee lassie, Bruce? What a fine tall girl. What age is she now?"

"Bruce! Is this the daughter we've been hearing about? She's quite a young lady, I must say!"

"Now where have you been hiding this young person? Surely this cannae be your daughter? I'd no idea you had such a grown-up daughter, Bruce."

"Well, I'm blowed, this must surely be your wee girl, Bruce. Why have we never met her before? That's fine long hair she's got there."

A very diminutive old fellow peered up at her,

"And what does the young girlie think of our old club? Is she going to be a golfer too? She's tall enough."

One croaked and wheezed as he spoke,

"I *never knew* you had any family, Bruce. She's like you, I think, except for the long fair hair. Can't imagine you with pigtails, Bruce. Ha, ha, ha."

He shuffled off down the long corridor, laughing and wheezing.

Helen kept a polite smile on her face but found the encounters almost insufferable. When would the golf lesson start?

Eventually, they went outside and Bruce showed her how to hold her new club. When she drove off, the ball went straight, but not very far. She did not improve with practice. Her putting was slightly better, but she found golf slow and boring and knew she would never enjoy it. How could golf compare with swimming and the delight of using every muscle to power through the water, or recreate the graceful movements of Esther Williams.

Only twice more did Helen return to Killermont.

Bobby Forster and his fat spaniel, Sandy, accompanied them on the seond visit, the dog plodding at Bobby's heels and sensibly staying well out of range when either man addressed the ball.

Bruce and Bobby were playing a proper game, for Helen had made little progress and her ball never travelled further than fif-teen yards. After driving off at each hole, she picked up her ball and trotted after her father. She was too warm in her tweed suit, she was missing a good BBC concert and it seemed a terrible and depressing waste of time.

Perhaps even Bruce was a little depressed at his daughter's lack of skill. At intervals, he spoke words of encouragement to her and she smiled brightly, but Annie would have recognised that smile as false.

Even Sandy looked depressed, but Helen was human and could dissemble.

At the tenth hole, Bruce said,

"Now, Tuppenny, I want you to remember all the things I've told you and all the tips I've given you. Ready now, a nice steady swing and be sure and *keep your eye on the ball."*

Helen adjusted her grip and tried to remember everything.

"Bravo! Great shot, my lass..."

Helen could not believe it. The ball went soaring down the fairway, perhaps not a wonderful shot, but so much better than any that had preceded it, but... disaster. Poor Sandy had mis-judged her ability and was confidently strolling in the distance when the ball hit him in the ribs. The unfortunate dog took to his heels, attaining a speed unknown to him for many years, and the air was rent by his pain-filled yelps,

Helen was aghast and remorsful. What if she had killed the poor thing?

How badly was Sandy hurt? He was still running, that was hopeful.

Perhaps she had cracked his ribs?

Bearing little love for dogs in general and even less for Sandy in particular, she hated the idea of hurting an animal.

She determined never to golf again.

Sandy returned, apparently unhurt. Bruce even joked about the incident, but Bobby did not smile. Nor did he accompany them on Helen's third and final visit to the elite golf club.

At the first tee, she tried to remember everything but some-how, her swing went really wrong.

Luckily, none of Bruce's fellow members was around to see Helen break her driver at the first hole. Her tears convinced Bruce that it was completely unintentional. He was very understanding and they immediately left the hallowed precincts for a restorative ice cream drink in the nearest Italian café.

Helen would never be a golfer.

◊

"Anyway, Mummy, when did he think I would have *time* to trail away out of Glasgow and walk round for hours, hitting a silly wee ball. I always knew it was daft."

"Well, you gave it a try and you did your best."

"Poor wee dog! And the driver was expensive and I wrecked it! I'll *never* go near a golf course again. And you should have heard those old men going on about my long plaits! I think it's time I put my hair up."

◊

Although Helen did not have a starring role at the Athenaeum this year, she was in four different dances and thoroughly enjoyed the evening.

For the fifth time, she was awarded honours in her ballet examinations and again they mentioned her *beautiful* feet and excellent mime. Perhaps she might have liked some more elegant attribute praised, but Miss Hopkins seemed terribly pleased and proud of her.

Helen was delighted that she had galloped through the early exams and would now work with girls of her own age.

Summer 1947 · First Kiss

In July Eileen and her new little sister Sheila were in Pittenweem with Willie. Helen found Sheila very different from her sister. Where Eileen had been quiet and biddable, Sheila was determined and much more liable to cry and complain. She had a loud voice. Was that what she herself had been like? That was a worrying thought. Perhaps Sheila would improve, she was still a baby.

Helen would have liked to spend more time with Eileen and teach her to swim, but the one-year-old could only play in the sand and must be looked after at all times. Their holidays overlapped by a week and though sorry to say goodbye to her older cousin, Helen was relieved to walk to the station with them and wave as the train disappeared under the little bridge.

Now she could go swimming by herself and stay in the water as long as she liked.

◊

Helen had been at the pool that morning but she had not stayed as long as usual. She burst into the bedroom where Annie was painting and blurted out,

"Oh, Mummy, I've done a terrible thing!"

Annie's heart leaped and her fear showed in her face.

"What is it? What happened? Tell me!"

Intuitively, Helen at once realised that her mother was worried about that strange unknown act between male and female, though Helen was still very hazy about the whole thing. How on earth could her mother make such a mistake? She almost laughed because it was absolutely nothing to do with *that sort of thing*, whatever *that* was. As she knew no boys at all and had not even been kissed, it was a very unlikely occurrence. In a way, her mother's obvious terror made it easier to confess to the stupid thing that she had done.

"I dived into the pool with grandma's watch on. I'd forgotten to take it off!" she explained unnecessarily. Bruce had given her his mother's gold wristlet watch last year and Helen had been wearing it daily while looking after her cousins.

Her mother's expression changed to one of relief immediately and Helen knew that, amazingly, there would be no reproaches about her carelessness.

"Oh well, that's a pity, but it can't be helped. I expect it can be fixed. It's a shame there's no watchmaker in Pittenweem now, but you can take it into Anstruther on Friday, when you go to the library. Don't worry, I'm sure it will be all right."

Helen could not believe how calmly her mother was taking it.

Unfortunately the watch never was all right again. The interval of a few days had been enough to ruin it, though the watchmaker said there might have been a chance of saving it, if it had been immediately immersed in oil, Helen was not particularly regretful, for jewellery was unimportant in her life, but she did feel remorse and hoped her father would never find out.

◊

Two weeks later, Helen made friends with a boy on holiday from Glasgow, who kissed her in a very sweet and innocent way, amongst the long grass on the hillside above the swimming pool.

She was quite happy to discuss it and make a good story of it to entertain her mother. Annie was amused and astonished at the rather business-like way the story was told and at the fact that Helen would consider her mother as a confidante. Annie had never confided in her own mother in this way.

There was not a great deal of romance about the encounter, but Helen said he was a very nice boy and was obviously glad that it had happened.

She had been swimming by herself that morning. The pool was deserted, except for the young fellow who was wandering up and down watching her. She had noticed him before, at the open air dancing, where he had hovered at the edge of the crowd, but never danced. Now he was hovering at the pool and not swimming. Nevertheless he was about sixteen and 'not bad-looking'.

The tide was in and, as usual, Helen dived into the deep water outside the pool and swam in the waves for a while. When she tried to climb back on to the rocks, the waves made it more difficult than usual and she was forced to make two or three attempts. The young man had come over and stretched his hand out to help her. They smiled and said a few words before she walked back to the changing boxes. While she was dressing, she noticed that his enthusiastic strength had caused her to graze her knee on the barnacles. Infuriatingly, it would not stop bleeding.

"Just my luck. The day I meet a possible boyfriend, I get a sore knee like a wee kid." she told Annie at lunchtime. "His name is John Smith."

"Are you sure that's his real name?"

Helen paused, then continued,

"Isn't it funny, every boy I meet seems to be called John, just like Daddy and grandad. Jack Waddell is John, and Campbell has John in his name too. It must be a very popular name. Anyway, this John was waiting for me to get dressed and then he walked me home, but it's the end of his holidays, so there's no future for us. He goes home tomorrrow. Anyway, he's got quite a strong Glasgow accent and he makes mistakes in his grammar. *And* he smokes. He's an apprentice carpenter and I'm meeting him at the pool this afternoon and going for a walk. He doesn't swim! Useless! Maybe we'll walk to Saint Monance."

◊

It was a hot airless day and the pool was crowded. Helen's knee was sore and bleeding again, much to her embarrassment. They did not walk far and could still hear the shouts and laughter from the swimmers, when they decided to sit on the hillside. The weeds smelled strong and rank in the fierce sunshine and Helen tried to ignore their sharpness on the back of her bare legs.

John talked about Blackhill where he lived and Helen spoke of Hyndland. Neither had any idea of where the other's home might be.

"D'ye know where there's two great big gasometers? I live near that."

She shook her head.

"Do you know where the University is? I live near that."

The university meant nothing to John.

"Aw, ye must have read about Blackhill an' the Garngad an' the gangs and the *knives* an' all that."

Helen shook her head, but she remembered what Lindsay Waddell had said about keeping the car windows closed in case of knives. She had believed that was just a little boy's fantasy. Could it really be true? In Glasgow? Knives?

Then John had described a serious accident which had happened to him at work. The ambulance had made a terrible noise, as it rushed him to hospital. That was almost the most frightening bit, he said, though there was 'an awful lot of blood".

With Helen's knee also oozing blood, it was not as romantic a scene as she would have wished. She tried to hide one knee behind the other.

At last, in a pleasantly shy way, John kissed her. He seemed as unpractised as she was. She could not exactly say she enjoyed the kisses. She was sensitive and protective about her broken front tooth. and the strength of John's tight-lipped kisses, which adhered closely to the Hollywood model, made her fearful. The length of the kisses left her breathless, it was rather like staying underwater for those few seconds too long. But it was certainly a great satisfaction to feel that she was no longer an un-kissed girl.

They exchanged addresses the following day, but Helen suspected that a correspondence was unlikely.

The rest of the summer was filled by chores, dancing in the market place, swimming twice a day and without dreams of John Smith or anyone else.

Anna Boyter

In August, Helen made friends with Anna Boyter, who was two years older and worked in the sweet shop in the High Street. Anna's brother Bill had been in Helen's class during the war. Anna was a very good swimmer and Helen would meet her at six o'clock, when she left work and they would swim together. It was pleasant swimming in the evening, the crowds had gone and the water seemed warmer. They had a favourite trick. Starting from a distance of about twenty-five yards apart, they would dive under the surface and swim towards each other through the murky water, hopefully meeting and shaking hands while still submerged. It did not always work, sometimes they missed each other altogether and came up laughing. Once, and this put an end to the practice, a glamorously long nail on Anna's extended hand painfully poked Helen in the eye. Anna was very contrite and insisted on leaving the pool there and then and buying Helen a fish supper. Usually they bought chips after their swim and often went to the cinema.

One night Anna suggested going to the dance in St John's Hall, the small community building in the Marygate. Although Helen enjoyed the open air dancing in the Market Place each week, she was less sure about the more adult indoor dance. However Anna was keen to go and persuaded her.

Helen had often accompanied her grandmother to sales of work in this little hall and also attended concerts. She had recited a poem on that stage during her short career as a Brownie. Now the three-piece band on the tiny platform was enthusiastic and noisy. The place seemed stuffy and intimidating, with milling crowds of people, mainly holiday makers.

Anna was hoping to meet a particular young man there, but as yet there was no sign of him.

The two girls danced together and Helen was beginning to enjoy herself, in spite of the crowds and the terrible heat, when suddenly she slipped and fell right down on her bottom. How humiliating!

Anna hauled her up again quickly and they carried on dancing.

"Oh, I'm so sorry, Anna. That was terrible…what a fathead I am!"

"Och, that disnae matter at a'! Folk are aye fa'in' doon here a' the time..and ye didnae hurt yersel, did ye?"

"No, I'm fine."

"Ach, they'll jist be thinkin' ye've hud a wee drink!"

"Oh no! Anna, surely not."

"Ah'm jist kiddin' ye, ma lass. They wouldnae be thinkin' that at a'. Never you worry aboot it, noo."

As Anna's young man did not put in an appearance and as they had entered without the inconvenience of paying (Anna's cousin being 'on the door') they left early.

There was one unfortunate result of that month of swimming twice a day. With the teenage assurance that she was stronger and tougher than adults seemed to think, Helen neglected to dry her hair. It was a nuisance to take it down and dry it after the morning swim, for it would just get wet again by evening. Nor at bedtime did she bother to dry it. For most of the time, two long thick wet plaits were wrapped around her head. In the morning when she took it down and loosened it to brush it, her hair would still be really damp and she would have a momentary qualm. She knew she was perhaps foolish, but time was short with so much to enjoy, as well as the many daily tasks. Confident of her own infallibility, she spent several weeks with her hair almost continuously damp.

◊

Annie painted five flower pieces that summer and sold three to friends in Pittenweem. Two of the pictures included Dresden china figures, which Mary had picked up at bazaars for a shilling or two. The figures were rather fine though slightly chipped, but Annie could rectify these flaws in her paintings. Mary now felt completely justified in constantly search for suitable antique figurines for Annie to paint.

To receive money for a picture and know that it would hang on a wall gave Annie a wonderful sense of achievement. She laughed at herself, for the ten or fifteen pounds she received were small sums, but nevertheless, it was satisfying. She felt painting was good for her, too. She felt less pain when painting, or perhaps she just did not notice it.

When Bruce came to collect them, Mary brought a large bunch of flowers from the garden to take home.

"You can paint another flower picture when you get home and I'll look out for any china figures. The buyers seem to like them."

Helen frowned to herself in the back seat. She preferred her mother's pictures without fancy china in them. Flowers and fruit seemed perfectly lovely to her, without any cupids or old fashioned gentlemen in breeches.

Bruce and Annie sat in front, talking about the newly formed National Health Service.

"Well, it's bound to be a good thing, Bruce, surely. There are four hundred hospitals taken over in Scotland and they're waging a battle against TB."

"Aye, maybe. We'll see. There's other things beside medicine an' hospitals, though. They'll need to get folk out of the terrible hovels they've been living in."

"I suppose you've seen a lot more of that than I have. We'll hope for the best."

In the back seat, Helen, uninterested in the conversation, withdrew into her own world, delighting in the strong fragrance of the flowers in the small car.

Dinners, Dances and Dirndls

Helen paid the penalty of ignoring her wet hair and was plagued with recurring sinusitis for the first few weeks of term. Several times, she seemed recovered, then the intense pain across her cheeks and brow would again flare up. Because of her irregular attendance, she missed several important new points in mathematics, points which she would never completely grasp.

Miss Crichton sent her a very sweet sympathetic letter which delighted her.

◊

By the end of October, Helen was fully recovered.

"I was thinking we should give a wee dinner party for grandma and grandad's wedding anniversary and we could have Mr and Mrs Horsland. Maybe their son, Campbell would come, too. D'ye think we could manage that between us?"

Helen thought it a very good idea.

Mary was delighted and the three Horslands also seemed pleased to accept the invitation.

It was an occasion for some of Annie's seldom used wedding presents and Helen enjoyed examinng them. She particularly liked a large silver plated tray which held six small square dishes.

"That's for serving hors d'oevres." Annie told her. "We could have that to start the meal if you like. I believe the Poly has a good delicatessen counter."

As they worked in the kitchen, carefully washing crystal glasses and bowls and polishing silver, Annie and Helen planned the meal, then indulged in their favourite amusement of imagining how things might go wrong. Their fantasies reached such nonsensical heights and hilarity that it became unsafe for the delicate job in hand.

On Saturday, the day of the party, Agnes came in specially to wash Annie's hair and give the house an extra polish.

Helen went into town to buy black olives, olives stuffed with pimento, small pickled onions, tiny sweet gherkins and anchovies, each one wrapped tightly round a caper in a perfect circle. It was the most exciting food shopping she had ever done.

Everything went smoothly and to plan. Annie's ruff puff pastry was always perfect and the steak pie was golden in the oven. The heavy crystal bowl held a trifle. The wheeled trolley on which the wireless usually sat, was requisitioned and held a bottle each of wine, sherry, fruit juice, also a jug of water and glasses.

Helen was enchanted.

How beautiful the table looked with sparkling crystal and silver on the white damask cloth. She particularly admired the carefully laid out hors d'oevres. They added that final touch of mysterious sophistication which seemed the norm for those London socialites whose photographs appeared in Tatler.

◊

Campbell politely helped Helen to clear the first course. Hardly a word was spoken between them. She was unhappy about allowing him to see their shabby kitchen, for no doubt the Kelvin Court kitchen would be modern and perfect.

Annie smiled to her father at the other end of the table. It was so nice to have John Mackay with them. Apart from an evening at the Art Club, he seldom went out much in the winter. How good to see him talking and laughing with Archie Horsland. Of course they were very old friends. She wondered how Helen was dealing with the potatoes and the pie in the kitchen. Perhaps she should go through and give a hand? With this resolution, Annie released her brakes and pushed herself strongly backwards, unhappily colliding with the drinks trolley as she did so. The trolley over-balanced and wine, juice, glasses and water cascaded to the floor.

It was worse than their worst imaginings.

There were fewer breakages than there might have been, nevertheless, it was a mess.

Campbell insisted on taking complete charge and was swift and competent. Though Annie felt an idiot, everyone made light of it and the meal proceeded almost without a break.

Later Annie and Helen would laugh about it.

"But another time, perhaps we shouldn't go thinking up those horrible possibilities!"

Annie sounded rueful, but Helen said,

"Och, I think it made the party more interesting and Campbell and I got on better afterwards. We weren't so shy after dealing with such a catastrophe."

◊

The girls in her class were talking of going to lessons in ballroom dancing.

"Would you like to go too, darling? You should. Ballroom dancing is part of your education."

"But I'm going to dancing already."

"Yes, but not social dancing. Miss Hopkins doesn't have many boys at her classes, does she?"

"None that I've ever seen. Could we afford it?'

"I'm sure your father would be pleased to pay for them. He and I both went to Roger McEwan's when we were growing up."

"That's the same place they're talking about at school! And there is Alice McEwan as well.

"Is that right, by jove? Nothing changes! The dances might have changed a bit. You'll still do foxtrots and waltzes, I expect."

"We do the waltz at ballet, but we do it in fifth position and it's really difficult. I had to be Miss Hopkins' partner last week and I had to be the man because I'm tall, though she's taller still. But I got a shock when I put my hand behind her back to support her. Her whole back was like *metal*! It was like holding a motor car in my arms."

"Surely not!" Annie laughed.

"It was! And she said, 'Hold me firmly, dear.' But it felt very strange."

"I suppose she must wear a steel corset. No wonder she can keep that upright posture from morning 'til night. Can't be comfy though, poor soul. I wonder what age she is now? She must be at least ten or twelve years older than I am."

There was no knowing what physical discomfort other people suffered in silence.

"What other dances did you do when you were young, Mummy?"

"Well we did the Charleston a lot, you've seen that in films haven't you? And we did the Black Bottom."

"*The Black Bottom*! You told me about that dance before, but I didn't believe you."

"I wish I could show you but.. .stand up and I'll tell you what to do...now put one foot forward and bend your knees in a little bob. No, don't stay down, bend, then come right up again and stick your hip out. Right, now the other foot forward and bob again. Dum *darum* de dum *darum* de dumdum *darum* de dum dum... that's the way, good. Black *bottom*, the black *bottom*, pa *pum* pum pum....Excellent, you've got it now."

Annie had been moving her shoulders in rhythm, as she sang and Helen was touched by this carefree echo of a younger, crazier woman, though the dance seemed very repetitive.

"Did you keep doing that all the time?"

"Can't quite remember now. I expect so. It was fun."

Helen would not find the ballroom classes fun.

Only two boys turned up for the first lesson, and their attendance would always be erratic. As there were ten girls, some must always take the boy's part and as Helen was taller than most, the teacher usually expected her to lead. She felt that unfair. How she would ever manage at a real dance with a real masculine partner? Once, when she insisted on taking the girl's part, her smaller partner had no idea of the steps and it was a disaster. Compared to ballet, the steps were simple, but Helen found no pleasure in them and she disliked the bland Victor Sylvester records. A glass of over-diluted Kia Ora juice and stale biscuits were served at the break, which was probably the highlight of the class.

The November nights were dark, wet and miserable. After a long day at school, it was tempting to jump on a tram and go home, rather than walk along Sauchiehall Street in the rain and climb that narrow, steep, uninviting stairway to the bare, chilly studio. Helen cut the class three times, feeling guilty at the waste of fees, but unable to face the boring hour and a half.

Of course, there was a reason for continuing. The class was organising a Christmas dance, with boys from the Boys High invited. It would take place in the same unexciting studio but there would be a three-piece band playing. Perhaps that would improve things.

Surely a real dance, with boys and a band and pretty dresses would be entirely different. More like those 'hops' in the Andy Hardy films, where Mickey Rooney jived like a mad thing and fell in love with many different girls.

Helen decided against the green scalloped dress that Annie had made. C&A had very nice party dresses for 35/6 and she chose one in a deep pink, patterned fabric and removed the shoulder pads.

◊

Strangely enough, Helen's health had improved as the days got darker and colder. By November, she no longer suffered the miserable aching across her cheeks and over her brows that had played havoc with her attendance.

Until her last science exam, the result of which had been disappointing, she had hoped that she might choose science as her main subject, though the family seemed always to have taken it for granted that she would choose art. As it was not possible to study both subjects, for each required many periods in the week, Helen had chosen to specialise in art.

Miss Meldrum, the art teacher was a sad, uninspiring old lady. Helen felt no affection for her and wondered why she had never been taught by the other teachers in the department, Miss Liston and Miss Dobson. They both seemed to give much more exciting lessons. They were younger and their colourful and unusual clothing showed they were artistic. Tessa had enjoyed their classes very much and had produced various craft work.

However, Miss Meldrum made sure that she kept those girls who were studying for Highers in her own ineffectual grasp.

If Helen wanted to attend Art School she must gain a pass in art in her Higher Leaving Certificate. Thus she must continue in Miss M's classes, uninspiring and uninformative as they had been for the previous three years. Luckily, the four other girls studying art, Margaret, Sheila, Pat and Jan, were good fun and the five of them could grumble together about their unhappy lot.

◊

Helen's ballet classes were becoming wonderful. Helen now had real blocked shoes and could hover en pointe in the magical way that had always been her goal. The exercises were now complex and interesting with the various arabesques, ports de bras, jetés, entrechats and the many different pirouettes. She loved the names almost as much as the movements. Dance was another world for her. It was interesting that her sinus trouble had not caused her to miss nearly as many dance classes as it might have done, for she often felt much better on a Wednesday and a Saturday.

Although she had been at home she had not been idle. She had been enjoying using the sewing machine and had made herself a skirt of fine brown wool. It was very simple, just a straight piece of cloth gathered to a waistband and was called a dirndl skirt. She had seen a picture of one in Woman, the magazine that Annie had bought since it was first published in the thirties. When Pat, who was also taking Higher art, had seen the skirt, she asked if Helen could make her one. Pat, who was a tiny slender-waisted girl, chose a deep rich red and looked stunning in it. Helen, whose spare figure had practically no waist, thought it suited Pat better than it suited her own shape, but it was good to wear brown rather than the never-ending navy blue of school uniform. She vowed she would never wear navy again, once she left school. When Tessa saw the skirts, she too wanted one. Helen found a beautiful deep blue wool and buying a larger amount, made another. Tessa was pleased with it, but Helen's fears that it was the wrong shape for her broad-beamed friend were realised, and she made no more dirndl skirts.

More Fog

T he days were short and that evening was slightly foggy. "I wonder if it will get thicker later on? And I wonder if grandma will risk coming over to see us?"

Helen listened with a face devoid of expression. She liked fog for several reasons and one of them was that Mary might not venture out. It was not that she truly disliked her grandmother, she accepted Mary as one of life's unavoidable duties, like making tea and buttering bread for other people or ironing your shirt or brushing your teeth. Sometimes Mary was very generous and kind. At others she was awfully difficult. It was boring when she spoke a lot, often repeating herself. *Always* she was critical. Helen wondered why her own mother worried about Mary so much. Annie was often concerned with how she might help or please her mother, constantly thinking of small acts or presents to please her. Sadly these tokens of love seldom succeeded completely. Mary could find fault with most things, even presents and never hesitated to express her thoughts. That idea of not hurting people's feelings that Annie had impressed so firmly into Helen's personality had obviously not been part of Mary's upbringing.

Helen also welcomed fog for the strangeness that it cast over everyday objects. That quality of magic, when the sound of passing trams was muffled and only the blur of their lighted windows floated up the hill, appealed to her. She specially enjoyed fog when it shrouded the familiar tram route to school in mystery. Although Helen was sorry for the driver, she enjoyed the sensation of travelling through the unknown. Near the Kelvin Hall and the Art Galleries, the swirling yellow mist became denser, because of the river. Then those two enormous buildings, plus the view down the river to the flour mills, as well as the Western Infirmary, the University, even the bowling greens and tennis courts, were completely obliterated. She could almost believe they no longer existed! For the next few stops, it was impossible to decide exactly where you were, because of the impenetrable atmosphere. The many divergent trams and buses that whirled round Charing Cross, made the air clearer at that busy junction. Nevertheless, it looked unfamiliar. With regret, Helen could always recognise the stop to alight for school. Perhaps one day the fog would be so bad that she would go past her stop and travel onwards through the city centre, on and on to the unknown South Side, completely lost until she reached the terminus in Clarkston.

Last year, after she had recovered from illness, she had been moping about the house, still weak and not quite fit for school, but restless.

"What d'ye want to do? Go back to bed?"

"NO. I've had enough bed."

'What about a nice wee walk around Kingsborough Gardens and home again, not too far."

"No, I feel so funny when I'm walking, as though I'm not even touching the ground."

"Well, how about just getting on the tram out there and asking for a ticket to the terminus. You could sit there and just look at the view. Then at the terminus you might get off and have a very short walk around, then just get on the tram again and come home."

"Are you sure it would come back to Hyndland?"

"Oh yes, the number twenty four trundles backwards and forwards all day, Clarkston via Cathcart the one way and Anniesland via Hyndland the other."

"It seems a kind of strange thing to do. Would the conductor not think it a bit funny, if I just stayed on and came all the way back again?"

"But if you get off and walk around for ten minutes, it would be the next tram you would get back. The conductor would never know and he wouldn't care anyway, even if he did notice."

"Right, I think I'll do that."

Helen had enjoyed her round trip. It took her out of the house and gave her some interest, without making demands on her energy. The other side of town seemed very different and the small adventure helped her regain the confidence needed to return to school.

◊

Mary arrived that night in spite of the fog.

"Och I really need to get out of the house on a Wednesday. Your father's coughing non-stop with the fog of course, and he'll be listening for an hour to that damned concert on the wireless tonight. Making himself miserable, I keep telling him."

Mary did not share her husband's interest in classical music.

Helen brought tea, then retired to the kitchen to practise her pirouettes. These were difficult and the old linoleum was a hazard, but she was improving.

Mary lit a cigarette and adjusted her ivory beads and silk scarf.

"I never seem to see Bruce these days. He must be extra busy."

She paused for a reply to her subtle questioning.

"I suppose ... maybe he's not here so much these days. I don't know. P'raps you've just always missed each other? Or p'raps he's found a ladyfriend?"

Mary grunted, signifying disbelief.

"And no word of putting in a telephone for you yet, I suppose."

"No."

"I don't expect he ever will. You don't make enough fuss. I would *insist*."

Annie knitted silently.

"That looks like excellent coal you've been given this time, anyway. It's fairly burning. Won't last 'til bedtime at that rate. Have you changed your coalman?"

"No, still Sprott. Not so easy to change and I expect there's always good and bad coal whoever you get it from."

"I daresay." This was a favourite phrase of Mary's.

"Anything exciting happening at the whist drive these days?"

The twice weekly whist drive was held in the Conservative Club premises in Royal Crescent.

"Nothing much. You know that old man that was the secretary for a while. I didn't like him. He had a right sour expression and his shirt collar was always filthy and I never trusted him. Now they've discovered he's been dipping into the funds."

"Are the police involved?"

"I don't think so. It wasn't much that he took and now he's been chucked out, of course. We'll not likely hear any more about it. It would have been bad if it got into the papers. Those damned Socialists are always trying to pin the blame on Conservatives for something or other. And they're even worse themselves, I expect."

"Maybe Communism is the answer?"

"Huh! You don't really believe that, do you?"

"Who can tell? I don't know much about it, but it seems a fair way of doing. But I don't suppose it can work. Stalin seems a funny bugger, too. But I think he was given a very raw deal during the war. The poor Russians were left to get on with it, without any Allied support and there was terrible famine and fearful casualties. There were dreadful newsreels, I remember. And I saw a picture of Stalin at the Yalta conference and he looked as though he would like to murder Churchill."

"Oh, most people think Churchill's a wonderful man. He really helped us win the war."

"He's certainly had an amazingly long history."

"Anyway Russsia's been suffering terrible famines as long as I can remember."

World events were then laid aside and they spoke of the few interesting household goods which were once more filtering into the shops.

◊

After Mary left, and Helen had put her mother to bed and fallen asleep herself, Annie lay thinking about Bruce and how true it was that they saw less of him these days. He stayed for shorter periods and seemed to see less of the Fosters. At least he hardly mentioned them. Annie thought this a good thing, for Bobby had encouraged Bruce to drink far more than he ever had previously. She considered Bobby an alcoholic or well on the way to becoming one.

Mrs Corning's death had hit Bruce very hard. For the first year her name came into every conversation. It was evident that Bruce terribly regretted not being with her at the end.

There was self-pity as well as regret and his descriptions of the three men alone in Doune Terrace and their rough and ready domestic arrangements sounded very sad to Annie. Betty still came to clean and make soup three times a week.

"But oh, Annie, it's not like my mother's soup, oh no. Hardly any flavour at all. Then after the soup we usually just make ourselves ham and eggs or macaroni cheese. Willie does it usually. He can cook those quite well, but you soon get bloody tired of the same old thing. On Saturday, I often nip out for a fish supper in Berkeley Street and get one of their specials, you know with breadcrumbs rather than batter and they give you plenty bread and butter. Or marge, I expect. I don't mind. It's tasty and it fills the gap. But it's not the way it used to be with mother looking after us. Oh no, not at all."

He had looked so sad that night that Annie said,

"Would you like to come round here for a meal with Helen and me some Saturday evening? We could make something a bit tastier than macaroni for you. A nice mixed grill, maybe."

As she spoke, she could picture Helen's expression at such a suggestion, but Bruce looked so thin, she felt sorry for him, though he seemed as energetic as usual, crossing and re-crossing his legs, kicking her chair and hardly ever sitting still for three minutes together. He was like an awkward adolescent.

"No, no, Annie. I wouldn't dream of putting the two of you to such trouble. No, I enjoy my fish supper and I can always get a snack up at Killie too. I think the Glasgow Golf Club must be in cahoots with the city butchers for they always do a nice steak lunch on a Sunday. Not sure if it's whale or horse," He laughed uproariously, "But it's tasty and there's potatoes and onions and I do fine. Yes, I do just fine. It's not the way it used to be at home, of course. Not that mother often cooked steak, but she was a *wonderful* home-maker, you know. Such a superb cook and everything about the house always so splendidly, spotlessly clean. And she did it all on a shoestring! Father always said she never asked for an extra penny! Aye, there's not many like her nowadays. And I'll tell you, the house isn't as clean now. Dust *everywhere*. You never liked Betty, did you, and I see now what you meant. You were quite right. There's stuff gone missing from the house, I'm sure about that. And she's always looking for money. Needing extra for this and that. Ach well, if you'll excuse me, I'll get along now. There's a fellow I'm meeting in Tennants round about now."

He stood and shrugged himself into his coat.

"You should get rid of Betty."

"Aye, I suppose I should, but you know, mother was so fond of her that somehow I just can't do it. It would seem disloyal to mother's memory."

"That's daft."

"Aye, I suppose it is. Right now, I'm off and I'll see you next week sometime."

◊

Annie lay thinking about that conversation of nearly a year ago. Bruce was much more cheerful these days. His mother was hardly ever mentioned nor his father or brother. The self-pity seemed to have disappeared. He was not as skeletally thin either, although Bruce would never be anything but lean. Annie had not realised it, but he certainly was coming less and less to the house, although he was very friendly when he did come. It was months since he had come on a Saturday afternoon and talked through Helen's concert. Helen had commented gleefully about that, several times.

Could it possibly be, as Annie had jokingly suggested to her mother, that Bruce had found a ladyfriend to comfort him?

It was not impossible. He was a personable and vital man in his mid-forties.

And how did she feel about it?

Not exactly ecstatic, of course. No wife would be happy to think of her husband with another woman.

Annie sighed. Her feelings for him were very mixed.

Did she care about him any more? Probably not. And as she was no longer a wife in any way, it would be very dog-in-the-mangerish to begrudge Bruce a normal life.

She should try and do the decent thing.

If he could find someone willing to share a sexual and domestic relationship with him, surely she should be glad and wish them luck. She wondered what sort of woman would put up with Bruce and his unpredictable ways.

And how would he find the money for a girlfriend? Wooing required investment and he often spoke of being 'short of cash' but Annie believed that was a defence to protect himself from any extra requirements that she might ask for. Apart from Helen's dance fees, she tried to be as independent as possible. Independence was her dream.

Perhaps Bruce's new ladyfriend would affect Helen financially?

That was a worry, for the two of them lived very sparingly as it was.

Then Annie smiled to herself. What an idiot she was to worry like this. It was all sheer speculation. She had absolutely no proof that there was such a person in Bruce's life. What was she getting herself worked up about? Fathead that she was! She must stop this nonsense.

Annie fell asleep, smiling at her own ridiculous imaginings.

Disastrous Dance

Only a few were in McEwan's studio when Helen arrived and the place was not much more welcoming in the evening than it was in the afternoon. Helen had expected that it would be somehow more festive for a dance. In Andy Hardy films. the school halls were lavishly decorated.

And it was cold. Helen shivered in her light short-sleeved dress.

A three piece band played, without much enthusiasm, on a small platform. At least that made a change from a Victor Sylvester record, though the less dependable beat might make dancing difficult.

In the cloakroom she met Jan, who was in a very bad mood. She had invited Harry as her partner for tonight and he had chivalrously called for her and brought her there in the tram car.

"Did he bring you flowers, Jan? They always do in films."

"Humph" or a sound as much like that as a pretty girl in a party frock can make.

"In the tram, *do you know what he did?* I still can't believe it! I was so embarrassed. He bought a full fare for himself and a *half fare* for me!"

Helen tried not to smile. Poor Jan, and also poor Tessa, for if Harry were here with Jan, all Tessa's hopes and dreams for the evening were demolished.

Helen had a very bad feeling about the whole thing as she sat beside a subdued and silent Tessa. There had been three dances so far and no one had yet asked either of them on to the floor. The faltering couples passed and re-passed. Helen thought it obvious that they had all just newly learned those simple steps. She had watched ballroom dancing in many a film and knew it could be flowing, graceful and exciting. Possibly that sort of accomplishment lay in the future of these young people, possibly not. For just now...oh dear, Helen could not pick out one person who was really dancing. Of course it must be difficult to perform well if you had a dud partner.

Neither she nor Tessa had had any partner so far! The fact that everyone was so bad at dancing was cold comfort.

They sat there until the 'interlude' when sandwiches and cream biscuits were served, with the usual weak Kia Ora.

They sat in the same seats until the last waltz.

Nobody had asked either of them to dance all night.

What a disaster.

They travelled home in the tram, giggling ruefully. Helen told of Jan's fury at Harry's meanness and though Tessa smiled, she obviously thought it a minor fault in her hero.

"I don't know what I'll say to Margaret about not dancing for the whole evening." Tessa called her mother by her first name, which seemed an affectation to the other girls. "I think I'll say I danced a few dances. What about you?"

"Oh, I'll tell Mummy the truth. We'll have a good laugh about it. Honestly, we're surely not such unattractive beasts that no one wants to come near us? I don't think so. It doesn't really worry me. I think they were stupid not to pick nice girls like us, probably better dancers than most, because we've studied ballet. Anyway, they were all such *rotten* danccrs."

"All the same, I don't think I'll tell Margaret."

◊

When the tale was told, Annie was astonished, disappointed for her daughter's sake and worried that Helen would be deeply depressed by such a failure.

She was much more upset than Helen was.

◊

Just after Christmas, the Horslands invited Helen to the ballet. It was in the Theatre Royal and they sat in the stalls. It seemed very grown-up and sophisticated to Helen, reminding her of those London socialites in the Tatler.

"Let the young ones sit together, Archie!" Mrs Horsland directed her husband, but Helen and Campbell had little to say to each other.

Helen listened in rapture to the exquisite music as she watched the dancers float across the stage. She was entranced, although once or twice, she found herself thinking that the movements did not match the music just as well as they should. She had studied Arnold Haskell's book for years now, but perhaps she was too ignorant to understand all the traditions. She particularly loved the perfectly repeated movements of the chorus. They were such wonderful dancers, yet only chorus girls.

When the four little swans entered with their staccato steps, clasped hands and wagging heads, Campbell chuckled as though it were funny!

Helen drew further away from him and her lips tightened.

"What a Philistine!" she thought.

More Entertaining

Was it the disaster of the school dance or was it the monster tin of tomato juice that generated the idea of a party? Who can tell?

Whether it was necessary or not, Annie had racked her brains for some way of restoring Helen's self-esteem. Not that Helen seemed unduly depressed. She had only spoken of that night once, when she had suddenly exclaimed,

"If John Hennington had been there, I bet he'd have danced with me."

Annie concluded that Helen had not been scarred for life, for she continued to attend the ballroom classes, though glumly. Presumably she meant to try again, next time.

Helen was not so sure.

At McEwan's, they were now attempting to learn the tango and the Sylvestor record of 'Jealousy'was played repeatedly, sounding sadder each time. It reminded Helen of her little cousin Eileen lisping the song when she was only three. How unfair it had seemed to smile at her serious performance. Would Eileen's little sister also be cajoled into unsuitable performances, just to keep grown-ups amused?

Helen and her fellow pupils found the tango difficult. It did not have the simple rhythm of a quickstep and it was hard to conjure up southern passion and grace at five o'clock on a cold, wet January afternoon. Especially with another girl clasped in your arms.

Besides, after observing the dancing skills of the young men of the High School, Helen suspected that few of them would *ever* tackle a tango. The one time that it was played, the floor had remained empty, as the boys talked loudly and looked in the other direction. With a bitter mental smile she remembered that, as far as she was concerned, they had looked in the other direction *all night*. The Grand Old Duke of York was the only dance into which the boys had instilled much vigour, galumphing up and down far too fast on the slippery floor. When caught in the 'kissing bridge' they would bend their partners

awkwardly backwards and hold up proceedings with uneces-
sarily prolonged kisses, until remonstrating shouts forced them
to stop.

Helen hoped that her first *real* kiss, for those holiday kisses
hardly counted, would be very different from these embarrassing
public displays. That first loving kiss should have sweetness,
romance and *privacy*.

In many ways Helen had been quite relieved not to be asked
to dance. Her too vivid imagination could picture herself slipping
and falling as she had in Pittenweem, tripping her partner up
and the two of them landing on the floor in an undignified
sprawl. And certainly not one boy at the dance could compare
with John Hennington for looks.

In fact, she was really *delighted* that no-one had asked her to
dance.

Yet again the mournful tango record broke into her thoughts.

How could time move so slowly? Helen longed for the tray of
weak juice to appear, for then it would be nearly time to go home.

◊

"D'ye know what I saw in the grocer's today. Milly pointed it
out to me. It was an *enormous* tin of tomato juice. I think there
were five or six pints in it! Who would want all that tomato
juice?"

"I suppose it's for a hotel or something. Did she say what
price it was?"

"Five and six, I think."

"I think you should just go back and get it."

Helen opened her mouth to protest, but Annie stopped her,

"Don't say a word, just go and get it. I have an idea."

Annie's idea was to have a birthday party for Helen with boys
and girls and dancing. Helen's initial reaction was disappointing.

"It'll be great, my pet, and you need to put all those ballroom
dancing skills you've learned into practice. We could shift all the
furniture out the front bedroom and into the back and put that
slippy stuff down...what d'ye call it?"

"Slipperene. It sounds an awful lot of work and the back room
would be crammed bung full."

"Oh I expect Bruce would be glad to help and we could make
some nice food, for them, sausage rolls with those miraculous
tinned sausages and sandwiches and desert. And for drinks

there's all that tomato juice and maybe ginger beer and diluting juice,"

"Not Kia Ora."

"How about lemon barley water with a syphon of soda? That's refreshing and…"

"Who would we ask? What boys, I mean."

"Well I'm sure Campbell Horsland would be delighted to come along."

Helen looked doubtful at that. He was a good bit older. Besides he had lost some of his gilt since that night he had guffawed at the little swans.

"He could bring a friend, I'm sure and there's Elizabeth's two brothers, maybe they could bring someone else too. D'ye you know anyone with a boyfriend to bring? I wonder if Jack Waddell would come through from Edinburgh? But I don't know where he'd sleep."

"I don't expect he dances and we've lost touch with them anyway. How many would we have altogether?"

"Twelve or fourteen would make a nice party. And you could ask John upstairs."

"Oh NO, no, no. He would never come to a party like that. No I couldn't ask him."

Annie knew Helen was unenthusiastic about the project and possibly it was too ambitious an idea. However, she felt she must help Helen find a social life somehow, and she persevered. Bruce agreed to bring a man along from the works to help shift the furniture. Mary offered to make ginger buns and jam tarts and Agnes was thrilled with the idea and promised all the help she could give.

"I'll give all the lino a good going over in the morning…then I'll come along that night and be your kitchen staff and heat the sausage rolls and see to everything. And you don't need to pay me a penny, that can be my birthday present to wee Helen. Are you going to have a dumpling? Everybody loves a dumpling. Oh, I'm so excited. It'll be just lovely. I know it. And, Helen, I definitely think you should ask John upstairs. It's a golden opportunity!"

Helen shook her head.

In the face of everyone's enthusiasm, she had agreed to the party, though stipulating that it should not be called a birthday party.

"If they had to bring a present, they might not come at all."

Though she still had reservations about the party's success, she enjoyed the preparations and planning.

As the Saturday neared she brightened up and on the Tuesday evening she suddenly announced,

"I'm going upstairs to ask John to the party."

Annie showed no surprise, agreeing it was a good idea.

Helen was back within five minutes. Only Mrs Beaton was at home, for John had gone to London this week to visit his parents. Mrs Beaton had said what a terrible pity, for she knew John would have loved to come to the party, which was kind of her.

Annie was surprised that her daughter did not seem to be at all disappointed.

Helen was glad she had found the courage to give the invitation. She hated to avoid a challenge. And it was good that he was truly unavailable and had not been forced into manufacturing some excuse. Most importantly, she could not imagine him as a guest and it was a relief to know he would not be there.

◊

On Friday night, when the furniture was shifted, the back room was indeed very full.

"I hope you can manoeuvre my chair amongst all these chests of drawers and dressing tables. I had no idea there'd be so little space left."

"I'll manage." And Helen managed, with only moderate swearing.

As they lay in bed, Helen said,

"I feel we're on holiday in some really cheap hotel."

"I know what you mean but *Courage, camarade! Le diable est mort!*"

Helen laughed for she was in the middle of reading *The Cloister and the Hearth*, that wonderful book of adventure by Charles Reade. The French phrase would be repeated several times over the next twenty four hours, when setbacks occurred, as they always do with a first party.

In later years Helen would have clearer and more positive memories of reading her fascinating book in the roomful of furniture than she did of the party.

The party got off to a slow start. Elizabeth had brought her two brothers, Jim and Harry. Jim had brought records, but was derogatory about the needles in the old gramophone and offered to go home to Jordanhill and bring his own superior long playing needle for the evening. That was kind except that he took Harry, Jan and Pat away with him. Elizabeth, Tessa, Campbell and Duncan were left to help Helen sprinkle and spread the Slipperene over the green linoleum.

The room looked spacious enough for twice as many people and Helen felt a sinking in her stomach. What if the party was a failure? How long would those folk take to get to Jordanhill and back? Would anyone dance when the music started? Duncan was short and bespectacled and had informed her on arrival that he never danced. She wondered why Jim had brought him. Perhaps it was impossible to have a dance with just five girls and four boys, one of whom did not dance. What would Campbell think of this disorganised party?

Why had Annie ever suggested a party in the first place and why had she agreed to it? Helen had to admit it had been fun preparing for it. Was the preparation going to be the best part?

Perhaps not a complete success, the party was hardly a disaster, except perhaps for Tessa. For a long time this clever friend had yearned in vain for the romantic attentions of Elizabeth's older brother, Harry. Cruel classmates did not hesitate to sing the first few lines of 'I'm just wild about Harry", then watch and comment on the scarlet flooding of Tessa's normally pale cheek. It never failed. Harry was a tall self-confident youth with a mop of brown curls. He played first violin in the Boys' High orchestra and a glance around the audience would have shown a number of girlish eyes resting pleasurably and longingly on his sensitive features.

Perhaps Tessa hoped that Helen's party might open his eyes to her charms. Helen hoped so too. It was not to be. Tessa's unquestioned intellectual ability together with those extra inches on her hips, were too great a handicap. The heart-throb of the Boy's High could take his pick of the prettiest girls. When the superior needle was brought and fitted, the two brothers spent the rest of the evening flirting with Pat and Jan, slender, giggling girls, who properly appreciated that appearance is much more important than passing examinations.

Tessa slumped disconsolately against the wall, trying not to look in the direction of the laughing group.

Campbell was a good dancer. He danced first with Helen and

she found it a superior experience to the stumbling of the McEwan classes. Unfortunately his voice was very low and muffled. Helen missed much of what he said and misheard the rest. Twice they talked at complete cross purposes. It was a relief when he danced with Tessa, though Helen recognised the strained and puzzled look on Tessa's face. She was obviously having just as much trouble making conversation with him. Elizabeth and Duncan chatted happily of hockey and football.

Annie joined them in the sitting room, when the meal was served. The party started to go with more of a swing. Annie was good at helping young people to talk and the food was appreciated. Soon there was more relaxed and general laughter than had been heard in the dancing room. Duncan came into his own and told some excellent jokes. Agnes, looking smart in a dark pink dress, handed sandwiches and sausage rolls and Campbell dealt with the tomato juice and lemon barley water. He was very efficient and Helen once more felt grateful and kindly towards him. He really was quite handsome. If only he would speak up!

He must be very shy.

Annie had advised buying three syphons of soda water, but with a deposit of five shillings on each syphon, Helen took cold feet and bought only two, which were not quite sufficient, but there was plenty of tap water.

When the savouries were eaten, Agnes brought in the steamed dumpling. Annie had wanted to make a traditional clooty dumpling, but Helen made a face.

"I just like it steamed in a bowl and then you don't have to wash out the horrible slimy cloth afterwards."

She had her way and the pudding turned out of the bowl perfectly.

Annie had insisted on having the traditional silver threepenny pieces in the dumpling. There were eight guests, fewer than they had hoped and ten silver pieces, each wrapped in grease proof paper.

Agnes presented the steaming pudding triumphantly to Annie, who had wheeled herself to the table to serve it. She was hoping to make sure that each portion contained a coin.

She might as well not have bothered. In spite of clear instructions and several warnings, the idea of coins hidden in a pudding seemed a difficult concept for the teenage minds. One threepenny bit was thrown in the fire, another caused a choking, fortunately not serious. Four were politely left, still wrapped in paper, at the side of the plate. Three remained in the uneaten pudding and one was unaccounted for. The pudding was voted delicious, but nobody said a word about the coins.

Bruce kindly popped in at ten to drive Agnes home.

There was more dancing after supper and the guests left at eleven o'clock. Campbell offered to escort Tessa home, as she lived in the opposite direction to the others. Helen was sure she would have liked that. Unfortunately, before they left the house, Tessa's father arrived to collect her and the poor girl was deprived of the one morsel of romance offered to her that evening.

◊

As Helen steered the chair around the unaccustomed furniture in the back room, Annie asked,

"Well, are you tired, my love?"

"No. I didn't really do enough dancing to be tired. But I have enjoyed myself. Thank you for suggesting it and all the work *and* the expense."

"As long as you enjoyed it, that's fine. Are you sure you did enjoy it all right?"

"Yes, although it wasn't a bit the way I thought it would be. The dancing was certainly much more fun than those awful classes and I can see it would be terrific, if you had the right man to dance with."

"But Campbell's not the right man?"

"No, I don't think so and I don't think he thinks he is either, but he's a pretty good dancer and he was a great help. I just wish I could hear what he was saying."

"Well we better struggle through this jungle of furniture in our cheap hotel and get away to bed."

Influenza

Two weeks after the party, Helen developed influenza and was really ill for more than a fortnight. With a high fever and slightly delirious, she sometimes believed herself still in that overcrowded back room, though everything had been replaced the following day. At other times she re-lived the adventures of the hero of Reade's novel, clambering up tree after tree, in a desperate attempt to escape the terrifying bear. More pleasantly, when music infiltrated her dreams, she danced on her toes like a real ballerina. Sometimes she flew through the upper space of the studio at 351, and she found that delightful, awakening to reality with regret.

It was difficult for Annie, who was very unwilling to ask her daughter for help. In the afternoon and evening, when Agnes was not there, she must rely on Helen at intervals. She would wait as long as possible, then waken the girl gently and apologetically. Helen would get out of bed, groggy and unsteady, protesting that she felt fine, not to worry, it was no trouble at all and afterwards fall back into bed to sleep once more. Annie felt tremendous guilt, contenting herself with bread and butter for supper and going to bed early. Helen took little of anything except lemon barley water.

When she ventured outside for the first time, Helen had the strange sensation of hovering ten inches above the pavement. It was rather pleasant, though un-nerving.

◊

Although she had not suffered another asthma attack like that first terrifying one in Pittenweem, Helen seemed to have a tendency to chest infections. After she recovered from the 'flu, another unusual and worrying symptom appeared, not frightening but embarrassing. When she became nervous or too hot, the fine skin on her neck and chest and on the inside of her arms and legs became rough, red and very itchy.

The first time it happened was in school just after a gym lesson which had not been a happy one. Miss Loudon, a short-tempered middle-aged teacher, had been particularly demanding and critical that day. As Helen walked along a narrow beam, testing her balance by lifting her arms above her head and believing she was doing it rather well, the teacher suddenly snapped loudly,

"Watch your arms, Helen! You're not in the ballet class now!"

Presumably classical grace was not in fashion in athletic circles at the time. Helen lost her concentration, then her balance and jumped to the floor. Probably the look which Helen turned on the teacher at that moment did not serve to improve Miss Loudon's mood, for she walked through the gym hall criticising and castigating other pupils. She was not a happy woman.

The changing room grumbles were silenced when Helen discovered her arms and legs disfigured by lumpy blotches which were quickly becoming unbearably itchy.

"What is it? Have you had it before?"

"Ooh, d'ye think it's catching?"

"Did it just happen suddenly?"

"That's really queer, I think you should go to the medical room."

"That looks really beastly! What is it?"

"Don't scratch it if you can help. That'll only make it worse."

"D'ye feel all right otherwise?"

"Here's a drink of water. Sit down for a minute. Maybe it'll go away."

"I don't think that'll go away quickly!"

"I've never seen anything like it *in my life*!"

"I really think you *should* go to the medical room."

Helen did not enjoy the attention and fuss. What if it were a serious disease and she had already infected the whole class? Her skin looked strange and ugly and the sudden way it had happened was inexplicable. It was similar to the heatspots which had afflicted her as a child, though much worse. As well as the itch, the entire affected area was burning with heat. Did heatspots pop out suddenly like this? She remembered they were most unbearable at night, when her mother would dab calamine lotion on each spot and tell stories to help take her mind off the problem.

Her grandmother used to blame her suffering on too many sweets or strawberries, but she had never believed that theory. It seemed like a good excuse to curtail her intake of those delicacies. Certainly her diet contained little of either item nowadays.

There were several ways that the girls could return from the gym to their classroom in the main building and they chose the longest one which led through the playground.

"Maybe the fresh air will help you."

"We'll pass the medical room on the way and I think you should go in and see what they say."

But in the cool air and with the sympathy of her friends, Helen knew the condition was beginning to fade. By the time they reached the classroom the unpleasant sensations were almost gone, though her skin took another twenty minutes to return to normal. She was relieved that no teacher need be apprised of her condition. It seemed so peculiar. It was hard to believe it had ever happened, though she felt rather tired by four o'clock.

That evening when Doctor Hamilton was called in to hear of this new affliction, he smiled,

"Oh yes, we have a sensitive wee lass here. It's an allergy! Allergies and asthma are often together. Yes, we meet them all the time with young folk nowadays. We don't know much about them, but we can do a wee bit to help. The good news is you'll likely just grow out of the whole problem. That's what usually happens. Anyway, you're allergic to something or other and you sneeze a lot too, do you? Right, we'll send you along to the Western and they'll do a few tests…try to find out exactly what it is that you're allergic *to* …"

He paused impressively,

"Then you'll know how to avoid it, won't you!"

He sat there, smiling kindly and packing his papers and stethoscope into his black valise. Then as he rose to go, he asked,

"And how are you keeping yourself, Mrs Corning? Never hear any complaints from you. Keeping fit and healthy are you? Appetite fine? Bowels regular?"

"Yes, I'm pretty good and fit all round, I suppose. Bit too much pain sometimes, but … it passes."

"Yes, yes. That's a pity, a great pity. Aspirin much help? Good, good. And the massage too, some benefit there?"

"Oh, the massage has been wonderful, just a shame it can't get my legs straightened out."

The doctor laughed kindly at her small joke and left.

Bruce's Other Life

Bruce had met Nan at the Foster's house a few times, though he had hardly exchanged ten words with her. He found her a rather unattractive young woman. Although her grammar and accent were careful and correct, her meagre figure, pale complexion and lack of confidence told of impoverished origins. She seemed out of her element in the comfortable Hyndland flat, sitting on the edge of her chair, taking little part in the quick, wise-cracking conversation, always refusing proffered alcohol and just smiling politely during the long bursts of loud laughter. Bruce had sometimes wondered how she came to be a friend of the Fosters, then almost at once lost interest in the question. It would be fair to say that he dismissed her from his mind as soon as he left the flat.

Nan often asked herself why she chose to spend her precious free evenings in that boisterous, rather vulgar household with its philosophy of 'What the hell? Let's have another drink!'. For, in spite of Bobby's constant cajoling, she refused even the smallest sherry. How she hated the very word alcohol. Drink had led to so many problems in her own large family.

"Och, come on, wee Nan. I cannae enjoy my own dram wi' you sippin' lemonade there. That stuff's poison on its own, ye know. Just have a wee dribble whisky in your glass. Look! Just that wee tate! Ye'll enjoy it, I'm telling you. You will!"

"Leave her alone, Bobby. D'ye hear what she's saying? *She doesn't want it.*"

Bobby never gave up, but his wife Peggy understood, for she knew more about Nan's background. Though Peggy also wondered why Nan came to the house, for the girl never seemed at ease. At the end of each visit, Nan promised herself it would be the last, but she kept returning for there was always the possibility of seeing Bruce.

Bruce seemed to her the perfect man. Mature, sure of himself, hearty and energetic, always hail-fellow-well-met with everyone. It was obvious that he was full of integrity and dedicated to his business. It was his life. He also seemed so affectionate and respectful to his old father. And he cared about his brother, too, though Willie seemed a queer fellow, almost a miser. But at least he did not spend half his life in Barlinnie, as her own brother Danny did.

An engineer in a long-established East End business, Bruce Corning always looked clean and newly shaved. He must be quite well off, for he had a car and was a member of at least two clubs. It was strange that his clothes were so shabby. His tweed jacket, well-worn and shapeless, must be pre-war, but then the gentry usually wore their old clothes for ever. Obviously Bruce had no vanity about his appearance and it was obvious that he did not have a woman to care for him. How attractive he was, somewhere between forty and fifty, lovely white teeth, no grey hairs, good slim figure. He was terribly strong, too. Though he was only of middle height, she had watched him manhandle a large wardrobe at the Foster's with ease. Bobby had just stood watching. Nan despised Bobby. Though he was a gym teacher, his potbelly told how little exercise he took and how greedy he was. Bruce obviously watched what he ate and kept himself in shape, with swimmimg and golf. How she admired a man that worked hard and yet had time for such pleasant hobbies. Danny's hobbies consisted of drink, more drink and getting into trouble. Her other brothers were heading the same way. It was because of not having a father, she supposed. Her father had abandoned the family when Nan was ten. With five children, her mother had struggled on valiantly while they were young but now she was getting older, failing. The frequent policeman's knock at the door sent her into hysterics. Nan had hardened her heart and escaped to her own life as a nurse. Living in the hospital, she could distance herself from the family to a certain extent and was able to help financially, though only a little. A large part of the pittance she received was retained by the hospital for her 'keep'. Nan suspected her small weekly sacrifice was probably spent in the pub, for she had learned that her mother now often joined her sons there on a Saturday night.

Sometimes Nan despaired of the future.

Would she eat that terrible hospital food all her life and never have her own nice sitting room, with pretty cushions on the couch and her own ornaments on the mantelpiece? She worked hard and conscientiously and it did not seem too much to ask.

In the meantime, one of her few pleasures was being in the same room as Bruce Corning. She harboured no foolish thoughts of romance. She was positive she only admired him as a fine example of a man. She knew he was married, but living apart from a crippled wife and an awkward daughter. Certainly neither of them could provide him with much happiness, yet he kept up such a cheerful appearance. How kind and noble he was to support them. He really was a wonderful man.

It was springtime in Glasgow and the rain poured down. Bruce stood up and jingled his keys in his pocket.

"Well, Bobby, time for me to hit the road. Must get home. Expecting a phone call tonight, very important one. Fellow from Singers promised me a big load o' wood. Hope it works out all right. Always a struggle to keep on top, aye, always a struggle, keep the men busy, keep the orders filled. Well, I'll see you Wednesday at the club, will I? Righty-ho."

Just then Peggy Foster came into the room,

"Is that you going now, Bruce? It's absolutely pissing down. D'ye have to go right now?"

"Aye, important phone call, y'know. Got to get back, I'm afraid. I was telling Bobby there. Can't afford to miss this one."

"Well, if you have to go, could you possibly give Nan a lift to the hospital? You've time for that, surely. It's a a hellish night."

"Aye, S'ppose I could do that. Which hospital is it? Not the Southern General, I hope. Wouldn't have time to go into town and way back out west again, I'm afraid.

"It's the Royal, I've told you often enough."

"Right, right. I remember now. Suppose I could do that, not much traffic this time o' night. Aye, if you hurry up, Nan, get your coat on. I'll get you there."

The drive into town took twenty minutes and a more foolish man than Bruce could hardly have failed to recognise the respect and admiration in Nan's attitude towards him. In the intimacy of the little car, as the rain dashed fiercely against the windscreen, she could not hide her feelings of hero-worship.

When she left the car, with a wave and a brighter smile than usual, Bruce's opinion of that 'skinny wee friend of the Fosters' had changed. She had a lot more sense than he had ever realised. Seemed a very intelligent girl and so dedicated to nursing. What a wonderful career that was. A vocation really. Tender and nurturing. Really, just what a woman should be.

He decided Nan was probably a very similar type of woman to his own mother.

Tests at the Western

T he appointment was made for Helen to go to the Western Infirmary on a Saturday morning. She was to wear a short sleeved blouse and might be there for at least two hours. It was quite exciting. What sort of tests? Why such a long time?

After waiting for twenty minutes in a little room that smelled clean and hospitally, Helen was interrupted in her daydreams by a tremendously tall young man, who put his head around the door.

"Are you Helen Corning? I'm Doctor Anderson."

He looked too young to be a doctor! Younger than Campbell or John Hennington. He looked like a very nice young man. In an instant, this hospital visit was transformed for Helen. The smell of disinfectant was overlaid by the perfume of Romance.

The doctor wheeled in a small trolley, which held some instruments and many little bottles. Placing two chairs opposite each other, he sat in one himself and silently indicated that Helen should sit in the other.

The chairs were so close that his very long thighs left no room for her moderately long thighs. Seeing her hesitation, he pushed his chair back a little. Helen felt nervous and rather surprised, for they were still terribly close to each other, so close that their knees bumped. It seemed very intimate to bump knees with a young attractive stranger. Not entirely unpleasant.

Next, with the air of a conjuring trick, he slowly and carefully lifted the trolley into the air and placed it between them. Helen felt some relief that she could no longer see their knees touching, though of course she still felt his bony warmth. Then, still without a word, he moved his chair forward some inches and Helen felt her knees clasped firmly between his knees. It was a shock! With the distance between them lessened, perhaps it was the only practical solution. Nevertheless it was very unexpected and she trembled slightly.

Without saying a word, he took her left wrist and turned her arm to show the underside. With a biro pen he then marked the numbers from one to eleven on the skin between her elbow and wrist.

"Now don't be frightened. This won't be a bit sore."

He had a very nice voice.

Next he stuck a needle into one of the bottles and choosing the appropriate number, delicately pushed the tip of the needle just below the surface of the skin. He worked slowly and exactly, using a different needle and bottle for each number. Helen wondered what sort of *stuff* these different test bottles contained, but was too shy to ask. Though not pleasant to watch, the process was fascinating and certainly not sore.

So involved in his work was the young man, that Helen soon stopped trembling and worrying about their knees and started to enjoy the whole experience. She liked watching the careful way that he did everything. He made her think of a small boy absorbed in a favourite hobby, perhaps making model aeroplanes for instance. She could imagine him doing that when he was ten or eleven. Each used needle was put into a container and every little bottle was replaced in its correct compartment. Sometimes he peered at a label twice to make sure he was right, cross-checking it with a printed list.

Next he took her right arm and marked it with numbers too.

"Now these last three might be just a little painful, but I expect you know that the best way to take an injection is to try and relax your muscles as much as possible. Did you know that?"

Helen smiled and shook her head.

"You'll have had an injection before, I'm sure."

"Yes, and a vaccination."

"Well one of these is quite like a vaccination, but I'm sure you'll deal with it fine." And he smiled a charming smile.

It was a smile which consigned John Hennington to oblivion.

This was certainly Helen's most exciting, romantic and pleasurable encounter with the opposite sex, yet.

She wished that, like an Indian goddess, she had several arms to be tested, that she might sit here all day, watching this dedicated young man, while his knees clasped hers so decorously below the table.

With vague disappointment, she watched him again lift the trolley high in the air and set it aside Then, pushing back his chair, he released her knees.

"I expect you'll hear from your own GP quite soon and we'll

arrange for you to come in to the Western a few times, for injections. Thank you for being so helpful and stoic. D'ye know what stoic means? You've been *very* stoic. A nurse will be along in a moment to see you out. Good-bye."

Spring 1948

"Surely the spring must soon be here. Don't you think you could do with a nice light coat? You've only got your navy school coat."

"Could we afford a coat? I don't suppose I *really* need one. I'd like one, but I don't need it."

"You could charge it. We'd scrape up the money somehow, no doubt. My Distillers dividend comes in next month. I think you should pop into Coplands on Saturday and see what they've got."

Not for the first time, Helen thought what a very unusual mother she had. Fancy insisting she should buy something that she herself had not even thought of wanting.

Annie had her reasons. She felt her daughter was still low after all the ill health she had suffered. A new coat might cheer her up.

Nowadays, there was more of a selection in the clothes departments and Helen very quickly found the perfect coat in Coplands. It was a princess style, in a subtle dark cream bouclé. Classically simple, with a satin lining, it fitted her beautifully. The shoulders were not too widely padded and the long full skirt swished around her ankles in a rich and satisfying manner. Her reflection showed something closely resembling those fashion drawings in the Herald.

Helen had not yet developed the sensible habit of looking at the price tag before falling in love with a purchase.

When the saleslady mentioned the price of sixteen pounds, four shillings and a penny, Helen almost stopped breathing. She had pretty well said she would take it! Anyway, after wearing this coat, no other would do.

She signed the sales slip and the assistant folded it and placed it in the little tube, to be sucked up to the accounting. The deed was done.

Annie had expected to pay five or six pounds and was a little taken back, but tried not to show it.

"It is a *really* beautiful coat, right enough, but, remember, it's to do you for a good few years!"

The coat taught Helen several lessons. Although it had a light summery aspect, the fabric was woollen and too warm for the summer. In winter, the style was too closely fitted to hang smoothly over bulkier clothing. Its light colour was easily soiled and seemed to be a magnet for accidental spills. It was a beautiful and stylish garment and hung in Helen's wardrobe for the next ten years, but it was not worn often enough to justify the price, and remained a constant reproach.

◊

Although it was obvious that Campbell did not find her attractive, his parents seemed anxious that they should be friendly. She believed that it was probably his mother who had forced him to come to her party, for he had not accepted immediately. In April, when she had delivered a birthday present from her mother to Mrs Horsland, Helen had been welcomed and made much of by both parents.

Their flat at Kelvin Court had been an experience for Helen. The décor was Moderne, the atmosphere luxurious. It was like stepping into a Fred Astaire film. On entering the building, one was immediately enfolded in enticing warmth. Apart from the womb-like warmth of the Arlington, such indoor comfort was unknown to her. The lift, carpeted like a little room, glided silently upwards, very different from those ancient rattling metal cages in department stores. The ceilings in the flat were much lower than she was used to in Glasgow, but the rooms were large. Thick carpeting covered every part of every floor and the upholstery was of pale satin damask, with pretty velvet cushions scattered here and there. Helen was not sure if she would like to live in such a place. Even without her cardigan, which she had removed along with her coat, she felt too warm and fervently hoped she would not have one of her strange itching attacks. Also, she thought, you would need to be *very* careful not to spill anything in this room. Although she was not fond of the sturdy leather furniture at home, it was easy to wipe and polish.

On that visit, she and Campbell had a short conversation about reading and he loaned her a book called *Borzoi* about a dog in Russia. She had enjoyed the book and felt their friendship had progressed a little, perhaps enough to ask him to the school dance. She felt she should take a partner this time. While she could remain stoic (she liked that word very much now) about the dance last Christmas, and joke about it, she was not prepared to repeat the experience.

As well as the extreme humiliation, Helen had particularly disliked *watching* rather than *doing*.

◊

"I'm going to ask Campbell to go the summer dance with me."

"That's a good idea. I'm sure he would love to go."

"I think that's probably a bit strong. He'll go because he's a friend of the family. I'm asking him because he's quite a good dancer and the only man I know to ask. And his mother will encourage him to go. We never know what to say to each other and I can never hear what he's saying when he does speak."

"That's tricky, isn't it. His father is a bit of a whisperer too, but very witty."

"Yes, well maybe Campbell is too, if I could hear him."

◊

Campbell came to the dance and the evening was not a failure.

There was no romance, but they danced reaonably well together, and enjoyed a little conversation. They talked about dogs and Russia because of the book.

When Campbell politely danced two or three times with Tessa, other boys asked Helen to dance. Their dancing skills were only just adequate and she realised how terribly lucky she was to have Campbell as a partner.

When the Grand Old Duke of York was announced, she was relieved that he sat back and lit a cigarette.

There was enthusiastic grabbing of partners for this dance and nearly everyone was on the floor. Tessa had been asked to dance though not by her adored Harry, but quite unexpectedly by Charles, whose sister was in their class. A dark, un-smiling boy, he stood silently opposite Tessa amongst the other dancers, who laughed and chatted as they waited expectantly for the music to begin. Charles looked remote and slightly bored as he gazed at the three-piece band. He had a superior air which suited Tessa's. They were the only couple not holding hands. Tessa, her cheeks faintly flushed, watched him apprehensively.

When the music started, the first couples raced up and down, then led the others round behind them to form the 'kissing bridge' which seemed to be the *raison d'etre* of the dance. It must be admitted that Helen felt slight disapproval. She found it far too public and unrestrained. Just as at Christmas, the boys bent the girls backwards and also kept their mouths clamped together for far too long. The girls seemed powerless, but perhaps they enjoyed that. In Helen's view, it was unseemly and not at all romantic.

Not every couple was caught after each gallop. The dance might have lasted all night, had that been the case. Charles showed no sign of enjoyment as he danced and did not smile or look at Tessa when they were the galloping couple. There was a lack of enthusiasm in his demeanour and their bridge caught only a few couples.

As Helen watched, Tessa and Charles always escaped being caught, until, at the very end of the dance, they were finally imprisoned. Charles seemed surprised and paused instead of pouncing. Then he announced, partly to Tessa, but loudly enough for many to hear,

"I do think kissing is *very unhygienic*."

And firmly releasing his partner and himself from the enclosing arms, he led Tessa back to the line.

Everybody looked puzzled. Tessa looked dazed but dignified. Helen admired her for that, but felt very sorry for her. What a humiliation! What an idiot boy! Why did he dance that ridiculous dance if he would not kiss? Not that she approved of such public kissing, but the dance had no point otherwise. What on earth would she say to Tessa? But the subject was never mentioned between them, although it was discussed by everyone else in the class for weeks.

Although they were still friends, Tessa was often critical of Helen and she had a talent amounting to genius for burying a bitchy comment in an apparently innocent remark. Sometimes Helen did not even appreciate quite how unpleasant the comment had been until some time later. Had Tessa carefully thought out the underlying meaning before she spoke? Or perhaps Helen herself was mistaken and Tessa did not really mean it. At other times, Tessa could be very complimentary and kind.

Her family had gone to Brittany on holiday last year, which had seemed very exciting for no one else in the class had ever been abroad. Tessa had brought back little gifts for several friends, but Helen's, a silver filigree bracelet, was by far the nicest. Helen was touched as well as delighted.

It was a strange friendship.

Tessa would take Latin and Greek for her main subjects after the summer. Helen wondered if she really wanted to do that, or was it her parents' idea.

What could she do with these subjects, except teach them to other people? Surely Tessa did not want to be like Miss McCullough the classics teacher? She was a little bird like woman who wore pince nez and *spats!* No one else that Helen had ever seen wore spats. And Tessa would never look little and bird-like.

Ariane in Pittenweem

Helen occasionally spoke to Annie about a girl in her class, Ariane. She seemed to be very interested in boys and had gone on dates with several of the popular boys in High School. She also went out with an older man.

Although her daughter adroitly avoided the subject of sex, Annie had the impression that Ariane was more advanced in her romantic adventures than others in the class.

Eventually, as Helen was again speaking of Ariane, Annie took the bull by the horns and asked,

"D'ye think Ariane is a bit...y'know...d'ye think she goes the whole hog with the boys? Is that why she's so popular, would you say?"

Helen blushed, smiled and nodded.

"Well, she says she does. Maybe it's just talk. And she's not even all that beautiful. She's attractive, with a nice figure, but..."

Helen shrugged.

"Perhaps she's got oomph?"

Helen looked puzzled.

"You know, attraction for the opposite sex. Like Betty Grable. You don't need to be pretty to have oomph, or 'it' as we used to say."

"She doesn't seem anything special to me, but she talks about boys a lot and all her adventures. And of course everyone likes to listen. Some folk don't believe her."

"Do you?"

Helen shrugged and walked to the window to watch the passengers alight from a tramcar. Then she returned to her chair and picked up her knitting

"Last month Ariane was up to high doh because her period was late. Everyone in fourth year was worried for her. Each different class we went to, we were asking each other 'Have you seen Ariane? Has it arrived yet?'. Then in the afternoon at history, I saw her and she was smiling and looking very relieved. So that was fine."

Annie's face had changed,

"That sounds very serious. What a silly girl! At first I wondered if she was perhaps making it up, just to make herself important, *but really!* Does she not consider how serious it would be to have a baby at sixteen. It would affect her whole life. What a little idiot."

"She certainly keeps the class entertained. Don't know what they would talk about without Ariane. But it *would* be awful if she had a baby wouldn't it? What a thought!"

◊

That year, Miss Hopkins' annual show had a circus theme and Helen would dance two solos. At first she would be a lion tamer, in a rather masculine outfit with a whip and four unlikely-looking lions. After a quick change, she would appear as a tightrope walker. Each dance made good use of her talent for mime and in the latter, she would dance *en pointe* for the first time on stage. As a surprise, Miss Hopkins had ordered the loveliest of tutus, in vivid pinks and purples, to be made for her. It was her first proper tutu and fitted her perfectly.

Annie and Bruce sat in the front row, where Helen glimpsed them momentarily, as she danced. Though they leaned away from each other, both smiled fondly and their eyes and teeth gleamed out of the surrounding darkness.

◊

As usual, the beautiful weather broke as soon as the Glasgow Fair holiday makers arrived in Pittenweem. After two weeks of hot sunshine, the blue sky was obliterated by heavy cloud and a bitter wind blew in from the North Sea. Only a few showers fell, but the raindrops were sharp and ice-cold. Groups of disconsolate visitors, heads bowed, wandered along Pittenweem High Street, wrapping their scarves more tightly around their throats.

"I said it would be like this, didn't I! It's a shame for the poor folk, but it's always the same. I don't know why they come, year after year." Mary had predicted this bad weather and once again she was proved right. Her apparent sympathy was diluted by a streak of satisfaction which irritated Helen.

John sighed and said,

"Aye, it's a strange phenomenon, isn't it. There was always a week or two at this time of year that I couldn't paint outside. Couldn't keep my easel from blowing over. Strange how Nature has her established patterns. You can't fight Nature, she's stronger than any of us,"

Smiling and nodding, he looked out at the windswept garden where hollyhocks, delphiniums and lupins were bending and breaking.

Mary tried to light a cigarette and struck the match with such vigour that the head broke off.

"*Damn!* That bloody wind, there won't be a flower left in the garden. Look at the studio too, it's swaying! Look at it! We'll need to get something done about the glass. It's not safe. I *hate* wind."

She puffed strenuously.

Annie said nothing, for the weather was affecting her badly. Knitting was impossible and she had laid it aside.

She struggled to conceal her extreme discomfort from the others. for she knew it upset Helen and her father, while it often seemed to make Mary irritable. Even now she could see that her mother's impatient foot was tapping. The waves of pain that accompanied each uncontrollable muscle spasm in her calves and thighs, finally became unbearable.

"Helen, I think I'll have to go to bed for a wee while."

But Helen's watchful eye had judged the situation and even as Annie spoke, her chair was tilted backwards ready to whirl it around and wheel her away to her bedroom.

"I'll just lie here for an hour or so."

"It seems awful bad today, poor wee Maw."

"It's that wind and those lowering clouds. I'd be better if the rain would just come on."

"And you don't even have a wireless here to listen to."

"Och, never mind, I'll just lie here and think. I'll think about my wee daughter dancing on the stage."

'Did you like my solo?"

"Wonderful. You know, I'm feeling *hellish* just now, but I haven't felt as bad as this for a long time. Maybe I'm improving? Getting over the worst of it anyway. And Miss Arthur's made a tremendous difference. I suppose I miss my weekly pummelling when I'm through here. But off you go and make them a cup of tea before you go for your swim. And don't worry about me, I'm feeling a bit better now, starting to relax. I bet the rain has come on."

"Yes, it's started and it's absolutely pelting."

"But I expect you'll go swimming just the same."

"I expect so."

◊

Annie had a chance to meet the notorious Ariane in July. Her family were on holiday in Elie, and quite unexpectedly, she visited Helen.

She seemed a very self-confident girl, certainly not a beauty but well-groomed and vivacious. She wore a great deal of bright red lipstick and possibly some mascara. Her tightly fitting clothes accentuated her shapely figure and she made good use of her large pale eyes and long lashes as she spoke.

Immediately after the introductions, Ariane seated herself in the garden and brought out a packet of Players.

"What a lovely garden and such a great view of the sea. It's gorgeous. You are lucky. D'you mind if I smoke, Mrs Corning?" she already had a cigarette withdrawn from the packet.

"Not at all. Go ahead."

"Can I offer you one?"

"No thank you. I stopped years ago."

"What about you, Helen? Have one?"

Annie was amused at the assumed sophistication of the girl. She might have been a woman of thirty.

Helen shook her head,

"No, thank you."

Then Annie proved her psychological wisdom.

"Go on Helen, try it if you like!"

Helen looked at her mother aghast. She had no desire to try a cigarette. That year of smoking string had been enough to satisfy any yearnings to use a cigarette in order to appear grown-up. She had no intention of ever smoking. It seemed a complete waste of money and she knew her mother thought it unhealthy.

"Go on, Helen, try one. You'll enjoy it!" Ariane held out the packet invitingly.

Helen looked at her mother, who nodded.

"Go ahead, try one if you want to."

With two people encourging her, it seemed impossible to refuse and Helen gingerly took one from the packet. Ariane lit it for her and Helen quickly withdrew it from her mouth and held it, looking at her mother in dismay.

Annie smiling benignly, commented,

"You're holding it in a very practised way there, darling. Are you sure that's your first fag!"

Helen felt furious with both of them, but especially her mother. She had no intention of telling them that she had practised with string last year.

She replaced the cigarette between her lips for a second or two, then removed it quickly.

"I've watched grandma smoking all my life, so I should know how to do it."

They were both watching her so closely. It was embarrassing.

A third time she placed the small papery tube between her lips momentarily. It tasted unpleasant and she felt a fool.

"Sorry, but I really don't think I like it."

Quickly she stubbed it out in the grass and threw it behind a shrub, determined that she would never again touch a cigarette.

Annie watched her with the familiar quizzical expression.

"Let's have a cup of coffee then, shall we!"

Helen was pleased to escape and recover her dignity.

Ariane invited Helen to come up to St Andrews with her parents for the afternoon.

First, they drove back to the Elie hotel, where Ariane spent an interminable time trying on different outfits. Helen sat on the bed and nodded as each new blouse was tried with a different skirt or shorts. Very short shorts, Helen noticed. The kind that Hollywood starlets wore and that she herself had never found in the shops. Ariane's mother shouted to them to hurry up several times, but was ignored. More and more clothes were brought from the wardrobe and tried on. Helen was bored. She had never met such a time-waster before and felt very irritated. Then Ariane wondered about her hair. It was in a perfect pageboy, but should she change it?

"No, no your hair's just great, Ariane. I was thinking it was like something in a magazine, so smooth. Don't change it at all. Let's get going, your folk are waiting for us."

Helen, always aware of time passing, wondered when they would return from this trip which had not even started yet. Her poor mother might be wanting to go to the bathroom even now. Or she might just want to come into the house. Helen felt less than friendly towards this girl, though she was glad that her mother had met her.

After another five minutes, a red spotted blouse with white shorts was chosen. As a last touch, Ariane applied more lipstick, then twisted the lower part of her blouse and tied it in a knot under her bosom, leaving her midriff bare.

"Ready now!" she announced pertly.

Helen felt faint with astonishment, for though this style might appear in film magazines, it was unknown on the streets of Fife.

Was she really going to go out looking like that?

The word 'sexy' had not yet become popular and was not in Helen's vocabulary, but she felt that Ariane looked a bit 'rude' to go out in public.

As the parents had shopping to do, the girls were dropped off near the putting green close to the venerable club house of the Royal and Ancient. They would return to collect the girls at the same place in an hour. Almost before the car was out of sight, two young men in their twenties had crossed the road and started speaking to them in a very friendly way. They were possibly students and seemed quite respectable but they stood uncomfortably close to the girls. Helen was very aware of her friend's bare midriff and tried to edge away as unobtrusively as possible.

Later, she described the incident to Annie.

"Honestly, Mummy, I don't know how they got there so quickly! Suddenly they were standing beside us and smiling as though they were old friends."

"Perhaps it was a previous arrangement?"

"Oh, no, they were complete strangers, I'm sure."

"She must have given them the glad eye!"

"What on earth is that?"

"You know! A come-hither glance, a 'come up and see me sometime' sort of look. And no doubt the way she was dressed was an attraction."

"Maybe. I suppose so. But she must have been awful quick with her glad eye. It was all so sudden and so *embarrassing*. I didn't know what to say or do, at all. It was awful. They seemed nice enough, but one of them was black and he had a strong accent and the other was very English, very la-de-da. I could hardly make out what either of them were saying. I think they were students. What an experience! I'm certainly *never* going out with that girl again."

"Yes that's probably a good idea."

"You know, they stood there talking for ages and all I did was smile sometimes. I felt an idiot and all the time I was worried that her folk would come back and find us there and think it was *my* fault that we'd picked up two strange men."

"I expect they know their daughter pretty well by this time."

"No, because when they did arrive and see the blokes, her mother looked daggers at me, as though it *was* my fault. Gosh I was glad to get back in the car and get home again."

"Was anything said in the car about your *rencontre?*"

"Never a word. I think her folk were angry with each other as well as with us."

"It's not been a happy day out, has it! And I don't think you cared much for your cigarette, did you?"

Helen looked at her mother reproachfully and did not deign to reply.

Northern Idyll

urther north in the seaside town of Nairn, Bruce and Nan sat on the beach, munching sandwiches, drinking ginger beer and smoking. The fact that they were both heavy smokers had cemented their relationship.

Though Nan's two-piece swimsuit did not flatter her thin body, her small face was glowing and pretty. Happiness and the fresh breeze had brought colour to her cheeks. Bruce gazed at the horizon with a wide grin. He had not once thought of the loss of his mother since the holiday began. Nor had he contemplated his aging and unreliable staff, nor the relentless demands of the charcoal furnace and certainly neither his wife or daughter was in his mind.

"My, it's a great life here, wee Nan, isn't it? Don't ye wish our holiday could go on forever. I remember when I was a wee lad, I used to cry at the end of the holidays. Cry real tears. Roar and howl! I never wanted to come home again. Did you not feel that terrible sadness at the end of your holidays. Nan? I bet you did."

He slung his arm around her shoulders and hugged her tightly. She winced at his strength though at the same time feeling happily protected by the gesture.

As so often happened, Nan made no reply and Bruce, who was always happy to talk, continued his monologue without noticing her silence.

The truth was that Nan had never had a seaside holiday. There had been no money for holidays in her life. This was her first and she did wish that they might never go home, but she was a realist and knew that they must. Besides, she loved her tiny flat in Athole Gardens with the cushions on the couch and ornaments on the mantelpiece, just as she had always imagined it. It was quiet and yet so convenient for subway, tram or bus and shopping in Byres Road.

She turned to look at Bruce. What a marvellous man he was. How brown and handsome he was with his sparkling white teeth and always so energetic and generous, too. He had bought her this swimsuit and two lovely dresses for their holiday together.

Though she would never have dared put it into words, she knew this was a sort of honeymoon and the future stretched charmingly, though rather mistily, ahead.

The sun and sea had also helped Nan rid her mind of unwanted images. The interminable walking back and forth in the infirmary and the continuous, intimate demands of querulous and difficult patients might never have existed. And as for any qualms of conscience concerning that unknown crippled wife and the lanky, un-loving daughter in Hyndland, they had faded into complete oblivion.

At that moment, Nan and Bruce experienced the perfection of happiness, one adoring, the other adored.

Transitions

That summer of 1948 marked a big change in Helen's experience of Pittenweem. Although she had attended the local school for years and had spent nearly every summer of her life in the town, she had always felt herself a visitor, an *incomer*. Perhaps these awkward feelings of 'not belonging' were partly her own fault and partly that of the small close-knit community.

The previous summer, she had formed the special intense friendship with local girl Anna Boyter. This year she was welcomed into a group of morning swimmers, which included Anna's brothers, Bill and Davy as well as Irene and Bill Black and another old school friend, Bunty Millet. This meant Helen became less reliant on the occasional visits of friends who were, like herself, incomers.

Not only was she welcomed, she was sought after. Suddenly and, as it seemed to her, inexplicably, Helen became popular. Perhaps her confidence bloomed, perhaps her looks improved, perhaps the local young people started to realise that she was shy, rather than stand-offish. Perhaps her close friendship with Anna helped. Whatever the reason, Helen suddenly found herself part of the local young community. Her jokes were laughed at, her clothes and her long hair were complimented and her swimming, especially, was admired.

Because the nearest indoor pools were inconveniently far away, in Dundee or Dunfermline, Helen had the great advantage of swimming throughout the winter and she was a more powerful swimmer than the local children. She was also able to impress with the various elegant strokes inspired by her celluloid heroine, Esther Williams. But she had always been a good swimmer and it was only this year that recognition came. To her utter astonishment, she found herself a sort of heroine. Old schoolfellows, who had seemed unaware of her existence for years, would shout 'hullo' across the street and her arrival at the swimming pool was greeted with some celebration.

It was an utterly new experience for Helen to be lionised. Of course she enjoyed it, but she wondered if they realised how differently they were treating her.

When contemporaries asked for tips on diving or swimming, Helen, always happy to teach, would demonstrate. She encouraged younger children to swim and was pleased to perform to amuse them. There was the 'submarine' where she floated on her back with one straight leg pointing in the air, then submerging, she would swim backwards for several yards and with only her foot showing above the surface like a periscope. It required strength and control and though others tried it, they failed. Another favourite was swimming animals, where she demonstrated the appropriate splashings of a mouse, a cat, a dog, a horse and lastly an elephant, starting with two index fingers and ending with four limbs thrashing wildly to make as much turbulence as possible. The younger children loved it and Helen enjoyed displaying that exhibitionist self which lies hidden in all of us.

Most embarrassing sign of her new popularity was the ice cream cone with which she was bestowed, gratis, each time she passed the newly opened Paterson's ice-cream shop.

"It's a present!" the young girl would exclaim with a lovely smile.

Helen realised it was a present that Mr Paterson was unaware of giving, but could not hurt her friend's feelings by spurning it.

◊

Archie Millett, an energetic local councillor, conceived the idea of re-instating a summer swimming gala, the first since 1939.

Only weeks before war started, Helen had been the only swimmer in the beginner's race and she remembered winning a box of soft, aging toffees which she had enjoyed, though her mother had been displeased, considering they were old stock that some shop had been glad to clear from its shelves.

This gala would be a much more sophisticated affair. Councillor Millett was ambitious. He organised the local coast guard to demonstrate their rocket and breeches buoy equipment. He bullied friends into performing a comedy sketch on the raft, which of course culminated in all fully clothed actors falling in the water. Most importantly he wrote to Nancy Riach, a young Olympic swimming champion, a Scottish girl, asking her to appear and swim at the gala. She accepted and he cleverly publicised her visit throughout Fife.

It would be the biggest event in the East Neuk that summer.

Mary was reading about it in the *East Fife Observer,* a modest local newsheet which appeared each Thursday and was also known as 'the two minutes' silence'.

"I see there's going to be a beauty contest at the Swimming Gala next week. That's something different, surely. Are you going to go in for that, my jewel? I think you should."

Helen looked unsure. Her friends had been talking about it and encouraging her to join them in entering.

The following day, Mary came down early, waving her Daily Express triumphantly.

"Would you just look at this! What a coincidence. It's a marvel! The Express has a free pattern for a two piece swimsuit and I've got just the right bit of material to make it up for my wee grand daughter. Then you'll go in for that beauty contest and knock spots off everyone else, I bet."

As would happen repeatedly throughout much of her life, though she had not yet quite realised it, Helen was caught in the floodtide of another person's enthusiasm and would be swept off in a direction which she herself would never have chosen.

Perhaps she was not entirely averse to her grandmother's plan, but if left to herself, she would have been unlikely to enter the contest.

In those days, it was taken for granted that sixteen-year-olds were malleable creatures and many of them acceped it.

Mary looked out the fabric immediately. The brightly patterned cretonne was pre-war. She had used some to cover a little couch last year but there was just the right amount left to make the two-piece. Mary loved to make use of things. She stayed at her sewing machine all that day.

The halter-neck top was simple and suited Helen, though the idea of showing her midriff was a bit daring. Only weeks ago, she had felt shocked at Ariane's bare midriff. But she comforted herself that perhaps the seaside was a more acceptable location for semi-nudity than the street. She was less sure about the success of the voluminous lower half. The baggy pants reminded her of the clothes worn by Shakespearean actors. It was certainly not a revealing swimsuit, and Helen did not feel as shy about wearing it as she had thought she might. The colourful pattern was pretty and eye-catching.

Mary and Annie were delighted with her appearance and positive that she would win.

When her friends saw it on the day of the gala, there was only a slight pause. It was certainly very different from the woollen jersey one-piece suits the other girls were wearing. Soon, they all decided her two-piece was great, wonderful, smashing and any other adjectives they could think of.

The natural amphitheatre overlooking the pool was crammed to capacity. More than two thousand people came to Pittenweem that fine sunny day, each one hoping to see the famous young Olympic champion.

No one had expected quite such a huge turn-out and the idea of a beauty parade before so many, was daunting for the participants.

First came the races. Helen had several competitors, but they were not of her calibre and somewhat shamefacedly she was first in the ladies' fifty yards crawl, fifty yards freestyle and the hundred yards freestyle, Her diving, though elementary by today's standards, was superior to the others and she won that too.

Then it was time for the beauty contestants to change from their workaday swimsuits to something more glamorous. Many applied sophisticated make-up. Some added a little judicious padding. Helen, her dark skin several shades browner than others, relied on her tan and her Daily Express two-piece. The competition was to be judged by general acclaim rather than a jury. The contestant who was awarded loudest applause from the immense audience, would win. To Helen, it seemed a rough and ready method, with infinite possibilities for an unfair judgement. Who would decide when the audience was at its loudest?

The girls walked self -consciously around three sides of the large swimming pool. It was an ordeal and Helen tried to concentrate on the view of sea, sky and North Berwick Law.

The audience had been asked to express their approval as the twelve contestants walked across the final twenty-five yards of beach. Helen felt angry at this, for after walking as tall and elegantly as possible on the concrete path, now at the most important moment, they must trudge and stumble through the stony and uneven sand as best they might. What idiot had organised such a situation?

Helen was last to walk across. She tried to walk smoothly and also to smile, but it was difficutl. The noise was deafening, overwhelming and it all seemed to come from a vociferous crowd of her Pittenweem friends. She would never know how well she was accepted by the vast crowds above on the hillside, because they were drowned out by the strong and determined roars of approval from her own friends.

Helen became Miss Pittenweem.

"But really I should never have won it!" she told her family later. "It was such nonsense. It was nice that my friends wanted me to win, but it wasn't at all fair. There were other girls far, far more glamorous then me."

"I bet there wasn't another swimsuit more glamorous though, was there?" Annie put in slyly and Mary looked pleased.

'No, that's true, but it was all a lot of rubbish. And all those people too and the Olympic girl never came. I don't know what happened, but she didn't turn up."

"What a shame! I bet they made plenty money selling tickets, too. The folk wouldn't be a bit pleased. It's a wonder Archie Millett wasn't lynched!" Mary enjoyed news of a disaster

"I heard people grumbling, but it was a lovely day and there were lots of other things to see. The rocket launch and rescue was exciting and the boys on the greasy pole, hitting each other with blown up bladders was great fun to watch. I've never seen it before and it looked really sore."

"And you won several prizes for races too. I hope they're something better than a box of rotten old sweeties this time." That still rankled with Annie.

"I got gift vouchers for local shops and they add up to seventeen and sixpence."

"*What!*" Annie could not believe her ears, "You won all those races and the beauty contest too, and it's not even a *pound*! Oh what greed, really. I can hardly believe it."

"And they must have taken an absolute *fortune* from that audience." Mary added indignantly

"Oh, I don't mind really. There's a nice nighty in the drapers I've had my eye on for ages and I need a new swim cap and a toothbrush and there's just the right amount for all those things. AND I am Miss Pittenweem, though I don't deserve it, but it's nice to know my friends thought so."

"Well we think you deserve it too, don't we, Maw?"

Mary agreed heartily.

"I'm sure it was the fancy swimsuit that did it." laughed Helen.

◊

Some weeks later, Mary was reading the Herald one afternoon.

"I see the skirts are getting really long these days. It says here the Paris fashion designers have been rebuked for using far too much fabric in their styles when things are so scarce. Can't say I want to go back to long trailing skirts again. And you have to wear high heels to look good."

Helen really liked the idea of long full skirts.

Suddenly Mary exclaimed in a loud voice,

"Oh, I say! What an awful shame. That's so sad. You know that young girl, the swimmer that was supposed to come to the Pittenweem Gala, and didn't turn up. Well, it says here she's *died suddenly*! Polio. They think she was training too hard and hadn't enough strength to fight the disease. Nancy Riach is her name and she was only a year or so older than Helen. Really awful, isn't it. I'm so sorry for her people."

Fifth Year

Back at school, there was more sad news. Miss Crichton had died suddenly. It was rumoured that because she had some important work to finish, she had ignored a painful appendix, until it was too late. For such a conscientious woman this was a reasonable explanation, but no one knew exactly. Many girls wept that day.

Elizabeth Crichton had been that wonderful mixture of lively intelligence, charm, humour and kindliness that makes a great teacher. She was a good-looking woman, with a complete and obvious lack of interest in clothes. Was she ever aware of the many hours her pupils spent in discussing how they might take her in hand and knock her into elegant shape?

No doubt she would have smiled her quiet smile at such an idea.

That first day, her register class sat desolate and silent exept for a quiet sob, now and again. It was too hard to believe. and there was little that other teachers could do or say. The whole school was in mourning.

Several girls tried to draw her portrait from memory and Tessa wrote a eulogistic poem, whose sincerity made up for any other deficiencies.

Helen sat and thought about the sympathetic letter she had received from Miss Crichton last year. It had thanked Helen for a pot of home-made damson jam, saying how delicious it had been and confessing that she had been greedy enough to sup it with a spoon. Probably no other girl in the class had such a precious memento and she knew she would treasure it always.

◊

This was the all important year of the Higher Leaving Certificate and both teachers and pupils talked of hard work ahead.

There was a big change at the High School. After so many distinguished years, Mrs Tebb, the headmistress had retired and a new one, Miss Boulter, had been appointed. Like all new brooms, she was determined to sweep the school clean.

No doubt it would have been difficult for any new headmistress to tread successfully in Mrs Tebb's adored and competent footsteps. Miss Boulter made too many changes too quickly and also several mistakes, and endeared herself to neither pupils nor staff.

Because Helen was taking art, she found herself no longer in the A class but grouped with others who were studying minority subjects. This section was designated Vv, standing for five variety. It sounded absurd and seemed like demotion.

Though she felt indignant, this small annoyance was diminished and placed in proper perspective by Helen's great sadness at the loss of Miss Crichton.

Ronnie

On a dusky Autumn evening, Helen sat typing at the table in the window,. The curtains were not yet pulled and she was as visible to the passers by in the street as they were to her. Pausing as she thought of her next sentence, she watched the Hyndland residents walking past, occasionally forming small groups and indulging in loud and vehement discussion. Extreme indignation was in the air. The small shop next to the fish shop was due to open shortly as an *ice cream shop and café* which would remain open until *nine pm!*

It was shocking! There had never been anything of this sort in Hyndland before.

Every shop had always closed respectably by six o'clock.

The residents were horrified and fearful. Dire possibilities of crime and disruption visiting the neighbourhood and the almost certain threat of gangs of youths hanging around and plotting vandalism, were discussed by the worried populace. Helen thought a cafe an excellent idea, though she must still pop along to Byres Road on the first Sunday of the month to spend her sweet coupons, for the Hyndland café would not open on Sundays. Strong local opinion had averted this danger.

She glanced up from her typewriter and saw two young men standing at the tram stop, watching her. They immediately waved to her in a friendly manner.

She lowered her eyes to the keyboard and resumed typing. After a few minutes, she again looked up and again the boys waved cheerily, as though they were old acquaintances.

"There are two boys out there at the tram stop, waving to me! What should I do?"

Annie who sat further back in the room smiled,

"D'ye know them?"

"No."

"Do they look nice fellows?"

"All right, I suppose. They're waving at me again."

"Maybe you should wave back."

However the boys had taken the initiative and climbed into

the garden and their heads and shoulders appeared above the window sill. They could now see Annie within the room and they smiled and waved to her.

"I think they seem to know you Helen. You'd better open the window and speak to them."

Duggie, the taller and younger of the two, immediately introduced himself and explained that he was a pupil at Hyndland school and for years he had seen Helen and her mother from the art room window.

"I feel I know the two of you and when I saw you sitting typing…well it was Ronnie said we should wave to you."

Helen thought they seemed very nice boys. She had wondered for years how she might get to know local boys and here they were chatting to her through the window! She blushed when she remembered the many times she had pushed back the furniture and danced wildly and spontaneously around the room. Had Duggie been watching her from the art room then? How embarrassing. If that were the case, she hoped she would never find out.

Ronnie was twenty and more assured than Duggie. He would be the first boy to take Helen on a real date.

The following week they went to the Grosvenor cinema and saw Bob Hope in *Paleface*.

The catchy tune of the film, 'Button and Bows' became perpetually enshrined in Helen's heart, for it had that power to evoke which only popular music possesses.

Even the crazy words of the song delighted her,

> *My bones denounce the buckboard bounce*
> *And the cactus hurt my toes*

What rubbish it was, but she loved it, because of Ronnie.

Ronnie seemed almost perfect as a boyfriend. How different from those foolish dreams of John Hennington, the unnattainable medical student.

Helen considered herself to be in love at last.

Ronnie Mackenzie lived around the corner in Polwarth Street and quite soon his mother spoke to Helen in the street. In a few weeks, Mrs Mackenzie was visiting Annie each week.

Not that there were any more outings to the cinema with Ronnie. Perhaps he could not afford it. Perhaps she should have asked him out? It did not occur to her, for Helen was quite content to join him in the Clarence Drive lock-up where he kept his motor bike, and watch him as he tinkered and polished.

Ronnie had served his National Service in the Navy and was a fastidious young man. He did not smoke or drink. His short curly hair was well cut, his tie well-tied and his shirts always pristine. He washed them himself.

"Don't think Mum takes enough care." He explained.

He was a salesman for a firm which sold cider, but he had greater ambitions for the future.

It was quite different from the youthful Hollywood romances that Helen had studied, but it was very pleasant. Ronnie arrived at different times to visit and kiss her, sometimes clambering in the kitchen window at six o'clock as she cleared up after the evening meal and sometimes arriving at the front door as late as ten and lounging against the storm door, chatting until Annie cooee-d from the sitting room.

"Do you two know it's nearly half past eleven? I want to go to bed soon, even if you don't."

Then Ronnie would pop in for a moment and apologise charmingly. He was a self-confident young man and he and Annie had a friendly relaxed relationship.

Helen was very, very fond of Ronnie. On several evenings each week, she joined him about eight thirty and would spend a blissful hour or two watching him as he worked on his motor bike. The chilly, winter fogginess added a magical quality to the walk down Clarence Drive, then under the railway bridge and past the advertisement hoardings to the little group of wooden lock-ups where he kept the bike.

The large advertisements were all very familiar. Like old friends, they changed little from year to year and the products were long established names. But about this time, something very strange and innovative appeared. A large otherwise blank poster with only the words,

IT'S COMING!

Nothing else was on the hoarding, It was mysterious. There was no picture to give a clue and it caused a lot of discussion, for everyone had noticed it and paid it more attention than usual. Helen thought it rather frightening, but Annie just said,

"What a ridiculous idea to spend money on something that no one understands."

"But what can it be?" Helen wondered.

"Och, it won't be anything very exciting, I don't suppose."

After two or three weeks another poster took its place.

IT'S COMING SOON!

It was intriguing. What on earth could it be?

After another two weeks, the billboard informed the public that,

WHITE RAIN IS COMING.

Quite soon it was common knowledge that White Rain was a new shampoo. Helen found that very disappointing.

◊

Helen had been seriously warned by her parents that she must *never on any account* accept a ride on Ronnie's motor bike. Bruce had driven one when young and knew only too well how dangerous they were, but as it happened, Ronnie never suggested that she should join him. This made life simple for she had not the slightest interest in the bike, but she enjoyed the intimate companionship of the little hut with her boyfriend busily employed. It seemed a proper way for a couple to enjoy themselves. There was never any kissing in the lock-up, for Ronnie wore his oily overalls. The kissing and the strong rib-cracking hugs were reserved for the kitchen or the front door.

◊

In November, when Helen was buying the Sunday papers in the newsagent, she noticed Miss Boulter beside her and was astonished to see the new headmistress buy the *News of the World*.

Helen was appalled. Her reading had become selective and rather snobbish since those long-ago fashion contests.

She and her schoolfriends were agreed that 'Fanny B', her disparaging nickname, would never be the headmistress that Mrs Tebb had been.

Helen bought a new dress at C&A for the Christmas dance.

"Are you taking Ronnie to the dance?"

"No, he doesn't dance."

Ronnie had been disappointing as far as dates were concerned. That first visit to the Grosvenor had not been repeated. Perhaps his emotional involvement was greater with his motorbike, than with Helen.

"How about Campbell?"

"No. Don't think he enjoyed it particularly the last time. He's really too *old* for a school dance. He must be twenty-one at least. I'll just go myself."

Annie secretly worried that the dance might be a repeat of the previous year. She thought it unlikely, but, if no boy was sensible enough to see what a lovely girl she was, what would that do to Helen's self-esteem? She hid her concern successfully and sat at the window to wave Helen off. As she watched her jump on the tram, she felt suddenly helpless. Even if some nice young fellow came along, Helen was handicapped by having no telelphone. All her girlfriends had telephones. How would a boy get in touch with her again? Really, she must speak to Bruce about that.

◊

That evening, Mary's visit coincided with Bruce's. As usual they greeted each other enthusiastically.

" And have you been very busy, Bruce?"

"To tell you the truth, I've had a *devil* of a time, Mrs Mackay. Men off sick, wood supplies cut, orders cancelled. It's hard times, I can tell you. Sometimes feel the business won't last. It's tough, very tough."

"I daresay. Pity you're not a dentist, isn't it?"

They all laughed. The introduction of the National Health Service seemed to have brought dentistry into a sort of financial paradise. They were reputed to be making many thousands a year.

"Yes, but that's all going to change," Annie said, "The government is going to take a fifty per cent cut of anything they earn above five thousand a year.

They laughed raucously. Five thousand a year was a salary undreamed of. Annie continued,

"Don't worry though, the poor dentists have formed a 'council of war' to protest at such cruelty."

Mary broke into the even louder laughter,

"Yes, and what d'ye think of Glasgow Corporation giving Princess Elizabeth a bedroom suite as a wedding present? I wonder what that cost? She's probably got *hundreds* of suites already. See that Royal family, I believe it's worth billions. *And it's our rates paying for another damned bedroom suite."*

◊

The dance could not have been more different from the fiasco of the previous Christmas. Almost as soon as Helen entered the chilly, little studio, she was asked to waltz. Then another boy asked her for the quickstep. Next, an impressively tall blonde fellow asked her for a military two-step. After exchanging names (his was the unusual one of Haig), he informed her that he would like to dance with her for the rest of the evening and to see her home. As he was a good dancer and was easily the tallest and best-looking man in the room, Helen agreed. It was a very satisfying evening altogether. Haig lived on the South Side of Glasgow but insisted on escorting her home to the West End and did not even expect to kiss her, which she thought charming, though slightly disappointing.

Annie immediately realised from the glow of pleasure and a certain air of triumph on Helen's face that the evening had been a success.

"My goodness, you're as tidy and perfect as when you went away! Did you have a good time, my jewel."

"Absolutely *great!* I met a really nice boy, Haig, and he came home with me all the way, though he lives in Eastwood. Heaven knows how he'll get home. He was a very good dancer. He could *reverse* in the old-fashioned waltz! Not many can do that."

"And are you seeing him again? I was worrying that we didn't have a phone for him to get in touch with you."

"Oh, don't worry, I've arranged for him to phone me at Grandma's next Sunday afternoon. Are you ready for bed now? Or would you like a wee drink of Horlicks first? Oh, I had such a *lovely* time tonight."

Annie was once again struck by her daughter's practical sense. The thought of using Mary's phone on Sunday had never occurred to her.

◊

By the end of January, the romance with Ronnie had faded and gone. Some other girl resembling, according to Ronnie, the gorgeous film star Hedy Lamarr, had stepped between them. Helen was terribly sad, but knew she must concentrate on her school work and obtain a pass in her Higher Leaving Certificate. In 1949 it was necessary to pass every main subject in order to achieve the 'group' necessary for tertiary education. Failure in one subject would cancel the passes in others and no certificate would be awarded. She dreaded the idea of failing. History was her weak subject and there was the absolute necessity of passing her history exam, perhaps for the first time in five years. Study, not one of Helen's skills, was imperative. Hard work might help her broken heart, for she still yearned for Ronnie.

First Ball

"I really don't think I could tackle a ballgown. That's just a bit beyond your old mother's capabilities, I'm afraid."

"Blethers! I bet you could do it *easily*. I saw the loveliest stuff in the Poly on Saturday. It'll just be a simple shape in lovely rich material."

"Well, I don't know. It seems very ambitious."

"What sort of dresses did you used to wear to go dancing?"

"Oh, often they were Mrs Horsland's cast-offs, but they were beautiful dresses. Models. Silk chiffon with beading or embroidery. Not down to the floor of course, quite short, really, in those far-off days. You needed a short dress to do the Charleston."

"And the Black Bottom."

"Yes, you needed lots of freedom of movement for those mad dances. But you want yours right down to the ground, I take it."

"*Oh yes!*" Helen shivered with delight at the thought.

"Like something in a film maybe?"

"Mm. Or something from Paris."

"*Paris!* You're no' greedy but ye like a loat. How d'ye think I can make anything like a Parisian gown."

"Just wait 'til you see the stuff, it's so *gorgeous!*"

"So you've got it all worked out, have you?"

"Yes and I've seen a Simplicity pattern I like. Off the shoulder and a full skirt with a frill."

"Well if you know what you want, you'd better go and buy it and we'll get started and see what we can do. It's not pink is it?"

"No, of course not. Its black and white checked taffeta, just a small check, like gingham, only silky and *so lovely!*"

"Well I never! You first evening dress is going to be black and white!"

"Yes. I don't want any peely-wally pale blues or pinks and this looks more like grey, because the checks are tiny. Wait 'til you see it, you'll love it!"

"And how much is this magnificent stuff per yard? And how many yards will we need for a Parisian gown?"

"It's five shillings a yard and we need eight yards. That's two pounds, d'ye think that's too dear? And I saw lovely silk roses in Coplands to wear in my hair. They were seven and six each but they were *so very nice*. Am I being greedy?"

"I certainly don't think you're being greedy. I bet you'd pay a lot more for a bought one."

"Yes, they're all about seventeen pounds in the shops and they're horrible. Not a bit smart. This one will be chic and....oh."

Helen closed her eyes and held her breath as she often did in moments of excitement.

"I think you mean superlative. Well, I just hope your faith in me is justified, but I'll do my best for my wee ewe lamb."

Helen made a face.

"I'm ain't goin' to look like no lamb in this dress, I betcha!"

◊

As soon as Helen returned from town on Saturday afternoon, she unwrapped the taffeta with a flourish and its folds flowed over an armchair and spilled across the carpet. There was a great deal of it. The sitting room seemed filled with its shining, rippling, rustling glory. The dazzle of the tiny glittering checks made Helen feel quite faint. It was an exciting moment and one she would never forget. Her very first evening dress.

"In the name of the wee man, how many yards did you get? Am I supposed to wrestle all that stuff into one garment. I'll never do it and I'll be blinded with all those checks. But it does look *lovely* and I'm dying to get started. Have you got your scissors there?"

"At the ready."

By bedtime, the bodice was taking shape and the wide skirt edged by a deep frill looked every bit as glamorous as Helen had dreamed.

Annie stretched her tired arms.

"I'm exhausted, but that's been one of the most exciting afternoons of my life!"

She felt that the dress might well come up to her daughter's high expectations. Helen's face was such a picture of delight that Annie would have worked all night to finish it, if there had been any necessity to do so.

"I must say I'd never have thought of choosing that fabric myself, but I have to congratulate you, for I think it suits the pattern and I think it's going to look just smashing. I hope Haig is properly astonished and appreciative of the work we've put into this creation."

"He will be. I just wish he lived on this side of town."

Helen and Haig had not yet had a proper date. Their friendship had relied entirely on Sunday telephone conversations, conducted when Helen was visiting Renfrew Street. As Haig was preparing for examinations, he was expected to stay in and study until the exams were safely behind him. If he had lived closer, they might have met for a coffee but Helen quite enjoyed the long distance friendship. They had got to know each other on the phone. Wee Eileen was always delighted when it rang on a Sunday afternoon,

"There's the phone! That's your boyfriend, Helen! Hurry up! Hurry, hurry! Does he know I'm here listening? Will I go away? Can I stay and listen? Can I speak to him?"

But she would run away giggling, if Helen handed the phone to her.

The dress was created for an eighteenth birthday party in March, which was unfortunately also the month of the exams.

Margaret Innes was an attractive self-contained girl, who seemed very mature. The other girls found it thrilling that she was engaged to a young man of twenty-four. They would be married as soon as Margaret finished school, and the couple would then take charge of the hotel on Loch Ard which his parents owned. The other girls held her in some awe. It seemed strange to know that your grown-up life, marriage and career were all mapped out and would start in the very near future.

"Fancy being engaged when you're only eighteen! And to a twenty-four year old man, Mummy!"

"You sound as though you disapprove. There's a bigger age difference between grandma and grandad."

"Is there? And they're going to run a hotel, too. It seems as though she's missing part of the fun of growing up. But she seems very happy. Very much in love."

"That's good."

"But she's so young."

"Yes, she is very young and I have to say I think she's too young to be so tied down. Where is it she's having her party, exactly? In town somewhere?"

"Yes, her parents own a place in Sauchiehall Street, I think Margaret called it a 'function suite', is that right? They have weddings and parties there. It's on the left when you're going into town, just past the High School hill and before the big grassy hill."

"Oh, her parents are in catering too, are they? Perhaps that's why they're quite happy for her to follow in the same line of business. Now, I'm just wondering, does this place have large curved windows on either side of the entrance?"

"Yes, that's right."

"Well, what an *amazing* coincidence! There was a girl in my class at school and *her* parents owned that shop too! They were bakers, Austrian I think, and I suppose they hired out the function rooms and catered as well. Their name was Kunzl and their daughter was Edelweiss Kunzl. I thought that was the loveliest name. She was such a nice girl, too, very pretty. And now you're friendly with Margaret whose folk have the same place! Fancy, how history repeats itself. It's incredible. And right up until the war started, you could buy little cakes called Kunzl cakes, though I don't suppose they're around any more."

◊

The taxi would arrive shortly.

Helen gazed in the mirror.

For the first time in her life, Helen felt entirely pleased with her own appearance. The dress transformed her.

Her bare shoulders seemed unusual and glamorous. The dark mole on her left shoulder might have been the beauty spot that Georgette Heyer often mentioned as her heroine's attribute.

Helen wore no jewellery. She felt the two roses in her hair, which added a sense of Parisian luxury, were sufficient.

She looked over her shoulder to check her back view. Yes, she was completely satisfied. and the sensation of the wide rustling skirt around her ankles spelled Romance.

She felt buoyant with a previously unknown confidence and she could not stop smiling.

Annie watched her daughter with pride and also a certain satisfaction. It was a great relief that the dress was finished and successful. It had evolved into a large unmanageable garment and the final stages had not been easy.

She felt a throb of joy that she could still be a useful mother.

The party was all that Helen hoped it might be, and Haig loved the dress.

While they enjoyed their evening together, dancing and laughing a lot, their romance had little future, partly because of the inconvenient distance between their homes, but more especially because of Haig's examinations. He was finding first year medicine very hard going.

Helen was asked to dance by other young men and amongst them was a very tall boy from Hyndland. There was an instant attraction between them. Douglas lived in Falkland Street, and was also an only child. He had brown curls, a ready smile and a relaxed charming manner and was a fairly good dancer. Finding that they were both keen swimmers and members of the Arlington Baths, they bemoaned the fact that they could never meet there, because of the club's policy of segregating the sexes. They fantasised about how wonderful it would be to have a swimming pool in Hyndland and agreed that the piece of waste land behind the little fruit shop would be a perfect place to build one. Surely it was possible?

Douglas had almost finished his accountancy training. He would then join the RNVR for his National Service.

As they were each with other partners, they made no future arrangements that night, but each promised to look out for the other in Hyndland.

Haig was a nice young man but the friendship had too many handicaps. The Sunday phone calls became sporadic and had stopped by the summer.

All thoughts of Ronnie were swept from Helen's mind by Douglas, who would drift in and out of Helen's life for the next eight years. Without considering herself 'in love' with him, or certainly not prepared to admit it, she would remain aware of his existence in the world, whether they were in touch or not. With his charm, his good looks and his personality, he would provide a bench mark against which Helen measured each young man that she met in those years.

Not one of them would quite measure up to Douglas.

Rationing

In April, Tate and Lyle announced a record turnover of £78,000,000 and shortly after the Minister for Food announced that sweet rationing would end on the 24th. Alas, he was too optimistic. The following day, shopkeepers were forced to introduce their own scheme of rationing and by the 26th, the demand was 'overwhelming'. Sweet coupons were reintroduced in July, with a promise of a bonus at Christmas.

◊

"Aye, Annie, they've invented a new type of putting green in New Zealand, made of sawdust! Can ye imagine. Seems to be like a big cork mat. It'll never catch on here, I'm thinking, never catch on here."

"We'll not need it here, I suppose. We've plenty rain to make the grass grow, although I thought it was quite wet out there too, with all the mountains. But what about this maximum charge of five shillings that they're getting rid of in the restaurants? Is that going to affect you?"

"Och, no, I go to the cheap dives, lovely fish supper for a couple o' bob."

"Poor teachers, too. I didn't know they were so badly paid. The paper says a de-mobbed man with two kids gets a government grant of three hundred and sixty quid a year to train as a teacher, but once he's through, his salary will be *less than that!* And the price of cheese is going up to *one and tuppence a pound*, though we're to get thruppence more on the meat ration. But that's still less than we got when the war was on *and* we're only to get tuppence worth of corned beef. It's all a bit of a scunner, isn't it."

"Aye, though there's a penny off a pint of beer. That's always something Annie."

"Yes I suppose so for some folk. But this new health service seems to be working. The Herald says Glasgow's infant mortality rate is the lowest ever."

◊

Slowly, there were small luxuries returning to the shops. Sweet shops started to stock remembered names. After the fiasco of de-rationing, Helen continued to visit the Byres Road ice cream shop on the first Sunday of each month to buy the new allowance of one pound per person. The second pound of sweets would be bought before the end of that week. Then there would be three sweet-free weeks. As Annie said,

"It's a hunger or a burst."

Otherwise Helen's shopping was mainly in Hyndland, as everything was available there. The grocer now stocked Primula cheese in a tube which, with the Spanish tomatoes one could now buy in winter, made a delicious sandwich. Heinz sandwich spread was still a favourite indulgence and Helen would stand in the kitchen, guiltily eating this by the spoonful, unable to stop herself. She felt hungry a lot of the time and though Annie suggested bread, she found it unexciting.

McKeans pork butchers in Byres Road now had various cold meats on offer, salt beef, gammon, tongue, jellied veal and liver sausage. The last was a spreading pate and was Annie's favourite. Helen liked jellied veal best.

Sometimes on a nice Saturday afternoon Annie would say,

"Away along to McKeans and get something tasty for the tea."

Helen enjoyed walking the mile quickly, choosing a different route each time. When she returned, Annie would say,

"Back already? Did you run all the way? I think you must have a pair of seven league boots."

Helen had always wondered exactly how seven league boots were supposed to work. Even fairy stories should be capable of logical explanation.

Helen was returning from Byres Road in April, nibbling a slice of jellied veal as she walked along a tree-lined lane, when she noticed that one of the parked cars belonged to her father. There was no doubt about it, CUS 767 was his car. She always joked that his number plate perfectly suited someone who swore as much as he did. There was his car and it seemed a strange place for it to be. Usually he was golfing at Killermont on a nice Saturday afternoon. Could he be shopping in Byres Road? Then why not park nearer the shops? She forgot to mention it to her mother.

Over the next few weeks, she saw the car parked in the same spot, four times. When she told her mother, Annie just said,

"I expect he's visiting someone."

Annie wondered who it was, but dismissed it from her mind and said nothing to Bruce about it.

Perhaps it was best not to know.

◊

Annie now used the old typewriter for all her letters and Helen had encouraged her to type out her poems and stories too.

Although Annie would always take infinite pains with knitting and sewing, her typing fell far short of perfection. Her fingers were not reliable and she developed a free and careless style. Also she was impatient. Bad mistakes were overprinted with XXXs and lesser mistakes were pushed, not always legibly, into shape.

"Och well, it'll take them all the longer to puzzle it out! Anyway they're lucky to get any letters from a poor invalid."

Perfection, that quality attributed to those born inder the sign of Virgo, was a quality that Annie, a Virgoan, could take or leave alone.

Helen occasionally typed a letter to Jean, who now worked as a dentist's receptionist in Dunfermline.

Her parents had taken over a working man's hostel called the Abbot's House, a medieval building close to Dunfermline Abbey. It sounded very romantic. Clare said it had a beautiful garden but was impossible to keep clean, for the floors were stone and ancient dust dropped down from the vaulted ceilings.

Examinations and Barnacle Bill

Spring came early that year. February was bright and mild and Helen thought swotting for exams might be more bearable outside in the sunshine.

She walked along the lane to the back green belonging to the Polwarth Street tenement which had been demolished by a land-mine during the war. It was not yet re-built and its garden afforded the only sunny spot amongst the tall buildings. There she would sit each day reading about the nineteenth century Reform Bills, perhaps also hoping to catch a glimpse of Ronnie.

The melancholy and untouched bomb site was one of the few results of the war with which Helen was familiar. She had read of the destruction throughout Europe and the devastation in Clydebank only five miles away, but here in front of her was the reality. Helen thought the empty space was as ugly and obvious as a huge tooth missing from an enormous mouth. Terrible to think that a whole building had been wiped away by a single bomb, dropped from a plane hurtling through the night. Incredible that eight families had once lived in large comfortable homes, where now there was nothing but emptiness. It was still possible to see where fireplaces had been and even some scraps of wallpaper fluttered in the spring breeze.

How important the war had seemed to everyone, always the main topic of any conversation. People listened to every news bulletin throughout the day, then discussed it endlessly. Now, apart from this great hole in the respectable line of tenements, the war was in the past. Just as much as these nineteenth century Reform Bills which she was studying. Helen found these social reforms more interesting than the endless parade of kings and battles that had filled so many history lessons. Now she seemed to learn about real people and a past which affected the present. Had those years of war affected the way that ordinary people would live now? She felt sure it could never be forgotten by those whose homes, familiar possessions, and personal treasures had dissolved into empty air. She could hardly imagine what it would be like to lose everything that she cherished. Did those unlucky people still think about chairs they had sat in and favourite pictures and all those little things which had other memories attached to them? Or were the things and the memories both forgotten? Helen could visualise objects clearly in her head and thought it must be heart-breaking to know they were lost forever.

Helen knew she was lucky. None of her relatives had suffered or died and her home was unscathed. She gazed up at the sky showing through the large gap. How strange to know that your home had once existed in that large empty space up there, perhaps just *there* on the third floor, where a triangular scrap of paper patterned with autumn leaves still remained on a wall. That would be their sitting room. How long had they lived in that home, with the elaborate plaster ceiling high above their heads and solid walls with fancy paper and light switches and wooden floors with linoleum and carpets to walk and dance and jump on? Now there was nothing but empty air.

Helen shivered in spite of the sun.

◊

The exams finished in April, with oral examinations, then results in June.

Helen tried not to think about June. She was preparing for dance exams and also thinking about summer clothes, for fashions were changing drastically. Skirts were much longer. The French fashions last year had caused lots of discussion, even uproar at their extravagance, but most women now agreed they could no longer wear knee length skirts. Helen hoped her mother would make her two or three of these longer dresses, graceful, romantic and rather French.

Margaret came to visit Helen, wearing a navy dress with white spots and an unusually wide skirt.

"What a lovely dress, Margaret." Annie said

"Yes isn't it gorgeous!" Helen breathed.

" Thank you. I love it too! We bought it in Daly's."

"Gosh, I bet it was expensive!"

"Mmm, I suppose so, but it's my favourite. It's for my trousseau, but I wanted to wear it sooner." She laughed self-consciously.

Annie looked carefully at the way it was made and nodded.

"That's very clever, the skirt is cut in three tiers of different widths, each gathered to the upper one, so that it's really wide at the hem, but not too full at the waist. I like it very much. Very elegant!"

"I think it's called a parasol skirt." Margaret volunteered.

As soon as she left, Annie said firmly,

"You've to do something for me! Away into town, right now, and go to the Poly. Choose some nice stuff that you like and get me six yards of it. I'm going to make you a dress with a parasol skirt."

Helen looked at her and giggled. Annie shook a dismissive hand.

"*Come on!* What are you waiting for? Don't waste a minute. Off you go."

Helen laughed as she hurried out the front door. She was sure no other girl had a mother quite like Annie.

Some French ginghams had 'just arrived' in Lewis's, at two shillings and sixpence a yard. Some were in rich jewel colours and others more delicate greys and blues. It was difficult to choose, for they were all lovely. As it seemed such a bargain, Helen bought six yards of a vivid check and six yards of a more subtle one.

Returning on the tram, she worried. Had she been too extravagant buying all that material? Perhaps two and six a yard was not such a bargain after all? Would her mother be angry? Counting the thread and zip fasteners, she had spent very nearly two pounds. She comforted herself that a dress in C&A's was nearly three pounds and the dress from Daly's almost certainly cost fifteen.

She need not have worried. Annie exclaimed with delight at the fact that there were two dresses to make.

"Aye, you've got your grandmother's eye for a bargain. Now, where are the scissors and which one will you cut out first? "

◊

"I wonder if the two of you could do me a bit of a favour, Annie."

Bruce was paying his usual fleeting visit before meeting someone at the Grosvenor cinema. Annie noticed he no longer mentioned the friend's name.

"I'm sure we could. What was it you were wanting us to do?"

"Well, I'd like you to offer some hospitality to a cousin of mine. You like doing that sort of thing, don't you? Cooking and

all that stuff. And Stewart and I couldn't have him at Doune
Terrace, the place is a dump these days. He's just a young chap,
terribly brainy sort of fellow, I believe. Went to Cambridge, did
his Tripos, whatever that is. Now he's in the RNVR and stationed
down at Helensburgh. Bill McKerracher is his name, grew up in
Bolton. I'd never heard of him. Maybe I did, but I'd forgotten.
Anyway this letter came from him, funny sort of letter, too. I'll let
you see it. Maybe you could ask him for his tea sometime, seeing
he's far from home and we're related and all that sort of thing.
Would ye do that for me?"

'Oh certainly, Bruce. We'll be delighted to have him for a meal,
won't we, Helen?"

She gave her daughter a strong meaning look which
conveyed the message, 'Buck up, agree with me and be nice to
your father'. Helen did her best. She was slowly learning to
hide her feelings.

When Bill arrived the following Saturday, tall, thin and very
presentable in his officer's uniform, Helen was pleasantly surprised. There was a faint family resemblance, his nose showing
the sharp bridge that Helen shared with her father. He seemed
shy and awkward, but very grateful for the home-cooked food,
and had brought four bars of chocolate and a little bunch of
flowers.

After he left, Annie commented,

"He's not a very usual young man, is he?"

Over the next few months, Bill came up to Glasgow whenever
he had leave. He and Helen visited the cinema, the museum, and
the parks. They danced once in Hillhead Town Hall, but that was
unsuccessful. Bill's dancing skills were as untried as his social
ones.

It was very pleasant to walk around Hyndland on the arm of a
handsome Naval officer and it certainly helped to deaden the
pain of Ronnie's desertion. It also gave her the chance to wear
that expensive bouclé coat.

Between his visits, they wrote letters to each other, Bill always
enclosing a bar of chocolate of an unusual type not yet available in
the shops, with plain chocolate sandwiched between two layers of
milk. They played old records one evening and one particularly
caught their fancy,

(Sound of knocking. Then small quavery voice asks)
  "Who's that knocking at my door?"
(More knocking, same voice)
  "Who's that knocking at my door?"
(Much more knocking, same voice)
  "Who's that knocking at my door?" cried the fair young maiden
(Large deep voice roars out)
  "IT'S ONLY ME FROM OVER THE SEA, SAID BARNACLE BILL THE SAILOR!
  "JUST GOT BACK FROM PORTUGEE ABOARD A BRITISH WHALER"

After that, letters were signed from Barnacle Bill and from the Fair Young Maiden.

Their cousinly friendship could hardly be called a romance, although kisses were exchanged, but they were 'practice' kisses and acknowledged as such.

The first kiss happened one night when they were sitting on either side of the fire, chatting decorously about the film they had seen that evening. Annie had gone off to bed to listen to a radio play and Bill must shortly catch the last bus to Helensburgh.

Suddenly Bill, stammering slightly, said,

"You know, I know really nothing much about girls and kissing and that sort of thing. I'm sure my technique is poor."

Helen looked at him astonished. He continued to speak.

"For instance, I've no idea how easily offended a girl might be, supposing you kissed her…"

Helen had no idea what to say. In her limited experience, kissing was not discussed, it just happened. She looked at him blankly.

Then he stood up,

"Stand up, please" he said, rather peremptorily. Helen stood up and he kissed her, not in an entirely unpractised way, she thought. Then he sat down again, leaving her standing on the hearthrug. Bill motioned her back to her seat and continued to talk about the technique and ethics of kissing in various environments and how offence might be avoided. Helen had no idea what he was going on about, but listened politely.

When he left to catch the bus, he gave her a cousinly peck on the cheek.

When Helen went to bed, Annie asked if she had enjoyed her evening with Bill.

"He's nice enough, but he certainly is strange."

"Ah, that's these intellectuals for you."

Over the next few months, practice helped them achieve a more relaxed and enjoyable, though passionless, kissing experience.

In the summer, Bill left the Gareloch to serve in more exotic seas and soon their correspondence petered out. Helen heard that he had emigrated to Australia and she would never meet him again.

◊

It was a Sunday night in June. The oral exams had passed with nobody being asked anything much at all. Now the final results were imminent. Mrs Connell, Miss Arthur and Helen's grandparents were all positive that Helen would pass with no trouble. Annie assured her it would be fine, but Helen knew there was the possibility of failing history, in which case she would not be awarded the qualification necessary for Art School, no matter how well she did in other subjects.. What would she do if she failed? She could not face another year at school. The University prelims took place in September, providing an alternative to those who had not passed Highers, but what a nightmare to do all that work again.

Annie had made the mistake of saying,

"Well, even if you don't pass this time, it's not the end of the world. You'll get them the next time!"

Helen had burst into tears. Even her mother believed it possible she might fail.

After the usual busy Sunday, Helen was making the roast beef dinner. The piece of meat looked pathetically small this week, but she would be extravagant and use more flour and two dried eggs in the Yorkshire pudding. Her bath was waiting for her and as she put Annie to bed she dashed back to the kitchen to keep an eye on the potatoes and turnip which would soon be ready to pour and mash. Somehow things had gone a little wrong tonight, everything was behind hand. Perhaps she had read for too long or perhaps procrastinated earlier. Her bath must be a hurried one tonight.

Annie was sitting up in bed when Helen, wrapped in a towel, damp and rather flushed, came into the bedroom and sat beside her.

"I've got one of those itchy attacks again. And I feel a bit strange. Woozy."

Then she lay down across the bed. Annie thought she had fainted, but she was still conscious though very distressed. She seemed to have difficulty speaking, for her voice was faint and hoarse.

"Inside my mouth seems all itchy too. It's horrible and I can't get a proper breath."

Her face was very pale, though the skin of her neck and inner arms was scarlet and roughened.

Annie tried to hide her panic.

"Try and keep calm, Helen."

Now Annie realised the terrible lack of a telephone. She felt assailed by guilt. Mary had been right. They should certainly have had a phone for emergencies, long before now. How could she get help? They were alone and she was useless. Why had she not demanded that they have a phone?

Helen's breathing was becoming more shallow and her eyes were wide and staring. It was obvious the girl was terrified of what was happening to her. Once again her body was out of control.

Annie felt agonisingly helpless. Should she leave her daughter and attempt to reach Mrs Unsworth next door? But by the time she could crawl slowly to her neighbour for help, it might be too late. What if Helen were dying? Annie turned herself over, preparatory to dropping down to the floor from the high bed. She had never done this before and must be careful to keep her balance and not injure herself.

When Helen realised her mother's intention, she shook her head wildly and whispered,

"Don't leave me."

Annie returned to her place and stroked Helen's hand, but the girl did not want to be touched and convulsively clutched the sheets.

After eight terrible minutes, Helen's breathing became slightly easier. In another twenty, the rash started to subside.

"Oh, that was really horrible, Mummy. Horrible. I couldn't get a breath in or out. I really thought I was dying this time. I wonder why it was so bad? It's never been as bad as that before. The itch was in my mouth and down my throat too and I was itchy all over. Look at my arms and my thighs. They're still itching but not so much now. But the worst thing is not being able to breathe properly. It all came on so quickly too, just as though I was bewitched."

"My poor wee girl. I wonder what brought it on like that?"

"My bath was quite hot, maybe too hot. And I was rushing a bit to get the dinner over before the play started on the wireless. And we've missed the beginning now, I'm afraid. I'm sorry."

"Oh that doesn't matter a damn. As long as you're all right, darling. I was so worried about you, my pet, and I could do nothing to help you. What a useless old mother. But I've made up my mind and *we're going to get a phone in as soon as possible*, This week if we can. I hope we never need it again, but we *must* have one."

"It'll be handy for boyfriends, anyway." Helen croaked with a weak smile.

Annie gazed at her daughter. How happy she was to think of Helen having boyfriends. It had seemed tonight that she might lose her forever.

"Well, I'll just go and heat up the dinner and make the gravy."

"Dinner! It'll be burned to a frazzle by this time? It doesn't matter."

"Oh no. I turned everything off when I started to feel funny. The Yorkshire might be a bit leathery, but that can't be helped."

Annie was astonished that her daughter had had the presence of mind to think of the dinner in the face of such an attack, but food had been precious all Helen's life and avoiding waste would always be a part of her philosophy.

◊

Helen's study had been effective. Even the dreaded history paper was passed. She gained her Higher Leaving Certificate and would start Art School in September.

Leaving High School

Nancy Little was the first person that Annie called on the shiny new black telephone. It really was very nice to get in touch with friends so easily and she was able to give the good news that Helen had passed her Highers.

Three days later, Nancy phoned back. She sounded excited.

"Have you seen the Glasgow Herald today, Ann?"

"No, I didn't get a paper today. Is there something of interest?"

Nancy's voice deepened and she spoke even more deliberately and dramatically than usual,

"There certainly is. I think you'll be tremendously pleased."

"Well, come on then, don't keep me in suspense!"

"You know the schoolchildren's art competition that's held annually at the Art Galleries? Well… *Helen has won a gold medal*! Isn't that wonderful. I do congratulate her. She's a clever girl."

"My goodness, that really is wonderful, isn't it. You've taken my breath away! They gave her a ' highly commended' once, but a *gold medal*! That really is something special. What an honour, right enough. I am delighted and she will be too, of course. And thank you so much for letting me know. I'm absolutely speechless!"

"Yes, you know there are only five gold medals awarded each year and about fourteen thousand children enter the competition. It's a wonderful start to her Art School studies, isn't it. I'm so proud of her."

Helen was less impressed.

"Fancy! I've no idea why. It was just a rough watercolour of a bunch of flowers. I wasn't all that pleased with it and I left early. Just luck, I think. Very nice of course, but just luck. Other kids do such wonderful drawings, things I couldn't begin to do. Miss Meldrum never helps us much and I know she wouldn't have liked my picture. She never likes what I do. Fancy them picking out my splashy watercolour. It's amazing."

Mrs Connell was quite overcome by the news and had to make herself a cup of tea to calm down and she could not stop smiling for the rest of that day.

Annie wrote to Mary in Pittenweem. She immediately informed the local newspaper and the following week forwarded this clipping from the East Fife Observer,

IN THE BLOOD
Helen Corning, granddaughter of John Mackay, the well-known Glasgow artist, has been awarded a Gold medal in the Glasgow Corporation Schoolchildren's Art Competition. Helen will be remembered as the attractive winner of the Miss Pittenweem beauty contest last year.

Helen did not know whether to be amused or offended.

"What a headline! It sounds like a *murder* report. It's maybe fine to see your name in the paper, but not under that sort of heading."

But it made a good story and her school friends laughed.

As Helen had not distinguished herself either academically or athletically at High School, it was nice to leave with a little trail of glory.

Her art teacher, the unloved Miss Meldrum, was most enthusiastic and shook Helen's hand, saying,

"Oh, I always knew you could do it, Helen."

Helen's face remained expressionless. What a hypocritical old besom! Helen had received little encouragement and knew her art education had been inadequate and boring.

The unexpected news was that Miss Meldrum was *leaving to get married!*

In her mid-fifties, the teacher seemed an old lady to her pupils, though as she made this astonishing announcement, her manner was girlish and coy. She confided that she was marrying her late sister's widower, a farmer in Aberdeen.

The girls discussed it later,

"What is she thinking of?"

"It's just bizarre. At her age!"

"Incredible."

"But it makes it seem better somehow, her keeping it in the family, so to speak."

They giggled.

"D'ye think so? I'm not sure if it's legal to marry your sister's widower."

"Surely she'd have made enquiries and found out if it's legal or not. But I do think it's a bit strange, all the same."

"No, I wouldn't like it at all, my sister's husband, ugh."

"Me neither. It gives me the creeps."

"I certainly call it very peculiar."

Only Margaret, whose own wedding would be very soon, had a kinder attitude.

"Well, she's not young and she's not what you'd call attractive. I think she's lucky to find anyone to marry her and I hope she'll be happy. At least she won't be lonely in her old age, poor soul."

Astonished outrage or condescending pity, which comment was least flattering?

Certainly Miss Meldrum was not a popular teacher.

As usual, June was warm and sunny. With the exams behind them, the fifth year pupils sat idly in the playground, chatting. It seemed a shame to come to school at all.

There was an option available of cookery lessons in another school, but Helen considered herself sufficiently experienced in that art.

◊

The main subject for Higher English had been Hamlet.

As in former years, Shakespeare's masterpiece had been deconstructed, minutely analysed, then put together again, several times, by every fifth year pupil in Scotland. First for the December examinations, then for the Preliminaries in February and finally for the certificate examination in March.

The confident girls could now discuss every subtle nuance of Hamlet's mental processes. But think of those poor teachers who, year after year open their worn copies, knowing that yet again they must listen to teenagers struggling to declaim the too-familiar speeches, must direct those young minds, many of them unwilling, to the complexities of the plot and the indecision of the prince. It is not only on the battlefield that heroes are to be found.

That was the year that Laurence Olivier brought his interpretation of Hamlet to the cinema, incidentally shocking everyone by bleaching his hair blonde for the lead role.

Helen and her friends watched it in the Cosmo cinema and were very impressed. It seemed marvellous, though some of the costumes were rather weird and Helen could not be completely happy with the blonde Olivier. Nearly everyone in the film was a well-known Shakespearean actor. The fact that the girls were steeped in the play was useful, for much of the action took place in gloomy darkness.

Before Annie was confined to a wheelchair, she and Helen had enjoyed the cinema enthusiastically and regularly, but Helen had lost the habit and only in summertime did she spend an evening watching ancient or unheard of movies in the small, grubby Pittenweem Picture House. She found the stylish and luxurious Cosmo a very different, sophisticated experience and determined to return soon. Perhaps next time she would watch one of those foreign films, only to be seen in this tiny art cinema.

◊

Unlike many of her friends, Helen had no regrets when her schooldays ended. It was the end of an era which had generated little affection in her breast. She would keep in touch with some friends, otherwise she was happy to shake off the dust of the Glasgow High School for Girls forever. Never again need she rush up that long steep hill and then half way down the other side!

She had scarcely realised that the Art School, situated further east on the Garnethill mountain, would also present a demanding daily climb, shorter but steeper.

On the last day, with several other pupils, she visited each teacher to say goodbye, and was surprised at how tenderly some of them spoke to her and wished her well. She could not remember finding much of that sort of friendliness in the preceding years. Perhaps then she might have felt more regret at leaving, but few of these forbidding spinsters in their black cloaks had seemed human or accessible. Only Miss Crichton had been loving and beloved and she was gone.

Miss Loudon, the unpopular gym teacher, was particularly fulsome to Helen, complimenting her on her smart skirt and slender figure. Helen smiled thinly, but found it hard to forget the day that same teacher had demolished her self-confidence with criticism. She still felt hot and humiliated at the memory. Usually, she replaced this memory with the more pleasant one of the concert given for the school's fiftieth anniversary when Helen had danced a Tarantella with seven other pupils. Afterwards the headmistress had spoken to her specially,

"You really love dancing, don't you, Helen!"

Not only had Mrs Tebb known the name and personal history of every girl in the school, she also had the knack of saying just the right thing.

East Neuk Again

Pittenweem seemed an anti-climax after the last exciting weeks in Glasgow. They arrived on a Tuesday, for Bruce had business in Dundee. After the car was unpacked, he waited only long enough for coffee and three rolls, spread with Mary's home-made rhubarb jam. With many enthusiastic compliments about the jam and questions about how it was made, together with excuses and apologies for leaving so soon, Bruce made his usual abrupt exit.

"I don't think he's got business in Dundee at all. I don't believe it for a minute." Mary pronounced as soon as he left, the gravel spurting under his back wheels. "I'm quite sure he's away to golf with those friends."

"Och well, what does it matter? He's brought us through and we're here earlier than we thought we would be. And it's great to be here. The garden looks effulgent and wonderful."

Mary was not to be mollified. Deprived of an audience. she was cross.

"I just think he's meeting that wee fat man, whatsisname, in St Andrews and I don't like people to be dishonest with me. Why could he not just say he was going to golf? Helen, did you notice if his golf bag was in the boot when you brought in the luggage?"

"I don't think so, but I didn't really notice."

Mary shook her head, unconvinced.

Annie had a different theory. She also believed there was no business meeting, nor yet a rendezvous with Bobby Forrester. Bruce hardly mentioned him these days. These meetings with an un-named friend were often used to excuse his hurried exits and Annie was pretty sure it was a female friend. She told herself she did not mind. Bruce deserved a normal life and she wished him luck, but there was more than a trace of loss and sadness behind her philosophical attitude.

◊

Helen had felt little enthusiasm for going to Fife this year, but it was taken for granted that they would join the Mackays and she knew the holiday was good for them both. Helen had a deep abiding faith in fresh air, believing it impossible to get too much of it. She would have stayed outside from morning to night, if practicable. Helen could not pinpoint exactly why she felt this way, for her family had certainly not enforced any such idea. Neither the Mackays nor the Cornings were interested in the great outdoors.

Perhaps the general climate of opinion still worshipped the ideal of the garden city and certainly the Spartan life was admired. Respectable people were careful to let it be known that they always slept with wide open windows, babies were put outside to sleep in their prams for most of the day, and all new schools had been built with draughty open corridors.

At the Arlington older members would finish off their hot shower with a few bracing moments under the stinging needles of a cold one, in order to 'close the pores'. Old dogmatic ladies advised younger members to folow their example, but Helen only tried it once. She did enjoy the painful, though rewarding, dive into the icy swimming pool in Pittenweem, preferring a sudden plunge, to the slow, agonising wade into ever-deepening water at the shallow end. Some bathers found it helpful to splash water on their arms and shoulders, gradually introducing their body to the knowledge of just how cold the water was. Helen liked to stride unhesitatingly to the deep end, step on to the diving board and launch herself into the water without a pause. There was more than a little bravado in this ritual and while flying through the air, she often wondered why she was doing it. Too late! The first three minutes of immersion were the worst, but vigorous swimming soon helped the body regain an acceptable temperature. Or, as grandad suggested, paralysis stopped the brain realising how extremely cold it was.

Masochistic or not, Helen longed to swim as soon as she smelled the pungent sea air.

The magical qualities of the Pittenweem garden also entranced Helen and the familiar perfumes of marigolds, lavender, honey-suckle and artemisia conjured up childhood memories.

As she sat in the little garden, she was fascinated anew each year by the immense sky overhead and enjoyed watching the ever-changing cloud formations imperceptibly travel out over the North Sea and disappear. The vivid expanse of restless blue sea stretching to the other shore of the Forth made hot, dusty, smelly

Glasgow seem very far away.

They had fish suppers that night and Mrs Taylor presented Helen with the usual beautiful bouquet for her mother.

"Well, my goodness, I'd better get up early tomorrow and get cracking on this. It's almost more than I can face." Annie laughed.

Such a splendid bouquet seemed to challenge the horticultural achievement of Mary's garden.

"It certainly is an enormous bunch and the colours are so very *intense*! That woman must have an astonishing garden." She paused to light a cigarette. "But you'd need to be careful what sort of picture you painted with such *very vivid* colours. They're not... what I would call exactly...artistic. Almost harsh, in fact. Wouldn't you agree, John?"

He laughed slightly,

"Well, they certainly are particularly bright flowers, very bright. Perhaps Annie might modify their brilliance, just a little. I expect she'll make a good job of it."

John had found the energy to agree with his wife, but soon his chin dropped back towards his chest and his gaze returned to the hearthrug. He was getting very old and tired. Still, he had enjoyed his fish and chips and Helen was glad about that.

At seven o'clock, there was the sound of distant music. The open air dancing was starting up in the Market Place.

"There's the music, my jewel. Are you going along to have a dance?" Mary asked.

Helen looked at her mother for approval. They had just arrived, perhaps she should be making herself useful.

"Yes, on you go, if you're not too tired."

Helen hardly knew the meaning of the word 'tired' and washed her face, tidied her hair and ran along to the Market Place to start the ruination of another pair of sandals.

◊

Not only dancers gathered in the Market Place when the music started. Visitors and locals, out for an evening stroll, were drawn to the sound from all parts of the town and a fair-sized audience quickly formed. Even the residents of the square enjoyed the twice-weekly session, sitting at their open windows and watching the charming scene with that avid interest in their neighbours which is found in small towns. It was not a late night for the music finished promptly at nine o'clock, and as the van drove off the noisy, laughing crowds quickly dispersed to form queues at the fish and chip shops.

Apart from the occasional brave fellow, local boys tended to stand and watch, rather than dance and the couples performing the St Bernard's waltz, the Highland Schottische or the Military Two-step were mainly female though this did not appear to detract from their enjoyment. Certainly Helen preferred to dance with a girl who knew what she was about, than with a boy who floundered. The uneven terrain made dancing difficult enough without a clumsy partner. More young men, usually visitors, would join the dancers for a quickstep or old fashioned waltz. Helen had no expectations of being asked to dance by a stranger and was just happy to enjoy the energetic and demanding exercise. She was aware that her dancing skills were not unremarked, for Alice Thomson the butcher had described Helen as a 'grand wee dancer' and hinted she was not alone in that opinion. Where other girls turned once in the St Bernard's waltz, Helen turned twice. She knew it was 'showing off' but it was fun and she might as well make use of all those ballet lessons.

Helen glanced up at the first floor window above the butcher's shop and was pleased to see her friend Alison waving madly. Wonderful! Alison was a great partner and they would not stop for the next two hours.

Ten minutes later, the compere announced 'Strip the Willow', that energetic dance which consists almost entirely of madly fast whirling around. Unexpectedly, two tall youths in kilts and Scout uniform stepped forward and claimed Helen and Alison as partners. Previously, Helen had danced this only with girls and she was unprepared for the strength and speed which the young men brought to the dance. The boys' kilts and the girls' full skirts flew out horizontally as they burled like dervishes.

Afterwards the boys thanked them politely and the two girls returned to their former place.

"That was *so* exciting!" Alison's cheeks were pink and her eyes sparkled. "Do you think they'll ask us to dance again."

Helen was looking over Alison's shoulder.

"Well, I see them asking other girls to dance this next one." Alison looked downhearted, "But never mind, Alison, we'll enjoy dancing it together."

Helen took the boy's part, but somehow it did seem less thrilling to dance with a girl.

The same two scouts soon invited them once more, this time for an old-fashioned waltz, which was a challenge on the uneven tarmac.

David, Helen's partner, was a splendid dancer who could reverse, that skill which Helen so appreciated. He came from Thornton and was in charge of a troop of scouts camping outside Anstruther. Helen told him she was from Glasgow and was starting Art School in September. Apart from this exchange of information, they said very little and danced together until nine o'clock. David's friend, James danced with Alison.

When the music van departed, David suggested they go to the British Legion Hall, where an informal 'hop' was about to start, with a proper band. Helen was unsure. A public hall seemed a step beyond open air dancing. Alison glanced nervously up at the window where her aunt sternly watched the girls talking with the two unknown boys.

"I think I'll go in now, Helen and I'll see you tomorrow. I'm a bit tired tonight."

Helen hardly believed that. No doubt Alison was unsure of her aunt's reaction, for the Legion Hall was adjacent to the butcher's shop and Alice regularly complained of the noisy dances next door.

Helen was not sure of the reaction she would meet with in her own home. What would her grandmother say?

Fortunately, Annie was enthusiastic.

"In charge of a troop of scouts, is he? Sounds a responsible young man, although he's obviously left them to their own devices tonight. And a good dancer too? Off you go and have a lovely time. No, I don't have to go to bed just now, if it ends at eleven thirty. I'll be fine 'til you get back. On you go and don't keep him waiting."

The Legion Hall was small and smoky and not at all what Helen had expected. Some of the men had obviously been drinking. No one was drunk, but their unpredictability made her nervous. When one of them asked her to dance, she was pleased that David very quickly said,

"Sorry, she's with me."

In spite of the boyish uniform, David's height and deep voice were intimidating and the man moved away immediately.

On the short walk back to her house, David admitted that he envied her going to Art School. He had taken Higher art and had won the school prize, but his father and two brothers were railway engineers.

"There wasn't much chance for me to break away from the family. I don't suppose I'll be painting much in the future, but I'll show you some of my work sometime, if you like. I'm coming back to Pittenweem in a fortnight to compete in the races. Would you like to come and watch? Then we could have a fish supper before I catch the train home."

He seemed an interesting boy and she said she would like that.

'Why don't you and your friend Alison come and visit the camp tomorrow afternoon? We'll get the kids to clean everything up nicely for you and we'll give you tea and biscuits."

Helen thought that would be fun and said goodnight. As she put her mother to bed, she told of tomorrow's plan and was unprepared for her mother's response.

"Oh I don't think you should go visiting the camp! I don't think that would be quite ... well you know, quite the 'done thing'."

"Why on earth d'ye say that?" Helen was astonished.

"Well, two girls and all those young men. No, I don't think so. And I'm sure Alice wouldn't approve of her niece gallivanting off to a scout camp."

Helen was more amused than angry. She could not believe her mother would seriously forbid the visit. It all seemed so terribly innocent. Besides she had made up her mind to go.

"We're two big strong women invited for tea and biscuits, very genteel, and they're not *men*, they're just boys of seventeen and eighteen and there's lots of wee boys running everywhere too. What on earth could happen?"

"Mmm. You never know, do you" Annie frowned. "And where is this camp, exactly?"

"At a farm, just outside Anstruther. You can see it from the road."

"Well, I suppose you can go, but don't tell grandma you're visiting a scout camp. She doesn't need to know and she'd be expecting the worst."

Helen was astonished that her mother was making such a

storm in a teacup. And hiding it from Mary. Next day she extended the invitation to Alison.

"Oh that's *so exciting*! I can't *wait* until this afternoon! But what will Aunt Alice say? *I'm sure she wouldn't approve.* But it's *such* fun. What will I tell her? I just won't say where we're going. Let's say we're going to see them at the Billowness swimming pool? That sounds respectable."

Helen found it incredible that Alison, as well as her own mother, saw something improper in the proposed visit. Neither Mary nor Alice was to know the truth! Helen hated the idea of deceit.

But could it be a foolish thing to do, after all?

Perhaps in her own ignorance she did not see the dangers?

David seemed a nice, quiet, well-behaved fellow. She was sure it was a perfectly straight forward invitation.

As the two girls walked towards the farm that afternoon, Helen began to have doubts about the visit. When she saw the tents in the distance, her nervousness increased. Would the boys expect kissing in the tents? Surely not. Or something more than kissing? Was that why her mother was worried?

The sight of several very young scouts scampering about, jumping over the guy ropes, reassured her. Those fears had been groundless, the afternoon was highly conventional, not to say quite dull. David poured very strong tea from a battered tin teapot and two nine year-olds handed round the plates of slightly broken digestive biscuits.

As if David realised the afternoon was not as entertaining as it might have been, he suggested a walk to the beach. Several of the younger boys accompanied them and David and James took the opportunity of giving the small boys a quick plunge in the sea, explaining,

"They're long overdue a bath!"

It was overcast, with a sharp east wind blowing and the young scouts screamed as they were forcibly dipped, fully dressed, into the cold water. Alison and Helen stood at a distance and watched disapprovingly. The shrieks were heart-rending and they thought it very cruel. Though the girls immersed themselves in the icy sea each day, it was different when it was your own choice.

"I wonder what their mothers would say if they saw their wee boys treated like that?" Helen sniffed.

"I don't think they would like it at all!" replied Alison.

The girls said a cold farewell and returned to Pittenweem.

It was difficult for David and James to understand this sudden coolness, but agreed that girls were often incomprehensible.

On Friday morning David presented himself at Helen's front door at nine thirty.

"There's a dance in Anstruther Town Hall tonight and we wondered if you and Alison would like to meet us inside. We'd really like to take you, but I'm afraid we're flat broke and you'd have to pay yourselves in. I'm sorry. But would you come? Please come. We'd have a great night's dancing and we've got to go home tomorrow and I have to get straight back to the camp now and see to breakfast."

"I'll see what Alison says about tonight, but haven't those poor kids had breakfast yet? They'll be starving!"

Alison was enthusiastic. Helen liked that about her friend, she was always happy to have an adventure and did not worry about gloomy things that might go wrong.

Anstruther Town Hall was enormous compared to the Legion Hall. They arrived at an interval and it was very quiet. The sound of conversation drifted upwards and disappeared into the dark ceiling which soared high above them. They crossed the intimidating expanse of empty dance floor to join the crowd of girls on what was obviously the 'female side' of the hall. There was subdued chatter and giggles amongst the brightly dressed girls as they tried to appear unconscious of the opposite masculine group. The men made no secret of the fact that they were inspecting the girls.

"It's a bit like a slave market, Alison! Not sure I like it. Which one of us will be chosen?"

Suddenly a quickstep was announced and the four piece band struck up loudly. Although the wailing electric guitar tended to drown out the other instruments, it also added a professional note, reminding Helen of B-movies set in Hawaii. Perhaps the echo of the tall chamber enhanced the resonance. Helen was not even sure she liked it, but it was a sound which entered deeply into her consciousness and would remain there for the rest of her life. That sad echo, common to all public dance halls, would always evoke that first nervous anticipation and those possibilities of meeting, or not meeting, someone attractive, someone who might dance superbly, even someone who might prove important in your future.

"I don't see those scouts anywhere! Do you? What if they don't come?" Alison was laughing, but also biting her lip.

"Oh, I'm sure they'll be here all right. Unless they haven't enough money to get in. David said they were 'flat broke'. Anyway, someone will ask us to dance, I expect."

"You don't see many girls dancing together here, do you?"

"No, it's a bit more sophisticated than the Market Place. But not much."

They both laughed.

Just then a young man asked Helen to dance. Quite soon Alison was also dancing.

"Oh, that was *such* a nice boy!" Alison enthused. "And quite a good dancer, too. *I wonder if he's going to ask me again.*" She giggled excitedly, as she watched him return to the masculine side.

"Well mine wasn't nearly as good a dancer as David and I'm not sure we should get involved with other boys. We're here to dance with David and James. We promised. And it's their last night."

"But they're not here, Helen," Alison said very sensibly,"so we'd better just enjoy ourselves, hadn't we."

"Mmm."

Helen was in a dilemma. How loyal should they be? Perhaps the scouts would not turn up at all.

The next dance was a slow foxtrot. Few couples took to the floor for this difficult dance. One or two optimists grabbed a partner and shuffled around much as they would to any other music. Helen pitied the girls who stumbled after such partners. One couple, however, was a pleasure to watch. Well-dressed, tall and elegant, their smooth well matched steps and skilled timing showed that they not only understood the subtleties of the dance, but were practised partners. As they left the floor, Helen heard them speak in a broad Glasgow accent which seemed incongruous for such a stylish pair. Perhaps they were regular patrons of the Locarno at Charing Cross. Throughout her schooldays, Helen had walked past that imposing dance hall daily. Large posters proclaimed the famous bands who played there, She had always wondered what the interior would be like. Perhaps everyone that went to the Locarno danced as well as this couple?

Just then the two kilted scouts arrived and Helen was relieved, not caring to dance with unknown men, smelling of beer and tobacco.

David was shy and quiet and yet an excellent and exciting dancer, madly whirling Helen round in her billowing skirt. If James was less accomplished, that was Alison's bad luck.

Helen thoroughly enjoyed her evening. The walk home was fun too, with the four of them telling stupid jokes and asking silly riddles.

◊

There was to be an auction of furniture in a large house on James Street next day and Annie asked rhetorically,

"Going up to the roup today, Maw?"

Mary hated to miss a roup.

"Yes, I thought I might as well just go and have a look around. It's old Captain Robertson's house and there's bound to be interesting foreign stuff. I'll go early and just stay an hour or so."

Mary's magpie propensities never ceased to amaze Annie. The house was already full of artefacts, some of them valuable, others of little worth, but interesting. Mary adored the thrill of searching for a bargain and if it were snatched from under the nose of a fellow hunter, then the achievement was most satisfying. If the nose in question was that of her friend Mrs Clark, another intrepid tracker of bargains, Mary's pleasure was complete.

"Will Mrs Clark be there?" Annie asked innocently.

"Oh I expect so, we didn't make any arrangements but she never lets anything go past her. I'll get away up now, quick as I can, though I expect she's pipped me at the post. I think she sets her alarm clock when there's an auction."

Annie and Helen glanced at each other. Mary and Chris Clark were deadly rivals in the way that close friends with common interests and character traits can often be.

The atmosphere of the house relaxed when Mary left. Unusually, John sat in the sunny garden with Helen and Annie.

"My, it's a wonderful view, isn't it." He was gazing at the sea and the distant shore where the Bass Rock glittered, pale against the blue mainland." Always changing. I never get tired of it. After all these years, I never tire of watching the sea in all its different moods."

Annie smiled at her father.

"You must love the sea very much."

"Yes, I do, I do."

"That's why you're so good at painting it."

"Aye, that might be right. I suppose that's the case. The sea's certainly always challenging. Fascinating is the word, I suppose. Or maybe enthralling is better."

He took a deep and enjoyable breath of the sea air and smiled.

It was unusual and very pleasant for Helen to hear her mother and grandfather speak so seriously and personally. She wished that she might add something to the conversation but could think of nothing to say.

Annie spoke,

"I believe I feel a bit the same way about flowers. When I see a nice bunch, I just want to paint it."

"Yes, I can believe that. And you paint them very well, Annie. Just look at what you see in Nature and practise, practise. Keep practising. Only Nature can teach us. Nothing like Nature. But that's a bit of a cold wind today and I'll just get away up to the studio, now."

Helen watched him slowly climb the stone steps, coughing slightly as he went.

"I don't think it's a bit cold today, do you?"

"Och well, I suppose when you're as old as Grandad, you feel the cold more, even the slightest draught. We're not all heat producing engines like yourself, y'know."

It was a long-standing joke between them that Annie might have frozen to death during the war years if she had not had Helen in bed with her, generating more heat than ten hot water bottles.

"How old is grandad now?"

"Let me think. My goodness, I believe he'll be eighty in October."

"*That is old* ! But grandma's much younger, isn't she."

'Yes, she's just sixty-six."

It still seemed immeasurably old to Helen.

"Talking of your grandma, I wonder how she's getting on up there. I think you should pop up and see if she needs a hand to bring back any ill-gotten gains."

Helen made a face.

"On you go and show Pittenweem that nice spotted dress you're wearing. Go on, you never know who you might meet."

Helen walked up to James Street, aware that this was a first outing for her fashionable dress. She felt particularly chic and was pleased to nod and smile to several acquaintances.

Mary was glad to see her.

"Thank goodness you've come up to help. I didn't know how I'd manage home. Wait until you see what I've bought. I'll bring the rest of the things, but I could never have carried this down the road as well. It's not really heavy, just awkward."

There was a twinkle in Mary's eye which was not mirrored in Helen's expression.

Lying at Mary's feet was a six foot long stuffed crocodile.

Refusing a task was not part of Helen's philosophy, but she was dismayed and displeased. She picked the creature up and clasped it to her. With a long tail and sharp claws, it certainly was awkward and very dusty. Her pale dress was instantly soiled. How fervently she hoped that she might *not meet anyone* on her return home.

The crocodile was taken straight into the garden and laid at Annie's feet.

Annie started to laugh and in a moment Helen had forgotten her humiliating walk and the two of them collapsed into that wonderful, helpless, cathartic laughter which comes so seldom.

And the crocodile proved to have been an excellent investment.

Kodak films were once more on the market and it was probably Annie that had the idea of taking photographs of Helen wrestling with the reptile.

"And you could dress yourself as Tarzan's Jane. Or maybe Dorothy Lamour would be more glamorous....?"

Nothing loth, Helen wrapped herself in an ad hoc sarong, loosened her long hair and placed a white flower behind her ear.

Mary brought out Annie's old pre-war box Brownie camera.

"Will it still work, d'ye think?'

Helen struggled with the crocodile in a variety of poses, using all her ingenuity to add some liveliness to the poor stuffed creature. Amazingly, the camera still worked and Mary proved to be an excellent photographer.

Two weeks later, Willie came through with Eileen and Sheila for a brief visit and again the crocodile was used as a prop. The two little girls rode on its back, then three-year old Sheila gazed into its gaping maw with an excellent expression of terror.

"Now I bet you folk wondered at me buying that stuffed crocodile. You'd be saying "What in the name of the wee man has she got this time?" And I know Helen was less than delighted to carry it down the road, but look at what an entertainment it's been. I bet you all thought 'the old girl's off her rocker this time!' But we've had *so much fun* and we've got those snapshots to remind us."

"Aye, but what are we going to do with it now?" Annie asked. When Mary was in a good mood, she was irrepressible.

"Oh, I'll think of something!" she replied confidently.

"I'm quite sure you will, my dear." John said laughing quietly under his moustache.

◊

The scouts had left. Alison and Helen, with many discussions of the pros and cons, decided they would return to the Anstruther Town Hall.

"There seemed to be lots of nice boys there." Alison chortled in her attractive way. "Really *very* nice, some of them. And good dancers, too, I'm sure."

"I don't know about that. David was *so good*. But yes, I'd like to go again. I really love dancing. Just as long as none of those drinkers ask me to dance. I wouldn't like to say an outright 'no', but… "

"Should we risk it?"

"I don't know, should we?"

"Yes."

"All right."

Dancing with lots of different partners was enjoyable, for though dancing skills were sometimes lacking, the conversation was varied and interesting.

Walking home together, they agreed it had certainly been worth the two shillings entry charge.

By the time Alison returned home to Dunfermline, Helen had met other Pittenweem girls that went dancing without a partner and she continued to dance each Wednesday, Friday and Saturday throughout the summer, sometimes in Anstruther, sometimes in the Legion Hall in Pittenweem. Nor did she neglect the open air dancing in the Market Place on Tuesday and Thursdays.

She also swam each day.

With hot water only available from a boiled kettle, washing her long hair daily was out of the question, In fact her flyaway hair with the two plaits pinned over the top of her head looked particularly neat with the daily rinsing of sea salt. For an evening in Anstruther, Helen washed her fringe in a little bowl. The short tendrils dried quickly, then her grandmother's metal curling tongs were heated on the gas ring and a slight curl added a touch of glamour for the evening. Olive oil on her lashes and lips completed her preparations. A natural look was always her aim. For she did not want to use cosmetics which would not be available if she found herself castaway on a desert island. Those old dreams of Robinson Crusoe and the three boys on Coral Island had never quite faded. She laughed at her own nonsensical fantasies, retaining them nevertheless.

As she was leaving to catch the bus one night, her grandfather commented,

"You're looking very festive tonight, Helen, that dress is a fine colour. Good to paint and it suits you very well."

Helen blushed with pleasure, then Mary exclaimed,

"Is that *another* new dress you're wearing? In heaven's name, how many new dresses have you got?"

Helen smiled and looked over at her mother.

"Och, it's my fault, Maw. The fashions have changed so quickly with the New Look and there are suddenly such nice fabrics in the shop. I felt I made quite a success of her ballgown and a summer dress is much easier. And I think it's good for me to sew. It's a sort of therapy and exercise. I really enjoy it. And you know Campbell Horsland is working in the fabric department in Coplands now and he puts aside any specially nice cottons for Helen and when he produces them, she can hardly say no, can she? And she can always charge it to the account, of course. So I've got into the habit of saying, just go and cut me out another summer dress. And she does! Then I run it up on the machine and she does the hand sewing. Anyway she's a bonnie wee thing to dress and she deserves spoiling and we're not extravagant in other ways, are we?"

Annie smiled fondly at her daughter.

"Well I think you're both very clever, for they're lovely dresses and she certainly does deserve it. I bet she's the belle of the ball at

Anstruther. And if you can afford it and you're enjoying the sewing, that's even better. But how many new dresses have the two of you made, exactly?"

Annie hesitated for a moment,

"I think it might be eleven or twelve!"

"Fourteen, actually." Corrected Helen.

Mary shook her head and laughed,

"I wasn't counting, but I was thinking I'd seen quite a few! Now away you go before you miss your bus. And have a good time."

◊

They were invited to visit the Forgies on their journey back to Glasgow. Although Bruce grumbled at the inconvenience, he appeared to enjoy the visit thoroughly. They ate in a large barrel-vaulted room where Helen could easily imagine tonsured monks sitting in silence, eating whatever it was that monks ate in the distant past.

Clare had provided a cold lunch with Spam and freshly picked salads from their garden. Bruce waxed lyrical about the lettuce.

"Now what could be more delicious than that, eh, Annie? Isn't that lettuce just the freshest you've ever tasted? It's wonderful, Mrs Forgie! Can't get anything like that in the shops now, can you. Oh dear, no. And did you really grow these tomatoes in your own greenhouse? That must be very satisfying. So sweet. I'm very impressed. Don't believe I've ever tasted a better tomato. But the lettuce now, it's *really special*. Perhaps I could have a little more, please? It's excellent! Helen, would you mind passing the lettuce up to yer old Dad, m'dear?"

Helen was in a quandary. As her father's voice had droned on, she had been gazing at the salad bowl in front of her, mesmerised by a large, well-nourished caterpillar cavorting on a lettuce leaf. Athletic and foolhardy, it had several times lost its footing and hung from the leaf by the skin of its teeth, so to speak, swinging precariously and apparently certain to drop to the table, but always hauling itself back to safety again.

Now she must pass the bowl to her father. What should she do?

It would be rude to draw attention to the caterpillar's presence, but it seemed cruel not to warn her voracious father.

She passed the bowl and cowardly looked the other way, as he helped himself to salad.

◊

Helen spent an active summer with swimming and dancing added to her domestic chores and her health remained good.

She thought little about the Art School, for she could not imagine what it would be like. It would be a different life and she was content to wait until she experienced it.

Glasgow School of Art

Helen started her studies at Glasgow School of Art in September 1949. That first day in the unique and exquisite building designed by Charles Rennie Mackintosh marked a milestone in her life.

Neither her relatives nor her teachers had prepared her for the mysterious fascination of the Art School. Helen was ignorant of the world-wide fame of this aesthetic structure, for the genius and importance of Mackintosh's work was markedly less acknowledged or appreciated locally at that time.

She found it incredible that neither her mother, who had studied there, nor her grandfather who had taught there, had ever spoken of what a strange and beautiful environment it provided. Nothing could have been more different from the dusty, dreary, echoing High School with its confusing corridors and staircases and its gloomy, intimidating basement cloakrooms.

From the moment that Helen mounted the elegant front steps and passed through the two sets of double swing doors which comprised the main entrance to the Art School, she fell in love with the building, appreciating its simple practicality as much as its poetic originality. For the next four years she would continue to find new corners and magical aspects and though she could not know this at the time, her studios, unlike those of less fortunate students, would always be located in the Mackintosh building.

Helen learned at the reception desk that she was in Section One of the four alphabetically divided quarters of first year, William Drummond Bone would be her tutor and his room was number 25, just around the corner from the office. She was given a little card with her name and matriculation number, 128. She looked at it rather stupidly. Her club number at the Arlington Baths was 128. How could she have the same number here? Could there be some connection? Of course not, it was just a strange coincidence. Helen prided herself on not being at all superstitious but this could be considered a good omen.

Sheila, the only other High School girl starting that day, was assigned to a different section in another building and they parted with promises to meet at lunchtime.

The main staircase, an elegant flight of 16 wooden stairs, lay directly ahead. It had soaring black banisters, reminiscent of those belonging to the studio staircase in 351, though twice as high.

A small office, rather like a cinema ticket box, was at the foot of the stairs. Two officials in formal dark green uniform conferred inside and nodded to Helen in a friendly way as she passed their open window.

Many young people were walking around, obviously not 'freshers' like herself for they walked fast and purposefully and almost all were laden with large portfolios, canvases, boxes and bags.

Helen turned the corner and came face to face with a classical statue on a plinth, much larger than life. This ancient goddess seemed enormous and appeared to gaze superciliously down at the row of workaday metal lockers which lined the other side of the corridor. Beyond the goddess were the double swing doors to Mr Bone's room.

Helen gently pushed the door and peeped in. No one was there. The studio was spacious with five large windows flooding it with a clear, unchanging northern light. Wooden stools and tables similar to school furniture were carelessly scattered about. In a corner, stood another classical statue, an archer, his arms poised and his muscles tensed, ready to release an invisible arrow from an invisible bow. Helen wondered if the weapon had ever existed. Timidly, she decided not to enter the room until the others arrived and stood waiting beside the towering goddess, whose plaster drapery fell in many realistic folds. Helen felt apprehensive, yet pleasurably so. Even the lockers in the corridor seemed thrilling. She had never owned a locker and would require a padlock for it. Even the thought of a padlock was exciting. She would get one that opened with a tumbled code word rather than a key. Each small detail was new and important.

No one seemed to be heading for room 25. Where was everyone?

The hall became busier as students deposited belongings in lockers.

One of the ladies' rooms was just along the hall. This room too had double swing doors and girls crowded in and out. Helen went in briefly to check that she was tidy, but could not get near the one mirror and returned to the draped cast.

Helen's keen sense of smell was delighted with the atmosphere, faintly and pleasantly perfumed with linseed oil, turpentine and some other unknown odour. The Art School smelled clean and artistic, very different from the depressing school aroma of chalk dust, science labs and stale cooking from the dining hall.

Young people continually brushed past her, talking and laughing. Helen envied their relaxed confidence. Some groups descended to the lower regions, others disappeared up the main staircase. There was another stairway to her left at the end of the corridor. So many stairscases all going in the same direction, so much better than the confusing High School.

Everything about her new life was going to be better!

A few students wore attractive smocks or utilitarian overalls. Many of the girls wore baggy corduroy trousers. Though trousers were unfashionable at that time in the outside world, they were almost *de rigeur* for female art students. Helen determined that she would *not* be wearing trousers. She had worn a uniform for six years and would never conform again.

Two young men and three girls checked the room number and joined Helen. They nodded and smiled shyly to each other, but did not speak.

Suddenly a small stout man in his early forties appeared around the corner and marched swiftly towards them. He wore a severe expression and an enormous moustache, known as a 'handlebar', almost certainly a sign that he had served in the RAF.

"Section one, I take it? In you come. I'm Mr Bone."

He did not smile as he counted them.

"There must be more than this, surely. What's happened to everyone?"

He seemed in rather a bad mood.

"Find a seat for yourselves. Sit down. As cheap sitting as standing. I'll go and round up the others."

While he was out of the room, they murmured to each other. The situation and the purity of the light seemed to daunt them.

One girl whispered to Helen,

'What d'ye think he's angry about? He seems very cross."

Helen shrugged.

Mr Bone soon returned with the others, who had been drinking coffee in the refectory. Some of these were men in their early twenties, who had chosen to do National Service before studying.

Mr Bone seemed even more irritated.

They all sat up very straight on their stools. Perhaps it was not so different from school after all.

Mr Bone's manner warmed somewhat as he welcomed them to the Glasgow School of Art.

He spoke pleasantly, but very seriously, impressing on them the *honour* of having been accepted as students at such a prestigious establishment and the *necessity* of working hard and making the very best use of their time while there.

"This is not a school room and I will not be in attendance every minute of the day, for I expect you to be responsible adults. I will not be there to nag if you slack, nor do you require my permission to leave the studio for a coffee, or for whatever other reason." He blinked twice and paused as though embarrassed. "But I do expect you to be here at nine thirty each morning and also at two pm on Tuesday and Thursday afternoons, in order that I may mark you present or otherwise. And I would advise you to use your time sensibly; time is a precious commodity and can slip through your fingers only too easily and fast, frighteningly fast. There is a great deal of work to be accomplished. A very, very great deal. I will expect each student to keep a sketchbook, which he or she will use diligently. Each Thursday, I'll inspect these books and comment and I would expect to see four or five well worked drawings each week. At least. Once a month you will be given a subject for a figure composition, usually this will be in your own choice of medium, though not always. There will be a deadline for handing in and *no late entries will be accepted*. Unless perhaps in the case of extreme illness or accident. These efforts will be displayed and given individual criticisms in class and the entire section should listen carefully, for you will learn much from the work of others, good or bad. It goes without saying that your attendance is desirable at this monthly crit and also on the handing-in day for sketchbooks. Any questions?"

The twenty five young faces looked silently up at him. He looked so very serious.

He had been inspiring, but would he always be so unbending?

"Nothing to say? Anyone? No questions at all? I'll remind you also that you are all *on probation*. If the standard of your work or attendance is unsatisfactory at the end of the December term, you will be asked to leave. And that will be that."

A shiver ran down Helen's spine and no doubt she was not alone.

"However, now I will turn to a more pleasant task."

To everyone's delight, a small twitching of the monstrous moustache seemed to indicate the possibility of a smile. Twenty five faces relaxed and smiled broadly and hopefully at each other. Yes, it appeared that Mr Bone could smile and was smiling, though the flowing facial adornment would always make it difficult to be sure.

"I should like to congratulate some of the members of my section. It seems we are fortunate enough to count four medallists in the Glasgow schools art competition among us today. Bill Buchanan, please stand up!"

A slight young boy, blushing furiously, stood up. He was obviously uncomfortable and looked almost near tears. He sat down almost immediately.

" No, no, stay standing, please, Mr Buchanan. We want to see our heroes. And Fred Baird, stand up!"

An enormous blonde Viking of a chap, well over six feet, stood and clasping his hands above his head like a victorious boxer, smiled vaingloriously at the others. Helen hoped it was just an act to hide his embarrassment.

"Now, two very clever young ladies, Margery Clinton and Helen Corning. Please stand up. And I think three cheers would be in order."

Although it was nice to be recognised, it was embarrassing to be the centre of attention. Helen bit her lip and exchanged a meaning glance with Margery and wondered if there was a cruel streak in their tutor.

"Sit down now, thank you. I am aware that you four chaps will be absent next week, when the Lord Provost presents you with your medals. And very nice medals they are, too. You'll be delighted and proud. Now I have timetables here for you, please help yourself, and then just one more thing. Tomorrow we will start DRAWING. I want you to bring a potato with you," There was a quiet mutter, to which Mr Bone immediately replied, "No, sir, *not* a cooked one, but an interesting raw one. It should not be *too* strangely shaped, no little manikins and no perfect spheres, but some little irregularity in its formation is probably desirable, *as you will be drawing it for the rest of this week.* That is everything for today. I think you have a class in design this afternoon with Mr Fleming, whose studio is on the top floor, room 58 and a very beautiful room too. You are free until lunchtime. I advise you to prowl around and make yourselves familiar with our splendid building, locate the rooms in which you will be studying. Nothing more irritating than folk getting lost and trailing in late. Good morning."

Mr Bone surveyed the stunned faces in front of him, seemingly satisfied at the effect he had made, then swept from the room with a surprising amount of dignity for a portly man. Was he smiling faintly? The moustache would always make that a moot point.

They were left to discover each other's names and who had won which medals and all the other things that young people want to learn about each other.

◊

At home that first day, Annie had mixed feelings: glad that Helen had started on the road to a career, hopeful that her daughter would take her studies more seriously than she herself had done. Annie's years at Art School had been enjoyed only too well and she regretted her wasted opportunities. Too many parties and not enough work. She sighed. Had she really been lazy, as her mother had so often suggested? Or had this rotten illness started long before she was aware of it? Or was that just an excuse?

Mrs Connell popped her head round the sitting room door,

"Are you all right in here, Mrs Corning? Can I get you anything? I wonder how wee Helen's getting on? It'll be awful new to her the first day."

"Yes, I was just thinking of her. I hope she enjoys it. I bet she does and I'd better find things to keep me busy, for it's a longer day now."

"Oh I'm sure our Helen'll be a big success. Now what can I pass you?"

"I'll come into the kitchen and do the totties and carrots and maybe make some gingerbread, will I?"

"Oh yes! I just love yer gingerbread, Mrs Corning."

Agnes, sensitive to Annie's worries, was particularly attentive that morning. She remembered her own mother's sadness when her daughter wanted to leave home and marry at eighteen and wondered what would happen when Helen met the 'right man'. Life would certainly change for Annie when Helen made her own life.

Of course Annie had also thought of that future problem. Like most mothers, she hoped to see her daughter become a happy wife and mother, and was determined that her own disability would not stand in Helen's way. Perhaps some sort of nursing home would be the answer. Her thoughts shied away from that unknown future. Helen had four years of study on which to concentrate.

As for Helen herself, she might have been dismayed to think of a future without marriage, but she considered it to be so remote that she gave no thought to the problem of what would happen to her mother.

◊

"Well how did your first day go? Did it come up to expectations? Was it more fun than school?"

But Annie could tell from her daughter's face that it had been a success.

"What a lot of interesting people in the class! There's Margery Clinton who won a gold medal, too. She lives in Jordanhill and I've invited her to come and have Russian tea with us some evening. Her dad's a sea captain and away from home a lot and her mother annoys her by fussing over her and you'll like her. She's a bit of a character with a big booming laugh and she doesn't seem a bit shy. Mattie is another nice girl. She's much quieter, quite shy like myself. She lives in Shawlands with her widowed mother who runs a plumber's business! I'd like to ask her and Margery for a meal some weekend. And there's lots of boys in the class, far more boys than girls. Some are quite old! About twenty two or three, probably."

"Oh, quite ancient!"

"No, but it's strange to be in a class with grown-ups. There's a very nice older man, Donald. He's a bit mysterious and doesn't say much but everyone listens when he does speak."

"I take it that he's the one that interests you most?'

"No, no! I don't know them properly yet and they all seem nice, though big Donald is rather fascinating. But there's another

Donald and he's quite wee, about the same height as me. He's English and he's got a moustache and talks a lot. He's *terribly* funny, quick and clever, y'know. You would get on well with him. He's been in the army and also studied at another art school down south. He lives in Milngavie with his sister who runs a baby linen shop." She paused for breath, " Our section's rather proud of itself for there are two others, boys, Fred and Buckie. who won medals in the competition. Fred is enormously tall and broad and *so self-confident*, almost conceited but quite nice too. comes from Coatbridge and has six sisters younger than him!"

"Well, no wonder he's conceited, he must be the prince of the household."

"Yes and his mother's a widow, too so he's the only male in the house."

"I don't envy any girl *he* takes home, with seven pairs of jealous eyes sizing her up and criticising her every move."

"Mmm, that hadn't struck me. Then Buckie is really different. His parents are in the West Indies and he stays with an old aunty in Greenock and has to travel up by train every day. I'm not sure that the aunt makes him very comfortable, from what he says. He's nice-looking, but terribly thin and nervous and quite young. He's not even seventeen yet. He can be very funny too. I like him. It would be nice to ask him for a meal sometime. He looks as though he could do with feeding."

Annie laughed,

"You're as bad as my mother, always wanting to feed people. How many is that you've marked down as guests so far?"

Annie found it touching that, no matter how enthralling Helen's new life was, she wanted to involve her mother in it. Was Helen consciously including her? Perhaps only out of kindness? Did she really want to bring these students home to meet an invalid? Perhaps Helen just felt motherly or hospitable towards these new friends. Whatever the reason, it was pleasant to know that her daughter was prepared, even anxious, to share her friends and invite them to her unconventional home.

Mr Bone's Section

Apart from five young men who had already completed their National Service, most of the group were aged seventeen or eighteen and straight from school. Though not necessarily more talented than the younger members, those older men would bring a sense of purpose and determination to the class, which, added to the high standards demanded by Mr Bone, inspired a dedication to work and a special self-confidence in the group. Perhaps the four medals added a sense of superiority. Within a fortnight, with their shared interests, youth and enthusiasm they had created something very like a family. Mr Bone, though a stern and strict disciplinarian, was a kind and encouraging father figure, and sometimes showed an unexpected and quirky sense of humour.

For Helen, straight from the strictly female High School, it was exciting and pleasant to be flung into this mixed group. The work was stimulating and demanding, the conversation witty and artistic. It was like the best kind of party, a party that lasted all day, every day of the week. It was a democratic group with a distinct lack of competition between the sexes, for girls were just as likely to produce a successful drawing or painting as boys were.

There would be flirtations and passing love affairs, even a broken heart or two in the future, but the general feeling was of hard work, comradeship and equality. Friendships were made and affection was more in evidence than rivalry or petty jealousies, though perhaps Helen hardly noticed these last, for she was entranced by her new life. For the first time, she became part of a group in which she did not feel an outsider. At school, the weekend had been the longed-for goal of freedom. Now, Friday was the depressing start of a two day separation from her friends.

Most importantly, she learned to work and study in a way that had never been presented to her at school. Sadly, she learned the inadequacies of her previous education with no introduction to any craft, lettering, design, technical drawing or three dimensional work. Her art education was about to start and she would find it difficult, but always she would be happy in her new environment.

After three weeks of drawing a potato, they drew the wooden studio furniture as though it were made of glass. Next they copied drawings by old masters, then drew plaster busts.

These exercises lasted until Christmas and though the stools and tables and casts were uninspiring, they learned to look and record information with care and understanding. They were advised to fill the home sketchbook with various subjects. Self portraits were encouraged and most people drew at least one each week. Helen grew very dissatisfied with her own face, for her features seemed different each time and she felt her draughtsmanship would never improve.

Each Thursday, Willie Bone, as they had learned to call him in private, stood at the side of the studio looking through their homework sketchbooks. His face expressionless as he turned the pages, he would pause now again to consider a particular drawing, gently stroking his chin with his left thumb as he pondered. Then with a fateful slap, he would drop each book either in the *good pile* or the *bad pile*. Anxious faces watched surreptitiously to see which pile they had attained that week. Helen was always in the bad pile.

She was more successful with the monthly figure composition, eliciting positive comments and occasional praise.

Unlike some of the other tutors, Willie gave many talks on composition and Helen would always be grateful to him. What she learned from him about composition she was later able to assimilate into her dance compositions and indeed to many other aspects of her life. In fact his rules of composition became an integral part of Helen's philosophy.

Willie Bone was a conscientious and kindly teacher who inspired love and respect. The class learned to treasure his infrequent, camouflaged smiles. No doubt there were times he did smile, for he had a subtle and sometimes mischievous sense of humour. Every student who was lucky enough to have him as a tutor for the two year General Course would remember him with gratitude and fondness.

Section One that year would also remember the violent rage which apparently consumed him one day. In Mr Bone's absence, a violin which had found its way into the studio had been playfully tucked under the chin of the Archer statue.

Willie saw it as soon as he entered the studio and immediately blew up. He was infuriated and for twenty minutes reproached them with infantile behaviour, lack of responsibility, downright vandalism. They stood around, hanging their heads like chastened children. Only one person had committed the crime, but they all took the brunt of their tutor's anger. How ashamed they felt, yet more than one of them considered it was not such a vile crime. Why was he so emotional? The statue was not hurt or damaged.

Contritely and sincerely, they promised that never again would they play tricks with the statues.

The potency of Mr Bone was much augmented by his display of fury that day. His students would always work hard because of the love and respect they felt for him, but that one occasion showed he had teeth and claws and they should also fear him.

◊

At first small sub-groups formed within Section One. Later they would dissolve and rearrange themselves. The older men sat together smoking while Claude and William, who knew each other from school, laughed and joked together. Fred and Buckie the silver and bronze medallists made friends. Margery, the other gold medallist who also lived in the West End, joined forces with Helen and Mattie.

For nearly six years, Helen's plentiful energies and enthusiasms had been mainly invested in the activities of her own home, along with dance and swimming, and recently her burgeoning social life. Until she became a student, these interests had been her reality, with school an unattractive interstitial necessity.

Now, the camaraderie of Mr Bone's section, allied to the demanding work ethic of the Art School, created an entirely new life for her. She loved everything about it. Each day brought some new interest and though she discovered uncomfortable areas of ignorance in herself, her work was stimulating and her surroundings were pleasing. She could dress as she wished and her companions were friendly and encouraging. The working week seemed too short and the weekend too long, so very different from her perception of schooldays.

Although she was one of the youngest students in the class, Helen had spent six years running a home and being responsible for her disabled mother. She had gained confidence and experience that few of the others had, for most still stayed at home. Even the National Servicemen still lived with parents.

Unlike other girls, Helen did not have the continuous close surveillance of a mother. Her duties were important and appreciated as such and she had freedom to accomplish them in her own way. She listened to Annie's advice, but often experimented in quicker or easier or just different ways of doing things when alone. No doubt she made mistakes, but she learned from them. Annie had suffered and struggled against her own mother's rigid ideas of '*how things should be done properly*' and understood her daughter's need to experiment.This life of freedom had given Helen a relaxed confidence in her own abilities, As with most young people, Helen considered her own life completely normal, However the reaction of her fellow students to one incident that she described awoke her to the fact that perhaps her life was a little unusual.

Early one November morning, Helen had been awakened by the sound of rushing water. Leaping out of bed, she discovered water flooding from the cistern high above the WC. Without any plumbing knowledge, she stood in her nightgown, balanced on the wooden seat and with arms high above her head, fumbled with the unseen and unfamiliar ball and cock mechanism, as the icy water poured down her arms and body. Eventually, by trial and error, she managed to switch off the flow. It was quite exciting and it made a good story to tell her friends at break. She had meant to be amusing because, after the water was stopped, she was able to laugh, but the faces around her did not smile. If she had told a story of derring-do and high adventure, they could not have looked more admiring and impressed. She felt embarrassed and wished she had not recounted the adventure. It might sound like boasting.

"That was *awful*."

"You must have been soaking wet!"

"Were you not *frozen stiff*?"

"What a heroine!"

After a pause, one of the older men asked,

"And was there no one else in the house to do it?"

And of course there was not.

It was a point that Helen had hardly considered before.

Work and Play

Students wishing to gain a Diploma at the school of art must take the two year General Course, which, though chiefly concerned with drawing and painting, covered a wide variety of other subjects. From Monday to Thursday, three hours were spent each morning, drawing with Mr Bone. Friday morning was spent in the basement, clay modelling. The afternoon period of the same length was devoted to various subjects: lettering, architectural drawing, the study and history of pure design, and a craft of their choice. Helen chose embroidery. The day started at 9 30 and finished at 4 30 except on Mondays, when they stayed until six o'clock for an art history lecture from the principal, Douglas Percy Bliss.

There was a remote other-worldly quality about Mr Bliss. He had a drawling English accent, coupled with that apparent supreme self-confidence of which his race is so often accused. His lectures were interesting, but marred by many nervous affectations. He continually removed and replaced his spectacles with a humorous but exhausted flourish. At regular intervals, he turned his profile to the class and dramatically swept his handsome hair back from his forehead. Helen wondered if these movements were for effect, or if he could not help himself.

His lecture took place in the basement lecture theatre and surely Rennie Mackintosh had allowed his malicious streak to surface when he designed such very uncomfortable seats. The extremely narrow benches were backed with an inexplicable wooden strut, which dug relentlessly into the middle of the sitter's back. Was his intention to ensure that students sat up and stayed awake? If it were, it was often defeated. In the last long twenty minutes of the lecture, projections of the discussed paintings were shown and as soon as lights were dimmed for the epidiascope, many tired young people relaxed and lost consciousness. It had been a long, demanding day. Helen prided herself on being able to take short refreshing naps at home, but her body could never overcome the discomfort of those benches. When nearby friends started snoring gently, she might usefully nudge them before they disgraced themselves.

Helen wondered if Mr Bliss was aware that part of his audience was dozing? What would happen if he found every student sound sleep when light was restored? Would he creep away, offended? Or would he match that fine flow of rage and vituperation which Mr Bone had so unexpectedly delivered?

A Friday morning, when they descended to the noisy and odorous basement to work with clay, was a favourite. Artificially lit and conceived on a smaller scale than the upper floors, it seemed like a different building altogether. Added to the damp smell of clay, there was the aroma of freshly carved wood from the sculpture studios and a faint sniff of leather and glue from the book-binding room. Interesting bangs and hammerings could be heard behind each fascinating door.

The class became more sociable in the clay room. Perhaps the small, low-ceiled room was less intimidating than the spacious studio upstairs. Possibly modelling requires less absolute concentration than drawing. Certainly the tutor, less conscientious than Mr Bone, generally left them alone to get on with it. Whatever the reason, clay modelling was a relaxed class with lots of joking and conversation.

For the first three months, the work consisted of copying. Each student was given a chunk of cold, soft, grey clay and a plaster cast of a large eye, ear, nose or mouth and asked to make an exact copy of it. The casts were about ten inches square and were of the facial features of Michelangelo's David.

Copying had never appealed to Helen and she viewed this exercise without enthusiasm. However, when she started she found it relatively easy. Much easier than trying to capture shapes in two dimensions with pencil and paper. In later years she would realise that she had learned a great deal from this study, becoming familiar with the subtle detailed structure of the facial features, details more difficult to observe in the smaller scale of nature.

When more clay was required, a few students would descend to the sub-basement to fetch it. The sub-basement, where the furnace and heating arrangements were, was dungeon-like and *really different* from the rest of the building.

The clay room contained a machine rather like an outsize mincer, into which used clay was continually returned, to be thoroughly mixed, then once more extruded into manageable pieces for the students upstairs to shape again into eyes, noses, ears and mouths. The clay lived a poetic circular existence.

With their armfuls of clay lumps, the students hurried quickly back upstairs. Helen would never have ventured down there on her own, nor did the boys seem keen to explore it, or even linger there.

Friday afternoons, spent in the department of architecture at the west end of the ground floor, were also fun, though certainly less productive as far as Helen was concerned. While many of the boys had studied technical drawing at school, none of the girls had and most found it exacting, repetitive and unimaginative. Helen certainly did and made a poor show of it.

It must be admitted that work was not pursued diligently by any students on a Friday afternoon.

Again, there was seldom a tutor present and singing foolish songs was a favourite and regular occupation. They invented a game in which songs were ruthlessly edited to provide amusement and never failed to cause helpless infantile laughter. One sentimental ditty, heard too frequently on the radio, was altered by removing the last three words.

In a shady nook,
By a babbling brook,
That's where I fell in love with you

And the daring word *sex* was substituted for *guard* in A. A. Milne's sentimental ditty:

'They're changing guard at Buckingham Palace'

Folk songs, new to Helen were sung. *Barbara Allen* and *Wrap me up in my Tarpaulin Jacket* were performed with mournful relish.

Helen was not blessed with a fine singing voice, none of the group was, but she was tuneful, though she seldom sang at home for Annie was not keen on the human voice. At school, Helen had been a member of the choir for a few months and had struggled with the difficulties of the ambiguously titled *Fall on me like a Gentle Dew*. When assigned to sing the descant, she had found it impossible to hold her own against the powerful voices of the adjacent singers of the melody. Eventually, content to act as a

barrier between the two halves of the choir, she had stopped producing sound, though continuing to mouth the words, for the look
of the thing. Now in this uninhibited company and the acoustically
excellent architecture rooms, she sang that strange song and the
laughing students appreciated its bizarre quality. Encouraged, she
sang a lush Victorian ballad with exaggerated pathos.

> *Less than the dust beneath thy chariot wheel,*
> *Less than the rust which never stains thy sword,*
> *Less than the trust thou hast in me, oh, L-o-o-ord,*
> *Even le-ess am I, even le-e-e-ss am I.*

That was a hilarious success, though probably due to Helen's
histrionic, rather than vocal, abilities.

She was certainly not the only person in the class to find that
the relaxed family atmosphere wiped away inhibitions and
encouraged performance skills that many of those creative young
people had not realised previously.

It was not only in the architecture room that songs echoed in
the high empty spaces. The acoustics of Room 25 were also found
to be excellent, when Mr Bone was not present.

Perhaps he occasionally heard his pupils rejoicing as he saun-
tered back along the corridor? Did the elusive smile peep out? To
give models privacy and protect them from draughts, a large canvas screen stood immediately in front of the studio door. Anyone
entering the studio would not immediately come into view, but
must walk around it. In spite of songs and laughter, sharp young
ears would detect the double swish of the swing doors long
before Mr Bone appeared around the screen. Did he make sure
that the faint creak of the swing door heralded his return – then
kindly pause for a moment, to allow them to regain the proper
silence of dedicated application?

◊

As the term advanced and the atmosphere of the imposing
building became familiar, more boisterous games took place. A
small spherical handbag belonging to one of the girls was regularly
passed back and forth for rugby practice. She did not seem to mind.
Sometimes a girl was picked up and handed, like a parcel, from one
tall young man to another for no particular reason. Helen found it
exciting and enjoyable, once she became used to it. Her self image

was of a strong, broad-shouldered person who was depended upon and it was rather nice to be treated as though she were petite and helpless though there was relief when she was returned safely to her feet again.

If anyone felt inclined to display their skills, the rest were ready to encourage and enjoy the spectacle.

Adam, a keen footballer, was demonstrating his control of the ball when it was noticed how much his toes turned inwards. Helen pointed out that as a ballet dancer her toes always turned outwards. By exaggerating their natural propensities, they entertained the class with a grotesque quickstep.

When enormously tall, burly Fred, acted the ventriloquist with diminutive Donald sitting on his knee, it was a spontaneous and masterly improvisation which brought the house down. It would be repeated at other times until, unfortunately, the chair broke.

Infantile and innocent as these games were, they provided an outlet for the youthful madness that drew the group ever closer together.

Separated from other sections by the undoubted honour of belonging to Mr Bone and also perhaps a little smug because of the four medallists, Section One considered itself *special*. Possibly other sections felt the same way about themselves.

Helen, for the first time, found herself an integral and valued unit of a close-knit and self-confident group.

◊

Helen dropped in to her grandparent's flat at lunchtime once or twice a week. Often there was some errand required and she would trot along to Coopers for groceries or perhaps collect a prescription at Boots.

Mary appreciated this help, for John was losing strength and staying in bed for longer each day.

He always seemed pleased to see Helen and would ask her about what she was studying at art school, but she felt that he was too tired to listen or find it interesting. He was pale and thin and had a bout of coughing if he said more than a few words.

The routine never varied, even Mary often made the same remarks.

"How d'ye think he looks today? He's had a very bad night, I heard him coughing all the time. But he's usually better in the evening and quite bright by nine o'clock. He listens to the news and last night he even suggested he might go along to the Art Club for a game of snooker. Of course I told him that was nonsense, but I was quite pleased he felt like it. I'm just dreading that fog starting. Now, I've made a wee sandwich for you, my jewel. D'ye want to eat it before you go out for the bread and milk?"

"I'll get the messages first, in case I don't have enough time. They like us to be there on the dot and I can always eat it as I go back up the hill, thank you."

Mary laughed. Feeding people was one of her favourite occupations. hardly trusting anyone to feed themselves properly. She would have been horrified to discover how seldom her granddaughter ate any lunch. Helen preferred to stay in the studio and socialise. On Tuesdays and Thursdays, Helen walked to the Arlington Baths. Quite often she found herself in Renfrew Street at the same time as another student, a man in fourth year. After the first smile, they had fallen into the habit of walking along Woodlands Road together. Ralph lived in Otago Street and looked like an archetypal artist, slender, blond and with fine aesthetic features. He had a pleasant voice and was obviously very serious about his work. Helen was always disappointed when their paths did not converge, though she felt rather in awe of someone in their final year. How far his skills must have progressed beyond potatoes and wooden tables, though he too must have struggled with those mundane objects at one time, for Willie Bone had been his tutor. They agreed that Willie was a marvellous man.

Ralph spoke of fire-watching on the roof, during the war. He had enjoyed it, but Helen thought how much his mother must have worried about her sixteen-year-old.

They parted company at the top of Arlington Street, outside a bakery where excitingly named cakes were sold. Eiffel Towers, with coconut sticking to their jammy sides and dry-as-dust Paris buns with a meagre scatter of sugar crystals. Helen's favourite, not always available, were piney cakes, pastries filled with ersatz cream and pineapple jam, topped with bright yellow icing,. Helen would buy two. Then, soaking in the uniquely deep and incomparably hot bath of the Arlington, she nibbled her vivid tarts and revelled in her own hedonism.

Problems with Fred

The four medallists looked very smart. Helen in an elegant tweed suit (£6.4s.6d and eighteen coupons from Coplands ladies' department), Margery in a pretty blue woollen dress which revealed her beautiful legs, normally hidden in baggy brown corduroys. The boys looked handsome in sparkling white shirts, neatly knotted ties and what were obviously their best tweed jackets and newest flannels. Helen wondered why they did not wear suits but probably suits were expensive and might not last long if they were still growing. When David had visited her in Glasgow, she had felt sorry for him in a suit, short in sleeve and leg. Boys seemed to suffer more unpredictable spurts of growth than girls. Buckie, at sixteen might still sprout a bit. She certainly hoped Fred, at enormous eighteen, had stopped growing.

The interior of the Kelvingrove Art Galleries, familiar to Helen since early childhood, looked strange and uninviting with an audience perched on uncomfortable folding seats. The Lord Provost was not in his robes of office, the speeches were interminable and the occasion was less impressive than Helen had imagined. When she received her medal, she was delighted to find it a very pretty piece of jewellery, small and oval, beautifully engraved with her name and achievement and unexpectedly heavy. Helen determined to wear it on a gold chain. No doubt her grandmother would have something of the sort in her jewellery box. Wearing it might be considered 'showing off' but the lettering was small and it was too attractive to keep hidden.

After the ceremony, the four students crossed the road to the Orlando Café, situated on the gusset where Sauchiehall Street and Argyle Street diverged. Helen was pleased to visit this unique café, which she had glimpsed daily on her journey to school, considering the unusual building to be like something in an American film. They ordered enormous ice cream drinks, and stirred the long spoon for only a short time, in order to have some ice cream left once the drink was finished.

The pleasant company, the kudos of their success and the Art Deco interior made the celebration very special.

◊

Next day, Fred asked Helen to go to the pictures with him and decorously held her hand throughout the show. It was apparent from his admiring glances and soft smiles that he was completely smitten. Helen realised this with dismay. Fred seemed a very nice fellow, but she was not particularly attracted to him and was too enchanted with her new environment to consider romance.

The following week, Fred asked her to come and have a meal with his family in Coatbridge on Saturday.

"What will I say to him? I'd like to meet his family with all those sisters, but I think he is keen and I don't feel that way about him. I've said you might need me at the weekend."

"Oh, so you're using me as an excuse, are you?"

"I suppose I am. And remember what you said about a girl friend going to his house and all those sisters inspecting her. It wouldn't be easy. *And* they're Catholics, too. They'd hardly be pleased to meet a Protestant girlfriend with a broken tooth."

Annie laughed.

"Och well, I think you should go. It's just puppy love and his mother will know that, I'm sure. It'll please the poor bloke and you'll enjoy yourself."

Helen went and was made very welcome. The prince of the house sat smiling at the top of the table, just as Annie had imagined, but his sisters were not too deferential and his mother was bossy and business-like with him. They admired Helen's dress and hair and laughed at her jokes and it was a very pleasant visit, though she was positive Fred would never be more than a friend.

In spite of the distance, Fred brought her home and gave her a gentle goodnight kiss.

He seemed inhumanly big at such close quarters, so much taller and with a nose and mouth of entirely different proportions from her own. Fred's features were strong and classical and not dissimilar to Michelangelo's David and Helen found herself uncomfortably reminded of those giant plaster casts on Friday mornings.

It was like kissing a statue!

◊

"So what will you wear to the Hallowe'en Howl?"

This was the first dance in the Assembly Hall that year. Earlier there had been a small 'Freshers' Hop' in the small ground floor hall. Informal and enjoyable, it had seemed like an extension of their daily life. Older students and staff would attend this larger fancy dress event and the marvellous Clyde Valley Stompers jazz band would be onstage.

"I'm going as Alice in Wonderland. I'll wear the French gingham dress and you can make me a little white apron and I'll have my hair loose with a ribbon holding my fringe back."

"And will you wear proper Tenniel stripey stockings and little black shoes?"

"I wish I could, but I've never seen any striped stockings, anywhere. It's always the problem with fancy dress, you can never find the right footgear. I'll wear my black leather ballet shoes I suppose."

"You don't think you'll look too girly? There are bound to be lots of witches and skeletons and ghosts that night."

"I suppose so, but those are so *predictable*! No, I want to go to a dance looking as good as I can. Anyway it must be awful difficult to get broken down buniony shoes that look right for a witch!"

Helen was vain enough to seize this opportunity of wearing her hair loose. Probably none of her friends realised how long it was and it was an attribute that no one else in the Art School possessed.

Though proud of it, there was an ambivalence in Helen's attitude towards her hair. Sometimes it seemed as though a change was desirable and she was tempted to grab scissors and put an end to the particular image presented by the two neat plaits severely binding her head. But there was always the fear that a whole new image must then be created. And what would she do with her fine fly-away hair? Useless for a short style, for it would never stay out of her eyes and a really short cut would make her more boyish-looking than ever. She had no admiration for the tightly permed curls that most girls wore. Her present style was brushed, plaited and pinned up in the morning and she need never think about it again until the next day. How many women could say that? Her hair was practical, tidy for dancing and swimming and she had no need of the services of a hairdresser. Also she knew her mother would be sad to see it shorn, while her father would be delighted.

At intervals, arguments for and against cutting her hair would jumble around in her mind, always reaching the same conclusion of keeping it long.

◊

Poor Fred slumped his immensity against the wall and watched Helen with mournful eyes. In love for the first time, he had hoped to be Helen's only partner that night and made no attempt to hide his misery when she danced with others. Fred's height made conversation difficult on the dance floor and he was less skilled in the art of dancing than smaller, neater men.

Dismayed to find him so seriously affected, Helen became cross. She had given him no reason to believe their friendship exclusive and such dramatic, unhidden sorrow seemed very like blackmail.

As they danced with her, Buckie and wee Donald gently reproached her for her cruelty to Fred.

When the Clyde Valley Stompers changed gear for the romantic last waltz at eleven o'clock, Helen smiled to Fred and he hurried over with a joyful expression. The honour of the final waltz was sufficient delight.

Donald stood there, nodding his head and smiling approvingly. 'Just like a benevolent little uncle' Helen thought bitterly.

Fred was a nice boy but she was not going to jump into his arms, just because his friends thought she should!

◊

The weeks of drawing inanimate objects were no doubt a good exercise, but terribly boring. In the last five weeks of term they drew 'from the antique'. Plaster casts of heads and torsos were brought into the studio and the complexities of using light and shade to delineate more subtle forms were studied. The elegant Archer was drawn by the more successful students. After Christmas, they would start life-drawing and were advised to buy and study Gray's Anatomy for Artists.

In December, the Cosmo was showing a French film which contained nudity, hardly ever seen in films at that time. Claude and William, the *enfants terribles* of the class cut Friday afternoon to visit the Cosmo protesting that they were preparing for future life classes.

On Monday, when asked if they had enjoyed the film, they giggled and admitted that just as the beautiful star was about to disrobe, Claude was unwrapping a caramel which he unfortunately let fall to the floor. Both boys bent to retrieve it. By the time they recovered the sweet, the scene had changed to a respectably clothed crowd scene.

"But we sat round again and saw it properly the next time!"

The following week Helen visited the Cosmo to watch the magical 'Les Enfants du Paradis', a film which Helen would remember all her life. She longed to comfort the sad hero, played by Jean Louis Barrault, and his sensitive features created an ideal in her mind.

Fred had less of her sympathy. His mooning calf love continued unabated until Christmas and Helen became irritated. Had he no pride!

One morning, in the middle of class, he lumbered to his feet, with a great sigh from the sole of his boots. Gazing at Helen reproachfully, he slowly walked to the door and left the studio. His demeanour suggesting that, should he encounter a deep lake or a high cliff in the next half hour, he would probably put an end to it all. After his melodramatic exit, some wag whistled a few bars of Leoncavallo's heart-breaking melody, now a popular song,

You're breaking my heart 'cos you're leaving,
You've fallen for somebody new.

Helen felt embarrassed, guilty and angry and rubbed out her drawing.

On the day of the Christmas Ball, poor Fred discovered that Big Donald would be Helen's partner. That evening, he took the tram to Hyndland and poured out his misery to Annie. She admitted later she had shed a few tears.

"He was so big and helpless and so sad and there was nothing I could say to cheer him up."

After leaving Annie, he headed for the Kelvin Hall carnival and drowned his sorrows in doughnuts, chips and roundabouts.

Helen was cross that he had involved Annie.

Even crosser the following morning when she saw written across the four window panes in her kitchen,

D E A D

The impeccable lettering was in mirror image, properly spaced within the pane and obviously not the work of a child or vandal. Calligraphy had been one of the subjects that term. She never mentioned it to Fred.

◊

Helen wore her black and white checked dress to the Christmas Ball and, though the evening was romantic and gratifying, she and big Donald had little to say to each other. His dancing was mediocre. After an outing to the cinema during the Christmas holidays, they went their separate ways.

◊

When Rennie Mackintosh designed the east and west staircases of the Glasgow Art School, he achieved the same wonderful airy light that pervades the rest of the building by opening archways through the central wall between each flight of stairs.

Helen realised the possibility of clambering through each archway to move directly from the middle of one flight to the middle of the next, and she could not resist the challenge. It speeded up the long climb to the top floor. Some of the boys followed her example. After pursuing this energetic route for three months, she missed her footing one day and fell, hurting her elbow. Only Adam was with her and, as the blood was trickling freely over her hand, he was worried.

'We'd better have a look at it, Helen."

Her sleeve proved too tight to roll above the elbow and hating a fuss and feeling a fool, she was ready to ignore it.

"It'll be fine, Adam."

"No, you'd better go the ladies room and take your dress off and get someone to look at it." He blushed as he made the suggestion.

Mattie went with her and cleaned it. Nothing seemed broken, but it was painful for some weeks. Helen stopped climbing through the arches, and started to mount the stairs sedately, two at a time, as other people did.

Life Drawing and Charity Week

O n the first day after the Christmas holidays, Mr Bone had introduced them to the art school skeleton. He warned that *no one must touch it* and they needed no second telling. After a short lecture about the general workings of the human frame, Willie talked them through the first pages of their anatomy book, discussing some of the major surface muscles with which they must become familiar. The names were in Latin, daunting at first for some, but within a fortnight, the phrases *orbicularis oris, erector spinae, latissimus dorsi* and *gluteus maximus* were bandied about with ease, the last usually with a self-conscious smirk.

Their first attempt at drawing the naked figure took place in the second week. Helen felt nervous and ill at ease and was probably not alone. Mrs Kelly was perhaps forty, with a plump and well-shaped figure, which had obviously bred and fed several children. Her head was classically beautiful, with a fine Italian profile and thick black hair swept smoothly back. During her 'rest', when she put on her robe and chatted naturally to the students, the class became very relaxed and at the second pose were able to concentrate on transferring the delineations of a three-dimensional human body to a two-dimensional piece of paper. She was a wonderful model, graceful, motionless and very *real*. Also a very nice person.

Various models would come and go in the next four years, but Mrs Kelly, Mr Snow and Jimmy would be most familiar to the students.

Jimmy was in his late fifties, of middle height and with a spare, muscular build. He had worked in the Clyde shipyards and although not a talkative man, his conversation could flash with typical Glasgow humour. He had lost his left hand in an accident and wore a neat leather cover over his wrist. Always in the studio at nine-thirty, still and steady as he posed, uncomplaining about a difficult position and ready to resume the pose as soon as his five minute 'rest' was up, Jimmy was an excellent model. Brief black bathing trunks protected his modesty.

Mr Snow (he was always given his title) was entirely different. Late, loud and dogmatic, ready to criticise and even offer advice when no teacher was present, he was happy to let conversation extend the rest period indefinitely.

He had been on the music halls when young, playing a strong-man act with his wife. As far as Helen could learn, he had walked onstage with his wife playing the violin as she stood on his outstretched arm. Helen pictured her in a tutu, while he wore a leopard skin, but that might have been her imagination. Sadly those glorious days were long behind him and now in his late fifties, his once powerful muscles had degenerated to shapeless fat. With string and what looked like an old paint rag, he had devised a *cache-sexe* for himself, grubby and scarcely decent.

Mr Snow was a character, but never a favourite model.

◊

The lollipop lady, recently introduced by the Government to help guide school children across the road, inspired Wee Donald with an idea for Charities' Week.

"How about we all dress up as St Trinian's schoolgirls? I'll make one of those signs they hold up for schoolkids and we'll wander back and forth across the roads, holding up the traffic. It'll make more impact if there's a crowd of us. Collect more money."

Donald was authoritative and organising and everyone assembled on Saturday in borrowed school uniforms, some better fitting than others. Only Big Donald opted out, preferring the dramatic robes and headdress of an Indian Chief.

Helen and Mattie were in their old uniforms, both aiming to look more attractive than in those far off schooldays. When Margery arrived, they both felt inadequate, for she had used her creativity to make herself look *incredibly awful*. With her tie under one ear, her hat over the other, one leg of her knickers hanging to the knee, black stockings laddered and ripped, pimples on her nose and two front teeth blacked out, she was unrecognisable. Helen admired her friend's uninhibited spirit, but could never have made herself look such a guy. Even the boys in their laughably ill-fitting feminine gear could not compete with Margery for awfulness.

Only wee Donald was absolutely beautifully turned out in his cousin's navy school hat, crisp spotless blouse, neatly knotted tie, gym slip and tightly suspendered black stockings. His appearance was perfect and only enhanced by his large dark moustache. Carrying the pole with the STOP sign, he stood between the tramlines in Sauchiehall Street, superbly brave, and directed the motley crowd of schoolgirls back and forth under the noses of unamused and glowering tram drivers.

At the Art School dance that night, Helen was relieved to see that Margery, like everyone else, had changed to more appropriate gear.

Breakfast Party

Margery and Mattie usually met on Saturday to go sketching together, but Helen had too many domestic duties, as well as her dance class. Annie guessed that Helen missed her new art school friends at the weekend and suggested,

"Would you like to invite some of your fellow students round for the evening on a Saturday or Sunday?"

"Quite a few of them live far away. Buckie's in Greenock. Mattie, Nan and Connie are on the south side, Fred's in Coatbridge."

Fred's love-lorn attitude had faded, allowing everyone to relax.

"And another thing," Helen continued, "I might have to offer them some sort of alcohol at night. Wee Donald and Jim might expect it. They were in the army."

"Would they really expect it?"

"Well, it's not that anyone drinks much, but maybe it would look funny to offer nothing at all. But it would be expensive and I don't want folk drinking here. What do you think?"

"I don't suppose they would get obstreperous, but it would cost money. I remember when I was young, we used to hear about artists in Paris having breakfast parties. What about one of those? That would solve the problem of getting home at night and no one would expect alcohol in the morning. You could give them a really nice breakfast."

Helen thought it a great idea. Annie had omitted to mention those long-ago orgiastic breakfasts were famous for unlimited champagne.

Ten fellow students and Drew, Jack's cousin, were invited and all accepted.

Douglas was in Glasgow and he too was invited. He asked if he could bring a friend, Sam, a young man who seemed a bit lonely, an orphan.

"Of course, bring him along, that's fine."

"I should tell you he's *very* wealthy! His grandfather invented a famous headache powder and now his folk are dead and he's inherited *a hundred thousand pounds*. Well worth setting your cap at!"

Helen laughed. Marriage was the last thing on her mind and such a vast sum meant very little, but it was unique to meet anyone described as wealthy. Sam would turn out to be a nice ordinary fellow and no one would have guessed his secret.

◊

The party started at 9 30am, just as art school did.

The food was a great success and consisted of crisp rolls, sausages, hard-boiled eggs, and a large bowl of curry, for which Annie had prepared many vegetables. There was also a steaming pot of mussels, but only Margery shared Helen's taste for shell-fish.

With story-telling, mimes, charades and songs, the rest of the morning was very much a re-creation of the enjoyable social interludes in the studio.

Only Douglas and Sam seemed faintly bemused, finding these students different from those in accountancy.

◊

The art school curriculum was demanding, with a considerable amount of 'homework'. Although Helen was more conscientious than she had been at school, the weekly sketchbook was a burden. Willie Bone expected his students to aim for an ideal classical style. Drawings by Michelangelo, Raphael and other old masters were studied and copied, but Helen disliked this exercise. Somehow she could not grasp exactly how she must change her drawing to please Willie, nor was she sure that she wanted to change. Her need and determination to solve problems in her own way was a drawback and her sketchbook was always in the *bad pile*.

Perhaps others had more exciting subjects in their sketchbook? Margery and Mattie sketched in Central Station and around town and travelled to Bowling to draw fishing boats. When the Agricultural Show opened at the Kelvin Hall, Helen visited it and drew cows and pigs. She enjoyed herself and liked her own drawings, but they did not qualify her for the good pile. She would never repeat those few hours away from the weekend's domestic duties but drew her family, furniture and endless self-portraits. Willie often said you could not do too many of the last and of course you, yourself, were always available.

◊

In April, Helen had influenza, followed by an attack of tonsillitis and was in bed for two weeks, unable to speak. Apart from the boredom and discomfort, Helen found ill health such a *terrible waste of time.*

After the utilitarian war years, the idea of attractive packaging was coming back into fashion and in Mr Fleming's lofty studio on the top floor, the students were asked to design a small decorative box suitable for sweets or biscuits. Helen was surprised that she had never questioned how such ingenious boxes were constructed and realised how ignorant and incurious she had been before coming to the art school.

Throughout the year, they studied history of design and compiled a comprehensive notebook, with drawings and illustrations dating from earliest times. When studying these artefacts and decorations Helen found that she easily learned and remembered other facts about the people who used them. Without trying, she acquired a clearer overview of the historical timescale than she had ever received from school lessons. A visualisation of world geography also became plainer through the design research. Why had those dull text books not referred to any of these beautiful things in their dry pages? Those interminable lists of kings and ancient battles, distant rivers and boring crops had meant little to her.

Helen's favourite subject was figure composition. Mr Bone obviously enjoyed teaching it, using the paintings of various masters to explain and demonstrate the rules of composition. A painting of laundry women by Degas, probably Willie's favourite artist, helped Helen realise the pictorial possibilities of clothes hanging on a pulley. Her next composition was a kitchen scene and Willie's criticism was particularly enthusiastic and complimentary, which was very pleasant after all those weeks of the bad pile.

◊

In May, Miss Hopkins suggested that Helen might like to create her own solo, perhaps incorporating some mime, for the Athenaeum show in June. Helen was breathless with delight as she spoke to Annie,

"I never thought she would allow me to do that. Isn't it exciting! I can't believe it! She's so kind, but you know… her dances are all written down and she refers to the book, then gets us to do them, but somehow they're not… exactly… they're all *right*, but…

it's like cooking from a recipe book and her dances aren't...
mmm"

"From the heart, d'ye mean?"

"I suppose so. When Miss Cleland teaches you a new movement, she's so graceful herself, you just know how to do it! But
she's often quite bad-tempered. Miss Hopkins is always kind and
knows exactly *how* anything should be done, but somehow she
doesn't or can't... mm... make it look lovely... and it's the same
with her dances."

"She doesn't inspire you?"

"No she doesn't and I'm *so happy* to be making up my own
dance."

"You'll need to get cracking on some ideas."

"Oh, I thought it up on the tram coming home. I'll be a
blanchisseuse with that nice little basket that I got in the fruit shop,
full of different articles of clothing and as I hang each piece up on
a clothes horse, I'll mime what it suggests to me, like a baby's
dress or a beautiful lady's evening shawl. Then I'll dance in
between times. *On the point* now of course."

"Hmm, I'll look forward to that, should certainly be
different."

Annie was glad to see her daughter happier and more confident since starting art school.

Tonsilitis struck again in May, just as the examinations were
finishing. Helen was too ill to finish her design exam and Doctor
Hamilton said her tonsils should come out.

Bruce booked Helen into a nursing home in Garnethill, close
to the High School and arrangements were made for Agnes to
come twice a day to help Annie.

Several people shook their heads, warning that a tonsillectomy
was *much worse* when you were as old as eighteen, but Bruce had
had his removed at the same age and pooh-poohed that idea.
Optimistic folk assured her she would have ice cream at every meal.

The actual illness had been so very painful and miserable that
the operation and recovery seemed relatively slight to Helen. She
found it very pleasant to lie in bed and be waited upon by cheerful
young nurses.

Apart from sucking an aspirin before each meal to deaden the
pain, it was like a hotel with a preponderance of boiled chicken
on the menu, though never a hint of ice cream.

She read the Glasgow Herald each morning, finding it heavy going. Only the Women's Page amused her, for it described a life of unrecognisable domestic gentility.

Her classmates sent her anemones, Douglas sent her irises, Mattie brought talcum powder and Margery loaned her Arnold Bennett's 'Clayhanger' novels, which she read avidly. At Annie's behest, Agnes bought wildly pink wool to knit a cardigan. Though not a colour Helen would have chosen herself, it became a favourite garment, always reminding her of that carefree interlude on Garnethill.

It was a little holiday and a turning point in Helen's health, for she would never again suffer influenza.

Unfortunately she had not attained a pass mark in design and had failed in architecture and in order to enter second year, she must bring these subjects up to standard before September.

Though it went against her independent principles, Helen decided to follow the example of the other girls and seek some masculine help with her architecture. Technical drawing seemed to come so easily to the boys.

Summer 1950

Throughout that summer in Pittenweem, Helen and Donald exchanged humorous letters. Donald's were long, playful and imaginative, adorned with many illustrations, so dense they might be read several times with enjoyment. Helen replied to him in kind. Their letters were a pleasant mixture of sophisticated and child-like fantasy, perhaps verging on love letters, though each would have denied feeling anything more than affection.

Months previously they had admitted their virginity to each other. The unpleasant knowledge Donald had gained as a records clerk in the army had stopped him from any sexual experimentation. They made a pact that, should they be in the same innocent state when Helen reach her fortieth birthday, they would meet some weekend and remedy the problem.

As before, Helen protected her first hour of privacy by providing her grandparents with an early cup of tea. Then, settled on the wheeled seat in the garden, and luxuriously warmed by the sun, she enjoyed her own breakfast and read Donald's latest bulletin. The correspondence amused and employed Helen and kept her in touch with that new confident self that she had discovered at Art School.

Helen swam and danced through that summer, making friends with a milkman, a joiner, who was champion of the local tennis club, and several fishermen. She danced one evening with a handsome young fellow on holiday from a Manchester dye works, and would have liked to find out more about his occupation, but their conversation was sadly handicapped by the difference in their accents. A local baker also had an incomprehensible accent which defeated conversation completely. He seemed such a nice shy boy and Helen *longed* to understand him. Even his Fife companions had difficulty. Helen could only nod and smile sympathetically as they danced around the floor of Anstruther town hall.

It was interesting to meet young men so very different from her fellow art students.

◊

Annie sat knitting in the garden, a wide brimmed straw hat shading her face. Her hands were as dark as mahogany and showed how many hours she had spent in the sunny fresh air.

For fifteen minutes, Mary had been dealing with the myriad snails that lived in the crevices of the old walls, stamping mercilessly and crushing shells with apparent savage pleasure.

"My, I've had a fine slaughter today. That'll teach them, the *brutes*, eating up all my new plants."

Annie smiled at Mary's violence.

"Well, there'd be nothing left growing at all if I didn't get rid of them! Tell me, d'ye ever hear from that big he-horse that used to work for you. Whatwasername? She went to Aberdeen, didn't she?"

Annie looked at her mother coldly,

"I suppose you mean Jessie Clark. No, I've never heard any more from her."

" I don't expect writing letters is much in her line. I wonder whatever happened to her?"

"I often think of her. She was an awful kind, decent soul and very good to me."

"Coarse, though, and a bit of a china-basher, I seem to remember."

Annie made no reply but looked out over the sea to North Berwick Law, blue and perfect on the distant coast.

◊

As usual, Helen accompanied Mary to various local bazaars to help carry home the fresh produce that was always available. Broad beans were cheap, perhaps only tuppence a pound, for local gardeners grew them, not for their own sake, but to protect their carrots from black fly.

Almost always, as they entered some church hall, the heady smell of sweet peas would greet Helen and perhaps it was worth tholing an hour's boredom for that heavenly perfume.

"Do'ye not see anything you'd like to buy yourself, Helen? You might. Here's something, in case you do."

Helen thought it unlikely, but accepted the half crown gratefully.

Almost at once, amongst some uninspiring bric-a-brac, she saw a pretty little cream coloured vase with a fluted edge. It was made of glass with a pearl-like finish and seemed unusual. She bought it for two shillings, the first antique she had ever bought, and nearly the last, for she would never pursue that hobby. One collector in the family was enough. Her remaining sixpence bought a book by James Thurber and Helen was delighted to discover this whimsical and humorous American author. Helen would always treasure these purchases, but could never understand her grandmother's obssessive delight in bargain hunting.

◊

John was getting very forgetful and thin. He seemed to be fading before Annie's eyes. Would he be with them next summer? She knew her mother's life with him must be difficult, but wished Mary were less impatient and irritable with the old, failing man. But possibly John might find that strange, for Mary had *always* been irritable.

He did not seem unhappy, only tired. What did he think about in those long hours he spent upstairs in the studio? He listened to the news and read the Glasgow Herald and often surprised her with his awareness of current events. He made mild little jokes and occasionally referred, quite correctly, to past events. Radio concerts still gave him great pleasure. Beethoven's music in particular would waft him to some other plane of happiness and satisfaction, though tears coursed down his cheeks.

Second Year

Helen looked forward to returning in September to her friends and the busy disciplined life of the Art School. Her architecture and design re-sits were handed in before term started, but the deputy director, Mr Barnes, had unfortunately not found time to consider them. Much to Helen's indignation and humiliation, she found her name on the lists to repeat first year.

Mr Bone sent her immediately to the office to straighten things out, but administration was busy and it would be Friday before Helen joined her friends in second year.

Those three days were just long enough for Alistair, a self-confident boy straight from school, to fall for Helen. In spite of her distinct lack of encouragement, he accompanied her at every opportunity. When she returned to her own section, Alistair joined the second year group at coffee time in the ref, pushing through closely packed chairs to be beside Helen, in spite of her uninviting expression. Alistair was a brash fellow, determined and courageous enough to weather the grim frowns of Helen's companions and loud remarks such as,

"Helen, can you not get rid of that first year bloke?"

"Who does that young squirt think he is?"

"Why don't you tell that fresher to take a walk?"

Helen felt unkind, but Alistair was irritating and persistent and the embarrassing situation lasted for weeks. Helen found it hard to forgive Mr Barnes.

◊

"I think I'll wear my ballet dress to the Hallowe'en Howl this year."

"Oh yes, and what will you call yourself?"

"I'll be a Degas ballet dancer."

"Will you be the Degastliest ballet dancer ever?"

Helen looked sternly at her mother. She would have raised one eyebrow, if she could. Really, sometimes Annie tried too hard to wrest a pun from unlikely material.

Helen's partners that night were Donald and Buckie, the first looking authentically Chinese with drooping moustache and hands tucked into the sleeves of his tunic, while the latter was unusually smart in tweed jacket, white shirt and striped tie, though lacking trousers.

◊

Their studies had so many interesting and different aspects that the busy hours in the art school hardly seemed like work. There was a variety of crafts to choose from and this year Helen chose leatherwork and made herself a large handbag. Heraldry suited Buckie's meticulous style. Margery decided on print-making and Mattie on embroidery, Connie and Nan took book-binding.

The written work this year was history of architecture and some students invested in a copy of Bannister Fletcher, the architect's bible.

How good it was to be back in the beautiful building and how lucky they were to be based in it. Some of the general course students had their tutor's room in the modern building on the other side of Renfrew Street and must cross back and forth for different classes. Fortunately it was a one-way street and no accidents occurred or none that Helen heard of.

Mr Bone was present most of the time, teaching conscientiously, but occasionally, perhaps for a staff meeting, he left them to themselves. Then the model would be asked to "Rest, please," and a social interlude would start. Each week the latest Goon Show was discussed by its aficionados, mainly boys. Scenarios were analysed and re-enacted, the bizarre voices mimicked and favourite surreal phrases recalled and chortled over. Helen was impressed by the almost total recall that they possessed. Though she often listened to the show, and enjoyed it, she could retain very little of the speedy, insane dialogue. Another topic that provoked gales of laughter, was the popular strip cartoon of Lobey Dosser the Glesca cowboy. He rode a two-legged horse, called El Fideldo and had unlikely adventures in the wilds of the city.

A song by James Bridie became popular with the class. Mattie introduced it, singing it with the throttled vowels of a Kelvinside accent,

It's long paist midnight, the streets are getting dairk,
The fairies aire a' dancing in the West End Pairk.

It was a ditty of some length. Helen particularly enjoyed the lines,

A deep and holy stillness broods the Gorbals o'er,
And softly blow the zephyrs down on Govan's peaceful shore.

◊

Because of some lack in the service provided at lunchtime, the student council decided to boycott the refectory. Traditionally, when they had any money, the art students had gone to M&A Brown's very pleasant tearoom in Sauchiehall Street for morning coffee, but another smaller tearoom at the foot of the hill had just opened and Helen's friends decided to take their custom there. It proved to be delightfully inexpensive. A slice of plain bread toasted and buttered cost only a penny or two. Even those who at first declined to be tempted changed their minds when the aromatic plateful was brought to the table. Helen had never thought of eating at eleven o'clock, but she too succumbed, persuaded, like the others, by her sense of smell, The entire section ate toast and many found that, as it was so cheap, one slice was hardly enough. Certainly Fred always had three and sometimes four slices.

Willie B was cross when his class arrived late, which now sometimes happened, for the hill seemed somehow steeper than before.

It took five weeks for the problems of the ref to be sorted and for five weeks, Section One munched hot buttered toast each morning. Perhaps gorged would be a better word.

One afternoon, as Helen sat drawing, she noticed her skirt waistband and bra elastic felt uncomfortably tight. She looked around the class and her friends seemed subtly changed. Their sharp young features had become softer and less defined. Some showed embryo double chins. Their clothes hung less loosely.

Like little pigs for market, they were being fattened up on that delicious buttered toast!

Fortunately the refectory was eventually cured of its sins and with the more Spartan food on offer there, the class soon regained its slender aspect.

The little teashop went out of business. Only Fred continued to eat rather more than was necessary, even for his large frame.

Annie had met most of Mr Bone's section by now and certainly knew all about them from Helen's anecdotes.

Margery often visited, dropping in later in the evening to play cards and drink a cup of Russian tea. Sometimes they made up limericks, some of them rather vulgar. Margery enjoyed the relaxed, Bohemian atmosphere, very different from her conventional home.

"I would love to bake and cook," Margery said one evening, "But my mother won't let me into the kitchen, in case I make a mess."

Neither Annie or Helen knew what to say to that.

◊

Helen was invited to Dunfermline to visit Jean and it was arranged that Agnes would come in and look after Annie for the weekend.

As Helen jumped on to the bus, a young man looked up and caught her eye. It was John Smith, the boy who had given her that first important kiss. Though both had changed in the three intervening years, they recognised each other immediately and spent a pleasant journey, describing their experiences since that summer and saying goodbye in the Dunfermline bus station. Helen was glad to have met him, but did not expect to see him again. Nor did she.

That night she and Jean climbed the smallest, narrowest stairway Helen had ever seen, then ducked down through a doorway four feet high to Jean's tiny bedroom. It made Helen think of Alice in Wonderland and the potions she drank. The ancient building seemed a perfect place for ghosts and they discussed the supernatural far into the night.

About 2am, Jean remembered a poem they had learned in Pittenweem and recited it with gusto,

The King sate in Dunfermline toun, drinkin the blude red wine

Helen had loved the verse,

I saw the new moon late yestreen, wi the auld moon in her airm
An' if we gang tae sea, maister, I fear we'll come to hairm

Briefly, it took their minds off the ghosts, then they recalled another verse,

Half-ower, half-ower frae Aberdour, 'tis fifty fathoms deep
And there lies guid Sir Patrick Spens wi' the Scots Lords at his feet

It was not a cheerful story and it took some time for them to get to sleep. Helen was glad that she need never sleep alone in that little room, and pitied Jean.

Days later, Helen suddenly realised the fire hazard of that enclosed space and shivered.

The girls had each bought red nail varnish in Woolworths. Helen soon put her bottle of Wild Flame in a cupboard, philosophically accepting that it was impossible to maintain manicured hands in a life of stoking fires, washing clothes and painting in oils.

One Friday evening, when Annie was in bed waiting for her weekly massage, she said,

"Helen, how about painting my toenails scarlet and giving Miss Arthur a laugh."

As usual, Annie's hands and arms were dealt with first, then the bedclothes were thrown back in order to start on her feet. Poor Miss Arthur! The older lady nearly had hysterics.

Annie was contrite.

"Poor old soul, I should never have suggested it, but I've no idea why she was so upset. Did she think someone had torn my toenails off? But I do feel rotten, giving her such a fright."

Nevertheless Annie laughed each time she thought of it.

◊

There was no doubt Nancy Little was an unlucky woman, an accident magnet.

"Oh, Ann, I had such a dreadful experience in school last week. The staffroom toilet was out of order, but the plumber was working on it. He popped his head into the staffroom and told me he was fixing the cistern and would be ready very soon. Now, I could have gone to another toilet on the other side of the gym hall, but when he said 'very soon', I decided just to wait and make a cup of coffee for myself. And right enough, only minutes later, he looked in again and said it was all fixed and ready now and would I care to try it?"

Helen loved to watch the fleeting expressions pass over her mother's face as she listened, apparently politely, to one of Nancy's long stories.

"So I went in to the little toilet and without using it, I pulled the plug. Well! The chain pulled the whole mechanism *right out of the cistern,* and of course a great deal of water *cascaded down* . It's a blessing I was not at all injured, but I was *absolutely* soaked. The man was apologetic, of course, but really it was a dreadful business and should never have happened. And I just could not get warm again until bedtime that night."

Helen swiftly left the room to make coffee leaving Annie to tut-tut sympathetically.

Later, after Nancy had gone, Annie said,

"What did you think of that story about the cistern? How on earth could that happen? I don't believe a word of it."

Helen thought her mother cynical, but neither could she understand how it had happened. But surely no one would make up a story like that.

◊

Just after the war there had been the possibility of buying surplus parachutes, some were silk and some nylon. Mary had bought a nylon one but the fabric was stiff and unyielding and the garments were unsuccessful. The top of the parachute, with its many flared sections still lay in a drawer. Helen had tried it on one rainy day and found it fitted her like a long skirt, but it was unattractive and seemed useless.

When Annie heard that the Christmas Ball would have an Oriental theme that year, she remembered the parachute.

"What about that parachute? I think you could paint it with bright patterns and make it wonderful. You could be a nautch girl.

"What on earth is a an ouch girl?"

"It's an Indian dancer."

At once, Helen visualised a magnificent outfit.

" I think there should be gold on the skirt and there's the gold lamé from grandma's heyday that would make a bra top."

"Get it out then and let's have a look at it. But of course you wouldn't go to a dance with a bare midriff, would you?"

"Wouldn't I?"

Helen had thought this a necessity for an eastern dancer and was taken aback by her mother's prudish attitude.

"No, no, Helen, you couldn't, but I think there's some gold lace that'll fill in the gap nicely."

Helen sometimes found Annie unpredictable.

Helen went alone to the Christmas Ball and had an excellent time dancing with lots of different partners, most of whom were good friends. One new partner was Trevor, a young tutor, recently moved north from London. He was tremendously polite and gentlemanly with a cultured southern accent similar to that of Miss Hopkins. That night, his luxuriant Sultan's beard and extravagant silk turban and robes disguised his appearance, but she would find that, even in everyday dress, Trevor's appearance was strange. He was tall and skeletally thin, with the large sharp nose, slightly protruding teeth and inadequate chin of the typical foolish aristocrat described in the books of PG Wodehouse. Trevor's clothes were expensive, impeccable and always a little out of place in Glasgow. At first, because he was a tutor, Helen found him rather awe-inspiring, but when she discovered he was the most marvellous dancer, energetic, lithe and flexible, completely uninhibited, she thought him the perfect partner.

Perfect for dancing, that is to say.

Mungo

Just before her nineteenth birthday, Helen and Margery went to a university dance in the Queen Margaret Union. The building was pleasant, though smaller than they had expected. Almost immediately, Margery met an old school friend and danced with him for the rest of the evening. The first young man to ask Helen to dance was Mungo, an engineering student from Inverness. His thick dark hair, large eyes and refined features reminded her of the delicate, tragic hero of *Les Enfants du Paradis* and made a good impression. But Mungo had been drinking a little, although he tried to hide it, and Helen was distant with him.

"Who was that?" Margery asked.

"He's called Mungo and he's studying engineering. He comes from Inverness, but he's a bit tight and I'm not interested."

"Well, here he comes again, I'm afraid."

After the second dance, Helen moved to another part of the hall in order to avoid this unacceptable partner. Later in the evening, Mungo again sought her out and invited her for a cup of coffee, apologising for having been drinking earlier. He now seemed sober and they had a pleasant conversation.

As they spoke, Helen decided he looked just as a university student should look, terribly thin, with long hair falling across his brow, and a shabby tweed jacket with leather elbow patches. When she found that he rowed for the university, he seemed stereotypical, though she laughed at herself for having this preconceived idea.

He was a competent dancer and his Highland voice was attractive. They danced till the last waltz and Mungo walked home with her. As he had a free pass, they arranged to meet inside the hall the next week, Mungo promising 'not to touch a drop'.

◊

Mungo lodged in Otago Street, sharing a room with another engineering student. When Helen discovered that his evening meal was not provided on a Saturday night, she was astonished and asked what he did.

"Oh, we get a sandwich in the pub or maybe a fish supper if we're feeling wealthy." He laughed self-consciously.

Helen had quickly realised that money was even scarcer for him than for most of her friends. His mother had been a widow for many years and living away from home was expensive.

"You could come and have dinner with us some Saturday, if you'd like, and you could meet my mother."

And so Mungo was introduced into Annie's life and would become very close to her.

About the time that Helen first met Mungo, the papers were full of a daring robbery. In spite of disorganisation and incredible naivety, Scottish students had managed to steal the Stone of Destiny from Westminster Abbey. The establishment was deeply shocked and the police even more deeply puzzled. The ancient stone, heavy and awkward to lift, had been spirited away and had disappeared into the infinite.

Nor would it surface for several years.

Though Mungo was not actively involved in the robbery, he shared digs with someone who was near the centre of the conspiracy and he knew every detail of the adventurous theft. It says much about Mungo's character that he did not breathe a word to Helen of his inside knowledge, until the Stone was restored to the light of day some months later.

◊

Douglas was home at Easter and borrowed his father's car to take Helen to a dinner dance at Forresthills Hotel on Loch Ard. It seemed sophisticated and unlike any other date she had experienced. The long drive there and back made it very special. To drink a sherry and eat a delicious dinner with dancing between the courses was as glamorous as any of those romantic evenings portrayed in films.

Another day, they went to Drymen on his motor bike and even this more ordinary outing had excitement and charm. No doubt Helen found something special about the time she spent in Douglas's company. He had an aura of affection, reliability and confidence which made her feel safe and cared for. With him she felt happy yet always slightly shy, a feeling she no longer experienced with other young men.

It was a pity that his studies were in London and after that he would go abroad with the RNVR.

Festival of Britain

"Wouldn't you like to go down to London, Helen and see all the excitement down there? It's going to be a wonderful show, apparently."

"I'd like to visit London sometime, of course, but not for the Festival. I'm not impressed with the furniture and architecture and stuff you see in the papers. I don't like it at all. I think it's poor design and it looks uncomfortable and downright peculiar."

"Do you really?" Annie was amused at her daughter's strongly expressed views." I thought you would like all those new fashions."

"*No!* I don't like it at all. I think those peculiar chairs and tables are ugly with their wee wiry legs sticking out, ready to trip you up. That's not practical, it's not 'fitness for purpose'. If it doesn't work well, it's not good design."

"Oh aye? Well I must say I don't care for them much myself. But I thought I was just old-fashioned. What do they say about it at the art school?"

"Not much! You know I still remember the Empire Exhibition when I was a kid. It was really exciting and I *loved* those buildings and there's still a few around. There's the Beresford Hotel at Charing Cross, that I pass every day. It's a wee bit shabby looking but I'm sure it could be painted up again."

"That would be a big job, I'm afraid. I'm surprised you still remember the Empire Exhibition after all these years."

"I could never forget it. And there are those Art Deco houses at the end of Leven. I'd love to see inside one of them and sit out on the flat roof. I think that Exhibition was a highpoint of my childhood."

"It was a highpoint of flooding rain as far as I can remember."

"I don't remember it being wet. I suppose I was wearing my red oilskin and sou'wester from the Cellardyke factory. I used to love that wee outfit."

"Sometimes you had a yellow set."

"But I liked the red one best."

"You could do with a new waterproof now, I suppose."

"Yes, as a matter of fact I saw a nice one in Coplands, but it was quite dear, nine pounds ten."

"*That's* a bit steep, but if you like it, just get it. Have to do you for several years, though, at that price."

"I don't mind. It'll never go out of date. It's a classic, the sort detectives and newspaper reporters wear in films. You know, tightly belted and with the collar turned up mysteriously. Oh, I'll just love it."

Helen went into town next day and bought her first Burberry.

That spring, the Art Galleries had an exhibition of a little known Norwegian artist, Edvard Munch. The picture titled *The Scream* had yet to acquire its iconic status. The students of the Glasgow Art School were much affected by the emotion and agony of his paintings and Helen found his pictures more fascinating and inspiring than the strange child-like work of Picasso. However her grandparents were so rigorous in denouncing *Modern Art,* that she did not say much about Munch at home.

Margery regularly complained that her parents were 'utter Philistines', but Helen thought it even more difficult to deal with an artistic, but determinedly prejudiced, family.

◊

Though Tessa was now at University, she and Helen met occasionally. Tessa had not been successful in meeting boyfriends. Though unusually pale, with almost silver hair, she was a very pretty girl though much plumper than she should have been. However, many larger and more shapeless girls than Tessa found social success, but her adult vocabulary and erudite way of discussing serious subjects told against her in her dealings with the ordinary young man. Fellows were frightened off by her intense and superior manner, for which her parents were totally to blame. She had been encouraged to air her knowledge and display her cleverness. It had separated her from her peers in school and it now stood in her way in everyday student society.

Although it was not spoken of, Helen knew her friend was unhappy. One young man had seemed interested, then had disappeared. Tessa had sent him a poem of sad farewell. Helen was too polite to say she thought that a bit 'over the top', after only three dates. Things were to change for Tessa that summer.

Waddell Family Again

A cool East Coast breeze was blowing from the North Sea as Helen walked towards the swimming pool one day. Her Burberry was tightly belted and the collar turned up mysteriously. As she passed the putting green, two young men were playing. One of them looked at her with keen interest. Without acknowledging him, she realised that it was Jack Waddell, over six feet tall and much improved. The other boy must be Lindsay.

That evening, just as she set off for Anstruther Town Hall, she bumped into the whole Waddell family and invited them home.

They crowded into the low ceiled sitting room, the two boys seeming terribly tall. Isobel had not changed and her fast words poured out, relentlessly as ever, her voice flying high at the end of every sentence.

"Oh my, it's awful nice to be back in this dear wee room and see you all again! And how well you're looking, Mrs Mackay! And Annie too! How are you, my dear?"

"Oh warstlin' awa, ye know, but..."

"Well, you're as brown as a berry, Annie, and not a day older. Neither of you look a bit different. Now we're not needing a cup of tea, no, no. Well if the kettle's on...but, Helen, you were going somewhere when we met you and we brought you back home again. What a *lovely* girl she is, Annie, isn't she? She was always lovely. Now where were you away to when we turned ye back. *Dancing?* Were you going *dancing?* Jack's awful fond of dancing, aren't you, Jack? You could go along to Anstruther with Helen and have a dance. Is there a bus soon? Well, run away the two of you and we'll stay here and blether while you go dancing. Isn't that right Mrs Mackay? And we'll have a laugh. Nothing like a good laugh is there? Well, off you go, you two. What are waiting for? You'll miss the bus."

Helen was glad to see her again but unhappy about her suggestion, which was really more of an order! What if Jack was a rotten dancer and she was stuck with him for the whole night?

However Jack, now a fully fledged lawyer, was a splendid ballroom dancer and they had a wonderful evening. By the time they walked home along the shore, with the moon shining across the sea, Jack was obviously strongly attracted to her.

Helen did not intend to reciprocate these feelings and had no desire to be a heart breaker. Nevertheless it was very nice to be adored by that same boy who had ignored her five years ago, when she had so longed to be noticed.

They had an excellent fortnight dancing, swimming, sometimes with the family, sometimes not. Jack held her hand in the street in full view of his mother, which surprised and embarrassed Helen but delighted Isobel.

Jack's humour, like his mother's, often tended to the bawdy, while Lindsay's was more akin to that of the Glasgow art students, with wordplay, unexpected quirky statements, and the development of surreal fantasies. Helen was very fond of Lindsay, and his father Abe, was a kind, patient man. It might be nice to be a part of that family, but Jack was certainly not her idea of that faraway future husband.

When Jack's cousin Drew arrived in Pittenweem, dark and handsome, a splendid swimmer and dancer, the intense situation was diffused. Helen had learned the pleasures of being part of a crowd. It was much more fun to be friendly and light-heartedly flirtatious with every one, rather than half of a serious couple.

Mungo and Helen corresponded in a friendly way throughout the summer. He was at home in Inverness, struggling with second year maths which he had not yet passed. He said he was sure Helen would be good at the advanced work which he found so difficult. She did like numbers but had no idea what basis he had for this remark, other than flattery.

◊

Annie painted, knitted and wrote poems and seemed to suffer less pain if she kept busy, though the vagaries of the weather affected her badly. Sometimes several days would pass without any of the muscle spasms and she hoped and believed that the disease might be settling down.

Visitors popped in to see Mary throughout the day and they were always welcomed, though it might be a meal time. It irritated Helen that they would sit and chat for two hours, with the meal forgotten. She found it hard to understand how people could find so much to say about relatively nothing. Often the same piece of gossip was related two or three times, yet Mary would show the proper astonishment even at the third hearing. Sometimes her questions and suggestions seemed actively to encourage a more sensational aspect to the drama. Helen wondered how the story might have changed by the next time it was told.

Annie took little part in this, but she enjoyed some of the old phrases that her mother's visitors used.

A local old lady, Jean Hughes, was liable to pop in at any hour. Often Mary would have a little pot of jam or some pancakes to give her, then Jean would say,

"Aye, a gaun fit's aye gettin'."

"What does that mean?" Helen asked her mother later.

"I suppose it's if you're always on the move, you're bound to acquire things."

"But that's just the opposite of a rolling stone gathers no moss."

"And a standing stone gets peed on. You just have to choose the saying that suits you best at the time. Jean came in the other day and looked up at the big dark lowering clouds and said, 'Whit's it gonnae be, the day? It's makkin' awfy faces!' I've never heard that one before, but I like the idea of the sky making faces at you."

Third Year

By third year students must choose a specialist subject and Glasgow Art School offered a wide choice of interesting departments. Fred had chosen sculpture, Big Donald murals, Wee Donald graphics, Moira embroidery and weaving, Jim would immerse himself in lettering and calligraphy. Others would study interior decoration, jewellery or fabric design. The last was a splendid department which almost certainly guaranteed an excellent salary in the thriving British textile industry.

Margery, Mattie, Buckie, Connie, Dan and Helen would move to the first floor and study Drawing and Painting under Davy Donaldson.

The windows of room 45, the third year studio, soared even higher than those of room 25 and the space was permeated by a magical light. Helen noticed how this intense reflection of the sky bestowed an otherworldly, angelic aspect to the faces of those students with blue eyes.

With only one or two additions, most of the class had been Mr Bone's students and the close family feeling that Helen so much appreciated, would continue until they graduated. If there were any rivalry or ill feeling amongst them, Helen was unaware of it. It also seemed that the age-old problem of the power struggle between the sexes hardly existed. Perhaps the creative mind lessened the differences between male and female. Male superiority was never taken for granted, though boys did enjoy conveying information. Helen learned interesting facts about machinery from Adam and about pigment from Buckie. In private, the girls joked about the phenomenon of Man the Teacher.

Students in this department were less clear about their future. How wonderful to make one's name as an artist, but hardly possible in the financial climate of the time. Those heady Edwardian days of wealth when John Mackay pursued his successful career seemed unlikely to return.

Teaching seemed the most likely option, but they did not speak about that.

◊

David Donaldson was very different from Willie Bone, both in personality and in teaching methods. Where Willie was explanatory, exacting, patient, conscientious, Davy was hardly ever present in the studio and then almost always irascible. His instructions were hazy and his advice was accompanied by a great deal of colourful language.

Though no doubt a brilliant painter, Donaldson exaggerated the flamboyance of his personality, swearing and stamping around as if permanently furious. Perhaps his small stature required these dramatics, perhaps he felt disappointment at not having been appointed head of the department. Whatever the reason, he almost always gave Helen the impression of irritation. Very occasionally he might exchange a few pleasant words with a couple of students, then whirl out through the swing doors, leaving astonished looks behind him.

His method of teaching for the next two years would be to storm into the studio unexpectedly, stop at a student's easel and look at the painting with a few muttered oaths.

"Stand aside! Gimme your brushes!"

Then he would paint over the student's work for the next twenty minutes, miraculously bringing reality, depths and spontaneity to the canvas. Other students would gather round to watch and marvel.

At last the brushes were thrown down as he growled,

"Scrape that effing… off and start again."

A few more oaths would be mumbled, as he glanced cursorily at the other easels, then he would disappear to his own studio and they might not see him for a couple of days.

One result of this method was that many of them, perhaps most, painted in a similar manner to Donaldson. However his laissez-faire attitude allowed others to develop their own style or draw inspiration from other masters, if they wished.

No doubt Helen's style was affected by her tutor's dashing technique but she was also influenced by Renoir and Mary Cassat. Her strong need to carve out her own interpretation of what she saw often created a difficulty in pleasing her teacher. It would be near the end of her final year before Davy, reluctantly started to nod approval of her paintings.

Willie Armour was a much less colourful personality. He was acting head of Drawing and Painting and could not have found it easy to work beside Donaldson. Willie's eccentric wife Mary was also on the staff and his competent work paled in comparison with her ebullient and acclaimed still life paintings.

The official head of department was Gilbert Spencer. There was a touch of royalty in his infrequent visits, which reduced Mr Armour's status. Helen did not particularly like Mr Armour, but she felt sorry for him, for he seemed to live in the shade of others.

Possibly Gilbert Spencer, whose brother Stanley was hailed as a genius, had his own problems of standing in the shade.

◊

"Mr Armour's wife Mary will take us for still life."

"Oh, I went to art school with her. Long, long ago."

"Did you? She seems a bit older than you and a bit of a mad-woman. She came into the studio the other day to tell us what to bring next week and she had a tube of green paint and she was going on and on about what a *wonderful, marvellous* colour it was! She told us we must all get some and she was *absolutely covered* in green, both her hands and up her arms too. And her smock as well. What a mess she was."

"Mmm, sounds a very enthusiastic lady. I think she always was a bit like that."

"And Trevor took the drawing class today."

"I hope you weren't dancing around the studio."

"No, very business-like. He sat down at my desk to demon-strate, but I don't like his style at all, sharp lines and hard edges. I'd *hate* to draw like that. I was standing there behind him and you've no idea how *terribly* thin he is. I knew that already, but his wrists are much narrower than mine and his ears are so paper-thin that the light shines right through them."

Annie laughed,

"You've certainly been examining the poor bloke."

"Honestly, they were pink and transparent, like a mouse's ears."

"So Trevor's not husband material."

"Oh definitely not."

◊

Studio 45 was adjacent to Rennie Mackintosh's dream-like library. Each time Helen entered the hushed, forest-like space, she was astonished anew, for it was unique and awe-inspiring.

Then there were the whimsical window seats in the corridor, used by the smokers and affectionately called *'the tramcar'*.

Inviting as these seats were for social tête-à-têtes, Helen seldom used them, for as the ancients so truly observed, art is long.

At the head of the main staircase on the first floor was the large exhibition area known as the museum, and interesting work was always on display there, either from the art school itself or from some other source.

The Glasgow School of Art was a very gracious and beautiful environment in which to work and Helen would never take it for granted or lose that secret feeling of delight in the many aspects of the building. As she strolled along the corridors or used her muscles to glide smoothly up and down the long staircase, she perceived herself inhabiting a place that was very special.

Students had long discovered the excellent acoustics of the staircase which started in the basement, led past the ground floor and finished in the immense and spacious sounding box of the Museum. A journey up or downstairs was often accompanied by Glasgow street cries.

These had been distant and unclear in Mr Bone's studio, now in 45 they were fully audible. The voice would start faintly in the basement, then grow in volume as the caller ascended to the museum where the still air took the cry and magnified it.

"Times, News, CirriZEN ….. Times News CirriZEN"

"FoierWID…… FoirWID"

"Cowl BriQUETTES! …… Cowl BriQUETTES!"

These resounding cries would remain an evocative memory for Helen.

Soon another cry was added, when *A Streetcar Named Desire* came to the Cosmo and the mesmerising hero's anguished cry of "STELLA..A.. A" echoed around those aesthetic black beams.

Edinburgh

Helen visited the Waddell family in their Morningside bungalow. It was always interesting for Helen to see other people's houses. Everyone had such a different idea of how to make a home. While she suspected her own flat was shabby and lacking in many ways, it worked well for her mother and herself and her friends all seemed to enjoy visiting and staying late.

What Helen liked about the house in Greenbank Road was the music. If Jack was not playing classical or jazz on the piano in the front room, Isobel was bashing out marvellous honky tonk there. Lindsay was in his bedroom, playing his recorder or listening to Mozart. Abe was in the kitchen with the radio on. They seemed to pursue their separate lives very happily, coming together to eat tasty, if haphazard, meals. Talking would always come before domesticity with Isobel. It was comforting to note that Isobel's kitchen sink was often plugged with vegetable peelings and dirty water, in fact worse than her own ever was.

When Isobel took Helen to the local shops, they met a neighbour and started to chat. Isobel told her friend a story about a young man going to the chemist's before going out with his girlfriend. The chemist suggested he buy a Durex, but the young man, as he had a hot date, said he probably needed a Pyrex. Then the two women went into screams of laughter. Helen, expected to share such a story with a woman she had never met before, was taken aback! Her student friends might make suggestive remarks or double entendres, but they did not indulge in vulgar stories. Perhaps the fact that they were faced with nudity each day created some sort of restraining influence.

Helen hoped Isobel did not think she and Jack were indulging in that sort of relationship.

Jack took her to the West End Café in Princes Street in the afternoon. What a spacious, charming place it was. It was unlicensed and was full of young people eating ice cream as they listened to a jazz band. Helen wished there was somewhere like it in Glasgow.

At night they went dancing at the Plaza and the household was asleep when they came home. After putting her coat away, Helen joined Jack in the kitchen, where she found him drinking from a bottle, glugging down the last of the ginger beer. It was uncouth, and also greedy, for she would have liked a little ginger beer herself.

Jack's family was very nice and he was a great dancer but that small incident convinced her she would never feel seriously about him.

She slept in the little-used front room and experienced the extreme cold of the capital city. Three times she arose and added more garments to her bedclothes, until every article of clothing she had brought with her was piled on top of the several blankets. Edinburgh was even colder than Pittenweem.

◊

Annie enjoyed her sewing machine and had made good use of it.

"I've been thinking, Helen, I've made all those skirts and jackets for you and my mother and neither of you needs anything more *for ages*. What about putting a postcard in a shop window advertising dress-making. I'm sure I could make a bit of cash with sewing. What about it? I'd need some help from you, of course, but not too much. What d'ye think?"

"We could try it, I suppose."

The first customer wanted a pair of jodhpurs made for her daughter.

Later Annie admitted,

"I wasn't thinking of anything quite so ambitious, but I told her I would do my best. She also told me she had sent for several ready cut-out garments from Woman's Own, but when they arrived they seemed far too difficult, so I said to bring them along. I bet there's lots of folk send for ready cut-outs, then find them beyond their capabilities. Perhaps I should advertise that as a speciality? And it would save you the bother of cutting out."

It cannot be said that Helen was very enthusiastic about the new venture, nor would Annie made her fortune from dress-making, but it kept her employed. She felt she was contributing to the slender family purse and she met some nice people.

Mungo was a regular visitor for supper on Saturday night. Generally, Helen made a mixed grill with a small piece each of steak and liver, sausage, black pudding, fried onions, tomato, served with boiled potatoes and cabbage or sprouts. Though there was little of each individual item, Helen thought the plate looked generous and quite sophisticated and Mungo seemed very pleased.

He and Annie were very relaxed with each other almost from the start.

"My landlady thinks she knows you, Mrs Corning. She's sure you went to Garnethill school together."

"Well, I was at Garnethill for a year or so before I went to the High. But that seems incredible!"

"I told her about your father and she remembered the famous artist's daughter being in her class. It's amazing, isn't it."

"I wonder what her name was, not that I would likely remember it at this distance of time."

"Her first name is Freda, but she said you might remember the crippled girl. She's quite lame."

"Oh, of course I remember her! She was a heroine. Did she tell you why she's lame?"

Mungo shook his head.

"Well, she lived on Garnethill Street, you know how fearfully steep it is and one day, a pram with a baby in it started to roll down the hill, Heaven knows how it happened, anyway Freda was able to throw her leg in front of the runaway pram and stop it."

Helen was listening with wide eyes for she had climbed that steep hill daily for six years,

"That was awful! How could anyone let a pram roll away like that? With a baby in it!" Helen wanted to know.

"Perhaps children were in charge of it and just forgot it for one vital moment. I don't know, but it happened and if Freda hadn't acted promptly, it would have been certain death for the baby. She must have just been eight or so when it happened and it damaged her leg very badly. Perhaps nowadays they could repair the damage. Probably her family had no money to pay for proper medical attention. Poor Freda, lame all these years. Fancy that. I have a class photo somewhere and she'll be in it. Must look it out. Would she like to come and have tea with me sometime?"

"That would be nice, Mrs Corning. She's a widow with three children, just like my mother. I don't think she's ever had it easy."

Christmas Ball Circus

A competition was held each year for the design of the Christmas Ball. The class was delighted when Margery and Buckie won it with a circus theme. Davy Donaldson was less pleased.

"Bugger that! Too bloody much work to do here in the studio without that effing nonsense. You'd better not neglect the curriculum or I'll…"

He grumbled and used several words under his breath that were new to the more innocent members of the class, before stamping from the room. Though small, he could disturb the atmosphere like an electric storm.

The class risked his wrath and helped paint the colourful canvas flats which decorated the Assembly Hall. Terrifyingly high ladders were required to hang them. Buckie dealt with technicalities and clambered around the rafters above the ceiling. The health and safety issue was either unknown or ignored.

As Helen was painting in the hall one day, Trevor was rehearsing the cabaret which would be performed for the annual visit from the Edinburgh art school.

He was singing in a perfect Noel Coward drawl,

Isn't it sickening, we've run out of strychnine
And the Borgias are coming to tea!

Helen was impressed and congratulated him. Someone asked if he had ever thought of going on the stage.

"Ah well, it had occurred, but I do think it so much better to be an admired amateur than a failed professional."

Helen wondered if this was a quotation. It sounded sensible.

The marvellous pianist from the Clyde Valley Stompers was playing a wide variety of music, and Trevor and Helen started to dance together. Graceful and uninhibited, Trevor made an excellent attempt at ballet. Soon an admiring audience gathered.

"I say, Helen, we really should put on an act at the Christmas Ball. What d'you think?"

Helen agreed it was a splendid idea.

"In fact, could you perform next Saturday for the Edinburgh chaps? I'm going to be that Toulouse Lautrec chap with the nose and the top hat and you could be La Goulue and do the can-can."

Helen cut the full frilled skirt from her ball gown and stuck penny-sized circles of white cloth to a red blouse to recreate the dancer in Toulouse Lautrec's famous poster. Trevor needed only a black suit and top hat to resemble Aristide closely. Helen's high kicks and final drop into the splits established them as the dancers of the Art School. After that cabaret, Mr Bliss and the various heads of departments started to nod and smile kindly to Helen in the corridors, though she regretted that their recognition was for her dancing rather than her painting.

◊

Jack wanted to come through to the Christmas Ball.

"I expect he thinks it's a kind of orgy. He'll be very disappointed."

"What about Mungo? He'll be disappointed if he's not your partner."

"He's not all that keen on dancing and I see him every weekend anyway. I'm sure he won't mind. Probably couldn't afford it."

Jack, blonde and handsome, was dressed as a ringmaster. He was predictably bowled over by the brightly decorated hall, the imaginative costumes and the great jazz band. He danced with each of Helen's friends and seemed permanently astonished, constantly repeating how *arty* everything was.

Trevor and Helen had decided their act for the cabaret would be a dramatic scene, danced to Gershwin's *Slaughter on Tenth Avenue*. Helen had always wanted to use this music. Trevor was gaunt and unrecognisable in terminally tattered trousers, jacket and cap while Helen wore a striped top and beret, her skirt split to the thigh. Their appearance was probably more redolent of the Paris underworld than New York.

Shortly before the cabaret started there had been an unusual problem. A drunk fellow, not an art student, had been making himself objectionable in various ways. No one seemed to know him. He had been asked to leave but had refused. The small elderly janitors could not be expected to act as 'bouncers'.

Shortly before Helen was about to dance, she saw him leering at three girls in ballet dresses, shaking a box of matches in a threatening way. When he struck one and held it near the tarlatan skirts, Helen ran to fetch help. She found Tony, a massive third year student, whose hobby was weightlifting and left him to deal with the situation as it was almost time for her cue.

She had arranged to start the dance alone, backing on to the stage from behind a large screen, with her arms raised in apparent dread at what was hidden from the audience. Trevor would then enter from the other side of the stage. The dance would finish with an apparent murder.

As Helen stood behind the screen, waiting to hear the first strains of the music, the drunk stepped through a door and stood in front of her, his face and the front of his shirt covered in blood. It was a terrible sight. Tony had been forced to use violence and had broken the drunk's nose. For several seconds, the injured man stood quite close to her, swaying, then the music started and Helen backed away from him into view of the audience, just as she had choreographed it, and needed none of her acting ability to convey fear. She wondered if he might follow her onstage, but he did not.

Trevor and Helen were both congratulated on their realistic performance, though Trevor would only learn later of the real life drama. Helen would never repeat that dance and the music would always conjure up that vivid and awful scene in her mind's eye.

◊

Mungo phoned Annie that night at eleven, apologetic because he had been drinking a little. He was terribly low.

"Mrs Corning, my girl's away with a lawyer."

He repeated this several times.

Annie tried to comfort him, telling him that Jack was just a friend who wanted to experience an art school dance. Mungo should buck up and not worry. Jack would be away back to Edinburgh tomorrow.

Nothing seemed to help poor Mungo.

Annie wondered if her role in life was to comfort Helen's rejected suitors.

When Helen heard of the call, she had little sympathy.

She was impatient with folk that drank.

Although Mungo had eaten his dinner in Clarence Drive for so many Saturdays and was friendly and comfortable with

Annie, Helen still did not know much about him. Perhaps it was his Highland personality, but he seemed almost secretive, very different from her student friends and from Helen herself. No doubt there was a hidden side to him. It was a year before she discovered he had served in a parachute regiment while on National Service or that his brother was a consultant paediatrician. She was positive that she was not and never would be in love with Mungo. He would never light that spark of joy and excitement that Douglas did. Mungo was humorous, kindly and undemanding, but perhaps a little ungenerous with his money and his emotions. It was accepted that he was hard up and they seldom went out, but he lacked enthusiasm and found it difficult to pay even the smallest compliment.

Helen decided the honourable thing to do was put a stop to their friendship, for he was serious and she knew they had no future together.

However, Mungo was determined to remain a part of her life and, as she liked him and was sorry for him, there was an unexpectedly emotional scene. Reluctantly, he finally accepted her edict that she would continue to see other young men.

Death of John Mackay

John Mackay died in January and the Glasgow Herald obituary, spoke of his fine portraits and bright, breezy sea paintings. John's condition had been particularly bad since November and in many ways death was a release from the terrible bouts of coughing which were exhausting him and distressing Mary. Though she found it difficult to show her sympathy with kind soft words, she nursed him devotedly, shaving him daily and making his favourite milk puddings.

After the funeral, Mary came to stay in Clarence Drive. She seemed stunned and unable to visualise a life without John. She had lost weight and wore black, which did not suit her as well as the usual warm shades. Her normal volubility and irascibility were quenched and she spoke quietly and sadly, smoking her cigarettes without style or enthusiasm

"And I've no idea what I'm going to do, Annie."

Helen thought her grandmother had changed almost overnight. from an energetic and dominating middle-aged lady to an unpredictable elderly one. Of course Mary must be very sad, but she and John had never shared a social life in Helen's memory and he had often seemed to be a nuisance and a burden to her. Surely life would now be easier for her and she could attend whist drives and bazaars as before?

Because Helen had watched John fade gently away in the last few years, she accepted the inevitability of his death. He was an old man of eighty-four. Death was what happened when you were old. Perhaps because she could not feel great sadness at his passing, there was a shadow of guilt, but this faded when childhood memories of him drifted through her mind at night as she waited for sleep. She visualised those long ago visits to the Art Galleries, the walks in the countryside, where he would use his penknife to cut a whistle from a hollow stemmed branch for her. She thought of listening to fairy stories in the studio and eating potatoes or chestnuts roasted in the ashes of the Dutch stove. The little pictures on the blue and white tiles of the stove had fascinated her. Her favourite mental picture was of John, again with his penknife, very carefully peeling an apple for her, removing the skin in one long perfect strip.

Annie was most deeply affected by his loss, though she said little. She sat quietly thinking, unusually idle. She regretted terribly that she had not seen her father since the summer, nearly six months ago. It would have been difficult, for he was unable to leave the house. No doubt Bruce would have arranged to have her carried up all those stairs if she had asked him, but the very fact of her going to see her father would have been an acceptance that he was dying. She had spoken to John on the phone once or twice, but speaking in the cold hallway had caused a coughing fit and each time the call had come to an abrupt, unsatisfactory end.

How could she help her mother, who seemed distraught and unable to contemplate the future? Mary was obviously worried about money and unable to decide what to do with two houses, each full of furniture and paintings. Annie had no idea what her parents' financial position was and she felt her powerlessness more than ever.

◊

The King died in February. Radio and newspapers were solemn and laudatory.

The new Queen was recalled from her tour abroad. Though she was terribly young to take on such responsibilities, it was pointed out that Victoria had been younger still. The new queen's husband, tall handsome Prince Philip, would be a magnificent support.

There was nothing much else spoken of in the press.

Princess Elizabeth and her sister Margaret had been in the news all Helen's lifetime. She had seen their photographs in the illustrated magazines at the Arlington, usually dressed in diaphanous ballgowns or perhaps patting shining horses at the races. Elizabeth was only a few years older than she was herself and it was strange to think of her as a queen.

In Scotland it all seemed very far away and Helen soon forgot about it.

She had plenty to occupy her thoughts, for Mary was going to stay with them until she decided what to do and their quiet companionable life would be disrupted until Mary made up her mind.

◊

The main entrance to Glasgow School of Art is through two sets of double swing doors, each clearly marked IN and OUT in embossed and beautiful brass lettering. This direction simply means 'keep to the left' and certainly students in those days invariably obeyed. No doubt the double doors protected the hothouse interior of the Art School from the invading winds of Garnethill, but it was never easy to pass through them if encumbered with drawing board or large canvas.

Dan Campbell was heading out of the main building one day with Helen just behind him. Dan politely held the first door open for her to follow. Once she was through, he let it shut and, turning quickly, kissed her. Then, without a word spoken on either side, he pushed open the second door and again held it for her. Then without a backward glance, he quickly descended the stairs and crossed Renfrew Street in the direction of the ref. Helen was puzzled. What was that about? She and Dan were friendly enough, but he had never asked her out or particularly sought her company. She decided it must have been a momentary impulse.

However these impulses became more frequent and might happen at any time that Dan found her in a quiet corner. It was only ever one short kiss that he would snatch, for she would push him away, laughingly at first. Later she became more irritated. What sort of disrespectful way was that to treat a girl? Other people in the class became aware of it and asked her why he did it. How was she to know? Anyway, why did he not come and speak to her? They had studied together for three years and she had a great respect for his work and would have been happy to know him better.

At the end of one afternoon, Helen was washing her brushes at the studio sink, She was rather late and the rest of the class had gone. Suddenly Dan was behind her, leaning over her shoulder, about to steal a kiss.

"Get *off*, Dan." She exclaimed crossly and pushed the handful of half-washed brushes over her shoulder in his direction.

Dan did not move quickly enough and the horrible oily, soapy brushes caught him in the eye. Helen was appalled. Meaning only to discourage him, she had inflicted quite extreme violence on him. He was in obvious and terrible pain. Perhaps his eye was seriously hurt!

Deeply contrite, she guided him to a chair, found the cleanest paintrag in sight to wipe his face and tried to assess the damage.

She patted him lovingly and kissed his cheek with relief as the pain slowly abated.

"Oh Dan, can you see all right? Are you sure?"

"A bit hazy still and no colour, but."

"Oh *Dan!*"

"Only kidding. It's fine, perfectly all right again. Just a bit nippy, that's all."

"I *am so sorry!*" Helen had forgotten it was Dan who had precipitated the incident,"How can I show you how sorry I am? What can I do to make it up to you?"

"You could let me paint your portrait. Would you do that?"

"Of course, if you'd like me to. Any time."

"That'll be fine, then. We'll start tomorrow."

The portrait of Helen won first prize in the students' end of term exhibition and Dan never kissed her again.

◊

Mary gave Helen a brooch of garnets set in gold, which had belonged to John's sister. Helen loved the elaborate Victorian piece. When Mungo invited her to a formal dance at the Men's Union, it seemed an opportunity to wear it. She chose dusky green taffeta and a Vogue dress pattern to create a ballgown which would properly show off her heirloom.

"This is a lot more complicated than your last one." Annie was reading the instructions, "I hope I can manage! And is that green not rather dark?"

"I have complete confidence in you and the brooch will look perfect against that colour."

"I expect you're right. As usual. Where are the scissors? You'd better get cracking and get it cut out for me."

Helen was delighted with her dress and brooch and even more pleased when Mungo arrived to collect her, for he wore tails and was transformed. He seemed taller, slimmer, more elegant and *almost* tremendously handsome.

They would spend the evening with Arthur, another engineering student, and Beth, a friend from ballet. Arthur was an impressive young man, tall and bearing more than a passing resemblance to Gregory Peck. When Mungo had first introduced them, Beth had immediately fallen madly in love. Helen felt a little guilty, for it was obvious that Arthur did not reciprocate her strong feelings and heartbreak almost certainly lay ahead for

Beth, who was a pretty girl but unfortunate in her romances.

The band was excellent, the floor uncrowded, and the two couples danced every dance. A photograph taken that night showed how evening dress had changed the four students into young aristocrats, quite worthy of appearing in the pages of the Tatler or the Sketch.

◊

In a tiny top flat in Athole Gardens, Bruce was speaking seriously and firmly,

"No, Nan, it's best. I've made up my mind, we'll need to move you out of here. Need to find another place."

"But we've been so happy here and it's so convenient for shopping and buses… and I feel I've made it so home-like… I really don't want to leave…. I'd just *hate* to leave" she wept a few tears.

"Aye, m'dear, I know, I know and I understand, but we'll find another place just as fine, just as comfy. You leave it to me, dearie. And ye'll get another place nice and homey with yer wee bit knick-knacks. But you've got to move. No two ways about it. I knew that as soon as Helen mentioned seeing my car out in the lane a coupla times. Y'see, she uses that lane as a shortcut to Byres Road, so she'd see it another time and she's a bright wee spark and she'd likely get curious. Never know. Can't risk it anyway. I'll look about. Don't you worry now, my lass. Give me a jiffey and I'll soon find another place."

Bruce, in fact, rather enjoyed the idea of fleeing to another love nest. Almost equal to the comfort, pleasure and adoration that Nan brought to his life was the delight he derived from having this tremendous secret. He approved and thoroughly enjoyed the idea of his own boyish naughtiness, revelling in the fact that no-one knew a thing about Nan. As he sat talking to Annie, or his father, or his friends, he chuckled inside to think of his secret. He had certainly pulled the wool over their eyes this time.

Problems of 351

It was a terrible wrench for Mary to sell the beautiful furniture that she and John had acquired throughout their long marriage. Interested in antiques from the start, they had many that were valuable and interesting, few of which had been expensive. Each piece had its history and seemed even more precious if purchased at bargain price. Most items were of generous proportions to suit the large flat, too large for the Pittenweem house and unfortunately not popular in the modern saleroom. Mary felt daunted by it all.

While helping to tidy, Helen found a length of that vivid pink Japanese silk that Mary had bought in such abundance before the war. There were five or six yards of the brilliant, gossamer-like fabric.

"Grandma, can I have a loan of this, please."

"Take it, my jewel, if it's any use to you. Maybe it's perished, it's years old."

Mary started to laugh. She remembered ridiculously large bloomers she had made of the silk, then worn to a golf match, ruining any chance of winning that afternoon by keeping Sonya, her partner, in recurring fits of giggles with quick glimpses of their incongruous pinkness under her tweed skirt.

Helen was glad to see Mary laughing.

She had decided not to take ballet class in her final year at Art School, but was determined that her solo at the Athenaeum in June should be spectacular. She would create a *Moth Dance* and this flowing, fluttering silk would be the flame which would at first attract, then finally consume the moth.

◊

Muirhead Moffat, one of the main Glasgow antique dealers, bought various items of the furniture at 351. Mary did not receive the prices she had hoped for.

"He said nobody wants the big pieces nowadays. I was very disappointed. I'm going to take some things through to Fife, rather than sell them for buttons."

Bruce was visiting that evening,

"Aye, Mrs Mackay, he's a slippery customer, that one, got to watch his every move. He's great friends with my brother Stewart, you know. Real pals. They go on holiday together. An unlikely pair if you ask me. Mind you, mean as all get out, the two of them. Every penny counts! Aye, watch him like a hawk, Mrs Mackay, that's my advice."

"Well, I wish you'd told me that sooner, Bruce. He's certainly not the man his father was."

When the unique flat was advertised in the Herald by the firm of Walker, Fraser and Steele, Annie could hardly believe the wording they had used.

FOR SALE
Charing Cross top flat, three rooms and kitchen, with attics.

"That's *ludicrous*! Anyone looking for an ordinary three roomed flat would be frightened off when they saw the studio. It's a luxury flat and there must be someone with money who would be only too delighted to buy it. There's not another place like it in Glasgow! Really, what *nonsense*! It's just a waste of everyone's time. And you've to pay good money for this."

"Well, how was I to know what they would put in the paper? They're very well thought of and they advertise all over the front page of the Herald."

Mary was sad, worried, furious with everyone. Worst of all, she lacked her usual energy to express that fury or turn it into action. Even Helen felt sorry for her.

Only two or three people came to look at 351 and Helen was detailed to show them round. Except for the piano, the main studio was empty and looked even larger than before. With the two staircases and the empty rooms, the house had an eerie silence and Helen, nervous, though ashamed of her cowardice, left the front door wide open while waiting and played the piano. Generally she left with the viewers, but one morning she stayed and danced in the studio. What a marvellous dance studio it would make, more spacious than Miss Hopkins and so much more beautiful. Of course the folk in the flat downstairs would hardly like it.

Annie had been right. Each potential buyer quickly said it was not what they were looking for.

◊

Mungo, finally passing the stumbling block of second year mathematics and graduating with a first class degree, immediately started practical training in the North British locomotive works in Springburn.

He spoke admiringly of the skills that the older men possessed in the sand moulding workshop. He was especially struck by the fact that everyone in Springburn seemed to identify with the NB works. Even bus conductors and shop assistants discussed the latest delivery of one of the mammoth engines and most families had at least one relative working for NB. It made Springburn seem like a village.

Helen had never heard Mungo speak so enthusiastically before and she felt fonder of him and proud of his achievement.

Walker, Fraser and Steele had advised Mary that a thousand pounds was all she could expect for 351, but even at that low price, there were no takers. Mary considered a modest two room and kitchen flat in Novar Drive, priced at five hundred pounds, but could not make up her mind.

Did she want to stay in Glasgow? She had never considered makng a permanent home in Pittenweem.

In the Hyndland flat, the furniture was rearranged in the large bedroom, the double bed relegated to the back room and replaced with twin beds. Then the piano was moved from Renfrew Street and placed in the bay window where the dressing table used to stand. Helen thought it looked a little strange in a bedroom but was very happy to have it in her house and determined to take lessons after the summer holiday.

◊

Though John had been the quietest of men, the Pittenweem house seemed silent without him, that summer.

Sometimes Helen went up to his studio and sat there in the calm atmosphere, thinking about him. His palette and brushes lay on the table and seemed waiting for him. She looked at his many books. John Mackay's reading was eclectic and Helen tried Ruskin, but did not appreciate his heavy style. Zane Grey's tales of the American West were more appealing. Surprisingly, John had enjoyed these adventurous stories, but he would be a young man when the waggons were rolling west and perhaps he had dreamed of going there?

The house was changed in other ways.

Mary had brought the unsold furniture to Pittenweem in May and had enjoyed travelling in the cabin of the furniture van.

"Best journey of my life! It was marvellous! I was sitting so high up. I could see everything."

The added funiture made the house terrribly crowded. The sitting room was absolutely crammed and maneuvring the wheelchair was more difficult than ever. If 'speed were required' there was likely to be a collision with some solid mahogany item and Annie would gasp at the jolt and Mary would tut-tut. Helen gritted her teeth and silently cursed the excess chairs and tables. The garden became even more desirable.

Mary was hovering over Annie and Helen as they sat outside, plucking a large cockerel, which lay on the table between them.

"Now don't break the skin, if you can help it and try not to let the feathers blow all over the garden."

The splendidly coloured bird had come from those unknown Aunts in the North, with only a label tied around its scaly ankles to direct it to the right address.

"Do you think we'll ever meet them?" Helen wondered.

"Oh, I don't suppose so. Strange isn't it. Ardgay seems so far away. I wonder what sort of wee cottage they stay in? You've met Bella, though, haven't you Maw."

"Perhaps long, long ago, when I was a child. They were both a lot younger than my mother and neither had any family and my mother was away in India for years. But Bella was quite a girl in her time, I believe she had three husbands, one of them French. He was the steward at Gullane Golf Club. Quite a swell place. Funny to think of her landing up in the Highlands. Kate, the older one, never came south and she had a hard life of it with an invalid husband. She was married twice and I believe they were *both* invalids. But I'm away inside, that's a chilly wind blowing. Bring the bird in when it's ready and I'll haul its guts out."

Helen relaxed. Mary's watchful presence always resulted in criticism of some sort.

◊

Beth, still yearning for the unattainable Arthur, was on holiday in Anstruther.

Cellardyke, the coastal town just beyond Anstruther, had a swimming pool with light classical music playing throughout the day. Like Pittenweem, it was a large natural pool amongst the rocks, kept clean and cold by the constant tide. Though rather a long distance to walk, it was so luxurious and unusual to swim to music that Helen added miles to her daily exercise. The three miles return journey to Pittenweem was often partly run, as she worried about being late for Annie's comfort. She had never enjoyed racing but found a steady trot very enjoyable.

Mrs Robson, Beth's mother was a strange middle-aged lady. She spoke at length of the two young men to whom she had been engaged before she met her present husband. Both fiancés had died in the first war, she still wore their rings, and extended a chubby hand to substantiate her story. When the tale was repeated and the rings again displayed on her next visit, Helen wondered if it upset Mr Robson, who sat silently smoking his pipe. At the third repetition, she supposed he must be used to it. Mrs Robson, engaged at sixteen and seventeen, also liked to emphasise the contrast between herself and her daughter for Beth, at nineteen, had *never yet* been engaged. This repeated comparison affected Beth for, in spite of the fact that her parents provided a sad example of connubial bliss, marriage was the girl's only aim in life.

"Oh, how I'd *love* to get married, Helen. Arthur would be my *perfect* husband, but maybe I'll meet someone at the dance tonight."

"Well, I want to earn some money and enjoy being grown-up before I tie myself down."

Helen felt lucky to have a sensible, normal mother. Poor Beth.

The following week, after the dance, the crowd went swimming in the Cellardyke pool. Helen had never swum in the dark before and found it thrilling. Surprisingly the water seemed rather warm!

One night, a young man with his arm in a cast asked Helen to dance. Harry had grown up in Elie and remembered her in his class at the Waid Academy, when she was eleven. She did not remember him. He was now at St Andrews University and ruefully admitted to having broken his arm at some drunken student jollification. He asked if he might visit her in Pittenweem the following day.

He arrived the next morning about ten, earlier than she had expected.

"Did you get an earlier bus?"

"No, I just walked down."

It was nine miles and Helen was impressed.

He had served his National Service in the Air Force and his conversation was very surprising. What a picture of depravity he painted of St Andrews University! It seemed that students drank to excess every week, took drugs and had abortions. Several had committed suicide. Helen's eyes were wide as he described an unrecognisable society. Nothing like that happened amongst the students of her acquaintance. Possibly one or two couples unobtrusively indulged in sex, but virtue's greatest ally was the ever-present terror of pregnancy. Last year, when a fourth year couple found they were expecting a baby, the father-to-be was at once offered a tutorship and they married quickly and respectably. That was the most sensational event in Helen's experience.

Harry expressed horror that Helen was still a virgin.

"You should try it! You would really enjoy it, you know. It's great fun!"

Apart from the humorous future pact with Wee Donald, hardly anyone had ever discussed sex with her and certainly not on such a personal level. At first she was embarrassed, then she started to laugh. He was so ridiculously persistent.

She waved Harry off on the bus and did not expect to see him again.

◊

Mungo wrote regularly and Helen enjoyed reading his letters, one or two came from Jack and also from Douglas. Guiltily she knew the last were her favourite. Douglas was in Japan and described it as looking very like Scotland!

Mungo wrote that the NB staff were organising an outing to the Military Tattoo at the Edinburgh Festival and he had booked tickets for them. It was not an event she would have chosen to see, but it was nice to know Mungo was learning to spend his money. Mungo was not exactly a spoiling boyfriend and all those Saturday night mixed grills deserved some mark of gratitude.

They sat cosily at the Tattoo with a rug over their knees, though the dark night was not cold. Helen found the whole evening unexpectedly marvellous and emotional, more wonderful than she could have imagined, and was surprised to find tears in her eyes several times.

Final Year

Margery's summer employment was always more adventurous than the others. She had slaved in a Torquay hotel, conducted on the Glasgow trams and last year had hitch-hiked in France with her friend Irene. The two girls returned, metamorphosed into existentialists, dressed entirely in black, with heavy black eye make-up and a thick copy of Simone de Beauvoir always to hand. It seemed a strange image for Margery, a blonde, athletic Scandinavian type, to assume. Predictably she soon tired of the idea and returned to her attractive, rather careless, natural self. Irene continued to look dramatic and hopeless for more than a year.

To celebrate her twenty-first, Margery invited Mattie and Helen to a dinner inspired by this year's travels in Italy and Greece. Margery loved cooking, had a real flair for it and had finally been allowed to use her mother's kitchen.

Helen and Mattie tasted spaghetti bolognese, sprinkled with grated Parmesan cheese for the first time. How *delicious* it was. Although macaroni cheese was a regular family meal, spaghetti was only known as the soft, tasteless, pink stuff in a Heinz tin, a wartime last resort when the cupboard was bare. Helen determined to make this tasty meat sauce herself, very soon.

For dessert, yogurt was another unknown dish. Margery had brought culture back from Greece and now made her own, but, apart from those dinner-school desserts, Helen did not care for milk dishes and would never enjoy yogurt.

Coplands had taffeta in a wide range of beautiful colours at 2/11 a yard. Annie had made a peacock blue cocktail dress for Helen and expressed a wish to use every colour in the range. As Margery had admired Helen's dress, Annie made a deep green one for her birthday present and would later make one for Mattie – Annie's dressmaking business was more remunerative at some times than at others. She enjoyed being busy, but was philosophical if no orders came in. There were always letters to type in her idiosyncratic style, vegetables to prepare and usually some knitting on the pins, though Fair Isle gloves were a thing of the past.

Douglas's mother, Rosemary, had ordered a dressing gown.

Rosemary, vivacious, almost flamboyant and smartly dressed at all times, was approaching fifty. A girlish black velvet bow decorated her prematurely white curls, though she threatened to 'go bright red' before old age arrived. She played golf and bridge and gave the impression of an adored, spoiled wife. She often bemoaned the good old days when she had a maid.

Her husband, Henry, was a quiet man, surprisingly unassuming to be Rosemary's husband and astonishingly short to have fathered six foot plus Douglas. They seemed to lead rather separate lives but both were friendly towards Helen.

After Rosemary's first visit to 46, Annie teased,

"I think she just wanted to give her future daughter-in-law the once-over."

"Rubbish! How many times do I have to tell you. *I don't expect to marry Douglas?*"

"But you do like him, don't you. He's tall and nice-looking, but what is it you find special about him, I wonder?"

Helen sighed and thought for a moment,

"I think Douglas is... debonair... in a way the others aren't."

"Mmm, debonair like Fred Astaire?"

"But better looking."

"Bet he can't dance like him, though."

◊

When Bruce installed Nan in the service flat in Partickhill Road, he advised her to shop in Hyndland Road rather than Clarence Drive.

"Now, I'm not saying you *mustn't* go into Clarence Drive, m'dear. I just think it's *best* to avoid it. Ye might want to go to the Post Office, I expect, but you're far better popping along to Hillhead for stamps. There's all the shops you need at the top of the hill and they're *nearer*, so just do as I say this time and oblige me, please."

When had she ever done other than oblige him? Nan quickly suppressed the thought.

Nevertheless she was disgruntled. Perhaps due to this edict of Bruce's or perhaps due to the fact that the new flat was darker and smaller than the first and the tenants noisier and not very friendly. She had so loved that bright top flat.

After a month, Nan put on her hat one Saturday and walked through the quiet precincts of Hyndland Park, past trees and quaint little cottages, then down Turnberry Road and along Lauderdale Gardens, past the school and the garages. Her heart was beating strongly when she reached Clarence Drive though she told herself it was nonsense to think she might see anyone belonging to Bruce. And how could they possibly recognise each other. She bought a five shilling postal order for her mother in the post office. Probably it would be spent in the pub, but it eased her conscience to send it. She seldom saw her family now.

She noticed fresh kippers in the fish shop window. Bruce was fond of a kipper and how silly to go to Byres Road. Perhaps next week.

Bruce had given her thirty shillings to buy a few things in town and she now crossed the road and headed downhill to the tram stop.

As Nan waited, she noticed a woman sitting knitting at an open ground floor window. After a few minutes, a young woman, carrying a large portfolio, walked down the hill and waved cheerfully and extravagantly to the woman, whose face broke into a pleased smile. Then, standing quite close to Nan, the smiling girl spoke clearly.

"I've forgotten my keys. Sorry."

The woman nodded and moving smoothly backwards, as if on wheels, disappeared. The girl ran up the flight of stairs and into the close.

Nan stood motionless. She could hardly breathe. Surely that must be Bruce's wife and daughter. She had never known their exact address. They did not look at all as she had imagine and it seemed an incredible coincidence. At that moment, a tram appeared under the bridge at the foot of the hill but she did not wait for it. Practically running up the hill, Nan knew that Bruce was right, all future postal orders and kippers must be purchased in Byres Road.

◊

In October Helen again tried to break things off with Mungo. Was she in love with anyone else? No, she wasn't. Why break it off then? She tried to explain that she did love him, but she was not 'in love' with him. He was a dear friend and if they parted, she would miss him, but there was no future for them. He was ready to take the risk, he said. He looked so miserable, yet determined. Helen wept most of the weekend. By Sunday night, there was no change in the status quo.

Next day, Margery and Irene agreed she looked like a tragic French actress.

◊

Mary had stayed on in Pittenweem after the summer and had almost decided that she would live there permanently. Installing electricity would make the house more liveable. Annie invited her to come to Glasgow for the worst of the winter, but Mary would not commit herself.

"I'll let you know." She said miserably, "I can't make any decisions until that flat is sold."

Later that month there were heavy rains and the roof at 351 leaked badly. Helen was called out at ten pm to deal with water dripping into the flat below.

Even at a knockdown price, no one seemed to want to buy the beautiful white elephant.

◊

Annie had become more ambitious with her sewing.

"Now I'd like to make you one of these soft dressmaker suits that are coming into fashion. Away down to Coplands and see if you can get me a nice pattern and some nubbly tweed."

"What on earth is nubbly tweed?"

"Rough, you know with little lumps in it."

"I've never seen anything like that."

"Well go and look for it. You'll know it when you see it. And I've a fancy to make a fur fabric coat. Look around and see if anything catches your eye."

Helen returned with patterns for suit and coat, nubbly tweed and fur fabric in a realistic ocelot print. Annie was delighted and ordered Helen to start cutting out right away.

◊

Helen liked to amuse her mother with art school anecdotes.

One very warm day, Helen had been standing painting in her bare feet, when her paint rag fell to the floor. Without thinking and without interrupting her concentration on the canvas, she picked up the rag with the toes of her right foot and transferred it to her left hand. Tom, who stood painting beside her, let out a yell of horror, that startled the whole class.

Annie laughed heartily at this story.

"Not everyone has prehensile toes, you know!"

In spite of the various demands which awaited her outside school hours, Helen worked hard. She felt happier about her work now. She had given up trying to draw with a pencil and now worked with a brush and dry oil paint. No one else did this, but the teachers found the results satisfactory. She knew what she was aiming for and occasionally the result even pleased Davy. She was particularly interested in portraiture and chose to write her thesis on the history of portrait painting. Her secondary subject was sculpture and she modelled a terracotta head of Mungo, whose strongly individual features made it easy to get a good likeness. She was rather taken aback when it came to the firing of the piece. First she must take a length of wire and cut this very familiar head in half, then scoop out as much clay as possible from the interior. It seemed a gruesome task and Helen was relieved when it was finished and stuck back together again for firing.

◊

The Christmas Ball had an Elizabethan theme that year.

Trevor drawled his suggestion for the cabaret.

"I suspect Elizabethan dance was rather slow and stately. It would hardly give full rein to our undoubted dramatic powers, Helen. But those Elizabethans had rather a lot to do with Spain in those days, didn't they? Trading and marrying and fighting and such-like. Why don't we do a Spanish gypsy dance? Flamenco, I think they call it. Always goes down well and probably hasn't changed much in five hundred years. What d'ye say?"

It sounded excellent to Helen. She had just evolved a new way of twisting her hair into a bun on the top of her head and towards the end of the dance, with a few quickly withdrawn hairpins, her hair would cascade to her waist for the dramatic finale.

Mungo would come to the Christmas Ball for the first time and Helen gave more attention to his outfit than to her own. She dyed tights dark red for him and made baggy little Sir Francis Drake shorts and a dashing cap with a feather. A short cloak completed the outfit.

Margery, Mattie and Buckie kept him company while she danced the flamenco with Trevor.

She thought Mungo looked well in his outfit, but the photographs showed an unhappy man. Was it the baggy pants or the mulberry tights?

◊

Annie was always enthusiastic about any new project, probably more so than her daughter.

"They're wanting models for the Charities' Fashion Show next month. D'ye think I should volunteer?"

"Most certainly! And I'll have time to make you one or two new things in the Christmas holidays."

It was two years since a bright student, Betty Stewart, had instigated a fashion show for Students' Charities week. It proved very popular and running for four nights, had raised impressive funds. Betty's own outfits had been outrageous and a big future was prophesied for her. Tragically, as she was returning from a travelling scholarship in Europe, she was badly injured in the terrible Harrow train crash, when three trains piled up and caused many deaths and injuries. News of Betty's condition was now better than at first, but there was a strong feeling that this show must be a special tribute to her.

As Leonie had done a modelling course in London, she was put in charge of the twelve volunteers, all pretty girls, though none with a figure quite as wisp-like as her own. Glaring critically at their hips, some of which were more curvaceous than others, Leonie declared,

"The first thing you must all definitely buy is a *girdle*. A girdle is *absolutely necessary.*"

Helen had slender hips and was positive that she most certainly would not be buying something as uncomfortable and middle-aged as a girdle.

Many other girls agreed and shook their heads.

Leonie continued,

"Yes, you really must. Even *I* wear a girdle at all times."

With this remark, she lost the goodwill of her pupils though, rather sulkily, they did learn to glide along the catwalk, then with feet in fifth position, accomplish a smooth turn. They learned to doff a coat or jacket as they turned, then drag it negligently along the floor as they walked offstage. That seemed to be about all that was needed to be a model.

There was great excitement when journalists from the Picture Post arrived to do an article on the show.

The photographers immediately picked out Helen because of her waist length hair. Then, carried away by the magnificent view from the top of the building, they discussed how they might pose her on the roof, with the smoky city dramatically filling the background. It would be superb for the cover picture.

While Helen was thrilled to think of being featured on the cover of Picture Post, she was alarmed at the thought of perching dangerously out on the roof. But like so many good ideas, the project was abandoned. The photographers had quite forgotten that Picture Post had recently returned to a brightly coloured front cover and, equipped only with black and white film, they had not the means, in those penurious days, to buy Kodak colour. Helen would never be a cover girl, but she was featured inside, her long hair flowing over a sedate beach dress and holding an incongruous palette and brushes.

She would have several nightmares about climbing out of that window in the henrun.

On the first night of the show, Betty Stewart arrived in her wheelchair to wish them good luck. She looked well and hoped to be walking in another two months. Her visit made everyone happy and excited.

On the last night of the Fashion Show, Helen received a polite and well written letter from a stranger in the audience. Bob Wright was an amateur photographer who would like her to model for him.

Helen met him and arranged to come to his house, bringing a friend and various different outfits.

Friends bombarded her with warnings about the perils of photographers.

"Don't worry, girls, Mattie will be my chaperone and anyway he's highly respectable and quite old, mid thirties at least."

The evening could not have been more circumspect and some very nice photographs were taken of both Mattie and Helen. There was much adjusting of lights and tea and biscuits were served.

"Well, how did you get on? Could Mr Wright be 'Mr Right'?" Annie asked.

"Oh no! Never! He's quite old and not at all good-looking. He's not well, either. He's been off work for months. Didn't quite catch what was wrong. A bad back or something. Oh no, he's definitely not boyfriend material. I hope he got some good photos."

Helen had taken along two evening dresses and the fake leopard skin coat as well as two gorgeous Indian shawls that

Mary had bought at an auction in Balcaskie House, one of the many aristocratic estates in Fife. The glamour photographs were rather good and Helen returned for a few more sessions.

◊

There had been a desperate plea for more entrants in the Charities' Week beauty queen competition and Irene and Helen decided they might as well enter. It was an opportunity to wear evening dress and inveigle their boyfriends into dress suits. Helen had thought Mungo so very handsome in his tails.

There were six entrants, all in ballgowns, in the Art School heat of the competition. Other students were informally dressed as usual and only Mungo, Gordon and Alasdair were formally dressed to match their partners. These three young men kept pathetically close company throughout the evening.

Walter Pritchard, head of the mural department, and his wife, who was herself a lovely woman, were the judges.

First prize went to a tall swan-necked beauty, Delni Goalen. She was easily the most glamorous and outstanding girl in the contest. It was easy to believe the rumour that she was related to Barbara Goalen, the most famous fashion model in Britain. Delni would go forward to become Charities Queen, beating contestants from Glasgow University and all the other colleges.

Later that evening the Pritchards were kind enough to say to Helen, in private, that if they had been looking for an interesting face to paint, they would have chosen her. She hardly believed them, but thought it a nice gesture. She found beauty contests rather embarrassing and would not again enter one.

Milestones

When Helen served supper that Saturday night, she could see that Annie and Mungo were sharing some secret. They both looked very pleased.

"Why are you both smiling like Cheshire cats?" she asked suspiciously.

"Mungo has something to tell you."

But Mungo said nothing.

"Well, eat your dinner while it's hot if I'm not to be told the secret."

Helen was not fond of silly secrets.

"You've to congratulate him, Helen. He passed his driving test today. Isn't that wonderful! First time."

Helen was astonished. He had never said a word about taking driving lessons.

Mungo looked sheepish.

"I know I don't have a car, or any hope of getting one for a long time, but I thought it would be handy for the future."

"Congratulations! That's wonderful. It's just so sudden and I didn't know anything about it."

"Well, I knew all about it, but we thought we would surprise you." Annie smiled kindly at Mungo as she spoke.

Helen's feelings were mixed, as she ate her fish cake and cabbage. She was pleased and impressed that he had passed, yet she felt excluded. It must be many weeks since he started driving lessons. Why had he said nothing to her? Why had he confided in her mother? Her doubts regarding a shared future with Mungo were strengthened by this incident.

◊

"I think I'll have another breakfast party for my twenty-first."

"You'd need something a bit more special than that, surely. It's a big milestone in your life."

"Is it? I didn't know it was all that special."

"Oh, *yes*. What about a night at the Plaza?"

"That sounds nice, but the breakfast party is fun and this is the last year we're all together. Anyway the Plaza is a bit predictable. "

"Why not have both?"

"Would that not be strange, breaking up in the middle of the day, then coming together again at night?"

"I don't see that as a problem, anyway you might do something in the afternoon. You could go to a theatre matinee."

"Maw! You're talking about an all day *orgy*."

"Well why not? As you say, it's the last year you're all together. You might as well make the most of it. Will you ask wee Eileen? She's only fourteen."

"Yes, but she's taller than I am and she looks so grown up. I'm sure she'd like to come to the Plaza, anyway."

◊

The breakfast party, with its charades and infantile jokes was as enjoyable as ever, though Helen secretly wondered if, the full beards worn by five of her guests indicated that they were growing out of that stage of youthful madness. The morning finished with a bowl of Scotch broth before they crowded on to the tram for Charing Cross.

Patrons of the Kings Theatre auditorium were depressingly scarce that Saturday afternoon and Helen's party were sole occupants of the gallery. Unenthusiastic actors were unable to bring much life to a poor play and eventually some of the twenty four young people in the gods started adding their comments to the performance. Helen found this enjoyable but hoped the actors were not too upset.

After the theatre, they separated to their own homes to dress for the evening, returning to Clarence Drive at six thirty for the buffet supper and birthday cake. The only alcohol consumed that day was champagne served with the birthday cake. Although alcohol was seldom drunk in the family, Annie was amused and impressed that Helen was so unwilling to provide it and wondered what the young men thought of the 'dry' breakfast parties, though they did not seem to complain.

"My goodness, you'd think you were a Rechabite!"

"I don't know what that is."

"Someone who's taken a pledge not to drink alcohol. Your great grandfather Mackay was a rabid teetotaller. It must be in the blood."

"We're not going to spend money on fools that like to drink too much. I've seen parties ruined by one idiot. Fred was really upset last year when a drunk started throwing his mum's plum pudding about the room."

Annie laughed at the picture this conjured up.

"He was really angry and insulted. Anyway, if you give folk lots of nice food, they're quite happy and don't need booze."

Nor was alcohol available at the Plaza Ballroom, scene of so many 'twenty-firsts'. The most extravagant order was a Knickerbocker Glory, a rich concoction of ice cream and fruit salad.

Wee Eileen easily passed as a seventeen-year old and had a wonderful time.

As Helen's party quick-stepped around the decorative fountain, the five beards, an almost unknown facial adornment, added a touch of the Bohemian to the sedate dance hall.

◊

It was Annie that saw the advertisement,

Dancers wanted, ballet, musical comedy and tap.
Auditions in the Green Room, Theatre Royal.

"Do you not fancy trying that? It would be an experience."

"I've got enough on my plate with the finals looming. Still, it would be interesting, I suppose. Don't know any tap though."

As usual, Helen was unable to resist nurturing any seed of suggestion planted by Annie. Her friends also encouraged her.

Davy Donaldson was predictably out of the studio and Helen was taken aback when Mr Snow came over to speak to her at the first 'rest'. Other models donned a dressing gown when not posing but he added nothing to his inadequate garment.

"Thinking of going for a job, are you, Helen? Needing a wee bit help with the tap dancing, are you? I could give you a few tips that would easy get you through an audition. You'd pick them up in no time. Look, try this."

And, undeterred by bare feet or inappropriate clothing, he proceeded to demonstrate the basic elements of tap dancing.

At close quarters, Mr Snow's elderly muscles were not a pleasant sight when stationary, but when demonstrating a buck and wing... oh, oh, oh!

Politeness compelled Helen to attend and attempt to copy his steps in her unsuitable crepe soles.

She was in an agony of embarrassment.

Why did no one call "Pose please", and release her from the torture?

Who had suggested the idea to Mr Snow in the first place?

Aware of sympathetic looks and amused glances, Helen longed to sink into the floor.

Next Saturday Helen arrived early at the theatre, finding fewer girls than she had expected. At first she felt daunted and unprofessional in her short linen tunic, for the others wore woollen practice gear and liberal make-up. Then, as she watched them stretch and jump to warm up, a few balancing unsteadily on their points, she regained her confidence. The standard of dance hardly matched their glamorous appearance.

The audition was disorganised, with small groups tested, then re-tested, then asked to wait. There was a lot of waiting. Helen was not required to display her ignorance of tap-dancing, Forty new applicants arrived as she left.

It had been an adventure and Annie laughed as Helen described it, but wondered if her daughter harboured unspoken dreams of a stage career.

Two weeks later, Helen received a letter offering her a place in the company, which would shortly leave to entertain troops in the American sector of Berlin.

"Isn't that *great!* Fancy them offering me a job! Of course Heaven knows what sort of dancing it would be and I'm certainly not going. But I'm just so pleased to be *chosen.*"

"Are you quite sure you don't want to go?" Annie had no idea how she would manage without Helen, but hated to think her daughter might have regrets.

"No, no. I never thought of it seriously. I just remember what Trevor said about admired amateurs and failed professionals. I love my dancing, but it's only a hobby. I've applied to Jordanhill now and I'll still dance when I'm a teacher and *earn money!* I hope I'll dance all my life until I'm an old lady. Miss Hopkins has asked me to teach some of the advanced classes next year, though I haven't passed that exam myself yet. Perhaps I'll do a ballet for them in the Athenaeum. I've got an idea for using a pantomime horse."

"Well if you're sure, my love. You certainly seem to have plenty of plans for the future."

Helen was completely honest in saying she had no regrets.

She loved performing and creating dance, but had never seriously considered the unpredictable life of a professional dancer. She had always enjoyed teaching, and this more dependable career would enable her to continue caring for her mother.

Matthew

Hyndland had an influx of mice. Neighbours discussed ways of combating the invasion, but Helen hated the idea of poison or traps.

"I know I'm useless, but I couldn't do that sort of thing. What we need is a cat, but there don't seem to be any around these days."

"That's why there are mice." Annie smiled ruefully.

These were noisy mice. Each night Annie and Helen wakened to the sound of woodwork being destroyed. A gang of energetic mice seemed intent on demolishing the very fabric of the building.

Inspired by a Thurber story, Helen placed several pairs of shoes beside her bed each night. When the gnawing started, she flung shoe after shoe at the cupboard door behind which they seemed most active. It was good fun and quietened them for an hour, but hardly solved the problem.

Providence intervened.

Helen was washing dishes at the open kitchen window one beautiful Saturday morning in April. Annie peeled potatoes at the table and Mungo leaned against the coal bunker. They discussed the Coronation, now only weeks away.

"D'ye think you'll get a television set to watch it, Maw Corning?" Mungo had picked up Annie's pet name for her own mother, "Mrs Thorpe is buying one. Everyone seems to be getting one."

"No I couldn't be bothered peering at that wee screen. I'm going to wait until it's in colour. They'll improve eventually, no doubt. Mind you, I think it'll be a terrible time-waster."

"There's going to be lots of different Coronation celebrations. The Union is having a dinner dance and I'm hoping your daughter will accompany me to that."

Helen smiled over her shoulder and nodded enthusiastically.

"Ho, hum, I expect that means I'll be chained to the sewing machine again, slaving over a new evening dress."

"You know you love it." Helen laughed.

As she spoke, she was looking across the five back greens of the Polwarth Street tenements. In the distance she saw a tabby cat, who caught sight of her at the same moment and immediately started to gallop towards her, leaping over the unkempt tufts of grass, squeezing through one set of railings after another, making a beeline for the open window.

"Here's a wee cat coming stooring towards me, as though he recognises me!" Helen exclaimed.

The cat erupted through the window, jumped to the floor and rubbed himself ecstatically around Helen's ankles. greeting her like a long-lost friend. Always fascinated and charmed by cats, she was delighted.

Mungo's legs and Annie's chair were also rubbed against, then the young cat, no longer quite a kitten, jumped up on the bunker, down again, up on the table, down again and returned to Helen for more caresses. The cat's purring was phenomenally loud and his agility and speed amazing. His joyously waving tail declared his delight and pleasure.

"He's too clean and well-fed for a stray." Annie commented, then added

"He's certainly a bright wee cat and look at that waving tail! You'd think it was on ball bearings."

Immediately, she realised her unconscious *double entendre*, for the cat was very obviously male. Conversation was usually circumspect in Mungo's presence but he laughed, then so did Annie.

Helen smiled as she stroked the cat,

"I think I'll call him Matthew after that boy I met in Millport, long ago."

Although Matthew was put out of the house at night for a week, he sat on the doorstep again every morning and was eventually accepted as a permanent member of the family. Matthew was an affectionate and clever animal *and a great mouser*. Within weeks, the mouse problem was solved for the whole tenement, with any few remaining mice very sensibly moving to other premises. Matthew became a hero, welcomed and regaled with tasty bites of sardine, salmon or mince in every flat at 46. He was devoted to Helen, seeing her off at the tram stop in the morning and, seated on the window sill, awaiting her arrival home in the evening. He liked an evening walk with Helen and Mungo, but would leave them to disappear into rough grass where hunting might be possible. He was good company for Annie and liked to sit on the table, watching her type. He was a wonderful, undemanding cat, domestic and streetwise. Helen had yearned for a cat ever since her Pittenweem childhood when Ecky, a neighbour's cat, had delighted her by standing on his hind legs on the window sill outside and beating his front paws on the pane for attention.

Matthew had exactly the same imperious, yet charming, habit.

◊

"Ye'd like to see the Coronation, wouldn't ye, Tuppenny?"

"Yes. It might be interesting."

Helen had learned to hide her feelings more with her father. But she was not going to pretend an interest in this Royal ceremony. She was in the middle of six long weeks of examination paintings, which seemed unfairly demanding compared with the few days' exams of the university student.

Ignoring her lack of enthusiasm, Bruce continued

"Yes, I thought ye might be keen on that sort of thing. Willie Low asked me round to watch it on his set, but you can go instead of me. Couldn't care less, myself. I'll be out on the golf course that day. This Coronation business, it's more a thing for ladies, isn't it, all that dressing up and fuss. However, ye'd like me to arrange for you to see it on television, wouldn't ye, wee one?"

Annie broke in before Helen could speak,

"I think that would be marvellous, Bruce. It's a historic occasion and shouldn't be missed. Elizabeth is so young, there might not be another Coronation for a very long time. You'd *love* to see it, *wouldn't* you, Helen."

This was a directive rather than a question and Helen nodded with assumed enthusiasm.

It was arranged that she would meet her father's friend, John Bruce, in Hyndland Road and take a taxi to Willie Low's bungalow in Bearsden, It was a beautiful day. Helen knew she looked smart in her bouclé coat, but found it depressing to walk with someone even older than her father. The directions were given to the taxi driver, who looked round with a knowing wink and said,

"I'd be away out to the country on a day like this, sir, if I had a nice blonde wi' me."

Helen was furious! Did that leering taxi driver believe she was *dating this old man*? Indignant and wrathful, she could hardly breathe.

The insult of that dreadful taxi driver would remain in her mind more clearly than any memories of the historic occasion. Of the Coronation she retained only a hazy impression of sitting for hours on a hard chair amongst a crowd of strangers, with every face fascinated by a small flickering screen, where a young girl, unfairly weighted down by elaborate clothing, underwent incomprehensible rituals. Occasionally interruptions of cacophonous trumpets gave her some respite.

◊

Helen and Mungo attended the very splendid dinner dance in the University Union to celebrate the Coronation. He was impeccable in dinner jacket. She was stylishly clad in a wonderful, close-fitting, sea green, strapless gown, with a 'fishtail' flare behind the knee, for which Annie had used a Vogue *Special Pattern*, expensive at five shillings, but worth it for the excellent cut.

More Milestones

The paintings had a simple frame of plain wood nailed to the stretcher. This was the suggested presentation, though Helen thought it amateurish. Ten drawings were mounted and many others placed in a folio. The terracotta head was set on a plinth, with the history of painting notebook beside it. She was not pleased with the last for her hand writing was only slightly better than previously and the postcards and other illustrations made the notebook unpleasantly lumpy. But all the notebooks were like this.

What a relief to have her diploma work finished and on display, but who knew what visiting examiners might like or dislike?

There was no differentiation in the passes, only a straight pass or fail.

Helen passed.

Bruce arranged to take Annie to the Art School to see the show. The familiar surroundings hardly seemed changed and were powerfully evocative. She was wheeled past the well remembered window seats where she and her friends had smoked and chatted thirty years ago. What a giddy young girl she had been in her linen smock, intent on enjoying herself and happily ignorant of the difficulties ahead. What an innocent young ass, but not alone, for the whole world was rejoicing that the 'war to end wars' had finally finished.

◊

The degree show was dismantled and her locker emptied. Helen's days at Glasgow Art school were over. It had taken several journeys to bring everything home. Drawing board, T-square, canvases and folios leaned against the sitting room walls. Beside them were baskets holding palette, brushes and paints. The table was piled with art books, sketchbooks, note-books, and the many various objects acquired over four years.

"What a stuff! And where will I put this?"

Helen brought the life-size terracotta head out of the last basket.

"Put it down on the hearth just now. The fire won't be on for months. I must say it's terribly realistic! Looks good against the dark green tiles."

Helen went off to make lunch. When she returned, Annie was laughing.

"Och, you missed yourself just now. Matthew came into the room and immediately caught sight of the head! In a flash his tail fluffed out to twice its size and he crouched down flat 'til his belly was on the carpet. Slowly, slowly, one paw after another, he crept towards the fireplace, trembling all over, with his whiskers pointing straight forwards and his eyes enormous. Then when he reached the hearthrug, he suddenly realised it wasn't the gruesome object he'd thought and he stood up straight and gave that little dismissive flick of his front paw, then walked purposefully to the window and jumped up and looked out, as though that's what he'd meant to to do all along. But his tail's not back to normal yet."

"Poor wee cat. Did he really think it was Mungo's head chopped off, I wonder?"

◊

Bruce drove Annie and Helen to Pittenweem as usual. Matthew slept calmly on the back seat, awakening briefly in Kirkcaldy, when the linseed oil fumes from linoleum factories filled the car and again lifting his head at Cameron Bridge, to inhale the yeasty smell of the distillery.

Mary greeted their arrival with excitement,

"*You'll need to come out to the garden.* There's a wee *miracle* out there!"

Thirty years ago Annie had planted an apple pip which had grown into a modest little tree, healthy but bearing only leaves. This year it had blossomed!

"It must be for the Coronation! We should write to the papers about it!" Annie laughed.

Helen privately thought it might celebrate her Diploma.

That summer seemed a curiously blank waiting period. Helen had no idea what the Jordanhil course might entail and she had nothing to anticipate or plan for. However it was good to swim and dance with Jack and Drew and her Pittenweem friends again. While Jack could be slightly overbearing, Helen still enjoyed spending time with his family, though she did not allow Isobel to claim so much of her time.

It was pleasant to receive Mungo's letters, but she found no wild delight in his repeated assurances of how much he missed her. She did not miss him as she should and again determined their friendship must come to an end, for she would never marry him.

Several of her Pittenweem friends were already married. Helen thought it a foolhardy and amazing thing to do. She examined the youthful, uncouth husbands with a critical eye and could not imagine trusting her life to one of these immature, untried boys.

Helen was invited to Jean's wedding in Dunfermline. Bride and groom both looked incredibly young. Getting married was so serious and final, so *grown up*. There were so many other things to do in life. Were Walter and Jean absolutely and utterly sure that they wanted to be together always? How could they be sure? Helen hoped they would be happy.

◊

Although Annie kept very good general health and had in many ways come to terms with her condition, heavy low-lying cloud would always cause painful muscle spasms. These episodes were less frequent in Pittenweem than in Glasgow, but often more severe and sometimes lasted for nearly two hours. Annie was left spent and exhausted. Helen could do little and felt terribly helpless although aspirin and sometimes a gentle massage gave slight relief. It seemed heartless to leave Annie alone at these times, though she wondered if her mother would prefer that, for Annie, aware that her pain distressed Helen, tried hard to hide it, smiling ruefully in the brief moments of relief and whispering 'it'll stop when the rain comes on'.

After the waves of pain finally abated, Helen noticed Annie would not refer to it again. Such an experience might well have been a justification for self-pity or demands for special treatment, but once the misery was past, it might never have happened as far as Annie was concerned. After a brief rest, she would take up her industrious life where she had left off, resuming her knitting, typing a letter or preparing vegetables for the next meal. She required no retrospective sympathy. The return to normality seemed recompense enough for what she had gone through.

Mary was recovering her energy and spirit. She no longer wore black and had attended several auctions and bazaars this summer. Her conversation was once again irate and critical, rather than morbid, and was spiced with her former wit. Casual visitors, perhaps only acquaintances had always been welcome in the Pittenweem house. They might drop in at any hour of the day, staying perhaps for only ten minutes or possibly settling in for two or three hours, enjoying a cup ot tea and a second cup, if the next arrivals overlapped. Mary now encouraged this continuous social interaction. She loved the endless flow of gossip and the opportunity to dazzle and entertain suited her perfectly.

Annie accepted the visitors as a necessity, sometimes amusing and sometimes 'a bit too much of a good thing'.

The unpredictable stream of guests often made it impossible to get a proper meal served and Helen found the constant tea-making irritating. She worked to a routine in Glasgow, less than strict perhaps, but which ennabled her to find time for her own work and leisure. Pittenweem had been different when John was alive. Mealtimes, though erratic, had provided some structure to each day and though John was the last person to realise he was hungry, Mary was wont to say,

"Is that the right time, Helen? I can't believe it's after six? Quick, get the kettle on right away! Your grandfather'll be *starved*. His belly will think his throat's cut. Hurry."

Nowadays, Mary seemed content to meander through each directionless day, living happily on cups of tea, cigarettes and gossip.

Helen found the small town conversation boring and started to observe these intruders in a cynical and unfriendly way.

If her mother were in the garden, the visitor would assume an expression of profound sympathy, tiptoe outside, then almost bending over Annie, ask in a voice deeper than normal,

"And *how are you*, Mrs Corning? *How* are you keeping these days, my dear?"

"Och well, I'm doing fine, thank you. As well as can be expected, I suppose. And what about yourself?"

The long struggle with pain that morning would be unmentioned! Helen found it hard to believe that Annie ignored such a recent experience. How could it be forgotten? Moreover, this answer immediately released the visitor from the duty of further sympathy, and left the field open for her own complaints. For twenty minutes, they would hear of the severe symptoms, the pain and sleeplessness, the lack of understanding shown by Doctor So and So and the various strangely named medications which had proved useless. Annie's face might show signs of weariness, but these went unnoticed by the visitor, who had found a captive audience. Helen sometimes walked away, but it seemed unfair to let Annie deal with the tedious recital herself. Helen yearned to inform the visitor of that morning's agony, but obviously Annie preferred to wipe it from her mind.

◊

Throughout her life, Helen had observed Mary sit by the fire, curling her hair with the old iron curling tongs. Helen occasionally used them herself, employing the more gentle heat of the gas cooker.

The well worn implement was plunged into the glowing depths of the fire, then quickly withdrawn, though not quickly enough, for the first testing on a piece of newspaper would invariably destroy it, with smoke pouring upwards and often a flame. Mary would screw her eyes against the acrid smoke, then holding the newspaper at arm's length, try again. The second test burned the paper to a crisp dark brown, with slightly less smoke. Mary would tut-tut to herself as though this was unexpected. Parallel testing was continued along the edge of the newspaper, curling it into six or seven waves of ever fading brown. When the paper no longer showed any discolouration, the tongs were ready for the first lock of hair. Even then, the first curl might send a wisp of steam and a faint singed aroma into the air.

Annie also watched the process, marvelling that, in spite of her seventy one years and the abuse of the tongs, Mary's hair was thick and hardly faded from its original warm brown.

"It's a wonder you've got any hair left, Maw."

"Och, I'm awful fed up with it. When I come through to Glasgow, I'll go to a good hairdresser and get a proper perm. That one I got here was useless."

Helen was unhappy to hear her plans of coming to Glasgow. When would she come and how long would she stay?

◊

After they returned to Glasgow, Helen decided to paint her mother's portrait. She had drawn her often, but this would be a life-size oil painting. Annie was happy to sit for her, reminded of the many hours she had sat for her father, when young.

When Tessa saw the portrait, she was unusually complimentary. She considered herself an authority on art and was always ready to speak knowledgeably about artists and techniques. Helen was quietly amused by her enthusiasm, detecting more than a grain of surprise in it. No doubt, university students often showed a polite condescension towards art students.

"Would you like me to paint you, too? I'd like to and there's still a couple of weeks before I start Jordanhill."

Tessa was also painted. There was some talk of buying, but the price of forty pounds proved too great and there was no sale.

New Skills

A rt and music students must attend a two-term course at Jordanhill Training College to obtain a teaching certificate. From September until Easter, two days of each week were spent in the college for theory, with practical teaching in schools filling the other three days.

Helen found the time spent in college a terrible trial. Every Monday and Tuesday seemed to be windy and rainy as she walked up the long exposed driveway. She hated the building itself. Compared to the Art School, warm, welcoming and aesthetic, Jordanhill struck her as cold, ugly and badly designed. With its endless white-tiled corridors, it resembled a monstrous public lavatory. She and her friends had read widely and considered the lectures elementary and boring.

"Honestly, it's like the stuff I used to read in the Reader's Digest before I grew up. It's puerile! You'd think we were straight out of school. For psychology, we've to buy a book called 'Teach Yourself to Think'. I'm embarrassed to ask for it. Our first exam is on the first two chapters. I ask you! I'm going to get myself some knitting to do while he drivels on."

"Surely he'll know you're knitting."

Her mother smiled.

"No, I'll sit away at the back and he'll never see me. He's too busy referring to his notes, the idiot."

And certainly Helen accomplished a lot of knitting while at Jordanhill.

"And then the speech lessons! I hope I *never* speak like that woman. She's awful! So affected! We can hardly keep our faces straight when she tells us how to say,

'What a to-do to die today at a minute or two to two'"

Annie could not help laughing as Helen recited the strange mantra with exaggerated facial movements.

"Honestly, that's what she's like! It's *ridiculous*. Fortunately the art lessons are great. Mr Black is really good. And funny too."

Jordanhill was redeemed by Sam Black. He introduced them to crafts that could be employed in the classroom. Helen made lino prints, papier mâché masks, colourful mobiles and a small stage set of paper sculpture and thoroughly enjoyed these new, light-hearted skills

They must make a short speech in Sam's class and this terrified Helen. Apart from reciting poetry in school, Helen had never stood on her legs to speak in public and knew her voice to be quiet and inadequate. People often asked her to repeat herself and she seldom spoke out in a crowd unless with very good friends. For Sam's five minute talk, she chose to speak about cats. It was daunting to stand up in front of forty well-known faces and she trembled as she started. Soon, however, with the pleasure she felt in her subject, her self-consciousness faded and she found she was enjoying herself.

Helen learned most from her teaching practice in schools and her excellent mentor, George Gavin. He was a confident and relaxed teacher, firm yet kindly towards the often disappointing pupils of Copland Road Junior Secondary School. Helen was impressed by the humour which tempered Mr Gavin's discipline. In later years, when she had more experience of the strengths and weaknesses of teaching staff, she would realise her tremendous luck in having him as a role model.

The junior secondary school was part of a far from perfect system, solving some problems while creating others. It provided education for those children who, unlikely to pass fourth or fifth year exams, would leave at the end of third year aged fifteen and find immediate employment in factory or shop, with the more ambitious apprenticed to a trade or attending night classes. Many would fill the lowliest jobs that society offers and some would grow familiar with the walls of Barlinnie Prison.

In Copland Road, which was a girls' school, Helen came face to face with a darker side of Glasgow than she had yet met. Some pupils were without proper clothing or footwear. A weekly card informed the teacher which of the children had head lice. Helen could feel her scalp itching when George explained this fact to her. She remembered her wartime childhood in Pittenweem and her horror of the creatures in her hair, caught from the evacuees. Annie had used paraffin to get rid of the bugs, then constant, *painful*, fine-tooth combing. Helen never wanted to suffer that again.

She noticed particularly that these impoverished, ill-clad, unwashed children all had beautiful teeth, protected by the long years of sweet rationing.

George's assistant, Cathy Macdonald, was young, pretty and engaged to be married shortly. She took Helen under her wing and they ate lunch in a nearby pub, with Cathy providing cider on payday. The purchase of perfume was another payday indulgence and on Cathy's advice, Helen bought one by Coty. Seven and sixpence seemed extravagant but Bruce had given her a pound towards lunches. *Chypre* was a unique woody scent which would remain Helen's favourite until it was withdrawn from the market many years later.

On Wednesdays, Helen taught in Broomloan Road Primary school. Here she was on her own with a class of nearly forty. Although nervous, she soon found great pleasure in teaching them, especially the nine-year olds. These children were true citizens of Govan, familiar with the docks, warehouses, ferries and shipyards and with Helen's encouragement, they used their pride and knowledge to paint interesting murals.

To the younger classes she told untrue stories of Matthew stealing fish which the children illustrated, thereafter demanding a weekly tale of the bad cat.

Govan was a fascinating and educational experience for the young teacher.

◊

Helen had settled into her new routine by November, complaining of the time spent in the college, but travelling cheerfully to Govan by subway on the other three days.

Between Partick and Govan, the subway dives underneath the Clyde, transferring workers from the north to the south side of the river in a few minutes. Helen's first journey on the well-used route was at the height of the rush hour and she was crushed claustrophobically. She made sure to leave home much earlier in future.

Nothing had been resolved with Mungo and he came for his meal every Saturday night as always. Sometimes on Fridays, they might go to a cinema or attend a student dance. Once, at Helen's request, they visited the Locarno Ballroom. Knowing it had started its long career as a roller skating rink and having walked past it all her life, she was curious about it. The interior was immense, but shabby and unprepossessing, much like the dance halls portrayed in British films, with a loud band and crowded floor. It had neither the period charm of the Plaza, nor the familiarity of student dances where you were certain to bump into friends. The Locarno was disappointing.

Margery very often popped round for Russian tea late on Fridays, staying until well after midnight, sharing grumbles with Helen about Jordanhill and playing cards with Annie. Sometimes the three of them still composed those rather vulgar limericks.

Margery had been offered a post graduate course in lithography at the Art School, but had turned it down. Though unenthusiastic about the idea of teaching, she had, like most of the others, opted to take the Jordanhill course, thus making sure of employment. Unlike Helen, Margery took no pleasure whatever in teaching as a skill or art.

◊

Helen was surprised to get a phone call from Trevor. He had been asked to provide a cabaret for an important dinner in the McLellan Galleries. Could he persuade her to join him in performing last year's Spanish dance? Helen agreed delightedly.

On the night of the performance, she was taken aback when she saw the changing room they must share. It was little more than a cupboard! Even when changing amongst girls, Helen was rather modest. There was no choice and they undressed and donned their costumes side by side, almost bumping into each other in the confined space. Helen concentrated on how she would make her mother laugh that night.

Unexpected Present

O ne Saturday, Helen answered the loudly jangling doorbell. Her father stood there, but made no move to enter. "Got a jiffy, have you? Something to show you out here!"

Bruce was smiling broadly, his shoulders twitching inside his jacket and his keys jingling in his pocket.

Helen nodded and, skipping to keep up with his fast stride, followed him out to the lane, where he always parked.

"Now, here's a wee present for you. I didn't pay too much for it, mind you, just a fiver, but I've been working on it for a coupla months. I think it'll get you started, do ye fine for a year or so anyway. I've put in a new engine, but I had to cobble the bloody exhaust pipe, it was a right bugger, but... I think it'll see you through. It's been a good car in its time, ye know, old but solid. D'ye like it, lass? Are ye surprised?"

Helen was much more than surprised. She was dismayed, almost aghast, but managed to say,

"A car! Thank you very much indeed, Daddy. It's very kind of you."

Of all the things that she might have dreamed of owning, a car was the very last. She was still a student. What need had she of a car? What would she do with it? Only wealthy folk owned cars, apart from her father. She was nervous when riding her bicycle and hardly used hers, always preferring to walk. A car would be *ten times* worse.

Although the pre-war saloon YS 1834 was nearly the same age as Helen, many of this particular model were still to be seen on British roads. Square, black and large, it had been a luxury car, with broad running boards, leather upholstery and synchromesh gear change between third and top. The two distinctive metal flashes along the bonnet proclaimed it a Vauxhall.

It was impossible for Bruce to realise his daughter's dismay.

"Get inside, wee yin. See how it feels behind the wheel."

For Helen, the open door to the driver's seat seemed like the door to a world which she had no desire to enter.

"It's enormous, isn't it, a bit like a taxi! I can hardly see over the wheel."

"Aye, we'll soon get ye a cushion to solve that problem.."

Helen could see how excited her father was and she truly wished she could show more enthusiasm. Not for the first time, she thought a son would have known what to say and would have shown the absolute delight which Bruce obviously expected.

She felt cold all over.

"We'll take her for a wee spin, will we?"

"Right now?" She tried to hide her reluctance.

"Aye! Not to worry! I know just the place to try her out. You jump out now, and I'll drive us there before ye know."

Relieved that she need not start driving immediately, Helen darted into the house to tell Annie they were going for a drive.

"And how d'ye like your exciting present, wee pet? Pretty good, eh?"

Helen smiled wanly. How could her mother think that owning a car was a good thing?

Bruce drove to a wasteland on the western edge of Glasgow. Obviously ambitious building works were about to start here. Large areas of ground had been cleared of vegetation and heavy machinery awaited the next phase.

"Aye, this'll be a fine place, dearie. We're off the road, 'cos you're not quite legal yet. You need a licence. I'll see about that for you. Now, the first thing I want to say is a *car is a lethal weapon.* Ye always have to remember that. *It can kill!* But I know you'll take care and be a good, sensible driver."

Helen's mouth became dry and her stomach contracted. Why had he said that? Had he no idea how terrified she already was by the thought of driving?

"First of all, I'll just explain to you a wee bit about how the gears work. It's not difficult."

His explanations were lengthy and complicated and might as well have been delivered in a foreign language. Helen, as she so often had in her history class when kings and battles were the subject, removed her attention and drifted into an unthinking dream. Convinced that she would never understand gears anyway, she stopped trying.

When it came to the practical side and she sat behind the wheel, she started to concentrate and learned the seemingly illogical and magical movements required to make the car move. Soon she was able to set it in motion comparatively smoothly and to change from first to second.

"Next time, I'll have to teach you how to double de-clutch. Now that's a tricky one. Not necessary nowadays of course, but I'm afraid you'll need to know how to use it between second and third in this old bugger. But you're doing just grand. You'll be a great wee driver yet and yer old Dad 'll be proud o' you."

Helen's mind was tired of machinery and exhausted by her father's relentless voice. She longed to get home to her knitting.

"Where is this place, anyway?"

"Aye, well I think the Corporation's got big plans here. Putting up lots of houses, council houses, of course, trying to prise the folk out the slums. Terrible crowding there, y'know. We're talking big money. God, it's a pity they couldn't raze the Gallowgate to the ground, some of those bloody awful closes. Pity the Jerries didn't bomb that lot. Aye and it's not even as bad as when I first went there! Not fit for pigs to live in, never mind human beings. This scheme here'll maybe help a bit. It's big enough anyway."

"And what's this place called?"

"This area? I suppose it's Drumchapel. Aye that'll be it. There's a wee village, Old Drumchapel, just over there."

"That's where my friend Olive stays."

"Aye that's a genteel wee place. They'll no' like what's happenin' here, I bet. There'll be big changes when this housing scheme's finished."

Back home, after Bruce had drunk a coffee and gone to 'meet a fellow in the pub', Annie said,

"Well! Are you excited about your new car?"

Helen thought for a moment before she replied. Obviously her mother also believed a car would delight her.

"It's very, very good of him to give it to me, I suppose."

"I think it's wonderful! My goodness, I'd have been *delirious* to have a car when I was your age."

"Would you?"

Helen remembered sitting in the backseat of the car, as a child, when Bruce was teaching her mother to drive. It had not seemed a happy experience for any of them and Annie had never sat the test.

"Are you not delighted?"

Helen huffed,

"Not really."

"But it'll be different when you learn to drive. Just imagine what fun you'll have. And you'll be able to take me about a wee bit. That'll be nice and we won't need to rely on Bruce to go to Pittenweem."

"Mhmm. Yes, I can see that would be good and it would be great to take you about. Not sure where I'd want to go, myself, though. I quite like sitting in the tram and reading or thinking. And there's trains for going further away."

"Oh, I'm quite sure you'll find lots of places to go in your car and you'll just *love* it. You're a lucky girl."

Even Annie did not understand.

Helen had the familiar feeling of being hurried along a street in a direction which she would never have chosen for herself, pushed by kindly people with the best of generous intentions. People who would be astonished and hurt, if she dug in her heels and refused to go another step.

◊

Now that the piano was in her own home, Helen was determined to take lessons. Elizabeth Main, a kenspeckle figure in Hyndland, was suggested as a teacher. Helen had long known her well by sight. Small and bosomy, Miss Main wore flamboyant cloaks. fluttering silk scarves and outsize Art Nouveau jewellery. Her features did not match the artistic grace of her clothing, With an excessively long upper lip, small peering eyes, close-set in a rather large face and dark hair severely middle-parted and dragged tightly back, she bore almost a threatening aspect. It was easy to see why the pupils of the Lambhill school where she taught music had nicknamed her Geronimo, for she bore a strong resemblance to the Red Indian warrior. Even her colourful and extravagant attire was reminiscent of a chieftain's gaudy outfit.

Fierce though she looked, Elizabeth was the kindest and most charming of women and a perfect teacher for Helen. Her looks were forgotten as one fell under her charm.

Helen knew nothing of reading music and at twenty-two, found it a hard skill to learn. Miss Main started with simple Bach and Mozart and was infinitely patient. Helen was determined and hard working, quite prepared to practice early and late for two or three hours each day. She would never achieve any true skill, but music would be a life-long pleasure, sometimes discarded for years when life was too demanding, then taken up, often as a solace, when difficulties seemed overpowering.

Miss Main was the driving power of the Glasgow Chamber Music Society and Helen attended the concerts in the McLellan Galleries. As she stood there in her smart woollen dress, selling programmes, her mind flicked through the various times she had been in this beautiful building; looking at her own portrait in the RGI when she was four; dancing that first simple Welsh dance as a teenager; more recently, dancing en pointe in her tutu; changing in the claustrophobic space with Trevor to perform the sensual Spanish dance.

Elizabeth rented rooms in a Sydenham Road mansion and after the concert, she entertained the Amadeus String Quartet in her magnificent sitting room. Helen had made salads and felt it a great honour to help serve supper to these famous musicians.

Like her personality, Elizabeth's figure and her choice of clothing did not conform to the conventional. Annie made several successful, though outré, outfits for her and they became friendly.

◊

Helen's driving lessons were much less enjoyable than her music. She had no desire to drive and was both bored and nervous behind the wheel.

The fact that she was not close to her father strangely made the lessons easier. Bruce was business-like, less teasing than normal. She admitted to herself that he taught her well. He suggested she should have five professional lessons prior to the test.

"That might help you to pass, for those blokes are up to all the dodges."

Once she had learned the basics, Mungo was happy to sit beside her for practice. Certain she would *never* enjoy driving, it was always a relief to hand the wheel back.

They planned a trip to Pittenweem in November. It would be Mungo's first visit. At the last minute, the temperamental old Vauxhall was deemed un-roadworthy for the long drive.

"Aye, better do a wee bit work on that camshaft before it goes on the road again. Never worry! You can take my car, but Mungo would need to do all the driving. Handbrake's buggered and the wee yin couldn't manage.

"*Bruce*! How d'ye drive it without a handbrake?"

"Oh, I'm pretty nippy with my feet. Mungo'll manage fine, I'm sure. He can pick it up at Doune Terrace on Saturday morning."

Bruce still lived with his father and brother, cherishing his secret.

Though Mungo was early to pick up the car, he was late arriving at Clarence Drive, for in Great Western Road, the little Austin Seven suffered a flat tyre, which Mungo must change in the rush hour traffic.

"Really, Mungo, I am sorry. I don't know what Bruce was thinking of, giving you such a broken down wreck to drive."

Mungo shook his head and smiled, pleased to demonstrate his ability to surmount difficulties.

◊

As they drove through Springburn, a second tyre went flat. Fortunately they were close to a garage.

While waiting for the tyre to be repaired, Helen suddenly realised she had left the suitcase of clothes behind. What an idiot! She hated to make stupid mistakes. As it was now after eleven and Mary expected them for lunch, they decided to forget the case. Helen sat silently in the back seat.

Recently, a large advertising campaign had trumpeted the amazing qualities of chlorophyll. Hoardings everywhere assured the public of the magic ability of this substance to banish all unpleasant smells when used in toothpaste, chewing gum or air fresheners. Across the road from the garage, unexpectedly, two tethered goats were munching on grassy Balgrayhill and Annie lightened the depressed mood by quoting a poem she had read,

"Why reeks the goat on yonder hill, he simply dotes on chlorophyll!"

The rest of the weekend was surprisingly successful. Mary was always ready to exert herself to charm one of the opposite sex, whether she liked him much or not.

◊

Tired of being rejected by the Glasgow Institute, Annie had submitted two paintings to the Paisley exhibition and was delighted to sell them both.

One buyer wrote a particularly nice letter to say how pleased she was and how well the painting looked in her sitting room.

Annie admitted to herself that the receipt of this letter seemed to give her energy. She was ready to paint another half dozen pictures!

"I've been thinking, Helen. I'm sure we could make money by renting out paintings. People could hang one on their walls for a few months and then have a change, if they wanted. Or maybe they would want to keep it permanently and the money they had paid could go towards buying it. D'ye not think that would be a good idea?"

Helen was noncommittal. She knew nothing about business and was not very interested in it. Quite soon she would earn her very first salary as a teacher and that seemed a sufficient goal in the meantime.

"How about this," Annie said another day, "when you pass your driving test…"

"If I pass my driving test!"

"Of course you'll pass it and when you do, wouldn't it be great to go up North and visit the old aunties?"

"Isn't Ardgay terribly far away?"

"Nowhere in Scotland is *terribly* far away. It would be an adventure and I'd love to see where they live with all their animals and they'd be so delighted to see us."

Helen had too many other things on her mind to feel enthusiastic, but the seed of the idea was planted.

◊

Jordanhill exams were passed and each of the hundred art students was placed in a primary school to await a secondary vacancy.

"Thank Heavens I need never go to that place again. I loathed it."

"Surely it couldn't have been as bad as all that?"

"Yes, it was."

"Well, you did fine in all the exams, even the speech exam which you worried about. She said nice things about your telling of the Elephant's Child story, didn't she?"

"Well, she described me as a natural storyteller and said I used colourful language, but you could take that two ways. She could have meant I was a good liar and I swore a lot. Anyway, *I never need to go there again!* Now I've to start in the Cowcaddens on the first of April! That doesn't seem like a good omen does it!

What a strange name, the Normal School. I wonder why it's called that?"

"I think it used to be a sort of training school for teachers."

"Like Jordanhill? That place was *never* normal."

◊

After only three weeks in the Normal School, Helen was transferred to St Cuthbert's Junior Secondary in Hamiltonhill in the north of the city. Her driving test was scheduled for the first day at the new school, which seemed disastrous to Helen, but Bruce was optimistic.

"Och we'll manage fine, Tuppenny. You just tell the headmaster you might be a wee bit late getting back from lunch. I'm sure he'll understandand. I'll drive you to St Vincent Crescent, then whizz you back up to the school, after you've passed."

Bruce had arranged for Helen to have five professional lessons and take the test in the driving school car. She had found the small modern car very different from her own, panicking one rainy day when the driving wheel was suddenly unresponsive. The tyres had become stuck in the tramlines! What might happen next? Dread was always a large part of her driving experience.

She had not expected to pass the test that over-stressful day and she did not.

St Cuthbert's was on top of a hill and the walk from the tram was exposed and bleak. Built in the thirties, Hamiltonhill may then have expressed the optimistic garden city ethos, but it was now a very depressed area. The council houses required maintenance and the shabby curtains at the grimy windows spoke of hopelessness. The ill-kempt front patches of weeds and rank grass were littered with rubbish. Mangy dogs sat on doorsteps, scratching and staring miserably at her as she passed, and emaciated cats would slink away when Helen spoke to them. Here and there an energetic tenant had spruced up their home with a lick of paint and some shrubs, but generally there was a feeling of defeat.

On her second day at the school, a small first year boy was thrown over a wall by older boys and taken to hospital with a broken leg and who knows how much psychological damage.

The following day, Bill Callaghan, her fellow art teacher, gleefully informed her that her class of third year boys was the worst in the school, but kindly added,

"If they're difficult and they will be, don't hesitate to send any troublemakers through to me, I'll deal with them."

Helen was determined to deal with the class herself and show no weakness. The boys were inattentive, noisy and cheeky but she struggled on, reaching the end of two periods without requiring Bill's intervention.

One tall fellow worried Helen. He seemed particularly dull, too dull to be much of a nuisance, for it was always the brighter boys who instigated trouble. But this boy did not interact with the others and grumbled to himself, obviously angry about something. She feared his unpredictability for he reminded her of the simple-minded character of great strength in one of Steinbeck's novels.

That was the most difficult class she had yet encountered and it was a relief when the bell sounded for lunch. Before she had collected all her things, she heard shouts and screams echoing from the nearby staircase. She ran out of her room and was horrified to see the large angry pupil grasping a much smaller pupil and attempting to stab him in the neck with a broken milk bottle. Sensibly putting aside any idea of independence, Helen ran for Bill, who was fortunately still in his room. Bill was a burly six-footer and able to deal with the violence on the staircase.

Helen was meeting a different side of life.

Teaching at St Cuthbert's was often a hard struggle, though there were no more dramatic incidents that term. There were new skills to acquire, skills ignored by the Jordanhill course. She learned to administer the belt, though she would never feel comfortable using it, and seldom used it on girls. Remembering her own horror of the 'strap', she felt sick when she wielded the heavy strip of leather for the first time, How hard should she strike? How capable was she of striking at all? Or of aiming correctly? What if she missed each time? However it was the accepted form of punishment, the victims were generally taller than she was and had spent half an hour baiting her. After their punishment, they returned to their seats and behaved properly for the rest of the afternoon. Occasionally, she would give lines for bad behaviour, but she was forgetful about demanding them when completed. Perhaps it was better to give the punishment at the moment of misdemeanour? She could never make up her mind.

Helen rather enjoyed collecting dinner money, accepting medical excuses and notes and filling in her register, neatly completing the percentages for the office each Friday afternoon. It reminded her of 'playing at schools'.

Most importantly, Helen learned to project her voice, sheer necessity succeeding where the Jordanhill elocution teacher had failed.

Not all classes were badly behaved. Helen met some very nice children, although their knowledge seemed incredibly narrow. She took in the old gramophone and played classical records while they worked and often used the art lesson to introduce other subjects. They seemed to listen with interest, for everything was new to them.

Soon, her art room looked colourful and productive, the walls adorned with papier mâché masks and bright repeat patterns on thin paper, which, when displayed in folds, looked like curtain fabric. The children were proud of their work and Helen gained confidence and found teaching generally satisfying, though there were always one or two difficult classes to darken the week.

Helen made friends with the science teacher, Margaret McGill, a quiet, pretty girl, also newly qualified. The staffroom was crowded with primary teachers endlessly discussing pupils and the two young women spent their free time in the art room or the science lab to indulge in more entertaining subjects, clothes, films, food and boyfriends.

On the last day of the month, Helen and Margaret queued with the other teachers outside the headmaster's room. The air was electric with expectation. The headmaster, Mr Hughes, a small, dour, man nearing retiral age, sat behind his desk, wearing overcoat, soft hat and a look of suspicion. Helen would never see him without these three attributes. In front of him lay the cash-filled paypackets. In a cathedral-like silence, each teacher stepped forward, signed where the unsmiling Mr Hughes indicated, then picked up the envelope and sidled sheepishly out of the office and past their colleagues.

The method of payment was undignified and after nearly five years of study, twenty eight pounds was hardly generous recompense for four weeks of work, but nevertheless Helen was delighted. At the age of twenty-two, this was her very first salary.

Poor Margaret had a problem pupil, Every teacher knew Cathy McGill was 'one to watch' and she had started to sabotage Margaret's science lessons, noisily knocking stools over, breaking test tubes, spilling potassium permanganate, Recently she had assured her friends that she was Miss McGill's cousin. It was outrageous and Helen and Margaret alternately fumed and laughed.

Bill Callaghan also admitted problems with Cathy. He was a fine-looking man of nearly forty and Cathy had taken to gazing soulfully at him wherever he was in the room. Bill came to Helen for help, one day.

"I was just sitting quietly at my desk when I heard her voice say, 'Och! Surr! Look surr, look at ma blowz." And when I turned my head, all I could see was her large left bosom, covered in red paint. I fled, muttering that you'd help clean it up. Is that all right?"

◊

Rod Berthoff, Tessa's American friend, was coming to Glasgow. It had been a most romantic encounter last summer in the Hebridean Islands and it now seemed Rod's intentions were serious. He was in his thirties, divorced and might even have children and though Helen looked forward to meeting him, she did not think him the right man for a girl of twenty one. Although Tessa had always said she wanted an experienced man, she had just graduated and might never use her degree to earn a living. Helen hated waste of any kind.

Helen invited Mungo, Tessa, Rod, Olive and her special boyfriend Jimmy for the evening. Annie went to bed to listen to a play on the wireless, leaving the three young couples to enjoy a particularly successful party. They all seemed to 'speak the same language' and laugh at the same jokes.

Olive was a beautiful girl with an elegant slender figure, dark colouring and classical features. Jimmy was nice-looking, clever and funny and very keen on Scottish Nationalism. Would they marry, Helen wondered?

Tessa was prettier and more vivacious than usual that evening. It seemed likely that she would move to America if this large self confident fellow asked her to go. Rod's Russian ancestry was apparent in his overpowering height and memorably deep voice. Although older, he was certainly good-looking, with magnificent American teeth and that air of having been well nourished and well washed since childhood. As he enjoyed wordplay, Helen suggested playing super ghosts, a spelling game described by James Thurber. Rod was familiar with it and soon they were all laughing helplessly. Helen was pleased to find Mungo just as quick and witty as the others.

That night it seemed as though the three couples had made their life choices.

Tessa had a party for her schoolfriends shortly before her wedding. Some were unexpectedly mature, others had hardly changed. Elizabeth, the archetypal schoolgirl, was still over-enthusiastic and giggly. Olive, always the most attractive girl in any group, had achieved an elegance not possible with school uniform. She would be Tessa's bridesmaid.

Ariane was there, well dressed and more subdued than previously. When she found herself beside Helen, she asked in a quiet, almost fearful voice,

"Tell me, Helen, is it really true that art students draw models without clothes?"

"Oh yes, every day. It's the best practice."

"Fancy that! And are there..." Ariane hesitated, "I mean are boys and girls together in the same room when they're drawing a naked person?"

"Yes, of course."

"Ooh, I don't think I'd like that. That must be *so embarrassing*. I can hardly believe it."

Ariane looked shocked and Helen was puzzled. Nothing could have been more innocent than the dedicated atmosphere of the life class. Ariane's prudish horror was surprising after all those stories of her early sexual romps. Had those stories been untrue? Had she reformed? Someone said she was unofficially engaged to a dentist and nothing could be more respectable, though Helen doubted if she herself would choose a husband who gazed into the wide open mouths of fearful patients all day. What a terrible strain that must be.

◊

In June, Helen was transferred for two days each week to St Agnes's, St Cuthbert's annexe. This small Lambhill school over-looked a large area of rough grassland and was close to the Forth and Clyde canal. The weather was spectacularly beautiful that month and at lunchtime she often walked to the canal and sat watching the determined, plodding horses pulling the barges, while she ate her sandwiches. It seemed another world. The area was familiar, for her mother's old art school friend Elsie had stayed in nearby Hillend Road. Helen had happy memories of entertaining Elsie's two little girls with plays enacted in their doll's house. Though younger than Helen, Maureen and Eleanor were allowed a great deal of freedom and had taken her to explore a dank mysterious tunnel called the Hallowe'en Pen, where Helen had felt very nervous. Annie was indignant when she learned of the children wandering in such a lonely place.

That family was now in London and they had practically lost touch.

One class had particularly nice girls in it, spruce, smart and diligent workers and Helen took them outside to draw. As they walked along in the sun, a pretty girl Anna, started to sing, "I love to go a-wandering". When the others joined in, their young voices drifted over the hillside in the fresh air and made teachng seem idyllic and delightful. St Agnes's seemed a small haven.

At the end of term Helen took the fifteen girls in her register class to Helensburgh for the day. Several came from impoverished backgrounds and not one had ever visited the resort. Surrounded by the excited, chattering noisy crowd on the bus, Helen wondered if she had bitten off more than she could chew. However the girls were unusually sedate as they walked along the front, any wilder spirits being quickly reprimanded by the others. After a swim in the open air pool, they demolished the picnic which Helen had brought. On the return journey everyone was quiet and exhausted and when they parted, Helen was very touched by the girls' gratitude.

Northern Adventure

As Helen was not yet qualified to drive and Mungo would spend the Fair fortnight with his mother in Inverness, he offered to take Annie and Helen to visit the two old aunts. He would drive them there, then have the use of the car until it was time to collect them and return to Glasgow. Ardgay, their postal address, was about eighty miles north of Inverness and Mrs Macaulay had kindly suggested they stay a night with her. Annie was delighted, Helen thought the project fraught with practical difficulties. The height of the bed and the space around it were so important in her dealings with Annie.

"What if I can't manage the wheelchair in their house? We would have to turn round and come right back home again."

"Och well, that wouldn't be the end of the world, would it. Don't worry, it will be an adventure." Annie was optimistic.

Helen considered her life quite adventurous enough. Her knowledge of Scotland was confined to the East Neuk and Ardgay seemed very far away.

They had a few days to wait until Mungo was free to start.

"I've been thinking, Helen."

"Uh huh! And what idea have you come up with this time, dear Mama?"

"Well... I've got my dividend and an unexpected bonus from Distillers' Company. I think I'll get one of these new Singer embroidery machines. They sound miraculous."

"That's a good idea, that old one must be nearly worn out by this time. You'll need to eat a double dose of yeast tablets and keep the profits up."

Annie believed yeast tablets kept her healthy, always buying the brand in which she held shares.

Matthew was very fond of them too and would be given half a tablet as a treat. One evening, Helen was summoned to the sitting room by a loud shout, conveying 'emergency'. As she was opening the bottle, Annie had fumbled and many tablets had spilled on the carpet. Matthew had immediately pounced on the feast.

"Thank heavens you were in the house! Or he might have eaten them all and exploded."

The swing needle embroidery machine was delivered and Annie and Helen enjoyed experimenting with the different stitches until Mungo's holiday started.

◊

The wheeled bucket seat had been fetched from Pittenweem and Matthew was placed in a cattery for a fortnight.

They left early in the morning, eating a picnic breakfast at Loch Lomond before eight o'clock. How lovely the still water and the purple mountains were, so different from the agricultural flatness of Fife.

Glencoe was a revelation, brooding and threatening even on a sunny day. What must it be like in winter?

The journey was long, but Helen was thrilled with each new scene and when it was her turn to drive, *almost* enjoyed skimming along the empty curving roads.

Mrs Macaulay, an old-fashioned Highland lady with her hair scraped into a little bun, seemed old to be Mungo's mother. Mary, five years older than her brother, was a nursing sister in the local hospital. She had travelled abroad more than anyone Helen knew. They were both very welcoming.

That balmy summer evening, Mungo and Helen strolled through the park. A band was playing beside a dancing platform and fairy lights were strung amongst the trees. Helen experienced the pleasure of being in an unknown environment and felt very close to Mungo.

Next day they travelled to Ardgay and after asking for directions several times, they followed the single track road leading to Strathcarron, finally locating the remote house which was perched on a hillside, a few hundred yards from the road. Annie, fearing it might be a tiny but and ben, was relieved to find it a two storey stone-built Highland house with three dormer windows.

"It's the rocky road to Dublin! I wonder how we're going to manage?" Annie mused as they bumped up the narrow, obviously unused track which led to the house.

Helen tried not to think of what might await them.

"Don't worry, Maw Corning. If it's impossible, we can always go back to Inverness. Anyway, I'm bringing my mother and Mary up on Sunday to see how you're getting on."

Annie thought what a kind, reliable young man Mungo was.

Suddenly, as if from nowhere, a thin old lady appeared in front of them. She was dressed in shapeless black garments and her long white hair flew out incongruously from a bright blue American baseball cap. Without a smile, she beckoned, indicating they should follow her, as she slowly climbed the last steep incline to the house. Mungo's driving skills were tested to the limit as he stayed carefully behind her over the rough ground. At the door of the house, another ancient lady, also with white witchlocks, stood smiling and nodding, with a crowd of cats clustering around her feet.

◊

After the tearful greetings, Helen was relieved to find the bed the right height and the house spacious enough to maneuvre the chair. They would 'manage' and Mungo could return to Inverness.

Bella, the younger and more dominant sister, was rather lame and kept to the house mostly. Cooking and feeding the chickens were her domain. In her youth she had lived in various parts of the world and with her third husband had managed various prestigious golf clubs. The meals she now cooked on the kitchen range were delicious and beautifully presented with wonderful scones and cakes baked in a battered tin biscuit box beside the fire. Like her niece in Pittenweem, Bella grumbled continuously, though with less real rancour than Mary. It was her method of conversing. Her favourite complaint concerned the 'terrible heavy traffic nowadays.'

Aunt Kate, of the baseball cap, (a present in a parcel from America) was eighty and the more active sister. She kept an impressive vegetable garden and a herd of five goats. The queen of the herd was a snow white nanny called Lily, whose tiny waving beard in no way detracted from her femininity. She received a daily tribute of two digestive biscuits while her silken coat was brushed. Lily would take her subjects foraging over the hillside, preferring the bark of young trees. When the nibbled trees eventually succumbed and fell over, Kate would drag them home for winter fuel. The plentiful goat's milk was made into cheese and butter, with the excess fed to the hens. Here was the secret of that unique creamy flavour which eggs and chickens from the north had always possessed.

A demanding pet lamb, now grown to strong adulthood, was ready to butt her way into the house if not placated by ginger snaps. She appeared to be the least useful member of the community but perhaps a sinister future awaited her.

Helen was charmed by the colony of seven cats, two of which were still kittens. The cats caught rabbits and brought them home for Bella to skin. Everyone seemed to have a busy life and Helen quickly assumed the duties of carrying water and sawing wood. She was particularly pleased when Kate commented,

"My goodness, you're awful strong for a city girl!"

But Helen knew there were a lot of things she could *never* do in that primitive life, such as skinning rabbits, or thrawing the necks of those chickens whose turn it was to provide dinner.

She took particular pleasure in collecting eggs. The first time she picked up a newly laid egg, still warm from the hen, seemed magical. She would have liked to learn to milk the goats, but Kate said they were unpredictable creatures. One day in the goat barn, a small black goat, in a burst of unexpected energy, injured Kate's hand with its horn.

"There now, you see what I mean, Helen. I think she's born of the deevil, that one!"

Kate's hand was bleeding freely and Helen offered to fetch the TCP.

"No, no, my dearie, don't bother, I'll use this."

To Helen's astonishment and horror, Kate reached up into the rafters of the ancient hut and brought down a handful of filthy cobwebs, then applied this to the deep cut.

Reared to worship cleanliness and antiseptic ointments, Helen felt slightly faint at this treatment of an open wound. Her face must have told the story.

"Don't you worry, now! Cobwebs are the very best thing and it will be healing in no time at all. You just wait and see."

Because of the many animals in the house and the fact that, for Bella, cookery was obviously more of a priority than house maintenance, Helen had been applyng TCP liberally to a small graze on Annie's leg and she shuddered at the idea of cobwebs.

The weather was incredibly hot and the garden and house baked each day in strong sunshine. Annie knitted happily in the doorway,

"It's very interesting sitting here and I couldn't sit outside in that heat anyway. One of the cats has just slipped past me carrying a rabbit almost as big as herself. And I watch the daft sheep forever losing and finding their lambs and that 'terrible traffic' that Bella complains about. I counted exactly eleven vehicles passing yesterday."

Nevertheless, the little dog Trixy now spent her life in the attic, earning her bread by barking at the approach of strangers, for, incredible as it seemed, she had recently lost a leg to one of those few passing cars. No doubt considering it an enemy, she had chased it. Helen took her walking on the hillside each evening, but Trixy longed to return to the road, perhaps to seek revenge.

One morning, Helen was sitting on the steps at Annie's feet, eating breakfast, when she felt a slight tug at her slice of bread and butter. A bold hen had helped herself to a sharp triangular bite.

What a terribly different, and fascinating life it was!

At night, white mist poured into the valley, filling it up, almost to the doorstep of the house, with a milky lake that blotted out burn, trees and fences. The landscape was transformed until nine the next morning, when the hot sun burned off the mist and restored the valley. Throughout the night, the muffled calls of sheep and their lost lambs could be heard. Then would come a short silence as though all were reunited, but quite soon the plaintive calls of half a dozen lambs echoed back and forth. Even the night noises had a charm for Helen.

In teaching, Helen had been introduced to the deprived side of Glasgow life. Here was another different way of living. The house was solid and in the summer it was possible to live there in comfort, even a degree of luxury. But with no gas, electricity or running water, what was it like in the winter?

"Our next door neighbout, Miss Clark, is coming to visit us tomorrow when your friends are here from Inverness. We'll have a nice afternoon tea for them." Bella was beating a cake as she spoke.

"Yes, she's a poor old soul, although she was a teacher once and she must have a pension, which is more than we do. But she's very careful. I always give her a potato or two and a wee drop milk and cheese. She doesn't need the eggs, for she has beautiful hens of her own. Oh, such a handsome big cockerel, you've never seen the like, but he's awful fierce and when she feeds the hens, she has to take her broomstick with her, He's better by far than any guard dog. But her house is very poor, it's still the stone walls inside and an earth floor. *And d'you know what she told me?* She gets a wee piece of hough every Monday from the van and cooks it very, very slowly and then she just eats a little bit each day. *And it lasts her all week!* Have you ever heard the like? And her with a pension!'

Such meanness with regard to food seemed criminal to Bella.

When Mungo and his mother and sister arrived, incredible circumstances came to light. The ancient, toothless Miss Clark had taught in Crianlarich primary school before the first World War and *Mrs Macaulay had been one of her pupils.* Before training as a teacher, the old lady had been in service in a Partickhill mansion. This was at a time prior to the building of the Hyndland tenements, though she vaguely remembered Hyndland Park.

Helen tried, but found it impossible to visualise that familiar area without the many streets of tall red sandstone tenements.

When Mungo returned the following week, the final leave-taking was very sad. The old aunties would have filled the car with farewell gifts of food and furniture. Eggs, vegetables, cheese, a horn spoon, two painted plates and a large engraved glass jug were brought to the car and stowed away. When a stuffed golden eagle (slightly moth-damaged) in a glass dome was brought down from the attic, Helen had to be firm. It was certainly a lovely thing but there was just no room for it in the car and what a shame if it were broken!

As they drove through Bonar Bridge, even the small rural town with its shops, railway station and pedestrians appeared busy and urban after the remote house in the strath. Annie marvelled,

"I feel I've been living in a dream for the last ten days."

"Or we've been acting in a film."

Mungo suggested that the house and the aunts with all their animals might now have disappeared, just like a fairy village.

Annie sat smiling for a few minutes, then her face clouded,

"It's all very well in beautiful summer weather, but it must be pretty hellish in the depths of winter. How do they manage? Having to bring in all the water and fuel? And the animals have to be looked after. What a hard life for two old buddies. I suppose they've been doing it for years, but it must be very tough. Yet Kate never grumbles."

Annie thought of her mother in Pittenweem and her many complaints. The house would soon have electricity installed and Mary would have an old age of comfort, even luxury, compared to her relatives.

"Well, I'm terribly grateful to you both for getting me up here to see these old souls. Strange to think that's the first time I've ever met them. Thank you both very much. It's been such an adventure and I thought my days for adventuring were over."

"Those days might be *just beginning*, Maw Corning!"

◊

In Pittenweem, Helen's car was the only one parked in the High Street and she made sure that she drove each day. It had been humiliating to fail and she was determined to pass the next time. Officially, she was required to have an experienced driver sitting beside her, but as no one was available and as there was practically no traffic in the East Neuk, she risked it. The layout of the small town helped her become very practised in three point turns. Sometimes Drew sat beside her, impersonating an experienced driver. The previous year she and Drew had often walked to the Anstruther funfair and amused themselves chasing and battering each other on the dodgem cars. Now she told him sadly,

"It's a pity, but when you learn to drive, you lose all pleasure in dodgems. Real driving knocks all that madness out of you, so enjoy it while you can. I'll never drive a dodgem again."

They dared to venture to St Andrews one day, forgetting that the Lammas Fair was in progress. In South Street, Helen was shocked to come face to face with a traffic policeman, an unknown phenomenon in Fife, and quickly left St Andrews by the shortest route.

Back in Glasgow, Helen took the test in her own car and passed.

It seemed a good omen when the examiner asked for a three point turn in Arlington Street, just outside the baths. Knowing the capabilities of her car, she told the examiner,

"I'm afraid it won't turn right round with three points in this narrow street."

"You just take as many as you want." He smiled kindly and she knew she had passed.

Operas and Ski-pants

Miss Hopkins had exciting news after the holidays. She had been asked to provide the dancing girls for the Glasgow Grand Opera Club's production of *Aida*. Although this was an amateur club, the performance would take place in the Theatre Royal, with Alexander Gibson conducting the Scottish Orchestra and the leading roles sung by professionals.

Annie was thrilled.

"On the stage of the Royal! How marvellous. I'll need to see that!"

"Of course you'll see it. It's on for a week."

"Do you think you'll have a solo?"

"Perhaps. I know I have a duet with Kate. We've started learning it."

"Now who is Kate? I don't think I've met her."

"She's an awfully nice girl who's just started coming to class recently. She's very slender and elegant, a sort of fairy-like creature. Wish I was like that. She was a pupil at the posh Helensburgh school where Miss Hopkins teaches. Kate's done all the work up to Intermediate standard, but her mother doesn't want her to do exams. And because she spends so much time on the train, she knits a lot. *She's knitted herself a pair of practice tights!* Isn't that amazing, but boring I'd think. I hope Miss Hopkins lets me choreograph some of the dances, but she hasn't said anything so far. The duet's *not* very exciting so far and we've to do an arabesque allongé. It's so easy to wobble in one of those, especially when you're nervous. I would never have used it myself. But I'm looking forward to it all *so much*!"

Kate and Helen became very good friends at the many rehearsals that Autumn.

One evening Kate's boyfriend came to collect her. A newly-fledged teacher, he was full of indignation. His headmaster, Mr Starker, insisted all male staff should wear a hat to school.

"I think it's ridiculous! I've never worn a hat in my life and I don't intend to start now."

Helen cheered him up by pointing out that with a name like that, the headmaster should keep quiet about how other folk dress.

Miss Hopkins did not ask Helen to provide any of the choreography. It was a disappointment and Helen also thought it a mistake. However, the experience was very special and she enjoyed her week at the Royal thoroughly. It was a taste of the 'might have been' but the exposure to greasepaint and footlights generated no yearnings for a stage career, for the repetition did not appeal to her.

The music was piped into each dressing room and *Aida* found a special place in Helen's heart, though piano and orchestral works would always appeal to her more than the human voice.

Annie was brought to the Theatre Royal on the Thursday evening and was happy to sit in the luxurious stalls and watch her daughter dance, though not very impressed with the rest of the performance. But then, she never was keen on the human voice.

What with teaching and the nightly performance, it was a demanding week, but the nerve-racking, *arabesque* was accomplished each night without a wobble and Helen was given her solo. Those few magical minutes, dancing alone on the stage of the Theatre Royal, with Gibson conducting the wonderful Scottish Orchestra were an important highlight of Helen's life.

◊

The flat at 351 lay empty and grew dusty. Mary was worried and Annie constantly wondered how she might help her. There seemed to be no hope of selling it.

Helen visited the flat regularly to check that it was weatherproof, and the quiet and loneliness of the empty rooms still made her nervous. It was always a relief to close the front door behind her and lock up with the massive key.

One weekend, she organised three of her pupils to come and clean the flat and the bustle and happy chatter of the girls transformed the atmosphere. When they had gone, she danced in the studio. What a lovely place it was, but what were they going to do with it?

Annie had been wondering if she and Helen might take it over and rent it out. It would take the burden off her mother's shoulders and at the same time make an income for themselves, eventually. She had four hundred pounds to make a down payment, but would Mary let them pay the rest up in monthly instalments? Annie had not yet discussed the idea with Helen. She would think it over more carefully before she did, as Helen would be faced with the practical responsibilities.

Annie was sad to let the beautiful flat deteriorate and eventually pass into other hands for a song.

◊

Bruce stood watching Annie as she sewed and wrestled with yards of ocelot-printed fur fabric, a coat for Helen.

"How d'ye like your fancy new machine, Annie?"

"It's wonderful, Bruce, so big and strong for this heavy stuff and the embroidery stitches are very pretty. I've had great fun with it."

"Aye, Singer's is a marvellous firm. Don't know what I'd have done without them during the war, manys the time I was desperate for wood and they could nearly always help me out. Don't know where they got it, but they always managed. Cost me, right enough. What about yerself? D'ye make many shekels with yer dress-making? Seems like a lot of work."

"Oh, I can't say I make much, but I make *something* and I enjoy doing it. I meet lots of people and we certainly *save* plenty, what with clothes getting dearer all the time. Helen hardly buys any-thing these days and I make things for myself and my mother and Mrs Connell, too. Mrs Connell hardly takes any wages these days, for she's paying off a suit and a cocktail dress. And I made dresses for three of Helen's friends last year."

"Aye, well as long as it pays you, that's fine. I can see you're busy. I was wondering if you were too busy to do a wee job for me?"

Annie stopped sewing in astonishment.

"For you, Bruce! What were you needing? I'm not tackling plus fours, mind you!"

Formerly, these had been Bruce's favourite garments and he had recently commented that they were no longer sold in the shops, but he laughed,

"No, no, my old ones'll last me another twenty years. No, it's wee Christian Turnbull. She's wanting a pair of these tight fitting trousers that the film stars are all wearing. I think Helen has tar-tan ones, does she not? Christian wants black velvet ones to go to a party and she's asked me to get them! Good God! Can ye see me trailing round town asking for ladies' black velvet trousers? I doubt they'd make them in her size anyway, she's such a wee skelf. Could ye help me out here, Annie, d'ye think? You could make them for me and save me one big bloody headache. Would you do that? I'd pay the going rate."

Annie was quite touched that Bruce should ask her help and though she wondered why he had been given such an errand, she replied,

"Och, I'd be pleased to do that for you and no payment required. Helen will give you a list of the measurements needed."

Just then, Helen came into the room wearing her tartan trews. At Art School, where most girls had worn trousers, she had preferred a skirt. Now that the elfin Audrey Hepburn had popularised these more fitted garments, Helen had discovered their warmth and convenience, as well as their allure.

"Aye, those are the ones I was meaning. Very smart. Just the ticket. Could you get them ready for her birthday at the end of Novenber?"

"Nae boather at a'! It'll be a pleasure. And I think you call them ski-pants."

No doubt there was still a bond between Annie and Bruce, for he had been her husband and was the father of her child. They were very different personalities and often irritated each other unbearably. Bruce no doubt resented the financial burden they still posed and Annie resented her dependence on him and sometimes dreamed of making enough money to tell him to go to hell. And yet, there was still affection and a feeling of mutual duty. Bruce had continuously given financial support, perhaps not generous but always dependable. He also fulfilled occasional extra commitments, such as the visit to *Aida*, without too much fuss. Much of his life was a mystery to Annie. Was there another woman? He seemed calmer and his shirts were well laundered but perhaps that was due to Mrs Wilson, the new housekeeper now employed by the three men in Doune Terrace. Nor did Bruce have much interest in the lives of Annie and Helen. The teaching of art or dance seemed a strange inexplicable business to him, though he was pleased his daughter earned a salary and often mentioned that she was a teacher to his friends at the club.

Annie felt a sympathy for Bruce that Helen never would.

Caution

Though Mungo had now been working for nearly a year, their lives had not changed. He came for dinner each week and they often walked in the evening, occasionally visiting a cinema. They never quarrelled or even argued seriously. Helen tried to analyse her dissatisfaction with Mungo. He earned a salary, but still dressed in his old patched tweed jacket and lived very carefully. She had no desire for luxurious gifts or expensive outings but dining out occasionally seemed a desirable treat. She had very little experience of restaurants and after all those Saturday dinners, surely Mungo should want to return the favour. To make the suggestion herself would spoil the delight of the event.

Bruce had taken her to the prestigious 101 restaurant when she was a schoolgirl. That had been at her own timid request and it would have been nicer if the invitation had come from him. Helen had not learned, as some daughters do, to wheedle a favour from her father and would always shy away from any suggestion of dependence.

Only Douglas had ever invited her out to eat, and both evenings had been glamorous and exciting.

Was Mungo mean?

He was cautious, certainly cautious with money, but he had been penurious for years and Helen could sympathise. She accepted a world where personal possessions were few and precious. But it was not only money, caution was a large part of his character. He was not generous with his praise, or opinions or emotions. He did not share his thoughts or ideas. Helen knew he was fond of poetry, but she did not know which poets he liked, or why. Helen would have liked to enjoy the same confiding relationship with Mungo as she had shared with her mother, but his reserved Highland personality precluded that and it was sometimes difficult for Helen to understand him. Perhaps, if their long relationship had been less chaste, they might have found a different basis of understanding, but chastity was the rule and Mungo had accepted that rule, where another less cautious man might not.

Annie was fond of Mungo, but she could see his faults. He had been very helpful and kind their journey north, but it was obvious that Helen was often disgruntled with him.

If he were to marry her daughter, Annie would almost certainly be accepted as part of the family, but her daughter must not marry for those reasons.

"You should tell him you'd like to go out a bit more, perhaps to the theatre or a restaurant." Annie advised.

"It wouldn't be the same if I asked him. It was fine when he had no money, I didn't mind just walking around, but I think he should want to spend a bit, now that he has it. I'm not wanting presents or anything, just a little bit more... I don't know what... excitement I suppose, luxury. Verve. There's not much verve in our lives."

No doubt Annie dropped a hint, for soon after this conversation, Mungo bought himself a new suit and organised an evening at the theatre, preceded by a meal in Ferrarri's restaurant.

It was a pleasant evening, but perhaps it came too late. Helen could not look ahead to a lifetime with Mungo. Without quite knowing the reasons herself, she had always tried to make this plain to him. Now she began to discover and understand some of her unwillingness. She hated the idea of hurting him and she knew that she had hurt him by allowing the friendship to continue. She had been stupidly weak in not breaking things off long ago. She should have been more determined. She had been cruel but not cruel enough. The break had to be made, She could never talk to him of that terrible caution, though surely his caution was only part of the story.

By the end of November, Helen had finally broken off with Mungo. They would meet again several times but never as a couple. Each, in their own way, was desolate. Annie was also sad. Mungo had been a familiar part of her life for years and she had been almost sure they would marry eventually. Of course the decision must be Helen's, but she seemed terribly depressed.

A Hard Winter

Mary came to Glasgow for Christmas. Helen was dreading the disruption, but the first week was enjoyable. Mary had great charm when she chose. The weather had been severe throughout December and Mary appreciated the comfort of the warmer house and complimented Helen on her cooking. For the first few days she told amusing stories and spoke interestingly with hardly a grumble.

The Queen mother had visited Pittenweem.

"She's related to some local bigwig and I suppose she was staying with him. As you can imagine, there was nothing else talked about for weeks beforehand and afterwards as well. Where she went and what she wore and what she said. When I knew she was actually in the town, I just put on my coat and hat and took your camera along the High Street. I think I got quite a few nice pictures, though I says it myself. No one else seemed to be photographing her."

"My mother, the roving reporter!" Annie quipped, delighted to find Mary in such good fettle. "I hope you've brought the photos with you."

"Yes, I've got them, I'll show you later. Of course not everyone was satisfied that day! Old Eck Reekie, he's evidently the oldest inhabitant, was wheeled out to meet the Queen. Then Jean Hughes pushed her way through the crowd and plonked herself down in the seat beside him, which was meant for his daughter. She's nearly eighty and a bit slow. Anyway, no doubt Eck is deaf and doddery for every time the Queen mother asked him a question, Jean leaned forward and answered it for him, before he got a chance to say a word. Then when the Queen mother was about to move away, Jean caught hold of her sleeve and said,

"Haste ye back, yer Majesty, now haste ye back!"

"My goodness, that was *lese majesty* and I expect the Reekies must have been furious."

"Absolutely raging! They'll never forget the insult. Of course Jean's always been mad keen on royalty and she grabbed her chance when she could."

They all laughed.

"I must say those are wonderful slippers you're wearing, Maw."

"D'ye like them? I wondered if you'd notice them.' Mary stretched her foot forward, pointing her toe.

"Could hardly ignore such exotic footwear, what with the velvet and gold lamé and fur trimming. Where on earth did you get them?"

"I made them! Don't you recognise the fabrics?"

"I believe I do! Have you been cutting up some of your old finery?"

"Yes that old cloak was just lying there in the drawer and the moths were gorging themselves on it. But they are rather nice aren't they?" She again extended her foot.

"They are *exquisite* and beautifully made, too. What a great idea. I'm very impressed."

Mary then explained exactly how she had made them and how she intended making more.

"I found some tweed scraps and I thought I might try a more masculine pair next time. Would Mungo wear slippers, d'ye think?"

It was explained that Mungo was no longer on the scene.

"Oh, that's a shame. He seemed a decent enough fellow. I quite liked him."

But Mary had seldom said a kind word about Mungo. Helen had no wish to renew their relationship, but there was still sadness and guilt about how she had treated him.

◊

Bruce kept the old car at his works for the three winter months. Starting it was a gamble in the cold, and icy roads were tricky for a new driver. Helen travelled by bus to Charing Cross, then took a tram to Keppochhill where she climbed the long flight of steps before trudging up to St Cuthberts.

The weather worsened and news reports told of food supplies airlifted to those living in remote areas and imprisoned by deep snow.

How were the aunts surviving? Annie and Helen discussed their plight. Kate bore all the responsibility and how could a woman of eighty continue the daily struggle through deep snow to tend animals and collect fuel? Annie wrote several letters, but there was no reply.

"I worry more now that we know how primitive their life is." Annie said sadly, " It was quite a paradise in that glorious summer weather, but what can it be like just now for those poor old souls? How do they keep warm enough?"

"Yes, our lives are hardly affected here, just slush to wade through some days. What could we do?"

Annie had sent off gloves, two shawls and some tea, but they received no reply.

Then Bruce arrived with shocking news. Christian Turnbull had died. She was only twenty.

"Aye, the bad weather had a hand in the tragedy, I'm afraid, but of course it was her own personality that was the problem. She's been spoilt all her life, very very spoilt." Bruce shook his head sadly. "It's a terrible thing, terrible. They'll never get over it, never."

Bruce sat with his head bowed over his clasped hands for several minutes. Helen had never seen him silent for so long. She tried to picture the girl. She had not seen her since that visit to the Kelvin Hall when Christian was still a child but it was only weeks since Helen had put the final stitches in the black velvet pants.

At last Annie quietly asked how it had happened.

"Well, she had been to the dentist and you know she always made a terrible fuss there, screaming and crying. I took her there once, but never again. Their dentist's an old man and evidently he got upset too, couldn't take it any more and just put in a temporary filling. She was to go back soon again but she kicked up a fuss and the roads were terrible, anyway they didn't go. A couple of weeks after that, Christian was in terrible pain, or said she was. That's the problem too, you see, you could never tell whether she was as bad as she said she was. The dentist was in Helensburgh and by this time they were pretty well snowed in at Rosneath. They asked the advice of a young woman next door, a medical student and she gave the kid a painkiller and said it would be all right to wait until the next day. But Christian died in the night. They think it was septicaemia. She was never a strong lass. The Turnbulls will never get over it."

Bruce left soon after that.

"That's hit Bruce hard. He's spent a lot of time with the poor girl over the years. Poor Christian, she had little enjoyment of her velvet trousers"

It was the first time that Helen had encountered the death of a young person. She had hardly known Christian but had heard of her all her life. How could such a final and dreadful end happen so very simply?

◊

No matter how bad the weather was, Mrs Connell arrived each morning at nine-thirty. She was always cheerful and often had some tale of interest to tell Annie. On the day that a blizzard was gusting throughout the city, she popped her head round the bedroom door as usual,

"Are you needing any messages, Mrs Corning? Will I take my boots off?"

"No. Come away in and make yourself a cup of tea. What a day, but you're here on the dot as usual. It must have been a struggle up from Partick. You're a wonderful wee woman. D'ye know that it's ten years since you first came to work for me?"

"Oh, Mrs Corning, I can hardly believe that. I just feel I've always known you!"

"Well I feel the same and here's a wee present to mark those ten years of loyal friendship."

Annie gave her an envelope with twenty pounds in it. Mrs Connel was speechless and wept a little.

Later that night Annie told Helen,

"If I had given her a thousand pounds, she couldn't have been more astonished or grateful. I wish I could have given her more."

◊

When Helen returned from school at four thirty, she first attended to her mother, next stoked the fire, washed her face, made coffee, then settled comfortably to read a book for an hour or so and thus recover from her day's teaching. Annie was quite content to read quietly too. Helen had known and enjoyed the space and calmness of this large square room ever since her childhood. She loved the familiarity of the furniture, the tall carved mantelpiece, the tree in the garden and the trams which regularly halted outside, filling the three windows with bright green, orange and yellow for a few moments, before trundling on up the hill. To return and sit quietly calmed her jangling nerves.

When Mary came to stay, this gentle ritual was dispelled. Mary was ready to help prepare dinner as soon as Helen's key was in the lock. Not necessarily hungry, Mary obviously felt the day long or perhaps thought it time for Helen to resume her household duties. After the meal there was no quiet time for reading. Silence was something Mary abhorred, unless it was the palpable silence she employed to show her displeasure, which was more unbearable than her determined conversation. Helen longed hopelessly for a sustaining hour of quiet reading. Mary's benevolence had gradually faded as the weeks of bad weather kept her indoors. She had a genius for finding items in the newspaper to anger her.

"I see the princess has put an end to that affair with Townsend. What a carry-on it's been."

"She's very young, Maw, and he's very dashing. Propinquity, you know. You'd think the powers-that-be would have taken more care of her."

"Of course I knew all along it would come to nothing. That wee besom would never give up her royal privileges."

Often Mary's conversation dwelt on worries about the house in Pittenweem. In her absence, she imagined catastrophes such as the tiles ripped from the roof by high winds, the studio blown out to sea, the pipes bursting and flooding out the front door.

"But you would have the water turned off when you left, didn't you?' Annie asked and had her nose snapped off.

"Of course I did. I'm not a bloody fool. But you can never tell what might happen when a house is empty."

Mary was also deeply concerned about 351.

At last, with some hesitation, Annie made her suggestion of buying the flat on the instalment system and renting it out in three apartments. She had already discussed the idea with Helen, who was less than enthusiastic but agreed something must be done about the neglected premises.

Mary was surprisingly agreeable, only too pleased to find some small part of its value and yet keep the flat in the family. The down payment would pay for installing electricity in the Pittenweem house.

Before Mary returned to Fife in April, Helen had become a property owner.

◊

Another important purchase was made at this time. A new folding wheelchair was bought for Annie. How compact and modern the tubular steel construction looked. It was simple to fold and light to lift into the boot of the car, and meant that they would be more independent on their travels. Annie said it was just as comfortable as the old ungainly chair. Helen intended to return to Ardgay and visit the aunts again in the summer, but in May the sad news came that Aunt Kate had died during the terrible winter.

◊

Helen had been very quiet since the break with Mungo. Although she was full of energy and seemed to enjoy many aspects of her teaching, she had little social life. Margery dropped in regularly for cards and had once or twice suggested going to an art school dance, but Helen always found some excuse. Annie encouraged her to go out.

"You should go and enjoy an evening's dancing. You can put me to bed early and leave me the wireless. I'll be perfectly happy. On you go, you never know who you might meet."

Annie now had a neat little portable radio to carry around the house.

Eventually Helen did go dancing with Margery and she did meet someone. Mario Picozzi was a lawyer, presumably successful, for he hailed a taxi to take them back to Hyndland! A taxi! An outrageous expense when buses and tramcars passed her door.

Mario was obviously of Italian extraction, though not beautiful as young Italian men can be. His face was dark and commanding and he was of middle height. His expensively cut suit and overcoat disguised a slight portliness, unusual in a man of twenty six. He had presence.

This self-assured young man practically invited himself in to meet her mother. Annie had not gone to bed that night and in no time at all, Mario was discussing religion with her. Was the family Protestant or Catholic? Annie admitted they were not anything very much, probably Protestant was nearest the mark.

"You must understand, Mrs Corning, that my mother is a very devout Catholic. Very, very devout. Do you know, I believe she would rather see me marry a prostitute than a Protestant."

After a slight pause, Annie politely asked

"That would be a Catholic prostitute, I take it."

"Naturally, yes, a Catholic prostitute."

Helen thought this was certainly the strangest fellow she had brought home yet.

Then Mario asked Annie if she was fond of music, opera in particular, for he was very fond of opera himself.

"Oh yes, I'm devoted to opera." Annie was enjoying herself, "The last opera I attended was *Aida*. It was really excellent. I did enjoy it and the dancing was particularly good, I thought."

Helen left the room to make coffee.

When she returned, Mario was describing his secret dream of meeting a girl with a wonderful voice, who would sing love songs to him.

That certainly counted Helen out.

Next, Mario explained that although his professional work was successful, he had thought it expedient have some other income and had recently invested in a fish and chip van. One of his many cousins was driving this through the outer suburbs and making a very good thing of it.

At last, he phoned for a taxi and left, promising to phone Helen very soon.

"Well, *where* did you find *him*?"

"Do you think he could have anything to do with the Mafia?"

"He certainly looks as though he might, but there's an innocence about him, too. You'd think he was seriously considering you for marriage."

"Heaven forbid. What an idea! It's time you were in your bed."

The following week, Mario took Helen to the Kings Theatre to see *Faust*. Their seats were in the grand circle and to Helen's embarrassment they arrived late and left early.

"I know the ending so well, let's leave now and have a bite of supper."

A taxi whisked them to Ferrari's where he was welcomed deferentially, obviously a regular customer. How very different from the meal with Mungo. Mario ordered *sole a la bonne femme* for both and a bottle of sparkling wine. The fish was delicious, though Helen might have liked to choose for herself. A taxi took them to Hyndland but Mario said that he would not come in, as he had important business to attend to.

"I'm glad I wore my leopardskin coat. Just right for a gangster's moll and that's what I felt like. Luxury all the way. He just chucks his money around like water. I suppose it was good fun, *as an experience,* but honestly... what d'ye make of him? I wonder what sort of important business he's doing at eleven o'clock at night? Sound suspicious."

"Could be sinister or maybe he's helping his cousin clean up the fish and chip van after a busy night? Are you going to see him again?"

"Yes, I'm going to paint his portrait. I'll never get another chance to paint a face like that. But I may not actually go out with him again."

◊

This year Helen was once more studying and teaching at Miss Hopkins's school. Inspired by Gene Kelly's joyous use of ballet in films and also by an old pantomime horse costume, she was preparing a short scene called the *'Milkman's Horse'*. The advanced class would perform it in the Athenaeum in June. Helen was pleased but somewhat surprised that Miss Hopkins seemed happy to give her carte blanche as far as choreography was concerned. Helen had no training in that art and had less dance training than the pupils she was directing. Miss Hopkins must have had great faith in her and never criticised or suggested any changes. After watching a piece for the first time she would always assure Helen that it was,

"Lovely as ever!"

Helen appreciated and certainly gained confidence from this unfailing approval.

Helen used music by Offenbach and Sullivan and tried to create movements best suited to the abilities of each dancer. As she experimented, she realised what a marvellous opportunity she had. All those years of transforming music into movement in her imagination could now be put into practice.

More Northern Adventures

On the second journey north, they left early in the morning, having previously arranged for the local policeman to help carry Annie out to the car.

Matthew was with Mary in Pittenweem.

They would drive all the way to Ardgay, with plenty of breaks to enjoy the scenery, and would arrive late in the long summer evening. Bella had arranged for a strong neighbour to help Annie into the house. They knew more of their destination this year, though without Kate the place would be changed.

In the boot was the folding wheelchair, a picnic and two undifferentiated thermos flasks, one with coffee, one with soup. After saying neevy-neevy nick-nack, they would drink which ever flask was chosen. It was Annie's idea and Helen liked this mad side of her mother. Most people in their fifties were very staid.

The house on the hill was sadly different. There was no vegetable patch and the goats and pet sheep had gone. The three-legged dog had died. Only a few chickens and two of the cats remained. Poor Bella was finding life hard, but was very unwilling to move into town, though everyone advised this before winter set in again.

"Now what would I do without my chickens? It would be no life at all, would it? Old Miss Clark along the way has been put in a home for old folk but I don't want that. I'm not even eighty yet. It could never be such a bad winter again, I'm sure. Yon was terrible but it'll never come again for years. You don't think I should give up the house do you, Annie?"

Annie was unwilling to upset her by agreeing too openly with the unacceptable advice, but a move to Bonar Bridge seemed inevitable.

"I'm sure you would meet some nice friends in the town, Bella. Surely it's a bit lonely for you here, all on your own. My mother has lots of visitors dropping in and it would be the same for you in Bonar Bridge. Would you not like that?"

As she spoke, she thought of the bitter comments and complaints that Mary made about her visitors. Bella would be just the same. There was not only a strong physical resemblance between the aunt and niece. Their personalities were similar, though Mary's less demanding life and financial comfort had allowed her an elegance and sophistication denied to her aunt.

The following week, when they drove, rather sadly, away from the house in the Strath, Bella was still determined to remain in her remote abode.

"I hate leaving Bella like that, Maw. She's not very happy, is she?"

"No, but I expect she'll have to move in the end and she's more forgetful than last year, too, isn't she? It must be rotten growing old when you're alone. I'm awfully glad we saw them both last year with the happy productive life they'd lived for years. I suppose it had to come to an end sometime."

They were silent until they reached Bonar Bridge.

Helen's intention had been to return to Glasgow, stay for a week, then go to Fife, taking Nancy Little with them.

Annie suddenly said,

"You know, we don't have to go straight home for any reason, Helen. Why don't we go a wee bit further north. Seeing we've come so far, we might as well go a bit further. Maybe just a few miles."

Helen was all in favour of the suggestion. They stopped after twenty miles and looked at their map. Who does not know the temptation of a map and unlimited time to spare?

"It doesn't look *all that far* up to John o' Groats." Helen suggested.

"Where would we sleep tonight, though."

"We'd surely find a bed and breakfast. Let's do it, let's have an adventure. We can always turn round if it seems too far."

"Well, I am in your hands and I'm game for anything."

Annie, knowing her daughter, thought it unlikely they would turn back before John o' Groats.

But perhaps that remote northern point had no accommodation. They decided to turn left at Latheron and head due north towards Thurso.

"We're quite near Castletown, where Kate and Bella and my mother's mother were born."

Helen was becoming anxious about where they would stay that night.

"Thurso is too towny. Let's go to Melvich. I like that name and we're sure to find a B&B in that area."

But the boarding house at Melvich was full and Helen was advised to try The Bungalow which turned out to be a workman's hostel. The warden's suggestion found them driving half a mile along a narrow causeway over marshland which stretched into the distance. Dusk was falling and the large house which was their destination was unlighted.

"It's a bit like one of those scary British films with the mists swirling, isn't it!"

Annie was only partly humorous when she added,

"D'you think that's a bog on either side of this wee road? I've always been terrified of sinking into the mud."

"Don't say that!" Helen laughed, but no doubt she was extremely careful as she manoeuvred the car back and forth in the small space in front of the apparently deserted house.

Eventually, about eleven o'clock, they found a warm welcome at the Bettyhill Post Office. Certainly, they must come in. There was a suitable ground floor room available and a ceilidh was just about to start. Perhaps the two ladies would like to join them for some entertainment?

Though it seemed a shame to miss such an opportunity, Helen was ready for bed. When she found unlimited hot water pouring from the tap she asked if she might take a bath. What luxury to find on this far northern coast!

The music and dancing continued throughout most of the night, but did not disturb the tired travellers.

Helen had a pleasant walk the following morning before the ten thirty breakfast served by a sleepy-eyed young woman.

Helen filled the thermos flasks before leaving Bettyhill and they drove along the spectacular North coast of Scotand, driving around the great and beautiful inlets of Tongue and Eriboll.

"D'ye think this is what a fiord is like, Maw?"

"I suspect they are even bigger and more terrifying."

In Durness, a sign pointed to Smoo Cave.

"I've always wanted to see a *real* cave." Helen sighed, "But we better keep going and find a place to sleep, That was hair-raising last night. P'raps we'll come here next year."

That night they slept in Kylesku, staying with the ferryman and his wife, a handsome young couple, with two beautiful little girls and a romantic history. The couple originally came from Glasgow. Twelve years ago, they had met on a day trip to Rothesay and married three weeks later. Almost immediately the husband left his Clydeside job and applied for the vacancy at Kylesku Ferry. They seemed terribly happy, though it sounded incredibly impulsive to Helen.

The third night of their travels found them in Tomintoul, again late at night. It was a beautiful clear night and the children were still playing in the streets at ten.

"This is one of the highest towns in Scotland. It's always first to be cut off when there's heavy snow." Annie commented.

"Can hardly believe that tonight. It's *so warm*."

"Amazingly mild and I can't be bothered finding a place that's suitable, why don't we just sleep in the car, tonight?"

"It would certainly be easier. I don't mind trying it, if you don't."

The smart little maid in Tomintoul Hotel brought a tray out to the car with a large silver pot of coffee (two cupfuls each and the thermos filled for the morning), china cups and saucers and many tea biscuits, all for a moderate three shillings, and a sixpenny tip.

They drove out of town, found a lay-by in which to park and slept soundly all night in the quiet countryside. When Helen wakened, she was charmed to find a cow gazing at her, the large damp nose almost pressed to the window. She had never been so close to a cow.

"Next time we go away, Maw, we'll take pillows and blankets with us because it won't always be as warm as this. But we never need to go into a bed and breakfast again! That 'll make it *so easy* and what a lot of money we'll save."

At the age of fifty-three, after eleven years in a wheelchair, Annie was offered the prospect of gypsying about the country. She smiled to herself and supposed she was game for anything.

◊

Helen suggested they go home via Pittenweem and see Willie's family who were visiting Mary.

By this time the old Vauxhall had accomplished many miles over rough and stony ways. Ascending and descending steep hills, pausing and backing in the dance of the single track roads (then predominant in the north) had taken its toll of the ancient vehicle. As Annie phrased it, the car was 'conking out, bit by bit'.

Fortunately Helen had received a fund of advice from didactic male friends. The loss of the starter was unimportant for Bruce had taught her always to park on a slope for a hill start. When the windscreen wipers went 'phut' she remembered Bill Callaghan had once mentioned that tram drivers, when their wipers failed, would spit on their window, then the rain would slide over the saliva and leave the glass clear. When the horn stopped making a sound, she recalled a friend's story. When the noise of the car horns became unendurable in the streets of Istanbul, they were banned. Now, drivers leaned out of their windows and beat violently on the door panel. Helen used this method to disperse a flock of sheep blocking the road.

In the Cairngorms, Helen became aware that her brakes were becoming less efficient. YS 1834 required Bruce's loving care. Nevertheless they continued to Pittenweem, arriving safely with something of the aura of explorers.

◊

The cousins were delighted to see each other for a few hours.

Eileen, nearly sixteen, was an exceptionally attractive young woman and Sheila had left her infant cantrips behind and was a very sweet little girl.

The holiday had been marred for the Mackays by Matthew's presence, for they had brought their budgie with them. Joey, reputedley a fluent conversationalist, was regarded as one of the family. Sadly, Joey had been terrified into silence by Matthew, who sat outside on the window sill all day, threatening the poor bird with bristling whiskers and glittering eyes.

Helen wondered why they had not taken the cage upstairs where that malign gaze could not follow.

In Glasgow three days later, after a quick turn around, Annie and Helen set off again for Fife, arranging to pick up Nancy Little in Byres Road. The rubbish collectors were emptying the bins and pleased to help carry Annie to the car for a small disbursement. Four rather puny little men picked her up in her chair and made a stately procession to the car. Annie muttered something about 'the hen's march to the midden'. As they drove past the end of Kingsborough Gardens Annie exclaimed with urgency,

"Helen, I smell burning and I think it's getting smoky in here."

Helen immediately stopped, leapt out, opened the back door of the car and dragged Annie unceremoniously into the gutter.

"I don't see any smoke myself," as she peered into the car, "but it smells funny. Better safe than sorry."

Helen looked ruefully at her mother kneelng there on the ground, then hailed the next passing driver, who, though somewhat unwilling, could hardly say no to helping. In moments they were back at the flat where the midden men were still working and happy to carry Annie in her chair back into the house.

Bruce was phoned and the car was taken off and returned to working order. Annie had been sitting on top of the battery and her continued bouncing over the rough northern roads had led to the trouble.

Poor Nancy was eventually rescued from Byres Road and they reached Pittenweem late that night.

◊

It was nearly eight months since the break with Mungo and although the cloud of sadness of the early weeks seemed to have dispersed, Helen had shown little interest in renewing a social life. Apart from Mario, and that friendship had finished when the portrait was painted, Helen hardly ever went out in the evenings. She had been busy, extraordinarily busy, with teaching, organising tenants for the flat at 351, helping with dress-making and creating the ballet for Miss Hopkins' summer show and of course their wonderful journey to the wilds of Scotland. Annie could still hardly believe that she had visited so many far-away places. She wondered if Helen regretted Mungo. She missed him herself, for they had shared a similar sense of humour, but Helen seemed to take life in her stride. Even the problems and setbacks of being a landlady, and there had been one problem tenant already, did not distress her unduly, although she had said with deep feeling.

"I'm learning plenty about life with this bloody renting business. How I hate writing cheques and paying bills and I never knew people could be so stupid or so difficult."

Annie wondered if she had been unfair to involve her daughter in such responsibilities for there was, as yet, no profit, but Helen would be the owner of a beautiful property by next year and Mary's problems had been solved. Perhaps Helen would enjoy a sociable summer.

Spy School?

Five miles along the coast from Pittenweem, in the old aerodrome at Crail, the Ministry of Defence had recently established the Joint Services School of Languages. Officially, this project taught Russian to men from all the services. The chosen men were university graduates, already fluent in one or two other languages. It seemed possible, in the climate of the Cold War, that these clever young men were being trained for *special purposes*. They appeared to be nice, ordinary, middle-class fellows but rumour described them as fledgling spies.

The JSSL boys were a welcome addition to the dances in Anstruther Town Hall. The conversation of these educated fellows was sophisticated and an occasional *spasibo* or *do svi daniya* added mystery.

And which skills of intrigue were they learning in the draughty aerodrome at Crail?

Helen had met Jerry at Easter and they had spoken on the phone several times. He had grown up in Turkey. He maintained he was English and his accent was perfect, but his looks had an attractive foreign quality and his manners and appearance were certainly more immaculate than those of the usual young Briton. His suit was sharply pressed, his crisp hair and moustache well-groomed and his shoes glittered with an unreal shine. A golden tie-pin, amusingly shaped like a safety pin, held his tie in perfect subjection.

He was ironic about their training in Crail. Classes were held in icy cold huts, text books were dog-eared and the tutors were an eccentric bunch. There was no reference to anything as exciting as espionage. He peeled his share of potatoes and enjoyed it. Jerry had previously been stationed in airforce bases in Yorkshire and Devon, where he had found the people suspicious and unfriendly. Since coming to Fife, he had experienced nothing but hospitality and generosity and thought the tradition of Scottish meanness a ridiculous myth and a calumny.

He admitted his tie-pin was an ordinary safety pin and his most precious possession was his bicycle.

Early in their friendship, Jerry decided to teach Helen the
elements of Turkish. He was sure she would be excellent at
learning languages. Russian would come later when he had
more command of it himself. He bought a thick notebook for
her and wrote out useful phrases, vocabulary and examples of
declensions and conjugation to study. It was like returning to
those Latin lessons which, by third year. had lost all charm for
Helen. She did try to learn the difficult language, but her heart
was not in it. Why were boys so determined to teach? And how
did they perceive those hidden talents, of which you yourself
were unaware?

She also made friends with a young local chemist, Ronnie, who
was amusing and an excellent dancer. He owned a brand new
Mini and on the first night they met, forced an unenthusiastic
Helen to take his modern little car for a spin. It handled very
differently from her own old monster and she was relieved to
return it to him unscathed.

They were probably the only two young car-owners in the East
Neuk until Jack's cousin Drew arrived from Glasgow, with his 1929
MG sportscar. He had bought the fragile little machine for a song.
With a manual to help, he had taken the engine to pieces then put it
together again. Now he had passed his test and immediately
rushed to Pittenweem. Helen was impressed and was allowed to
drive the classic to St Andrews, though she found driving with legs
extended straight in front rather awkward. In less than a week the
ancient machine slowly rolled downhill and found its last resting
place in a convenient garage. With no possibility of finding spares,
the MG was abandoned. Drew accepted its demise philosophically,
for he had learned a lot.

It was a beautiful autumn and because their stay in Pittenweem
had been shorter than usual, Helen drove through every second
weekend. Friday lunch-time, she would return to Hyndland and
pack her mother into the car. With only the first period to teach in
the afternoon, they were well on their way to Fife by four o'clock.
Officially, Helen should have remained in school until four, but
there was a laissez faire attitude in the Lambhill annexe.

After a pleasantly social weekend, they would leave
Pittenweem at six am on Monday morning, giving Helen time to
drive to Glasgow, find a policeman to help carry Annie into the
flat, then reach the school for nine. It was a demanding schedule.

Luckily, Helen was free for the first period and often dozed in the staff room.

Annie enjoyed the unconventional hours spent in the car and felt that Mary appreciated the company, for she worried about her mother.

Jerry was very much a part of these weekends though Helen assured Annie that he was just a 'good friend'.

"I think he's pretty keen, is he not?"

"Well, perhaps, but I don't take it seriously. He's due for a transfer soon and doesn't know where he'll be posted."

"Perhaps this will be the start of his real espionage training, secret codes and revolvers and that sort of thing!"

"I shouldn't think so. They all swear there's absolutely nothing like that going on at Crail."

"But if something *were* going on, that's just what they would say, wouldn't they? They'd be sworn to secrecy!"

"Mm, I doubt if Jerry could ever be a spy. He likes talking too much."

Jerry came through to Glasgow one weekend, bringing his bike on the train. He loved the large city, so different from the other places he had encountered in Britain. They walked around town, crossed the Clyde on the Finnieston ferry, visited the Art Galleries, the People's Palace and the Botanic Gardens. It was an energetic two days.

Helen had expected he would return by train, but at eleven o'clock on Sunday night, after five minutes' steady perusal of a road map, he bicycled back to Crail through the night. He phoned in the early morning to tell her that after a short nap in a phone box, he was now safely back in camp. To Helen, it seemed an amazing achievement. The route across Scotland was complicated, unfamiliar, rainy and dark. Had he memorised the map in those few minutes? Perhaps he did have the ability to be a spy.

When his new posting came through, Helen drove him to Kirkcaldy to catch the London train. The parting was sad and they promised to write, but both knew their paths were unlikely to cross again.

Annie sighed and shook her head,

"And we'll never know if he was a spy or not !"

Douglas Comes Home

Shortly before Christmas, Agnes Connell had finished work on Friday and Annie handed over the modest wages. "Now don't forget to take that packet of tea and the wee cake I made for the kids."

Agnes had put on her coat, but still stood there.

"Was there something else you wanted, Agnes?"

"Oh, Mrs Corning, I've got... something to tell you."

"Good news, I hope." Instinctively, Annie guessed what the news would be.

"Oh, Mrs Corning I don't know if it's good or bad. I'm that upset, but I'm going to have another baby."

"Agnes, I think that's *lovely* news. I adore babies. Congratulations."

"But after all these years, Mrs Corning. And Rena's nearly fourteen now, she'll soon be leaving school and I haven't even told her and wee John yet. I'm frightened."

"What about big John?"

"Oh he's delighted, so he is. He doesn't have to get big and fat and look after a wean for years and years. I hope it'll not make any difference to my work here with you, for I know my mother'll be a good help to me. But Mrs Corning, d'ye not think I'm too *old* to be having a baby?"

"Och away with you, what are you now, thirty-four? And you look like twenty-four. I know you're just going to love this baby when it arrives and so will I."

Agnes looked more cheerful as she left, but Annie knew she must expect changes in her own life.

◊

Helen drove to Pittenweem and collected Mary just before Christmas. Although the house now had electricity installed, Mary was peculiarly careful about using it. The sitting room fire always burned brightly, but as the winter set in, the rest of the house became ice-cold as usual. The East Neuk juts out into the North Sea and the damp, bitter air from Scandinavia scourges the unprotected coast.

"If it's extra cold when I go upstairs, I might put on the wee radiator for a couple of minutes." Mary would say, "But I've got my electric blanket and I'm fine and cosy when I get into bed. Don't worry about me."

But Annie did worry, remembering how miserable the house had been in the war years. She could not understand her mother's apparent meanness. Now in her seventies, surely Mary did not need to watch every penny. Ruefully she discussed this with Helen,

"I've no idea what her financial position is. She doesn't have an old age pension, for my father didn't believe in it and never paid into the scheme."

When Helen smiled at this, Annie laughed and added,

"He didn't believe in the internal combustion engine either. Considered it just a passing fancy that would never take on."

Mary seemed happy to come to Glasgow for the three winter months and Helen accepted it as one of life's duties, though she would never enjoy the visit and wondered if Mary enjoyed it, for she was always critical. Helen had been trained from an early age to show kindness and respect to older people, no matter how difficult they were. At twenty-four, she had never 'spoken back' to her grandmother, though possibly she was not always successful at hiding her feelings.

As Mary re-told a well-known anecdote, Annie's mind wandered. She realised her own health had stabilised in the last year or two. Low pressure weather still caused painful cramps, but other symptoms, tingling, numbness and exhaustion seemed to have disappeared. Her physical condition seemed less affected by her emotions. Perhaps she was less emotional than previously? But her mother often made her furious, yet she had certainly suffered less pain this winter. She no longer needed six aspirin each day, an occasional two were sufficient. Perhaps her hands were slightly less deft, but she could knit, sew, type, peel potatoes and generally make herself useful, so she would not complain.

Was the improvement due to Miss Arthur, who still came faithfully each week? She looked frail these days, but her hands still squeezed and pummelled mercilessly.

Perhaps some of the improvement was due to that wonderful sewing machine and all those tweed suits, ballgowns and fur-coats she had hauled about on it? Surely that was good exercise for an old invalid and it was great fun! Annie liked nothing better than to puzzle out the intricacies of a new garment.

How astonishing that she was no longer housebound and had in fact travelled more than she ever did in those far off days when able to walk. How kind of Bruce to provide the car and keep it in good order. And Helen was such a marvellous daughter, happy to drag her mother around everywhere. She was talking of going to London next, where they could visit Annie's old school friend Elsie.

Annie gave a small sigh and smiled happily to herself and Mary returned the smile, accepting it as proper appreciation of the story she had just told.

Helen's mind also drifted away as Mary spoke.

More often than she would have admitted to anyone, her thoughts centred on Douglas, who would finish his naval service and return from the far East in June.

Ever since meeting him nine years ago at Margaret's birthday ball, Douglas had held a special place in Helen's heart. Other young men seemed lacking, when compared to Douglas, less handsome, less charming, less confident. Was it only his height, grace and personality that appealed to her? Helen wondered if she were unrealistically romantic about him. Each time they met, Helen felt sure there was something deeper than affection between them, though they had never discussed the future on a serious level.

Over the years, whenever Douglas was in Glasgow, they had gone swimming, dancing, into the country on the back of his motor bike or in his father's car. Helen had always found these outings very special. She knew there were other girls in his life, just as there were other boys in her life. They had corresponded throughout his years in the RNVR but the affectionate, light hearted letters were not numerous and certainly not love letters. Did they vaguely suggest some happy shared future? Helen found it difficult to know and, unwilling to read too much into them, replied in similar light vein. Perhaps Douglas's attitude was his biggest asset, for Helen had no strong desire to marry. Marriage would mean a complete upheaval of her present life. No doubt her mind shied away from the insoluble problem of Annie's dependence on her. Anyway few of her female friends were married, although several were engaged. Helen enjoyed her demanding life and, after five years of student poverty, it was pleasant to earn a salary and enjoy some of the small luxuries which were slowly becoming available. She was pleased to enjoy male companionship and admiration without worrying about breaking hearts. Never again would she treat someone as she had treated Mungo. The emotional turmoil had been terrible and she was still guilt-ridden. Why were young men so serious, when no one had any money to start a home?

Sometime in the future, no doubt, she would marry and possibly that shadowy, unknown husband in her mind's eye bore a strong resemblance to Douglas.

Picnic at Loch Lomond

D ouglas's parents had always been very friendly towards Helen and as Douglas's return to Glasgow approached, they became even friendlier. Rosemary dropped in to visit Annie several times and if Helen bumped into her or Henry in the street, she was invited back to their flat for coffee, where most of the conversation concerned the return of their son.

"I think there's no doubt they see you as their future daughter-in-law." Annie pronounced one day when Helen had been visiting Rosemary.

"Then they may be disappointed, because I'm not at all sure that Douglas has any thoughts of marriage or whether I would accept him if he did ask me. We've never had that sort of conversation."

"But you like him, don't you?"

"Oh yes, we've always got on well and I always have a great time with him. But somehow, I don't really know him as well as I know lots of other folk, Drew and Donald and even Ronnie and Jerry."

"And Mungo?"

"Poor Mungo. I suppose we were good friends in a way, but he had a secret side. We were terribly different from each other, Perhaps I was too young to understand or appreciate him.

"I liked Mungo fine but I know what you mean, he had a hidden side. Nor do I feel I know Douglas as well as some of your other friends. He's always very polite and courteous, but we never seem to have a relaxed *blether*. He hardly ever sits down."

"That might be because of the cat."

"Mmm, of course, the cat. You must find his dislike of cats a bit of a drawback, when you're so daft about them yourself. But perhaps you intend to convert him to feline adoration, eventually. Mind you, I'm quite surprised that Rosemary is enthusiastic about the idea of her son getting married! Mothers don't usually welcome their only son's choice of a bride."

"*We don't know I'm his choice!* Anyway, I'd like to remind you she's not the first mother to consider me a suitable wife for her son! Isobel Waddell did too, and Drew's mother and there's another one I can't remember. But it's not very exciting to be viewed as good daughter-in-law material. Domestic, boring and biddable."

"Och, that's not it at all. These mothers see you as strong and sensible, well educated and self sufficient and they think you'll be able to knock their sons into some sort of proper shape. Something they failed to do themselves!"

Helen laughed,

"Is that what wives are expected to do? I don't fancy that much."

◊

Douglas returned from the Far East on a Tuesday and Helen was invited to his house the following evening. She was surprised to be the only guest.

He looked tanned and healthy, even more handsome than she remembered.

After a welcome home toast was drunk, Douglas produced various exotically wrapped parcels. There was a length of bright silk and a string of pink pearls for Rosemary, a carved box containing a splendid watch for Henry and for Helen, exquisite earrings of jade set in gold. She had not expected to receive a present and felt almost overpowered by such a valuable one. She stammered her thanks and gave him a swift kiss. His parents admired the earrings extravagantly and looked meaningfully at the two young people. Then, outspoken and practical as always, Rosemary advised Helen to insure them at once.

Annie also made it obvious she thought such an expensive present significant.

"Absolutely lovely, my pet! I expect it'll be a ring next."

It troubled Helen that both families took an imminent engagement for granted. Perhaps Douglas had no such intention and she was certainly far from sure of her own feelings.

Douglas and Helen arranged to take a picnic to Loch Lomond on Saturday. Helen would drive.

"Let's go to Balmaha and take a boat out to one of the islands." Douglas suggested.

Helen agreed they should start early.

It was a wonderful early summer's day, soft and warm. Their conversation was stilted as they drove through Bearsden for they had not seen each other for months, nor had she driven Douglas before. Yet she also felt terribly happy to be with him again. How handsome and familiar his tanned face was. How *right* it seemed to have him sitting there beside her. Eventually they relaxed into a more companionable silence.

As they came in sight of the mountains, Helen started to speak of her music studies and her difficulties with reading it. Douglas had studied the piano as a boy and offered to give Helen some of his sheet music. They laughingly agreed that no-one could touch Beethoven.

"Your music is probably too advanced for me. Anyway you might start playing again yourself."

"Oh I only did the first few grades and I don't suppose I'll have a piano in London and I'll be too busy earning the shekels, I expect."

Helen had not known he would leave for London soon and she could not bring herself to ask about his plans. She did not want to seem too curious about his future, as though wondering if she might be part of it. But perhaps he would think she was uninterested? Suddenly the day was fraught with difficulties. Their previous outings had been unself-conscious and relaxed and now the air was full of unknown possibilities. She blamed the earrings. They were beautiful, but much too fine. They unbalanced the situation. Besides, she preferred to wear pendant earrings rather than studs. This thought made her feel ungrateful and boorish and did not help her state of mind.

They parked the car and found a boat to hire.

Too early in the year for holiday makers, the boatman was the only person in sight.

Apart from intermittent birdsong, it was quiet, with that wonderful palpable silence only found near a stretch of still water. As they walked along the jetty, the sound of their foot-steps and the gentle lap of water against wood reminded Helen of some pleasurable past experience, which she could not quite place.

Each fresh green tree was reflected in the tranquil loch, though an occasional puff of wind briefly ruffled the perfect image.

Douglas rowed to a small secluded landing place on an island, then hauled the boat ashore.

"I like watching you row and handle the boat. You're so competent."

"I should hope so, after all these years at sea! Would have lost my gold braid and been keel-hauled, otherwise."

Helen would have liked to tell him how she had loved reading books about the sea from her early teens and knew exactly what keel-hauling was, but that seemed a bit coy. How she wished she felt less self-conscious. She was like a foolish teenager.

Douglas carried the picnic basket and led the way through some bushes and trees to a sunny little bay, surrounded by shrubbery. With a view over a large empty expanse of the loch, it was remote and lonely, like a stage set for a desert island.

He had seemed to know exactly where to find this perfect private spot and Helen wondered if he had brought other girls here, but tried to dismiss the thought.

Was it her imagination that the atmosphere was filled with expectations?

Did she expect him to propose? Did she want him to propose? Did he think that she expected him to do so? And did he perhaps feel pressured and trapped? Marriage had never been mentioned in their previous light-hearted years of friendship.

But he had brought her to this romantic, lonely place?

Why?

Perhaps his expectations were far removed from a marriage proposal?

It must be obvious that Helen admired him and he was a very attractive fellow who probably did not find it difficult to fascinate any girl. Were those expensive earrings only a lure?

Their previous kisses and caresses had been conducted in less private surroundings, but Douglas had never been an importunate lover.

Perhaps he expected her to fall into his embrace on this completely deserted shore?

She smiled as the old fashioned phrase occurred to her.

Did she want to fall into his embrace?

As she had made up the sandwiches this morning, had she considered the possibility of losing her virginity on Loch Lomondside?

No. She knew the answer to that question and it was no. Those twin fears of pregnancy and sexual disease were too potent.

What, as she was making up the sandwiches, had she expected to happen at Loch Lomond?

Helen had no idea.

Though it was hardly eleven, they decided to eat.

◊

Helen drove back to Glasgow with more vivacity than on the outward journey, but with an inner emptiness, a feeling of finality.

No setting could have been more propitious for a romantic proposal, yet nothing had been said. Did Douglas, overwhelmed by the pressure to propose, take cold feet? Or had he never considered it? Perhaps the problem of Helen's mother seem insurmountable or did marriage seem financially out of reach, at this stage of his career? Nor had there been any need to defend her virginity or even discuss her attitude towards sex. Had Douglas not expected to make love? Or was he experienced enough to judge that Helen was not a girl to accept casual sex?

As they had relaxed in the sun in those magnificent and very private surroundings, there had been the usual compliments, chaste kisses and shared pleasure of the beautiful day. It was all very enjoyable, but nothing more. Their conversation was superficial. The future might not have existed.

As Helen smiled and chatted, she realised a part of her life had ended. What she had felt for Douglas was a sort of hero worship. She hardly knew him and would never know what he felt for her. It was sad that they had never met on a deeper level and perhaps it was as much her fault as his. He had appeared in her life at infrequent intervals and had always charmed her and no doubt his good looks and attractive self-confidence had cast a shadow over other, more real friendships.

Helen had a clear mental picture of every previous outing with Douglas, every detail of the clothes she had worn, the food they had eaten, the things they had said and the places they had been. Memories that were visualised and enjoyed in retrospect. But she would remember no such details of that Loch Lomond picnic, not the dress she had worn, nor the sandwich fillings. Even Douglas's face seemed vague. Only a pale image of the beautiful landscape, like a washed out watercolour, remained in her mind.

It was the end of a chapter in Helen's life.

Saturday Morning

Two ladies stood chatting outside the newsagent's shop in Clarence Drive one Saturday morning. Amy Smilie was a tall pretty woman in her mid thirties, elegantly and expensively dressed. Originally trained as an architect, she had now moved into the comparatively new profession of town planning. Jan Borden was ten years older, an architect's wife with no family. Jan had never been a beauty, though her face was kindly and often expressed concern for others.

Both had lived in Hyndland for most of their lives.

A young woman in a tweed suit walked quickly down the hill, smiling and nodding to Amy as she passed, including Jan in her greeting, though they knew each other only by sight.

Both women turned to watch the girl as she crossed the road.

"Isn't that a very smart suit she's wearing." Amy commented.

"That's the girl that lives in the next close down from you, isn't it?"

"Yes, that's right. She and her mother make all her clothes, too, I believe. She's always very up to the minute."

"And her mother's in a wheelchair, isn't she, and I sometimes see her painting."

"Yes she's very good. I've seen her work in the Paisley Institute. Bright flower pieces, mainly."

"I'm just so sorry for the daughter, though... I've watched the mother sitting at her window for years, ever since that young woman was just a child. I believe she's an only child and I suppose she's had the burden of looking after her mum all these long years. Poor thing! Such a terrible tie for a young girl to have so much responsibility, isn't it! What a shame! I do pity her."

Amy smiled and shook her head slightly,

"Well, you needn't pity her one little bit, Mrs Borden, for she lives a very full life indeed...I think she does more than most girls. She studied at Art School and Jordanhill and teaches now. She dresses well and drives her own car and she and her mother travel all over Scotland. And I have to tell you she has *loads* of boyfriends, all very personable young men. No, you certainly need not feel *one little bit* sorry for that young woman!"

How much Annie would have appreciated that conversation, had she overheard it.

The Rennie Mackintosh Dress

Ever since the swing needle sewing machine had arrived in the house three years ago, Helen had spoken of using it to make a piece of applique.

"When are you going to start this wonderful embroidery? I'm dying to see what you're going to do with the magic machine." Annie asked.

She realised Helen was sometimes in the doldrums these days.

She suspected that the final break with Douglas had hurt her. Perhaps not broken her heart, but it had removed something important from her life. Douglas had never been a large presence in their lives, he was often out of Glasgow, but they had written for years and Helen had always welcomed him home with great pleasure. Had he held a special place in her daughter's heart? Annie was never quite sure. There had been no new young men in Helen's life since Douglas's departure for London eighteen months ago. She sometimes attended a Friday night Art School dance and most probably danced all evening with her friend Trevor, whom Annie had never met. Helen had assured her that, though a brilliant dancer, he was most certainly *not a boyfriend*. In this last year, he had invited her to Daft Friday, the Glasgow University's all-night Christmas dance, and to one or two concerts and films. Though Annie had never met Trevor, she knew he was always beautifully and expensively dressed, quite a dandy in fact.

"I do like going out with him, because it means I can get dressed up too! And when we first walk into a theatre or anywhere, it's like steppng out on stage, for everyone turns and looks at us. Though he's really quite strange-looking, so terribly tall and thin. He is exactly like that fellow with the top hat in Toulouse Lautrec's poster. He gets more like him every day."

Annie was intrigued and would certainly have liked to meet this man.

"Perhaps you should make yourself a stunning embroidered dress to go dancing with Trevor. I'm sure he would appreciate something unusual like that."

"I suppose so. Mmm, Trevor."

Perhaps Helen was inspired by the thought of dancing with Trevor. More likely she felt her usual compulsion to turn a good idea into a reality. Next day in Coplands, she bought vivid green silk and a Vogue pattern for a simple low-backed shift. Using rich blue, purple and black silks, she appliqued a bold Rennie Mackintosh-inspired design around the slightly gathered knee-level frill. It was a unique dress, and very different from the voluminous, petticoat supported skirts that were in fashion.

Annie looked at her daughter as she modelled her new frock. As usual, she had previously had unexpressed doubts about Helen's idea, but now she thought it looked wonderful.

"I think it's marvellous, Helen. It suits you and I love it. Very *different* though. I thought you didn't like to be too different?"

"That was when I was at *school*. I do like to be different now."

"Well I'm sure Trevor will certainly appreciate it."

"I hope there'll be others who like it, too. Poor Trevor, he's a nice friend, but dancing and dressing up are about all we have in common. To tell you the truth, I don't think he's really interested in girls."

Annie waited for Helen to say more. Did she mean that Trevor was homosexual? It was not a subject they had ever discussed. Annie was forced to accept that her curiosity on this point might never be satisfied.

The following Friday, Helen wore her new dress to the Art School. Though it was a student dance, Helen, at twenty-five, was quite likely to meet people of her own age. Graduates and tutors attended and there were also still many older students, those who had finished National Service before studying. She enjoyed dancing and certainly did not expect to meet any romantic interest. She hardly seemed to have time for romance. She would probably finish the evening leaping madly around with Trevor. Then he would bring her home and give her the usual chaste kiss on the forehead.

It was particularly busy that night, with no sign of Trevor.

◊

The first man to ask her to dance was standing slightly behind her when he spoke. Helen turned and her first impression was that he was tall, burly and self assured, with a mass of curls which, in the dimness of the Assembley Hall might have been red. His ready smile showed teeth so evenly spaced and perfect that momentarily, she wondered if they were false. After a couple of dances, they went for a coffee and she saw that his hair was dark blonde, his teeth were his own and he was young and very thin. His strong face explained that first suggestion of power. His name was Thomson McLean. One of his friends joined them and immediately started to flirt with Helen. At first she replied politely then a glance showed that Thomson was dejectedly staring into his coffee. Helen soon brushed away the interloper and Thomson cheered up at once. They spent the evening together, enjoying each other's company and finding they had much in common. Helen thought their conversation unusually interesting and philosophic. Thomson admitted that his background was humble. He lived with his parents in a two-roomed flat in Clydebank and must take his bath in the local public baths.

As they waited for Helen's bus, Thomson wrote down her telephone number.

"Honestly, we don't have a telephone at home or I would give you mine."

Helen smiled. He seemed so knowledgeable and serious-minded, but so naive to think that she might make the first call. Nevertheless, there was charm in his boyishness.

"So, will you come out with me next week? We could go to the Cosmo, maybe. This week I've got to work non-stop, I'm afraid. I'm really, *really* sorry we can't meet sooner, but this project is awful important."

"Yes, that's fine. I'd like that. You can phone me.

She was amused that he was so apologetic. She could wait.

However Helen was surprised to find an unexpected emotional intensity in their good-night kiss.

"Well, did you have a good time?"Annie smiled at her daughter. As usual, Annie marvelled that her daughter was as well-groomed as when she left home and showed no signs of energetic dancing.

"And did Trevor appreciate your Rennie Mackintosh dress?"

"He wasn't there, but I met someone else who liked it."

"Somebody interesting?"

"Well, very nice… a bit on the youthful side for me, I'm afraid. Don't know what age exactly, but young. Still a student. Final year architecture."

"But that's a long course, isn't it? Might not be much younger than you. Has he done his National Service yet?"

"I wouldn't expect so. But he seems very sensible and serious-minded and terribly enthusiastic about architecture. Not handsome but he had a very nice expression, honest and full of integrity somehow. Idealistic, I suppose. Quite funny too. And I could make him laugh, as well."

"Will you see him again, d'ye think?"

"I expect so. He has my phone number."

"Was he 'smitten', d'ye think?"

Helen shrugged. Then frowning slightly, shook her head.

"He's too young for anything...serious."

"So it's the old story, is it. My daughter, the baby snatcher."

"Oh, don't say that, please.

They laughed and Helen put her mother to bed.

Before falling asleep, Helen remembered her teenage assertion that 'she would *never* go out with anyone smaller or younger than she was. But Wee Donald had been part of her life for many months. Now here was Thomson.

Perhaps she would just say 'no' when he phoned next week.

He phoned next day and they arranged to meet on Monday evening at Charing Cross, perhaps go to the Cosmo where a French film was showing.

◊

Agnes brought in the Daily Express on Monday morning.

Enormous black headlines and a blurred, enlarged photo of two toddlers on the front page told a sad story.

"Oh Mrs Corning, just look at this terrible thing that's happened to two wee boys in Lanarkshire. Their mother must be half mad with grief. Oh, I don't know how she'll ever live with herself again, that poor woman. Read it yourself, it's just the saddest thing."

The two-year-old twins had gone missing from the garden on Sunday morning and were later found in a nearby pond, drowned and clasped in each others' arms.

"The wee souls must have been trying to save each other." Annie blinked away a tear. "But the mother has two other children and is also expecting a baby. That's all for the best, I suppose. She'll have something to live for."

It is human to identify with any tragedy and Annie could not help but think of the even greater horror of losing an only child and finding oneself completely bereft.

Helen seldom read newspapers, but glanced at the dramatic front page story on her return from school that day.

She noticed that McLean was the name of the bereaved Lanarkshire family. On reading further she discovered that one of the twins was called Thomson. Thomson Mclean! Surely it was an impossible coincidence.

Thomson's face told the whole story when they met that evening. Helen stammered,

"I saw in the paper today, the same name... was that...?"

"Yes, my two wee cousins."

There were tears in his eyes.

"You should have phoned to cancel."

"No, I *had* to get out the house. My mother's weeping and father's angry... och it's terrible... and what can I do, anyway? What can I say? I hardly knew the twins... and I wanted to see you, I needed to see you."

They linked arms and walked slowly along Sauchiehall Street.

"We don't need to go to the pictures tonight, Thomson."

"I think we should. What d'ye think? It would take my mind off the whole sad business for a while. Let's go."

It would have been hard to find a more tragically dramatic and emotionally disturbing film than *Gervaise,* an adaptation of Emil Zola's novel, *'L'Assommoir'*. Almost too realistically the dark tale of Parisian poverty and misery was recreated. The exquisite actress Maria Schell played the pathetic, ill-fated heroine and from the first moment that she limped across the screen, Thomson and Helen were enthralled, sitting closely and tensely together, their four hands tightly intertwined.

The early scene of a violent fight amongst the women in a Parisian public wash-house seemed particularly vivid to Helen. She had never visited a Glasgow 'steamie', but had heard them described. Surely this was how they looked in the last century and perhaps similar female brawls were not unknown in Glasgow? The story relentlessly followed the downward spiral of the main characters until they reached destitution.

When Thomson and Helen left the cinema, the harrowing effect of the film faded and sad reality once more poured into their minds. They gazed at each other. There was nothing to say.

It seemed as though they had shared more emotion than many couples meet with in years.

The following week, after a pleasant walk, they suddenly disagreed and quarrelled furiously. Helen had never experienced an outright quarrel with a boyfriend. Perhaps she had never cared enough to waste her energy before. They parted coldly.

Two days later, a white box lay on the front doormat. Inside was a delicate paper sculpture of a ballet dancer in her final deep curtsy. It was really beautiful and a perfect apology. Helen was touched and impressed by his skill.

The following week Thomson took the tram to Lambhill and they picnicked on the banks of the canal. Thomson brought a touch of celebration to the occasion with two bottles of Babycham, a slightly alcoholic and well-advertised drink which Helen had not tasted before.

It was beautiful autumn weather and they watched a shaggy horse tread heavily along the tow path. The man on the barge waved cheerfully to them.

It was a memorable day.

On Friday Thomson visited Annie and almost at once they were talking like old friends. Annie's comment was,

"I would say he's a natural gentleman."

On Saturday, Thomson proposed marriage.

"I've thought it all out. My uncle has a farm in East Lothian and he's getting older now. I'm sure he needs help. I'll give up my studies and get a job with him. And I expect there's a cottage we could rent somewhere and we can get married quite soon. And your mother can live with us. I'd like that. I think she's great."

How, with kindness, could she tell this impulsive young man, this *very* young man, (for she had found there was more than four years difference in their ages), what nonsense he was talking? Although he seemed so widely read and mature in his conversation, yet here he was talking like a teenage boy! How might she save his pride, while letting him know what a foolish idea it was and how unready they both were to make such a commitment? True, they did seem to be strongly attracted and they had many interests in common. They had survived strong disagreements and had shared deep emotions. He was clever, she had found that he had won a prestigious scholarship that year and no doubt he had a successful career ahead of him as an architect. But really, this idea of giving up his studies to marry was just a fantasy. It was impractical and it was silly. She tried to hide this opinion as she replied in a quiet thoughtful voice.

"First of all, I think it would be a great shame if you gave up your studies. Secondly and very importantly, though I might just think of being an architect's wife, I'd never, under any circumstances, consider being a farmer's wife. I have no interest in farming. I like visiting the country, but I'd never want to live there. And Thomson, we hardly know each other yet. Let's see what happens in the future."

Flattered by his impetuosity, she was shaken by his lack of common sense, that necessary attribute that experience had taught her. It made her realise how terribly young he was. To fall deeply and romantically in love, with the natural outcome of marriage hovering somewhere in the misty distance was charming, but life had made Helen a realist, with more than sufficient demands on her time and energy and with cost always the most important consideration. She had no illusions that marriage would bring perfect happiness and she must also think of her mother's welfare.

Mungo would have included Annie in their household, but Helen had known he could never be her husband.

Now Thomson, this madly impulsive young man, was taking it for granted that her mother would be part of their joint future. It was far too soon to make such a far-reaching decision, though no doubt their mutual attraction was strong. Was Helen prepared to marry someone who was not yet established in his profession and who came from a penniless background? She did not tell Annie of the proposal, for it seemed too ridiculous to mention.

Perhaps the age difference was insurmountable?

Certainly they must all get to know each other much better before Helen could consider the serious step of marriage.